Masterpieces of Terror and the Unknown

Anthologies edited by Marvin Kaye

Devils & Demons
Frantic Comedy
Ghosts
Haunted America
Masterpieces of Terror and the Supernatural
Sweet Revenge
13 Plays of Ghosts and the Supernatural
Weird Tales™: The Magazine that Never Dies
Witches & Warlocks
Lovers and Other Monsters

Masterpieces

# of Terror

and the Unknown

Selected by Marvin Kaye

GUILDAMERICA BOOKS®

DOUBLEDAY BOOK & MUSIC CLUBS
Garden City, New York

Book Design by Randall Mize
Copyright © 1993 by Marvin Kaye
All Rights Reserved
Printed in the United States of America

GuildAmerica Books® is a registered trademark of Doubleday Book & Music Clubs, Inc.
Acknowledgments on pages 571–73.
The author and publisher have made a thorough effort to locate all persons having any rights or interests in the material presented in this book and to secure all necessary reprint permissions. If any required acknowledgments have been omitted inadvertently or any rights overlooked, we regret the error and will correct the oversight in future editions of the book.

ISBN 1-56865-043-4

Contents

Introduction

Gather Ye Nosegays

Masterpieces of Terror and the Unknown, the ninth Doubleday Book & Music Clubs (DBMCI) anthology I have edited since 1981, is a companion volume to *Masterpieces of Terror and the Supernatural*, which *The New York Times* reported to be one of DBMCI's all-time best-selling books.

Not long ago, I shared a chuckle with my colleague David Hartwell over editors who repeatedly proclaim that "anthologies don't sell." Fortunately, no such pundits work at DBMCI. Still, there is a degree of truth to the bromide. It takes more than a clever title and a few "name" authors to justify a lackluster assortment of overly familiar, second-rate stories.

"Anthology" derives from the Greek *anthologia*, meaning a gathering of blossoms to form a bouquet. Since considerations of balance and selection govern the art of flower arrangement, to paraphrase the Lord Chancellor in Gilbert and Sullivan's *Iolanthe*, "I fancy the same might apply to the book."

Now since *Masterpieces of Terror and the Unknown* consists of both new and reprinted literature, its titular claim is admittedly difficult to substantiate. I may consider a contributor's writing style, skill at characterization and/or insight into the human condition altogether superior, yet to label any new story a masterpiece is an act of hubris. My defense is that as my enthusiasm for genre literature has been hardened by decades of promiscuous reading, any tale still capable of haunting my jaded imagination may have something special to recommend it.

This ego-driven rationale is partially offset by the principle of balance that suggests that in any compendium as sizable as *Masterpieces of Terror and the Unknown* a variety of reading tastes ought to be accommodated. So if a story embodies some strikingly original theme and/or plot, I may set aside my personal stylistic preferences in favor of its inclusion. Happily, I have not had to make any such compromise in choosing the contents of *this* volume.

Masterpieces of Terror and the Unknown is divided into five parts that deliberately mirror-image *Masterpieces of Terror and the Supernatural*. Thus, the first section of this book, "Ghosts and Miscellaneous Nightmares," echoes the final group in the earlier volume, and so on. The sole exception is "Lovers and Other Monsters," which became the title of my 1992 DBMCI anthology. In its place, I have substituted "Contes Cruelles."

Of Terror and the Unknown

In the Afterword to *Masterpieces of Terror and the Supernatural*, I wrote, "When a great artist turns to the terror genre, he or she elevates the exorcism process to the level of catharsis: that working-out of pity commingled with terror that the Greeks experienced at the close of a Sophoclean trilogy—a massive cultural purging that permitted the participants to leave the sacred theatre uplifted and better equipped to deal with the everyday fears of life itself."

A minor British journalist, Hugh Barnacle, recently scoffed at this concept by proclaiming that "Greek tragedy derived from religious ritual and folk tradition, and both priest and storyteller had the same motive as those adolescent boys who enthrall their friends late at night with sick hitchhiker or haunted-house tales which they swear to be true: they use fear to subject and dominate the audience, not to instruct it." Though worthless as scholarship, this curiously unsubstantiated opinion provides a valid insight into morbid psychology and, perhaps, the felicitously named reviewer's own childhood.

Several times in print and repeatedly in public debate I have articulated the difference—and my preference—for the literature and cinema of terror as opposed to horror. My position is epitomized in the following paragraph from the Introduction to *Masterpieces of Terror and the Supernatural:*

In spite of their common confusion in the media, the terms "terror" and "horror" are not interchangeable. Boris Karloff once delineated between them by dismissing horror as mere insistence on the gory and otherwise repugnant—the numbingly banal atrocities seen on the Six O'Clock News (and in Hollywood's dreary splatter films). Terror, according to Karloff, is rooted in cosmic fear of the unknown. It is the more dreadful experience . . . but its very profundity makes it more difficult to achieve artistically. That is surely why most of our contemporary horror writers are *nothing more* than horror writers. The liberal use of ghastly murders and decaying corpses is the stuff of pornography. The psychology of terror, like true erotica, demands far more technique to comprehend and employ.

While I do not deny that horror has its proper place in the genre, I conceive of it as one dab on the artist's palette, to be used sparingly and only when absolutely necessary. There is very little of it in the ensuing pages, but I do not think its absence undercuts (pun absolutely unintended) the capacity of most of these fifty-three tales and five poems to invoke chills and a sense of wonder.

—MARVIN KAYE
New York, 1993

Masterpieces of Terror and the Unknown

Ghosts and Miscellaneous Nightmares

Like most aficionados of the literature of the weird and strange, I became addicted at an early age, only to discover that the price of overindulgence is satiety. Vampires and werewolves and many other standard trappings of horror literature and cinema strike me as spiritualistically anachronistic at best . . . at worst, appallingly juvenile. They fail to wring my withers or raise a single hackle.

Ghosts are altogether another matter. Though I deeply distrust the tendency of many occultists to interpret every unexplained phenomenon in terms of whole-cloth survival of the human spirit, over the years I've had a few too many unsettling experiences to remain skeptical. Thus, though I can't be positive that a ghost once frightened me out of an East Side Manhattan theatre, I do know that it would take a sizable fortune to get me to spend a whole night there alone.

The following dozen selections include traditional (more or less) hauntings offset by several decidedly offbeat excursions into the occult.

JOYCE CAROL OATES

The Others

The condescending attitude of certain critics and academics toward imaginative literature is exasperating. The significant prosodists who have assayed fantasy is virtually a roll call of Western belles lettres; for instance, a far from exhaustive American list must include Ray Bradbury, Theodore Dreiser, William Faulkner, Robert Frost, Nathaniel Hawthorne, Shirley Jackson, Henry James, Ring Lardner, Percy MacKaye, Edgar Allan Poe, Damon Runyon, Wilfred Sheed, Vincent Starrett, John Steinbeck, Mark Twain, Edith Wharton, Thornton Wilder, Tennessee Williams, Alexander Woollcott and Herman Wouk. To this list may now be added JOYCE CAROL OATES, *one of America's most respected novelists (including* Because It Is Bitter and Because It Is My Heart *and* You Must Remember This). *Ms. Oates is Distinguished Professor in the Humanities at Princeton University, but—literary snobs, please note—the following eerie tale appeared in the solidly genre periodical* Twilight Zone *magazine,* not The Atlantic Monthly *or* The New Yorker!

Early one evening in a crowd of people, most of them commuters, he happened to see, quite by accident—he'd taken a slightly different route that day, having left the building in which he worked by an entrance he rarely used—and this, as he'd recall afterward, with the fussy precision which had characterized him since childhood, and helped to account for his success in his profession, because there was renovation being done in the main lobby—a man he had not seen in years, or was it decades: a face teasingly familiar, yet made strange by time like an old photograph about to disintegrate into its elements.

Spence followed the man into the street, into a blowsy damp dusk, but did not catch up to him and introduce himself: that wasn't his way. He was certain he knew the man, and that the man knew him, but how, or why, or from what period in his life the man dated, he could not have said. Spence was forty-two years old and the other seemed to be about that age, yet oddly, older: his skin liverish, his profile vague as if seen through an element transparent yet dense, like water; his clothing—handsome tweed overcoat, sharply creased gray trousers—hanging slack on him, as if several sizes too large.

Outside, Spence soon lost sight of the man in a swarm of pedestrians crossing the street; and made no effort to locate him again. But for most of the ride home on the train he thought of nothing else: who was that man, why was he certain the man would have known him, what were they to each other, resembling each other only very slightly, yet close as twins? He felt stabs of excitement that left him weak and breathless but it wasn't until that night, when he and his wife were undressing for bed, that he said, or heard himself say, in a voice of bemused wonder, and dread: "I saw someone today who looked just like my cousin Sandy—"

"Did I know Sandy?" his wife asked.

"—my cousin Sandy who died, who drowned, when we were both in college."

"But did I know him?" his wife asked. She cast him an impatient sidelong glance and smiled her sweet-derisive smile. "It's difficult to envision him if I've never seen him, and if he's been dead for so long, why should it matter so much to you?"

Spence had begun to perspire. His heart beat hard and steady as if in the presence of danger. "I don't understand what you're saying," he said.

"The actual words, or their meaning?"

"The words."

She laughed as if he had said something witty, and did not answer him. As he fell asleep he tried not to think of his cousin Sandy whom he had not seen in twenty years and whom he'd last seen in an open casket in a funeral home in Damascus, Minnesota.

The second episode occurred a few weeks later when Spence was in line at a post office, not the post office he usually frequented but another, larger, busier, in a suburban township adjacent to his own, and the elderly woman in front of him drew his attention: wasn't she, too, someone he knew? Or had known, many years ago? He stared, fascinated, at her stitched-looking skin, soft and puckered as a glove of some exquisite material, and unnaturally white; her eyes that were small, sunken, yet shining; her astonishing hands—delicate, even skeletal, discolored by liver spots like coins, yet with rings on several fingers, and in a way rather beautiful. The woman appeared to be in her mid-nineties, if not older: fuzzy, anxious, very possibly addled: complaining ceaselessly to herself, or to others by way of herself. Yet her manner was mirthful; nervous bustling energy crackled about her like invisible bees.

He believed he knew who she was: Miss Reuter, a teacher of his in elementary school. Whom he had not seen in more years than he wanted to calculate.

Miss Reuter, though enormously aged, was able, it seemed, to get around by herself. She carried a large rather glitzy shopping bag made of a silvery material, and in this bag, and in another at her feet, she was rummaging for her change purse, as she called it, which she could not seem to find. The post office clerk waited with a show of strained patience; the line now consisted of a half-dozen people.

Spence asked Miss Reuter—for surely it was she: while virtually unrecognizable she was at the same time unmistakable—if she needed some assistance. He did not call her by name and as she turned to him, in exasperation, and gratitude—as if she knew that he, or someone, would come shortly to her aid—she did not seem to recognize him. Spence paid for her postage and a roll of stamps and Miss Reuter, still rummaging in her bag, vexed, cheerful, befuddled, thanked him without looking up at him. She insisted it must be a loan, and not a gift, for she was, she said, "Not yet an object of public charity."

Afterward Spence put the incident out of his mind, knowing the woman was dead. It was purposeless to think of it, and would only upset him.

After that he began to see them more frequently. The Others, as he thought of them. On the street, in restaurants, at church; in the building in which he worked; on the very floor, in the very department in which his office was located. (He was a tax lawyer for one of the largest of American "conglomerates"—yes and very well paid.) One morning his wife saw him standing at a bedroom window looking out toward the street. She poked him playfully in the ribs. "What's wrong?" she said. "None of this behavior suits you."

"There's someone out there, at the curb."

"No one's there."

"I have the idea he's waiting for me."

"Oh yes, I do see someone," his wife said carelessly. "He's often there. But I doubt that he's waiting for you."

She laughed, as at a private joke. She was a pretty, freckled, snub-nosed woman given to moments of mysterious amusement. Spence had married her long ago in a trance of love from which he had yet to awaken.

Spence said, his voice shaking. "I think—I'm afraid I think I might be having a nervous breakdown. I'm so very, very afraid."

"No," said his wife, "you're the sanest person I know. All surface and no cracks, fissures, potholes."

Spence turned to her. His eyes were filling with tears.

"Don't joke. Have pity."

She made no reply; seemed about to drift away; then slipped an arm around his waist and nudged her head against his shoulder in a gesture of camaraderie. Whether mocking, or altogether genuine, Spence could not have said.

"It's just that I'm so afraid."

"Yes, you've said."

"—of losing my mind. Going mad."

She stood for a moment, peering out toward the street. The elderly gentleman standing at the curb glanced back but could not have seen them, or anyone, behind the lacy bedroom curtains. He was well dressed, and carried an umbrella. An umbrella? Perhaps it was a cane.

Spence said, "I seem to be seeing, more and more, these people—people I don't think are truly there."

"*He's* there."

"I think they're dead. Dead people."

His wife drew back and cast him a sidelong glance, smiling mysteriously. "It does seem to have upset you," she said.

"Since I know they're not there—"

"*He's* there."

"—so I must be losing my mind. A kind of schizophrenia, waking dreams, hallucinations—"

Spence was speaking excitedly, and did not know exactly what he was saying. His wife drew away from him in alarm, or distaste. "You take everything so personally," she said.

One morning shortly after the New Year, when the air was sharp as a knife, and the sky so blue it brought tears of pain to one's eyes, Spence set off on the underground route from his train station to his building. Beneath the city's paved surface was a honeycomb of tunnels, some of them damp and befouled but most of them in good condition, with, occasionally, a corridor of gleaming white tiles that looked as if it had been lovingly polished by hand. Spence preferred aboveground, or believed he should prefer aboveground, for reasons vague and puritanical, but in fierce weather he made his way underground, and worried only that he might get lost, as he sometimes did. (Yet, even lost, he had only to find an escalator or steps leading to the street—and he was no longer lost.)

This morning, however, the tunnels were far more crowded than usual. Spence saw a preponderance of elderly men and women, with here and there, startling, and seemingly unnatural, a young face. Here and there, yet more startling, a child's face. A few of the faces had that air, so disconcerting to him in the past, of the eerily familiar laid upon the utterly unfamiliar; and these he resolutely ignored.

He soon fell into step with the crowd, keeping to their pace—which was erratic, surging faster along straight stretches of tunnel and slower at curves; he found it agreeable to be borne along by the flow, as of a tide. A tunnel of familiar tearstained mosaics yielded to one of the smart gleaming tunnels and that in turn to a tunnel badly in need of repair—and, indeed, being noisily repaired, by one of those crews of workmen that labor at all hours of the day and night beneath the surface of the city—and as Spence hurried past the deafening vibrations of the air hammer he found himself descending a stairs into a tunnel unknown to him: a place of warm, humming, droning sound, like conversation, though none of his fellow pedestrians seemed to be talking. Where were they going, so many people? And in the same direction?—with only, here and there, a lone, clearly lost individual bucking the tide, white-faced, eyes snatching at his as if in desperate recognition.

Might as well accompany them, Spence thought, and see.

JOHN GREGORY BETANCOURT

Tap Dancing

JOHN GREGORY BETANCOURT, *a partner of the new publishing firm Bleak House, plays poker nearly as well as he writes, and that makes him a formidable penny-ante opponent. A resident of New Jersey, John, a former principal at* Weird Tales *magazine, is currently an editor at Byron Preiss Visual Publications. His novels include* Johnny Zed, Rememory *and* The Blind Archer.

Martha Peckinpah sat alone in the back of the theatre, watching a dress rehearsal for *Stardust Whammy*. Floodlights bathed the stage in silvers and blues, glittering the sparkle-sewn tuxedos on both dancers. Moog-synthesized Brahms swelled to dizzying peaks as the men rat-tat-tatted to a stop.

Brilliant. That's what the critics would say, Martha thought. Only she knew better. There hadn't been anything new or fresh in the choreography, and the kid on the left had been a half-beat slow on at least a dozen of his repartees. But nobody else had noticed. Standards had fallen, and tap had died a lingering death. This revival was the best she'd seen in the last five years, though, and it might last all of a week before closing. She felt a hollowness inside as she thought of how television and movies and glittery, shallow theatrics like *Cats* had replaced dance and theatre as *the* American performing arts.

But the house lights would be coming on in a minute and the dancers might see her. She had to hurry. If the manager caught her again—

It would be: *Miss Peckinpah, you know you can't come in here and bother people. You'll make the dancers nervous.* Or: *Don't you ever learn? If you don't leave, I'll have to call the police. Again.* Or, if he was in a kind mood: *Miss Peckinpah, sneaking in during rehearsals isn't proper. I know you used to dance here—but that was forty years ago, for crying out loud. Things have changed. You're no longer a star.*

Pity. That was the worst. If it hadn't been for the car crash—

Shuddering, she seized her silver-handled cane and levered herself from the seat, cursing under her breath. Her left knee buckled. The dress she wore, with its faded cherry-blossom print, tangled around her like some monstrous python.

She grabbed for the chair in front of her—and missed. Teetering, arms flailing, she fell. Sharp, fiery pain shot through her left leg. She pressed hands to mouth and managed to stifle her cry . . . thankfully what noise trickled out sounded more like the whimper of some distant, wounded animal than the shriek of a woman in agony.

Carefully she eased forward. Grabbing her purse, she searched for her pain pills. She found the bottle and ripped off its cap, only to have her shaking hand scatter the contents across the floor. Pills tap-tap-tapped downhill toward the stage.

The lights began to brighten. Her leg throbbed. *No time.* Bending, she ducked down and prayed nobody would see her.

The dancers walked up the aisle, laughing and joking, the little steel taps on their shoes muffled by the worn red carpet. The manager and two stagehands followed, muttering gloomily about potential box office. She pressed her eyes shut and held her breath. At last the doors squeaked and she was alone.

Why me, oh God why me? In a rare moment of introspection it struck her how pathetic she must seem, a crazy old woman nobody remembered, sneaking into theatres just to criticize the young, just to say to herself, *Oh, how much greater we were back then.* Better she had never come back to this theatre. Better she had died in that car crash forty years before. Better she had never been born.

"Not so." It was a soft voice, a man's voice, and the words held a strange inflection—a trace of a Southern accent, and something else, something more.

"Who said that?" she called.

"I did."

She became aware of light—a soft blue-gray glow that seemed to surround her. A man dressed all in black leather sat beside her. He had shoulder-length black hair and wore dark glasses, an old-fashioned pair with round lenses and wire rims. A silver cross dangled from his left ear. He smiled and there was an aliveness about him that surprised her.

"You're not Mr. Lipshitz, the manager," Martha said. "You can't throw me out—"

"Did I say I wanted to?"

"No." There was something naggingly familiar about him, she thought. She'd seen him before, somewhere. Perhaps on television?

"I'm just a visitor. If you need a name, Johnny will do."

"Can you help me up?"

"If that's what you want, yes." He took her hand—his touch was cool, his grip strong—and he pulled her to her feet with little effort. The pain in Martha's leg seemed gone. She stood with no trouble for the first time since her accident.

"Who—what?"

"Did you like their dance?" he asked softly.

"It could have been better."

He shook his head slowly. "And what are you going to do to fix it?"

"Me?"

"Why not you?"

"Son, I'm old, and I'm sick, and I don't have time for this nonsense. They don't have the talent. They're not as good as we were, that's all there is to it."

"You're right, of course. A big star like you—I should just let you go on about your life. Whatever it is. Whatever it's worth."

Martha winced. "You're cruel," she whispered.

"I used to watch your movies," he continued. "You and Fred, you were the best. It's a shame to let all that go to waste. I *know*. It's too late for me—I never shared my gifts, I hoarded them—and now I've got to work to make up for it. There's a balance. You get some, you share some. Don't hide it all away. There's so much you know, so much you can still *do*—"

"Don't lecture me!" she said. "I don't need your pity!" She couldn't make herself look at him. Guilt? Did she feel . . . *guilt?* "That was such a long time ago."

"Have you forgotten?"

Had she forgotten? She could have laughed. *Had she forgotten?* Of course not. She couldn't forget, not ever. Tap had been her whole life. Nothing else had mattered. Until those screaming brakes, that tree rushing at her—

"Please," he said, taking her hand, squeezing it reassuringly. "Dance with me?"

"What do you mean?" She finally met his gaze. There was hope there, and faith. He knew she could dance—he remembered!

"Come," he said. He took her elbow gently and led her down to the stage. She was halfway there before she noticed she wasn't using her cane.

"I left my—" she began.

"Do you need it?" he asked.

"No. No!" She said it with conviction, then laughed. "No!" She stepped ahead of him, courage and confidence welling up inside her. Her stride was jaunty. The years seemed to be melting away. She could see the theatre as it had once been: the red velvet seats, the plush carpeting, the crowds—

Then somehow she was on the stage. The lights shone bright and hot like always, like she'd never been away. She felt a heady rush of elation. Then she looked down, saw her scarred, treelike legs jutting out, those old woman's legs with their sagging muscles—

"Oh no!" she cried.

"It doesn't matter," Johnny said.

And he was right, it didn't. Martha took a deep breath. Suddenly she was no longer old Martha Peckinpah but Desiree Diamond again —star of stage and screen. She'd danced with the best of them, Fred Astaire, Gene Kelly, Ray Bolger—

Tap-tap-tap. *Rat-ta-ta*-tap-*ta-tap*. Her feet moved on their own. They remembered. The opening number from *Bound for Broadway*—

Johnny now wore a black tux with tails. He took her hand, spun her slowly, and they moved into all the old dances, up and across the stage, tapping away, faster and faster, around and around and around. Her red silk dress swirled. The tails of his tux whipped by. Martha was laughing and tears streamed down her face like they would never stop. Around and around and around they went, and the orchestra played as though their lives depended on it. *Tap-a-tap-ratta-tap*-tap!

Martha came to a stop, quivering. Her breath came in short gasps. She looked down. Her faded dress with its cherry-blossom print had returned. Johnny, smiling, gave her a little bow.

"You haven't forgotten," he said.

"No," she agreed, "I haven't."

"Then I thank you," he said, turning to go. "Thank you, and goodbye."

"Wait!" Martha called. She took a step and the pain shot through her leg. She gasped, stumbled.

Johnny paused. "I'm sorry. I can't stay any longer."

"But *why?*" she cried.

"Purgatory isn't a place, it's a process. You have to work off your debt." Then he turned and hopped down from the stage, melting off into the darkness. His voice seemed to carry back like an echo of an echo. *"Remember . . ."*

By the time Martha reached the aisle, the theatre was deserted.

She limped back to her apartment and collapsed in her overstuffed armchair, all her shattered dreams coming back to haunt her. *Bound for Broadway*, closed in mid-run because of her accident. Her canceled contract with Sam Goldwyn. All her ruined plans.

A tear traced a path down the creases of her cheek. Angrily she brushed it away. *I don't owe them anything*, she thought. *They never came to see me. They never wrote. They just swept me under the carpet and kept going with their lives like nothing had happened, nothing had changed.*

She stabbed the remote control with one finger. The television flickered to life.

And she found herself looking at Johnny's face.

"—dead tonight, Johnny Devlin, head singer of the heavy metal rock group Cruel Blade. A drug overdose is suspected, and an autopsy has been ordered. Fans are already mourning Johnny's loss. Cruel Blade's first album, a groundbreaking mix of heavy metal, jazz, and reggae, is currently topping the charts in both the U.S. and England—"

Martha hurriedly flicked the television off. Johnny's words came back to her, and she shuddered. *That's the way of things when you're working off your debt.*

Martha poured herself a brandy, downed it, had a second. Her hands were shaking again. *You get some, you share some.*

She spent a sleepless night wondering.

The next morning, bright and early, she donned her good dress—the one she always wore to funerals—and had another drink. Then, spirit girded, she set off for the theatre.

Rather than sliding her trusty old butter knife into the firedoor's lock, lifting the latch, and sneaking in the way she usually did, she went straight to the stage entrance.

Adam Lipshitz, the manager, saw her coming and came out to

meet her. "For the thousandth time, Miss Peckinpah," he began, "I don't want you coming here and—"

Martha cut him off with a curt gesture. "I watched the show last night. Your dancers are good this time, Lipshitz. Really good. But their routines stink."

"I choreographed it myself!"

She snorted. "It shows! You need a professional. How long till opening? A week?"

He nodded.

"Then there's still time . . ." She smiled, and focused on him once more. "I want to help you," she said kindly, in her best grandmotherly voice. "I think this time you could really have something here, something important, something *great* instead of merely adequate. Will you let me restage the routines for you?"

"Why should I listen to you?"

"I'm the best."

"You *were* the best."

"I still am," she said. "I still remember . . ."

"How much will it cost?" he asked, eyes narrowing.

"You really don't understand, do you? I'm an old woman. I don't need more than I already have. This isn't for *money*, Lipshitz, it's for *art*. For *tap*. That's why you couldn't get it right."

He threw up his hands. "Okay, already! It doesn't hurt to look. Come in, I'll get the dancers. Then we'll see what you suggest."

Martha followed him, cane tap-tap-tapping the way to the stage. She began to smile. Backstage, with the smell of makeup, with the tiny dressing rooms and the clutter of props—it felt like coming home. How long had it been? Too long.

And when Lipshitz opened the curtain onto the side of the stage, when she saw the dancers fumbling their way through routines that should have come like water flowing down a river, she finally knew that this was good, this was right. Perhaps she'd been meant for this in the cosmic order of things. Perhaps her accident had happened merely to guide her here, to this particular moment, to make her a director instead of a star.

When *Stardust Whammy* opened, it would be magic, it would be art, and it would be beauty.

And she knew she'd be happy for the first time in forty years.

"This is for you, Johnny," she whispered. "Thank you . . . I *do* remember."

RABINDRANATH TAGORE

The Hungry Stones

RABINDRANATH TAGORE *(1861–1941) was an important Indian critic, composer, essayist, novelist, playwright and poet. Author of the internationally renowned play* The King of the Dark Chamber *and an esteemed novel,* The Home and the World, *Tagore was fluent in English but chose to write in his native Bengali. My colleague Jessica Amanda Salmonson first introduced me to his ghostly and erotic story, "The Hungry Stones." According to Ms. Salmonson, Tagore probably did the English translation himself.*

My kinsman and myself were returning to Calcutta from our Puja trip when we met the man in a train. From his dress and bearing we took him at first for an up-country Mahomedan, but we were puzzled as we heard him talk. He discoursed upon all subjects so confidently that you might think the Disposer of All Things consulted him at all times in all that He did. Hitherto we had been perfectly happy, as we did not know that secret and unheard-of forces were at work, that the Russians had advanced close to us, that the English had deep and secret policies, that confusion among the native chiefs had come to a head. But our newly-acquired friend said with a sly smile: "There happen more things in heaven and earth, Horatio, than are reported in your newspapers." As we had never stirred out of our homes before, the demeanour of the man struck us dumb with wonder. Be the topic ever so trivial, he would quote science, or comment on the *Vedas,* or repeat quatrains from some Persian poet; and as we had no pretence to a knowledge of science or the *Vedas* or Persian, our admiration for him went on increasing, and my kinsman, a theosophist, was firmly convinced that our fellow-passenger must have been supernaturally inspired by some strange "magnetism" or "occult power," by an "astral body" or something of that kind. He listened to the tritest saying that fell from the lips of our extraordinary companion with devotional rapture, and secretly took down notes of his conversation. I fancy that the extraordinary man saw this, and was a little pleased with it.

When the train reached the junction, we assembled in the waiting-room for the connection. It was then 10 P.M., and as the train, we heard, was likely to be very late, owing to something wrong in the lines, I spread my bed on the table and was about to lie down for a comfortable doze, when the extraordinary person deliberately set about spinning the following yarn. Of course, I could get no sleep that night.

When, owing to a disagreement about some questions of administrative policy, I threw up my post at Junagarh, and entered the service of the Nizam of Hyderabad, they appointed me at once, as a strong young man, collector of cotton duties at Barich.

Barich is a lovely place. The *Susta* "chatters over stony ways and babbles on the pebbles," tripping, like a skilful dancing girl, in through the woods below the lonely hills. A flight of 150 steps rises from the river, and above that flight, on the river's brim and at the foot of the hills, there stands a solitary marble palace. Around it there is no habitation of man—the village and the cotton mart of Barich being far off.

About 250 years ago the Emperor Mahmud Shah II had built this lonely palace for his pleasure and luxury. In his days jets of rose-water spurted from its fountains, and on the cold marble floors of its spray-cooled rooms young Persian damsels would sit, their hair dishevelled before bathing, and, splashing their soft naked feet in the clear water of the reservoirs, would sing, to the tune of the guitar, the *ghazals* of their vineyards.

The fountains play no longer; the songs have ceased; no longer do snow-white feet step gracefully on the snowy marble. It is but the vast and solitary quarters of cess-collectors like us, men oppressed with solitude and deprived of the society of women. Now, Karim Khan, the old clerk of my office, warned me repeatedly not to take up my abode there. "Pass the day there, if you like," said he, "but never stay the night." I passed it off with a light laugh. The servants said that they would work till dark, and go away at night. I gave my ready assent. The house had such a bad name that even thieves would not venture near it after dark.

At first the solitude of the deserted palace weighed upon me like a nightmare. I would stay out, and work hard as long as possible, then return home at night jaded and tired, go to bed and fall asleep.

Before a week had passed, the place began to exert a weird fascination upon me. It is difficult to describe or to induce people to believe; but I felt as if the whole house was like a living organism slowly and imperceptibly digesting me by the action of some stupefying gastric juice.

Perhaps the process had begun as soon as I set my foot in the house, but I distinctly remember the day on which I first was conscious of it.

It was the beginning of summer, and the market being dull I had no work to do. A little before sunset I was sitting in an arm-chair near the water's edge below the steps. The *Susta* had shrunk and sunk low; a broad patch of sand on the other side glowed with the hues of evening; on this side the pebbles at the bottom of the clear shallow waters were glistening. There was not a breath of wind anywhere, and the still air was laden with an oppressive scent from the spicy shrubs growing on the hills close by.

As the sun sank behind the hill-tops a long dark curtain fell upon the stage of day, and the intervening hills cut short the time in which light and shade mingle at sunset. I thought of going out for a ride, and was about to get up when I heard a footfall on the steps behind. I looked back, but there was no one.

As I sat down again, thinking it to be an illusion, I heard many footfalls, as if a large number of persons were rushing down the steps. A strange thrill of delight, slightly tinged with fear, passed through my frame, and though there was not a figure before my eyes, methought I saw a bevy of joyous maidens coming down the steps to bathe in the *Susta* in that summer evening. Not a sound was in the valley, in the river, or in the palace, to break the silence, but I distinctly heard the maidens' gay and mirthful laugh, like the gurgle of a spring gushing forth in a hundred cascades, as they ran past me, in quick playful pursuit of each other, towards the river, without noticing me at all. As they were invisible to me, so I was, as it were, invisible to them. The river was perfectly calm, but I felt that its still, shallow, and clear waters were stirred suddenly by the splash of many an arm jingling with bracelets, that the girls laughed and dashed and spattered water at one another, that the feet of the fair swimmers tossed the tiny waves up in showers of pearl.

I felt a thrill at my heart—I cannot say whether the excitement was due to fear or delight or curiosity. I had a strong desire to see them more clearly, but naught was visible before me; I thought I could catch all that they said if I only strained my ears; but however hard I strained them, I heard nothing but the chirping of the cicadas in the woods. It seemed as if a dark curtain of 250 years was hanging before me, and I would fain lift a corner of it tremblingly and peer through, though the assembly on the other side was completely enveloped in darkness.

The oppressive closeness of the evening was broken by a sudden gust of wind, and the still surface of the *Susta* rippled and curled like the hair of a nymph, and from the woods wrapt in the evening gloom there came forth a simultaneous murmur, as though they were awakening from a black dream. Call it reality or dream, the momentary glimpse of that invisible mirage reflected from a far-off world, 250 years old, vanished in a flash. The mystic forms that brushed past me with their quick unbodied steps, and loud, voiceless laughter, and threw themselves into the river, did not go back wringing their dripping robes as they went. Like fragrance wafted away by the wind they were dispersed by a single breath of the spring.

Then I was filled with a lively fear that it was the Muse that had taken advantage of my solitude and possessed me—the witch had evidently come to ruin a poor devil like myself making a living by collecting cotton duties. I decided to have a good dinner—it is the empty stomach that all sorts of incurable diseases find an easy prey. I sent for my cook and gave orders for a rich, sumptuous *moghlai* dinner, redolent of spices and *ghi*.

Next morning the whole affair appeared a queer fantasy. With a light heart I put on a *sola* hat like the *sahebs*, and drove out to my work. I was to have written my quarterly report that day, and expected to return late; but before it was dark I was strangely drawn to my house—by what I could not say—I felt they were all waiting, and that I should delay no longer. Leaving my report unfinished I rose, put on my *sola* hat, and startling the dark, shady, desolate path with the rattle of my carriage, I reached the vast silent palace standing on the gloomy skirts of the hills.

On the first floor the stairs led to a very spacious hall, its roof stretching wide over ornamental arches resting on three rows of massive pillars, and groaning day and night under the weight of its own intense solitude. The day had just closed, and the lamps had not yet been lighted. As I pushed the door open a great bustle seemed to follow within, as if a throng of people had broken up in confusion, and rushed out through the doors and windows and corridors and verandas and rooms, to make its hurried escape.

As I saw no one I stood bewildered, my hair on end in a kind of ecstatic delight, and a faint scent of *attar* and unguents almost effaced by age lingered in my nostrils. Standing in the darkness of that vast desolate hall between the rows of those ancient pillars, I could hear the gurgle of fountains plashing on the marble floor, a strange tune on the guitar, the jingle of ornaments and the tinkle of anklets, the clang of bells tolling the hours, the distant note of *nahabat*, the din of the crystal pendants of chandeliers shaken by the breeze, the song of *bulbuls* from the cages in the corridors, the cackle of storks in the gardens, all creating round me a strange unearthly music.

Then I came under such a spell that this intangible, inaccessible, unearthly vision appeared to be the only reality in the world—and all else a mere dream. That I, that is to say, Srijut So-and-so, the eldest son of So-and-so of blessed memory, should be drawing a monthly salary of Rs. 450 by the discharge of my duties as collector of cotton duties, and driving in my dog-cart to my office every day in a short coat and *sola* hat, appeared to me to be such an astonishingly ludicrous illusion that I burst into a horse-laugh, as I stood in the gloom of that vast silent hall.

At that moment my servant entered with a lighted kerosene lamp in his hand. I do not know whether he thought me mad, but it came back to me at once that I was in very deed Srijut So-and-so, son of So-and-so of blessed memory, and that, while our poets, great and small, alone could say whether inside or outside the earth there was a region where unseen fountains perpetually played and fairy guitars, struck by invisible fingers, sent forth an eternal harmony, this at any rate was certain, that I collected duties at the cotton market at Barich, and earned thereby Rs. 450 per mensem as my salary. I laughed in great glee at my curious illusion, as I sat over the newspaper at my camp-table, lighted by the kerosene lamp.

After I had finished my paper and eaten my *moghlai* dinner, I put out the lamp, and lay down on my bed in a small side-room. Through the open window a radiant star, high above the Avalli hills skirted by the darkness of their woods, was gazing intently from millions and millions of miles away in the sky at Mr. Collector lying on a humble camp-bedstead. I wondered and felt amused at the idea, and do not know when I fell asleep or how long I slept; but I suddenly awoke with a start, though I heard no sound and saw no intruder—only the steady bright star on the hilltop had set, and the dim light of the new moon was stealthily entering the room through the open window, as if ashamed of its intrusion.

I saw nobody, but felt as if some one was gently pushing me. As I awoke she said not a word, but beckoned me with her five fingers bedecked with rings to follow her cautiously. I got up noiselessly, and, though not a soul save myself was there in the countless apartments of that deserted palace with its slumbering sounds and waking echoes, I feared at every step lest any one should wake up. Most of the rooms of the palace were always kept closed, and I had never entered them.

I followed breathless and with silent steps my invisible guide—I cannot now say where. What endless dark and narrow passages, what long corridors, what silent and solemn audience-chambers and close secret cells I crossed!

Though I could not see my fair guide, her form was not invisible to my mind's eye—an Arab girl, her arms, hard and smooth as marble, visible through her loose sleeves, a thin veil falling on her face from the fringe of her cap, and a curved dagger at her waist! Methought that one of the thousand and one Arabian Nights had been wafted to me from the world of romance, and that at the dead of night I was wending my way through the dark narrow alleys of slumbering Bagdad to a trysting-place fraught with peril.

At last my fair guide stopped abruptly before a deep blue screen, and seemed to point to something below. There was nothing there, but a sudden dread froze the blood in my heart—methought I saw there on the floor at the foot of the screen a terrible Negro eunuch dressed in rich brocade, sitting and dozing with outstretched legs, with a naked sword on his lap. My fair guide lightly tripped over his legs and held up a fringe of the screen. I could catch a glimpse of a part of the room spread with a Persian carpet—some one was sitting inside on a bed—I could not see her, but only caught a glimpse of two exquisite feet in gold-embroidered slippers, hanging out from loose saffron-coloured *paijamas* and placed idly on the orange-coloured velvet carpet. On one side there was a bluish crystal tray on which a few apples, pears, oranges, and bunches of grapes in plenty, two small cups and a gold-tinted decanter were evidently awaiting the guest. A fragrant intoxicating vapour, issuing from a strange sort of incense that burned within, almost overpowered my senses.

As with trembling heart I made an attempt to step across the out-stretched legs of the eunuch, he woke up suddenly with a start, and the sword fell from his lap with a sharp clang on the marble floor.

A terrific scream made me jump, and I saw I was sitting on that camp-bedstead of mine sweating heavily; and the crescent moon looked pale in the morning light like a weary sleepless patient at dawn; and our crazy Meher Ali was crying out, as is his daily custom, "Stand back! Stand back!!" while he went along the lonely road.

Such was the abrupt close of one of my Arabian Nights; but there were yet a thousand nights left.

Then followed a great discord between my days and nights. During the day I would go to my work worn and tired, cursing the bewitching night and her empty dreams, but as night came my daily life with its bonds and shackles of work would appear a petty, false, ludicrous vanity.

After nightfall I was caught and overwhelmed in the snare of a strange intoxication. I would then be transformed into some unknown personage of a bygone age, playing my part in unwritten history; and my short English coat and tight breeches did not suit me in the least. With a red velvet cap on my head, loose *paijamas*, an embroidered vest, a long flowing silk gown, and coloured handker-chiefs scented with *attar*, I would complete my elaborate toilet, sit on a high-cushioned chair, and replace my cigarette with a many-coiled *narghileh* filled with rose-water, as if in eager expectation of a strange meeting with the beloved one.

I have no power to describe the marvellous incidents that un-folded themselves, as the gloom of the night deepened. I felt as if in the curious apartments of that vast edifice the fragments of a beauti-ful story, which I could follow for some distance, but of which I could never see the end, flew about in a sudden gust of the vernal breeze. And all the same I would wander from room to room in pursuit of them the whole night long.

Amid the eddy of these dream-fragments, amid the smell of *henna* and the twanging of the guitar, amid the waves of air charged with fragrant spray, I would catch like a flash of lightning the momentary glimpse of a fair damsel. She it was who had saffron-coloured *paijamas*, white ruddy soft feet in gold-embroidered slippers with curved toes, a close-fitting bodice wrought with gold, a red cap, from which a golden frill fell on her snowy brow and cheeks.

She had maddened me. In pursuit of her I wandered from room

to room, from path to path among the bewildering maze of alleys in the enchanted dreamland of the nether world of sleep.

Sometimes in the evening, while arraying myself carefully as a prince of the blood-royal before a large mirror, with a candle burning on either side, I would see a sudden reflection of the Persian beauty by the side of my own. A swift turn of her neck, a quick eager glance of intense passion and pain glowing in her large dark eyes, just a suspicion of speech on her dainty red lips, her figure, fair and slim, crowned with youth like a blossoming creeper, quickly uplifted in her graceful tilting gait, a dazzling flash of pain and craving and ecstasy, a smile and a glance and a blaze of jewels and silk, and she melted away. A wild gust of wind, laden with all the fragrance of hills and woods, would put out my light, and I would fling aside my dress and lie down on my bed, my eyes closed and my body thrilling with delight, and there around me in the breeze, amid all the perfume of the woods and hills, floated through the silent gloom many a caress and many a kiss and many a tender touch of hands, and gentle murmurs in my ears, and fragrant breaths on my brow; or a sweetly-perfumed kerchief was wafted again and again on my cheeks. Then slowly a mysterious serpent would twist her stupefying coils about me; and heaving a heavy sigh, I would lapse into insensibility, and then into a profound slumber.

One evening I decided to go out on my horse—I do not know who implored me to stay—but I would listen to no entreaties that day. My English hat and coat were resting on a rack, and I was about to take them down when a sudden whirlwind, crested with the sands of the *Susta* and the dead leaves of the Avalli hills, caught them up, and whirled them round and round, while a loud peal of merry laughter rose higher and higher, striking all the chords of mirth till it died away in the land of sunset.

I could not go out for my ride, and the next day I gave up my queer English coat and hat for good.

That day again at dead of night I heard the stifled heart-breaking sobs of some one—as if below the bed, below the floor, below the stony foundation of that gigantic palace, from the depths of a dark damp grave, a voice piteously cried and implored me: "Oh, rescue me! Break through these doors of hard illusion, deathlike slumber and fruitless dreams, place me by your side on the saddle, press me to your heart, and, riding through hills and woods and across the river, take me to the warm radiance of your sunny rooms above!"

Who am I? Oh, how can I rescue thee? What drowning beauty,

what incarnate passion shall I drag to the shore from this wild eddy of dreams? O lovely ethereal apparition! Where didst thou flourish and when? By what cool spring, under the shade of what date-groves, wast though born—in the lap of what homeless wanderer in the desert? What Bedouin snatched thee from thy mother's arms, an opening bud plucked from a wild creeper, placed thee on a horse swift as lightning, crossed the burning sands, and took thee to the slave-market of what royal city? And there, what officer of the Bad-shah, seeing the glory of thy bashful blossoming youth, paid for thee in gold, placed thee in a golden palanquin, and offered thee as a present for the seraglio of his master? And O, the history of that place! The music of the *sareng*,* the jingle of anklets, the occasional flash of daggers and the glowing wine of Shiraz poison, and the piercing flashing glance! What infinite grandeur, what endless servitude! The slave-girls to thy right and left waved the *chamar*,* as diamonds flashed from their bracelets; the Badshah, the king of kings, fell on his knees at thy snowy feet in bejewelled shoes, and outside the terrible Abyssinian eunuch, looking like a messenger of death, but clothed like an angel, stood with a naked sword in his hand! Then, O, thou flower of the desert, swept away by the blood-stained dazzling ocean of grandeur, with its foam of jealousy, its rocks and shoals of intrigue, on what shore of cruel death wast thou cast, or in what other land more splendid and more cruel?

Suddenly at this moment that crazy Meher Ali screamed out: "Stand back! Stand back!! All is false! All is false!!" I opened my eyes and saw that it was already light. My *chaprasi* came and handed me my letters, and the cook waited with a *salam* for my orders.

I said: "No, I can stay here no longer." That very day I packed up, and moved to my office. Old Karim Khan smiled a little as he saw me. I felt nettled, but said nothing, and fell to my work.

As evening approached I grew absent-minded; I felt as if I had an appointment to keep; and the work of examining the cotton accounts seemed wholly useless; even the *Nizamat*,* of the Nizam did not appear to be of much worth. Whatever belonged to the present, whatever was moving and acting and working for bread seemed trivial, meaningless, and contemptible.

I threw my pen down, closed my ledgers, got into my dog-cart, and drove away. I noticed that it stopped of itself at the gate of the

* A sort of violin.
* *Chamar*: chowrie, yak-tail.
* Royalty.

marble palace just at the hour of twilight. With quick steps I climbed the stairs, and entered the room.

A heavy silence was reigning within. The dark rooms were looking sullen as if they had taken offence. My heart was full of contrition, but there was no one to whom I could lay it bare, or of whom I could ask forgiveness. I wandered about the dark rooms with a vacant mind. I wished I had a guitar to which I could sing to the unknown: "O fire, the poor moth that made a vain effort to fly away has come back to thee! Forgive it but this once, burn its wings and consume it in thy flame!"

Suddenly two tear-drops fell from overhead on my brow. Dark masses of clouds overcast the top of the Avalli hills that day. The gloomy woods and the sooty waters of the *Susta* were waiting in terrible suspense and in an ominous calm. Suddenly land, water, and sky shivered, and a wild tempest-blast rushed howling through the distant pathless woods, showing its lightning-teeth like a raving maniac who had broken his chains. The desolate halls of the palace banged their doors, and moaned in the bitterness of anguish.

The servants were all in the office, and there was no one to light the lamps. The night was cloudy and moonless. In the dense gloom within I could distinctly feel that a woman was lying on her face on the carpet below the bed—clasping and tearing her long dishevelled hair with desperate fingers. Blood was trickling down her fair brow, and she was now laughing a hard, harsh, mirthless laugh, now bursting into violent wringing sobs, now rending her bodice and striking at her bare bosom, as the wind roared in through the open window, and the rain poured in torrents and soaked her through and through.

All night there was no cessation of the storm or of the passionate cry. I wandered from room to room in the dark, with unavailing sorrow. Whom could I console when no one was by? Whose was this intense agony of sorrow? Whence arose this inconsolable grief?

And the mad man cried out: "Stand back! Stand back!! All is false! All is false!!"

I saw that the day had dawned, and Meher Ali was going round and round the palace with his usual cry in that dreadful weather. Suddenly it came to me that perhaps he also had once lived in that house, and that, though he had gone mad, he came there every day, and went round and round, fascinated by the weird spell cast by the marble demon.

Despite the storm and rain I ran to him and asked: "Ho, Meher Ali, what is false?"

The man answered nothing, but pushing me aside went round and round with his frantic cry, like a bird flying fascinated about the jaws of a snake, and made a desperate effort to warn himself by repeating: "Stand back! Stand back!! All is false! All is false!!"

I ran like a mad man through the pelting rain to my office, and asked Karim Khan: "Tell me the meaning of all this!"

What I gathered from that old man was this: That at one time countless unrequited passions and unsatisfied longings and lurid flames of wild blazing pleasure raged within that palace, and that the curse of all the heart-aches and blasted hopes had made its every stone thirsty and hungry, eager to swallow up like a famished ogress any living man who might chance to approach. Not one of those who lived there for three consecutive nights could escape these cruel jaws, save Meher Ali, who had escaped at the cost of his reason.

I asked: "Is there no means whatever of my release?" The old man said: "There is only one means, and that is very difficult. I will tell you what it is, but first you must hear the history of a young Persian girl who once lived in that pleasure-dome. A stranger or a more bitterly heart-rending tragedy was never enacted on this earth."

Just at this moment the coolies announced that the train was coming. So soon? We hurriedly packed up our luggage, as the train steamed in. An English gentleman, apparently just aroused from slumber, was looking out of a first-class carriage endeavouring to read the name of the station. As soon as he caught sight of our fellow-passenger, he cried, "Hallo," and took him into his own compartment. As we got into a second-class carriage, we had no chance of finding out who the man was nor what was the end of his story.

I said: "The man evidently took us for fools and imposed upon us out of fun. The story is pure fabrication from start to finish." The discussion that followed ended in a lifelong rupture between my theosophist kinsman and myself.

MARY E. WILKINS FREEMAN

The Southwest Chamber

According to the stodgily mainstream Oxford Companion to English Literature, MARY E. WILKINS FREEMAN *(1852–1930) is "distinguished for her realistic stories of New England life." How curious, therefore, that her fiction turns up repeatedly in my anthologies. Ms. Freeman, who once served as secretary to Oliver Wendell Holmes, wrote many excellent ghost stories, including "The Vacant Lot," "The Wind in the Rosebush" and "Luella Miller." The following grim drama of spiritual corruption invites favorable comparison with Nathaniel Hawthorne's darker morality tales.*

"That school-teacher from Acton is coming to-day," said Miss Sophia Gill. "I have decided to put her in the southwest chamber."

Amanda looked at her sister with an expression of mingled doubt and terror. "You don't suppose she would—" she began hesitatingly.

"Would what!" demanded Sophia sharply. Both were below the medium height and stout, but Sophia was firm where Amanda was flabby. Amanda wore a baggy old muslin (it was a hot day), and Sophia was uncompromisingly hooked up in a starched and boned cambric over her high shelving figure.

"I didn't know but she would object to sleeping in that room, as long as Aunt Harriet died there such a little while ago," faltered Amanda.

"Well," said Sophia, "of all the silly notions! If you are going to pick out rooms where nobody has died you'll have your hands full. I don't believe there's a room or a bed in this house that somebody hasn't passed away in."

"Well, I suppose I am silly to think of it, and she'd better go in there," said Amanda.

"I know she had. Now I guess you'd better go and see if any dust has settled on anything since it was cleaned, and open the west windows and let the sun in, while I see to that cake."

Amanda went to her task in the southwest chamber.

Nobody knew how this elderly woman with the untrammeled imagination of a child dreaded to enter the southwest chamber, and yet she could not have told why she had the dread. She had occupied rooms which had been once tenanted by persons now dead. But this was different. She entered and her heart beat thickly in her ears. Her hands were cold. The room was a very large one. The four windows were closed, the blinds also. The room was in a film of green gloom. The furniture loomed out vaguely. The white counterpane on the bed showed like a blank page.

Amanda crossed the room, opened one of the windows, and threw back the blind. Then the room revealed itself an apartment full of an aged and worn, but no less valid state. Pieces of old mahogany swelled forth; a peacock-patterned chintz draped the bedstead. The closet door stood ajar. There was a glimpse of purple drapery floating from a peg inside. Amanda went across and took down the garment hanging there. She wondered how her sister had happened to leave it when she cleaned the room. It was an old loose gown which had belonged to her aunt. She took it down shuddering, and closed the closet door after a fearful glance into its dark depths. It was a long closet with a strong odor of lovage. Aunt Harriet had had a habit of eating lovage and had carried it constantly in her pocket.

Amanda received the odor with a start as if before an actual presence. She was always conscious of this fragrance of lovage as she tidied the room. She spread fresh towels over the washstand and the bureau; she made the bed. Then she thought to take the purple gown from the easy chair where she had just thrown it and carry it to the garret and put it in the trunk with the other articles of the dead woman's wardrobe which had been packed away there; *but the purple gown was not on the chair!*

Amanda Gill was not a woman of strong convictions even as to her own actions. She directly thought that possibly she had been mistaken and had not removed it from the closet. She glanced at the closet door and saw with surprise that it was open, and she had thought she had closed it, but she instantly was not sure of that. So she entered the closet and looked for the purple gown. *It was not there!*

Amanda Gill went feebly out of the closet and looked at the easy chair again. The purple gown was not there! She looked wildly around the room. She went down on her trembling knees and peered under the bed, she opened the bureau drawers, she looked again in the closet. Then she stood in the middle of the floor and fairly wrung her hands.

There is a limit at which self-refutation must stop in any sane person. Amanda Gill had reached it. She knew that she had seen that purple gown in that closet; she knew that she had removed it and put it on the easy chair. She also knew that she had not taken it out of the room.

Then the thought occurred to her that possibly her sister Sophia might have entered the room unobserved while her back was turned and removed the dress. A sensation of relief came over her. Her blood seemed to flow back into its usual channels; the tension of her nerves relaxed.

"How silly I am!" she said aloud.

She hurried out and downstairs into the kitchen where Sophia was making cake, stirring with splendid circular sweeps of a wooden spoon a creamy yellow mass. Sophia looked up as her sister entered.

"Have you got it done?" said she.

"Yes," replied Amanda. Then she hesitated. A sudden terror overcame her. It did not seem as if it were at all probable that Sophia had left that foamy cake mixture a second to go to Aunt Harriet's chamber and remove that purple gown.

"Did you come up in Aunt Harriet's room while I was there?" she asked weakly.

"Of course I didn't. Why?"

"Nothing," replied Amanda.

Suddenly she realized that she could not tell her sister what had happened. She knew what Sophia would say if she told her. She dropped into a chair and began shelling the beans with nerveless fingers.

For the next hour or two the women were very busy. They kept no servant. When they had come into possession of this fine old place by the death of their aunt it had seemed a doubtful blessing. There was not a cent with which to pay for repairs and taxes and insurance. There had been a division in the old Ackley family years before. One of the daughters had married against her mother's wish, and had been disinherited. She had married a poor man by the name of Gill, and shared his humble lot in sight of her former home and her sister and mother living in prosperity, until she had borne three daughters; then she died, worn out with overwork and worry.

The mother and the elder sister had been pitiless to the last. Neither had ever spoken to her since she left her home the night of her marriage. They were hard women.

The three daughters of the disinherited sister had lived quiet and poor but not actually needy lives. Jane, the middle daughter, had married, and died in less than a year. Amanda and Sophia had taken the girl baby she left when the father married again. Sophia had taught a primary school for many years; she had saved enough to buy the little house in which they lived. Amanda had crocheted lace, and embroidered flannel, and made tidies and pincushions, and now in their late middle life had come the death of the aunt to whom they had never spoken, although they had often seen her, who had lived in solitary state in the old Ackley mansion until she was more than eighty. There had been no will, and they were the only heirs, with the exception of young Flora Scott, the daughter of the dead sister.

Sophia had promptly decided what was to be done. The small house was to be sold, and they were to move into the old Ackley house and take boarders to pay for its keeping. She scouted the idea of selling it. She had an enormous family pride.

Sophia and Amanda Gill had been living in the old Ackley house a fortnight, and they had three boarders: an elderly widow with a comfortable income, a young Congregationalist clergyman, and the middle-aged single woman who had charge of the village library. Now the school-teacher from Acton, Miss Louisa Stark, was expected for the summer.

Flora, their niece, was a very gentle girl, rather pretty, with large, serious blue eyes, a seldom smiling mouth, and smooth flaxen hair. She was delicate and very young—sixteen on her next birthday.

She came home soon now with her parcels of sugar and tea from the grocer's. She entered the kitchen gravely and deposited them on the table by which her Aunt Amanda was seated stringing beans. Flora wore an obsolete turban-shaped hat of black straw which had belonged to the dead aunt; it set high like a crown, revealing her forehead. Her dress was an ancient purple-and-white print, too long and too large, except over the chest, where it held her like a straight waistcoat.

"Flora," said Sophia, "you go up to the room that was your Great-aunt Harriet's and take the water-pitcher off the washstand and fill it with water."

"In *that* chamber?" asked Flora. Her face changed a little.

"Yes, in that chamber," returned her Aunt Sophia sharply. "Go right along."

Flora went. Very soon she returned with the blue-and-white water-pitcher and filled it carefully at the kitchen sink.

"Now be careful and not spill it," said Sophia as she went out of the room carrying it gingerly.

Then the village stage-coach was seen driving round to the front of the house. The house stood on a corner.

"Here, Amanda, you look better than I do, you go and meet her," said Sophia. "Show her right up to her room."

Amanda removed her apron hastily and obeyed. Sophia hurried with her cake. She had just put it in the oven, when the door opened and Flora entered carrying the blue water-pitcher.

"What are you bringing down that pitcher again for?" asked Sophia.

"She wants some water, and Aunt Amanda sent me," replied Flora.

"For the land sake! She hasn't used all that great pitcher full of water so quick?"

"There wasn't any water in it," replied Flora.

Her high, childish forehead was contracted slightly with a puzzled frown as she looked at her aunt.

"Didn't I see you filling the pitcher with water not ten minutes ago, I want to know?"

"Yes, ma'am."

"Let me see that pitcher." Sophia examined the pitcher. It was not only perfectly dry from top to bottom, but even a little dusty. She turned severely on the young girl. "That shows," said she, "you did not fill the pitcher at all. You let the water run at the side because you didn't want to carry it upstairs. I am ashamed of you. It's bad enough to be lazy, but when it comes to not telling the truth!"

The young girl's face broke up suddenly into piteous confusion and her blue eyes became filmy with tears.

"I did fill the pitcher, honest," she faltered. "You ask Aunt Amanda."

"I'll ask nobody. The pitcher is proof enough. Water don't go off and leave the pitcher dusty on the inside if it was put in ten minutes ago. Now you fill that pitcher quick, and carry it upstairs, and if you spill a drop there'll be something besides talk."

Flora filled the pitcher, with the tears falling over her cheeks. She snivelled softly as she went out, balancing it carefully against her slender hip. Sophia followed her up the stairs to the chamber where Miss Louisa Stark was waiting for the water to remove the soil of travel.

Louisa Stark was stout and solidly built. She was a masterly woman inured to command from years of school-teaching. She carried her swelling bulk with majesty; even her face, moist and red with the heat, lost nothing of its dignity of expression.

She was standing in the middle of the floor with an air which gave the effect of her standing upon an elevation. She turned when Sophia and Flora, carrying the water-pitcher, entered.

"This is my sister Sophia," said Amanda, tremulously.

Sophia advanced, shook hands with Miss Louisa Stark and bade her welcome and hoped she would like her room. Then she moved toward the closet. "There is a nice large closet in this room—" she said, then she stopped short.

The closet door was ajar, and a purple garment seemed suddenly to swing into view as if impelled by some wind.

"Why, here is something left in this closet," Sophia said in a mortified tone.

She pulled down the garment with a jerk, and as she did so Amanda passed her in a weak rush for the door.

"I am afraid your sister is not well," said the school-teacher from Acton. "She may be going to faint."

"She is not subject to fainting spells," replied Sophia, but she followed Amanda.

She found her in the room which they occupied together, lying on the bed, very pale and gasping. She leaned over her.

"Amanda, what is the matter? Don't you feel well?" she asked.

"I feel a little faint."

Sophia got a camphor bottle and began rubbing her sister's forehead.

"Do you feel better?" she asked.

Amanda nodded.

"I guess if you feel better I'll just get that dress of Aunt Harriet's and take it up garret."

Sophia hurried out, but soon returned.

"I want to know," she said, looking sharply and quickly around, "if I brought that purple dress in here? It isn't in that chamber, nor the closet. You aren't lying on it, are you?"

"I lay down before you came in," replied Amanda.

"So you did. Well, I'll go and look again."

Presently Amanda heard her sister's heavy step on the garret stairs. Then she returned with a queer defiant expression on her face.

"I carried it up garret after all and put it in the trunk," said she. "I declare, I forgot it. I suppose your being faint sort of put it out of my head."

Sophia's mouth was set; her eyes upon her sister's scared, agitated face were full of hard challenge.

"I must go right down and see to that cake," said she, going out of the room. "If you don't feel well, you pound on the floor with the umbrella."

Amanda looked after her. She knew that Sophia had not put that purple dress of her dead Aunt Harriet's in the trunk in the garret.

Meantime Miss Louiss Stark was settling herself in the southwest chamber. She unpacked her trunk and hung her dresses carefully in the closet. She was a very punctilious woman. She put on a black India silk dress with purple flowers. She pinned her lace at her throat with a brooch, very handsome, although somewhat obsolete—a bunch of pearl grapes on black onyx, set in gold filigree.

As she surveyed herself in the little swing-mirror surmounting the old-fashioned mahogany bureau she suddenly bent forward and looked closely at the brooch. Instead of the familiar bunch of pearl grapes on the black onyx, she saw a knot of blond-and-black hair under glass surrounded by a border of twisted gold. She felt a thrill of horror. She unpinned the brooch, and it was her own familiar one, the pearl grapes and the onyx. "How very foolish I am," she thought. She thrust the pin in the lace at her throat, and again looked at herself in the glass, and there it was again—the knot of blond-and-black hair and twisted gold.

Louisa Stark looked at her own large, firm face above the brooch and it was full of terror and dismay which were new to it. She straightway began to wonder if there could be anything wrong with her mind. She remembered that an aunt of her mother's had been insane. A sort of fury with herself possessed her. She stared at the brooch in the glass with eyes at once angry and terrified. Then she removed it again and there was her own old brooch. Finally she thrust the gold pin through the lace again, fastened it, and, turning a defiant back on the glass, went down to supper.

At the supper table she met the other boarders. She viewed the elderly widow with reserve, the clergyman with respect, the middle-aged librarian with suspicion. The latter wore a very youthful shirt-waist, and her hair in a girlish fashion, which the school-teacher, who twisted hers severely from the straining roots at the nape of the neck to the small, smooth coil at the top, condemned as straining after effects no longer hers by right.

The librarian, who had a quick alertness of manner, addressed her.

"What room are you in, Miss Stark?" said she.

"I am at a loss how to designate the room," replied Miss Stark stiffly.

The librarian, whose name was Eliza Lippincott, turned abruptly to Miss Amanda Gill, over whose delicate face a curious color compounded of flush and pallor was stealing.

"What room did your aunt die in, Miss Amanda?" asked she abruptly.

Amanda cast a terrified glance at her sister, who was serving a second plate of pudding for the minister.

"That room," she replied feebly.

"That's what I thought," said the librarian with a certain triumph. "I calculated that must be the room she died in, for it's the best room in the house, and you haven't put anybody in it before. Somehow the room that anybody has died in lately is generally the last room anybody is put in."

The young minister looked up from his pudding. He was very spiritual, but he had had poor picking in his previous boarding place, and he could not help a certain abstract enjoyment over Miss Gill's cooking.

"You certainly, Miss Lippincott," he remarked with his gentle, almost caressing inflection of tone, "do not for a minute believe that a higher power would allow any manifestation on the part of a disembodied spirit—who we trust is in her heavenly home—to harm one of His servants?"

"Oh, Mr. Dunn, of course not," replied Eliza Lippincott with a blush. "Of course not. I never meant to imply—"

"Of course dear Miss Harriet Gill was a professing Christian," remarked the widow, "and I don't suppose a professing Christian would come back and scare folks if she could. I wouldn't be a mite afraid to sleep in the room; I'd rather have it than the one I've got." Then she turned to Miss Stark. "Any time you feel timid in that room, I'm ready and willing to change with you," said she.

"Thank you. I have no desire to change. I am perfectly satisfied with my room," replied Miss Stark with freezing dignity, which was thrown away upon the widow.

Miss Louisa Stark did not sit down in the parlor with the other boarders after dinner. She went straight to her room. She felt tired after her journey, and meditated a loose wrapper and writing a few letters quietly before she went to bed. When she entered the southwest chamber she saw against the wall paper directly facing the door the waist of her best black satin dress hung over a picture.

"That is very strange," she said to herself, and a thrill of vague horror came over her. She knew or thought she knew, that she had put that black satin dress waist away nicely folded between towels in her trunk.

She took down the black waist and laid it on the bed preparatory to folding it, but when she attempted to do so she discovered that the two sleeves were firmly sewed together. Louisa Stark stared at the sewed sleeves. "What does this mean?" she asked herself. She examined the sewing carefully; the stitches were small, and even, and firm, of black silk.

She moved toward the door. For a moment she thought that this was something legitimate, about which she might demand information; then she became doubtful. Suppose she herself had done this absurd thing, or suppose that she had not, what was to hinder the others from thinking so—what was to hinder a doubt being cast upon her own memory and reasoning powers?

Louisa Stark had been on the verge of a nervous breakdown in spite of her iron constitution and her great will power. No woman can teach school for forty years with absolute impunity. She was more credulous as to her own possible failings than she had ever been in her whole life. She was cold with horror and terror, and yet not so much horror and terror of the supernatural as of her own self. The weakness of belief in the supernatural was nearly impossible for this strong nature. She could more easily believe in her own failing powers.

She started toward the mirror to unfasten her dress, then she remembered the strange circumstance of the brooch, and stopped short. Then she straightened herself defiantly and marched up to the bureau and looked in the glass. She saw reflected therein, fastening the lace at her throat, the old-fashioned thing of a large oval, a knot of fair and black hair under the glass, set in a rim of twisted gold. She unfastened it with trembling fingers and looked at it. It was her own brooch, the cluster of pearl grapes on black onyx. Louisa Stark placed the trinket in its little box on the nest of pink cotton and put it away in the bureau drawer. Only death could disturb her habit of order.

Her fingers were so cold they felt fairly numb as she unfastened her dress; she staggered when she slipped it over her head. She went to the closet to hang it up and recoiled. A strong smell of lovage came to her nostrils, a purple gown near the door swung softly against her face as if impelled by some wind from within. All the pegs were filled with garments not her own, mostly of somber black.

Suddenly Louisa Stark recovered her nerve. This, she told herself, was something distinctly tangible. Somebody had been taking liberties with her wardrobe. Somebody had been hanging someone else's clothes in her closet. She hastily slipped on her dress again and marched straight down stairs.

She found Sophia Gill standing by the kitchen table kneading dough with dignity.

"Miss Gill," said Miss Stark, with her utmost school-teacher manner, "I wish to inquire why you have had my clothes removed from the closet in my room and others substituted?"

Sophia Gill stood, with her hand fast in the dough, regarding her. Her own face paled slowly and reluctantly, her mouth stiffened.

"I'll go upstairs with you, Miss Stark," said she, "and see what the trouble is." She spoke stiffly, with constrained civility.

Sophia and Louisa Stark went up to the southwest chamber. The closet door was shut. Sophia threw it open, then she looked at Miss Stark. On the pegs hung the school-teacher's own garments in orderly array.

"I can't see that there is anything wrong," remarked Sophia grimly.

Miss Stark sank down on the nearest chair. She saw her own clothes in the closet. She knew there had been no time for any human being to remove those which she thought she had seen and put hers in their places. She knew it was impossible. Again the awful horror of herself overwhelmed her.

She muttered something, she scarcely knew what. Sophia then went out of the room. In the morning Miss Stark did not go down to breakfast, and left before noon.

Directly the widow, Mrs. Elvira Simmons, knew that the school-teacher had gone, and the southwest room was vacant, she begged to have it in exchange for her own. Sophia hesitated a moment.

"I have no objections, Mrs. Simmons," said she, "if—"

"If what?" asked the widow.

"If you have common sense enough not to keep fussing because the room happens to be the one my aunt died in," said Sophia bluntly.

"Fiddlesticks!" said the widow.

That very afternoon she moved into the southwest chamber.

The widow was openly triumphant over her new room. She talked a deal about it at the dinner-table.

"You are sure you don't feel afraid of ghosts?" said the librarian. "I wouldn't sleep in that room after—" She checked herself with an eye on the minister.

"After what?" asked the widow.

"Nothing," replied Eliza Lippincott in an embarrassed fashion.

"You did see or hear something—now what was it, I want to know?" said the widow that evening when they were alone in the parlor. The minister had gone to make a call.

"Well," said Eliza hesitatingly, "if you'll promise not to tell."

"Yes, I promise; what was it?"

"Well, one day last week just before the school-teacher came, I went into that room to see if there were any clouds. I wanted to wear my gray dress, and I was afraid it was going to rain, so I wanted to look at the sky at all points, and— You know that chintz over the bed, and the valance? What pattern should you say it was?"

"Why, peacocks on a blue ground. Good land, I shouldn't think anyone who had ever seen that would forget it."

"Well, when I went in there that afternoon it was not peacocks on a blue ground; it was great red roses on a yellow ground."

"Did Miss Sophia have it changed?"

"No. I went in there again an hour later and the peacocks were there."

The widow stared at her a moment, then she began to laugh rather hysterically.

"Well," said she, "I guess I shan't give up my nice room for any such tomfoolery as that. I guess I would just as soon have red roses on a yellow ground as peacocks on a blue; but there's no use talking, you couldn't have seen straight. How could such a thing have happened?"

"I don't know," said Eliza Lippincott, "but I know I wouldn't sleep in that room if you'd give me a thousand dollars."

When Mrs. Simmons went to the southwest chamber that night, she cast a glance at the bed-hanging. There were the peacocks on the blue ground. She gave a contemptuous thought of Eliza Lippincott.

But just before Mrs. Simmons was ready to get into bed she looked again at the hangings, and there were the red roses on the yellow ground instead of the peacocks on blue. She looked long and sharply. Then she crossed the room, turned her back to the bed, and looked out at the night from the east window. It was clear, and the full moon had just risen. She watched it a moment sailing over the dark blue in its nimbus of gold. Then she looked around at the bed hangings. She still saw the red roses on the yellow ground.

Mrs. Simmons was struck in the most vulnerable point. This apparent contradiction of the reasonable as manifested in such a commonplace thing as the chintz of a bed-hanging affected this ordinary, unimaginative woman as no ghostly appearance could have done. Those red roses on the yellow ground were to her much more ghastly than any strange figure clad in the white robes of the grave entering the room.

She took a step toward the door, then she turned with a resolute air. "As for going downstairs and owning up I'm scared and having that Lippincott girl crowing over me, I won't for any red roses instead of peacocks. I guess they can't hurt me, and as long as we've both of us seen 'em I guess we can't both be getting loony," she said.

Mrs. Elvira Simmons blew out her light and got into bed. After a little she fell asleep.

But she was awakened about midnight by a strange sensation in her throat. She had dreamed that someone with long white fingers was strangling her, and she saw bending over her the face of an old woman in a white cap. When she waked there was no old woman, the room was almost as light as day in the full moonlight, and looked very peaceful; but the strangling sensation continued, and besides that, her face and ears felt muffled. She put up her hand and felt that her head was covered with a ruffled nightcap tied under her chin so tightly that it was exceedingly uncomfortable. A great qualm of horror shot over her. She tore the thing off frantically and flung it from her with a convulsive effort as if it had been a spider. She sprang out of bed and was going toward the door when she stopped.

It suddenly occurred to her that Eliza Lippincott might have entered the room and tied on the cap while she was asleep. Then she tried to open the door, but to her astonishment found that it was bolted on the inside. "I must have locked it after all," she reflected with wonder, for she never locked her door.

She went toward the spot where she had thrown the cap—she had stepped over it on her way to the door—but it was not there. She searched the whole room, lighting the lamp, but she could not find the cap. Finally she gave it up. She extinguished her lamp and went back to bed. She fell asleep again, to be again awakened in the same fashion. That time she tore off the cap as before, but she did not fling it on the floor. Instead, she held to it with a fierce grip. Her blood was up.

Holding fast to the flimsy white thing, she sprang out of bed, ran to the window which was open, slipped the screen, and flung it out; but a sudden gust of wind, though the night was calm, arose and it floated back in her face. She clutched at it. It eluded her clutching fingers. Then she did not see it at all. She examined the floor, she lighted her lamp again and searched, but there was no sign of it.

Mrs. Simmons was then in such a rage that all terror had disappeared for the time. To be baffled like this and resisted by something which was nothing to her straining senses filled her with intensest resentment.

Finally she got back into bed again; she did not go to sleep. She felt strangely drowsy, but she fought against it. She was wide awake, staring at the moonlight, when she suddenly felt the soft white strings of the thing tighten round her throat and realized that her enemy was again upon her. She seized the strings, untied them, twitched off the cap, ran with it to the table where her scissors lay and furiously cut it into small bits. She cut and tore, feeling an insane fury of gratification.

She tossed the bits of muslin into a basket and went back to bed. Almost immediately she felt the soft strings tighten round her throat. Then at last she yielded, vanquished. This new refutal of all the laws of reason by which she had learned, as it were, to spell her theory of life was too much for her equilibrium. She pulled off the clinging strings feebly, drew the thing from her head, slid weakly out of bed, caught up her wrapper and hastened out of the room. She went noiselessly along the hall to her own old room, entered it, got into her familiar bed, and lay there the rest of the night shuddering and listening, and if she dozed, waking with a start at the feeling of the pressure upon her throat—to find that it was not there, yet still unable to shake off entirely the horror.

She went down to breakfast the next morning with an imperturbable face. When asked by Eliza Lippincott how she had slept, she replied with an appearance of calmness which was bewildering that she had not slept very well. She never did sleep very well in a new bed, and she thought she would go back to her old room.

Eliza Lippincott was not deceived, however; neither were the Gill sisters, nor the young girl Flora. Eliza Lippincott spoke out bluntly.

"You needn't talk to me about sleeping well," said she. "I know something queer happened in that room last night by the way you act."

They all looked at Mrs. Simmons inquiringly—the librarian with malicious curiosity and triumph, the minister with sad incredulity, Sophia Gill with fear and indignation, Amanda and the young girl with unmixed terror. The widow bore herself with dignity.

"I saw nothing nor heard nothing which I trust could not have been accounted for in some rational manner," said she.

"What was it?" persisted Eliza Lippincott.

"I do not wish to discuss the matter any further," replied Mrs. Simmons shortly. Then she passed her plate for more creamed potato. She felt that she would die before she confessed to the ghastly absurdity of that nightcap, or to having been disturbed by the flight of peacocks off a blue field of chintz. She left the whole matter so vague that in a fashion she came off the mistress of the situation.

That afternoon the young minister, John Dunn, went to Sophia Gill and requested permission to occupy the southwest chamber that night.

"I don't ask to have my effects moved there," said he, "for I could scarcely afford a room so much superior to the one I now occupy, but I should like, if you please, to sleep there to-night for the purpose of refuting in my own person any unfortunate superstition which may have obtained root here."

Sophia Gill thanked the minister gratefully and eagerly accepted his offer.

That night about twelve o'clock the Reverend John Dunn essayed to go to his nightly slumber in the southwest chamber. He had been sitting up until that hour preparing his sermon.

He traversed the hall with a little night-lamp in his hand; he opened the door of the southwest chamber and essayed to enter. He might as well have essayed to enter the solid side of a house. He could look into the room full of soft lights and shadows under the moonlight which streamed in at the windows. He could see the bed in which he had expected to pass the night, but he could not enter. Whenever he strove to do so, he had a curious sensation as if he were trying to press against an invisible person who met him with a force of opposition impossible to overcome. The minister was not an athletic man, yet he had considerable strength. He squared his elbows, set his mouth hard, and strove to push his way through into the room. The opposition which he met was as sternly and mutely terrible as the rocky fastness of a mountain in his way.

For a half-hour John Dunn, doubting, raging, overwhelmed with spiritual agony as to the state of his own soul rather than fear, strove to enter the southwest chamber. He was simply powerless against this uncanny obstacle. Finally a great horror as of evil itself came over him. He was a nervous man and very young. He fairly fled to his own chamber and locked himself in like a terror-stricken girl.

The next morning he went to Miss Gill and told her frankly what had happened.

"What it is I know not, Miss Sophia," said he, "but I firmly believe, against my will, that there is in that room some accursed evil power at work of which modern faith and modern science know nothing."

Miss Sophia Gill listened with grimly lowering face.

"I think I will sleep in that room myself to-night," she said, when the minister had finished.

There were occasions when Miss Sophia Gill could put on a manner of majesty, and she did now.

It was ten o'clock that night when Sophia Gill entered the southwest chamber. She had told her sister what she intended doing and had been proof against her tearful entreaties. Amanda was charged not to tell the young girl, Flora.

"There is no use in frightening that child over nothing," said Sophia.

Sophia, when she entered the southwest chamber, set the lamp which she carried on the bureau, and began moving about the room, pulling down the curtains, taking the nice white counterpane off the bed, and preparing generally for the night.

As she did so, moving with great coolness and deliberation, she became conscious that she was thinking some thoughts that were foreign to her. She began remembering what she could not have remembered, since she was not then born: the trouble over her mother's marriage, the bitter opposition, the shutting the door upon her, the ostracizing her from heart and home. She became aware of a most singular sensation of bitter resentment, and not against the mother and sister who had so treated her own mother, but against her own mother herself, and then she became aware of a like bitterness extended to her own self. She felt malignant toward her mother as a young girl whom she remembered, though she could not have remembered, and she felt malignant toward her own self, and her sister Amanda, and Flora. Evil suggestions surged in her brain—suggestions which turned her heart to stone and which still fascinated her. And all the time by a sort of double consciousness she knew that what she thought was strange and not due to her own volition. She knew that she was thinking the thoughts of some other person, and she knew who. She felt herself possessed.

But there was tremendous strength in the woman's nature. She had inherited strength for good and righteous self-assertion from the evil strength of her ancestors. They had turned their own weapons against themselves. She made an effort which seemed more than human, and was conscious that the hideous thing was gone from her. She thought her own thoughts. Then she scouted to herself the idea of anything supernatural about the terrific experience. "I am imagining everything," she told herself.

She went on with her preparations; she went to the bureau to take down her hair. She looked in the glass and saw, instead of her own face, middle-aged and good to see, with its expression of a life of honesty and good-will to others and patience under trials, the face of a very old woman scowling forever with unceasing hatred and misery at herself and all others, at life and death, at that which had been and that which was to come. She saw, instead of her own face in the glass, the face of her dead Aunt Harriet, topping her own shoulders in her own well-known dress!

Sophia Gill left the room. She went into the one which she shared with her sister Amanda. Amanda looked up and saw her standing there with her handkerchief pressed to her face.

"Oh, Sophia, let me call in somebody. Is your face hurt? Sophia, what is the matter with your face?" fairly shrieked Amanda.

Suddenly Sophia took the handkerchief from her face.

"Look at me, Amanda Gill," she said.

Amanda looked, shrinking.

"What is it? Oh, what is it? You don't look hurt. What is it, Sophia?"

"What do you see?"

"Why, I see you."

"Me?"

"Yes, you. What did you think I would see?"

Sophia Gill looked at her sister.

"Never as long as I live will I tell you what I thought you would see, and you must never ask me," said she. "I am going to sell this house."

FITZ-JAMES O'BRIEN

The Lost Room

FITZ-JAMES O'BRIEN *(1828–1862) was an Irish writer who died of an infected wound while fighting on the Union side in the American Civil War. His well-known shivery tales and poems (some of them precursors of modern science fiction) include "What Was It?," "The Demon of the Gibbet," "The Diamond Lens" and "The Wonder-Smith." Difficult to describe and, once read, impossible to forget, "The Lost Room" is indeed a Miscellaneous Nightmare!*

It was oppressively warm. The sun had long disappeared, but seemed to have left its vital spirit of heat behind it. The air rested; the leaves of the acacia-trees that shrouded my windows hung plumb-like on their delicate stalks. The smoke of my cigar scarce rose above my head, but hung about me in a pale blue cloud, which I had to dissipate with languid waves of my hand. My shirt was open at the throat, and my chest heaved laboriously in the effort to catch some breaths of fresher air. The noises of the city seemed to be wrapped in slumber, and the shrilling of the mosquitoes was the only sound that broke the stillness.

As I lay with my feet elevated on the back of a chair, wrapped in that peculiar frame of mind in which thought assumes a species of lifeless motion, the strange fancy seized me of making a languid inventory of the principal articles of furniture in my room. It was a task well suited to the mood in which I found myself. Their forms were duskily defined in the dim twilight that floated shadowily through the chamber; it was no labor to note and particularize each, and from the place where I sat I could command a view of all my possessions without even turning my head.

There was, *imprimis*, that ghostly lithograph by Calame. It was a mere black spot on the white wall, but my inner vision scrutinized every detail of the picture. A wild, desolate, midnight heath, with a spectral oak-tree in the centre of the foreground. The wind blows fiercely, and the jagged branches, clothed scantily with ill-grown leaves, are swept to the left continually by its giant force. A formless wrack of clouds streams across the awful sky, and the rain sweeps almost parallel with the horizon. Beyond, the heath stretches off into endless blackness, in the extreme of which either fancy or art has conjured up some undefinable shapes that seem riding into space. At the base of the huge oak stands a shrouded figure. His mantle is wound by the blast in tight folds around his form, and the long cock's feather in his hat is blown upright, till it seems as if it stood on end with fear. His features are not visible, for he has grasped his cloak with both hands, and drawn it from either side across his face. The picture is seemingly objectless. It tells no tale, but there is a weird power about it that haunts one.

Next to the picture comes the round blot that hangs below it, which I know to be a smoking-cap. It has my coat of arms embroidered on the front, and for that reason I never wear it; though, when properly arranged on my head, with its long blue silken tassel hanging down by my cheek, I believe it becomes me well. I remember the time when it was in the course of manufacture. I remember the tiny little hands that pushed the colored silks so nimbly through the cloth that was stretched on the embroidery-frame—the vast trouble I was put to get a colored copy of my armorial bearings for the heraldic work which was to decorate the front of the band—the pursings up of the little mouth, and the contractions of the young forehead, as their possessor plunged into a profound sea of cogitation touching the way in which the cloud should be represented from which the armed hand, that is my crest, issues—the heavenly moment when the tiny hands placed it on my head, in a position that I could not bear for more than a few seconds, and I, king-like, immediately assumed my royal prerogative after the coronation, and instantly levied a tax on my only subject, which was, however, not paid unwillingly. Ah, the cap is there, but the embroiderer has fled; for Atropos was severing the web of life above her head while she was weaving that silken shelter for mine!

How uncouthly the huge piano that occupies the corner at the left of the door looms out in the uncertain twilight! I neither play nor sing, yet I own a piano. It is a comfort to me to look at it, and to feel that the music is there, although I am not able to break the spell that binds it. It is pleasant to know that Bellini and Mozart, Cimarosa, Porpora, Gluck, and all such—or at least their souls—sleep in that unwieldy case. There lie embalmed, as it were, all operas, sonatas, oratorios, notturnos, marches, songs, and dances, that ever climbed into existence through the four bars that wall in a melody. Once I was entirely repaid for the investment of my funds in that instrument which I never use. Blokeeta, the composer, came to see me. Of course his instincts urged him as irresistibly to my piano as if some magnetic power lay within it compelling him to approach. He tuned it, he played on it. All night long, until the gray and spectral dawn rose out of the depths of the midnight, he sat and played, and I lay smoking by the window listening. Wild, unearthly, and sometimes insufferably painful, were the improvisations of Blokeeta. The chords of the instrument seemed breaking with anguish. Lost souls shrieked in his dismal preludes; the half-heard utterances of spirits in pain, that groped at inconceivable distances from anything lovely or harmonious, seemed to rise dimly up out of the waves of sound that gathered under his hands. Melancholy human love wandered out on distant heaths, or beneath dank and gloomy cypresses, murmuring its unanswered sorrow, or hateful gnomes sported and sang in the stagnant swamps, triumphing in unearthly tones over the knight whom they had lured to his death. Such was Blokeeta's night's entertainment; and when he at length closed the piano, and hurried away through the cold morning, he left a memory about the instrument from which I could never escape.

Those snowshoes that hang in the space between the mirror and the door recall Canadian wanderings—a long race through the dense forests, over the frozen snow, through whose brittle crust the slender hoofs of the caribou that we were pursuing sank at every step, until the poor creature despairingly turned at bay in a small juniper coppice, and we heartlessly shot him down. And I remember how Gabriel, the *habitant*, and François, the halfbreed, cut his throat, and how the hot blood rushed out in a torrent over the snowy soil; and I recall the snow *cabane* that Gabriel built, where we all three slept so warmly; and the great fire that glowed at our feet, painting all kinds of demoniac shapes on the black screen of forest that lay without; and the deer-steaks that we roasted for our breakfast; and the savage drunkenness of Gabriel in the morning, he having been privately drinking out of my brandy-flask all the night long.

That long, haftless dagger that dangles over the mantelpiece makes my heart swell. I found it, when a boy, in a hoary old castle in which one of my maternal ancestors once lived. That same ancestor —who, by the way, yet lives in history—was a strange old sea-king, who dwelt on the extremest point of the southwestern coast of Ireland. He owned the whole of that fertile island called Inniskeiran, which directly faces Cape Clear, where between them the Atlantic rolls furiously, forming what the fishermen of the place call "the Sound." An awful place in winter is that same Sound. On certain days no boat can live there for a moment, and Cape Clear is frequently cut off for days from any communication with the mainland.

This old sea-king—Sir Florence O'Driscoll by name—passed a stormy life. From the summit of his castle he watched the ocean, and when any richly laden vessels, bound from the south to the industrious Galway merchants, hove in sight, Sir Florence hoisted the sails of his galley, and it went hard with him if he did not tow into harbor ship and crew. In this way, he lived; not a very honest mode of livelihood, certainly, according to our modern ideas, but quite reconcilable with the morals of the time. As may be supposed, Sir Florence got into trouble. Complaints were laid against him at the English court by the plundered merchants, and the Irish viking set out for London, to plead his own cause before good Queen Bess, as she was called. He had one powerful recommendation: he was a marvelously handsome man. Not Celtic by descent, but half Spanish, half Danish in blood, he had the great northern stature with the regular features, flashing eyes, and dark hair of the Iberian race. This may account for the fact that his stay at the English court was much longer than was necessary, as also for the tradition, which a local historian mentions, that the English Queen evinced a preference for the Irish chieftain, of other nature than that usually shown by monarch to subject.

Previous to his departure, Sir Florence had intrusted the care of his property to an Englishman named Hull. During the long absence of the knight, this person managed to ingratiate himself with the local authorities, and gain their favor so far that they were willing to support him in almost any scheme. After a protracted stay, Sir Florence, pardoned of all his misdeeds, returned to his home. Home no longer. Hull was in possession, and refused to yield an acre of the lands he had so nefariously acquired. It was no use appealing to the law, for its officers were in the opposite interest. It was no use appealing to the Queen, for she had another lover, and had forgotten the poor Irish knight by this time; and so the viking passed the best portion of his life in unsuccessful attempts to reclaim his vast estates, and was eventually, in his old age, obliged to content himself with his castle by the sea and the island of Inniskeiran, the only spot of which the usurper was unable to deprive him. So this old story of my kinsman's fate looms up out of the darkness that enshrouds that haftless dagger hanging on the wall.

It was somewhat after the foregoing fashion that I dreamily made the inventory of my personal property. As I turned my eyes on each object, one after the other—or the places where they lay, for the room was now so dark that it was almost impossible to see with any distinctness—a crowd of memories connected with each rose up before me, and, perforce, I had to indulge them. So I proceeded but slowly, and at last my cigar shortened to a hot and bitter morsel that I could barely hold between my lips, while it seemed to me that the night grew each moment more insufferably oppressive. While I was revolving some impossible means of cooling my wretched body, the cigar stump began to burn my lips. I flung it angrily through the open window, and stooped out to watch it falling. It first lighted on the leaves of the acacia, sending out a spray of red sparkles, then, rolling off, it fell plump on the dark walk in the garden, faintly illuminating for a moment the dusky trees and breathless flowers. Whether it was the contrast between the red flash of the cigar-stump and the silent darkness of the garden, or whether it was that I detected by the sudden light a faint waving of the leaves, I know not; but something suggested to me that the garden was cool. I will take a turn there, thought I, just as I am; it cannot be warmer than this room, and however still the atmosphere, there is always a feeling of liberty and spaciousness in the open air, that partially supplies one's wants. With this idea running through my head, I arose, lit another cigar, and passed out into the long, intricate corridors that led to the main staircase. As I crossed the threshold of my room, with what a different feeling I should have passed it had I known that I was never to set foot in it again!

I lived in a very large house, in which I occupied two rooms on the second floor. The house was old-fashioned, and all the floors communicated by a huge circular staircase that wound up through the centre of the building, while at every landing long, rambling corridors stretched off into mysterious nooks and corners. This palace of mine was very high, and its resources, in the way of crannies and windings, seemed to be interminable. Nothing seemed to stop anywhere. Cul-de-sacs were unknown on the premises. The corridors and passages, like mathematical lines, seemed capable of indefinite extensions, and the object of the architect must have been to erect an edifice in which people might go ahead forever. The whole place was gloomy, not so much because it was large, but because an unearthly nakedness seemed to pervade the structure. The staircases, corridors, halls, and vestibules all partook of a desert-like desolation. There was nothing on the walls to break the sombre monotony of those long vistas of shade. No carvings on the wainscoting, no moulded masks peering down from the simply severe cornices, no marble vases on the landings. There was an eminent dreariness and want of life—so rare in an American establishment—all over the abode. It was Hood's haunted house put in order and newly painted. The servants, too, were shadowy, and chary of their visits. Bells rang three times before the gloomy chambermaid could be induced to present herself; and the Negro waiter, a ghoul-like looking creature from Congo, obeyed the summons only when one's patience was exhausted or one's want satisfied in some other way. When he did come, one felt sorry that he had not stayed away altogether, so sullen and savage did he appear. He moved along the echoless floors with a slow, noiseless shamble, until his dusky figure, advancing from the gloom, seemed like some reluctant afreet, compelled by the superior power of his master to disclose himself. When the doors of all the chambers were closed, and no light illuminated the long corridor save the red, unwholesome glare of a small oil lamp on a table at the end, where late lodgers lit their candles, one could not by any possibility conjure up a sadder or more desolate prospect.

Yet the house suited me. Of meditative and sedentary habits, I enjoyed the extreme quiet. There were but few lodgers, from which I infer that the landlord did not drive a very thriving trade; and these, probably oppressed by the sombre spirit of the place, were quiet and ghost-like in their movements. The proprietor I scarcely ever saw. My bills were deposited by unseen hands every month on my table, while I was out walking or riding, and my pecuniary response was intrusted to the attendant afreet. On the whole, when the bustling wideawake spirit of New York is taken into consideration, the sombre, half-vivified character of the house in which I lived was an anomaly that no one appreciated better than I who lived there.

I felt my way down the wide, dark staircase in my pursuit of zephyrs. The garden, as I entered it, did feel somewhat cooler than my own room, and I puffed my cigar along the dim, cypress-shrouded walks with a sensation of comparative relief. It was very dark. The tall-growing flowers that bordered the path were so wrapped in gloom as to present the aspect of solid pyramidal masses, all the details of leaves and blossoms being buried in an embracing darkness, while the trees had lost all form, and seemed like masses of overhanging cloud. It was a place and time to excite the imagination; for in the impenetrable cavities of endless gloom there was room for the most riotous fancies to play at will. I walked and walked, and the echoes of my footsteps on the ungravelled and mossy path suggested a double feeling. I felt alone and yet in company at the same time. The solitariness of the place made itself distinct enough in the still-ness, broken alone by the hollow reverberations of my step, while those very reverberations seemed to imbue me with an undefined feeling that I was not alone. I was not, therefore, much startled when I was suddenly accosted from beneath the solid darkness of an im-mense cypress by a voice saying, "Will you give me a light, sir?"

"Certainly," I replied, trying in vain to distinguish the speaker amidst the impenetrable dark.

Somebody advanced, and I held out my cigar. All I could gather definitely about the individual who thus accosted me was that he must have been of extremely small stature; for I, who am by no means an overgrown man, had to stoop considerably in handing him my cigar. The vigorous puff that he gave his own lighted up my Havana for a moment, and I fancied that I caught a glimpse of a pale, weird countenance, immersed in a background of long, wild hair. The flash was, however, so momentary that I could not even say certainly whether this was an actual impression or the mere ef-fort of imagination to embody that which the senses had failed to distinguish.

"Sir, you are out late," said this unknown to me, as he, with half-uttered thanks, handed me back my cigar, for which I had to grope in the gloom.

"Not later than usual," I replied, dryly.

"Hum! you are fond of late wanderings, then?"

"That is just as the fancy seizes me."

"Do you live here?"

"Yes."

"Queer house, isn't it?"

"I have only found it quiet."

"Hum! But you *will* find it queer, take my word for it." This was earnestly uttered; and I felt at the same time a bony finger laid on my arm, that cut it sharply like a blunted knife.

"I cannot take your word for any such assertion," I replied, rudely, shaking off the bony finger with an irrepressible motion of disgust.

"No offence, no offence," muttered my unseen companion rapidly, in a strange, subdued voice, that would have been shrill had it been louder; "your being angry does not alter the matter. You will find it a queer house. Everybody finds it a queer house. Do you know who live there?"

"I never busy myself, sir, about other people's affairs," I answered sharply, for the individual's manner, combined with my utter uncertainty as to his appearance, oppressed me with an irksome longing to be rid of him.

"O, you don't? Well, I do. I know what they are—well, well, well!" and as he pronounced the three last words his voice rose with each, until, with the last, it reached a shrill shriek that echoed horribly among the lonely walks. "Do you know what they eat?" he continued.

"No, sir—nor care."

"O, but you will care. You must care. You shall care. I'll tell you what they are. They are enchanters. They are ghouls. They are cannibals. Did you never remark their eyes, and how they gloated on you when you passed? Did you never remark the food that they served up at your table? Did you never in the dead of night hear muffled and unearthly footsteps gliding along the corridors, and stealthy hands turning the handle of your door? Does not some magnetic influence fold itself continually around you when they pass, and send a thrill through spirit and body, and a cold shiver that no sunshine will chase away? O, you have! You have felt all these things! I know it!"

The earnest rapidity, the subdued tones, the eagerness of accent, with which all this was uttered, impressed me most uncomfortably. It really seemed as if I could recall all those weird occurrences and influences of which he spoke; and I shuddered in spite of myself in the midst of the impenetrable darkness that surrounded me.

"Hum!" said I, assuming, without knowing it, a confidential tone, "may I ask how you know these things?"

"How I know them? Because I am their enemy; because they

tremble at my whisper; because I follow upon their track with the perseverance of a bloodhound and the stealthiness of a tiger; because—because—I was *of* them once!"

"Wretch!" I cried excitedly, for involuntarily his eager tones had wrought me up to a high pitch of spasmodic nervousness, "then you mean to say that you—"

As I uttered this word, obeying an uncontrollable impulse, I stretched forth my hand in the direction of the speaker and made a blind clutch. The tips of my fingers seemed to touch a surface as smooth as glass, that glided suddenly from under them. A sharp, angry hiss sounded through the gloom, followed by a whirring noise, as if some projectile passed rapidly by, and the next moment I felt instinctively that I was alone.

A most disagreeable feeling instantly assailed me—a prophetic instinct that some terrible misfortune menaced me; an eager and overpowering anxiety to get back to my own room without loss of time. I turned and ran blindly along the dark cypress alley, every dusky clump of flowers that rose blackly in the borders making my heart each moment cease to beat. The echoes of my own footsteps seemed to redouble and assume the sounds of unknown pursuers following fast upon my track. The boughs of lilac-bushes and syringas, that here and there stretched partly across the walk, seemed to have been furnished suddenly with hooked hands that sought to grasp me as I flew by, and each moment I expected to behold some awful and impassable barrier fall across my track and wall me up forever.

At length I reached the wide entrance. With a single leap I sprang up the four or five steps that formed the stoop, and dashed along the hall, up the wide, echoing stairs, and again along the dim, funereal corridors until I paused, breathless and panting, at the door of my room. Once so far, I stopped for an instant and leaned heavily against one of the panels, panting lustily after my late run. I had, however, scarcely rested my whole weight against the door, when it suddenly gave way, and I staggered in headforemost. To my utter astonishment the room I had left in profound darkness was now a blaze of light. So intense was the illumination that, for a few seconds while the pupils of my eyes were contracting under the sudden change, I saw absolutely nothing save the dazzling glare. This fact in itself, coming on me with such utter suddenness, was sufficient to prolong my confusion, and it was not until after several minutes had elapsed that I perceived the room was not only illuminated, but occupied. And such occupants! Amazement at the scene took such possession of me that I was incapable of either moving or uttering a word. All that I could do was to lean against the wall, and stare blankly at the strange picture.

It might have been a scene out of Faublas, or Grammont's Memoirs, or happened in some palace of Minister Fouque.

Round a large table in the centre of the room, where I had left a studentlike litter of books and papers, were seated a half a dozen persons. Three were men and three were women. The table was heaped with a prodigality of luxuries. Luscious eastern fruits were piled up in silver filigree vases, through whose meshes their glowing rinds shone in the contrasts of a thousand hues. Small silver dishes that Benvenuto might have designed, filled with succulent and aromatic meats, were distributed upon a cloth of snowy damask. Bottles of every shape, slender ones from the Rhine, stout fellows from Holland, sturdy ones from Spain, and quaint basket-woven flasks from Italy, absolutely littered the board. Drinking-glasses of every size and hue filled up the interstices, and the thirsty German flagon stood side by side with the aerial bubbles of Venetian glass that rest so lightly on their threadlike stems. An odor of luxury and sensuality floated through the apartment. The lamps that burned in every direction seemed to diffuse a subtle incense on the air, and in a large vase that stood on the floor I saw a mass of magnolias, tuberoses, and jasmines grouped together, stifling each other with their honeyed and heavy fragrance.

The inhabitants of my room seemed beings well suited to so sensual an atmosphere. The women were strangely beautiful, and all were attired in dresses of the most fantastic devices and brilliant hues. Their figures were round, supple, and elastic; their eyes dark and languishing; their lips full, ripe, and of the richest bloom. The three men wore half-masks, so that all I could distinguish were heavy jaws, pointed beards, and brawny throats that rose like massive pillars out of their doublets. All six lay reclining on Roman couches about the table, drinking down the purple wines in large draughts, and tossing back their heads and laughing wildly.

I stood, I suppose, for some three minutes, with my back against the wall staring vacantly at the bacchanal vision, before any of the revellers appeared to notice my presence. At length, without any expression to indicate whether I had been observed from the beginning or not, two of the women arose from their couches, and, approaching, took each a hand and led me to the table. I obeyed their motions mechanically. I sat on a couch between them as they indicated. I unresistingly permitted them to wind their arms about my neck.

"You must drink," said one, pouring out a large glass of red wine, "here is Clos Vougeot of a rare vintage; and here," pushing a flask of amber-hued wine before me, "is Lachryma Christi."

"You must eat," said the other, drawing the silver dishes toward her. "Here are cutlets stewed with olives, and here are slices of a *filet* stuffed with bruised sweet chestnuts"—and as she spoke, she, without waiting for a reply, proceeded to help me.

The sight of the food recalled to me the warnings I had received in the garden. This sudden effort of memory restored to me my other faculties at the same instant. I sprang to my feet, thrusting the women from me with each hand.

"Demons!" I almost shouted, "I will have none of your accursed food. I know you. You are cannibals, you are ghouls, you are enchanters. Begone, I tell you! Leave my room in peace!"

A shout of laughter from all six was the only effect that my passionate speech produced. The men rolled on their couches, and their half-masks quivered with the convulsions of their mirth. The women shrieked, and tossed the slender wine-glasses wildly aloft, and turned to me and flung themselves on my bosom fairly sobbing with laughter.

"Yes," I continued, as soon as the noisy mirth had subsided, "yes, I say, leave my room instantly! I will have none of your unnatural orgies here!"

"His room!" shrieked the woman on my right.

"His room!" echoed she on my left.

"His room! He calls it his room!" shouted the whole party, as they rolled once more into jocular convulsions.

"How know you that it is your room?" said one of the men who sat opposite to me, at length, after the laughter had once more somewhat subsided.

"How do I know?" I replied, indignantly. "How do I know my own room? How could I mistake it, pray? There's my furniture—my piano—"

"He calls that a piano!" shouted my neighbors.

The peculiar emphasis they laid on the word "piano" caused me to scrutinize the article I was indicating more thoroughly. Up to this time, though utterly amazed at the entrance of these people into my chamber, and connecting them somewhat with the wild stories I had heard in the garden, I still had a sort of indefinite idea that the whole thing was a masquerading freak got up in my absence, and that the bacchanalian orgy I was witnessing was nothing more than a portion of some elaborate hoax of which I was to be the victim. But when my eyes turned to the corner where I had left a huge and cumbrous piano, and beheld a vast and sombre organ lifting its fluted front to the very ceiling, and convinced myself, by a hurried process of memory, that it occupied the very spot in which I had left my own instrument, the little self-possession that I had left forsook me. I gazed around me bewildered.

In like manner everything was changed. In the place of that old haftless dagger, connected with so many historic associations personal to myself, I beheld a Turkish yataghan dangling by its belt of crimson silk, while the jewels in the hilt blazed as the lamplight played upon them. In the spot where hung my cherished smoking-cap, memorial of a buried love, a knightly casque was suspended, on the crest of which a golden dragon stood in the act of springing. That strange lithograph by Calame was no longer a lithograph, but it seemed to me that the portion of the wall which it had covered, of the exact shape and size, had been cut out, and, in place of the picture, a *real* scene on the same scale, and with real actors, was distinctly visible. The old oak was there, and the stormy sky was there; but I saw the branches of the oak sway with the tempest, and the clouds drive before the wind. The wanderer in his cloak was gone; but in his place I beheld a circle of wild figures, men and women, dancing with linked hands around the bole of the great tree, chanting some wild fragment of a song, to which the winds roared an unearthly chorus. The snowshoes, too, on whose sinewy woof I had sped for many days amidst Canadian wastes, had vanished, and in their place lay a pair of strange upcurled Turkish slippers.

All was changed. Wherever my eyes turned they missed familiar objects, yet encountered strange representatives. Still, in all the substitutes there seemed to me a reminiscence of what they replaced. They seemed only for a time transmuted into other shapes, and there lingered around them the atmosphere of what they once had been. Thus I could have sworn the room to have been mine, yet there was nothing in it that I could rightly claim.

"Well, have you determined whether or not this is your room?" asked the girl on my left, proffering me a huge tumbler creaming over with champagne, and laughing wickedly as she spoke.

"It is mine," I answered, doggedly, striking the glass rudely with my hand, and dashing the aromatic wine over the white cloth.

"Hush! hush!" she said, gently, not in the least angered at my rough treatment. "You are excited. Alf shall play something to soothe you."

At her signal, one of the men sat down at the organ. After a short, wild, spasmodic prelude, he began what seemed to me to be a symphony of recollections. Dark and sombre, and all through full of quivering and intense agony, it appeared to recall a dark and dismal night, on a cold reef, around which an unseen but terribly audible ocean broke with eternal fury. It seemed as if a lonely pair were on the reef, one living, the other dead; one clasping his arms around the tender neck and naked bosom of the other, striving to warm her into life, when his own vitality was being each moment sucked from him by the icy breath of the storm. Here and there a terrible wailing minor key would tremble through the chords like the shriek of sea-birds, or the warning of advancing death. While the man played I could scarce restrain myself. It seemed to be Blokeeta whom I listened to, and on whom I gazed. That wondrous night of pleasure and pain that I had once passed listening to him seemed to have been taken up again at the spot where it had broken off, and the same hand was continuing it. I stared at the man called Alf. There he sat with his cloak and doublet, and long rapier and mask of black velvet. But there was something in the air of the peaked beard, a familiar mystery in the wild mass of raven hair that fell as if wind-blown over his shoulders, which riveted my memory.

"Blokeeta! Blokeeta!" I shouted, starting up furiously from the couch on which I was lying, and bursting the fair arms that were linked around my neck as if they had been hateful chains— "Blokeeta! my friend! speak to me, I entreat you! Tell these horrid enchanters to leave me. Say that I hate them. Say that I command them to leave my room."

The man at the organ stirred not in answer to my appeal. He ceased playing, and the dying sound of the last note he had touched faded off into a melancholy moan.

"Why will you persist in calling this your room?" said the woman next me, with a smile meant to be kind, but to me inexpressibly loathsome. "Have we not shown you by the furniture, by the general appearance of the place, that you are mistaken, and that this cannot be your apartment? Rest content, then, with us."

"Rest content?" I answered, madly; "live with ghosts! eat of awful meats, and see awful sights! Never, never!"

"Softly, softly!" said another of the sirens. "Let us settle this amicably. This poor gentleman seems obstinate and inclined to make an uproar.

"Now," she continued, "I have a proposition to make. It would be ridiculous for us to surrender this room simply because this gentleman states that it is his; and yet I feel anxious to gratify, as far as may be fair, his wild assertion of ownership. A room, after all, is not much to us; we can get one easily enough, but still we should be loath to give this apartment up to so imperious a demand. We are willing, however, to *risk* its loss. That is to say"—turning to me—"I propose that we play for the room. If you win, we will immediately surrender it to you just as it stands; if, on the contrary, you lose, you shall bind yourself to depart."

Agonized at the ever-darkening mysteries that seemed to thicken around me, and despairing of being able to dissipate them by the mere exercise of my own will, I caught almost gladly at the chance thus presented to me.

"I agree," I cried, eagerly; "I agree. Anything to rid myself of such unearthly company!"

The woman touched a small golden bell that stood near her on the table, and it had scarce ceased to tinkle when a Negro dwarf entered with a silver tray on which were dice-boxes and dice. A shudder passed over me as I thought in this stunted African I could trace a resemblance to the ghoul-like black servant to whose attendance I had been accustomed.

"Now," said my neighbor, seizing one of the dice-boxes and giving me the other, "the highest wins. Shall I throw first?"

I nodded assent. She rattled the dice, and I felt an inexpressible load lifted from my heart as she threw fifteen.

"It is your turn," she said, with a mocking smile; "but before you throw, I repeat the offer I made you before. Live with us. Be one of us."

My reply was a fierce oath, as I rattled the dice with spasmodic nervousness and flung them on the board. They rolled over and over again, and during that brief instant I felt a suspense, the intensity of which I have never known before or since. At last they lay before me. A shout of the same horrible, maddening laughter rang in my ears. I peered in vain at the dice, but my sight was so confused that I could not distinguish the amount of the cast. This lasted for a few moments. Then my sight grew clear, and I sank back almost lifeless with despair as I saw that I had thrown but *twelve!*

"Lost! Lost!" screamed my neighbor, with a wild laugh. "Lost!

Lost!" shouted the deep voices of the masked men. "Leave us, coward!" they all cried; "you are not fit to be one of us. Remember your promise; leave us!"

Then it seemed as if some unseen power caught me by the shoulders and thrust me toward the door. In vain I resisted. In vain I screamed and shouted for help. In vain I screamed and twisted in despair. In vain I implored them for pity. All the reply I had was those mocking peals of merriment, while, under the invisible influence, I staggered like a drunken man toward the door. As I reached the threshold the organ pealed out a wild, triumphal strain. The power that impelled me concentrated itself into one vigorous impulse that sent me blindly staggering out into the echoing corridor, and, as the door closed swiftly behind me, I caught one glimpse of the apartment I had left forever. A change passed like a shadow over it. The lamps died out, the siren women and masked men had vanished, the flowers, the fruits, the bright silver and bizarre furniture faded swiftly, and I saw again, for the tenth of a second, my own old chamber restored.

The next instant the door closed violently, and I was left standing in the corridor stunned and despairing.

As soon as I had partially recovered my comprehension I rushed madly to the door, with the dim idea of beating it in. My fingers touched a cold and solid wall. There was no door! I felt all along the corridor for many yards on both sides. There was not even a crevice to give me hope. No one answered. In the vestibule I met the Negro; I seized him by the collar, and demanded my room. The demon showed his white and awful teeth, which were filed into a saw-like shape, and, extricating himself from my grasp with a sudden jerk, fled down the passage with a gibbering laugh. Nothing but echo answered to my despairing shrieks.

Since that awful hour I have never found my room. Everywhere I look for it, yet never see it. Shall I ever find it?

W. S. GILBERT

The Ghost
to His Ladye Love

Important elements of H.M.S. Pinafore, Patience, The Gondoliers, Trial
by Jury *and other of the fourteen comic operettas of Arthur Sullivan and*
WILLIAM S. GILBERT *(1836–1911) derive from the series of humorous poems
that Gilbert wrote for* Fun *and other British periodicals. As a devoted G&S
scholar, I am enormously grateful to James Ellis who, in his 1980 Harvard
University Press edition of "The Bab Ballads" (as these lyrics are collectively
known), republished some fifty forgotten Gilbertian verses, including "The
Ghost to His Ladye Love," whose sole earlier appearance was in* Fun *on
August 14, 1869. It seems to be the indirect source for Sir Roderic's famous
song, "When the Night Wind Howls," from the G&S "ghost operetta," Rud-
digore.*

Fair Phantom, come! The moon's awake.
The owl hoots gaily from its brake.
　　The blithesome bat's a-wing.
Come, soar to yonder silent clouds;
The ether teems with peopled shrouds:
We'll fly the lightsome spectre crowds,
　　Thou cloudy, clammy thing!

Though there are others, spectre mine,
With eyes as hollow, quite, as thine,
　　That thrill me from above—
Whose lips are quite as deathly pale,
Whose voices rival thine in wail

When, riding on the joyous gale,
    They breathe sepulchral love.

Still, there's a modest charm in thee,
That causes thee to seem to be
    More pure than others are—
Though rich in calico and bone,
Thou art not beautiful alone—
For thou art also *good*, my own!
    And that is better, far.

United, we'll defy alarms:
A death-time in each other's arms
    We'll pass—and fear no dearth
Of jollity: when Morpheus flits
O'er mortal eyes, we'll whet our wits,
And frighten people into fits
    Who did us harm on earth!

Come, essence of a slumb'ring soul.
Throw off thy maidenly control
    Un-shroud thy ghastly face!
Give me thy foggy lips divine.
And let me press my mist to thine.
And fold thy nothingness in mine,
    In one long damp embrace.
                                    [*She does.*]

ARTHUR MACHEN

The Happy Children

The great Welsh fantasist Arthur Llewellyn Jones is better known as ARTHUR
MACHEN *(1863–1947). Born in Caerleon-on-Usk, which historians believe to
be the factual counterpart of King Arthur's Camelot, Machen penned some of
England's most remarkable fantasy fiction, including "The Novel of the Black
Seal," "The Bowmen," "The Novel of the White Powder" and the following
gentle "historical" ghost story.*

A day after the Christmas of 1915, my professional duties took me
up north; or to be as precise as our present conventions allow, to
"the north-eastern district." There was some singular talk; mad gossip of the Germans having a "dug-out" somewhere by Malton Head.
Nobody seemed to be quite clear as to what they were doing there or
what they hoped to do there; but the report ran like wildfire from
one foolish mouth to another, and it was thought desirable that the
whole silly tale should be tracked down to its source and exposed or
denied once and for all.

   I went up, then, to that north-eastern district on Sunday, December 26, 1915, and pursued my investigations from Helmsdale Bay,
which is a small watering-place within a couple of miles of Malton
Head. The people of the dales and the moors had just heard of the
fable, I found, and regarded it all with supreme and sour contempt.
So far as I could make out, it originated from the games of some
children who had stayed at Helmsdale Bay in the summer. They had
acted a rude drama of German spies and their capture, and had
used Helby Cavern, between Helmsdale and Malton Head, as the

60 ARTHUR MACHEN

scene of their play. That was all; the fools apparently had done the rest; the fools who believed with all their hearts in "the Russians," and got cross with anyone who expressed a doubt as to "the Angels of Mons."

"Gang oop to beasten and tell them sike a tale and they'll not believe it," said one dalesman to me; and I have a suspicion that he thought that I, who had come so many hundred miles to investigate the story, was but little wiser than those who credited it. He could not be expected to understand that a journalist has two offices—to proclaim the truth and to denounce the lie.

I had finished with "the Germans" and their dug-out early in the afternoon of Monday, and I decided to break the journey home at Banwick, which I had often heard of as a beautiful and curious old place. So I took the one-thirty train, and went wandering inland, and stopped at many unknown stations in the midst of great levels, and changed at Marishes Ambo, and went on again through a strange land in the dimness of the winter afternoon. Somehow the train left the level and glided down into a deep and narrow dell, dark with winter woods, brown with withered bracken, solemn in its loneliness. The only thing that moved was the swift and rushing stream that foamed over the boulders and then lay still in brown pools under the bank.

The dark woods scattered and thinned into groups of stunted, ancient thorns; great grey rocks, strangely shaped, rose out of the ground; crenellated rocks rose on the heights on either side. The brooklet swelled and became a river, and always following this river we came to Banwick soon after the setting of the sun.

I saw the wonder of the town in the light of the afterglow that was red in the west. The clouds blossomed into rose-gardens; there were seas of fairy green that swam about isles of crimson light; there were clouds like spears of flame, like dragons of fire. And under the mingling lights and colours of such a sky Banwick went down to the pools of its land-locked harbour and climbed again across the bridge towards the ruined abbey and the great church on the hill.

I came from the station by an ancient street, winding and narrow, with cavernous closes and yards opening from it on either side, and flights of uneven steps going upward to high terraced houses, or downward to the harbour and the incoming tide. I saw there many gabled houses, sunken with age far beneath the level of the pavement, with dipping roof-trees and bowed doorways, with traces of grotesque carving on their walls. And when I stood on the quay, there on the other side of the harbour was the most amazing confusion of red-tiled roofs that I had ever seen, and the great grey Norman church high on the bare hill above them; and below them the boats swinging in the swaying tide, and the water burning in the fires of the sunset. It was the town of a magic dream. I stood on the quay till the shining had gone from the sky and the waterpools, and the winter night came down dark upon Banwick.

I found an old snug inn just by the harbour, where I had been standing. The walls of the rooms met each other at odd and unexpected angles; there were strange projections and juttings of masonry, as if one room were trying to force its way into another; there were indications as of unthinkable staircases in the corners of the ceilings. But there was a bar where Tom Smart would have loved to sit, with a roaring fire and snug, old elbow chairs about it and pleasant indications that if "something warm" were wanted after supper it could be generously supplied.

I sat in this pleasant place for an hour or two and talked to the pleasant people of the town who came in and out. They told me of the old adventures and industries of the town. It had once been, they said, a great whaling port, and then there had been a lot of shipbuilding, and later Banwick had been famous for its amber-cutting. "And now there's nowt," said one of the men in the bar; "but we get on none so badly."

I went out for a stroll before my supper. Banwick was now black, in thick darkness. For good reasons not a single lamp was lighted in the streets, hardly a gleam showed from behind the closely curtained windows. It was as if one walked a town of the Middle Ages, and with the ancient overhanging shapes of the houses dimly visible I was reminded of those strange, cavernous pictures of mediaeval Paris and Tours that Doré drew.

Hardly anyone was abroad in the streets; but all the courts and alleys seemed alive with children. I could just see little white forms fluttering to and fro as they ran in and out. And I never heard such happy children's voices. Some were singing, some were laughing; and peering into one black cavern, I made out a ring of children dancing round and round and chanting in clear voices a wonderful melody; some old tune of local tradition, as I supposed, for its modulations were such as I had never heard before.

I went back to my tavern and spoke to the landlord about the number of children who were playing about the dark streets and courts, and how delightfully happy they all seemed to be.

He looked at me steadily for a moment and then said:

"Well, you see, sir, the children have got a bit out of hand of late; their fathers are out at the front, and their mothers can't keep them in order. So they're running a bit wild."

There was something odd about his manner. I could not make out exactly what the oddity was, or what it meant. I could see that my remark had somehow made him uncomfortable; but I was at a loss to know what I had done. I had my supper, and then sat down for a couple of hours to settle "the Germans" of Malton Head.

I finished my account of the German myth, and instead of going to bed, I determined that I would have one more look at Banwick in its wonderful darkness. So I went out and crossed the bridge, and began to climb up the street on the other side, where there was that strange huddle of red roofs mounting one above the other that I had seen in the afterglow. And to my amazement I found that these extraordinary Banwick children were still about and abroad, still revelling and carolling, dancing and singing, standing, as I supposed, on the top of the flights of steps that climbed from the courts up the hill-side, and so having the appearance of floating in mid air. And their happy laughter rang out like bells on the night.

It was a quarter past eleven when I had left my inn, and I was just thinking that the Banwick mothers had indeed allowed indulgence to go too far, when the children began again to sing that old melody that I had heard in the evening. And now the sweet, clear voices swelled out into the night, and, I thought, must be numbered by hundreds. I was standing in a dark alleyway, and I saw with amazement that the children were passing me in a long procession that wound up the hill towards the abbey. Whether a faint moon now rose, or whether clouds passed from before the stars, I do not know; but the air lightened, and I could see the children plainly as they went by singing, with the rapture and exultation of them that sing in the woods in springtime.

They were all in white, but some of them had strange marks upon them which, I supposed, were of significance in this fragment of some traditional mystery-play that I was beholding. Many of them had wreaths of dripping seaweed about their brows; one showed a painted scar on her throat; a tiny boy held open his white robe, and pointed to a dreadful wound above his heart, from which the blood seemed to flow; another child held out his hands wide apart and the palms looked torn and bleeding, as if they had been pierced. One of the children held up a little baby in her arms, and even the infant showed the appearance of a wound on its face.

The procession passed me by, and I heard it still singing as if in the sky as it went on its steep way up the hill to the ancient church. I went back to my inn, and as I crossed the bridge it suddenly struck me that this was the eve of the Holy Innocents'. No doubt I had seen a confused relic of some mediaeval observance, and when I got back to the inn I asked the landlord about it.

Then I understood the meaning of the strange expression I had seen on the man's face. He was sick and shuddering with terror; he drew away from me as though I were a messenger from the dead.

Some weeks after this I was reading in a book called *The Ancient Rites of Banwick*. It was written in the reign of Queen Elizabeth by some anonymous person who had seen the glory of the old abbey, and then the desolation that had come to it. I found this passage:

> And on Childermas Day, at midnight, there was done there a marvellous solemn service. For when the monks had ended their singing of Te Deum at their Mattins, there came unto the altar the lord abbot, gloriously arrayed in a vestment of cloth of gold, so that it was a great marvel to behold him. And there came also into the church all the children that were of tender years of Banwick, and they were all clothed in white robes. And then began the lord abbot to sing the Mass of the Holy Innocents. And when the sacring of the Mass was ended, then there came up from the church into the quire the youngest child that there was present that might hold himself aright. And this child was borne up to the high altar, and the lord abbot set the little child upon a golden and glistering throne afore the high altar, and bowed down and worshipped him, singing "Talium Regnum Coelorum, Alleluya. Of such is the Kingdom of Heaven. Alleluya," and all the quire answered singing, "Amicti sunt stolis albis, Alleluya, Alleluya; They are clad in white robes, Alleluya, Alleluya." And then the prior and all the monks in their order did like worship and reverence to the little child that was upon the throne.

I had seen the White Order of the Innocents. I had seen those who came singing from the deep waters that are about the *Lusitania;* I had seen the innocent martyrs of the fields of Flanders and France rejoicing as they went up to hear their Mass in the spiritual place.

HERMINIE T. KAVANAGH

Darby O'Gill and the Good People

In 1945, Walt Disney first encountered Darby O'Gill and the Good People *by* HERMINIE TEMPLETON KAVANAGH *(1876–1933), a delightful collection of six fantasies about an elderly Irish shanachie (storyteller) and his adventures among the leprechauns living in the heart of the nearby mountain, Sleive-na-mon. The tales so delighted Disney that he flew to Ireland and fell in love with the land and the people. In 1959, his studio released the wonderful film* Darby O'Gill and the Little People. *However, the movie did not spark the reappearance of the 1915 book, perhaps because Dell Books instead chose to publish a pleasant novelization of the film by Lawrence Edward Watkin, author of the popular fantasy play/film* On Borrowed Time. *Therefore, it is a real pleasure to present—perhaps for the first time in over seventy-five years—the first Darby O'Gill story.*

Foreword

This history sets forth the only true account of the adventures of a daring Tipperary man named Darby O'Gill among the Fairies of Sleive-na-mon.

These adventures were first related to me by Mr. Jerry Murtaugh, a reliable car-driver, who goes between Kilcuny and Ballinderg. He is a first cousin of Darby O'Gill's own mother.

Although only one living man of his own free will ever went among them there, still, any well-learned person in Ireland can tell you that the abode of the Good People is in the hollow heart of the great mountain, Sleive-na-mon. That same one man was Darby O'Gill, a cousin of my own mother.

Right and left, generation after generation, the fairies had stolen pigs, young childher, old women, young men, cows, churnings of butter from other people, but had never bothered any of our kith or kin until, for some mysterious rayson, they soured on Darby, and took the eldest of his three foine pigs.

The next week a second pig went the same way. The third week not a thing had Darby left for the Balinrobe fair. You may aisly think how sore and sorry the poor man was, an' how Bridget, his wife, an' the childher carried on. The rent was due, and all left was to sell his cow Rosie to pay it. Rosie was the apple of his eye; he admired and rayspected the pigs, but he loved Rosie.

Worst luck of all was yet to come. On the morning when Darby went for the cow to bring her into market, bad scrans to the hoof was there; but in her place only a wisp of dirty straw to mock him. Millia murther! What a howlin' and screechin' and cursin' did Darby bring back to the house!

Now Darby was a bould man, and a desperate man in his anger as you soon will see. He shoved his feet into a pair of brogues, clapped his hat on his head, and gripped his stick in his hand.

"Fairy or no fairy, ghost or goblin, livin' or dead, who took Rosie'll rue the day," he says.

With those wild words he boulted in the direction of Sleive-na-mon.

All day long he climbed like an ant over the hill, looking for hole or cave through which he could get at the prison of Rosie. At times he struck the rocks with his black-thorn, cryin' out challenge.

"Come out, you that took her," he called. "If ye have the courage of a mouse, ye murtherin' thieves, come out!"

No one made answer—at laste, not just then. But at night, as he turned, hungry and footsore, toward home, who should he meet up with on the cross-roads but the ould fairy doctor, Sheelah Maguire; well known was she as a spy for the Good People. She spoke up:

"Oh, then, you're the foolish, blundherin'-headed man to be saying what you've said, and doing what you've done this day, Darby O'Gill," says she.

"What do I care!" says he, fiercely. "I'd fight the divil for my beautiful cow."

"Then go into Mrs. Hagan's meadow beyant," says Sheelah, "and wait till the moon is up. By an' by ye'll see a herd of cows come down from the mountain, and yer own'll be among them."

"What I'll I do then?" asked Darby, his voice thrembling with excitement.

"Sorra a hair I care what ye do! But there'll be lads there, and hundreds you won't see, that'll stand no ill words, Darby O'Gill."

"One question more, ma'am," says Darby, as Sheelah was moving away. "How late in the night will they stay without?"

Sheelah caught him by the collar and, pulling his head close, whuspered:

"When the cock crows the Good People must be safe at home. After cock-crow they have no power to help or to hurt, and every mortal eye can see them plain."

"I thank you kindly," says Darby, "and I bid you good evening, ma'am." He turned away, leaving her standing there alone looking after him; but he was sure he heard voices talkin' to her and laughin' and tittherin' behind him.

It was dark night when Darby stretched himself on the ground in Hagan's meadow; the yellow rim of the moon just tipped the edge of the hills.

As he lay there in the long grass amidst the silence there came a cowld shudder in the air, an' afther it had passed the deep cracked voice of a near-by bullfrog called loudly an' ballyraggin':

"The Omadhaun! Omadhaun! Omadhaun!" it said.

From a sloe three over near the hedge an owl cried, surprised and thrembling:

"Who-o-o? who-o-o?" it axed.

At that every frog in the meadow—an' there must have been tin thousand of them—took up the answer, an' shrieked shrill an' high together. "Darby O'Gill! Darby O'Gill! Darby O'Gill!" sang they.

"The Omadhaun! The Omadhaun!" cried the wheezy masther frog again. "Who-o? Who-o?" axed the owl. "Darby O'Gill! Darby O'Gill!" screamed the rollicking chorus; an' that way they were goin' over an' over agin until the bould man was just about to creep off to another spot whin, sudden, a hundred slow shadows, stirring up the mists, crept from the mountain way toward him. First he must find was Rosie among the herd. To creep quiet as a cat through the hedge and raich the first cow was only a minute's work. Then his plan, to wait till cock-crow, with all other sober, sensible thoughts, went clane out of the lad's head before his rage; for cropping eagerly the long, sweet grass, the first baste he met, was Rosie.

With a leap Darby was behind her, his stick falling sharply on her flanks. The ingratichude of that cow almost broke Darby's heart. Rosie turned fiercely on him with a vicious lunge, her two horns aimed at his breast. There was no suppler boy in the parish than Darby, and well for him it was so, for the mad rush the cow gave would have caught any man the laste trifle heavy on his legs and ended his days right there.

As it was, our hayro sprang to one side. As Rosie passed his left hand gripped her tail. When one of the O'Gills takes hould of a thing he hangs on like a bull-terrier. Away he went, rushing with her.

Now began a race the like of which was never heard of before or since. Ten jumps to the second and a hundred feet to the jump. Rosie's tail standing straight up in the air, firm as an iron bar, and Darby floating straight out behind; a thousand furious fairies flying a short distance after, filling the air with wild commands and threatenings.

Suddenly the sky opened for a crash of lightning that shivered the hills, and a roar of thunder that turned out of their beds every man, woman, and child in four counties. Flash after flash came the lightning, hitting on every side of our hayro. If it wasn't for fear of hurting Rosie the fairies would certainly have killed Darby. As it was, he was stiff with fear, afraid to hould on and afraid to lave go, but flew, waving in the air at Rosie's tail like a flag.

As the cow turned into the long, narrow valley which cuts into the east side of the mountain the Good People caught up with the pair, and what they didn't do to Darby in the line of sticking pins, pulling whiskers, and pinching wouldn't take long to tell. In troth, he was just about to let go his hould and take the chances of a fall when the hillside opened and—whisk! the cow turned into the mountain. Darby found himself flying down a wide, high passage which grew lighter as he went along. He heard the opening behind shut like a trap, and his heart almost stopped beating, for this was the fairies' home in the heart of Sleive-na-mon. He was captured by them!

When Rosie stopped, so stiff were all Darby's joints that he had great trouble loosening himself to come down. He landed among a lot of angry-faced little people, each no higher than your hand, every one wearing a green velvet cloak and a red cap, and in every cap was stuck a white owl's feather.

"We'll take him to the King," says a red-whuskered wee chap. "What he'll do to the murtherin' spalpeen'll be good and plenty!"

With that they marched our bould Darby, a prisoner, down the long passage, which every second grew wider and lighter and fuller of little people.

Sometimes, though, he met with human beings like himself, only the black charm was on them, they having been stolen at some time by the Good People. He saw lost people there from every parish in Ireland, both commoners and gentry. Each was laughing, talking, and divarting himself with another. Off to the sides he could see small cobblers making brogues, tinkers mending pans, tailors sewing cloth, smiths hammering horse-shoes, every one merrily to his trade, making a diversion out of work.

To this day Darby can't tell where the beautiful red light he now saw came from. It was like a soft glow, only it filled the place, making things brighter than day.

Down near the centre of the mountain was a room twenty times higher and broader than the biggest church in the worruld. As they drew near this room there arose the sound of a reel played on bag-pipes. The music was so bewitching that Darby, who was the gracefullest reel-dancer in all Ireland, could hardly make his feet behave themselves.

At the room's edge Darby stopped short and caught his breath, the sight was so entrancing. Set over the broad floor were thousands and thousands of the Good People, facing this way and that, dancing to a reel; while on a throne in the middle of the room sat ould Brian Connors, King of the Fairies, blowing on the bagpipes. The little King, with a goold crown on his head, wearing a beautiful green velvet coat and red knee-breeches, sat with his legs crossed, beating time with his foot to the music.

There were many from Darby's own parish; and what was his surprise to see there Maureen McGibney, his own wife's sister, whom he had supposed resting dacintly in her own grave in holy ground these three years. She had flowers in her brown hair, a fine colour in her cheeks, a gown of white silk and goold, and her green mantle raiched to the heels of her purty red slippers.

There she was gliding back an' forth, ferninst a little gray-whus-kered, round-stomached fairy man, as though there was never a care nor a sorrow in the worruld.

As I tould you before, I tell you again, Darby was the finest reel-dancer in all Ireland; and he came from a family of dancers, though I say it who shouldn't, as he was my mother's own cousin. Three things in the worruld banish sorrow—love and whisky and music.

So, when the surprise of it all melted a little, Darby's feet led him in to the thick of the throng, right under the throne of the King, where he flung care to the winds and put his heart and mind into his two nimble feet. Darby's dancing was such that purty soon those around stood still to admire.

There's a saying come down in our family through generations which I still hould to be true, that the better the music the aisier the step. Sure never did mortal men dance to so fine a chune and never so supple a dancer did such a chune meet up with.

Fair and graceful he began. Backward and forward, side-step and turn; cross over, thin forward; a hand on his hip and his stick twirling free; side-step and forward; cross over agin; bow to his partner, and hammer the floor.

It wasn't long till half the dancers crowded around admiring, clapping their hands, and shouting encouragement. The ould King grew so excited that he laid down the pipes, took up his fiddle, came down from the throne, and, standing ferninst Darby, began a finer chune than the first.

The dancing lasted a whole hour, no one speaking a word except to cry out, "Foot it, ye divil!" "Aisy now, he's threading on flowers!" "Hooroo! hooroo! hooray!" Then the King stopped and said:

"Well, that bates Banagher, and Banagher bates the worruld! Who are you and how came you here?"

Then Darby up and tould the whole story.

When he had finished, the King looked sayrious. "I'm glad you came, an' I'm sorry you came," he says. "If we had put our charm on you outside to bring you in you'd never die till the ind of the worruld, when we here must all go to hell. But," he added, quickly, "there's no use in worrying about that now. That's nayther here nor there! Those willing to come with us can't come at all, at all; and here you are of your own free act and will. Howsomever, you're here, and we darn't let you go outside to tell others of what you have seen, and so give us a bad name about—about taking things, you know. We'll make you as comfortable as we can; and so you won't worry about Bridget and the childher, I'll have a goold sovereign left with them every day of their lives. But I wish we had comeither on you," he says, with a sigh, "for it's aisy to see you're great company. Now, come up to my place and have a noggin of punch for friendship's sake," says he.

That's how Darby O'Gill began his six months' stay with the Good People. Not a thing was left undone to make Darby contented and happy. A civiller people than the Good People he never met. At first he couldn't get over saying, "God save all here" and "God save you kindly," and things like that, which was like burning them with a hot iron.

If it weren't for Maureen McGibney, Darby would be in Sleive-na-mon at this hour. Sure she was always the wise girl, ready with her crafty plans and warnings. On a day when they two were sitting alone together she says to him:

"Darby, dear," says she, "it isn't right for a dacint man of family to be spending his days cavortin' and idlin' and fillin' the hours with sport and nonsense. We must get you out of here; for what is a sovereign a day to compare with the care and protection of a father?" she says.

"Thrue for ye!" moaned Darby, "and my heart is just splittin' for a sight of Bridget an' the childher. Bad luck to the day I set so much store on a dirty, ongrateful, treacherous cow!"

"I know well how you feel," says Maureen, "for I'd give the world to say three words to Bob Broderick, that ye tell me that out of grief for me he has never kept company with any other girl till this day. But that'll never be," she says, "because I must stop here till the Day of Judgment, then I must go to ———," says she, beginning to cry, "but if you get out, you'll bear a message to Bob for me, maybe?" she says.

"It's aisy to talk about going out, but how can it be done?" asked Darby.

"There's a way," says Maureen, wiping her big, gray eyes, "but it may take years. First, you must know that the Good People can never put their charm on anyone who is willing to come with them. That's whay you came safe. Then, agin, they can't work harm in the daylight, and after cock-crow any mortal eye can see them plain; nor can they harm anyone who has a sprig of holly, nor pass over a leaf or twig of holly, because that's Christmas bloom. Well, there's a certain evil word for a charm that opens the side of the mountain, and I will try to find it out for you. Without that word all the armies in the worruld couldn't get out or in. But you must be patient and wise and wait."

"I will so, with the help of God," says Darby.

At these words Maureen gave a terrible screech.

"Cruel man!" she cried, "don't you know that to say pious words to one of the Good People, or to one undher their black charm, is like cutting him with a knife?"

The next night she came to Darby again.

"Watch yerself now," she says, "for to-night they're goin' to have the door of the mountain open to thry you; and if you stir two steps outside they'll put the comeither on you," she says.

Sure enough, when Darby took his walk down the passage after supper, as he did every night, there the side of the mountain lay wide open and no one in sight. The temptation to make one rush was great; but he only looked out a minute, and went whustling down the passage, knowing well that a hundred hidden eyes were on him the while. For a dozen nights after it was the same.

At another time Maureen said:

"The King himself is going to thry you hard the day, so beware!" She had no sooner said the words than Darby was called for, and went up to the King.

"Darby, my sowl," says the King, in a sootherin' way, "have this noggin of punch. A betther never was brewed; it's the last we'll have for many a day. I'm going to set you free, Darby O'Gill, that's what I am."

"Why, King," says Darby, putting on a mournful face, "how have I offended ye?"

"No offence at all," says the King, "only we're depriving you."

"No depravity in life!" says Darby. "I have lashins and lavings to ate and to drink and nothing but fun an' divarsion all day long. Out in the worruld it was nothing but work and throuble and sickness, disappointment and care."

"But Bridget and the childher?" says the King, giving him a sharp look out of half-shut eyes.

"Oh, as for that, King," says Darby, "it's aisier for a widow to get a husband or for orphans to find a father than it is for them to pick up a sovereign a day."

The King looked mighty satisfied and smoked for a while without a word.

"Would you mind goin' out an evenin' now and then, helpin' the boys to mind the cows?" he asked at last.

Darby feared to trust himself outside in their company.

"Well, I'll tell ye how it is," replied my brave Darby. "Some of the neighbours might see me, and spread the report on me that I'm with the fairies and that'd disgrace Bridget and the childher," he says.

The King knocked ashes from his pipe.

"You're a wise man, besides being the height of good company," says he, "and it's sorry I am you didn't take my word, for then we would have you always, at laste till the Day of Judgment, when—but that's nayther here nor there! Howsomever, we'll bother you about it no more."

From that day they thrated him as one of their own.

It was nearly five months afther that Maureen plucked Darby by the coat and led him off to a lonely spot.

"I've got the word," she says.

"Have you, faith! What is it?" says Darby, all of a thrimble.

Then she whispered a word so blasphaymous, so irrayligious that Darby blessed himself. When Maureen saw him making the sign, she fell down in a fit, the holy emblem hurt her so, poor child.

Three hours after this me bould Darby was sitting at his own fireside talking to Bridget and the childher. The neighbours were hurrying to him down every road and through every field, carrying armfuls of holly bushes, as he had sent word for them to do. He knew well he'd have fierce and savage visitors before morning.

After they had come with the holly, he had them make a circle of it so thick around the house that a fly couldn't walk through without touching a twig or leaf. But that was not all.

You'll know what a wise girl and what a crafty girl that Maureen was when you hear what the neighbours did next. They made a second ring of holly outside the first, so that the house sat in two great wreaths, one wreath around the other. The outside ring was much the bigger, and left a good space between it and the first, with room for ever so many people to stand there. It was like the inner ring, except for a little gate, left open as though by accident, where the fairies could walk in.

But it wasn't an accident at all, only the wise plan of Maureen's; for nearby this little gap, in the outside wreath, lay a sprig of holly with a bit of twine tied to it. Then the twine ran along up to Darby's house, and in through the window, where its ind lay convaynient to his hand. A little pull on the twine would drag the stray piece of holly into the gap and close tight the outside ring.

It was a trap, you see. When the fairies walked in through the gap the twine was to be pulled, and so they were to be made prisoners between the two rings of holly. They couldn't get into Darby's house because the circle of holly nearest the house was so tight that a fly couldn't get through without touching the blessed tree or its wood. Likewise, when the gap in the outer wreath was closed, they couldn't get out agin. Well, anyway, these things were hardly finished and fixed when the dusky brown of the hills warned the neighbours of twilight, and they scurried like frightened rabbits to their homes.

Only one amongst them all had courage to sit inside Darby's house waiting the dreadful wisitors, and that one was Bob Broderick. What vengeance was in store couldn't be guessed at all, at all, only it was sure to be more turrible than any yet wreaked on mortal man.

Not in Darby's house alone was the terror, for in their anger the Good People might lay waste the whole parish. The roads and fields were empty and silent in the darkness. Not a window glimmered with light for miles around. Many a blaggard who hadn't said a prayer for years was down on his marrow bones among the dacint members of his family, thumping his craw and roaring his Pather and Aves.

In Darby's quiet house, against which the cunning, the power, and the fury of the Good People would first break, you can't think of half the suffering of Bridget and the childher as they lay huddled together on the settle-bed; nor of the strain on Bob and Darby, who sat smoking their dudeens and whispering anxiously together.

For some rayson or other the Good People were long in coming. Ten o'clock struck, thin eleven, afther that twelve, and not a sound from the outside. The silence, and then no sign of any kind, had them all just about crazy, when suddenly there fell a sharp rap on the door.

"Millia murther," whispered Darby, "we're in for it. They've crossed the two rings of holly and are at the door itself."

The childher begun to cry, and Bridget said her prayers out loud; but no one answered the knock.

"Rap, rap, rap," on the door, then a pause.

"God save all here!" cried a queer voice from the outside.

Now no fairy would say "God save all here," so Darby took heart and opened the door. Who should be standing there but Sheelah Maguire, a spy for the Good People. So angry were Darby and Bob that they snatched her within the threshold, and before she knew it they had her tied hand and foot, wound a cloth around her mouth, and rolled her under the bed. Within the minute a thousand rustling woices sprung from outside. Through the window, in the clear moonlight, Darby marked weeds and grass being trampled by inwisible feet beyond the farthest ring of holly.

Suddenly broke a great cry. The gap in the first ring was found. Signs were plainly seen of uncountable feet rushing through and spreading about the nearer wreath. Afther that a howl of madness from the little men and women. Darby had pulled his twine and the trap was closed, with five thousand of the Good People entirely at his mercy.

Princes, princesses, dukes, dukesses, earls, earlesses, and all the quality of Sleive-na-mon were presoners. Not more than a dozen of the last to come escaped, and they flew back to tell the King.

For an hour they raged. All the bad names ever called to mortal man were given free, but Darby said never a word. "Pickpocket!" "Sheep-stayler!" "Murtherin' thafe of a blaggard!" were the softest words trun at him.

By an' by, howsumever, as it begun to grow near to cock-crow, their talk grew a great dale civiller. Then came beggin', pladin', promisin', and enthratin', but the doors of the house still stayed shut an' its windows down.

Purty soon Darby's old rooster, Terry, came down from his perch, yawned, an' flapped his wings a few times. At that the terror and the screechin' of the Good People would have melted the heart of a stone.

All of a sudden a fine clear voice rose from beyant the crowd. The King had come. The other fairies grew still listening.

"Ye murtherin' thafe of the worruld," says the King, grandly, "what are ye doin' wid my people?"

"Keep a civil tongue in yer head, Brian Connors," says Darby, sticking his head out the window, "for I'm as good a man as you, any day," says Darby.

At that minute Terry, the cock, flapped his wings and crowed. In a flash there sprang into full view the crowd of Good People—dukes, earls, princes, quality and commoners, with their ladies—jammed thick together about the house; every one of them with his head trun back bawling and crying, and tears as big as pigeon-eggs rouling down their cheeks.

A few feet away, on a straw-pile in the barnyard, stood the King, his goold crown tilted on the side of his head, his long green cloak about him and his rod in his hand, but thremblin' all over.

In the middle of the crowd, but towering high above them all, stood Maureen McGibney in her cloak of green an' goold, her purty brown hair fallin' down her chowlders, an' she—the crafty villain—cryin' an' bawlin' an' abusin' Darby with the best of them.

"What'll you have an' let them go?" says the King.

"First an' foremost," says Darby, "take yer spell off that slip of a girl there, an' send her into the house."

In a second Maureen was standing inside the door, her both arms about Bob's neck and her head on his collar-bone.

What they said to aich other, an' what they done in the way of embracin' an' kissin' an' cryin' I won't take time in telling you.

"Next," says Darby, "send back Rosie and the pigs."

"I expected that," says the King. And at those words they saw a black bunch coming through the air, and in a few seconds Rosie and the three pigs walked into the stable.

"Now," says Darby, "promise in the name of Ould Nick" ('tis by him the Good People swear) "never to moil nor meddle agin with anyone or anything from this parish."

The King was fair put out by this. Howsomever, he said at last: "You ongrateful scoundrel, in the name of Ould Nick I promise."

"So far, so good," says Darby; "but the worst is yet to come. Now you must raylase from your spell every sowl you've stole from this parish; and besides, you must send me two hundhred pounds in goold."

Well, the King gave a roar of anger that was heard in the next barony.

"Ye high-handed, hard-hearted robber," he says, "I'll never con-sent!" says he.

"Plase yeself," says Darby. "I see Father Cassidy comin' down the hedge," he says, "an' he has a prayer for ye all in his book that'll burn ye up like wisps of sthraw if he ever catches ye here," says Darby.

With that the roaring and bawling was pitiful to hear, and in a few minutes a bag with two hundhred goold sovereigns in it was trun at Darby's threshold; and fifty people, young an' some of them ould, flew over an' stood beside the King. Some of them had spent years with the fairies. Their relatives thought them dead and buried. They were the lost ones from that parish.

With that Darby pulled the bit of twine again, opening the trap, and it wasn't long until every fairy was gone.

The green coat of the last one was hardly out of sight when, sure enough, who should come up but Father Cassidy, his book in his hand. He looked at the fifty people who had been with the fairies standin' there—the poor crathures—thremblin' an' wondherin' an' afeard to go to their homes.

Darby tould him what had happened.

"Ye foolish man," says the priest, "you could have got out every poor presoner that's locked in Sleive-na-mon, let alone those from this parish."

One could have scraped with a knife the surprise off Darby's face.

"Would yer Reverence have me let out the Corkonians, the Connaught men, and the Fardowns, I ask ye?" he says, hotly. "When Mrs. Malowney there goes home and finds that Tim has married the Widow Hogan, ye'll say I let out too many, even of this parish, I'm thinkin'."

"But," says the priest, "ye might have got two hundred pounds for aich of us."

"If aich had two hundhred pounds, what comfort would I have in being rich?" axed Darby agin. "To enjoy well being rich there should be plenty of poor," says Darby.

"God forgive ye, ye selfish man!" says Father Cassidy.

"There's another rayson besides," says Darby. "I never got betther nor friendlier thratement than I had from the Good People. An' the divil a hair of their heads I'd hurt more than need be," he says.

Some way or other the King heard of this saying, an' was so mightily pleased that the next night a jug of the finest poteen was left at Darby's door.

After that, indade, many's the winter night, when the snow lay so heavy that no neighbour was stirrin', and when Bridget and the childher were in bed, Darby sat by the fire, a noggin of hot punch in his hand, argying an' getting news of the whole worruld. A little man with a goold crown on his head, a green cloak on his back, and one foot trun over the other, sat ferninst him by the hearth.

ALGERNON BLACKWOOD

Keeping His Promise

ALGERNON BLACKWOOD *(1869–1951), one of England's great writers of the macabre and supernatural, is best known for "The Willows" and similarly terrifying stories set in the Canadian woods and other wild spots. "Keeping His Promise," one of Blackwood's less common tales of urban terror, is set in one of Europe's bloodiest metropolises, Edinburgh, hometown of the body snatchers Burke and Hare, as well as Deacon Brodie, historic counterpart of Robert Louis Stevenson's Dr. Jekyll and Mr. Hyde.*

It was eleven o'clock at night, and young Marriott was locked into his room, cramming as hard as he could cram. He was a "Fourth Year Man" at Edinburgh University and he had been ploughed for this particular examination so often that his parents had positively declared they could no longer supply the funds to keep him there.

His rooms were cheap and dingy, but it was the lecture fees that took the money. So Marriott pulled himself together at last and definitely made up his mind that he would pass or die in the attempt, and for some weeks now he had been reading as hard as mortal man can read. He was trying to make up for lost time and money in a way that showed conclusively he did not understand the value of either. For no ordinary man—and Marriott was in every sense an ordinary man—can afford to drive the mind as he had lately been driving his, without sooner or later paying the cost.

Among the students he had few friends or acquaintances, and these few had promised not to disturb him at night, knowing he was at last reading in earnest. It was, therefore, with feelings a good deal stronger than mere surprise that he heard his door-bell ring on this particular night and realised that he was to have a visitor. Some men would simply have muffled the bell and gone on quietly with their work. But Marriott was not this sort. He was nervous. It would have bothered and pecked at his mind all night long not to know who the visitor was and what he wanted. The only thing to do, therefore, was to let him in—and out again—as quickly as possible.

The landlady went to bed at ten o'clock punctually, after which hour nothing would induce her to pretend she heard the bell, so Marriott jumped up from his books with an exclamation that augured ill for the reception of his caller, and prepared to let him in with his own hand.

The streets of Edinburgh town were very still at this late hour—it was late for Edinburgh—and in the quiet neighbourhood of F—— Street, where Marriott lived on the third floor, scarcely a sound broke the silence. As he crossed the floor, the bell rang a second time, with unnecessary clamour, and he unlocked the door and passed into the little hallway with considerable wrath and annoyance in his heart at the insolence of the double interruption.

"The fellows all know I'm reading for this exam. Why in the world do they come to bother me at such an unearthly hour?"

The inhabitants of the building, with himself, were medical students, general students, poor Writers to the Signet, and some others whose vocations were perhaps not so obvious. The stone staircase, dimly lighted at each floor by a gas-jet that would not turn above a certain height, wound down to the level of the street with no pretence at carpet or railing. At some levels it was cleaner than at others. It depended on the landlady of the particular level.

The acoustic properties of a spiral staircase seem to be peculiar. Marriott, standing by the open door, book in hand, thought every moment the owner of the footsteps would come into view. The sound of the boots was so close and so loud that they seemed to travel disproportionately in advance of their cause. Wondering who it could be, he stood ready with all manner of sharp greetings for the man who dared thus to disturb his work. But the man did not appear. The steps sounded almost under his nose, yet no one was visible.

A sudden queer sensation of fear passed over him—a faintness and a shiver down the back. It went, however, almost as soon as it came, and he was just debating whether he would call aloud to his invisible visitor, or slam the door and return to his books, when the cause of the disturbance turned the corner very slowly and came into view.

It was a stranger. He saw a youngish man short of figure and very broad. His face was the colour of a piece of chalk and the eyes, which were very bright, had heavy lines underneath them. Though the cheeks and chin were unshaven and the general appearance unkempt, the man was evidently a gentleman, for he was well dressed and bore himself with a certain air. But, strangest of all, he wore no hat, and carried none in his hand; and although rain had been falling steadily all the evening, he appeared to have neither overcoat nor umbrella.

A hundred questions sprang up in Marriott's mind and rushed to his lips, chief among which was something like "Who in the world are you?" and "What in the name of heaven do you come to me for?" But none of these questions found time to express themselves in words, for almost at once the caller turned his head a little so that the gas light in the hall fell upon his features from a new angle. Then in a flash Marriott recognised him.

"Field! Man alive! Is it you?" he gasped.

The Fourth Year Man was not lacking in intuition, and he perceived at once that here was a case for delicate treatment. He divined, without any actual process of thought, that the catastrophe often predicted had come at last, and that this man's father had turned him out of the house. They had been at a private school together years before, and though they had hardly met once since, the news had not failed to reach him from time to time with considerable detail, for the family lived near his own and between certain of the sisters there was great intimacy. Young Field had gone wild later, he remembered hearing about it all—drink, a woman, opium, or something of the sort—he could not exactly call to mind.

"Come in," he said at once, his anger vanishing. "There's been something wrong, I can see. Come in, and tell me all about it and perhaps I can help—" He hardly knew what to say, and stammered a lot more besides. The dark side of life, and the horror of it, belonged to a world that lay remote from his own select little atmosphere of books and dreamings. But he had a man's heart for all that.

He led the way across the hall, shutting the front door carefully behind him, and noticed as he did so that the other, though certainly sober, was unsteady on his legs, and evidently much exhausted. Marriott might not be able to pass his examinations, but he at least knew the symptoms of starvation—acute starvation, unless he was much mistaken—when they stared him in the face.

"Come along," he said cheerfully, and with genuine sympathy in his voice. "I'm glad to see you. I was going to have a bite of something to eat, and you're just in time to join me."

The other made no audible reply, and shuffled so feebly with his feet that Marriott took his arm by way of support. He noticed for the first time that the clothes hung on him with pitiful looseness. The broad frame was literally hardly more than a frame. He was as thin as a skeleton. But, as he touched him, the sensation of faintness and dread returned. It only lasted a moment, and then passed off, and he ascribed it not unnaturally to the distress and shock of seeing a former friend in such a pitiful plight.

"Better let me guide you. It's shamefully dark—this hall. I'm always complaining," he said lightly, recognising by the weight upon his arm that the guidance was sorely needed, "but the old cat never does anything except promise." He led him to the sofa, wondering all the time where he had come from and how he had found out the address. It must be at least seven years since those days at the private school when they used to be such close friends.

"Now, if you'll forgive me for a minute," he said, "I'll get supper ready—such as it is. And don't bother to talk. Just take it easy on the sofa. I see you're dead tired. You can tell me about it afterwards, and we'll make plans."

The other sat down on the edge of the sofa and stared in silence, while Marriott got out the brown loaf, scones, and huge pot of marmalade that Edinburgh students always keep in their cupboards. His eyes shone with a brightness that suggested drugs, Marriott thought, stealing a glance at him from behind the cupboard door. He did not like yet to take a full square look. The fellow was in a bad way, and it would have been so like an examination to stare and wait for explanations. Besides, he was evidently almost too exhausted to speak. So, for reasons of delicacy—and for another reason as well which he could not exactly formulate to himself—he let his visitor rest apparently unnoticed, while he busied himself with the supper. He lit the spirit lamp to make cocoa, and when the water was boiling he drew up the table with the good things to the sofa, so that Field need not have even the trouble of moving to a chair.

"Now, let's tuck in," he said, "and afterwards we'll have a pipe and a chat. I'm reading for an exam, you know, and I always have something about this time. It's jolly to have a companion."

He looked up and caught his guest's eyes directed straight upon his own. An involuntary shudder ran through him from head to foot. The face opposite him was deadly white and wore a dreadful expression of pain and mental suffering.

"By Gad!" he said, jumping up, "I quite forgot. I've got some whisky somewhere. What an ass I am. I never touch it myself when I'm working like this."

He went to the cupboard and poured out a stiff glass which the other swallowed at a single gulp and without any water. Marriott watched him while he drank it, and at the same time noticed something else as well—Field's coat was all over dust, and on one shoulder was a bit of cobweb. It was perfectly dry; Field arrived on a soaking wet night without hat, umbrella, or overcoat, and yet perfectly dry, even dusty. Therefore he had been under cover. What did it all mean? Had he been hiding in the building . . . ?

It was very strange. Yet he volunteered nothing; and Marriott had pretty well made up his mind by this time that he would not ask any questions until he had eaten and slept. Food and sleep were obviously what the poor devil needed most and first—he was pleased with his powers of ready diagnosis—and it would not be fair to press him till he had recovered a bit.

They ate their supper together while the host carried on a running one-sided conversation, chiefly about himself and his exams and his "old cat" of a landlady, so that the guest need not utter a single word unless he really wished to—which he evidently did not! But, while he toyed with his food, feeling no desire to eat, the other ate voraciously. To see a hungry man devour cold scones, stale oatcake, and brown bread laden with marmalade was a revelation to this inexperienced student who had never known what it was to be without at least three meals a day. He watched in spite of himself, wondering why the fellow did not choke in the process.

But Field seemed to be as sleepy as he was hungry. More than once his head dropped and he ceased to masticate the food in his mouth. Marriott had positively to shake him before he would go on with his meal. A stronger emotion will overcome a weaker, but this struggle between the sting of real hunger and the magical opiate of overpowering sleep was a curious sight to the student, who watched it with mingled astonishment and alarm. He had heard of the pleasure it was to feed hungry men, and watch them eat, but he had never actually witnessed it, and he had no idea it was like this. Field ate like an animal—gobbled, stuffed, gorged. Marriott forgot his reading, and began to feel something very much like a lump in his throat.

"Afraid there's been awfully little to offer you, old man," he managed to blurt out when at length the last scone had disappeared, and the rapid, one-sided meal was at an end. Field still made no reply, for he was almost asleep in his seat. He merely looked up wearily and gratefully.

"Now you must have some sleep, you know," he continued, "or you'll go to pieces. I shall be up all night reading for this blessed exam. You're more than welcome to my bed. To-morrow we'll have a late breakfast and—and see what can be done—and make plans— I'm awfully good at making plans, you know," he added with an attempt at lightness.

Field maintained his "dead sleepy" silence, but appeared to acquiesce, and the other led the way into the bedroom, apologising as he did so to this half-starved son of a baronet—whose own home was almost a palace—for the size of the room. The weary guest, however, made no pretence of thanks or politeness. He merely steadied himself on his friend's arm as he staggered across the room, and then, with all his clothes on, dropped his exhausted body on the bed. In less than a minute he was to all appearances sound asleep.

For several minutes Marriott stood in the open door and watched him; praying devoutly that he might never find himself in a like predicament, and then fell to wondering what he would do with his unbidden guest on the morrow. But he did not stop long to think, for the call of his books was imperative, and happen what might, he must see to it that he passed that examination.

Having again locked the door into the hall, he sat down to his books and resumed his notes on *materia medica* where he had left off when the bell rang. But it was difficult for some time to concentrate his mind on the subject. His thoughts kept wandering to the picture of that white-faced, strange-eyed fellow, starved and dirty, lying in his clothes and boots on the bed. He recalled their schooldays together before they had drifted apart, and how they had vowed eternal friendship—and all the rest of it. And now! What horrible straits to be in. How could any man let the love of dissipation take such hold upon him?

But one of their vows together Marriott, it seemed, had completely forgotten. Just now, at any rate, it lay too far in the background of his memory to be recalled.

Through the half-open door—the bedroom led out of the sitting-room and had no other door—came the sound of deep, long-drawn breathing, the regular, steady breathing of a tired man, so tired that even to listen to it made Marriott almost want to go to sleep himself.

"He needed it," reflected the student, "and perhaps it came only just in time!"

Perhaps so; for outside the bitter wind from across the Forth howled cruelly and drove the rain in cold streams against the window-panes, and down the deserted streets. Long before Marriott settled down again properly to his reading, he heard distantly, as it were, through the sentences of the book, the heavy, deep breathing of the sleeper in the next room.

A couple of hours later, when he yawned and changed his books, he still heard the breathing, and went cautiously up to the door to look round.

At first the darkness of the room must have deceived him, or else his eyes were confused and dazzled by the recent glare of the reading lamp. For a minute or two he could make out nothing at all but dark lumps of furniture, the mass of the chest of drawers by the wall, and the white patch where his bath stood in the centre of the floor.

Then the bed came slowly into view. And on it he saw the outline of the sleeping body gradually take shape before his eyes, growing up strangely into the darkness, till it stood out in marked relief—the long black form against the white counterpane.

He could hardly help smiling. Field had not moved an inch. He watched him a moment or two and then returned to his books. The night was full of the singing voices of the wind and rain. There was no sound of traffic; no hansoms clattered over the cobbles, and it was still too early for the milk carts. He worked on steadily and conscientiously, only stopping now and again to change a book, or to sip some of the poisonous stuff that kept him awake and made his brain so active, and on these occasions Field's breathing was always distinctly audible in the room. Outside, the storm continued to howl, but inside the house all was stillness. The shade of the reading lamp threw all the light upon the littered table, leaving the other end of the room in comparative darkness. The bedroom door was exactly opposite him where he sat. There was nothing to disturb the worker, nothing but an occasional rush of wind against the windows, and a slight pain in his arm.

This pain, however, which he was unable to account for, grew once or twice very acute. It bothered him; and he tried to remember how, and when, he could have bruised himself so severely, but without success.

At length the page before him turned from yellow to grey, and there were sounds of wheels in the street below. It was four o'clock. Marriott leaned back and yawned prodigiously. Then he drew back the curtains. The storm had subsided and the Castle Rock was shrouded in mist. With another yawn he turned away from the dreary outlook and prepared to sleep the remaining four hours till breakfast on the sofa. Field was still breathing heavily in the next room, and he first tip-toed across the floor to take another look at him.

Peering cautiously round the half-opened door his first glance fell upon the bed now plainly discernible in the grey light of morning. He stared hard. Then he rubbed his eyes. Then he rubbed his eyes again and thrust his head farther round the edge of the door. With fixed eyes he stared harder still, and harder.

But it made no difference at all. He was staring into an empty room.

The sensation of fear he had felt when Field first appeared upon the scene returned suddenly, but with much greater force. He became conscious, too, that his left arm was throbbing violently and causing him great pain. He stood wondering, and staring, and trying to collect his thoughts. He was trembling from head to foot.

By a great effort of the will he left the support of the door and walked forward boldly into the room.

There, upon the bed, was the impress of a body, where Field had lain and slept. There was the mark of the head on the pillow, and the slight indentation at the foot of the bed where the boots had rested on the counterpane. And there, plainer than ever—for he was closer to it—was *the breathing!*

Marriott tried to pull himself together. With a great effort he found his voice and called his friend aloud by name!

"Field! Is that you? Where are you?"

There was no reply; but the breathing continued without interruption, coming directly from the bed. His voice had such an unfamiliar sound that Marriott did not care to repeat his questions, but he went down on his knees and examined the bed above and below, pulling the mattress off finally, and taking the coverings away separately one by one. But though the sounds continued there was no visible sign of Field, nor was there any space in which a human being, however small, could have concealed itself. He pulled the bed out from the wall, but the sound *stayed where it was*. It did not move with the bed.

Marriott, finding self-control a little difficult in his weary condition, at once set about a thorough search of the room. He went through the cupboard, the chest of drawers, the little alcove where the clothes hung—everything. But there was no sign of anyone. The small window near the ceiling was closed; and, anyhow, was not large enough to let a cat pass. The sitting-room door was locked on the inside; he could not have got out that way. Curious thoughts began to trouble Marriott's mind, bringing in their train unwelcome sensations. He grew more and more excited; he searched the bed again till it resembled the scene of a pillow fight; he searched both rooms, knowing all the time it was useless—and then he searched again. A cold perspiration broke out all over his body; and the sound of heavy breathing, all this time, never ceased to come from the corner where Field had lain down to sleep.

Then he tried something else. He pushed the bed back exactly into its original position—and himself lay down upon it just where his guest had lain. But the same instant he sprang up again in a single bound. The breathing was close beside him, almost on his cheek, and between him and the wall! Not even a child could have squeezed into the space.

He went back into his sitting-room, opened the windows, welcoming all the light and air possible, and tried to think the whole matter over quietly and clearly. Men who read too hard, and slept too little, he knew were sometimes troubled with very vivid hallucinations. Again he calmly reviewed every incident of the night; his accurate sensations; the vivid details; the emotions stirred in him; the dreadful feast—no single hallucination could ever combine all these and cover so long a period of time. But with less satisfaction he thought of the recurring faintness, and curious sense of horror that had once or twice come over him, and then of the violent pains in his arm. These were quite unaccountable.

Moreover, now that he began to analyse and examine, there was one other thing that fell upon him like a sudden revelation: *During the whole time Field had not actually uttered a single word!* Yet, as though in mockery upon his reflections, there came ever from that inner room the sound of the breathing, long-drawn, deep, and regular. The thing was incredible. It was absurd.

Haunted by visions of brain fever and insanity, Marriott put on his cap and macintosh and left the house. The morning air on Arthur's

Seat would blow the cobwebs from his brain; the scent of the heather, and above all, the sight of the sea. He roamed over the wet slopes above Holyrood for a couple of hours, and did not return until the exercise had shaken some of the horror out of his bones, and given him a ravening appetite into the bargain.

As he entered he saw that there was another man in the room, standing against the window with his back to the light. He recognised his fellow-student Greene, who was reading for the same examination.

"Read hard all night, Marriott," he said, "and thought I'd drop in here to compare notes and have some breakfast. You're out early?" he added, by way of a question. Marriott said he had a headache and a walk had helped it, and Greene nodded and said "Ah!" But when the girl had set the steaming porridge on the table and gone out again, he went on with rather a forced tone, "Didn't know you had any friends who drank, Marriott?"

This was obviously tentative, and Marriott replied drily that he did not know it either.

"Sounds just as if some chap were 'sleeping it off' in there, doesn't it, though?" persisted the other, with a nod in the direction of the bedroom, and looking curiously at his friend. The two men stared steadily at each other for several seconds, and then Marriott said earnestly—

"Then you hear it too, thank God!"

"Of course I hear it. The door's open. Sorry if I wasn't meant to."

"Oh, I don't mean that," said Marriott, lowering his voice. "But I'm awfully relieved. Let me explain. Of course, if you hear it too, then it's all right; but really it frightened me more than I can tell you. I thought I was going to have brain fever, or something, and you know what a lot depends on this exam. It always begins with sounds, or visions, or some sort of beastly hallucination, and I—"

"Rot!" ejaculated the other impatiently. "What *are* you talking about?"

"Now, listen to me, Greene," said Marriott, as calmly as he could, for the breathing was still plainly audible, "and I'll tell you what I mean, only don't interrupt." And thereupon he related exactly what had happened during the night, telling everything, even down to the pain in his arm. When it was over he got up from the table and crossed the room.

"You hear the breathing now plainly, don't you?" he said. Greene said he did. "Well, come with me, and we'll search the room together." The other, however, did not move from his chair.

"I've been in already," he said sheepishly; "I heard the sounds and thought it was you. The door was ajar—so I went in."

Marriott made no comment, but pushed the door open as wide as it would go. As it opened, the sound of breathing grew more and more distinct.

"*Someone* must be in there," said Greene under his breath.

"*Someone* is in there, but *where?*" said Marriott. Again he urged his friend to go in with him. But Greene refused point-blank; said he had been in once and had searched the room and there was nothing there. He would not go in again for a good deal.

They shut the door and retired into the other room to talk it all over with many pipes. Greene questioned his friend very closely, but without illuminating result, since questions cannot alter facts.

"The only thing that ought to have a proper, a logical, explanation is the pain in my arm," said Marriott, rubbing that member with an attempt at a smile. "It hurts so infernally and aches all the way up. I can't remember bruising it, though."

"Let me examine it for you," said Greene. "I'm awfully good at bones in spite of the examiners' opinion to the contrary." It was a relief to play the fool a bit, and Marriott took his coat off and rolled up his sleeve.

"By George, though, I'm bleeding!" he exclaimed. "Look here! What on earth's this?"

On the forearm, quite close to the wrist, was a thin red line. There was a tiny drop of apparently fresh blood on it. Greene came over and looked closely at it for some minutes. Then he sat back in his chair, looking curiously at his friend's face.

"You've scratched yourself without knowing it," he said presently. "There's no sign of a bruise. It must be something else that made the arm ache."

Marriott sat very still, staring silently at his arm as though the solution of the whole mystery lay there actually written upon the skin.

"What's the matter? I see nothing very strange about a scratch," said Greene, in an unconvincing sort of voice. "It was your cuff links probably. Last night in your excitement—"

But Marriott, white to the very lips, was trying to speak. The sweat stood in great beads on his forehead. At last he leaned forward close to his friend's face.

"Look," he said, in a low voice that shook a little. "Do you see that red mark? I mean *underneath* what you call the scratch?"

Greene admitted he saw something or other, and Marriott wiped the place clean with his handkerchief and told him to look again more closely.

"Yes, I see," returned the other, lifting his head after a moment's careful inspection. "It looks like an old scar."

"It *is* an old scar," whispered Marriott, his lips trembling. "*Now* it all comes back to me."

"All what?" Greene fidgeted on his chair. He tried to laugh, but without success. His friend seemed bordering on collapse.

"Hush! Be quiet, and—I'll tell you," he said. "*Field made that scar.*"

For a whole minute the two men looked each other full in the face without speaking.

"Field made that scar!" repeated Marriott at length in a louder voice.

"Field! You mean—last night?"

"No, not last night. Years ago—at school, with his knife. And I made a scar in his arm with mine." Marriott was talking rapidly now.

"We exchanged drops of blood in each other's cuts. He put a drop into my arm and I put one into his—"

"In the name of heaven, what for?"

"It was a boys' compact. We made a sacred pledge, a bargain. I remember it all perfectly now. We had been reading some dreadful book and we swore to appear to one another—I mean, whoever died first swore to show himself to the other. And we sealed the compact with each other's blood. I remember it all so well—the hot summer afternoon in the playground, seven years ago—and one of the masters caught us and confiscated the knives—and I have never thought of it again to this day—"

"And you mean—" stammered Greene.

But Marriott made no answer. He got up and crossed the room and lay down wearily upon the sofa, hiding his face in his hands.

Greene himself was a bit non-plussed. He left his friend alone for a little while, thinking it all over again. Suddenly an idea seemed to strike him. He went over to where Marriott still lay motionless on the sofa and roused him. In any case it was better to face the matter, whether there was an explanation or not. Giving in was always the silly exit.

"I say, Marriott," he began, as the other turned his white face up to him. "There's no good being so upset about it. I mean—if it's all an hallucination we know what to do. And if it isn't—well, we know what to think, don't we?"

"I suppose so. But it frightens me horribly for some reason," returned his friend in a hushed voice. "And that poor devil—"

"But, after all, if the worst is true and—and that chap *has* kept his promise—well, he has, that's all, isn't it?"

Marriott nodded.

"There's only one thing that occurs to me," Greene went on, "and that is, are you quite sure that—that he really ate like that—I mean that he actually *ate anything at all?*" he finished, blurting out all his thought.

Marriott stared at him for a moment and then said he could easily make certain. He spoke quietly. After the main shock no lesser surprise could affect him.

"I put the things away myself," he said, "after we had finished. They are on the third shelf in that cupboard. No one's touched 'em since."

He pointed without getting up, and Greene took the hint and went over to look.

"Exactly," he said, after a brief examination; "just as I thought. It was partly hallucination, at any rate. The things haven't been touched. Come and see for yourself."

Together they examined the shelf. There was the brown loaf, the plate of stale scones, the oatcake, all untouched. Even the glass of whisky Marriott had poured out stood there with the whisky still in it.

"You were feeding—no one," said Greene "Field ate and drank nothing. He was not there at all!"

"But the breathing?" urged the other in a low voice, staring with a dazed expression on his face.

Greene did not answer. He walked over to the bedroom, while Marriott followed him with his eyes. He opened the door, and listened. There was no need for words. The sound of deep, regular breathing came floating through the air. There was no hallucination about that, at any rate. Marriott could hear it where he stood on the other side of the room.

Greene closed the door and came back. "There's only one thing to do," he declared with decision. "Write home and find out about him, and meanwhile come and finish your reading in my rooms. I've got an extra bed."

"Agreed," returned the Fourth Year Man; "there's no hallucination about that exam; I must pass that whatever happens."

And this was what they did.

It was about a week later when Marriott got the answer from his sister. Part of it he read out to Greene—

"It is curious," she wrote, "that in your letter you should have enquired after Field. It seems a terrible thing, but you know only a short while ago Sir John's patience became exhausted, and he turned him out of the house, they say without a penny. Well, what do you think? He has killed himself. At least, it looks like suicide. Instead of leaving the house, he went down into the cellar and simply starved himself to death. . . . They're trying to suppress it, of course, but I heard it all from my maid, who got it from their footman. . . . They found the body on the 14th and the doctor said he had died about twelve hours before. . . . He was dreadfully thin. . . ."

"Then he died on the 13th," said Greene.

Marriott nodded.

"That's the very night he came to see you."

Marriott nodded again.

CAROLE BUGGÉ

A Day in the Life
of Comrade Lenin

A wildly talented actress, poet, singer and composer, CAROLE BUGGÉ *has
contributed two other excellent fantasies, "Laura" and "Miracle at Chimayo,"
to my Doubleday anthologies. In the following bizarre tale, Ms. Buggé inflicts
a richly deserved "miscellaneous nightmare" on the late unlamented Russian
revolutionary leader Vladimir Ilyich Ulyanov, who ultimately came to be
known by his pen name, Lenin.*

Comrade Lenin is the Father of his Country. Comrade Lenin gets
up in the morning and puts in his wooden teeth. Can he not afford
real teeth? Yes, but the peasant's bed is made of wood so Comrade
Lenin will eat with wood. Comrade Lenin goes outside. There he
sees a tree—an oak tree. He chops it down. Could he not afford a
cherry tree? Yes, he could, but the peasants have only oak trees—
except Chekhov who was not really a peasant and therefore doesn't
count. Comrade Lenin decides, in fact, to chop down Chekhov's
orchard, and he does. The Cherry Orchard is the aristocracy. The
oak tree is the bourgeois. When Comrade Lenin is asked who
chopped down all the trees, he says, "I cannot tell a lie. It was the
proletariat, and I am the proletariat." When asked why he chopped
down all the trees, Comrade Lenin is not so sure. "Because they
were there"? Wrong answer. He is not a mountain climber, nor is he
an explorer. Why? "Because revolution cannot take place in a cherry
orchard." Who will now plant the new trees? "The proletariat will
now plant only the trees they want in the cherry orchard," says
Comrade Lenin. He is smiling. He has found all the answers to all

the questions—he has justified his actions in the eyes of others. He is a great man. He understands the nature of social order, and he understands the nature of metaphors.

A tiny doubt takes seed in his mind and begins to grow. Which are the right questions? Who knows what questions to ask; who decides on the right answers? This gives Lenin a metaphorical headache. This headache is only a figure of speech and therefore shouldn't bother him, but it does. He is a philosopher. This tiny doubt begins to eat like a small bird in his ear, and it wakes him up at night. One night he stands at his doorway looking at the cherry orchard in the white Russian moonlight, and he feels he cannot find the answers here. He must leave—but where to go? Norway? They have no use for a philosopher—they have Ibsen. England? Warm beer and Shaw. Lenin shudders. In the courtyard, an owl swoops down upon a mouse with a screech. Lenin admires the efficiency of this bird of prey. What does it remind him of, though? Something, but he cannot quite grasp it. He turns, wraps himself closely in his fur robe, and goes to bed. That night he sleeps soundly, and dreams he is an eagle on a cliff looking over the ocean. The next morning he knows what he must do; he packs his trunk and leaves on a steamer for America.

Comrade Lenin Goes to Bloomingdale's

Comrade Lenin is lost in New York City. He has wandered into the Upper East Side. He is looking for some proletarians to talk to, but he cannot find any here. He is walking up and down Madison Avenue. He gets a strange look from a thin woman who is walking a poodle. He looks back. Barbarians, these Americans, he thinks. He finds someone who looks like he may be a proletarian but it is only a Dutch tourist. In desperation, he begins to talk to a wino, who listens for a while but then moves on. Lenin envies the wino—he can have a conversation with no one at all. Lenin tries this—he practices talking to his reflection in a store window, but a policeman tells him to move on. Lenin begins to see that America has very little use for a philosopher, and he moves on.

Lenin sees a building—is it a shrine? It is full of people coming and going and they all look very reverent and serious. Cautiously, he enters. Immediately he is astonished—he has never seen so many different colors of socks in his entire life. There are colors here that most Russians will never see. Shyly, he reaches out to fondle a chartreuse pair with metallic threads. Instantly, he is aware of someone hovering. He turns around. A woman with vermilion cheeks is expressing what he takes to be a smile.

"Would you like to try them on?" she asks.

Lenin cannot speak. He nods, dumbly. He is led to a small room with the whitest lights he has ever seen. Trembling, he removes his shoes. Carefully, he pulls the socks over his feet, taking care not to pull the threads. The socks, when they are on his feet, make his feet dance. He dances out of the little room, into the cosmetics department. There he is stared at. A small crowd begins to gather, but he dances, past the L'Oreal and Charles of the Ritz display, past the perfume counter, and out into the candy department. He dances through it, eating one of every kind of candy, doing pirouettes and pas de chats through the Swiss chocolate Easter bunnies. He does a balance on the head of Famous Amos, and jetés out into the street. He dances for a minute in front of the store, for which he is given several quarters by pedestrians. He takes off in the direction of Park Avenue. But now he is very hungry so he buys some pizza on the way, doing the mambo in place while he eats it, and reaches Park Avenue with a quick little fox-trot. There a limousine is waiting for him.

"Mr. Lenin?" asks the black driver, who might be a proletarian, but Lenin has never seen a chauffeur before. Lenin nods and bunny-hops into the car. He is tired—it has been a long day. He falls asleep instantly, snoring loudly. The limousine, a black silent stork, bears him away on its rubber wheels.

Comrade Lenin and the Punk Rockers

Comrade Lenin has come to see Soho. He is wandering around, feeling very lonely. There are people walking very fast in all directions but he does not know any of them. He is too embarrassed to speak to them, afraid they will not understand his accent. He peers in the window of a store called The Look. An advertisement shows a girl with a grin like a piano keyboard. "Do *you* have The Look?" it asks. Lenin stares at it. He sees his reflection: shaggy dark hair, rumpled hat, round eyeglasses hiding his myopic eyes, clipped triangular beard, shapeless black overcoat. He ponders the girl in the advertisement. She glows, sleek as a seal, standing on a beach under a beach umbrella. He could almost reach out and touch her moist skin. His hand flaps at his side, a fish out of water.

Comrade Lenin is aware of a body close to his; one out of the sea of movement has come to rest for a moment beside him. He is afraid to turn and look at it, so he remains looking in the window. A girl, tall with purple hair and matching tights, is looking at the same display. She is smoking a cigarette and its smell reminds Lenin of home. His eyes fall on the box in her breast pocket: it is a box of Sobranie Black Russians. Comrade Lenin sighs deeply, feeling very sad and homesick. This causes the girl to look at him. Without speaking, she offers him a cigarette. This touches him deeply, and he begins to cry. She is distressed by this, and does not know what to do. He would like to explain to her that it is all right, that he is just homesick, but he knows no English except for "restaurant" and "toilet." He looks at her earnestly, shaking his head.

"Toilet," he says through his tears. She continues to stare at him.

"Restaurant," he says thickly.

Understanding passes over her face like a neon light. She takes his hand in hers, purple fingernails pressing into his flesh, and leads him through the narrow streets. Lenin does not resist; he follows meekly behind her, staring like a child at the people with green hair and yellow eye shadow and fluorescent stockings. She leads him to the doorway of an underground restaurant. It is very dark inside, and as they go down the concrete steps Lenin blinks rapidly. The room smells of garlic and cigarettes, and his mouth begins to water. He is embarrassed by the low rumble which emanates from his stomach; he clenches his muscles hard to stop it, but no one seems to have noticed it anyway. They are all sitting at tables with white cloths, laughing and drinking and eating and talking. Several young women have kerchiefs around their heads, but they wear them in a very different fashion from the Russian women Lenin is accustomed to. The Russian women look submissive, dowdy in their kerchiefs, but these women look defiant and brash. Their scarves are maroon, orange, neon pink, yellow; bright, warm colors, and they are worn for decoration, like jewelry, Lenin decides. He feels warm, almost drunk with the nearness of these people and the sweat of their clean American bodies.

The girl has found a table and is motioning Lenin toward it. A wave of panic rises in his throat, a tightening vise on his breath. Can he do this? He feels any minute someone at one of these cheerful tables will stand up and call him a fraud. He will be pointed at, singled out, shamed before all these beautiful strangers. They will all see that he is not one of them, and his humiliation will be complete.

Lenin can feel the blood rising to his cheeks, but he is saved once again by the girl, who pulls him into a chair and thrusts a menu before him. Relief sweat pops out on his forehead—here, sitting down, he is much less conspicuous. He hunches a bit in his chair and stares at the menu. It is covered with English words, and again he feels the panic rising. He looks to the girl for help—she is talking with a tall, thin man who has just come in. He is dressed in shiny black pants and a pink shirt. He does not seem to notice Lenin, but as he talks to the girl his eyes wander restlessly around the crowded room. Then, with a swing of his thin black hips, he is gone, moving between the tables with the grace of a panther. Lenin admires his sleek slimness, painfully aware of his own bulky awkwardness.

But now a waiter has appeared: the girl is ready to order and she is looking at Lenin, who stares at the waiter pleadingly. The waiter is a lithe blond with a coral-red napkin around his neck. He stands on one hip, looking bored, as if giving Lenin only the minimum amount of attention he can possibly give. Lenin clears his throat and points at random to something on the menu. The waiter bends over to look at it, and Lenin is startled by the scent rising from his neck—sweet and soft, like apple blossoms. He watches the waiter make his way through the sea of linen and kerchiefs—for all his insolence, Lenin finds him a dashingly attractive figure.

The girl has lit a cigarette and is holding the pack out to Lenin. He takes one and lights it, drawing deeply, too deeply, for it makes his head feel hollow and weak. The last time he had a cigarette was his niece's wedding in Volensk, when he had been so drunk on cider and vodka that he took Olga Smollensk out into the horse barn. The next day he couldn't remember what they had done out there, but from the way Olga looked at him for weeks afterward he knew it must have been something neither of them had any control over. He remembered her dress; it was thick red wool with black flecks, and her eyes were green with yellow flecks in them, and he remembered that, drunk as he was, he enjoyed the symmetry of that.

The girl is now pouring wine for both of them from a teardrop decanter. She lifts her glass to Lenin, smiling, and he lifts his, suddenly feeling a rush of happiness so intense it brings tears to his eyes. His glasses begin to fog, and he takes them off to wipe them on his napkin. As he wipes his glasses, he looks around the room. Everything is a soft blur; the tables are like ships in a fog, and the prints of the headbands are no longer discernible to him. He enjoys this out-of-focus version of the restaurant, and delays putting on his glasses.

The thin red candle on their table is surrounded by a halo, and it reminds him of crucifixes he saw in church as a child. He looks at the girl—she is laughing in response to something someone at the table next to them has said. Her head is thrown back, swimming in cigarette smoke and candlelight. Looking at her, looking at these animated shapes at their separate tables, Lenin feels a sense of long-sought-after recognition: these people are the proletariat! He is so excited he almost chokes on his wine. These people are his vision of the proletariat as he wants them to become: free, joyous, unselfconscious in their appreciation of the life of the senses. Not bogged down with centuries of repression like the aristocracy; for them it is too late to find liberation, but for the proletariat the summer of life is rising before them. Lenin finishes his wine and pours another glass, wishing to prolong this happy meditation. How can he bring this revelation of his back to his country? He finds a Sobranie and lights it, being careful not to inhale deeply.

Their food has arrived, and the girl is eating rapidly. Lenin looks at his plate: some unidentified meat sits between two round pieces of bread with a large onion slice on the side. Lenin likes onions, and he places it on top of the bread. This causes the girl to laugh at him, but he is not distressed by that, and lifts the whole thing carefully to his mouth. The first bite causes an explosion of saliva in his mouth such as he has never felt before—it has been days since he has eaten a meal, and this is the best meal he has ever tasted, it seems. Impulsively, he grabs the girl's hand and squeezes it. She squeezes his hand, smiling at him.

After the waiter takes away the dishes, they sit, smoking cigarettes. Lenin is gloriously happy; he feels a part of the scene now, he feels that he shares many things with these blithe, laughing people. The girl has taken a pen out of her purse and is sketching on the back of a napkin; Lenin peers over her shoulder to see: it is him she is drawing! He feels inexpressibly flattered and grateful to her, and again he squeezes her hand. She stops drawing and looks at him. Her eyes are green, with flecks in them like Olga Smollensk had, only her flecks are brown instead of yellow. Something in the way she looks at him causes his spine to tingle.

Abruptly, she picks up her purse, takes his hand firmly in hers, and begins to lead him, winding through the maze of tables. Lenin stumbles a bit; his boots are too heavy for such intricate footwork. She waves to someone as she leads him up the gray painted steps; Lenin turns around to see who it is, but she tugs him firmly forward.

He relinquishes all control to her, and allows himself to be tugged along the street. It is night now, and the street lights cast circles of light which they move in and out of as they stride along. People pass by them, also striding. What a city of striders this is—Lenin is astounded by all the energy.

Finally they have reached their destination, it seems: up some steps with ivy-covered wrought-iron railings, and in front of a red door she pauses, looks through her purse, and produces some keys. As she does this, Lenin looks around the street. A young couple approaches hand in hand—both of them are short-haired and supple, dressed in tight jeans and open white shirts. As they approach Lenin looks earnestly at their faces. Is he imagining things, or does the girl have a small blond moustache? He squints, peers harder, but it is too late, they are past him now, moving in and out of the circles of light, their thin thighs swinging forward.

The girl has opened the red door and motions him inside the building. He enters the hallway, which has a musty smell of boiled eggs. He follows her up some linoleum stairs which lean to the left; he grasps the rail to pull himself erect. He is panting heavily by the time they reach her apartment on the fifth floor. When she opens the door, he sees a note on the carpet just beyond the door jamb; she picks it up quickly and puts it in her purse without reading it.

She beckons him inside and closes the door after him. The room is small and cozy, with a faint smell of sandalwood. An upright piano in the corner is draped with a tasseled cream-colored shawl, on top of which is strewn sheet music of Schubert, Brahms, Beethoven. The girl is at the stereo, searching through the records. Her feet keep time to an imaginary beat as she does this. Finding a record, she puts it on the turntable. Lenin recognizes it as the Brahms Piano Quintet in D and grins broadly at her, but she has already gone to the small sink in the corner and is pouring a clear liqueur into two tiny glasses. She hands one to Lenin, smiling. Her front teeth are crooked and slightly crowded, and her lips are full and pink. He is glad she has not put on any more of the purple lipstick; it gave her an eerie, deathly look. He sips the liqueur, which tastes of licorice. She sits on the floor, leaning her back against a large red armchair. She looks up at him, beckoning him to sit. There is no more room in the armchair so he sits on the floor with a thud. His feet are very hot now and he would like to take off his boots. But how to do that without being rude? He points to his boots and grimaces. This causes a whoop of laughter from her, which startles him. She scoots over to him and begins to undo his laces. Lenin does not know what to do; he has never had a woman take off his boots before, let alone a woman with purple hair. She pulls gently and stands the boots in the corner by the window, next to a painted red radiator. Lenin is aware that his feet do not smell good, and to his horror, a fly is buzzing happily around his boots. The girl is not looking at his boots, however; she has begun to massage his feet. Lenin stares at her. No one has ever massaged his feet. He feels he should move, tell her to stop this, but he also feels helpless to move or even try to talk. Slowly, he leans back on his elbows. He is aware of how silly he looks, sitting there in his overcoat and socks, but now he does not care. In fact, he thinks he would kill anyone who tried to stop this right now. He closes his eyes, concentrating on feeling her fingers digging into his soles. He thinks of his mother, standing in the snow, waving to him as he goes back to the University after Christmas. She is wearing a green woolen scarf and the snow completely covers her feet and shins. He wishes she were still alive so he could show her how good this feels. He would massage her feet until he had rubbed away the snows of all those winters. He would massage her feet until she was a young girl again, running through spring buttercups instead of the frozen wasteland of a Russian winter.

The girl's face is concentrated, bending over his feet. A small wisp of purple hair has fallen over her face. Lenin bends forward stiffly and lifts it off her forehead; she looks at him with solemn brown-flecked eyes. Leaning over his outstretched legs, she takes his face in her hands, pulling his beard gently, and kisses him on the lips. Lenin is overcome. A deep splotch of red appears on both his cheeks, which feel hot and icy all at once, as if frostbitten. He stares at her, his throat constricted in mid-swallow. Her smile reminds him of Olga's mysterious smile, of the smile of the Mona Lisa, the smile of Womankind. This girl, he thinks, knows the secret of all Womankind, as surely as Olga knew it. She carries it in her body, as surely as the proletariat carry the fate of the world in their hands. He tells his arms to embrace her, but they remain at his sides, fingers digging into the braided rug. With one clean movement the girl stands and turns off the overhead light, so that only the blue-white light of the street lamp shining through the lace curtains illuminates the room. It falls on the floor in lace patterns, and Lenin stares at it. Swaying, the girl stands above him and rubs his shoulders with one hand, undoing the buttons of his black overcoat with the other.

Lenin begins to tremble. His legs are shaking visibly. He clenches his muscles to make them stop, but this only worsens the trembling. The girl pulls gently on his overcoat and in so doing pulls him over onto his back, so that he is lying outstretched on the rug. He stares at the ceiling, noticing the water stains from where the roof leaks. One of the patterns looks like the Ukraine. Weakly, he points to it, but she is on top of him now, kissing his beard, pulling gently at it with her sharp white teeth. Lenin feels as if he is going to faint. He doesn't faint, though, and closing his eyes, he begs his body to take over. He invokes his strong Russian ancestors, his virile Ukrainian uncles, his father whose wrists were as thick as horses' hooves. Gradually, he feels the strength return to his body. He struggles to sit up, lifting the girl off him. Clenching his jaw, he takes her by the wrist and holds her at arm's length. Then, taking a deep breath, he takes her in his arms, staggers to his feet and carries her to the couch under the window, plopping her on its red and green afghan covering. With as much determination as he can muster, he places his hands on her shoulders and kisses her. He wants to say something to her, but his meager English fails him and so he murmurs "Comrade" into her ear in Russian. Gaily, she seizes his face with both hands and, drawing it to her, bites his earlobe. This is worth a thousand Russian winters, Lenin thinks as he sinks back into the couch, green and yellow flecks swimming before his eyes.

Later, they lie on the braided rug, smoking the last two of her Sobranie cigarettes. Lenin meditates on the ceiling stain. It seems like weeks ago since he noticed it, and yet it is only an hour ago; there is the same fly buzzing around his boots. Lenin feels timeless, ageless, universal. He has found the proletariat, but he has found so much more. He feels expansive; he regards the fly on his boot with magnanimous benevolence. The girl is lying on her stomach, blowing smoke rings over her head.

Lenin reaches out to touch her shoulder, and the front door explodes. Lenin throws himself over the girl in a protective gesture, covering his head. He feels hands grabbing him by his undershirt. Uncovering his eyes, he is in time to see black-clad arms tossing him across the room. He lands on the couch, rolling off into the corner, where he sits in a daze regarding his assailant, who has already turned his back on Lenin and is yelling at the girl, who is staring off into space, her lower lip jutting out. The man is tall, hairy and dressed entirely in black. His head has been shaved, except for a strip of black hair down the middle of his skull. He seems to have forgotten Lenin and is concentrating his anger on the girl. It is obvious to Lenin that he is an interloper in their relationship. He would like to fight for the girl, but he doesn't have the heart. No doubt this large, well-fed American would grind him into a pulp.

Lenin pulls himself to his feet. The girl is talking now, quietly angry, stubbing her cigarette out on the hearth. Lenin begins timidly to collect his clothing; pulling on his boots without tying them, he buttons his shirt and looks for his coat. He wants simply to get away from these confusing, glamorous people. To get to his coat he must cross the living room, which he does on his hands and knees. He is suddenly aware that they have stopped arguing—that they are both staring at him. Sweat prickling on his forehead, he ignores their stare and fetches his coat, pulling it on hurriedly. To his horror, the girl begins to giggle, and after a moment the man joins in. They both shake with laughter, leaning against each other for support. Lenin is more devastated by the laughter than by the man's anger. Miserably, he gathers the remainder of his things and, casting a bitter, tragic look at the girl, he slides through the door and into the hall. Followed by their intolerable laughter, he hurries down the stairs, cupping his hands over his ears.

Outside, he leans against the big red door to catch his breath. A light rain has started to fall, turning the circles of light under the street lamps into faint rainbows in the dark. Lenin pulls his collar up to his chin.

A solitary figure approaches him on the pavement. It is a young man with close-cropped blond hair and tight green jeans culminating in pointed leather boots. He holds a cigarette in his hand, smiling warmly.

"Light?" he asks Lenin.

With a flush of pleasure, Lenin remembers he has matches from the restaurant still in his coat pocket. Gratefully, he produces them, his hands shaking a little. The young man lights his cigarette and with a friendly smile begins to walk away. After two or three paces he stops underneath a circle of light. Looking at Lenin solemnly, he jerks his head in a quizzical manner. Lenin understands this to be an invitation to accompany him. Lenin's melancholy changes to joy with the swiftness of a swallow in flight. Joyfully, he accepts, almost springing toward the young man. What a wonderful country this is where one meets new friends so easily. A cigarette, a smile under street lamps, and you have a friend. The young man smiles into Lenin's face. He is very young and has no beard growth. Slipping his arm through Lenin's, he draws him down the deserted street. Arm in arm, they pass through the rainbow-colored circles of light.

DARRELL SCHWEITZER and JASON VAN HOLLANDER
The Throwing Suit

Transients and Other Strange Travellers *is the most recent collection of "disquieting" tales by* DARRELL SCHWEITZER, *a prolific Pennsylvania fantasist who currently edits* Weird Tales *magazine. Mr. Schweitzer has collaborated several times with* JASON VAN HOLLANDER, *whose popular fantasy illustrations have been seen in* Weird Tales *as well as in books published by Arkham House Publishers, Inc.*

Jeffrey Quilt's paintings were muted, desolate things: curiously disturbing patterns of grays and browns mostly, with a very rare burst of some bright color so brilliant it came as a shock. "*Etudes*" he called his works. They sold well; they were affordable. I am sure he made a comfortable living from them, for all his house and studio always seemed on the verge of being condemned by either the Board of Health, the building inspectors, or both.

"The artistic temperament," he used to joke, "makes a wonderful excuse for many sorts of otherwise unacceptable behavior, including simple laziness."

"But far more, too," I said, on this particular occasion. "Far, far more."

"You're quite right," he said as he led me through the obstacle course of the living room, amid boxes of papers, old canvases, a broken TV set which now served as a repository for old and sometimes only half-emptied TV dinner trays, and boxes upon boxes of old, lurid paperback novels and magazines he always called his "reference library," but which, as far as I could tell, bore no relevance whatever to his painting.

"For who," I went on in this mock-pretentious mode, "can possibly know the soul of a true artist?"

He had reached the base of the steps, and he turned to me, sharply. The look on his face was puzzling. At first I thought he was actually angry with me, and I wondered what I'd said wrong. Then, for less than a second he seemed *afraid*, as if remembering for something, or even *listening*. I listened too, but all I heard was the strident chirping of Fido, his pet parakeet and sole housemate.

At last he laughed, not very convincingly. "I suppose that is why we'll never know the reason Hemingway cut off his ear."

I said nothing as we ascended, past the strange little miniatures that lined the stairwell, pictures of not-quite cute animals and animal-headed humans doing frequently less than cute things to one another amid teetering, vaguely medieval cityscapes.

The entire second story of the house was devoted to his "garret," four rooms' worth. Here was one of the great treasure-repositories of the United States, little known by mainstream art critics, but to the devotee a curious mixture of the Louvre and King Tut's tomb. Small oils were hung everywhere, on all the walls of all the rooms, on the doors, in the hall, in the closet-sized bathroom. ("I am considering the expansion potential of the ceiling," he said virtually every time I visited him.) Still more paintings stood upright in boxes in the middle of the floor.

As always, he followed me around wraithlike as I browsed, making his inevitable joke about discounts and saving his "admirers" gallery fees and sales tax. Then he went on, as he sometimes did, to philosophize upon *de morbis artificum,* the artist's sedentary ways and the morbidity that often attended such an existence.

Over the years I had acquired three Jeffrey Quilt oil paintings, and now, on this blustery December evening, after a good deal of searching, I believed I had found a fourth: one to match the season, a drab but intricate depiction of a costumed, ghostly figure seen from behind, looking out the window of a tower on what seemed to be a winter evening exactly like the present one.

I lifted it out of a box from between two others and held it up to Quilt.

"Ah, *The Throwing Suit.* There is a story behind that one. A truly horrible story."

Once more he seemed to be *listening*. Then he looked at me, awaiting my indication that he should continue.

"I will buy the painting," I said, "on the strict condition that the story isn't true. I don't want a painting with a bad history."

"Like the Hope Diamond."

"Yes, like that."

"Then I am afraid that I cannot sell the painting to you," he said evenly. "Come, there are others in the next room which may interest you, a new series I call *Revenants of the Living*."

He gestured to the door. But I couldn't stop staring at the ghostly figure. It must have been a trick of the light, but the shrouded man (I think it was a man) looked smaller now, more overwhelmed by shadows, and by the hugeness of the room in which he stood. The point of view was perhaps from a doorway, and at the full length of the room this figure stood gazing out another doorway, or perhaps a large window, at . . . what? Only the foreground details were clear: chipping paint, stains, exposed and rotting boards behind broken plaster. As far as I could make out, the standing figure's costume made no sense at all. It was sort of a shroudlike coat, with some of the characteristics of a straitjacket, only with too many straps and arms.

A *throwing suit* he had called it.

"Now you've got me curious," I said. "You *must* tell me the story."

"Very well, I will, but only on the *strict condition* that you buy the painting. Only then."

Adamant, he stared at me until I agreed—which I was reluctant to do since I'm more than a little superstitious. I handed him a check. Then we went downstairs into the kitchen, he cleared off two chairs, and we sat over paper cups of Pabst Blue Ribbon while he told me how autobiographical this particular painting was.

"That's half the reason I want to get rid of it," he said. Just then the wind whistled through the back door. The sound startled him. He knocked over the half-empty bottle, then righted it, but didn't bother to clean up the mess before beginning his story.

I have my own little audience, [*Quilt declared*] consisting of aficionados of a similar stripe to myself, who collect my work and have troubled themselves to make personal contact with me.

Five years ago, a collector of my work, a friend, put me in touch with a wealthy man with a great interest in otherworldly phenomena. I hasten to emphasize—I believe it is important—that I never saw my patron in the flesh. I met his go-betweens, servants, employees or whatever, and I spoke with him on the phone a few times. I got the impression that he was a recluse, perhaps a cripple. He offered me a commission. The amount was such that I didn't ask very many questions. For this extravagant sum, I was to execute an oil painting of a house, a property he owned in rural Chester County. Haunted, needless to say. I emphasized that my artwork is seldom pleasant to look at, and this seemed only to encourage him in his belief that he had chosen the right artist.

"For reasons of health," he said, "I must avoid this ghostly haven. But I am intensely eager to know what it *feels* like to be there. The videotapes I've already had made were unremarkable; you'd never know it was a haunted house. I dismissed a local portraitist who proposed to work from photographs: he insisted on completing the painting in his studio. He could not possibly capture—I suppose you would call it—the authentic atmosphere of the place without being there all the time he worked. Therefore I have chosen you, Jeffrey Quilt, an artist who specializes in macabre subject matter. If you accept, you will stay in the house and work there. The kitchen will be stocked with food. The electricity will be on. When the painting is complete, you will call me. There is a telephone on the first floor. My man will come for the painting within the hour. Further, although I don't insist on it, I would appreciate it very much if you would call me periodically to describe your impressions."

"You are a man whose interests mirror my own," I said, almost frivolously.

Very grimly, he said, "Hear me out. If we are to proceed, then you must agree to one *strict condition:* in order for me to be sure you are not working from photographs, a member of my staff will personally drive you to the house and lock you inside. Ten thousand dollars shall be yours, Jeffrey Quilt, if you abide by these terms and if you have a finished painting at the end of your stay."

The wealthy man went on to explain that the house was in a remote area ("No neighbors for miles in any direction") and that the windows were boarded up ("To discourage vandals!").

I was intrigued, to say the least. An authentic *haunted* house. This was my métier, after all. And working from photographs, I had to agree, would sacrifice the whole point.

I accepted. My patron insisted we begin at once. I began to pack my bags and painting supplies. A half an hour later the doorbell rang, and there was the millionaire's man, in a chauffeur's uniform no less, but I soon understood that he was more than just a driver.

"My employer insists that the painting be utterly *realistic*," this fellow said. "Nothing made up. Nothing fanciful."

"Certainly not. I have a reputation to maintain. Like a certain distinguished predecessor, I paint what I see."

". . . And the completion date of the painting?"

I hedged. "Perhaps a week. Longer if I need it. But I must insist on a down payment in any case."

He looked at me sternly, but was ready for this. He drew a fat envelope out of his pocket.

"Would twenty-five hundred be acceptable?"

A few minutes later I was the passenger in a Lincoln Continental, whizzing through the Pennsylvania countryside as twilight came on. My companion stared at the road ahead as if determined to pretend I didn't exist.

"It's a shame your boss can't come along," I said. "This really sounds like his kind of thing."

The driver said nothing.

"I *said* I wish I could meet your employer."

The response was one of barely controlled rage. "Because of his infirmity, he is unable to travel."

"So, what does he do with his time?"

The veins on his forehead stood out as he pondered my question. "He studies . . . mysteries."

"You mean like Ellery Queen and Sherlock Holmes?"

"*Sir*, if you are unable to take this any more seriously than you seem to show, I shall be forced to tell my employer that he has made the wrong choice for a painter."

"Now wait a minute," I said. "I'm your man, all right. I just want to know, what do you mean by mysteries?"

"You would not understand."

"Try me."

He all but spat the word. "Gnosticism."

It was hopeless. Once or twice further during the ride I tried to initiate conversation with him, but was curtly rebuffed. The driver was a complete enigma to me, his manner, both bland beyond my ability to describe and at the same time definitely hostile, was offensive in the extreme. Worse, it made no sense. It was as if service to his employer had all but erased him, and what remained was not his own personality, but an extension of his superior's, those parts of the inner mind the outer shell of custom and propriety keep hidden. My very nearness seemed to be an unforgivable violation of privacy.

As we drove, the countryside grew ever more desolate: the dun-colored, sloping hillsides stubbled with dead cornstalks, the occasional weathered house with its western-facing windows faintly gleaming in the last glimmer of sunlight. The December landscape and darkening sky were a lesson for me, a reminder of seasonal mortality, of mortalities everywhere.

I cherished such scenes. I was eager to paint.

Down a sloping country road we continued until we finally arrived, gravel rattling in an unpaved driveway; we pulled up in front of a solid-looking stone and wood farmhouse surrounded by milkweed.

The driver helped me with my luggage. He let the motor run. I stood in the gathering darkness and gazed up at what was more than a simple farmhouse.

"What a mélange!" I said aloud, eying the weird combination of architectural styles: a round tower with a conical roof (an allusion to a castle or a chateau), a broad, single-span porch supported on two pairs of columns, the spindle work and detailing on the porch an even more curious mixture of foliate faces, serpents, Colonial revival Tuscan columns, Romanesque revival with Prussian inflections; an awkward, uneasy blend. "The architect must have been *on* something. No wonder the place is haunted."

"The house was built in 1892," the driver sniffed as if that explained something. He jammed the key into the door, turned it. The door creaked open.

"Once you are inside, you are to call my employer."

"I thought he only wanted my impressions, and it was optional."

"Those are his *specific* instructions, sir."

Shuffling inside with my gear, I found myself in a large, unlit foyer. I couldn't see much, but the driver flicked on a switch with something like familiarity.

"Mr. Quilt," he intoned as he stood in the doorway, "I am to remind you that you forfeit the commission if you try to leave on your own." (Here, for the first time, a little, ingratiating smile.) "Leaving would be difficult in any event, for the windows are boarded up, the door is sturdy, and there are no tools."

As per our agreement, he ransacked my luggage and materials in search of a camera. While watching him do this, I became apprehensive. "What if there's a fire?"

"There is a volunteer fire company in the nearest town. You could make the call, then run up to the tower, which has a balcony, or perhaps you might consider it a porch, just under the roof. Wait there. It would be a simple matter to fetch you down with a ladder."

"Have you ever been up there?"

"Alas, the view is best appreciated by someone with the sensibility possessed by you or . . . my master."

Another strange facet to this strange character: for the first time his voice seemed tinged with *regret*. And for the first time he referred to his boss as his master. But things were too hurried for me to question him further. Satisfied I had not smuggled a camera along, he smiled again—a mocking smile—then let himself out. I heard the key turning in the keyhole, and a minute later the car rumbling away.

Alone in the house, I admired the furniture, the antique fixtures. There is the comforting but false belief that by possessing things—books, curios, paintings—we can somehow arrest the flow of time. A treasured photograph seems to freeze a scene or a loved one like an insect in amber; there it is on the shelf, never fading. I thought that this was what the wealthy man had done. Perhaps he was dying of some strange disease. Therefore he had purchased a house where the stream of time did not flow, where the dust and the smells and the passing hours were utterly stagnant, *here*.

It was an odd notion. Almost at once, I got out my sketchbook and began to draw as I wandered from room to room in the downstairs of the house: here a drapery, there a chair, again a coffin-shaped grandfather clock which had long since stopped ticking. I thought: Time is the artist's silent assistant. The artist stands back and watches time at work; as the pencil strokes accumulate, the sketch seems to fill in by itself. There are seasons in each moment.

The phone was ringing. I continued sketching, unmindful of it. All at once the ringing stopped. Only the sudden silence alerted me. Only then did it occur to me that I was hours overdue with my first phone call.

Behind the telephone was a huge pier mirror. A slip of paper with phone numbers on it had been placed between the mirror and the wall. As I dialed, I winced at the reflection of myself, at the day-dreaming expression of a man who took no notice of time except to rhapsodize about it in morbid reveries.

My call finally went through. An enfeebled voice answered, my patron's without a doubt, but fainter, muttering something about the lateness of the hour and my discourtesy. But his words faded away as I thought about the essential quality of this mansion, about the compost of the days here, gathering slowly like falling leaves the rich humus of hours.

"I lost track of time," I heard myself saying over the phone.

"Quilt! Tell me what you see!"

I tried to describe the vaulting foyer, the spiral staircase winding to the second floor. I mentioned the sketches I had made so far. "I haven't been upstairs yet," I said. Then I told him about the kitchen, which was frightening only in its banality.

"Have you located the *bad place* in the house?"

I joked: "I *am* the bad place."

"Eh—?"

"Which way I fly is Hell; myself am Hell."

"Have you found it or not?" he demanded.

Relenting, I suggested that the *bad place* might be upstairs. My sketches thus far were rather like seismographic recordings of a quakeless land: no "jolts" yet.

"It would be a lot easier," I complained, "if you'd stop playing games with me and just *tell* me where the hauntings occurred." I noticed a closet behind me, reflected in the pier mirror.

"As I've already explained, Quilt, I do not wish to plant any suggestion in your mind which could lead to bias."

"For instance, I am in the kitchen. Across from me is a closet—"

"Which should be firmly sealed shut."

"Actually, the door is ajar."

"What?"

I walked across to the closet, trailing phone wire. Even as I did the door swung outward, releasing air that smelled of damp earth long confined.

"It's opening," I said. "The door is open all the way now. Is this it? Am I getting warmer?"

"No. Stay away from that closet, Quilt. That's an order. *Stay away.* It's off limits. The door may swing shut on you. It can't be opened from the inside. You would suffocate. There's no one to hear you."

Even as he spoke I nudged the door open more. Inside was what looked like a canvas costume drooped over a black portfolio. I saw a colorfully paint-smeared box on the floor.

"The door's completely open," I said innocently. "Is that a box of pastels on the floor?"

"Close the door, Quilt. Close it *now.*"

I knelt down and opened the box. "Art supplies. And some kind of artist's smock with a hood. I've never seen anything quite like it."

"Jeffrey, please. Leave that closet alone."

I handled the smock. The weave was very coarse, like sailcloth. It was yellowed with great age, but still very strong. Its purpose and design I couldn't immediately figure out. There were a lot of buckles in places that didn't make any sense, and more straps than there were buckles. Strangest of all, the hood did not open to allow the wearer any view out at all, or even breathing room. What I took to be the front had a solid oval of metal riveted into it, like a heavy, featureless mask.

"This is really weird," I said. "It's sort of a straitjacket. It's very old—"

"God *damn* you, Quilt! The age has no bearing on your assignment. Leave that closet alone and concentrate on your painting."

Just then an almost inexplicable impulse came over me. While little admonitions were spewing out of the telephone—grumbles and threats and pleadings from a possibly invalid man many miles away ("Those items are personal property. They are irreplaceable. You have no right")—it seemed to me that the only possible course of action was to *put the smock on.*

I slid it over my head. The smell of old canvas was overwhelming. And there was something else, distinctly unpleasant, like rotting meat. The feel of the cloth, too, was quite nasty, at first as rough as steel wool, then warm and soft and firm, as if the thing were alive, as if I were inside a huge and toothless mouth which clamped down on me harder and harder.

I struggled to breathe. Somewhere, very far away, a voice was screaming, "Put it away, Quilt! Put it away!"

I still had the phone receiver with me, inside the smock, or bag, or whatever it was.

". . . the throwing suit . . ." he seemed to be saying. "Damn you, Quilt. Damn you."

My mind wasn't right then. My perceptions were distorted. It seemed to take hours, and only with the utmost concentration of will could I wriggle out of the thing, as if indeed it were a dark mouth filled with slime, holding me tighter and tighter.

Then I was sitting on the kitchen floor, the "throwing suit" crumpled in my lap. I fumbled for the phone.

"Hello . . . ?" I gasped for breath.

"Put it *back*, Quilt."

Without hesitation, I obeyed, and kicked the closet door shut.
"If it will be any comfort to you, I could always nail the door shut."
"There aren't any tools, Quilt. Remember?"
"I could block it with something heavy."
"Yes, you do that, Quilt. Then get back to your painting." He
excused himself, pleading that his blood pressure was soaring, and
hung up.
  I sat there for a long time, bewildered. Bingo, I thought. The
spectral seismograph has recorded its first tremor. Time indeed
seemed to stand still. I sat, trying to focus my thoughts, feeling
vaguely ill. I don't know how long it was. Eventually a full bladder
forced me to get up and find the bathroom.

I slept late the following morning and only fitfully attempted breakfast. I couldn't remember any dreams, but was left with the impression of having dreamed. Only a hint remained, a pseudo-memory of
endless grayness, like a world filled with ash.
  I spent much of the afternoon wandering through the first and
second stories of the house, sketching, absorbing the congested stillness that is the characteristic of such places: the curious density of
rooms left unoccupied, of objects untouched and unused for decades. Stale-smelling sheets covered the furniture and gray dust—
yes, like that in my forgotten dream—covered everything. Amid this
ghostly furniture I sat and sketched, then rose, went to another
room, sketched again, everywhere stirring up swirls of dust. Sunlight
sliced through the cracks of the boarded windows. I savored the
motes that sparkled in the brilliant beams.
  My attention wandered. I mused on time and death and the
enigma of my unseen patron. None of my sketches amounted to
anything. Frustrated, I gave up and started rummaging. I found a
cache of old magazines in a trunk in one of the rooms, mystery pulps
from the 1930s, *Police Gazette* from the '40s. I have no idea how they
got there, but they were just the thing for the moment. I sat paging
through them happily, for hours. At times I need pure trash, to
rescue me from the sublime. Life is short and Art is long, too long,
sometimes.
  In truth, all the rooms I had been in were harmless and even
agreeable. They radiated a certain antique charm. But then it somehow became completely clear to me, as I sat reading the pulp magazines, that my true subject matter, the *bad place* which would earn my

ten thousand dollars, was not in the closet below, but, inevitably, above me, on the unexplored third floor, in the tower.

So my ambition and plain greed propelled me, and the fascination of the prospect drove me, but my better judgment—call it my artist's sense of proportion, of *form*—bade me wait until the evening, when the light through the window slats deepened to red and twisted into the musty carpet at sharp angles. Then, and only then, would it be time for me to ascend.

For it is in the fading of the day, when the last traces of sunlight remind us of death, that hauntings manifest themselves. Somehow I was utterly sure. My patron was paying me for my impressions, and *that* was my impression.

But first I went down into the kitchen and got the "throwing suit" out of the closet. I was afraid of it—yes, afraid of an inanimate thing of canvas and metal—but it was again my impression—I *knew*—that I would need it, that despite my patron's hope that I could draw the essence of this place out with sheer artistic perception, the "throwing suit" was the key to the whole puzzle.

Haunted, I had been assured this house was. . . . *I hear there are such things. They hold the talk of spirits, their mirth and sorrowings.*

No, merely silent. As I searched the antique chambers of the third floor, I found nothing worthy of my brush. I made a few sketches, but only of old rooms, atmospheric but devoid of the resonating *torment* which makes a true haunted place.

It came to me that my commission was at stake, that if I didn't find anything more definite, I would have to fabricate some strangeness which would surely fail to satisfy my patron.

He knew what he wanted. He just wasn't telling me. He was waiting for me to find it myself, so he could *recognize* it.

I still could not discern his motives. He was no connoisseur. I was sure of that. My impression of him, over the phone and through the actions of his intermediaries, was of a greedy, grasping, perhaps desperate man, but insensitive to the point of vulgarity. He was a man who had *lost* something, perhaps, and was expecting me to find it.

Still it puzzled me that he did not come here himself, even if he were an invalid, even if he had to be carried. A painting, no matter how brilliant, could only be a secondhand thing, a sensation conveyed rather than experienced directly.

Why had he even purchased this house?

Filled with questions, seeking answers, seeking, let me admit it, something *horrible* which would inspire a suitably impressive "haunted house" painting, I did the one thing I knew I had to: I put the "throwing suit" on again.

The smell was not nearly as bad, as if the thing were accustomed to me. I stood, more puzzled than afraid as it slithered over me, as some of the buckles seemed to fasten themselves of their own accord, as the sleeves found my arms and the straps bound my arms tightly to my sides. I thought briefly, *How am I going to paint anything tied up like this?* but the thought passed, as did the sensation of being restricted. All was numbness and I was floating in the dark; and it occurred to me that the real purpose of this device might not be restraint, that it was instead the Victorian equivalent of a sensory-deprivation tank, into which one could withdraw to contemplate the inner mysteries—

Then the metal oval settled over my face. I had a hand free somehow. I explored the mask, as if through gloves, and it was, as I had recalled, featureless and solid; *yet I could see through it.*

I did not question. At first there were only drifting globules of light before my eyes, but then I could see, clearly, the twilit staircase that led into the attic and into the tower. There was something *wrong* about this vision. It was all shades of gray, utterly devoid of color, and devoid of most textures, like a crude attempt to shade in the world with a lead pencil.

Somehow I stumbled up the stairs. The dust there was so rancid that I was grateful for my awkward costume, since it filtered the air. I bumped into a mummified bat, a leathery, pendulant thing. At no time did I feel afraid of the supernatural, of ghosts and hauntings and monsters from the dark, for inside the "throwing suit" I was curiously immune from such influences.

I came to a circular room which had to be the main chamber of the tower. I saw that it had once been set up as an artist's studio. A canvas still stood on an easel. Something had been painted there, or attempted, but I could only make out random daubings of gray and black; no colors at all.

What little light there was came from skylights set in the ceiling, and from a curtain, through which gray light strained.

I moved toward the curtain. The easel behind me crashed to the floor. I turned back, dully, and only slowly figured out that one of the trailing straps of my suit, something like a three-pronged grappling hook, had caught the easel by one of its legs.

The curtains parted for me of their own accord. Or perhaps it was the wind. The porch was much larger than I'd imagined. I was puzzled that I hadn't noticed it at all from the outside when I'd arrived. But nothing seemed frightening while I wore the suit, somehow. I was content to leave unanswered questions unanswered.

I stumbled into a vase; a drowned squirrel poured out.

I stood in the open air, unassailable in a stiff breeze, surveying the leaden December landscape.

No, it wasn't even that. It was like a black and gray ink-wash by Paul Klee, a world stripped of even the most essential details, barely there at all, flat as a map, without texture, without life. The only features at all were leafless trees twitching into a white sky like blind optic nerves.

But where was the horror?

Even as I stood there, gazing, I was answered.

The horror was sheer emptiness, a measureless nothing, a sky without even stars, a world without even dust, decayed beyond all possibility of decay, still, silent, eternal.

The horror was that I was drawn inexorably to that place, by some force I could not explain, by the perverting of my own will, by the writhing action of the "throwing suit" itself, and ultimately by a kind of *lust.*

I tried to scream, but my mouth was filled with cloth. I tried to turn away, but my body seemed floating in a gray haze. I looked out, through the metal mask, onto that ultimate *death,* the death of sensation and experience, a death beyond the cessation of life. I was able to fold my knees, to make my legs buckle.

But the "throwing suit" dragged me on of its own volition. Helplessly I wriggled like a huge, enshrouded worm to the edge of the porch, and up, over the stone railing, then down, into space.

I was falling, it seemed forever. There were no points of reference, only nausea, a feeling of weightlessness, of no longer having a body.

For an instant I thought I saw something moving among the trees. I wasn't afraid. It was a flash of hope. What a relief to encounter any animate creature, any being at all, among such devouring emptiness.

I tried to call out once more, but my voice was muffled.

Yet the thing heard me, and answered, and drew nearer.

I heard it, its voice fainter than the wind, calling my name.

Jeffrey Quilt, here I am, it seemed to say.

I could almost make out a form, shoulders, arms, but not really. I had to imagine them, to fabricate.

But I could see the face, an old man's face, pocked, shriveled, wrinkled, twisted with cruelty and greed and desperate, almost pathetic terror.

Help me, it said. *Bring me back, into death, at least into clean death.*

Damn you, Quilt, it said. *I'll keep you here with me, forever. You deserve it.*

I cannot weep, it said. *Even that is forbidden me.*

As I watched the face decayed into a bare skull no thicker than gray, dirty paper; a dull red glow throbbed within, lighting it like a pulsating paper lantern.

Jeffrey Quilt—

It touched me. I felt frigid fingers on my cheeks, closing behind my head.

Jeffrey Quilt—

I *recognized* the voice then. That was my *impression,* for which I was to be so richly paid.

I knew that I had at last met my patron, there, in the *bad place.*

My recollections beyond this point are confused. I cannot say what it was precisely that provoked me to terror, thence to action. Perhaps it was the prospect of remaining in this void forever. Perhaps it was the way the apparition caressed my forehead *lovingly* while alternately threatening and pleading.

Somehow I struggled, and sensation returned. I felt the restraints of the suit and fought against them, desperately, as if far more than my life depended on escape.

And I felt myself sliding free, the abrasive cloth tearing at my face and arms and thighs as if I were completely unprotected, naked.

I was far less afraid of falling three and more stories from the tower balcony than I was of remaining inside the suit.

I was fortunate. My hands caught in the various straps and I dangled in the air as I swung back and forth, scraping against the stone of the tower's outer wall. Fortunately, too, I somehow managed to climb up the outside of the "throwing suit," grasping the straps, then the trailing cord that led to the grappling hook, and at last the porch railing, *all the while with my eyes tightly closed.*

I crawled through the curtain, then lay still on the studio floor, gasping for breath, exhausted.

Downstairs the phone was ringing endlessly. I just lay there and listened to it ring. The sound was comforting, as was the simple sensation of a solid floor beneath me.

Only after a very long while was I able to go downstairs, answer

the phone, and tell my patron that I had failed, that there would be
no painting.

He sent the driver for me. But before the man arrived I screwed
up all my courage and returned to the tower room, and even to the
porch. I stood there, looking out into the darkness, the "throwing
suit" still dangling from the railing before me. I saw only the normal
winter sky, and the Pennsylvania countryside. Then I noticed head-
lights coming up the driveway and I hurried downstairs again.

"My master sincerely hoped," the chauffeur said, "that you would be
able to rely entirely on your artistic skills and sensibilities, and avoid
the temptation of the throwing suit, which, as you have seen, proved
so disastrous for him." He did not accuse; and he was not speculat-
ing. He merely knew.

I made no reply.

As we left, he eyed me—ironically, I think—and said, "You are not
the first."

"Not the first," I said wearily.

"My master is the first. He was the first and only inhabitant of this
house."

My foggy brain could not put the pieces together. "Wait a minute.
That's . . . no, you must be mistaken. 1892. That would make your
boss at least a hundred."

"My master was elderly when he built the house," the driver said.
"He was seventy when he began what he called his *project*. He is now
one hundred and sixty-seven years of age. His problem, sir, which
he had hoped that you would solve, is that he is unable to die."

[Jeffrey Quilt stopped speaking.]

I sat there in the half-lit kitchen. My beer had lost all its foam. The
house was quiet, but for occasional pingings and creakings. Even the
parakeet was silent.

"You can't expect me to believe that story," I said at last. "It's
rubbish and you know it."

He raised his hand to silence me. I couldn't read his face. He was
completely inscrutable then.

"No, it is not. It is true. Every word of it. As my patron insisted, I
fabricated nothing."

"But it doesn't make any sense."

"True. It doesn't. Or it doesn't seem to. I returned the advance
money. I *insisted* on giving it back. I had forfeited the contract. But I

hadn't wasted my time. My *impressions* were superbly trained. It is the secret of my art. It brought on a sudden blossoming of the bizarre, the necrotic, which my admirers have, well, admired. Sure, I enjoyed a certain reputation *before* my adventure took place, but the difference, afterwards, was a whole order of magnitude."

"But how could that man be a hundred and sixty-seven? What was *going on* in that house?"

"I can only guess."

"But your *impression*—"

"Yes," said Quilt. "My impression. I learned from the driver that his master had been an artist once, or had tried to be. He was a brutal and ruthless man, very rich, but he wanted to be something more. He thought he could *take* what he wanted from nature, snatch it, like a thing off a shelf. Those were *his* paints in the closet and it was his studio in the tower room. But he failed. Perhaps he simply had no talent. Inspiration did not come. The harder he tried the more he drove himself into something like madness, beyond madness, into something altogether indescribable. Quite possibly he had achieved *gnosis*, the inner truth. He had delved too far into himself and found, in the end, only desolation. How can any of us be sure it is not the same for us?"

"What was the throwing suit?"

"I think it was a device, designed to function as it had for me. By its twistings and turnings, but the strange stresses and stranger sensations, it somehow slides the wearer outside of space and time as we know it, into—I don't know where. Wherever, he lost himself there. It was the wretched residue of his soul which I had encountered. Perhaps he too had wriggled out of the suit, but failed to catch the straps, and had fallen. Had he also crippled himself physically? I never found out. But one evening, after such experiments, he left the house forever, a changed man, utterly changed, neither dead nor alive, for he lacked an essence, whatever it is that makes us human."

I didn't know how to take this. Was Jeffrey Quilt drawing me into the most elaborate gag of all time? Or had he decided to stimulate sales by building a *mystique* around each of his paintings?

"I get it," I said. "He then went on to make a yet another pile in big business, where not having a soul was a definite advantage."

Quilt slammed his fist onto the tabletop. My beer cup hopped onto the floor and splattered.

"Forgive me," was all I could think to say.

"My purpose," he said slowly, "the reason my patron hired me, was to create a painting so effective, so vivid, so much the embodiment of the essence of that terrible place, that by staring into it he could recover his scattered soul, enough of it so that he could be human again, so he could die. I do not think he has ever succeeded, or ever will. If you don't believe me, you can ask him yourself. I'll give you his phone number. But then again, I doubt he'll want to talk about it."

We sat in silence for a while. I glanced at the painting of *The Throwing Suit*, then stared as something I couldn't define caught and held my attention.

It was only after a few minutes that I knew what I was looking at. The picture had changed. The shrouded figure, the wearer of the throwing suit, was facing me now, its featureless mask gazing directly at me.

"Good *God* . . ."

"What is it?" said Quilt, alarmed.

"Nothing."

He didn't believe me, obviously. We stared at one another in silence.

"I don't understand," I said at last. "If you didn't do the painting, what is this?"

"This isn't *the* painting. I made this for myself, to commemorate the adventure." He took the painting from me, looked at it closely—I am certain he trembled slightly before he assumed a lighter, almost jovial tone and handed it back. "It's yours now. According to our bargain, you've heard the story and now you must accept the artwork."

I held it again, then looked away.

"Yours," he insisted. "You paid for it."

What terrible secret would be revealed, I wondered, when the features of that masked figure finally became clear?

"Do I have a choice?" I said after a pause.

He told me that choice didn't enter into it. Smiling sadly, more than a little drunk, he explained that Art, if it has any power at all, is revelatory and therefore it "gives knowlege; yields experiences that can't be forgotten. So in that sense there is no choice." He paused, considering something. "But I'll tell you what: if you keep the painting I'll refund your money."

Nervously, I protested, insisting he keep both the money *and* the painting.

He laughed. "That won't be necessary." Then he returned the check. He agreed to keep *The Throwing Suit* on the strict condition that I refuse to believe the story.

"Besides," he said, shivering from the cold that I could barely feel, "there are a dozen new paintings upstairs that might interest you."

JOHN JAKES

The Man Who Wanted to Be in the Movies

JOHN JAKES, *a native of Chicago, resides with his wife, Rachel, in Greenwich, Connecticut, and also on South Carolina's Hilton Head Island. Author of the best-selling eight-volume* Kent Family Chronicles *and* The North and South Trilogy, *Mr. Jakes is also a playwright, actor and director. His weirdly offbeat short story, "The Man Who Wanted to Be in the Movies," first appeared in an anthology edited by August Derleth, cofounder of the legendary Wisconsin fantasy publishing firm, Arkham House.*

George Rollo stepped away from the mirror and surveyed his scrupulous grooming. His hair was neatly brushed back, his suit freshly pressed, and his maroon tie with the white polka dots was artfully knotted. His face was almost eclipsed by the carefully planned sartorial perfection.

George Rollo was in love. He happened to be in love with a young woman who received his attention with reserve. But he went right on pursuing her, doing anything within his power to win her affections. Because of her, he dressed carefully.

He picked up the expensive box of candy secured from the drug store. He was able to afford a large box because he was a pharmacist in the drug store and could get the candy wholesale.

He locked the door of his room soundly behind him and clattered down the stairs. On the second landing a young and rather pretty woman with big amber eyes stood leaning on the doorjamb, next to a sign that announced, *Yolanda Fox, Licensed Thaumaturgist, Helpful and Benevolent Spells of All Types.*

"Hello, George," she said warmly as he came banging down the stairway.

"Oh. Hello, Yolanda, how are you?" His voice was strained, absent.

A large furry white thing rushed past the girl's legs and began lapping affectionately at the young man's shoes.

"Down, Faust," Yolanda said sharply. "Come here."

The familiar, who resembled a large and pugnacious bull dog with amber eyes quite like the girl's, crept back to a position at the side of his mistress, whining helplessly.

"Going out?" Yolanda asked yearningly.

"Yes," George replied in a nervous tone, "with Mabel."

"Oh." Sadness dropped like a curtain across her face.

"Well," he said nervously, "well, I guess I'd better be going."

He hurried off down the stairs. Yolanda caught a glimpse of the candy box and her amber eyes narrowed with faint jealous anger.

Faust growled, displaying bulldog teeth.

She shrugged then, as if winning out against an impulse to injure George, who shot a hasty glance at her from the bottom of the stairs just as she returned to her apartment.

Out in the street, George shivered. He knew Yolanda liked him, even though he had a distinct fear of witches. Even white witches licensed by the State Thaumaturgy Board. They could only conjure helpful spirits or make hexes to ward off illness. The law said they could do no more, but George was certain many of them had darker, half-forgotten powers.

He put Yolanda from his thoughts and hurried on down the street.

Miss Mabel Fry sat in her dirty armchair, surrounded by piles of magazines. Their glazed covers blanketed the rugs, made colorful landscapes even in the small dinette. The walls of the apartment were covered with pictures of male movie idols, wearing houndstooth jackets or holding a golf club or smiling at starlets.

The doorbell clacked with a noise of sad disrepair.

Mabel reached for another peppermint, shoved it into her red mouth and went on reading her magazine: *It's the Simple Home Girl For Me, by Rodney de Cord, Rising Young Parafilm Star.*

The doorbell clacked a second time.

Mabel lifted her large body and moved disconsolately to the alcove. She opened the door and said in a bored manner, "Oh. George."

"Hello . . . uh . . . Mabel."

He burst eagerly into the room, presenting his candy. She accepted it with mumbled thanks. She was a perfume clerk in a local department store, but she didn't much like the idea of accepting candy from an ordinary druggist.

"Where are we going tonight?" she asked, slipping into her coat.

"Anyplace," George replied casually. "There's a fine concert at the Music Hall . . ."

She ignored him. "The Royal has a wonderful new picture. *I'll Slay My Love,* with Todd St. Bartholomew. He's *so* masculine. When he played a private detective and slapped Lona Lawndale in *Bodies to Burn,* I just couldn't stand it, it was so thrilling."

George didn't argue. "Anything you say," he mumbled.

As they walked to the theatre she babbled about the latest gossip from Hollywood. Who was marrying whom. Who was divorcing whom. Who was in bed with whom when who came home with whose perfume all over him. George listened with resignation.

Mabel waited under the glaring lights of the marquee while he bought the tickets. She rolled her eyes ecstatically at Todd St. Bartholomew staring belligerently from the poster, gun in hand. A caption balloon from his lithographed lips announced, *I'll Slay My Love.*

As they passed through the door, Terry Silver, the aging owner of the theatre, waved to Mabel.

"Evening," he called affably. "Next week we're showing *Husbands and Paramours* with Michale Yarven."

"Ooooooo," Mabel exclaimed loudly. "How wonderful!"

She allowed George to take her hand as they approached the main aisle. Just then a young man in a bright red sport coat sauntered over.

" 'Lo, Mabel," said Bertie Wallen.

George swore in a whisper. Bertie Wallen was a bit actor on local television shows. He dressed and looked like a movie actor.

"Thought I might find you here," Bertie said to Mabel. "Got big news. Friend of mine in Hollywood just wired me that I should fly out there right away. Metropole wants to test me."

Mabel squealed with delight.

George stood by impotently, glaring at Bertie as if he were a liar.

"Like to see the wire?" Bertie asked in broadly humorous tones.

"Sure, Bertie," Mabel cooed.

"Come on out to my car. Only take a minute."

Mabel started away, then turned to George. "Be a sweetie and go inside and wait for me. I'll be right in. The usual seats."

He started to protest feebly, hesitated, and stumbled into the auditorium. He found the customary seats, saving the adjacent chair for Mabel.

For two hours he sat woodenly, alone, watching Todd St. Bartholomew consuming quarts of alcohol and being pounded by assorted mobsters. George rather enjoyed the picture. One of Hollywood's better character actors, a man named Tab something or other, played a kindly old judge. George liked Tab whatever-it-was, although he doddered a bit. He must have been at least seventy-five. He had a sympathetic rugged face. He did not impress George as a professional lover.

George tapped on Yolanda Fox's door at eleven-thirty that evening. The door opened after a moment and she invited him in, surprised and pleased. Slipping out of a black robe and erasing a chalk pentagram from the floor, she turned up the lights.

"Just practicing a hay fever prevention spell," she explained. "Pollen season coming on."

He sank down on her sofa, staring moodily at the floor. Faust nuzzled his leg.

"Yolanda," he said at last as she bustled out of the kitchen with two steaming cups of tea, "you're the one for me."

She almost dropped the cups. Quickly she set them down and hurried to his side. "Oh, George . . ."

"Yes sir," he added gloomily, "you're the one to help me get Mabel."

"Oh."

Her face smoothed out. She seemed quite calm. She served the tea and inquired in a helpful tone, "What can I do?"

"I love Mabel Fry. I'll do anything to make her love me. But she . . . well . . . she likes movie stars. Isn't there any kind of a spell to make me lucky?" He paused, deliberated and plunged on. "Can't you get me into the movies?"

"I don't know," she answered, thinking.

"I'll pay anything," he offered. "That is, anything I can."

"It won't be necessary to pay me," she replied carefully. "I'll be glad to help you. In fact, I think I can get you into the movies tonight."

"You . . . can?" He was startled.

"Certainly." She picked up a valise, began to stuff it with the paraphernalia of demonology. "But we must have the right atmosphere."

"Atmosphere?"

"A theatre. The Royal is near. I guarantee that before morning you'll be in the movies. Come, Faust."

They hurried through the dark streets.

The Royal was a mound of shadow, closed for the night. The street was relatively deserted. Only a drunk reeled from a cocktail lounge opposite the theatre.

"Sssssh," Yolanda cautioned, finger to lips. "We've got to get inside."

They crept through the vacant lot adjoining the theatre. Before the brick wall, Yolanda halted and made several passes in the air, murmuring something about Asmodeus, and a cold wind shoved George forward through gray fog.

He looked about. They were in the middle of the darkened theatre lobby.

Faust yipped with satanic glee. His large amber eyes glowed with strange delight. Yolanda's eyes glowed in the same fashion. George didn't notice.

They made their way down one aisle of the auditorium. Above them, the screen was a formless patch of silver-white.

Yolanda opened her valise, pulling forth her black robe. She lit two small braziers that gave off pungent fumes. She drew circles on the rug, remembering all of the bits of black magic the law had forced her to forget.

George watched the screen in fascination, because if Yolanda proved successful, he would be up there, and soon!

Yolanda moaned and waved her hands in the air and chanted. The braziers smouldered with oily bronze fire. Faust capered up and down the aisle, barking. And then Yolanda tapped George on the shoulder. Her face was illuminated by some unholy light.

"All right, George," she whispered. "Here you go."

He was strangely lifted.

Yolanda erased her marks, put out her braziers, repacked her valise and departed. Faust cavorted behind her, bulldog face aglow with strange humor.

For a long time George Rollo didn't know what had happened, or where he was. If this was the way to get into the movies, it was certainly a peculiar way.

When he tried to move his hands or feet he found it was impossible. In fact, he was unable even to feel them at the ends of his arms or legs. That is, he amended in his thoughts, he would have been, if he could have felt his arms or legs.

Everything was strangely dark. Then suddenly it was as though a curtain had been swept away from his eyes.

He saw rows of white staring faces. Two of them belonged to Mabel Fry and Bertie Wallen. Suddenly it began to dawn on him just what Yolanda had done. Blinding lights hit him. He screamed.

The only sound that came out was a ruffle of drums and a snatch of vaguely familiar music.

He wasn't George Rollo. *Christ in heaven!* . . . he wasn't even a *man! He was flat . . . and from one end of him to the other, in* gigantic letters, he said IN CINEMASCOPE. . . .

The Beast Within

With the sole exception of the risible folk tale of Tim Finnegan's accidental death and riotous resurrection, the next sequence of grisly narratives features as brutal a set of villains as ever stalked the night. Bloody torturers, poisoners, rapists, fetishists, Nazis and other human monsters infest these pages.

Let the reader beware . . .

W. J. STAMPER

Fidel Bassin

In my earlier anthology Weird Tales: The Magazine that Never Dies, *I included a remarkable horror story, "Ti Michel" by W. J.* STAMPER, *one of the finest contributors to* Weird Tales *in the 1920s (and, unfortunately, one of the most obscure). Here is another of Stamper's six gruesome "weird" tales. Like "Ti Michel," it is also concerned with the early bloody history of the Haitian Republic.*

"It cannot be done. It would be the most dastardly deed in the annals of Haiti. Send all prisoners to Port au Prince with the utmost celerity. The general orders. The general be damned!"

Thus spoke Captain Vilnord of the Haitian army as he finished reading the latest dispatch from headquarters. He was the most gentle and by far the most humane officer yet sent to Hinche to combat the ravages of the Cacos, the small banditry that continually terrorized the interior. Although he realized that many a brave comrade had lost his head for words not half so strong as those he had just uttered, he did not care, for he had almost reached the breaking point. For months he had observed the cruelty with which the government at the capital dealt with the ignorant and half-clothed peasantry of the Department of the North. His nature revolted at the execution of the commands of General La Falais, the favorite general of the administration at Port au Prince. Hardly a day came but brought an order directing the imprisonment of some citizen, the ravage of some section with fire and sword, the wanton slaughtering of cattle or the burning of peaceful homes. He was a servant of the people and he had obeyed orders; but this last was too much.

"Any news of my captaincy?" inquired the rotund lieutenant, Fidel Bassin, as his chief finished the dispatch.

For answer Vilnord crumpled the message in his hand, threw it in the face of his subordinate and strode angrily out of the office. He went straight to the prison and entered without even returning the salute of the sentinel on duty.

He had viewed that noisome scene every day for weeks, powerless to aid or ameliorate the suffering. No food, no clothing, no medicine had arrived from Port au Prince, despite his urgent and repeated appeals. As he passed through the gloomy portal, a resolve was taking root in his bosom, and another sight of the victims would launch him upon the hazardous course he had seen opening for months.

The prison was a long, low adobe structure with three small grated windows but a foot from the roof. These furnished little ventilation, for the heat was stifling and the odors sickened him. Two hundred helpless men and women were crammed into this pesthouse of vermin and disease, and all under the pretext of their being friendly to the Cacos. Old men lay writhing on the floor with dirty rags bound tightly about their shriveled black skulls, and as Vilnord passed they held up their skinny arms and pleaded for food. Withered old women sat hunched against the walls and rocked back and forth like maniacs. The younger men who yet had strength to stand, paced restlessly up and down with sullen and haggard faces. From every dusky corner shone eyes staring with horror. Ineffable despair overhung them all.

Vilnord stooped over an emaciated old man, who seemed striving to speak through his swollen lips, and asked, "What is it, papa?"

"It is the dread scourge, *Capitaine*," he rasped, "the black dysentery. I must have medicine or I go like my poor brother, Oreste."

He pointed to a mass of rags beside him.

Without fear of the disease whose odor pervaded the whole room, Vilnord gently lifted the remains of a filthy shirt under which Oreste had crept to die.

No man who has never looked upon a victim of tropical dysentery after life has fled can imagine the horror of the thing. The lips were so charred with the accompanying fever that they had turned inside out, and from the corners of the gaping mouth there oozed a thick and greenish fluid. The skin was drawn tightly over the bony cheeks, and the eyes had entirely disappeared, leaving but dark and ghastly holes. He had been dead for hours. With a scream like a wounded animal, Vilnord rushed from the charnel-house and to his office, where Fidel was still waiting.

He opened the drawer of his desk, pulled out a parchment neatly bound with ribbon, and to the amazement of his subordinate tore it in pieces. It was his commission in the army, just such a paper as Fidel had desired for many years.

"Fidel, I am through," he roared. "I will stand this wanton murder no longer. Do as you like about those orders, for you are in command. I leave for Pignon tonight to join Benoit, the Caco chief."

"But, *Capitaine*," remonstrated Fidel, "you must not do such a thing. La Falais will send all his regiments to seek you out. He will camp in Hinche for ten years or capture you."

"I defy La Falais and his murderers! Let him camp in Hinche for ten years. I will stay in the deep mountains of Baie Terrible for ten years. With Benoit I will fight to the death."

With these words Vilnord strode to the door, Krag-Jorgensen in hand, and mounted his waiting horse.

Fidel followed him out, and as he was adjusting his saddle bags, inquired, "Would La Falais promote me if I failed to carry out those orders? Would he not stand me up before a firing squad?"

"You may pursue the same course which I have chosen, the only honorable course," answered Vilnord.

"But I am due for promotion."

Vilnord tore the captain's insignia from his collar and hurled them into the dust.

"You will never be a captain. *Au revoir*," he cried back to Fidel as he fled toward the bald mountains of Pignon.

A blazing sun beat down upon the grief-stricken village of Hinche. There was bustle and commotion outside the prison. Fidel was preparing to execute the orders of his superior. There in the dusty road was forming as sorry and pitiable a cavalcade as ever formed under the skies of Africa in the darkest days of slavery.

Men and women filed out the door between two rows of sentinels whose bayonets flashed and sparkled in the sunlight. There were curses and heavy blows as some reeling prisoner staggered toward his place in line. The prisoners formed in two lines facing each other. Handcuffs were brought out and fastened above the elbows, for their hands and wrists were so bony that the cuffs would slip over. Two prisoners were thus bound together with each set, one link above the elbow of each. A long rope, extending the full length of the line, was securely lashed to each pair of handcuffs so that no two prisoners could escape without dragging the whole line. Many were so weak with hunger and disease that they could not stand without great difficulty. None of them had shoes, and they must walk over many miles of sharp stones and thorns before arriving at Port au Prince. The trip would require many days, and no food was taken except that which was carried in the pouches of the sentries who were to act as guards.

Suddenly there arose a hoarse and mournful cry from assembled relatives, as two soldiers emerged from the barracks, each with a pick and shovel. Fidel knew that most of the prisoners would never see the gates of Port au Prince, and he had made provision.

"Corporal," he said as he passed down the line inspecting each handcuff, "you will bury them where they fall. If they tire out, do not leave them by the roadside."

Weeping friends and relatives surged up to the points of the bayonets begging that they might be allowed to give bread and bananas to the prisoners, for they well knew there was no food between Hinche and the capital except a few sparse fields of wild sugarcane.

"Back, vermin! Forward, march!" commanded the corporal.

His voice could scarcely be heard for the screams and moans of the relatives as they shrieked:

"Goodbye, papa! Goodbye, brother!"

Down the yellow banks of the Guyamouc wound the cavalcade, into the clear waters many of them would never see again.

Hinche mourned that day, and when the shades of night descended upon the plains there was nought to be heard save the measured beat of the tom-tom and the eerie bray of the burros.

Sleek, well-fed Fidel sat calmly smoking with his feet propped up on the very desk vacated by his chief the day before and mused upon the prospect of his captaincy, which he felt confident would be forthcoming. He had carried out the orders of La Falais and he knew that crafty general would not be slow to reward him when news of the desertion of Vilnord reached the capital. He muttered half aloud: "A captain within a month. Not so bad for a man of thirty."

But his face twisted with a frown as he recalled the solemn, almost prophetic words of Vilnord: "You will never be a captain."

There came a voice from the darkness outside.

"May I enter, *Capitaine?*"

He liked the title, "Captain." It sounded so appropriate.
"Come in," he commanded.

It was the aged and withered old magistrate of Hinche, who had seen his people maltreated for years and who, no doubt, would have joined the Cacos long before had his age permitted.

"I have come to make a request of you in the name of the citizens," he said, and there was a strange light in his eyes.

"In the name of the citizens!" Fidel repeated sneeringly, and added: "Anything you ask in that august name, no man could refuse. What is it?"

"We beg that you release the remaining prisoners, those who are unable to walk because of hunger and disease, and allow them to return to their homes where they can be cared for. They are dying like hogs in that pesthouse. Will you let them out?"

"Never," was the firm reply. "I will bury every festering Caco-breeder back of the prison with the rest of his kind."

The magistrate folded his arms and with shrill but steady voice cried out: "La Falais, and you too, Fidel, shall render an account before history for this foul action, this heartless torture, this wanton murder of your own people. We, who are left, have arms, and we shall oppose you to the last drop. This very night has settled upon the fresh graves of our best people. Along the trail to Ennery and Maissade they have died, and over the graves your vicious troopers have put up forked sticks and placed on them a skirt, a shoe, or a hat in derision of the dead. To what purpose did the immortal Dessalines and Petion fight and wrest our liberty from the foreigner when it is snatched from us by our own bloody government?"

"Be careful of your words, old man," replied Fidel. "I have but to command and my soldiers will shoot down every living thing and lay this Caco nest in ashes."

"I have been very busy today, *mon capitaine*. Your soldiers at this very moment have scattered among the bereaved families of those who lie dead by your hand. You have no troops—they have become the troops of Haiti."

With a curse Fidel snatched his pistol from the holster. But before he could use it, a half dozen burly blacks leapt from the darkness outside where they had been waiting, and bore him to the floor. His hands were bound behind his back, and two of his own soldiers stood over him with drawn revolvers.

"I'll have the last man of you court-martialed and shot!" he stormed. "Release me immediately."

"Small fear of that," answered the soldier. "We go to join Benoit, the Caco chief, when we have finished with you."

The magistrate walked to the door and spoke a few whispered words to one of the blacks, who hurried away into the darkness.

Every shack sent forth its avenger. Torches flared up, and soon the house was surrounded by a writhing, howling mob, eager for the blood of the man who had sent their loved ones to die on the blistering plains of Maissade, and all because he wanted to be a captain. The soldiers had cast away their uniforms, but their glittering bayonets could be seen flashing in the red torchlight. Wild screams rent the night as the brutishness of the mob-will gained ascendency.

"Let us skin him alive and cover our tom-toms with his hide!" shrieked an old hag as she squirmed through the crowd.

"Let us burn him or bury him alive!" yelled another.

By what magic the old magistrate gained control of that wild multitude, who may say? Standing in the doorway facing the mob, he lifted his withered hand and began: "Countrymen, for ten years I have meted out justice among you. Have I not always done the proper thing?"

"Always," they answered with one voice.

"Then," he continued, "will you not trust me in this hour when the future of Hinche hangs in the balance?"

"Leave it to the magistrate!" someone yelled, and the whole mass took up the cry.

"Norde, do you and Pilar bring along the prisoner. Follow me."

The two designated seized Fidel roughly, lifted him to his feet and preceded by the magistrate, hurried him across the road toward the prison. The mob followed, and the pale light of the torches shone on horrible faces, twisting with anger and deep hatred.

What could the magistrate have in mind?

The procession moved up to the prison door, and as the odors struck Fidel in the face, he drew back with a shudder, his eyes wild and rolling with terror. One torch was thrust inside the door, and its red light threw fantastic shadows over the yellow walls. All the prisoners had been removed, and there was nothing in sight save a mass of rags in a corner at the far end.

"Yonder," said the magistrate, "is Mamon. He died last night. But before we leave you, you must see the face of your bedfellow." As the mob grasped the intent of the speaker, loud cheers filled the night: "Leave it to the magistrate! He will do the right thing."

Fidel shivered with fear, not so much the fear of the dead as of the terrible malady which had burned out the life.

Norde pushed the shaking Fidel through the door, and the mob, forgetting the dread disease in their desire to see him suffer, followed him up to the pile of rags.

"Now," said the magistrate, when Fidel's hands were loosed, "uncover the face of your victim."

With trembling fingers Fidel lifted a filthy rag from the face of the corpse. Did human ever look on sight so horrible? The eyes were gone, sunken back into their sockets, leaving but dark and ghastly holes. The tongue was lolling out, black and parched, furrowed as if it had been hacked. Out of the corners of the gaping mouth there oozed a thick and greenish fluid.

The skin was drawn tightly over the cheeks, and the bones had cut through. There was a sparse and needlelike growth of beard standing up straight on the pointed and bony chin.

Fidel dropped the rag and screamed with terror. Norde picked it up, and, with the aid of Pilar, smothered his screams by wrapping it around his head. He hushed presently and when, at length, the rag was removed, the magistrate commanded: "Uncover that!" and he pointed to the stomach of the corpse. Fidel obeyed.

The stomach was black and flabby like a tire, and the skin had pulled loose from the supporting ribs.

"Here, *mon capitaine*," said the magistrate, "you will live with this dead man until the black dysentery has claimed you."

With a wild shriek Fidel fell fainting across the festering body of Mamon.

The magistrate barked out his commands quickly and sharply.

"Norde, bind him fast where he lies!"

In a moment Fidel was lashed to the fast decomposing body, his hair tied to that of the corpse; and cheek to cheek they left him with the dead.

It was high noon when a strange cavalcade headed toward Pignon, the lair of the Cacos. The old magistrate was leading. Men, women and children carried their few belongings on their heads. Hinche was deserted.

At the same time there entered Hinche by another trail two horsemen, who, after stopping at the office of Fidel, moved on to the prison. They were Vilnord and Benoit, the Caco chief. The prison door was ajar.

They entered, and what they saw was this—*the dead, cheek to cheek, slowly sinking into each other.*

Outside, Vilnord whispered to his companion as they mounted their horses, "I told him he would never be a captain"; and they rode away toward the bald mountains of Pignon.

PARKE GODWIN

Unsigned Original

PARKE GODWIN *is the author of such excellent historical novels as* Sherwood, Beloved Exile *and* The Last Rainbow; *the World Fantasy Award–winning novella "The Fire When It Comes"; the tongue-in-cheek science-fantasy novels* Waiting for the Galactic Bus *and* The Snake Oil Wars; *two "cult classic" science-fiction epics he wrote with me,* The Masters of Solitude *and* Wintermind, *and a popular occult horror novel that he and I also collaborated on,* A Cold Blue Light. *Parke and I began our careers as novelists within a few years of one another. One of his earliest short stories, "Unsigned Original," always struck me as his droll speculation on the possible future of our intertwined careers.*

Renquist's back was presented to me and heaved with eloquent regret as he poured the brandy.

"Murder as a literary art is quite dead, of course," he said. "There remains only refinement of the act itself."

He brought the Martell flanked by our poured snifters on a silver tray to the chess table between us. So we settled for the wet evening in Renquist's quiet house, sixtyish and solitary, given to brandy and reminiscence and precious little else anymore.

"You'll have to stay the night," Renquist told me. "You can't order a cab. My phone's out and there's no bus until morning."

"Why not?" I eased back in the well-upholstered chair. "I've nothing else to do."

"There you have it," Renquist nodded forlornly. "Like our art, we're superfluous—dead, dead, dead. At best, black-veiled mourners at a pulp-paper bier."

It might be said, if not already obvious, that there was always something *de trop* about Renquist. He overpresented himself like someone aspiring to an exclusive club and not altogether secure in his qualifications. "Florid" would describe his complexion and, more often than not, his prose. As his person, so his house. The bookshelves were punctuated with studiedly outré prints and drawings, a few Beardsleys, mostly the renounced monstrosities from *Lysistrata*, an original Bok worth quite a bit now, several of the darker Goyas and what appeared to be a Clarke, though subtly altered.

"There are more murders than ever," I said.

"I said *art*," Renquist grumbled, tugging his vest over an expanding middle. "Not a mere statistic. More murders, yes; more bloody-minded amateurs cluttering the streets with their plebian passions, shooting, cutting—mere ballistic and surgical demonstrations. But where," Renquist deplored, "is the *style*, the originality, the development of the puzzle?"

His gesture of regret sharpened to an index finger jabbed at the rows of books along one wall. "There they lie, all of them. Poe, Conan Doyle, James, Bulwer-Lytton. All the gothics. Christie, Sayers, Rinehart and their trim little tea-with-the-vicar mysteries. The master mechanics: Carr and Gardner. Stout's brilliant obesity issuing *dictums* from the house on Thirty-fifth Street. The less skillful moderns with their banal penchant for hustling a wench into bed rather than an early grave. There you are, Tarking." His hand reverenced my seven slim volumes like funerary urns in a special compartment, then the full, tight-wedged bottom shelf. "And finally myself. This isn't a bookcase, Tarking, it's a damned mortuary. We still live in a murdering world, but to write a superb mystery for its edification today is like serving an exquisitely sautéed shad roe to a redneck raised on grits; like one voice pronouncing 'murder' correctly in a crowd of homicidal harelips!"

I hid my jaded smile. In thirty years, I had written seven mysteries while he'd ground out twenty, all of them direct descendants of mine, varied and—admittedly—developed to their last possible plot ramification, but originality was beyond him. He was a pianist rendering endless variations on a given theme without the ability to pen one honest note of his own. The knowledge made Renquist by turns solicitous and patronizing toward me, as a goldsmith fashioning high art from the element I merely mined. He read my thought as my eye rested on the fat shelf of his books and the handful of my own.

"Yes, I've copied you, Tarking. Say rather improved. You were brilliant but lazy and wasteful. Could have gotten five books from the ideas you poured into one."

"I lose interest." I swirled the brandy in my glass, musing on its color. "The difference between research and development. One is fascinating, the other mere drudgery."

"Touché." Despite the home shot, Renquist was genial. "Still, we've remained friends. In memoriam, then. To a lost art."

I frowned at the amber liquid in my snifter and touched it to my lips.

"There *is* a glimmer of hope." Renquist eased back in the Chippendale. "The Muldauer murder. Surely you've read the papers."

"Yes, the commissioner of police. He won't be missed. Heart-warmingly venal, I hear."

"Passionately. And exquisitely dispatched. Broad daylight, a dozen people near, drilled in his driveway, probably with a silencer."

"Suspects?"

"Thousands!" Renquist hooted. "A neat thousand with as many motives. Needle in a bushel of needles. Result: zero, blank. Immaculate."

"You look as satisfied as if you'd done it yourself."

I was granted a look that only Renquist would have called enigmatic. "No," he admitted, "but I damn well wish I had."

His glance followed mine to the picture on the wall just behind him that I'd thought earlier was a Clarke. There was an alien element in the elongated figures, a vitality that Clarke would have avoided on principle. I leaned forward to it.

"That print; is that . . . ?"

Renquist beamed with pleasure. "I wondered when you'd notice it." He rose and bustled around to the picture. "Not Clarke. My own improvement on him. His figures look as if they'd lived all their two-dimensional lives in that uncomfortable position. Mine have all his macabre aura, but at least they give you the impression they might have gone to the bathroom once in a while."

With a careful fingertip he brushed imaginary dust from the picture. "I should have been a critic, Tarking. Improvement is my ruling passion."

Renquist sighed stagily. "But there are no new plots, no unique methods, the revels ended, the puzzles all undone, charted, catalogued . . . dead. I can no longer create paper mayhem to titillate a world grown numb with crass genocide. *Ergo* . . ."

He turned back to me and picked up the snifter with a flourish. "Therefore, Tarking, I've thought to take up the act itself as an art form, select one prominent person at a time and dispose of him with no clues whatever." He raised his glass. "To a new career."

My laugh hurt him, I think.

"I'm serious, Tarking."

"You're nothing of the sort," I boshed him. "You're fifty-eight and sedentary and, bless you, you couldn't cut your finger without telling the world about it, with a note to your agent to retain the film rights."

Renquist laughed with me, conceding the point. "Well, then: to me."

We drank to him.

"Actually," he said, "the idea was yours to begin with."

"Weren't they all?"

"Oh, don't be pettish, Tarking! What have I stolen that I've not improved a hundredfold? Your second book, *No Darker Art*, held the whole system: murder as a hobby for a retired author of murder mysteries. The goal—"

"Yes, I remember."

"—to accumulate a series of unsolved and unsolvable crimes to stand as a monument of enigma. And for my first," Renquist caressed the phrase with his tongue, "for my auspicious first, I'd choose someone fairly well in the public eye, yet sufficiently reclusive not to be missed for some time. Perhaps someone I know."

He took another satisfied sip of his brandy. We looked at each other across the ticking of the clock.

"The implication is a bit broad-footed."

"A bit," Renquist purred.

"Myself."

"Just so." His smile was sugared Machiavelli. "A night chosen when my telephone decides to take a siesta, the body buried in a pit already yawning in a corner of my large, dark cellar. Police annoyed at widening intervals about my dear friend, who hasn't even called. Think, Tarking: a series of such baroque leave-takings over, say, three years—researched, annotated, published, lauded. My *magnum opus*."

"A bit sick," I judged, "but not without merit of its kind. And the method?"

"Brandy," he smiled. "An excellent bottle. I wouldn't swing off a friend and connoisseur on rotgut, Tarking. A snifter of Martell envenomed with a swift and painless demise."

I winced. " 'Envenomed,' Renquist?"

"Aye, sirrah. 'Twas my word."

"It reeks of First Folio."

He glared at my breech of decorum. "I *am* serious, damn your *sang-froid*. It's rummaging your vitals right now, very efficiently up to no good. And you, dear Tarking, are my first—perhaps my most poetically original—chapter."

From his expression, I was expected to say something; perhaps to applaud. "Well, Tarking?"

I put down the glass. "Not quite original, not entirely without holes. First: I may have told someone I'd be here tonight."

Renquist chuckled. "Not you; you're gregarious as a clam. What reason would you have?"

"Any number, even casual."

"Your own phone is turned off eight days out of ten. Even your cleaning woman thinks you're a myth. The odds are with me," Renquist concluded happily. "What else?"

"Second: to a connoisseur, a good brandy is too clear to contain any toxin you could procure without clouding even slightly."

"Rot. You drank it."

"Looked like the results of bad plumbing."

"But . . . you drank it!" Renquist's features were a rapidly paling caricature of triumph.

"Did I?"

"I saw you." Renquist tried to rise. The inability surprised him, the high furrows of astonishment on his brow glistening with sudden perspiration. His breathing had accelerated. "I didn't take my eyes off you."

"Except for one moment to admire your improvement on Clarke, to which I directed your egotistical attention. Ample time for the light of hand. If I was wrong, no harm done." I shrugged. "As it is . . ."

He was sinking fast, horror-struck, his hand jittering at his laboring heart. "Tarking . . . a doctor . . ."

"Your phone," I reminded him tactfully. "I really didn't plan it this way. Here you are, my second chapter, and—"

Renquist wheezed hideously and ceased breathing.

—And he was supposed to be number *three*.

WILLA CATHER

The Clemency of the Court

In this era of renewed interest in Russian political history, it is interesting to examine the following grim, atypical early story by Virginian WILLA CATHER *(1873–1947), whose literary output includes such acclaimed novels as* Death Comes to the Archbishop, The Professor's House *and* O Pioneers!, *and the frequently anthologized short story "Paul's Case."*

"Damn you! What do you mean by giving me hooping like that?"

Serge Povolitchky folded his big workworn hands and was silent. That helpless, doglike silence of his always had a bad effect on the guard's temper, and he turned on him afresh.

"What do you mean by it, I say? Maybe you think you are some better than the rest of us; maybe you think you are too good to work. We'll see about that."

Serge still stared at the ground, muttering in a low, husky voice, "I could make some broom, I think. I would try much."

"O, you would, would you? So you don't try now? We will see about that. We will send you to a school where you can learn to hoop barrels. We have a school here, a little, dark school, a night school, you know, where we teach men a great many things."

Serge looked up appealingly into the man's face and his eyelids quivered with terror, but he said nothing, so the guard continued:

"Now I'll sit down here and watch you hoop them barrels, and if you don't do a mighty good job, I'll report you to the warden and have you strung up as high as a rope can twist."

Serge turned to his work again. He did wish the guard would not watch him; it seemed to him that he could hoop all right if he did not feel the guard's eye on him all the time. His hands had never done anything but dig and plow and they were so clumsy he could not make them do right. The guard began to swear and Serge trembled so he could scarcely hold his hammer. He was very much afraid of the dark cell. His cell was next to it and often at night he had heard the men groaning and shrieking when the pain got bad, and begging the guards for water. He heard one poor fellow get delirious when the rope cut and strangled him, and talk to his mother all night long, begging her not to hug him so hard, for she hurt him.

The guard went out and Serge worked on, never even stopping to wipe the sweat from his face. It was strange he could not hoop as well as the other men, for he was as strong and stalwart as they, but he was so clumsy at it. He thought he could work in the broom room if they would only let him. He had handled straw all his life, and it would seem good to work at the broom corn that had the scent of outdoors about it. But they said the broom room was full. He felt weak and sick all over, someway. He could not work in the house, he had never been indoors a whole day in his life until he came here.

Serge was born in the western part of the State, where he did not see many people. His mother was a handsome Russian girl, one of a Russian colony that a railroad had brought West to build grades. His father was supposed to be a railroad contractor, no one knew surely. At any rate by no will of his own or wish of his own, Serge existed. When he was a few months old, his mother had drowned herself in a pond so small that no one ever quite saw how she managed to do it.

Baba Skaldi, an old Russian woman of the colony, took Serge and brought him up among her own children. A hard enough life he had of it with her. She fed him what her children would not eat, and clothed him in what her children would not wear. She used to boast to *baba* Konach that she got a man's work out of the young rat. There was one pleasure in Serge's life with her. Often at night after she had beaten him and he lay sobbing on the floor in the corner, she would tell her children stories of Russia. They were beautiful stories, Serge thought. In spite of all her cruelty he never quite disliked *baba* Skaldi because she could tell such fine stories. The story told oftenest was one about her own brother. He had done something wrong, Serge could never make out just what, and had been sent to Siberia. His wife had gone with him. The *baba* told all about the journey to Siberia as she had heard it from returned convicts; all about the awful marches in the mud and ice, and how on the bound-

ary line the men would weep and fall down and kiss the soil of
Russia. When her brother reached the prison, he and his wife used
to work in the mines. His wife was too good a woman to get on well
in the prison, the *baba* said, and one day she had been knouted to
death at the command of an officer. After that her husband tried in
many ways to kill himself, but they always caught him at it. At last,
one night, he bit deep into his arm and tore open the veins with his
teeth and bled to death. The officials found him dead with his teeth
still set in his lacerated arm.

When she finished the little boys used to cry out at the awfulness
of it, but their mother would soothe them and tell them that such
things could not possibly happen here, because in this country the
State took care of people. In Russia there was no State, only the great
Tsar. Ah, yes, the State would take care of the children! The *baba* had
heard a Fourth-of-July speech once, and she had great ideas about
the State.

Serge used to listen till his eyes grew big, and play that he was that
brother of the *baba*'s and that he had been knouted by the officials
and that was why his little legs smarted so. Sometimes he would steal
out in the snow in his bare feet and take a sunflower stalk and play
he was hunting bears in Russia, or would walk about on the little
frozen pond where his mother had died and think it was the Volga.
Before his birth his mother used to go off alone and sit in the snow
for hours to cool the fever in her head and weep and think about her
own country. The feeling for the snow and the love for it seemed to
go into the boy's blood, somehow. He was never so happy as when
he saw the white flakes whirling.

When he was twelve years old a farmer took him to work for his
board and clothes. Then a change came into Serge's life. That first
morning as he stood, awkward and embarrassed, in the Davis
kitchen, holding his hands under his hat and shuffling his bare feet
over the floor, a little yellow cur came up to him and began to rub its
nose against his leg. He held out his hand and the dog licked it.
Serge bent over him, stroking him and calling him Russian pet
names. For the first time in his lonely, loveless life, he felt that something liked him.

The Davises gave him enough to eat and enough to wear and they
did not beat him. He could not read or talk English, so they treated
him very much as they did the horses. He stayed there seven years
because he did not have sense enough to know that he was utterly
miserable and could go somewhere else, and because the Slavonic

instinct was in him to labor and keep silent. The dog was the only thing that made life endurable. He called the dog Matushka, which was the name by which he always thought of his mother. He used to go to town sometimes, but he did not enjoy it, people frightened him so. When the town girls used to pass him dressed in their pretty dresses with their clean, white hands, he thought of his bare feet and his rough, tawny hair and his ragged overalls, and he would slink away behind his team with Matushka. On the coldest winter nights he always slept in the barn with the dog for a bedfellow. As he and the dog cuddled up to each other in the hay, he used to think about things, most often about Russia and the State. Russia must be a fine country but he was glad he did not live there, because the State was much better. The State was so very good to people. Once a man came there to get Davis to vote for him, and he asked Serge who his father was. Serge said he had none. The man only smiled and said, "Well, never mind, the State will be a father to you, my lad, and a mother."

Serge had a vague idea that the State must be an abstract thing of some kind, but he always thought of her as a woman with kind eyes, dressed in white with a yellow light about her head, and a little child in her arms, like the picture of the virgin in the church. He always took off his hat when he passed the court house in town, because he had an idea that it had something to do with the State someway. He thought he owed the State a great deal for something, he did not know what; that the State would do something great for him some day, because he had no one else. After his chores he used to go and sit down in the corral with his back against the wire fence and his chin on his knees and look at the sunset. He never got much pleasure out of it, it was always like watching something die. It made him feel desolate and lonesome to see so much sky, yet he always sat there, irresistibly fascinated. It was not much wonder that his eyes grew dull and his brain heavy, sitting there evening after evening with his dog, staring across the brown, windswept prairies that never lead anywhere, but always stretch on and on in a great yearning for something they never reach. He liked the plains because he thought they must be like the Russian steppes, and because they seemed like himself, always lonely and empty-handed.

One day when he was helping Davis top a haystack, Davis got angry at the dog for some reason and kicked at it. Serge threw out his arm and caught the blow himself. Davis, angrier than before, caught the hatchet and laid the dog's head open. He threw down the bloody hatchet and, telling Serge to go clean it, he bent over his work. Serge stood motionless, as dazed and helpless as if he had been struck himself. The dog's tail quivered and its legs moved weakly, its breath came through its throat in faint, wheezing groans and from its bleeding head its two dark eyes, clouded with pain, still looked lovingly up at him. He dropped on his knees beside it and lifted its poor head against his heart. It was only for a moment. It laid its paw upon his arm and then was still. Serge laid the dog gently down and rose. He took the bloody hatchet and went up behind his master. He did not hurry and he did not falter. He raised the weapon and struck down, clove through the man's skull from crown to chin, even as the man had struck the dog. Then he went to the barn to get a shovel to bury the dog. As he passed the house, the woman called out to him to tell her husband to come to dinner. He answered simply, "He will not come to dinner today. I killed him behind the haystack."

She rushed from the house with a shriek and when she caught sight of what lay behind the haystack, she started for the nearest farm house. Serge went to the barn for the shovel. He had no consciousness of having done wrong. He did not even think about the dead man. His heart seemed to cling to the side of his chest, the only thing he had ever loved was dead. He went to the haymow where he and Matushka slept every night and took a box from under the hay from which he drew a red silk handkerchief, the only "pretty thing," and indeed, the only handkerchief he had ever possessed. He went back to the haystack and never once glancing at the man, took the dog in his arms.

There was one spot on the farm that Serge liked. He and Matushka used often to go there on Sundays. It was a little, marshy pool, grown up in cattails and reeds with a few scraggy willows on the banks. The grass used to be quite green there, not red and gray like the buffalo grass. There he carried Matushka. He laid him down and began to dig a grave under the willows. The worst of it was that the world went on just as usual. The winds were laughing away among the rushes, sending the water slapping against the banks. The meadow larks sang in the corn field and the sun shone just as it did yesterday and all the while Matushka was dead and his own heart was breaking in his breast. When the hole was deep enough, he took the handkerchief from his pocket and tied it neatly about poor Matushka's mangled head. Then he pulled a few wild roses and laid them on its breast and fell sobbing across the body of the little yellow cur. Presently he saw the neighbors coming over the hill with Mrs. Davis, and he laid the dog in the grave and covered him up.

About his trial Serge remembered very little, except that they had taken him to the court house and he had not found the State. He remembered that the room was full of people, and some of them talked a great deal, and that the young lawyer who defended him cried when his sentence was read. That lawyer seemed to understand it all, about Matushka and the State, and everything. Serge thought he was the handsomest and most learned man in the world. He had fought day and night for Serge, without sleeping and almost without eating. Serge could always see him as he looked when he paced up and down the platform, shaking the hair back from his brow and trying to get it through the heads of the jurymen that love was love, even if it was for a dog. The people told Serge that his sentence had been commuted from death to imprisonment for life by the clemency of the court, but he knew well enough that it was by the talk of that lawyer. He had not deserted Serge after the trial even, he had come with him to the prison and had seen him put on his convict clothing.

"It's the State's badge of knighthood, Serge," he said, bitterly, touching one of the stripes. "The old emblem of the royal garter, to show that your blood is royal."

Just as the six o'clock whistle was blowing, the guard returned.

"You are to go to your cell tonight, and if you don't do no better in the morning, you are to be strung up in the dark cell, come along."

Serge laid down his hammer and followed him to his cell. Some of the men made little bookshelves for their cells and pasted pictures on the walls. Serge had neither books nor pictures, and he did not know how to ask for any, so his cell was bare. The cells were only six by four, just a little larger than a grave.

As a rule, the prisoners suffered from no particular cruelty, only from the elimination of all those little delicacies that make men men. The aim of the prison authorities seemed to be to make everything unnecessarily ugly and repulsive. The little things in which fine feeling is most truly manifest received no respect at all. Serge's bringing up had been none of the best, but it took him some time to get used to eating without knife or fork the indifferent food thrust in square tin bowls under the door of his cell. Most of the men read at night, but he could not read, so he lay tossing on his iron bunk, wondering how the fields were looking. His greatest deprivation was that he could not see the fields. The love of the plains was strong in him. It had always been so, ever since he was a little fellow, when the brown grass was up to his shoulders and the straw stacks were the golden mountains of fairyland. Men from the cities on the hills never understand this love, but the men from the plain country know what I mean. When he had tired himself out with longing, he turned over and fell asleep. He was never impatient, for he believed that the State would come some day and explain, and take him to herself. He watched for her coming every day, hoped for it every night.

In the morning work went no better. They watched him all the time and he could do nothing. At noon they took him into the dark cell and strung him up. They put his arms behind him and tied them together, then passed the rope about his neck, drawing his arms up as high as they could be stretched, so that if he let them "sag" he would strangle, and so they left him. The cell was perfectly bare and was not long enough for a man to lie at full length in. The prisoners were told to stand up, so Serge stood. At night his arms were let down long enough for him to eat his bread and water, then he was roped up again. All night long he stood there. By the end of the next day the pain in his arms was almost unendurable. They were paralyzed from the shoulder down so that the guard had to feed him like a baby. The next day and the next night and the next day he lay upon the floor of the cell, suffering as though every muscle were being individually wrenched from his arms. He had not been out of the bare cell for four days. All the ventilation came through some little auger holes in the door and the heat and odor were becoming unbearable. He had thought on the first night that the pain would kill him before morning, but he had endured over eighty-four hours of it and when the guard came in with his bread and water he found him lying with his eyes closed and his teeth set on his lip. He roused him with a kick and held the bread and water out to him, but Serge took only the water.

"Rope too tight?" growled the guard. Serge said nothing. He was almost dead now and he wanted to finish for he could not hoop barrels.

"Gittin so stuck up you can't speak, are you? Well, we'll just stretch you up a bit tighter." And he gave the stick in the rope another vicious twist that almost tore the arms from their sockets and sent a thrill of agony through the man's whole frame. Then Serge was left alone. The fever raged in his veins and about midnight his thirst was intolerable. He lay with his mouth open and his tongue hanging out.

The pain in his arms made his whole body tremble like a man with a chill. He could no longer keep his arms up and the ropes were beginning to strangle him. He did not call for help. He had heard poor devils shriek for help all night long and get no relief. He suffered, as the people of his mother's nation, in hopeless silence. The blood of the serf was in him, blood that has cowered beneath the knout for centuries and uttered no complaint. Then the State would surely come soon, she would not let them kill him. His mother, the State!

He fell into a half stupor. He dreamed about what the *baba* used to tell about the bargemen in their bearskin coats coming down the Volga in the spring when the ice had broken up and gone out; about how the wolves used to howl and follow the sledges across the snow in the starlight. That cold, white snow, that lay in ridges and banks! He thought he felt it in his mouth and he awoke and found himself licking the stone floor. He thought how lovely the plains would look in the morning when the sun was up; how the sunflowers would shake themselves in the wind, how the corn leaves would shine and how the cobwebs would sparkle all over the grass and the air would be clear and blue, the birds would begin to sing, the colts would run and jump in the pasture and the black bull would begin to bellow for his corn.

The rope grew tighter and tighter. The State must come soon now. He thought he felt the dog's cold nose against his throat. He tried to call its name, but the sound only came in an inarticulate gurgle. He drew his knees up to his chin and died.

And so it was that this great mother, the State, took this wilful, restless child of hers and put him to sleep in her bosom.

EDWARD D. HOCH
The Empty Zoo

The staggeringly prolific EDWARD D. HOCH, *who resides in Rochester, New York, has had at least one short story published in every issue of* Ellery Queen's Mystery Magazine *since May 1973. Early in his career, Mr. Hoch wrote three horror stories for the late lamented* Magazine of Horror. *Two of these tales, "The Faceless Thing" and "The Maze and the Monster," appeared, respectively, in my earlier anthologies,* Masterpieces of Terror and the Supernatural *and* Devils & Demons. *The last of this dark trio is "The Empty Zoo," which is offered here for the first time in print since its sole appearance in November 1965.*

He used to play there often as a child, especially on those summer days when the muggy heat drove others to the beach. Then, scorning their imagined friendships, he hurried over the hill to the grove of towering leafy trees that sheltered the single whitewashed building.

"Why would any boy want to play in an empty zoo?" his mother had asked once; but she never asked it again because she didn't really care about the answer. She didn't really care about him.

Once, of course, the zoo had not been empty. It had sheltered a score of various animals during the depression-ridden years, when the city could afford nothing better. Tommy had been so young he could hardly remember those years; hardly remember being pulled along screaming between his father and mother to see the animals he feared and thus hated.

Perhaps that was why he started going there alone once the animals had been moved to the new, larger zoo across town. He soon learned that the fence was easy to scale, and that a watchman patrolled the grounds periodically at best. Thus he established himself easily as king of the place, walked unafraid between the rows of empty cages with their gradually rusting bars, and even occasionally swung from the bars themselves in an open gesture of defiance.

He was always careful not to vandalize the place openly, and he left as little evidence as possible of his comings and goings. If the city fathers ever suspected that the empty zoo was becoming a playground, they did nothing about it. A brief opposition flurry about the deserted building faded into growing years of forgotten neglect.

The grass grew taller where the occasional power mower from the city failed to cut, and the watchman's job had been given over in time to routine checks by a police patrol car. Tommy grew with the grass, and sometimes with the coming of high school whole months would pass when he did not venture into the forbidden territory. But always, in the bleakness of a broken date or the tension of a tough examination, there was something to drive him back.

He didn't need to climb the fence any more, because smaller children had discovered the place and trampled a path across the worn wire links. One night, long after the early autumn dark, he found that they'd imprisoned a cat in one of the ancient cages. He freed the frightened beast, though for a moment his own fear had almost stampeded him.

Grown, he no longer prowled and crept in the cages, no longer swung on the bars. But still there was that overwhelming, driving urge to visit the place. He still lived at home, though his father had died, and often on a night when his mother hounded him, he would leave the house to walk once more over the hill to the old building.

It was on such a night, with the moon full but obscured by breeze-driven clouds, that he encountered another trespasser for the first time. Her name, he learned later, was Janet Crown—and she was eleven years old.

The bars were like the zoo and they closed him in on all sides until he could no longer think or feel or breathe. And always under the glare of the unshaded overhead bulb there was the rasping voice of the detective, and the milder voice of the assistant district attorney, and later the mildest voice of all which belonged to the prison psychiatrist.

"The girl will live," they told him first. "You're lucky."

Lucky.

His mother never came to see him in prison, but then he didn't really care. He passed the time thinking of the zoo, imagining himself now as one of those caged animals he'd feared so much. It was easy to think of animals in general, but he found it sometimes more difficult to concentrate on a particular one. A lion, perhaps? Or a prowling jaguar? Or maybe only a feathered owl to fly by night.

It was a long time before he came back to the city that was home. A decade had passed and the very contours of the city had changed. He'd changed, too, because prison and the hospital were certain to change anyone. Toward the end, he hardly ever thought about the zoo, and they said that was good. But he wondered sometimes if it was, wondered if the hours of staring blankly out the window without a thought in his head really meant he was cured.

He was past thirty now, a grown man who was far from unattractive. He'd been in town only two weeks when he met Carol Joyce.

She was tall and blonde and very beautiful, and when she spoke, he listened. He'd met her one day in the toy department of the store where they both worked, and since then a noon-day friendship had gradually blossomed.

"Tommy Lambert," she said, repeating his name one day in that soft velvet voice he'd come to love.

"That's me."

"I think you might have gone to school with my brother, Bob. Are you from the city?"

"Yes," he admitted, "but I don't remember your brother."

"Of course he was lots older than me. And better looking."

"I doubt that," he offered honestly.

She flushed a bit at the compliment. "How do you like it at the store?"

"It's a job," he answered with a shrug. "What department have they got you in today?"

"Sportswear," she said, making a face that was expressively cute. "I wish I were in toys with you. I like working with children."

"I hardly ever see them, Carol. All I do is move stock around. Stuffed animals, toy trains. All day long."

Finally the daily chats blossomed into lunch, and that was really the beginning of it. He started seeing Carol Joyce one or two nights a week, on outings that were almost—but not quite—dates. When she celebrated her twenty-first birthday (only twenty-one?) a month later he sent her an orchid and took her out to dinner. She was making him feel young again, making him forget the past.

"Have you lived here all your life?" she asked him one night, over an after-theater drink.

"Most of it. All my childhood. I was away for ten years, almost."

"In the army?"

"No. I was sick."

Her face reflected concern, but it quickly passed. "You're the healthiest sick man I ever saw."

"I'm cured, I guess."

In the week that followed, he was drawn to her by a feeling very much like love. He found himself watching the clock until their noontime meetings, planning little surprises that he knew would please her. But then something happened to bring back all the old doubts. She'd come up to the toy department to meet him after work one day, and when he returned from washing up he found her playing with a stuffed giraffe in the stockroom.

"Having fun?" he asked with a smile, always pleased to see her happy.

She nodded, turning her tanned, eternally expectant face toward him. "I love animals. Always have. We should go to the zoo some Saturday."

"Zoo? I thought it was closed." The words came tumbling out before he fully realized what he was saying. He was back there, among the empty cages.

"*Closed?* Whatever gave you that idea?" And then, after a moment, "Oh, you must be thinking of the old place. I keep forgetting you were away from here for ten years. Come to think of it, though, that old zoo's been closed longer than that."

"I used to go to the old place when I was a child. I still think of that as the real zoo."

"Well, we can go there if you like. But there aren't any animals."

His blood seemed to freeze at the unexpected words. What was she saying? Was she actually suggesting a visit to that place? "Oh, I don't know," he mumbled.

"It would be a fun place for a picnic, before they tear it down."

"Tear it down?"

"They've been fighting about it in the city council for years. Now it's going to be the site of a low-rent housing project. They'll start tearing down the old zoo next month."

"So soon?"

"It's been empty for twenty years, Tommy."

"Yes, I suppose so. I suppose I just hate to see the old things going."

And that Saturday, after further urging from Carol, they packed a picnic lunch, and a few cans of cool beer, and went off to the place that had once been so important to him. They went off to the empty zoo.

It stood much as he remembered it, lonely in a field of summer weeds, with blue wildflowers growing about in clusters. Even from a distance, the whitewashed walls were spiderwebbed with cracks, and the bars of the outdoor cages had taken on a permanent reddish-rust color. Otherwise, the only change was in the disappearance of the wire fence, which had been replaced by a high board barricade bearing the elaborately painted announcement: *Future Site of Spring Gardens Low-Rent Housing Development—Another Sign of Community Progress!*

The general area, though, seemed even more remote and isolated than he remembered. From the top of the hill overlooking the zoo he could see for miles in every direction, and what he saw was a soiled spot on the suburban landscape. Preliminary work of clearing trees for the approaches to the development had already been completed; and on the city side, where shoddy rows of apartments had been creeping toward the zoo for years, there was now only a massive field of rubble.

"No one ever comes here any more," Carol told him. "Not even the children to play. They don't even bother with the guards since they put up the new fence."

"How will we get in?" he asked a bit doubtfully.

"There's always a way," she reassured him. And there was. A door in the wooden fence stood partly ajar, its padlock broken loose by some vandal with a rock.

They picnicked on the side of a grassy slope, lolling away the afternoon with tales of half-remembered childhood adventures. It was a summer sort of day, perfect for reminiscing with the softness of uncut grass against their faces. "I used to play here a lot as a child," he said.

She looked down at the crumpling building with distaste. "I think there's nothing more horrible in the whole world than an empty zoo."

"Unless it's a full one."

She looked up, startled. "You feared the animals?"

"I suppose I did. And the place itself, with its thick walls and iron bars and musty odor. I suppose that's why I went there so often after the animals were gone. I was the king then, the king of the whole place. And I didn't fear it any more."

She shifted slightly in the grass, and her bare legs beneath the shorts were firm and tanned. "But you still seemed almost afraid when I suggested this place the other day."

Had he shown his feelings that openly? "I had a terrible experience here once. I don't like to talk about it."

"Not even to me, Tommy?"

"I'm afraid you'd understand least of all." And yet, looking into her pale eyes just then, he felt as if he'd always known her. As if he could tell her anything. She leaned over to kiss him then, and he thought it was the happiest moment of his life.

She rarely wore jewelry, but this day he noticed a little-girl bracelet on her left wrist in place of her watch. "When I'm with you, time doesn't matter," she whispered in his ear. "Daddy gave me that bracelet a long time ago, when I was in school. See—the jeweler got my initials backwards. *J.C.* instead of *C.J.*"

"You're a big girl now, Carol."

"I'm a woman now."

The sky darkened too soon with the coming of evening; he hadn't realized it was so late. "Perhaps we should be going," he volunteered.

"Before we've looked inside?"

"One last time?"

"All right," he consented. "It'll be gone in another month."

The door was trustingly unlocked, and as they stepped across the threshold he might have been stepping into the past. Suddenly, it was ten years ago, all too clearly, with the dimness of the outer twilight playing once more through the mesh-covered upper skylights, casting its uncertain illumination on the empty rows of open cages.

"A horrible place!" she said with distaste.

"Did you come here often, too?"

"Some," she answered. "But for me the fear wasn't the animals. I never knew the animals here."

He led her along, brushing away cobwebs, squeezing her hand a bit too tightly. "Maybe we all have to come back to the thing we fear," he said quietly.

The musty smell of long disuse was in the air, and when Carol

bravely touched an open cage, the barred door screeched with protesting age. The sound sent a shiver through him.

"I'd forgotten how it was," she said.

"Let's get out of here."

"Wait! Come here!" She'd climbed into one of the open cages, and
now she beckoned him to join her. "Kiss me first, Tommy. In here!"
He followed her in and her lips closed on his. He felt himself
pressed backward against the inner bars. In that moment it was as if
he'd known her all his life, and perhaps he had.

"Carol . . ."

Suddenly she shoved away from him and was out of the cage. The
rusty bars swung shut in his face, and he saw her click a shiny new
padlock into place. "Not Carol," she whispered in a different voice, a
voice he hardly recognized. "I'm Janet, Tommy. Remember? Janet
Crown. I've waited ten years for you to come back."

"*Janet!*" The word was a scream of sudden, blinding terror.

She was a little girl once more, and the zoo was the world, and life
was death. "Perhaps they'll hear your screams," she said through the
bars that separated them. "Perhaps you'll still be alive in a month,
when they come to tear the building down."

"*Janet!*"

He screamed her name again, and kept screaming it until she was
gone and he was alone in the empty zoo.

BARRY N. MALZBERG

Beyond Sleep

BARRY N. MALZBERG, *writer, editor, literary agent and New Jersey resident, is the prolific author of* Herovit's World, The Tactics of Conquest, Overlay, The Last Transaction, Beyond Apollo, *which won the coveted John W. Campbell Memorial Award, and many other highly respected science-fiction novels and stories. The ensuing excursion into morbid psychology first appeared in the November 1970 issue of* Ellery Queen's Mystery Magazine.

In the bed I dream that I have killed my wife, moving on her with an entirety of purpose which somehow vaults past circumstance, past memory, past even desire, the knife held high and gleaming in my hand, her eyes wide and open underneath me, my hand darting to her throat as she realizes—ah, it must be for the very first time—that I am capable of doing it.

"You've wrecked everything," I say to her, "our dreams, our hopes, everything that we worked toward, all illusion of romance, all mystery, all connection, everything dissolved in the hard bright core of your corruptibility"—and then the knife is fully upon her and with a grunt I drive it in and through, past tissue, past bone, into the rotting center of her, and she explodes underneath me like swollen fruit, blood to the side of her, blood on the floor, blood on the matting and sofa, small twists and threads of blood on the ceiling, and she falls away, away from the knife to my feet, and I stand over her poised, triumphant, easy at last but still cautious, cautious.

"There had to be an end to it," I say, "otherwise, you see, it just would have gone on and on and at the end only wreckage or hatred, but now you're free, I'm free, we're torn loose of one another"—and indeed it is true; I feel somehow not only free of her but of my own difficult history. It is as if I am no longer the man who killed her but a stronger, more integrated version of the man I was when I married her, and it is a good feeling, a good feeling, because it is almost possible to conceive of going back to the beginning and doing it right —but then I am falling, falling, through layers and levels of sensation, codes seeming to wink to me in lights bouncing off the graying walls and I wake up in my bed, gray on the pillow, gray on the walls, all languid within and turning to confront the place on the bed next to me where my living wife should be.

In the cell, after the interrogation, I fall into a thick doze; I dream that I have not killed my wife, not touched her at all but have in that horrid stricken instant the knife between us, and have turned to say, "You wrecked it, you wrecked everything—your corruptibility, your selfishness, your nagging have destroyed everything that could have been; but I won't have it any more, I tell you, I won't have it"—and raising the knife between us, the light bounces and flickers off the blade, and then I draw it very quickly, very cleanly across my throat, and blood burbles.

I can feel my life coming out of me in uneven pulses but there is time enough, time enough to say, "I didn't have the guts, the only person I really could kill was myself and maybe that's the way I always wanted it"—and in her eyes then comes a light of full understanding and she opens her mouth to say something, opens her mouth, for all I know, to issue the words which will grant me peace if not redemption; but it is too late and everything fades from me and everything is very dark and I wake up in the cell, hunched over my stomach, my shoes scrappling into the floor, a clanging of iron down the line, and realize that never, never, as long as I live, will I be able to get hold of this insight again.

In the hospital I dream that none of this has happened, that all is blank and gray and protected outside as well as inside. In this dream my wife bends over me, soft and limpid in her best dress, and runs a hand over my forehead and says, "It could have been different, you must believe that it could have been different"—and I reach toward her to hold her and moan my penitence into her ear and tell her that I truly see this now, but I only know about change that it is always beyond the next turning—which is too late; but before I can tell her this I feel the wrench of exit again and rising, falling, heaving, collapsing, I feel myself moving through all those layers of self into an awakening which I know will be so enormous and final and this time so far beyond the possibility of sleep that I do everything I can to keep it away. And then suspended in some infinite cove of possibility, halfway between dream and meaning, loss and renewal, I turn slowly in the orbit of purposes, as stark and bleak, trapped and isolated, as the spinning face of the moon itself which casts light through the window, summoning me toward the next sleeping tablet . . .

TRADITIONAL
Finnegan's Wake

Eyah, this is indeed the same Tim Finnegan that the great Irish writer James Joyce mentions in the title of his final comic masterpiece. According to scholars, Joyce borrowed the plot of the folk song as a symbol of the resurrection of green Eire itself. It is, perhaps, a cynical reference, considering the means by which revenant Tim returns. . . .

Tim Finnegan lived in Waukis Street,
A gentle Irishman, mighty odd,
With a lovely brogue, so rich and sweet.
To rise in the world he carried a hod.
   Now you'd see he'd a sort of a tippling taste;
   With a love of the liquor old Tim was born . . .
   To help him through his work each day,
   A drop of the creature every morn.
      Aah, whackerah, blood and brew!
      Won't the floor your trotters shake?
      Isn't it the truth I'm telling you?
      Lots of fun at Finnegan's Wake!

One day old Tim felt rather full.
His head felt heavy, which made him shake.
He fell from a ladder, which broke his skull.
They carried him home his corpse to ache.
   They rolled him up in a nice clean sheet
   And laid poor Tim out on the bed

With a candle or two around his feet
And a couple of dozen around his head.

The guests assembled at the wake
And Mrs. Finnegan called for lunch.
First they brought in tea and cake
And pipes, tobacco and whisky punch.
　　Miss Biddy O'Brien began to cry,
　　"Sich a nice clean corpse did y' niver see?
　　Tim, mavourneen, why did y' die?"
　　"Hold your gab!" said Paddy McGee.

Then Mrs. O'Connor took up the job:
"Biddy," she said, "you're wrong, I'm sure!"
But Biddy gave her a belt in the gob
And left her sprawling on the floor.
　　Well, then the war did fair engage!
　　'Twas woman and woman and man to man;
　　Shillelagh law was all the rage,
　　And a rousing ruction then began!
　　　Aah, whackerah, blood and brew!
　　　Won't the floor your trotters shake?
　　　Isn't it the truth I'm telling you?
　　　Lots of fun at Finnegan's Wake!

Then Mickey Maloney raised his head
And a noggin of whisky flew at him.
It missed him sprawling on the bed—
The liquor spattered over Tim.
　　Then Tim revived and began to rise,
　　And the corpse emerging from the bed, said,
　　"Hand me that likker, damn yer eyes!
　　I'll outdrink yez all, alive or dead!"
　　　Aah, whackerah, blood and brew!
　　　Won't the floor your trotters shake?
　　　Isn't it the truth I'm telling you?
　　　Lots of fun at Finnegan's Wake!

THEODORE STURGEON

Bianca's Hands

According to anthologist Groff Conklin, "Bianca's Hands" was turned down by every United States magazine it was originally submitted to, so THEODORE STURGEON *(1918–1985), author of such acclaimed science-fiction and fantasy tales as* More Than Human, The Cosmic Rape *and* E Pluribus Unicorn, *sent it to the British edition of* Argosy, *where it won first prize in a short story contest, edging out that esteemed author of espionage thrillers, Graham Greene.*

Bianca's mother was leading her when Ran saw her first. Bianca was squat and small, with dank hair and rotten teeth. Her mouth was crooked and it drooled. Either she was blind or she just didn't care about bumping into things. It didn't really matter because Bianca was an imbecile. Her hands . . .

They were lovely hands, graceful hands, hands as soft and smooth and white as snowflakes, hands whose colour was lightly tinged with pink like the glow of Mars on snow. They lay on the counter side by side, looking at Ran. They lay there half closed and crouching, each pulsing with a movement like the panting of a field creature, and they looked. Not watched. Later, they watched him. Now they looked. They did, because Ran felt their united gaze, and his heart beat strongly.

Bianca's mother demanded cheese stridently. Ran brought it to her in his own time while she berated him. She was a bitter woman, as any woman has a right to be who is wife of no man and mother to a monster. Ran gave her the cheese and took her money and never noticed that it was not enough, because of Bianca's hands. When Bianca's mother tried to take one of the hands, it scuttled away from the unwanted touch. It did not lift from the counter, but ran on its fingertips to the edge and leaped into a fold of Bianca's dress. The woman took the unresisting elbow and led Bianca out.

Ran stayed there at the counter unmoving, thinking of Bianca's hands. Ran was strong and bronze and not very clever. He had never been taught about beauty and strangeness, but he did not need that teaching. His shoulders were wide and his arms were heavy and thick, but he had great soft eyes and thick lashes. They curtained his eyes now. He was seeing Bianca's hands again dreamily. He found it hard to breathe . . .

Harding came back. Harding owned the store. He was a large man whose features barely kept his cheeks apart. He said, "Sweep up, Ran. We're closing early today." Then he went behind the counter, squeezing past Ran.

Ran got the broom and swept slowly.

"A woman bought cheese," he said suddenly. "A poor woman, with very old clothes. She was leading a girl. I can't remember what the girl looked like, except— Who was she?"

"I saw them go out," said Harding. "The woman is Bianca's mother, and the girl is Bianca. I don't know their other name. They don't talk to people much. I wish they wouldn't come in here. Hurry up, Ran."

Ran did what was necessary and put away his broom. Before he left he asked, "Where do they live, Bianca and her mother?"

"On the other side. A house on no road, away from people. Good night, Ran."

Ran went from the shop directly over to the other side, not waiting for his supper. He found the house easily, for it was indeed away from the road, and stood rudely by itself. The townspeople had cauterized the house by wrapping it in empty fields.

Harshly, "What do you want?" Bianca's mother asked as she opened the door.

"May I come in?"

"What do you want?"

"May I come in?" he asked again. She made as if to slam the door, and then stood aside. "Come."

Ran went in and stood still. Bianca's mother crossed the room and sat under an old lamp, in the shadow. Ran sat opposite her, on a three-legged stool. Bianca was not in the room.

The woman tried to speak, but embarrassment clutched at her voice. She withdrew into her bitterness, saying nothing. She kept peeping at Ran, who sat quietly with his arms folded and the uncertain light in his eyes. He knew she would speak soon, and he could wait.

"Ah, well . . . ." She was silent after that, for a time, but now she had forgiven him his intrusion. Then, "It's a great while since anyone came to see me; a great while . . . it was different before. I was a pretty girl—"

She bit her words off and her face popped out of the shadows, shrivelled and sagging as she leaned forward. Ran saw that she was beaten and cowed and did not want to be laughed at.

"Yes," he said gently. She sighed and leaned back so that her face disappeared again. She said nothing for a moment, sitting looking at Ran, liking him.

"We were happy, the two of us," she mused, "until Bianca came. He didn't like her, poor thing, he didn't, no more than I do now. He went away. I stayed by her because I was her mother. I'd go away myself, I would, but people know me, and I haven't a penny—not a penny . . . They'd bring me back to her, they would, to care for her. It doesn't matter much now, though, because people don't want me any more than they want her, they don't . . . ."

Ran shifted his feet uneasily, because the woman was crying. "Have you room for me here?" he asked.

Her head crept out into the light. Ran said swiftly, "I'll give you money each week, and I'll bring my own bed and things." He was afraid she would refuse.

She merged with the shadows again. "If you like," she said, trembling at her good fortune. "Though why you'd want to . . . still, I guess if I had a little something to cook up nice, and a good reason for it, I could make someone real cosy here. But—why?" She rose. Ran crossed the room and pushed her back into the chair. He stood over her, tall.

"I never want you to ask me that," he said, speaking very slowly. "Hear?"

She swallowed and nodded. "I'll come back tomorrow with the bed and things," he said.

He left her there under the lamp, blinking out of the dimness, folded round and about with her misery and her wonder.

People talked about it. People said, "Ran has moved to the house of Bianca's mother." "It must be because—" "Ah," said some, "Ran was always a strange boy. It must be because—" "Oh, *no!*" cried others, appalled. "Ran is such a good boy. He wouldn't—"

Harding was told. He frightened the busy little woman who told him. He said, "Ran is very quiet, but he is honest and he does his work. As long as he comes here in the morning and earns his wage, he can do what he wants, where he wants, and it is not my business to stop him." He said this so very sharply that the little woman dared not say anything more.

Ran was very happy, living there. Saying little, he began to learn about Bianca's hands.

He watched Bianca being fed. Her hands would not feed her, the lovely aristocrats. Beautiful parasites they were, taking their animal life from the heavy squat body that carried them, and giving nothing in return. They would lie one on each side of her plate, pulsing, while Bianca's mother put food into the disinterested drooling mouth. They were shy, those hands, of Ran's bewitched gaze. Caught out there naked in the light and open of the table-top, they would creep to the edge and drop out of sight—all but four rosy fingertips clutching the cloth.

They never lifted from a surface. When Bianca walked, her hands did not swing free, but twisted in the fabric of her dress. And when she approached a table or the mantelpiece and stood, her hands would run lightly up and leap, landing together, resting silently, watchfully, with that pulsing peculiar to them.

They cared for each other. They would not touch Bianca herself, but each hand groomed the other. It was the only labour to which they would bend themselves.

Three evenings after he came, Ran tried to take one of the hands in his. Bianca was alone in the room, and Ran went to her and sat beside her. She did not move, nor did her hands. They rested on a small table before her, preening themselves. This, then, was when they really began watching him. He felt it, right down to the depths of his enchanted heart. The hands kept stroking each other, and yet they knew he was there, they knew of his desire. They stretched themselves before him, archly, languorously, and his blood pounded hot. Before he could stay himself he reached and tried to grasp them. He was strong, and his move was sudden and clumsy. One of the hands seemed to disappear, so swiftly did it drop into Bianca's lap. But the other—

Ran's thick fingers closed on it and held it captive. It writhed, all but tore itself free. It took no power from the arm on which it lived, for Bianca's arms were flabby and weak. Its strength, like its beauty, was intrinsic, and it was only by shifting his grip to the puffy forearm that Ran succeeded in capturing it. So intent was he on touching it, holding it, that he did not see the other hand leap from the idiot girl's lap, land crouching at the table's edge. It reared back, fingers curling spiderlike, and sprang at him, fastening on his wrist. It clamped down agonizingly, and Ran felt bones give and crackle. With a cry he released the girl's arm. Her hands fell together and ran over each other, feeling for any small scratch, any tiny damage he might have done them in his passion. And as he sat there clutching his wrist, he saw the hands run to the far side of the little table, hook themselves over the edge and, contracting, draw her out of her place. She had no volition of her own—ah, but her hands had! Creeping over the walls, catching obscure and precarious holds in the wainscoting, they dragged the girl from the room.

And Ran sat there and sobbed, not so much from the pain in his swelling arm, but in shame for what he had done. They might have been won to him in another, gentler way . . .

His head was bowed, yet suddenly he felt the gaze of those hands. He looked up swiftly enough to see one of them whisk round the doorpost. It had come back, then, to see . . . Ran rose heavily and took himself and his shame away. Yet he was compelled to stop in the doorway, even as had Bianca's hands. He watched covertly and saw them come into the room dragging the unprotesting idiot girl. They brought her to the long bench where Ran had sat with her. They pushed her on to it, flung themselves to the table, and began rolling and flattening themselves most curiously about. Ran suddenly realized that there was something of his there, and he was comforted, a little. They were rejoicing, drinking thirstily, revelling in his tears.

Afterwards, for nineteen days, the hands made Ran do penance. He knew them as inviolate and unforgiving; they would not show themselves to him, remaining always hidden in Bianca's dress or under the supper table. For those nineteen days Ran's passion and desire grew. More—his love became true love, for only true love knows reverence . . . and the possession of the hands became his reason for living, his goal in the life which that reason had given him.

Ultimately they forgave him. They kissed him coyly when he was not looking, touched him on the wrist, caught and held him for one sweet moment. It was at table . . . a great power surged through him, and he gazed down at the hands, now returned to Bianca's lap. A strong muscle in his jaw twitched and twitched, swelled and fell. Happiness like a golden light flooded him; passion spurred him, love imprisoned him, reverence was the gold of the golden light. The room wheeled and whirled about him and forces unimaginable flickered through him. Battling with himself yet lax in the glory of it, Ran sat unmoving, beyond the world, enslaved and yet possessor of all. Bianca's hands flushed pink, and if ever hands smiled to each other, then they did.

He rose abruptly, flinging his chair from him, feeling the strength of his back and shoulders. Bianca's mother, by now beyond surprise, looked at him and away. There was that in his eyes which she did not like, for to fathom it would disturb her, and she wanted no trouble. Ran strode from the room and outdoors, to be by himself that he might learn more of this new thing that had possessed him.

It was evening. The crooked-bending skyline drank the buoyancy of the sun, dragged it down, sucking greedily. Ran stood on a knoll, his nostrils flaring, feeling the depth of his lungs. He sucked in the crisp air and it smelled new to him, as though the sunset shades were truly in it. He knotted the muscles of his thighs and stared at his smooth, solid fists. He raised his hands high over his head and stretching, sent out such a great shout that the sun sank. He watched it, knowing how great and tall he was, how strong he was, knowing the meaning of longing and belonging. And then he lay down on the clean earth and he wept.

When the sky grew cold enough for the moon to follow the sun beyond the hills, and still an hour after that, Ran returned to the house. He struck a light in the room of Bianca's mother, where she slept on a pile of old clothes. Ran sat beside her and let the light wake her. She rolled over to him and moaned, opened her eyes and shrank from him. "Ran . . . what do you want?"

"Bianca. I want to marry Bianca."

Her breath hissed between her gums. "No!" It was not a refusal, but astonishment. Ran touched her arm impatiently. Then she laughed.

"To—marry—Bianca. It's late, boy. Go back to bed, and in the morning you'll have forgotten this thing, this dream."

"I've not been to bed," he said patiently, but growing angry. "Will you give me Bianca, or not?"

She sat up and rested her chin on her withered knees. "You're right to ask me, for I'm her mother. Still and all— Ran, you've been good to us, Bianca and me. You're—you are a good boy but— Forgive me, lad, but you're something of a fool. Bianca's a monster. I say it though I am what I am to her. Do what you like, and never a word will I say. You should have known. I'm—sorry you asked me, for you have given me the memory of speaking so to you. I don't understand you; but do what you like, boy."

It was to have been a glance, but it became a stare as she saw his face. He put his hands carefully behind his back, and she knew he would have killed her else.

"I'll—marry her, then?" he whispered.

She nodded, terrified. "As you like, boy."

He blew out the light and left her.

Ran worked hard and saved his wages, and made one room beautiful for Bianca and himself. He built a soft chair, and a table that was like an altar for Bianca's sacred hands. There was a great bed, and heavy cloth to hide and soften the walls, and a rug.

They were married, though marrying took time. Ran had to go far afield before he could find one who would do what was necessary. The man came far and went again afterwards, so that none knew of it, and Ran and his wife were left alone. The mother spoke for Bianca, and Bianca's hand trembled frighteningly at the touch of the ring, writhed and struggled and then lay passive, blushing and beautiful. But it was done. Bianca's mother did not protest, for she didn't dare. Ran was happy, and Bianca—well, nobody cared about Bianca.

After they were married Bianca followed Ran and his two brides into the beautiful room. He washed Bianca and used rich lotions. He washed and combed her hair, and brushed it many times until it shone, to make her more fit to be with the hands he had married. He never touched the hands, though he gave them soaps and creams and tools with which they could groom themselves. They were pleased. Once one of them ran up his coat and touched his cheek and made him exultant.

He left then and returned to the shop with his heart full of music. He worked harder than ever, so that Harding was pleased and let him go home early. He wandered the hours away by the bank of a brook, watching the sun on the face of the chuckling water. A bird came to circle him, flew unafraid through the aura of gladness about him. The delicate tip of a wing brushed his wrist with the touch of the first secret kiss from the hands of Bianca. The singing that filled him was part of the nature of laughing, the running of water, the sound of the wind in the reeds by the edge of the stream. He yearned for the hands, and he knew he could go now and clasp them and own them; instead he stretched out on the bank and lay smiling, all lost in the sweetness and poignancy of waiting, denying desire. He laughed for pure joy in a world without hatred, held in the stainless palms of Bianca's hands.

As it grew dark he went home. All during that nuptial meal Bianca's hands twisted about one of his while he ate with the other, and Bianca's mother fed the girl. The fingers twined about each other and about his own, so that three hands seemed to be wrought of one flesh, to become a thing of lovely weight at his arm's end. When it was quite dark they went to the beautiful room and lay where he and the hands could watch, through the window, the clean, bright stars swim up out of the forest. The house and the room were dark and silent. Ran was so happy that he hardly dared to breathe.

A hand fluttered up over his hair, down his cheek, and crawled into the hollow of his throat. Its pulsing matched the beat of his heart. He opened his own hands wide and clenched his fingers, as though to catch and hold this moment.

Soon the other hand crept up and joined the first. For perhaps an hour they lay there passive with their coolness against Ran's warm neck. He felt them with his throat, each smooth convolution, each firm small expanse. He concentrated, with his mind and his heart on his throat, on each part of the hands that touched him, feeling with all his being first one touch and then another, though the contact was there unmoving. And he knew it would be soon now, soon.

As if at a command, he turned on his back and dug his head into the pillow. Staring up at the vague dark hangings on the wall, he began to realize what it was for which he had been working and dreaming so long. He put his head back yet farther and smiled, waiting. This would be possession, completion. He breathed deeply, twice, and the hands began to move.

The thumbs crossed over his throat and the fingertips settled one by one under his ears. For a long moment they lay there, gathering strength. Together, then, in perfect harmony, each co-operating with the other, they became rigid, rock-hard. Their touch was still light upon him, still light . . . no, now they were passing their rigidity to him, turning it to a contraction. They settled to it slowly, their pressure measured and equal. Ran lay silent. He could not breathe now, and did not want to. His great arms were crossed on his chest, his knotted fists under his armpits, his mind knowing a great peace. Soon, now . . .

Wave after wave of engulfing, glorious pain spread and receded. He saw colour impossible, without light. He arched his back, up, up . . . the hands bore down with all their hidden strength, and Ran's body bent like a bow, resting on feet and shoulders. Up, up . . . Something burst within him—his lungs, his heart—no matter. It was complete.

There was blood on the hands of Bianca's mother when they found her in the morning in the beautiful room, trying to soothe Ran's neck. They took Bianca away, and they buried Ran, but they hanged Bianca's mother because she tried to make them believe Bianca had done it, Bianca whose hands were quite dead, drooping like brown leaves from her wrists.

FREDERICK LAING

The Iron Man

FREDERICK LAING's *writing credits include more than a hundred published short stories and several critically acclaimed novels, including* The Giant's House, *which major reviewers listed among the year's best books, and* Six Seconds a Year, *which the Chicago* Daily News *called a "hard-hitting, swift-moving novel . . . a brilliantly dramatized indictment." Fred tells me that the following grim little World War II tale "brought a remarkable number of letters" when first published in the New York* Herald Tribune's This Week *magazine.*

You ask how I managed to escape, to reach your country alive. But perhaps my story is one which you have heard before. You may even have grown a little weary of it.

A guard is taken by surprise, killed. A gray-haired fugitive plunges into the edge of the forest, near the concentration camp. For days he hides there, nibbling wretchedly at the pieces of bread he has stuffed into his shirt.

Then on the first starless night he dashes past the sentries and jumps into the river, with the bullets zipping and splashing as he swims for the opposite shore.

I was such a man. I did these things. But to me these very dramatic details, they do not seem of great importance in the story of my escape.

I did these things, but what gave me the strength, and the courage? That is what seems important to me now.

My life had been quiet, peaceful. I was a teacher, a professor of psychology in a university.

Please do not ask me for names.

And you will not, I am sure, ask what was the nature of my crime. You know that in my country, today, it is a crime for some people to be born. A very serious crime for some people.

For this crime, they came and dragged me from my desk. And the fat sergeant—this sergeant I am going to tell you about—he was with them. "Herman," is the name I sometimes call him in my thoughts. Not, you understand, that I have anything against the name "Herman."

From the start, he seemed to take pleasure in abusing me. We psychologists had, of course, names for such pleasures. I did not hate him, because I understood. But Herman—he did not understand much of anything. And he hated me, because he had been taught to hate me.

He was just an ordinary man, in an abnormal country. And because I was a former professor, it was natural that he should be curious about my opinions.

So at first he would ask me questions, pretending that he was, as you say, pulling my leg. I would answer them honestly, and the truth would send him into a rage.

"I will make you crawl!" he would yell. "What do you say to that, Professor?"

"You will debase yourself," I answered. "You will despise yourself."

"We will destroy you and your kind," he said.

I did not say anything.

"Say something!" he screamed. "What is your answer to that?"

"You will make us as hard as iron," I said, and I bowed my head for the blow I expected.

"You will learn," he told me. "You will learn more important things here than you taught in your university."

He could not have realized the full truth of his words.

But every day he would help, as he said, with my education. I would go through what tortures his mind could invent.

"Crawl on your knees, Professor." And I would crawl. "Pick up that sandbag, Professor." And I would lift the heavy bag of sand. "Again—pick it up, put it down." Up, down. Up, down.

"And now," he would say, "who is right, you or me?"

"You are right," I would gasp.

And he would laugh. "As tough as iron," he would say, laughing. But he could see the truth in my eyes, and it drove him hysterical with hatred.

He had me trained, finally, like an intelligent animal. When I saw him I was to run for the sandbag.

"Speak, Professor," he would say. "Speak like a dog."

And I would speak. "Pick it up, put it down," I would say. I would gasp these words until my voice grew faint.

He knew the limits of my strength. "Lift it twelve times," he would tell me, knowing that the most I could manage was nine or ten. There were three lashes for every time less than twelve that I could lift the sandbag from the ground to my shoulder.

When I was finally able to lift it twelve times, there were no beatings for a few days. Then the order was raised to sixteen. From sixteen it went to twenty, and at last to forty. In two years, thirty-eight was the most I was ever able to do.

"I hope you have a strong heart," he kept saying. "I want you to die a little at a time." Yes, I think he wanted to keep me alive. It was only while he watched my ridiculous performance with the sandbag that he was able to forget some of the things I had told him.

Some nights I would lie awake thinking. Thinking of the other prisoners who were there because they had been born, or because they had the courage to speak the truth. Thinking of the secret discussions we had, and of the things we were pledged to do—those of us who got out alive. It was when I thought of the others that I felt sure my heart was strong.

One day a number of us prisoners were sent to the edge of the forest, to make a clearing for the enlargement of our camp.

It seemed that many new arrivals were expected.

We were under a heavy guard, of course. Herman never took his eyes off me for a moment.

"You are enjoying your work?" he asked. He was watching me with that greedy look. It meant trouble. "Cutting down bushes, a change from lifting sandbags, yes?"

"Yes," I said.

"Then you must quit it," he told me. "Come along. I will give you some lifting to do. A nice pile of rocks. Your two years of lifting experience should not be wasted, my friend."

He led me to a path in the forest. And he started talking. He was going to miss me, he said. He was being transferred to other work. I tried not to show the relief I felt.

"So you will not have to lift sandbags any more," he said. The tone of his voice—I can not forget it: "No, my good Professor, that is all over," he said. "You are going to be shot for trying to escape."

There was a rifle in his hands. He glanced quickly over his shoulder. I looked, too. There was no one in sight.

"On the whole, you have been a good pupil these two years," he said.

It was then that I knocked the rifle out of his hands and got his neck in the crook of my arm.

"I have tried to be," I answered.

I can still see his eyes bulging with strangulation, and amazement. While he was conscious, I spoke to him.

"You are surprised," I said. I wanted also to say some fine words about the strength of people who have been oppressed, but the words that came out were the words he had taught me.

"Pick it up, put it down," I said, as I felt him growing limp.

I think he understood, in a way, before he died.

For my arm was like a band of iron, and his body slumped like a bag of sand.

RAY RUSSELL

Sagittarius

RAY RUSSELL, *novelist, essayist, screenwriter and former fiction editor of* Playboy, *is the 1991 recipient of the prestigious World Fantasy Life Achievement Award. While my favorite Russell story is probably whichever one I've just read, I am particularly fond of his three gothic pastiches, the first two of which—"Sardonicus" and "Sanguinarius"—appeared, respectively, in my earlier collections,* Masterpieces of Terror and the Supernatural *and* Witches & Warlocks. *Now it is my privilege to present the author's expanded version of his third novella, a tale of murder, madness, the theatre and . . . well, you'll find out.*

I. The Century Club

"If Mr. Hyde had sired a son," said Lord Terry, "do you realize that the loathsome child could be alive at this moment?"

It was a humid summer evening, but he and his guest, Rolfe Hunt, were cool and crisp. They were sitting in the quiet sanctuary of the Century Club (so named, say wags, because its members all appear to be close to that age) and, over their drinks, had been talking about vampires and related monsters, about ghost stories and other dark tales of happenings real and imagined, and had been recounting some of their favorites. Hunt had been drinking martinis, but Lord Terry—The Earl Terrence Glencannon, rather—was a courtly old gentleman who considered the martini one of the major barbarities of the Twentieth Century. He would take only the finest, driest sherry before dinner, and he was now sipping his third glass. The conversation had touched upon the series of mutilation-killings that were currently shocking the city, and then upon such classic mutilators as Bluebeard and Jack the Ripper, and then upon murder and evil in general; upon certain works of fiction, such as *The Turn of the Screw* and its alleged ambiguities, *Dracula,* the short play *A Night at an Inn,* the German silent film *Nosferatu,* some stories of Blackwood, Coppard, Machen, Montague James, Le Fanu, Poe, and finally upon *The Strange Case of Dr. Jekyll and Mr. Hyde,* which had led the Earl to make his remark about Hyde's hypothetical son.

"How do you arrive at that, sir?" Hunt asked, with perhaps too much deference, but after all, to old Lord Terry, Hunt must have seemed a damp fledgling for all his thirty-five years, and the younger man could not presume too much heartiness simply because the Earl had known Hunt's father in the old days back in London. Lord Terry entertained few guests now, and it was a keen privilege to be sitting with him in his club—"The closest thing to an English club I could find in this beastly New York of yours," he once had granted, grudgingly.

Now, he was deftly evading Hunt's question by tearing a long, narrow ribbon from the evening paper and twisting it into that topological curiosity, the Möbius strip. "Fascinating," he smiled, running his finger along the little toy. "A surface with only one side. We speak of 'split personalities'—schizophrenes, Jekyll-and-Hyde, and whatnot—as if such persons were cleanly divided, marked off, with lines running down their centers. Actually, they're more like this Möbius strip—they *appear* to have two sides, but you soon discover that what you thought was the upper side turns out to be the under side as well. The two sides are one, strangely twisting and merging. You can never be sure which side you're looking at, or exactly where one side becomes the other . . . I'm sorry, did you ask me something?"

"I merely wondered," said Hunt, "how you happened to arrive at that interesting notion of yours: that Mr. Hyde's son—if Hyde had been a real person and if he had fathered a son—might be alive today?"

"Ah," Lord Terry said, putting aside the strip of paper. "Yes. Well, it's simple, really. We must first make a great leap of concession and, for sake of argument, look upon Bobbie Stevenson's story not as a story but as though it were firmly based in *fact.*"

It certainly was a great leap, but Hunt nodded.

"So much for that. Now, the story makes no reference to specific years—it uses that eighteen-followed-by-a-dash business which writers were so fond of in those days, I've never understood why—but we *do* know it was published in 1886. So, still making concessions for sake of argument, mind you, we might say Edward Hyde was 'born' in that year—but born a full-grown man, a creature capable of reproducing himself. We know, from the story, that Hyde spent his time in pursuit of carnal pleasures so gross that the good Dr. Jekyll was pale with shame at the remembrance of them. Surely one result of those pleasures might have been a child, born to some poor Soho wretch, and thrust nameless upon the world? Such a child, born in '86 or '87, would be in his seventies today. So you see it's quite possible."

He drained his glass. "And think of this now: whereas all other human creatures are compounded of both good and evil, Edward Hyde stood alone in the roster of mankind. For he was the first— and, let us hope, the last—human being who was *totally* evil. Consider his son. He is the offspring of one parent who, like all of us, was part good and part evil (the mother) and of one parent who was *all* evil (the father, Hyde). The son, then (to work it out arithmetically, if that is possible in a question of human factors), is three-quarters pure evil, with only a single thin flickering quarter of good in him. We might even weight the dice, as it were, and suggest that his mother, being most likely a drunken drab of extreme moral looseness, was hardly a person to bequeath upon her heir a strong full quarter of good—perhaps only an eighth, or a sixteenth. Not to put too fine a point on it, Hyde's son—if he is alive—is the second most evil person who has ever lived; and—since his father is dead—*the* most evil person on the face of the earth today!" Lord Terry stood up. "Shall we go in to dinner?" he said.

The dining room was inhabited by men in several stages of advanced decrepitude, and still-handsome Lord Terry seemed, in contrast, rather young. His bearing, his tall, straight body, clear eye, ruddy face, and unruly shock of thick white hair made him a vital figure among a room full of near-ghosts. The heavy concentration of senility acted as a depressant on Hunt's spirits, and Lord Terry seemed to sense this, for he said, as they sat down, "Waiting room. The whole place is one vast waiting room, full of played-out chaps waiting for the last train. They tell you age has its compensations. Don't believe it. It's ghastly."

Lord Terry recommended the red snapper soup with sherry, the Dover sole, the Green Goddess salad. "Named after a play, you know, *The Green Goddess*, George Arliss made quite a success in it, long before your time." He scribbled their choices on the card and handed it to the hovering waiter, also ordering another martini for Hunt and a fourth sherry for himself. "Yes," he said, his eye fixed on some long-ago stage, "I used to go to the theatre quite a lot in the old days. They put on jolly good shows then. Not all this rot . . . ." He focussed on Hunt. "But I mustn't be boorish—you're somehow involved in the theatre yourself, I believe you said?"

Hunt told him he was writing a series of theatrical histories, that his histories of the English and Italian theatres had already been published and that currently he was working on the French.

"Ah," the old man said. "Splendid. Will you mention Sellig?"

Hunt confessed that the name was new to him.

Lord Terry sighed. "Such is fame. A French actor. All the rage in Paris at one time. His name was spoken in the same breath with Mounet-Sully's, and some even considered him the new Lemaître. Bernhardt nagged Sardou into writing a play for him, they say, though I don't know if he ever did. Rostand left an unfinished play, *Don Juan's Last Night, La Dernière Nuit de Don Juan*, which some say was written expressly for Sellig, but Sellig never played it."

"Why not?"

Lord Terry shrugged. "Curious fellow. Very—what would you say —pristine, very dedicated to the highest theatrical art, classic stuff like Corneille and Racine, you know. The very highest. Wouldn't even do Hugo or Dumas. And yet he became a name not even a theatrical historian is familiar with."

"You must make me familiar with it," Hunt said, as the drinks arrived.

Lord Terry swallowed a white lozenge he took from a slim gold box. "Pills," he said. "In our youth we sow wild oats; in our dotage we reap pills." He replaced the box in his weskit pocket. "Yes, I'll tell you about Sellig, if you like. I knew him very well."

II. The Dangers of Charm

We were both of an age (said Lord Terry), very young, twenty-three or four, and Paris in those days was a grand place to be young in. The Eiffel Tower was a youngster then, too, our age exactly, for this was still the first decade of the century, you see. Gauguin had been dead only six years, Lautrec only eight, and although that Parisian Orpheus, Jacques Offenbach, had died almost thirty years before, his music and his gay spirit still ruled the city, and jolly *parisiennes* still danced the can-can with bare derrières to the rhythm of his *Galop Infernal*. The air was heady with a wonderful mixture of *ancien régime* elegance (the days of which were numbered and which would soon be dispelled forever by the War) combined with a forward-looking curiosity and excitement about the new century. Best of both worlds, you might say. The year, to be exact about it, was 1909.

It's easy to remember because in that very year both Coquelin brothers—the actors, you know—died. The elder, more famous brother, Constant-Benoît, who created the role of Cyrano, died first, and the younger, Alexandre Honoré, died scarcely a fortnight later. Here's a curious tidbit about Coquelin's Cyrano which you may want to use in your book: he played the first act wearing a long false nose, the second act with a shorter nose, and at the end of the play, wore no false nose at all—the really odd thing being that the audience never noticed it! Sir Cedric told me that just before he died. Hardwicke, you know. Where was I? Oh, yes. It was through a friend of the Coquelin family—a minor *comédien* named César Baudouin—that I first came to know Paris and, consequently, Sébastien Sellig.

He was appearing at the Théâtre Français, in Racine's *Britannicus*. He played the young Nero. And he played him with such style and fervor and godlike grace that one could *feel* the audience's sympathies being drawn toward Nero as to a magnet. I saw him afterward, in his dressing room, where he was removing his make-up. César introduced us.

He was a man of surpassing beauty: a face like the Apollo Belvedere, with classic features, a tumble of black curls, large brown eyes, and sensuous lips. I did not compliment him on his good looks, of course, for the world had only recently become unsafe for even the most innocent admiration between men, Oscar Wilde having died in Paris just nine years before. I did compliment him on his performance, and on the rush of sympathy which I've already remarked.

"Thank you," he said, in English, which he spoke very well. "It was unfortunate."

"Unfortunate?"

"The audience's sympathies should have remained with Britannicus. By drawing them to myself—quite inadvertently, I assure you —I upset the balance, reversed Racine's intentions, and thoroughly destroyed the play."

"But," observed César lightly, "you achieved a personal triumph."

"Yes," said Sellig. "At irreparable cost. It will not happen again, dear César, you may be sure of that. Next time I play Nero, I shall do so without violating Racine."

César, being a professional, took exception. "You can't be blamed for your charm, Sébastien," he insisted.

Sellig wiped off the last streak of paint from his face and began to draw on his street clothes. "An actor who cannot control his charm," he said, "is like an actor who cannot control his voice or his limbs. He is worthless." Then he smiled, charmingly. "But we mustn't talk shop in front of your friend. So very rude. Come, I shall take you to an enchanting little place for supper."

It was a small, dark place called L'Oubliette. The three of us ate an enormous and very good omelette, with crusty bread and a bottle of white wine. Sellig talked of the differences between France's classic poetic dramatist, Racine, and England's, Shakespeare. "Racine is like —" he lifted the bottle and refilled our glasses—"well, he is like a very fine vintage white. Delicate, serene, cool, subtle. So subtle that the excellence is not immediately enjoyed by uninitiated palates. Time is required, familiarity, a return and another return and yet another."

As an Englishman, I was prepared to defend our bard, so I asked, a little belligerently: "And Shakespeare?"

"Ah, Shakespeare!" smiled Sellig. *"Passionel, tumultueux!* He is like a mulled red, hot and bubbling from the fire, dark and rich with biting spices and sweet honey! The senses are smitten, one is overwhelmed, one becomes drunk, one reels, one spins . . . it can be a most agreeable sensation."

He drank from his glass. "Think of tonight's play. It depicts the first atrocity in a life of atrocities. It ends as Nero murders his brother. Later, he was to murder his mother, two wives, a trusted tutor, close friends, and untold thousands of Christians who died horribly in his arenas. But we see none of this. If Shakespeare had written the play, it would have *begun* with the death of Britannicus. It would then have shown us each new outrage, the entire chronicle of Nero's decline and fall and ignoble end. *Enfin,* it would have been *Macbeth.*"

I had heard of a little club where the girls danced in shockingly indecorous costumes, and I was eager to go. César allowed himself to be persuaded to take me there, and I invited Sellig to accompany us. He declined, pleading fatigue and a heavy day ahead of him. "Then perhaps," I said, "you will come with us tomorrow evening? It may not tempt a gentleman of your lofty theatrical tastes, but I'm determined to see a show at this Grand Guignol which César has told me of. Quite bloody and outrageous, I understand—rather like Shakespeare." Sellig laughed at my little joke. "Will you come? Or perhaps you have a performance . . ."

"I do have a performance," he said, "so I cannot join you until later. Suppose we plan to meet there, in the foyer, directly after the last curtain?"

"Will you be there in time?" I asked. "The Guignol shows are short, I hear."

"I will be there," said Sellig, and we parted.

III. Stage of Torture

Le Théâtre du Grand Guignol, as you probably know, had been established just a dozen or so years before, in 1896, on the Rue Chaptal, in a tiny building that had once been a chapel. Father Didon, a Dominican, had preached there, and in the many incarnations the building was to go through in later years it was to retain its churchly appearance. Right up to the day of its demolition in 1962, I'm told, it remained exactly as it had always been: quaint, small, huddled inconspicuously in a cobble-stone nook at the end of a Montmartre alley; inside, black-raftered, with gothic tracery writhing along the portals and fleurs-de-lis on the walls, with carved cherubs and a pair of seven-foot angels—dim with the patina of a century —smiling benignly down on the less than three hundred seats and loges . . . which, you know, looked not like conventional seats and loges but like church pews and confessionals. After the good Father Didon was no longer active, his chapel became the shop of a dealer specializing in religious art; still later, it was transformed into a studio for the academic painter, Rochegrosse; and so on, until, in '96, a man named Méténier—who had formerly been secretary to a *commissaire de police*—rechristened it the Théâtre du Grand Guignol and made of it the famous carnival of horror. Méténier died the following year, aptly enough, and Max Maurey took it over. I met Maurey briefly—he was still operating the theatre in 1909, the year of my little story.

The subject matter of the Guignol plays seldom varied. Their single acts were filled with girls being thrown into lighthouse lamps . . . faces singed by vitriol or pressed forcibly down upon red hot stoves . . . naked ladies nailed to crosses and carved up by gypsies . . . a variety of surgical operations . . . mad old crones who put

out the eyes of young maidens with knitting needles . . . chunks of
flesh ripped from victims' necks by men with hooks for hands . . .
bodies dissolved in acid baths . . . hands chopped off; also arms,
legs, heads . . . women raped and strangled . . . all done in a
hyper-realistic manner with ingenious trick props and the Guignol's
own secretly formulated blood—a thick, suety, red gruel which was
actually capable of congealing before your eyes and which was kept
continually hot in a big cauldron backstage.

Some actors—but especially actresses—made spectacular careers
at the Guignol. You may know of Maxa? She was after my time,
actually, but she was supposed to have been a beautiful woman, generously endowed by Nature, and they say it was impossible to find
one square inch of her lovely body that had not received some variety of stage violence in one play or another. The legend is that she
died ten thousand times, in sixty separate and distinct ways, each
more hideous than the last; and that she writhed in the assaults of
brutal rapine on no less than three thousand theatrical occasions.
For the remainder of her life she could not speak above a whisper:
the years of screaming had torn her throat to shreds.

At any rate, the evening following my first meeting with Sellig,
César and I were seated in this unique little theatre with two young
ladies we had escorted there; they were uncommonly pretty but uncommonly common—in point of fact, they were barely on the safe
side of respectability's border, being inhabitants of that peculiar
demimonde, that shadow world where several professions—actress,
model, barmaid, bawd—mingle and merge and overlap and often
coexist. But we were young, César and I, and this was, after all,
Paris. Their names, they told us, were Clothilde and Mathilde—and
I was never quite sure which was which. Soon after our arrival, the
lights dimmed and the Guignol curtain was raised.

The first offering on the programme was a dull, shrill little boudoir farce that concerned itself with broken corset laces and men
hiding under the bed and popping out of closets. It seemed to
amuse our feminine companions well enough, but the applause in
the house was desultory, I thought, a mere form . . . this fluttering
nonsense was not what the patrons had come for, was not the sort of
fare on which the Guignol had built its reputation. It was an hors
d'oeuvre. The entrée followed:

It was called, if memory serves, *La Septième Porte*, and was nothing
more than an opportunity for Bluebeard—played by an actor wearing an elaborately ugly make-up—to open six of his legendary seven

doors for his new young wife (displaying, among other things, realistically mouldering cadavers and a torture chamber in full operation). Remaining faithful to the legend, Bluebeard warns his wife never to open the seventh door. Left alone on stage, she of course cannot resist the tug of curiosity—she opens the door, letting loose a shackled swarm of shrieking, livid, rag-bedecked but not entirely unattractive harpies, whose white bodies, through their shredded clothing, are crisscrossed with crimson welts. They tell her they are Bluebeard's ex-wives, kept perpetually in a pitch-dark dungeon, in a state near to starvation, and periodically tortured by the vilest means imaginable. Why? the new wife asks. Bluebeard enters, a black whip in his hand. For the sin of curiosity, he replied—they, like you, could not resist the lure of the seventh door! The other wives chain the girl to them, and cringing under the crack of Bluebeard's whip, they crawl back into the darkness of the dungeon. Bluebeard locks the seventh door and soliloquizes: Diogenes had an easy task, to find an honest man; but my travail is tenfold—for where is she, or does she live, the wife who does not pry and snoop, who does not pilfer her husband's pockets, steam open his letters, and when he is late returning home, demand to know what wench he has been tumbling?

The lights had been dimming slowly until now only Bluebeard was illumined, and at this point he turned to the audience and addressed the women therein. *"Mesdames et Mademoiselles!"* he declaimed. *"Écoute! En garde! Voici la septième porte*—Hear me! Beware! Behold the seventh door!" By a stage trick the door was transformed into a mirror. The curtain fell to riotous applause.

Recounted baldly, *La Septième Porte* seems a trumpery entertainment, a mere excuse for scenes of horror—and so it was. But there was a strength, a power to the portrayal of Bluebeard; that ugly devil up there on the shabby little stage was like an icy flame, and when he'd turned to the house and delivered that closing line, there had been such force of personality, such demonic zeal, such hatred and scorn, such monumental threat, that I could feel my young companion shrink against me and shudder.

"Come, come, *ma petite*," I said, "it's only a play."

"Je le déteste," she said.

"You detest him? Who, Bluebeard?"

"Laval."

My French was sketchy at that time, and her English almost nonexistent, but as we made our slow way up the aisle, I managed to glean that the actor's name was Laval, and that she had at one time had some offstage congress with him, congress of an intimate nature, I gathered. I could not help asking *why*, since she disliked him so. (I was naïf then, you see, and knew little of women; it was somewhat later in life I learned that many of them find evil and even ugliness irresistible.) In answer to my question, she only shrugged and delivered a platitude: *"Les affaires sont les affaires*—Business is business."

Sellig was waiting for us in the foyer. His height, and his great beauty of face, made him stand out. Our two pretty companions took to him at once, for his attractive exterior was supplemented by waves of charm.

"Did you enjoy the programme?" he asked of me.

I did not know exactly what to reply. "Enjoy? . . . Let us say I found it fascinating, M'sieu Sellig."

"It did not strike you as tawdry? cheap? vulgar?"

"All those, yes. But, at the same time, exciting, as sometimes only the tawdry, the cheap, the vulgar, can be."

"You may be right. I have not watched a Guignol production for several years. Although, surely, the acting . . ."

We were entering a carriage, all five of us. I said, "The acting was unbelievably bad—with one exception."

"Really? And the exception?"

"The actor who played Bluebeard in a piece called *La Septième Porte*. His name is—" I turned to my companion again.

"Laval," she said, and the sound became a viscous thing.

"Ah yes," said Sellig, "Laval. The name is not entirely unknown to me. Shall we go to Maxime's?"

We did, and experienced a most enjoyable evening. Sellig's fame and personal magnetism won us the best table and the most efficient service. He told a variety of amusing—but never coarse—anecdotes about theatrical life, and did so without committing that all-too-common actor's offense of dominating the conversation. One anecdote concerned the theatre we had just left:

"I suppose César has told the story of the Guignol doctor. No? Ah then, it seems that at one point it was thought a capital idea to hire a house physician—to tend to swooning patrons and so on, you know. This was done, but it was unsuccessful. On the first night of the physician's tour of duty, a male spectator found one particular bit of stage torture too much for him, and he fainted. The house physician was summoned. He could not be found. Finally, the ushers revived the unconscious man without benefit of medical assistance, and naturally they apologized profusely and explained they had not been able to find the doctor. 'I know,' the man said, rather sheepishly, '*I am the doctor*.' "

At the end of the evening, César and I escorted our respective (but not precisely respectable) young ladies to their dwellings, where more pleasure was found. Sellig went home alone. I felt sorry for him, and there was a moment when it crossed my mind that perhaps he was one of those men who have no need of women—the theatrical profession is thickly inhabited by such men—but César privately assured me that Sellig had a mistress, a lovely and gracious widow named Lise, for Sellig's tastes were exceedingly refined and his image unblemished by descents into the dimly lit world of the sporting house. My own tastes, though acute, were not so elevated, and thus I enjoyed myself immensely that night.

Ignorance, they say, is bliss. I did not know that my ardent companion's warmth would turn unalterably cold in the space of a single night.

IV. Face of Evil

The *commissaire de police* had never seen anything like it. He spoke poor English, but I was able to glean his meaning without too much difficulty. "It is how you say . . ."

"Horrible?"

"*Ah, oui, mais . . . étrange, incroyable . . .*"

"Unique?"

"*Si! Uniquement monstrueux! Uniquement dégoûtant!*"

Uniquely disgusting. Yes, it was that. It was that, certainly.

"The manner, M'sieu . . . the method . . . the—"

"Mutilation."

"*Oui, la mutilation . . . est irrégulière, anormale . . .*"

We were in the morgue—not that newish Medico-Legal Institute of the University on the banks of the Seine, but the *old* morgue, that wretched, ugly place on the quai de l'Archevêché. She—Clothilde, my *petite amie* of the previous night—had been foully murdered; killed with knives; her prettiness destroyed; her very womanhood destroyed, extracted, bloodily but with surgical precision. I stood in the morgue with the *commissaire*, César, Sellig, and the other girl, Mathilde. Covering the corpse with its anonymous sheet, the *commissaire* said, "It resembles, does it not, the work of your English killer . . . Jacques?"

"Jack," I said. "Jack the Ripper."

"*Ah oui.*" He looked down upon the covered body. "*Mais pour-quoi?*"

"Yes," I said, hoarsely. "Why indeed? . . ."

"*La cause . . . la raison . . . le motif,*" he said; and then delivered himself of a small, eloquent, Gallic shrug. "*Inconnu.*" Motive unknown. He had stated it succinctly. A girl of the streets, a *fille de joie,* struck down, mutilated, her femaleness cancelled out. Who did it? *Inconnu.* And why? *Inconnu.*

"*Merci, messieurs, mademoiselle . . .*" The *commissaire* thanked us and we left the cold repository of Paris' unclaimed dead. All four of us—it had been "all five of us" just the night before—were strained, silent. The girl Mathilde was weeping. We, the men, felt not grief exactly—how could we, for one we had known so briefly, so imperfectly?—but a kind of embarrassment. Perhaps that is the most common reaction produced by the presence of death: embarrassment. Death is a kind of nakedness, a kind of indecency, a kind of *faux pas.* Unless we have known the dead person well enough to experience true loss, or un-less we have wronged the dead person enough to experience guilt, the only emotion we can experience is embarrassment. I must con-fess my own embarrassment was tinged with guilt. It was I, you see, who had used her, such a short time before. And now she would never be used again. Her warm lips were cold; her knowing fingers, still; her cajoling voice, silent; the very stronghold and temple of her treasure was destroyed.

In the street, I felt I had to make some utterance. "To think," I said, "that her last evening was spent at the Guignol!"

Sellig smiled sympathetically. "My friend," he said, "the Grand Guignol is not only a shabby little theatre in a Montmartre alley. This—" his gesture took in the world "—this is the Grandest Guignol of all."

I nodded. He placed a hand on my shoulder. "Do not be too much alone," he advised me. "Come to the Théâtre tonight. We are playing *Cinna.*"

"Thank you," I said. "But I have a strange urge to revisit the Guignol . . ."

César seemed shocked or puzzled, but Sellig understood. "Yes," he said, "that is perhaps a good thought." We parted—Sellig to his rooms, César with the weeping girl, I to my hotel.

I have an odd infirmity—perhaps it is not so odd, and perhaps it is no infirmity at all—but great shock or disappointment or despair do not rob me of sleep as they rob the sleep of others. On the contrary, they rob me of energy, they drug me, they send me into the merciful solace of sleep like a powerful anodyne. And so, that afternoon, I slept. But it was a sleep invaded by dreams . . . dreams of gross torture and mutilation, of blood, and of the dead Clothilde—alive again for the duration of a nap—repeating over and over a single statement.

I awoke covered with perspiration, and with that statement gone just beyond the reach of my mind. Try as I did, I could not recall it. I dashed cold water in my face to clear my head, and although I had no appetite, I rang for service and had some food brought me in my suite. Then, the theatre hour approaching, I dressed and made my way toward Montmartre and the Rue Chaptal.

The Guignol's *chef-d'oeuvre* that evening was a bit of white supremacy propaganda called *Chinoiserie*. ("The yellow menace" was just beginning to become a popular prejudice.) A white girl, played by a buxom but ungifted actress, was sold as a slave to a lecherous Chinese mandarin, and after being duly ravished by him and established as his most favored concubine, fell into the clutches of the beautiful but jealous Chinese woman who had hitherto occupied that honored post. The Woman Scorned, taking advantage of the temporary absence of her lord, seized the opportunity to strip her rival naked and subject her to the first installment of The Death of a Thousand Slices, when her plans were thwarted by the appearance of a handsome French lieutenant who freed the white girl and offered her the chance to turn the tables on the Asian witch. The liberated victim, after first frightening her tormentress with threats of the Thousand Slices, proved a credit to her race by contenting herself with merely tickling the soles of the Chinese girl's bared feet with a plume. Although I had been told that *l'épisode du chatouillement* —"the tickling scene"—was famed far and wide, going on for several minutes of shrieking hysterics until the tickled lady writhed herself out of her clothing, I left before its conclusion. The piece was unbearably boring, though it was no worse than the previous evening's offering. The reason for its tediousness was simple: Laval did not appear in the play. On my way out of the theatre, I inquired of an usher about the actor's absence. "Ah, the great Laval," he said, with shuddering admiration. "It is his—do you say 'night away'?"

"Night off . . ."

"*Oui*. His night off. He appears on alternate nights, *M'sieu* . . ."

Feeling somehow cheated, I decided to return the following night. I did so; in fact, I made it a point to visit the Guignol every night that week on which Laval was playing. I saw him in several little plays—shockers in which he starred as the monsters of history and legend—and in each, his art was lit by black fire and was the more admirable since he did not rely upon a succession of fantastic make-ups—in each, he wore the *same* grotesque make-up (save for the false facial hair) he had worn as Bluebeard; I assumed it was his trademark. The plays—which were of his own authorship, I discovered—included *L'Inquisiteur*, in which he played Torquemada, the merciless heretic-burner (convincing flames on the stage) and *L'Empoisonneur*, in which he played the insane, incestuous Cesare Borgia. There were many more, among them, a contemporary story, *L'Éventreur*, in which he played the currently notorious Jack the Ripper, knifing pretty young harlots with extreme realism until the stage was scarlet with sham blood. In this, there was one of those typically Lavalesque flashes, an infernally inspired *cri de coeur*, when The Ripper, remorseful, sunken in shame, enraged at his destiny, surfeited with killings but unable to stop, tore a rhymed couplet from the bottom of his soul and flung it like a live thing into the house:

> *La vie est un corridor noir*
> *D'impuissance et de désespoir!*

That's not very much in English—"Life is a black corridor of impotence and despair"—but in the original, and when hurled with the ferocity of Laval, it was Kean's Hamlet, Irving's Macbeth, Salvini's Othello, all fused into a single theatrical moment.

And, in that moment, there was another fusion—a fusion, in my own mind, of two voices. One was that of the *commissaire de police*—"It resembles, does it not, the work of your English killer . . . Jacques?" The other was the voice of the dead Clothilde, repeating a phrase she had first uttered in life, and then, after her death, in that fugitive dream—"*Je le déteste.*"

As the curtain fell, to tumultuous applause, I sent my card backstage, thus informing Laval that "*un admirateur*" wished to buy him a drink. Might we meet at L'Oubliette? The response was long in coming, insultingly long, but at last it did come and it was affirmative. I left at once for L'Oubliette.

Forty minutes later, after I had consumed half a bottle of red wine, Laval entered. The waitress brought him to my table and we shook hands.

I was shocked, for I looked into the ugliest and most evil face I had ever seen. I immediately realized that Laval never wore make-up on the stage.

He had no need of it.

V. *An Intimate Knowledge of Horrors*

Looking about, Laval said, "L'Oubliette," and sat down. "The filthy place is aptly named. Do you know what an *oubliette* is, M'sieu'?"

"No," I said; "I wish my French were as excellent as your English."

"But surely you know our word, *oublier?*"

"My French-English lexicon," I replied, "says it means 'to forget, to omit, to leave.' "

He nodded. "That is correct. In the old days, a variety of secret dungeon was called an *oubliette*. It was subterranean. It had no door, no window. It could be entered only by way of a trap door at the top. The trap door was too high to reach, even by climbing, since the walls sloped in the wrong direction and were eternally slick with slime. There was no bed, no chair, no table, no light, and very little air. Prisoners were dropped down into such dungeons to be—literally—forgotten. They seldom left alive. Infrequently, when a prisoner was fortunate enough to be freed by a change in administration, he was found to have become blind—from the years in the dark. And almost always, of course, insane."

"You have an intimate knowledge of horrors, Monsieur Laval," I said.

He shrugged. *"C'est mon métier."*

"Will you drink red wine?"

"Since you are paying, I will drink whisky," he said; adding, "if they have it here."

They did, an excellent Scotch and quite expensive. I decided to join him. He downed the first portion as soon as it was poured—not waiting for even a perfunctory toast—and instantly demanded another. This, too, he flung down his throat in one movement, smacking his bestial lips. I could not help thinking how much more graphic than our "he drinks like a fish" or "like a drainpipe" is the equivalent French figure of speech: "he drinks like a hole."

"Now then, M'sieu . . . Pendragon? . . ."

"Glencannon."

"Yes. You wished to speak with me."

I nodded.

"Speak," he said, gesturing to the barmaid for another drink.

"Why," I began, "I'm afraid I have nothing in particular to say, except that I admire your acting . . ."

"Many people do."

What a graceless boor, I told myself, but I continued: "Rightfully so, Monsieur Laval. I am new to Paris, but I have seen much theatre here these past few weeks, and to my mind yours is a towering talent, in the front rank of contemporary *artistes*, perhaps second only to—"

"Eh? Second?" He swallowed the fresh drink and looked up at me, his unwholesome eyes flaming. "Second to—whom, would you say?"

"I was going to say, Sellig."

Laval laughed. It was not a warming sound. His face grew uglier. "Sellig! Indeed. Sellig, the handsome. Sellig, the classicist. Sellig, the noble. *Bah!*"

I was growing uncomfortable. "Come, sir," I said, "surely you are not being fair . . ."

"Fair. That is oh so important to you English, is it not? Well, let me tell you, M'sieu Whatever-your-name-is—the lofty strutting of the mountebank Sellig makes me sick! What he can do, fools can do. Who cannot pompously declaim the cold, measured alexandrines of Racine and Corneille and Molière? Stop any schoolboy on the street and ask him to recite a bit of *Phèdre* or *Tartuffe* and he will oblige you, in that same stately classroom drone Sellig employs. Do not speak to me of this Sellig. He is a fraud; *worse*—he is a bore."

"He is also," I said, "my friend."

"A sorry comment on your taste."

"And yet it is a taste that can also appreciate you."

"To some, champagne and seltzer water taste the same."

"You know, sir, you are really quite rude."

"True."

"You must have few friends."

"Wrong. I have none."

"But that is distressing! Surely—"

He interrupted. "There is a verse of the late Rostand's. Perhaps you know it. '*A force de vous voir vous faire des amis . . .*' et cetera?"

"My French is poor."

"You need not remind me. I will give you a rough translation. 'Seeing the sort of friends you others have in tow, I cry with joy: send me another foe!' "

"And yet," I said, persisting, "all men need friends . . ."

Laval's eyes glittered like dark gems. "I am no ordinary man," he said. "I was born under the sign of Sagittarius. Perhaps you know nothing of astrology? Or, if you do, perhaps you think of Sagittarius as merely the innocuous sign of the Archer? Remember, then, just who that archer is—not a simple bear or bull or crab or pair of fish, not a man, not a natural creature at all, but a very unnatural creature half human, half bestial. Sagittarius: the Man-Beast. And I tell you this, M'sieu . . ." He dispatched the whisky in one gulp and banged the empty glass on the table to attract the attention of the barmaid. "I tell you this," he repeated. "So potent was the star under which I was born, that I have done what no one in the world has done—nor ever *can* do!"

The sentence was like a hot iron, searing my brain. I was to meet it once again before I left Paris. But now, sitting across the table from the mad—for he indeed seemed mad—Laval, I merely said, softly, "And what is it you have done, Monsieur?"

He chuckled nastily. "That," he said, "is a professional secret."

I tried another approach. "Monsieur Laval . . ."

"Yes?"

"I believe we have a mutual friend."

"Who may he be?"

"A lady."

"Oh? And her name?"

"She calls herself Clothilde. I do not know her last name."

"Then I gather she is not, after all, a lady."

I shrugged. "Do you know her?"

"I know many women," he said; and his face clouding with bitterness, he added, "Do you find that surprising—with this face?"

"Not at all. But you have not answered my question."

"I may know your Mam'selle Clothilde; I cannot be certain. May I have another drink?"

"To be sure." I signalled the waitress, and turned again to Laval. "She told me she knew you in her—professional capacity."

"It may be so. I do not clot my mind with memories of such women." The waitress poured out another portion of Scotch and Laval downed it. "Why do you ask?"

"For two reasons. First, because she told me she detested you."

"It is a common complaint. And the second reason?"

"Because she is dead."

"Ah?"

"Murdered. Mutilated. Obscenely disfigured."

"Quel dommage."

"It is not a situation to be met with a platitude, Monsieur!"

Laval smiled. It made him look like a lizard. "Is it not? How must I meet it, then? With tears? With a clucking of the tongue? With a beating of my breast and a rending of my garments? Come, M'sieu . . . she was a woman of the streets . . . I scarcely knew her, if indeed I knew her at all . . ."

"Why did she detest you?" I suddenly demanded.

"Oh, my dear sir! If I knew the answers to such questions, I would be *clairvoyant*. Because I have the face of a Notre Dame gargoyle, perhaps. Because she did not like the way I combed my hair. Because I left her too small a fee. Who knows? I assure you, her detestation does not perturb me in the slightest."

"To speak plainly, you relish it."

"Yes. Yes, I relish it."

"Do you also relish—" I toyed with my glass. "—blood, freshly spilt?"

He looked at me blankly for a moment. Then he threw back his head and roared with amusement. "I see," he said at last. "I understand now. You suspect I murdered this trollop?"

"She is dead, sir. It ill becomes you to malign her."

"This *lady*, then. You really think I killed her?"

"I accuse you of nothing, Monsieur Laval. But . . ."

"But?"

"But it strikes me as a distinct possibility."

He smiled again. "How interesting. How very, very interesting. Because she detested me?"

"That is one reason."

He pushed his glass to one side. "I will be frank with you, M'sieu. Yes, I knew Clothilde, briefly. Yes, it is true she loathed me. She found me disgusting. But can you not guess why?"

I shook my head. Laval leaned forward and spoke more softly. "You and I, M'sieu, we are men of the world . . . and surely you can understand that there are things . . . certain little things . . . that an imaginative man might require of such a woman? Things which—if she were overly fastidious—she might find objectionable?" Still again, he smiled. "I assure you, her detestation of me had no other ground than that. She was a silly little *bourgeoise*. She had no flair for her profession. She was easily shocked." Conspiratorially, he added: "Shall I be more specific?"

"That will not be necessary." I caught the eye of the waitress and paid her. To Laval, I said, "I must not detain you further, Monsieur."

"Oh, am I being sent off?" he said, mockingly, rising. "Thank you for the whisky, M'sieu. It was excellent." And, laughing hideously, he left.

VI. The Monster

I felt shaken, almost faint, and experienced a sudden desire to talk to someone. Hoping Sellig was playing that night at the Théâtre Français, I took a carriage there and was told he could probably be found at his rooms. My informant mentioned an address to my driver, and before long, Sébastien seemed pleasantly surprised at the appearance of his unannounced guest.

Sellig's rooms were tastefully appointed. The drapes were tall, classic folds of deep blue. A few good pictures hung on the walls, the chairs were roomy and comfortable, and the mingled fragrances of tobacco and book leather gave the air a decidedly masculine musk. Over a small spirit lamp, Sellig was preparing a simple ragout. As he stood in his shirt sleeves, stirring the food, I talked.

"You said, the other evening, that the name Laval was not unknown to you."

"That gentleman seems to hold you fascinated," he observed.

"Is it an unhealthy fascination, would you say?" I asked, candidly.

Sellig laughed. "Well, he is not exactly an appealing personage."

"Then you do know him?"

"In a sense. I have never seen him perform, however."

"He is enormously talented. He dominates the stage. There are only two actors in Paris who can transfix an audience in that manner."

"The other is . . . ?"

"You."

"Ah. Thank you. And yet, you do not equate me with Laval?"

Quickly, I assured him: "No, not at all. In everything but that one quality you and he are utterly different. Diametrically opposed."

"I am glad of that."

"Have you known him long?" I asked.

"Laval? Yes. For quite some time."

"He is not 'an appealing personage,' you said just now. Would you say he is . . . morally reprehensible?"

Sellig turned to me. "I would be violating a strict confidence if I told you any more than this: if he is morally corrupt (and I am not saying that he is), he is not reprehensible. If he is evil, then he was evil even in his mother's womb."

A popular song came to my mind, and I said, lightly, "More to be pitied than censured?"

Sellig received this remark seriously. "Yes," he said. "Yes, that is the point precisely. 'The sins of the father . . .' " But then he broke off and served the ragout.

As he ate, I—who had no appetite—spoke of my troubled mind and general depression.

"Perhaps it is not good for you to stay alone tonight," he said. "Would you like to sleep here? There is an extra bedroom."

"It would inconvenience you . . ."

"Not at all. I should be glad of the company."

I agreed to stay, for I was not looking forward to my lonely hotel suite, and not long after that we retired to our rooms. I fell asleep almost at once, but woke in a sweat about three in the morning. I arose, wrapped myself in one of Sellig's robes, and walked into the library for a book that might send me off to sleep again.

Sellig's collection of books was extensive, although heavily overbalanced by plays, volumes of theatrical criticism, biographies of actors, and so forth, a high percentage of them in English. I chose none of these: instead, I took down a weighty tome of French history. Its pedantic style and small type, as well as my imperfect command of the language, would combine to form the needed sedative. I took the book to bed with me.

My grasp of written French being somewhat firmer than my grasp of the conversational variety, I managed to labor through most of the first chapter before I began to turn the leaves in search of a more interesting section. It was quite by accident that my eyes fell upon a passage that seemed to thrust itself up from the page and stamp itself upon my brain. Though but a single sentence, I felt stunned by it. In a fever of curiosity, I read the other matter on that page, then turned back and read from an earlier point. I read in that volume for about ten minutes, or so I thought, but when I finished and looked up at the clock, I realized that I had read for over an hour. What I had read had numbed and shaken me.

I have never been a superstitious man. I have never believed in the existence of ghosts, or vampires, or other undead creatures out of lurid legend. They make excellent entertainment, but never before that shattering hour had I accepted them as anything more than entertainment. But as I sat in that bed, the book in my hands, the city outside silent, I had reason to feel as if a hand from some sub-zero hell had reached up and laid itself—oh, very gently—upon my heart. A shudder ran through my body. I looked down again at the book.

The pages I had read told of a monster—a real monster who had lived in France centuries before. The Marquis de Sade, in comparison, was a mischievous schoolboy. This was a man of high birth and high aspirations, a marshal of France who at the peak of his power had been the richest noble in all of Europe and who had fought side by side with Joan of Arc, but who had later fallen into such depths of degeneracy that he had been tried and sentenced to the stake by a shocked legislature. In a search for immortality, a yearning to avoid death, he had carried out disgusting experiments on the living bodies of youths and maidens and little children. Seven or eight hundred had died in the laboratory of his castle, died howling in pain and insanity, the victims of a "science" that was more like the unholy rites of the Black Mass. "The accused," read one of the charges at his trial, "has taken innocent boys and girls, and inhumanly butchered, killed, dismembered, burned and otherwise tortured them, and the said accused has immolated the bodies of the said innocents to devils, invoked and sacrificed to evil spirits, and has foully committed sin with young boys and in other ways lusted against nature after young girls, while they were alive or sometimes dead or even sometimes during their death throes." Another charge spoke of "the hand, the eyes, and the heart of one of these said children, with its blood in a glass vase . . ." And yet this madman, this miscreant monster, had offered no resistance when arrested, had felt justified for his actions, had said proudly and defiantly under the legislated torture: *"So potent was the star under which I was born that I have done what no one in the world has done nor ever can do."*

His name was Gilles de Laval, Baron de Rais, and he became known for all time and to all the world, of course, as Bluebeard.

I was out of bed in an instant, and found myself pounding like a madman on the door of Sellig's bedroom. When there was no response, I opened the door and went in. He was not in his bed. Behind me, I heard another door open. I turned.

Sellig was coming out of yet another room, hardly more than a closet: behind him, just before he closed the door and locked it, I caught a glimpse of bottles and glass trays—I remember surmising, in that instant, that perhaps he was a devotee of the new art of photography, but I had no wish to dwell further on this, for I was bursting with what I wanted to say. "Sébastien!" I cried. "I must tell you something . . ."

"What are you doing up at this hour, my friend?"

". . . Something incredible . . . terrifying . . ." (It did not occur to me to echo his question.)

"But you are distraught. Here, sit down . . . let me fetch you some cognac . . ."

The words tumbled out of me pell-mell, and I could see they made very little sense to Sellig. He wore the expression of one confronted by a lunatic. His eyes remained fixed on my face, as if he were alert for the first sign of total disintegration and violence. At length, out of breath, I stopped talking and drank the cognac he had placed in my hand.

Sellig spoke. "Let me see if I understand you," he began. "You met Laval this evening . . . and he said something about his star, and the accomplishment of something no other man has ever accomplished . . . and just now, in this book, you find the same statement attributed to Bluebeard . . . and, from this, you are trying to tell me that Laval . . ."

I nodded. "I know it sounds mad . . ."

"It does."

". . . But consider, Sébastien: the names, first of all, are identical —Bluebeard's name was Gilles de *Laval*. In the shadow of the stake, he boasted of doing what no man had ever done, of succeeding at his ambition . . . and are you aware of the nature of his ambition? To live forever! It was to that end that he butchered hundreds of innocents, trying to wrest the very riddle of life from their bodies!"

"But you say he was burned at the stake . . ."

"No! *Sentenced* to be burned! In return for not revoking the crimes he confessed under torture, he was granted the mercy of strangulation before burning . . ."

"Even so—"

"Listen to me! His relatives were allowed to remove his strangled body from the pyre before the flames reached it! That is a historical fact! They took it away—so they *said!*—to inter it in a Carmelite church in the vicinity. But don't you see what they really did?"

"No . . ."

"Don't you see, Sébastien, that this monster had found the key to eternal life, and had instructed his helots to revive his strangled body by use of those same loathesome arts he had practised? Don't you see that he went on living? That he lives still? That he tortures and murders still? That even when his hands are not drenched in human blood, they are drenched in the mock blood of the Guignol? That the actor Laval and the Laval of old are one and the same?"

Sellig looked at me strangely. It infuriated me. "I am not mad!" I said. I rose and screamed at him: *"Don't you understand?"*

And then—what with the lack of food, and the wine I had drunk with Laval, and the cognac, and the tremulous state of my nerves— the room began to tilt, then shrink, then spin, then burst into a star-shower, and I dimly saw Sellig reach out for me as I fell forward into blackness.

VII. A Transparent Cryptogram

The bedroom was full of noonday sunlight when I awoke. It lacerated my eyes. I turned away from it and saw someone sitting next to the bed. My eyes focussed, not without difficulty, and I realized it was a woman—a woman of exceptional beauty. Before I could speak, she said, "My name is Madame Pelletier. I am Sébastien's friend. He has asked me to care for you. You were ill last night."

"You must be . . . Lise . . ."

She nodded. "Can you sit up now?"

"I think so."

"Then you must take a little bouillon."

At the mention of food, I was instantly very hungry. Madame Pelletier helped me sit up, propped pillows at my back and began to feed me broth with a spoon. At first, I resisted this, but upon discovering that my trembling hand would not support the weight of the spoon, I surrendered to her ministrations.

Soon, I asked, "And where is Sébastien now?"

"At the Théâtre. A rehearsal of *Oedipe*." With a faintly deprecatory inflection, she added, "Voltaire's."

I smiled at this, and said, "Your theatrical tastes are as pristine as Sébastien's."

She smiled in return. "It was not always so, perhaps. But when one knows a man like Sébastien, a man dedicated, noble, with impeccable taste and living a life beyond reproach . . . one climbs up to his level, or tries to."

"You esteem him highly."

"I love him, M'sieu."

I had not forgotten my revelation of the night before. True, it seemed less credible in daylight, but it continued to stick in my mind like a burr. I asked myself what I should do with my fantastic theory. Blurt it out to this charming lady and have her think me demented? Take it to the *commissaire* and have him think me the same? Try to place it again before Sébastien, in more orderly fashion, and solicit his aid? I decided on the last course, and informed my lovely nurse that I felt well enough to leave. She protested; I assured her my strength was restored; and at last she left the bedroom and allowed me to dress. I did so quickly, and left the Sellig rooms immediately thereafter.

By this time, they knew me at the Théâtre Français, and I was allowed to stand in the wings while the Voltaire tragedy was being rehearsed. When the scene was finished, I sought out Sellig, drew him aside, and spoke to him, phrasing my suspicions with more calm than I had before.

"My dear friend," he said, "I flatter myself that my imagination is broad and ranging, that my mind is open, that I can give credence to many wonders at which other men might scoff. But *this*—"

"I know, I know," I said hastily, "and I do not profess to believe it entirely myself—but it is a clue, if nothing more, to Laval's character; a solution, perhaps, to a living puzzle . . ."

Sellig was a patient man. "Very well. I will have a bit of time after this rehearsal and before tonight's performance. Come back later and we will . . ." His voice trailed off. "And we will talk, at least. I do not know what else we can do."

I agreed to leave. I went directly to the Guignol, even though I knew that, being midafternoon, it would not be open. Arriving there, I found an elderly functionary, asked if Monsieur Laval was inside, perhaps rehearsing, and was told there was no one in the theatre. Then, after pressing a bank note into the old man's hand, I persuaded him to give me Laval's address. He did, and I immediately hailed a passing carriage.

As it carried me away from Montmartre, I tried to govern my thoughts. Why was I seeking out Laval? What would I say to him once I had found him? Would I point a finger at him and dramatically accuse him of being Gilles de Laval, Baron de Rais, a man of the Fifteenth Century? He would laugh at me, and have me committed as a madman. I still had not decided on a plan of attack when the carriage stopped, and the driver opened the door and said, "We are here, M'sieu."

I stepped out, paid him, and looked at the place to which I had been taken. Dumbfounded, I turned to the driver and said, "But this is not—"

"It is the address M'sieu gave me." He was correct. It was. I thanked him and the carriage drove off. My mind churning, I entered the building.

It was the same one which contained Sellig's rooms. Summoning the concierge, I asked the number of Laval's apartment. He told me no such person lived there. I described Laval. He nodded and said, "Ah. The ugly one. Yes, he lives here, but his name is not Laval. It is De Retz."

Rayx, Rays, Retz, Rais—according to the history book, they were different spellings of the same name. "And the number of his suite?" I asked, impatiently.

"Oh, he shares a suite," he said. "He shares a suite with M'sieu Sellig . . ."

I masked my astonishment and ran up the stairs, growing more angry with each step. To think that Sébastien had concealed this from me! Why? For what reason? And yet Laval had not shared the apartment the night before . . . . What did it mean?

Etiquette discarded, I did not knock but threw open the door and burst in. "Laval!" I shouted. "Laval, I know you are here! You cannot hide from me!"

There was no answer. I stalked furiously through the rooms. They were empty. "Madame?" I called. "Madame Pelletier?" And then, standing in Sellig's bedroom, I saw that the place had been ransacked. Drawers of chiffoniers had been pulled out and relieved of their contents. It appeared very much as if the occupant had taken sudden flight.

Then I remembered the little room or closet I had seen Sellig leaving in the small hours. Going to it, I turned the knob and found it locked. Desperation and anger flooded my arms with strength, and yelling unseemly oaths, I broke into the room.

It was chaos.

The glass phials and demijohns had been smashed into shards, as if someone had flailed methodically among them with a cane. What purpose they had served was now a mystery. Perhaps a chemist could have analyzed certain residues among the debris, but I could not. Yet, somehow, these ruins did not seem, as I had first assumed, equipment for the development of photographic plates.

Again, supernatural awe turned me cold. Was this the dread laboratory of Bluebeard? Had these bottles and jars contained human blood and vital organs? In this Paris apartment, with Sellig as his conscripted assistant, had Laval distilled, out of death itself, the inmost secrets of life?

Quaking, I backed out of the little room, and in so doing, displaced a corner of one of the blue draperies. Odd things flicker through one's mind in the direst of circumstances—for some reason, I remembered having once heard that blue is sometimes a mortuary color used in covering the coffins of young persons . . . and also that it is a symbol of eternity and human immortality . . . blue coffins . . . blue drapes . . . Bluebeard . . .

I looked down at the displaced drape and saw something that was to delay my return to London, to involve me with the police for many days until they would finally judge me innocent and release me. On the floor at my feet, only half hidden by the blue drapes, was the naked, butchered, dead body of Madame Pelletier.

I think I screamed. I know I must have dashed from those rooms like a possessed thing. I cannot remember my flight, nor the hailing of any carriage, but I do know I returned to the Théâtre Français, a babbling, incoherent maniac who demanded that the rehearsal be stopped, who insisted upon seeing Sébastien Sellig.

The manager finally succeeded in breaking through the wall of my hysteria. He said only one thing, but that one thing served as the cohesive substance that made everything fall into place in an instant.

"He is not here, M'sieu," he said. "It is very odd . . . he has never missed a rehearsal or a performance before today . . . he was here earlier, but now . . . an understudy has taken his place . . . I hope nothing has happened to him . . . but M'sieu Sellig, believe me, is not to be found."

I stumbled out into the street, my brain a kaleidoscope. I thought of that little laboratory . . . and of those two utterly opposite men, the sublime Sellig and the depraved Laval, living in the same suite . . . I thought of Sagittarius, the Man-Beast . . . I thought of the phrase "The sins of the fathers," and of a banal tune, "More to be Pitied than Censured." . . . I realized now why Laval was absent from the Guignol on certain nights, the very nights Sellig appeared at the Théâtre Français . . . I heard my own voice, on that first night, inviting Sellig to accompany us to the Guignol: "Will you come? Or perhaps you have a performance?" And Sellig's answer: "I do have a performance" (yes, but *where?*) . . . I heard Sellig's voice in other scraps: *I have not watched a Guignol performance for several years; I have never seen Laval perform* . . .

Of course not! How could he, when he and Laval . . .

I accosted a gendarme, seized his lapels, and roared into his astounded face: "Don't you see? How is it possible I overlooked it? It is so absurdly simple! It is the crudest . . . the most childish . . . the most transparent of cryptograms!"

"*What* is, M'sieu?" he demanded.

I laughed—or wept. "*Sellig!*" I cried. "One has only to spell it backward!"

VIII. *Over the Precipice*

The dining room of the Century Club was now almost deserted. Lord Terry was sipping a brandy with his coffee. He had refused dessert, but Hunt had not, and he was dispatching the last forkful of a particularly rich *baba au rhum*. His host produced from his pocket a massive, ornate case—of the same design as his pill box—and offered Hunt a cigar. It was deep brown, slender, fragrant, marvelously fresh. "The wizard has his wand," said Lord Terry, "the priest his censer, the king his sceptre, the soldier his sword, the policeman his nightstick, the orchestra conductor his baton. I have these. I suppose your generation would speak of phallic symbolism."

"We might," Hunt answered, smiling; "but we would also accept a cigar." He did, and a waiter appeared from nowhere to light them for the two men.

Through the first festoons of smoke, Hunt said, "You tell a grand story, sir."

"Story," the Earl repeated. "By that, you imply I have told a—whopper?"

"An extremely entertaining whopper."

He shrugged. "Very well. Let it stand as that and nothing more." He drew reflectively on his cigar.

"Come, Lord Terry," Hunt said. "Laval and Sellig were one man? The son of Edward Hyde? Starring at the Guignol in his evil personality and then, after a drink of his father's famous potion in that little laboratory, transforming himself into the blameless classicist of the Théâtre Français?"

"Exactly, my boy. And a murderer, besides, at least the Laval part of him; a murderer who felt I was drawing too close to the truth, and so fled Paris, never to be heard from again."

"Fled where?"

"Who knows? To New York, perhaps, where he still lives the

double life of a respectable man in constant fear of involuntarily becoming a monster in public (Jekyll came to that pass in the story), and who must periodically imbibe his father's formula simply to remain a man . . . and who sometimes fails. Think of it! Even now, somewhere, in this very city, this very *club*, the inhuman Man-Beast, blood still steaming on his hands, may be drinking off the draught that will transform him into a gentleman of spotless reputation! A gentleman who, when dominant, loathes the dormant evil half of his personality—just as that evil half, when *it* is dominant, loathes the respectable gentleman! I am not insisting he is still alive, you understand, but that is precisely the way it was in Paris, back in the early Nineteen Hundreds."

Hunt smiled. "You don't expect me to believe you, sir, surely?"

"If I have given you a pleasant hour," Lord Terry replied, "I am content. I do not ask you to accept my story as truth. But I do inquire of you: why *not* accept it? Why couldn't it be the truth?"

"He is teasing me, of course," Hunt told himself, "luring me on to another precipice of the plot, like any seasoned storyteller. And part of his art is the dead seriousness of his tone and face."

"Why couldn't it?" Lord Terry repeated.

Hunt was determined not to be led into pitfalls, so he did not trot out lengthy rebuttals and protestations about the fantastic and antinatural "facts" of the tale—he was sure the Earl had arguments woven of the best casuistry to meet and vanquish anything he might have said. So he simply conceded: "It could be true, I suppose."

But a second later, not able to resist, he added, "The—story—does have one very large flaw."

"Flaw? Rubbish. What flaw?"

"It seems to me you've tried to have the best of both worlds, sir, tried to tell two stories in one, and they don't really meld. Let's say, for the sake of argument, that I am prepared to accept as fact the notion that Gilles de Rais was not burned at the stake, that he not only escaped death but managed to live for centuries, thanks to his unholy experiments. All well and good. Let's say that he was indeed the Guignol actor known as Laval. Still well, still good. But you've made him something else—something he could not possibly be. The son of Dr. Henry Jekyll, or rather, of Jekyll's alter ego, Edward Hyde. In my trade, we would say your story 'needs work.' We would ask you to make up your mind—was Laval the son of Edward Hyde, or was he a person centuries older than his own father? He could not be both."

Lord Terry nodded. "Oh, I see," he said. "Yes. I should have made myself clearer. No, I do not doubt for a moment that Laval and Sellig were one and the same person and that person the natural son of Edward Hyde. I think the facts support that. The Bluebeard business is, as you say, quite impossible. It was a figment of my disturbed mind, nothing more. Sellig could not have been Gilles."

"Then—"

"You or I might take a saint as our idol, might we not, or a great statesman—Churchill, Roosevelt—or possibly a literary or musical or scientific genius. At any rate, some lofty benefactor of immaculate prestige. But the son of Hyde? Would he not be drawn to and fascinated by history's great figures of evil? Might he not liken himself to Bluebeard? Might he not assume his name? Might he not envelop himself in symbolic blue draperies? Might he not delight in portraying his idol upon the Guignol stage? Might it not please his fiendish irony to saddle even his 'good' self with a disguised form of Gilles's name, and to exert such influence over that good self that even as the noble Sellig he could wallow in the personality of, say, a Nero? Of *course* he was not actually Bluebeard. It was adulation and aping, my dear sir, identification and a touch of madness. In short, it was hero worship, pure and simple."

He had led Hunt to the precipice, after all, and the younger man had neatly tumbled over the edge.

"There is something else," Lord Terry said presently. "Something I have been saving for the last. I did not wish to inundate you with too much all at once. You say I've tried to tell two stories. But it may be—it just possibly may be—that I have not two but three stories here."

"Three?"

"Yes, in a way. It's just supposition, of course, a theory, and I have no evidence at all, other than circumstantial evidence, a certain remarkable juxtaposition of time and events that is a bit too pat to be coincidence . . ."

He treated himself to an abnormally long draw on his cigar, letting Hunt and the syntax hang in the air; then he started a new sentence: "Laval's father, Edward Hyde, may have left his mark on history in a manner much more real than the pages of a supposedly fictional work by Stevenson. Certain criminal deeds that are matters of police record may have been his doing. I think they were. Killings that took place between 1885 and 1891 in London, Paris, Moscow, Texas, New York, Nicaragua, and perhaps a few other places, by an unknown, unapprehended monster about whom speculation varies greatly but generally agrees on one point: the high probability that he was a medical man. Hyde, of course, was a medical man; or rather, Jekyll was; the same thing, really.

"What I'm suggesting, you see, is that Laval was—is?—not only the son of Hyde but the son of a fiend who has been supposed an Englishman, a Frenchman, an Algerian, a Polish Jew, a Russian, and an American; whose supposed true names include George Chapman, Severin Klosowski, Neill Cream, Sir William Gull, Aleksandr Pedachenko, Ameer Ben Ali, and even Queen Victoria's grandson, Eddy, Prince Albert Victor Christian Edward. His sobriquets are also legion: Frenchy, El Destripador, L'Éventreur, The Whitechapel Butcher, and, most popularly—"

Hunt snatched the words from his mouth: "Jack the Ripper."

IX. The Suspension of Disbelief

"Exactly," said Lord Terry. "The Ripper's killings, without exception, resembled the later Paris murders, and also the earlier massacres of Bluebeard's, in that they were obsessively sexual and resulted in 'wounds of a nature too shocking to be described,' as the London *Times* put it. The Bluebeard comparison is not exclusive with me—a Chicago doctor named Kiernan arrived at it independently and put it forth at the time of the Whitechapel murders. And the current series of perverted butcheries here in New York are, of course, of that same stripe. Incidentally, may I call your attention to the sound of Jekyll's name? Trivial, of course, but it would have been characteristic of that scoundrel Hyde to tell one of his victims his name was Jekyll, which she might have taken as 'jackal' and later gasped out in her last throes to a passerby, who mistook it for 'Jack.' And the dates fit, you know. We've placed Hyde's 'birth' at 1886 for no better reason than because the Stevenson story was published in that year . . . but if the story is based in truth, then it is a telling of events that took place before the publication date, perhaps very shortly before. Yes, there is a distinct possibility that Jack the Ripper was Mr. Hyde."

Hunt toyed with the dregs of his coffee. "Excuse me, Lord Terry," he said, "but another flaw has opened up."

"Truth cannot be flawed, my boy."

"Truth cannot, no." This time, it was Hunt who stalled. He signalled the waiter for hot coffee, elaborately added sugar and cream, stirred longly and thoughtfully. Then he said, "Jack the Ripper's crimes were committed, you say, between the years 1885 and 1891?"

"According to the best authorities, yes."

"But sir," Hunt said, smiling deferentially all the while, "in Stevenson's story, published in 1886, Hyde *died*. He therefore could not have committed those crimes that took place after 1886."

Lord Terry spread his arms expansively. "Oh, my dear boy," he said, "when I suggest that the story was based in truth, I do not mean to imply that it was a newspaper report, a dreary list of dates and statistics. For one thing, many small items, such as names and addresses, were surely changed for obvious reasons (Soho for Whitechapel, perhaps). For another thing, Stevenson was a consummate craftsman, not a police blotter. The unfinished, so-called realistic story is stylish today, but in Stevenson's time a teller of tales had to bring a story to a satisfying and definite conclusion, like a symphony. No, no, I'm afraid I can't allow you even a technical point."

"If names were fabricated, what about that Jekyll-jackal business?"

"Quite right—I retract the Jekyll-jackal business. Trivial anyway."

Hunt persisted. "Was Hyde's nationality a fabrication of Stevenson's, too, then?"

"No, I'm inclined to believe he was actually English . . ."

"Ah! But Laval and Sellig—"

"Were French? Oh, I rather think not. Both spoke English like natives, you know. And Laval drank Scotch whisky like water—which I've never seen a Frenchman do. Also, he mistook my name for Pendragon—a grand old English name out of Arthurian legend, not the sort of name that would spring readily to French lips, I shouldn't think. No, I'm sure they—he—were compatriots of mine."

"What was he—they—doing in France?"

"For the matter of that, what was I? But if you really need reasons over and above the mundane, you might consider the remote possibility that he was using an assumed nationality as a disguise, a shield from the police. That's not *too* fanciful for you, I hope? Although this may be: might not a man obsessed with worship of Gilles de Rais, a man who tried to emulate his evil idol in all things, also put on his idol's nation and language, like a magic cloak? But I shan't defend the story any further." He looked at his gold pocket watch, the size of a small potato and nearly as thick. "Too late, for one thing. Time for long-winded old codgers to be in their beds."

It was dismissal. He was, after all, an earl, and accustomed to calling the tune. Hunt hoped, however, that he hadn't offended him.

As they walked slowly to the cloakroom to redeem Hunt's hat, the Earl's guest thought about truth and fiction and Byron's remark that the first was stranger than the second. He thought, too, about that element so essential to the reception of a strange tale whether it be true or false—the element of believability; or, if not believability, at least the suspension of disbelief. Lord Terry had held him spellbound with his story, then had covered his tracks and filled the chinks in his armor pretty well. If Hunt were disposed to be indulgent and generous, he could believe—or suspend disbelief—in the notion that Hyde was an actual person, that he was the maniac killer known as Jack the Ripper, even that he had sired a son who'd lived and died under the names of Laval and Sellig around the turn of the century, in a glamorous Paris that exists now only in memories and stories. All that was comfortably remote. But it was the other idea of Lord Terry's—that Hyde's son might still be alive today—that strained Hunt's credulity, shattered the pleasant spell, and somewhat spoiled the story for him. By any logical standard, it was the easiest of all to believe, granted the other premise; but belief does not depend upon logic, it is a delicate and fragile flower that draws nourishment from intuition and instinct and hunch. There was something about this latter half of the Twentieth Century—with its sports cars and television and nuclear bombs and cold wars and payola and bustplasty and brain washing and motivation research— that just did not jibe with the flamboyant alchemy, the mysterious powders, the exotic elixirs, the bubbling, old-fashioned retorts and demijohns of Dr. Jekyll's and Mr. Hyde's. The thought of Laval, a monster "three-quarters pure evil, with only a single thin flickering quarter of good in him," alive now, perhaps in New York, perhaps the perpetrator of the current revolting crimes; the thought of him rushing desperately through crowded Manhattan streets to some secret laboratory, mixing his arcane chemicals and drinking off the churning, smoking draught that would transform him in to the eminently acceptable Sellig—no, that was the last straw. It was the one silly thing that destroyed the whole story for Hunt. He expressed these feelings, cordially and respectfully, to Lord Terry.

The Earl chuckled good naturedly. "My story still—needs work?"

Hunt's hat was on and he stood at the door, ready to leave his host and allow him to go upstairs to bed. "Yes," he said, "just a little."

"I will take that under advisement," Lord Terry said. Then, his eyes glinting with mischief, he added, "As for those old-fashioned demijohns and other outmoded paraphernalia, however—modern science has made many bulky pieces of apparatus remarkably compact. The transistor radio and whatnot, you know. To keep my amateur standing as a raconteur, I must continue to insist that my story is true—except for one necessary alteration. Good night, my boy. It was pleasant to see you."

"Good night, sir. And thanks again for your kindness."

Outside, the humidity had been dispelled, and the air, though warm, was dry and clear. The sky was cloudless, and dense with the stars of summer. From among them, Hunt picked out the eleven stars that form the constellation Sagittarius. The newspapers were announcing the appearance of another mutilated corpse, discovered in an alley only a few hours before. Reading the headlines, Hunt recalled a certain utterance—"*This* . . . is the Grandest Guignol of all." And another—"*La vie est un corridor noir/ D'impuissance et de désespoir.*" He bought a paper and hailed a taxi.

It was in the taxi, three blocks away from the club, that he suddenly "saw" the trivial, habitual action that had accompanied Lord Terry's closing remark about modern compactness. The old man had reached into his pocket for that little gold case and had casually taken a pill.

MICHAEL MOORCOCK

Wolf

MICHAEL MOORCOCK, *one of England's most prolific science-fantasists, has written such "mainstream" novels as* Mother London; *juvenile (yet eminently readable) adventurous homages to Edgar Rice Burroughs; a multilayered "swords and sorcery" series about a Byronic Eternal Champion; an astonishingly inventive comic science-fiction trilogy, "The Dancers at the End of Time"; the International Fantasy Award–winning* Behold the Man, *which, in an earlier century, surely would have branded Moorcock a heretic— the list goes on and on. For many years overlooked by "serious critics," the overwhelming quantity* and *quality of Moorcock's literary endeavors at last is drawing the attention it deserves. In his spare time (?!), Mr. Moorcock is a musician. Elements of musical structure may be traced in his prose, as, for instance, in the following offbeat nightmare.*

Whose little town are you, friend? Who owns you here? Wide and strong, you have an atmosphere of detached impermanence as you sit in the shallow valley with your bastion of disdainful pines surrounding you; with your slashed, gashed earth roads and your gleaming graveyards, cool under the sun. Here I stand in your peaceful centre, among the low houses, looking for your owner. Night is looming in my mind's backwaters.

I stop a long-jawed man with down-turned, sensuous lips. He rocks on his feet and stares at me in silence, his grey eyes brooding.

"Who owns this town?" I ask him.

"The people," he says. "The residents."

I laugh at the joke, but he refuses to join me, does not even smile. "Seriously—tell me. Who owns this town?"

He shrugs and walks off. I laugh louder: "Who owns this town, friend? Who owns it?" Does he hate me?

Without a mood, what is a man, anyway? A man has to have some kind of mood, even when he dreams. Scornfully, I laugh at the one who refused to smile and I watch his back as he walks stiffly and self-consciously over a bridge of wood and metal which spans soft water, full of blossom and leaves, flowing in the sunlight.

In my hand is a cool silver flask loaded with sweet fire. I know it is there. I lift it to my mouth and consume the fire, letting it consume me, also. Blandly, we destroy each other, the fire and I.

My stomach is full of flame and my legs are tingling, as soft as soda water, down to where my feet ache. *Don't leave me, sweetheart, with your hair of desire and your mockeries hollow in the moaning dawn. Don't leave me with the salt rain rushing down my cold face.* I laugh again and repeat the man's words: "The people—the residents!" Ho ho ho! But there is no one to hear my laughter now unless there are inhabitants in the white town's curtained dwellings. *Where are you, sweetheart—where's your taunting body, now, and the taste of your fingernails in my flesh?*

Harsh smoke drowns my sight and the town melts as I fall slowly down towards the cobbles of the street and a pain begins to inch its way through my stinging face.

Where's the peace that you seek in spurious godliness of another man—a woman? Why is it never there?

I regain my sight and look upwards to where the blue sky fills the world until it is obscured by troubled sounds which flow from a lovely face dominated by eyes asking questions which make me frustrated and angry, since I cannot possibly answer them. Not one of them. I smile, in spite of my anger and say, cynically: "It makes a change, doesn't it?" The girl shakes her head and the worried noises still pour from her mouth. Lips as red as blood—splashed on slender bones, a narrow, delicate skull. "Who—? Why are you—? What happened to you?"

"That's a very personal question, my dear," I say patronizingly. "But I have decided not to resent it."

"Thank you," says she. "Are you willing to rise and be helped somehow?"

Of course I am, but I would not let her know just yet. "I am seeking a friend who came this way," I say. "Perhaps you know her?

She is fat with my life—full of my soul. She should be easy to recognize."

"No—I haven't . . ."

"Ah—well, if you happen to notice her, I would appreciate it if you would let me know. I shall be in the area for a short while. I have become fond of this town." A thought strikes me; "Perhaps you own it?"

"No."

"Please excuse the question if you are embarrassed by it. I, personally, would be quite proud to own a town like this. Is it for sale, do you think?"

"Come, you'd better get up. You might be arrested. Up you get."

There is a disturbing reluctance on the part of the residents to tell me the owner of the town. Of course, I could not afford to buy it—I asked cunningly, in the hope of discovering who the owner was. Maybe she is too clever for me. The idea is not appealing.

"You're like a dead bird," she smiles, "with your wings broken."

I refuse her hand and get up quickly. "Lead the way."

She frowns and then says: "Home I think." So off we go with her walking ahead. I point upwards: "Look—there's a cloud the shape of a cloud!" She smiles and I feel encouraged to such a degree that I want to thank her.

We reach her house with its green door opening directly on to the street. There are windows with red and yellow curtains and the white paint covering the stone is beginning to flake. She produces a key, inserts it into the large black iron lock and pushes the door wide open, gesturing gracefully for me to enter before her. I incline my head and walk into the darkened hallway of the house. It smells of lavender and is full of old polished oak and brass plates, horse-brasses, candlesticks with no candles in them. On my right is a staircase which twists up into gloom, the stairs covered by dark red carpet.

There are ferns in vases, placed on high shelves. Several vases of ferns are on the window-sill by the door.

"I have a razor if you wish to shave," she informs me. Luckily for her, I am self-critical enough to realize that I need a shave. I thank her and she mounts the stairs, wide skirt swinging, leading me to the upstairs floor and a small bathroom smelling of perfume and disinfectant.

She switches on the light. Outside, the blue of the sky is deepening and the sun has already set. She shows me the safety-razor, soap, towel. She turns a tap and water gushes out into her cupped hand. "Still hot," she says, turning and closing the door behind her. I am tired and make a bad job of shaving. I wash my hands as an afterthought and then go to the door to make sure it isn't locked. I open the door and peer out into the lighted passage. I shout: "Hey!" and her head eventually comes into sight around another door at the far end of the passage. "I've shaved."

"Go downstairs into the front room," she says. "I'll join you there in a few minutes." I grin at her and my eyes tell her that I know she is naked beneath her clothes. They all are. Without their clothes and their hair, where would they be? *Where is she? She came this way—I scented her trail right here, to this town. She could even be hiding inside this woman—fooling me. She was always clever in her own way. I'll break her other hand, listen to the bones snap, and they won't catch me. She sucked my life out of me and they blamed me for breaking her fingers. I was just trying to get at the ring I gave her. It was hidden by the blaze of the others.*

She turned me into a sharp-toothed wolf.

I thunder down the stairs, deliberately stamping on them, making them moan and creak. I locate the front room and enter it. Deep leather chairs, more brass, more oak, more ferns in smoky glass of purple and scarlet. A fireplace without a fire. A soft carpet, multicoloured. A small piano with black-and-white keys and a picture in a frame on top of it.

There is a white-clothed table with cutlery and plates for two. Two chairs squat beside the table.

I stand with my back to the fireplace as I hear her pointed-heeled shoes tripping down the stairs. "Good evening," I say politely when she comes in, dressed in a tight frock of dark blue velvet, with rubies around her throat and at her ears. There are dazzling rings on her fingers and I shudder, but manage to control myself.

"Please sit down." She repeats the graceful gesture of the hand, indicating a leather chair with a yellow cushion. "Do you feel better now?" I am suspicious and will not answer her. It might be a trick question, one never knows. "I'll get dinner," she tells me, "I won't be long." Again I've defeated her. She can't win at this rate.

I consume the foreign meal greedily and only realize afterwards that it might have been poisoned. Philosophically I reflect that it is too late now as I wait for coffee. I will test the coffee and see if it smells of bitter almonds. If it does, I will know it contains poison. I try to remember if any of the food I have already eaten tasted of bitter almonds. I don't think so. I feel comparatively safe.

She brings in the coffee smoking in a big brown earthenware pot. She sits down and pours me a cup. It smells good and, relievedly, I discover it does not have the flavour of bitter almonds. Come to think of it, I am not altogether sure what bitter almonds smell like.

"You may stay the night here, if you wish. There is a spare room."

"Thank you," I say, letting my eyes narrow in a subtle question, but she looks away from me and reaches a slim hand for the coffee pot. "Thank you," I repeat. She doesn't answer me. What's her game? She takes a breath, is about to say something, looks quickly at me, changes her mind, says nothing. I laugh softly, leaning back in my chair with my hand clasped around my coffee cup.

"There are wolves and there are sheep," I say, as I have often said. "Which do you think you are?"

"Neither," says she.

"Then you are sheep," say I. "The wolves know what they are—what their function is. I am wolf."

"Really," she says and it is obvious that she is bored by my philosophy, not understanding it. "You had better go to bed now—you are tired."

"If you insist," I say lightly. "Very well."

She shows me up to the room overlooking the unlit street and bids me good night. Closing the door, I listen carefully for the sound of a key turning, but the sound doesn't come. The room contains a high, old-fashioned bed, a standard lamp with a parchment shade with flowers pressed between two thicknesses, an empty bookcase and a wooden chair, beautifully carved. I feel the chair with my fingertips and shiver with delight at the sensation I receive. I pull back the quilt covering the bed and inspect the sheets which are clean and smell fresh. There are two white pillows, both very soft. I extract myself from my suit, taking off my shoes and socks and leaving my underpants on. I switch off the light and, trembling a little, get into the sheets, I am soon asleep, but it is still very early. I am convinced that I shall wake up at dawn.

I open my eyes in the morning and pale sunshine forces its way between gaps in the curtains. I lie in bed trying to go back to sleep, but cannot. I push away the covers, which have slipped partly off the bed, and get up. I go to the window and look down into the street.

Incredibly, a huge hare is loping along the pavement, its nose twitching. A lorry roars past, its gears grating, but the hare continues its imperturbable course. I am tensed, excited. I open my door and run along the passage to the woman's room, entering with a rush. She is asleep, one arm sprawled outwards, the hand dangling over the edge of her bed, her shoulders pale and alive. I take hold of one shoulder in a strong grip designed to hurt her into wakefulness. She cries out, sits up quivering.

"Quick," I say—"Come and see. There is a hare in the street!"

"Go away and let me sleep," she tells me, "let me sleep."

"No! You must come and look at the big hare in the street. How did it get there?"

She rises and follows me back to my room. I leap towards the window and see with relief that the hare is still there. "Look!" I point towards it and she joins me at the window. She, too, is amazed. "Poor thing," she gasps. "We must save it."

"Save it?" I am astounded. "Save it? No, I will kill it and we can eat it."

She shudders. "How could you be so cruel?" The hare disappears around a corner of the street. I am furious and all the nerves of my body are taut. "It has gone!"

"It will probably be all right," she says in a self-conciliatory tone and this makes me more angry. I begin to sob with frustration. She puts a hand on my arm. "What is the matter?" I shrug off the hand, then think better of it, I begin to cry against her breast. She pats me on the back and I feel better. "Let me come to bed with you," I plead.

"No," she says quietly. "You must rest."

"Let me sleep with *you*," I insist, but she breaks from my grasp and backs towards the door. "No! Rest."

I follow her, my eyes hot in my skull, my body full. "You owe me something," I tell her viciously. "You all do."

"Go away," she says threateningly, desperate and afraid of me. I continue to move towards her, beyond the door, along the passage. She starts to run for her room but I run also, and catch her. I catch her before she reaches the room. She screams. I clutch at her fingers. I bend them back slowly, putting my other hand over her mouth to stop her horrible noises. The bones snap in the slim, pale flesh. Not all at once.

"You made me wolf." I snarl. "And sheep must die." My teeth seek her pounding jugular, my nose scents the perfume of her throat. I

214   MICHAEL MOORCOCK

slide my sharp teeth through skin and sinew. Blood oozes into my mouth. As I kill her, I sob.

Why did she suck the soul of me from the wounds she made? Why am I wolf because of her? Or did it always lurk there, needing only the pain she made to release the ferocity?

But she is dead.

I had forgotten. I had sought her in this pleasant town.

Ah, now the other is dead, too.

Let murder drown me until I am nothing but a snarling speck, harmless and protected by my infinitesimal size.

Oh, God, my bloody darling . . .

STEPHEN CRANE

An Illusion in Red and White

The brief life and career of STEPHEN CRANE *(1871–1900) was highlighted by such popular stories as "The Blue Hotel," "The Bride Comes to Yellow Sky," "The Upturned Face" and "The Open Boat." He achieved international fame with his second novel,* The Red Badge of Courage, *acclaimed in America and England as a significant war novel, though Crane had never seen a battle. Subsequently hired as a war correspondent, he went to England, where he befriended Joseph Conrad but soon contracted tuberculosis. Crane died a few years later in Baden-Baden.*

Nights on the Cuban blockade were long, at times exciting, often dull. The men on the small leaping dispatch-boats became as intimate as if they had all been buried in the same coffin. Correspondents who, in New York, had passed as fairly good fellows sometimes turned out to be perfect rogues of vanity and selfishness, but still more often the conceited chumps of Park Row became the kindly and thoughtful men of the Cuban blockade. Also each correspondent told all he knew, and sometimes more. For this gentle tale I am indebted to one of the brightening stars of New York journalism.

"Now, this is how I imagine it happened. I don't say it happened this way, but this is how I imagine it happened. And it always struck me as being a very interesting story. I hadn't been on the paper very long, but just about long enough to get a good show, when the city editor suddenly gave me this sparkling murder assignment.

"It seems that up in one of the back counties of New York State a farmer had taken a dislike to his wife; and so he went into the kitchen with an axe, and in the presence of their four children he just casually rapped his wife on the nape of the neck with the head of this axe. It was early in the morning, but he told the children they had better go to bed. Then he took his wife's body out in the woods and buried it.

"This farmer's name was Jones. The widower's eldest child was named Freddy. A week after the murder, one of the long-distance neighbors was rattling past the house in his buckboard when he saw Freddy playing in the road. He pulled up, and asked the boy about the welfare of the Jones family.

" 'Oh, we're all right,' said Freddy, 'only ma—she ain't—she's dead.'

" 'Why, when did she die?' cried the startled farmer. 'What did she die of?'

" 'Oh,' answered Freddy, 'last week a man with red hair and big white teeth and real white hands came into the kitchen, and killed ma with an axe.'

"The farmer was indignant with the boy for telling him this strange childish nonsense, and drove off much disgruntled. But he recited the incident at a tavern that evening, and when people began to miss the familiar figure of Mrs. Jones at the Methodist Church on Sunday mornings, they ended by having an investigation. The calm Jones was arrested for murder, and his wife's body was lifted from its grave in the woods and buried by her own family.

"The chief interest now centered upon the children. All four declared that they were in the kitchen at the time of the crime, and that the murderer had red hair. The hair of the virtuous Jones was grey. They said that the murderer's teeth were large and white. Jones only had about eight teeth, and these were small and brown. They said the murderer's hands were white. Jones's hands were the colour of black walnuts. They lifted their dazed, innocent faces, and crying, simply because the mysterious excitement and their new quarters frightened them, they repeated their heroic legend without important deviation, and without the parroty sameness which would excite suspicion.

"Women came to the jail and wept over them, and made little frocks for the girls, and little breeches for the boys, and idiotic detectives questioned them at length. Always they upheld the theory of the murderer with red hair, big white teeth, and white hands. Jones sat in his cell, his chin sullenly on his first vest-button. He knew nothing about any murder, he said. He thought his wife had gone on a visit to some relatives. He had had a quarrel with her, and she had said that she was going to leave him for a time, so that he might have proper opportunities for cooling down. Had he seen the blood on the floor? Yes, he had seen the blood on the floor. But he had been cleaning and skinning a rabbit at that spot on the day of his wife's disappearance. He had thought nothing of it. What had his children said when he returned from the fields? They had told him of a man with red hair, big white teeth, and white hands. To questions as to why he had not informed the police of the county, he answered that he had not thought it a matter of sufficient importance. He had cordially hated his wife, anyhow, and he was glad to be rid of her. He decided afterward that she had run off; and he had never credited the fantastic tale of the children.

"Of course, there was very little doubt in the minds of the majority that Jones was guilty, but there was a fairly strong following who insisted that Jones was a coarse and brutal man, and perhaps weak in his head—yes—but not a murderer. They pointed to the children and declared that children could never lie, and these kids, when asked, said that the murder had been committed by a man with red hair, large white teeth, and white hands. I myself had a number of interviews with the children, and I was amazed at the convincing power of their little story. Shining in the depths of the limpid upturned eyes, one could fairly see tiny mirrored images of men with red hair, big white teeth, and white hands.

"Now, I'll tell you how it happened—how I imagine it was done. Some time after burying his wife in the woods Jones strolled back into the house. Seeing nobody, he called out in the familiar fashion, 'Mother!' Then the kids came out whimpering. 'Where is your mother?' said Jones. The children looked at him blankly. 'Why, pa,' said Freddy, 'you came in here, and hit ma with the axe; and then you sent us to bed.' 'Me?' cried Jones. 'I haven't been near the house since breakfast-time.'

"The children did not know how to reply. Their meagre little sense informed them that their father had been the man with the axe, but he denied it, and to their minds everything was a mere great puzzle with no meaning whatever, save that it was mysteriously sad and made them cry.

" 'What kind of a looking man was it?' said Jones.

"Freddy hesitated. 'Now—he looked a good deal like you, pa.'

" 'Like me?' said Jones. 'Why, I thought you said he had red hair?'

" 'No, I didn't,' replied Freddy. 'I thought he had grey hair, like yours.'

" 'Well,' said Jones, 'I saw a man with kind of red hair going along the road up yonder, and I thought maybe that might have been him.'

"Little Lucy, the second child, here piped up with intense conviction. 'His hair was a little teeny bit red. I saw it.'

" 'No,' said Jones. 'The man I saw had very red hair. And what did his teeth look like? Were they big and white?'

" 'Yes,' answered Lucy, 'they were.'

"Even Freddy seemed to incline to think it. 'His teeth may have been big and white.'

"Jones said little more at that time. Later he intimated to the children that their mother had gone off on a visit, and although they were full of wonder, and sometimes wept because of the oppression of an incomprehensible feeling in the air, they said nothing. Jones did his chores. Everything was smooth.

"The morning after the day of the murder, Jones and his children had a breakfast of hominy and milk.

" 'Well, this man with red hair and big white teeth, Lucy,' said Jones. 'Did you notice anything else about him?'

"Lucy straightened in her chair, and showed the childish desire to come out with brilliant information which would gain her father's approval. 'He had white hands—hands all white—'

" 'How about you, Freddy?'

" 'I didn't look at them much, but I think they were white,' answered the boy.

" 'And what did little Martha notice?' cried the tender parent. 'Did she see the big bad man?'

"Martha, aged four, replied solemnly, 'His hair was all red, and his hand was white—all white.'

" 'That's the man I saw up the road,' said Jones to Freddy.

" 'Yes, sir, it seems like it must have been him,' said the boy, his brain now completely muddled.

"Again Jones allowed the subject of his wife's murder to lapse. The children did not know that it was a murder, of course. Adults were always performing in a way to make children's heads swim. For instance, what could be more incomprehensible than that a man with two horses, dragging a queer thing, should walk all day, making the grass turn down and the earth turn up? And why did they cut the long grass and put it in a barn? And what was a cow for? Did the water in the well like to be there? All these actions and things were grand, because they were associated with the high estate of grownup people, but they were deeply mysterious. If, then, a man with red hair, big white teeth, and white hands should hit their mother on the nape of the neck with an axe, it was merely a phenomenon of grownup life. Little Henry, the baby, when he had a want, howled and pounded the table with his spoon. That was all of life to him. He was not concerned with the fact that his mother had been murdered.

"One day Jones said to his children suddenly, 'Look here: I wonder if you could have made a mistake. Are you absolutely sure that the man you saw had red hair, big white teeth, and white hands?'

"The children were indignant with their father. 'Why, of course, pa, we ain't made no mistake. We saw him as plain as day.'

"Later young Freddy's mind began to work like ketchup. His nights were haunted with terrible memories of the man with the red hair, big white teeth, and white hands, and the prolonged absence of his mother made him wonder and wonder. Presently he quite gratuitously developed the theory that his mother was dead. He knew about death. He had once seen a dead dog; also dead chickens, rabbits, and mice. One day he asked his father, 'Pa, is ma ever coming back?'

"Jones said: 'Well, no; I don't think she is.' This answer confirmed the boy in his theory. He knew that dead people did not come back.

"The attitude of Jones towards this descriptive legend of the man with the axe was very peculiar. He came to be in opposition to it. He protested against the convictions of the children, but he could not move them. It was the one thing in their lives of which they were stonily and absolutely positive.

"Now that really ends the story. But I will continue for your amusement. The jury hung Jones as high as they could, and they were quite right: because Jones confessed before he died. Freddy is now a highly respected driver of a grocery wagon in Ogdensburg. When I was up there a good many years afterwards people told me that when he ever spoke of the tragedy at all he was certain to denounce the alleged confession as a lie. He considered his father a victim to the stupidity of juries, and some day he hopes to meet the man with the red hair, big white teeth, and white hands, whose image still remains so distinct in his memory that he could pick him out in a crowd of ten thousand."

Acts of God
and Other Horrors

In the following selections by a dozen modern (mostly) American and British authors, dark hints of cosmic power abound. Here there be disasters natural and unnatural, hellish entities, nameless creatures of the night and even a few examples of divine(?) intervention.

How the reader chooses to interpret these marvels and horrors is a matter of private conscience. As for me, I have long contended that the need to believe is an almost inescapable trap of the ego.

Acts of God
and Other Horrors

WINSTON CHURCHILL

Man Overboard

Though he won the Nobel Prize in 1953 and is respected for the nonfiction works he penned, including The World Crisis, *the four-volume* A History of the English-Speaking Peoples *and the six-volume history of* The Second World War, WINSTON CHURCHILL *(1874–1965) is best known for a life of public service that culminated in his serving as British Prime Minister from 1940 to 1945 and 1951 to 1955. Churchill's earlier writing career has been all but forgotten. "Man Overboard," a cynical testament to the efficacy of true prayer, appeared in 1898 in* Harmsworth, *a British family magazine, and was first "unearthed" by anthologist Peter Haining.*

It was a little after half-past nine when the man fell overboard. The mail steamer was hurrying through the Red Sea in the hope of making up the time which the currents of the Indian Ocean had stolen.

The night was clear, though the moon was hidden behind clouds. The warm air was laden with moisture. The still surface of the waters was only broken by the movement of the great ship, from whose quarter the long, slanting undulations struck out like the feathers from an arrow shaft, and in whose wake the froth and air bubbles churned up by the propeller trailed in a narrowing line to the darkness of the horizon.

There was a concert on board. All the passengers were glad to break the monotony of the voyage and gathered around the piano in the companion-house. The decks were deserted. The man had been listening to the music and joining in the songs, but the room was hot and he came out to smoke a cigarette and enjoy a breath of the wind which the speedy passage of the liner created. It was the only wind in the Red Sea that night.

The accommodation-ladder had not been unshipped since leaving Aden and the man walked out on to the platform, as on to a balcony. He leaned his back against the rail and blew a puff of smoke into the air reflectively. The piano struck up a lively tune and a voice began to sing the first verse of "The Rowdy Dowdy Boys." The measured pulsations of the screw were a subdued but additional accompaniment. The man knew the song, it had been the rage at all the music halls when he had started for India seven years before. It reminded him of the brilliant and busy streets he had not seen for so long, but was soon to see again. He was just going to join in the chorus when the railing, which had been insecurely fastened, gave way suddenly with a snap and he fell backwards into the warm water of the sea amid a great splash.

For a moment he was physically too much astonished to think. Then he realised he must shout. He began to do this even before he rose to the surface. He achieved a hoarse, inarticulate, half-choked scream. A startled brain suggested the word, "Help!" and he bawled this out lustily and with frantic effort six or seven times without stopping. Then he listened.

"Hi! hi! clear the way
For the Rowdy Dowdy Boys."

The chorus floated back to him across the smooth water for the ship had already completely passed by. And as he heard the music a long stab of terror drove through his heart. The possibility that he would not be picked up dawned for the first time on his consciousness. The chorus started again:

"Then—I—say—boys,
Who's for a jolly spree?
Rum—tum—tiddley—um,
Who'll have a drink with me?"

"Help! Help! Help!" shrieked the man, now in desperate fear.

"Fond of a glass now and then,
Fond of a row or noise;
Hi! hi! clear the way
For the Rowdy Dowdy Boys!"

The last words drawled out fainter and fainter. The vessel was steaming fast. The beginning of the second verse was confused and broken by the ever-growing distance. The dark outline of the great hull was getting blurred. The stern light dwindled.

Then he set out to swim after it with furious energy, pausing every dozen strokes to shout long wild shouts. The disturbed waters of the sea began to settle again to their rest and widening undulations became ripples. The aerated confusion of the screw fizzed itself upwards and out. The noise of motion and the sounds of life and music died away.

The liner was but a single fading light on the blackness of the waters and a dark shadow against the paler sky.

At length full realisation came to the man and he stopped swimming. He was alone—abandoned. With the understanding the brain reeled. He began again to swim, only now instead of shouting he prayed—mad, incoherent prayers, the words stumbling into one another.

Suddenly a distant light seemed to flicker and brighten.

A surge of joy and hope rushed through his mind. They were going to stop—to turn the ship and come back. And with the hope came gratitude. His prayer was answered. Broken words of thanksgiving rose to his lips. He stopped and stared after the light—his soul in his eyes. As he watched it, it grew gradually but steadily smaller. Then the man knew that his fate was certain. Despair succeeded hope; gratitude gave place to curses. Beating the water with his arms, he raved impotently. Foul oaths burst from him, as broken as his prayers—and as unheeded.

The fit of passion passed, hurried by increasing fatigue. He became silent—silent as was the sea, for even the ripples were subsiding into the glassy smoothness of the surface. He swam on mechanically along the track of the ship, sobbing quietly to himself in the misery of fear. And the stern light became a tiny speck, yellower but scarcely bigger than some of the stars, which here and there shone between the clouds.

Nearly twenty minutes passed and the man's fatigue began to change to exhaustion. The overpowering sense of the inevitable pressed upon him. With the weariness came a strange comfort—he need not swim all the long way to Suez. There was another course. He would die. He would resign his existence since he was thus abandoned. He threw up his hands impulsively and sank.

Down, down he went through the warm water. The physical death took hold of him and he began to drown. The pain of that savage grip recalled his anger. He fought with it furiously. Striking out with arms and legs he sought to get back to the air. It was a hard struggle, but he escaped victorious and gasping to the surface. Despair awaited him. Feebly splashing with his hands, he moaned in bitter misery:

"I can't—I must. O God! let me die."

The moon, then in her third quarter, pushed out from behind the concealing clouds and shed a pale, soft glitter upon the sea. Upright in the water, fifty yards away, was a black triangular object. It was a fin. It approached him slowly.

His last appeal had been heard.

A. MERRITT

The People of the Pit

A. MERRITT *(1884–1943), born in Beverly, New Jersey, wrote eight novels that, though not without flaws, are still properly regarded as American fantasy classics:* The Moon Pool, The Metal Monster, The Ship of Ishtar, Seven Footprints to Satan, The Face in the Abyss, Dwellers in the Mirage, Burn Witch Burn *and its sequel,* Creep Shadow Creep. *The unprolific Merritt was editor of* American Weekly *magazine and regarded fiction as a sideline. "The People of the Pit" is one of the first and best of the scant handful of short stories that Merritt wrote.*

North of us a shaft of light shot half way to the zenith. It came from behind the five peaks. The beam drove up through a column of blue haze whose edges were marked as sharply as the rain that streams from the edges of a thunder cloud. It was like the flash of a searchlight through an azure mist. It cast no shadows.

As it struck upward, the summits were outlined hard and black and I saw that the whole mountain was shaped like a hand. As the light silhouetted it, the gigantic fingers stretched, the hand seemed to thrust itself forward. It was exactly as though it moved to push something back. The shining beam held steady for a moment; then broke into myriad little luminous globes that swung to and fro and dropped gently. They seemed to be searching.

The forest had become very still. Every wood noise held its breath. I felt the dogs pressing against my legs. They, too, were silent; but every muscle in their bodies trembled, their hair was stiff along their backs and their eyes, fixed on the falling lights, were filmed with the terror glaze.

I looked at Anderson. He was staring at the north where once more the beam had pulsed upward.

"It can't be the aurora," I spoke without moving my lips. My mouth was as dry as though Lao T'zai had poured his fear dust down my throat.

"If it is I never saw one like it," he answered in the same tone. "Besides, who ever heard of an aurora at this time of the year?"

He voiced the thought that was in my own mind.

"It makes me think something is being hunted up there," he said, "an unholy sort of hunt—it's well for us to be out of range."

"The mountain seems to move each time the shaft shoots up," I said. "What's it keeping back, Starr? It makes me think of the frozen hand of cloud that Shan Nadour set before the Gate of Ghouls to keep them in the lairs that Eblis cut for them."

He raised a hand—listening.

From the north and high overhead there came a whispering. It was not the rustling of the aurora, that rushing, crackling sound like the ghosts of winds that blew at Creation racing through the skeleton leaves of ancient trees that sheltered Lilith. It was a whispering that held in it a demand. It was eager. It called us to come up where the beam was flashing. It drew. There was in it a note of inexorable insistence. It touched my heart with a thousand tiny fear-tipped fingers and it filled me with a vast longing to race on and merge myself in the light. It must have been so that Ulysses felt when he strained at the mast and strove to obey the crystal sweet singing of the Sirens.

The whispering grew louder.

"What the hell's the matter with those dogs?" cried Anderson savagely. "Look at them!"

The malamutes, whining, were racing away toward the light. We saw them disappear among the trees. There came back to us a mournful howling. Then that too died away and left nothing but the insistent murmuring overhead.

The glade we had camped in looked straight to the north. We had reached, I suppose, three hundred miles above the first great bend of the Koskokwim toward the Yukon. Certainly we were in an untrodden part of the wilderness. We had pushed through from Dawson at the breaking of the spring, on a fair lead to the lost five peaks between which, so the Athabasean medicine man had told us, the gold streams out like putty from a clenched fist. Not an Indian were we able to get to go with us. The land of the Hand Mountain was accursed, they said. We had sighted the peaks the night before, their tops faintly outlined against a pulsing glow. And now we saw the light that had led us to them.

Anderson stiffened. Through the whispering had broken a curious pad-pad and a rustling. It sounded as though a small bear were moving toward us. I threw a pile of wood on the fire and, as it blazed up, saw something break through the bushes. It walked on all fours, but it did not walk like a bear. All at once it flashed upon me—it was like a baby crawling upstairs. The forepaws lifted themselves in grotesquely infantile fashion. It was grotesque but it was—terrible. It drew closer. We reached for our guns—and dropped them. Suddenly we knew that this crawling thing was a man!

It was a man. Still with the high climbing pad-pad he swayed to the fire. He stopped.

"Safe," whispered the crawling man, in a voice that was an echo of the murmur overhead. "Quite safe here. They can't get out of the blue, you know. They can't get you—unless you go to them—"

He fell over on his side. We ran to him. Anderson knelt.

"God's love!" he said. "Frank, look at this!"

He pointed to the hands. The wrists were covered with torn rags of a heavy shirt. The hands themselves were stumps! The fingers had been bent into the palms and the flesh had been worn to the bone. They looked like the feet of a little black elephant! My eyes traveled down the body. Around the waist was a heavy band of yellow metal. From it fell a ring and a dozen links of shining white chain!

"What is he? Where did he come from?" said Anderson. "Look, he's fast asleep—yet even in his sleep his arms try to climb and his feet draw themselves up one after the other! And his knees—how in God's name was he ever able to move on them?"

It was even as he said. In the deep sleep that had come upon the crawler, arms and legs kept raising in a deliberate, dreadful climbing motion. It was as though they had a life of their own—they kept their movement independently of the motionless body. They were semaphoric motions. If you have ever stood at the back of a train and had watched the semaphores rise and fall you will know exactly what I mean.

Abruptly the overhead whispering ceased. The shaft of light dropped and did not rise again. The crawling man became still. A gentle glow began to grow around us. It was dawn, and the short

Alaskan summer night was over. Anderson rubbed his eyes and turned to me a haggard face.

"Man!" he exclaimed. "You look as though you have been through a spell of sickness!"

"No more than you, Starr," I said. "What do you make of it all?"

"I'm thinking our only answer lies there," he answered, pointing to the figure that lay so motionless under the blankets we had thrown over him. "Whatever it was—that's what it was after. There was no aurora about that light, Frank. It was like the flaring up of some queer hell the preacher folk never frightened us with."

"We'll go no further today," I said. "I wouldn't wake him for all the gold that runs between the fingers of the five peaks—nor for all the devils that may be behind them."

The crawling man lay in a sleep as deep as the Styx. We bathed and bandaged the pads that had been his hands. Arms and legs were as rigid as though they were crutches. He did not move while we worked over him. He lay as he had fallen, the arms a trifle raised, the knees bent.

"Why did he crawl?" whispered Anderson. "Why didn't he walk?"

I was filing the band about the waist. It was gold, but it was like no gold I had ever handled. Pure gold is soft. This was soft, but it had an unclean, viscid life of its own. It clung to the file. I gashed through it, bent it away from the body and hurled it far off. It was— loathsome!

All that day he slept. Darkness came and still he slept. That night there was no shaft of light, no questing globes, no whispering. Some spell of horror seemed lifted from the land. It was noon when the crawling man awoke. I jumped as the pleasant, drawling voice sounded.

"How long have I slept?" he asked. His pale blue eyes grew quizzical as I stared at him.

"A night—and almost two days," I said.

"Was there any light up there last night?" He nodded to the north eagerly. "Any whispering?"

"Neither," I answered. His head fell back and he stared up at the sky.

"They've given it up, then?" he said at last.

"Who have given it up?" asked Anderson.

"Why, the people of the pit," replied the crawling man quietly.

We stared at him.

"The people of the pit," he said. "Things that the Devil made before the Flood and that somehow have escaped God's vengeance. You weren't in any danger from them—unless you had followed their call. They can't get any further than the blue haze. I was their prisoner," he added simply. "They were trying to whisper me back to them!"

Anderson and I looked at each other, the same thought in both our minds.

"You're wrong," said the crawling man. "I'm not insane. Give me a very little to drink. I'm going to die soon, but I want you to take me as far south as you can before I die, and afterwards I want you to build a big fire and burn me. I want to be in such shape that no infernal spell of theirs can drag my body back to them. You'll do it too, when I've told you about them—" He hesitated. "I think their chain is off me?" he said.

"I cut it off," I answered shortly.

"Thank God for that, too," whispered the crawling man.

He drank the brandy and water we lifted to his lips.

"Arms and legs quite dead," he said. "Dead as I'll be soon. Well, they did well for me. Now I'll tell you what's up there behind that hand. Hell!

"Now listen. My name is Stanton—Sinclair Stanton. Class of 1900, Yale. Explorer. I started away from Dawson last year to hunt for five peaks that rise like a hand in a haunted country and run pure gold between them. Same thing you were after? I thought so. Late last fall my comrade sickened. Sent him back with some Indians. Little later all my Indians ran away from me. I decided I'd stick, built a cabin, stocked myself with food and lay down to winter it. In the spring I started off again. Little less than two weeks ago I sighted the five peaks. Not from this side, though—the other. Give me some more brandy.

"I'd made too wide a detour," he went on. "I'd gotten too far north. I beat back. From this side you see nothing but forest straight up to the base of the Hand Mountain. Over on the other side—"

He was silent for a moment.

"Over there is forest, too. But it doesn't reach so far. No! I came out of it. Stretching miles in front of me was a level plain. It was as worn and ancient looking as the desert around the ruins of Babylon. At its end rose the peaks. Between me and them—far off—was what looked like a low dike of rocks. Then—I ran across the road!"

"The road!" cried Anderson incredulously.

"The road," said the crawling man. "A fine smooth stone road. It ran straight on to the mountain. Oh, it was road all right—and worn as though millions and millions of feet had passed over it for thousands of years. On each side of it were sand and heaps of stones. After a while, I began to notice these stones. They were cut, and the shape of the heaps somehow gave me the idea that a hundred thousand years ago they might have been houses. I sensed man about them and at the same time they smelled of immemorial antiquity. Well—

"The peaks grew closer. The heaps of ruins thicker. Something inexpressibly desolate hovered over them; something reached from them that struck my heart like the touch of ghosts so old that they could be only the ghosts of ghosts. I went on.

"And now I saw that what I had thought to be the low rock range at the base of the peaks was a thicker litter of ruins. The Hand Mountain was really much farther off. The road passed between two high rocks that raised themselves like a gateway."

The crawling man paused.

"They were a gateway," he said. "I reached them. I went between them. And then I sprawled and clutched the earth in sheer awe! I was on a broad stone platform. Before me was—sheer space! Imagine the Grand Canyon five times as wide and with the bottom dropped out. That is what I was looking into. It was like peeping over the edge of a cleft world down into the infinity where the planets roll! On the far side stood the five peaks. They looked like a gigantic warning hand stretched up to the sky. The lip of the abyss curved away on each side of me.

"I could see down perhaps a thousand feet. Then a thick blue haze shut out the eye. It was like the blue you see gather on the high hills at dusk. And the pit—it was awesome; awesome as the Maori Gulf of Ranalak, that sinks between the living and the dead and that only the freshly released soul has strength to leap—but never strength to cross again.

"I crept back from the verge and stood up, weak. My hand rested against one of the pillars of the gateway. There was carving upon it. It bore in still sharp outlines the heroic figure of a man. His back was turned. His arms were outstretched. There was an odd, peaked headdress upon him. I looked at the opposite pillar. It bore a figure exactly similar. The pillars were triangular and the carvings were on the side away from the pit. The figures seemed to be holding something back. I looked closer. Behind the outstretched hands I seemed to see other shapes.

"I traced them out vaguely. Suddenly I felt unaccountably sick. There had come to me an impression of enormous upright slugs. Their swollen bodies were faintly cut—all except the heads which were well-marked globes. They were—unutterably loathsome. I turned from the gates back to the void. I stretched myself upon the slab and looked over the edge.

"A stairway led down into the pit!"

"A stairway!" we cried.

"A stairway," repeated the crawling man as patiently as before. "It seemed not so much carved out of the rock as built into it. The slabs were about six feet long and three feet wide. It ran down from the platform and vanished into the blue haze."

"But who could build such a stairway as that?" I said. "A stairway built into the wall of a precipice and leading down into a bottomless pit!"

"Not bottomless," said the crawling man quietly. "There was a bottom. I reached it!"

"Reached it?" we repeated.

"Yes, by the stairway," answered the crawling man. "You see—I went down it!

"Yes," he said. "I went down the stairway. But not that day. I made my camp back of the gates. At dawn I filled my knapsack with food, my two canteens with water from a spring that wells up there by the gateway, walked between the carved monoliths and stepped over the edge of the pit.

"The steps ran along the side of the rock at a forty-degree pitch. As I went down and down I studied them. They were of a greenish rock quite different from the granitic porphyry that formed the wall of the precipice. At first I thought that the builders had taken advantage of an outcropping stratum, and had carved from it their gigantic flight. But the regularity of the angle at which it fell made me doubtful of this theory.

"After I had gone perhaps half a mile I stepped out upon a landing. From this landing the stairs made a V-shaped turn and ran on downward, clinging to the cliff at the same angle as the first flight; it was a zigzag, and after I had made three of these turns I knew that the steps dropped straight down in a succession of such angles. No strata could be so regular as that. No, the stairway was built by hands! But whose? The answer is in those ruins around the edge, I think—never to be read.

"By noon I had lost sight of the five peaks and the lip of the abyss.

Above me, below me, was nothing but the blue haze. Beside me, too, was nothingness, for the further breast of rock had long since vanished. I felt no dizziness, and any trace of fear was swallowed in a vast curiosity. What was I to discover? Some ancient and wonderful civilization that had ruled when the Poles were tropical gardens? Nothing living, I felt sure—all was too old for life. Still, a stairway so wonderful must lead to something quite as wonderful, I knew. What was it? I went on.

"At regular intervals I had passed the mouths of small caves. There would be two thousand steps and then an opening, two thousand more steps and an opening—and so on and on. Late that afternoon I stopped before one of these clefts. I suppose I had gone then three miles down the pit, although the angles were such that I had walked in all fully ten miles. I examined the entrance. On each side were carved the figures of the great portal above, only now they were standing face forward, the arms outstretched as though to hold something back from the outer depths. Their faces were covered with veils. There were no hideous shapes behind them. I went inside. The fissure ran back for twenty yards like a burrow. It was dry and perfectly light. Outside I could see the blue haze rising upward like a column, its edges clearly marked. I felt an extraordinary sense of security, although I had not been conscious of any fear. I felt that the figures at the entrance were guardians—but against what?

"The blue haze thickened and grew faintly luminescent. I fancied that it was dusk above. I ate and drank a little and slept. When I awoke the blue had lightened again, and I fancied it was dawn above. I went on. I forgot the gulf yawning at my side. I felt no fatigue and little hunger or thirst, although I had drunk and eaten sparingly. That night I spent within another of the caves, and at dawn I descended again.

"It was late that day when I first saw the city—"

He was silent for a time.

"The city," he said at last; "there is a city, you know. But not such a city as you have ever seen—nor any other man who has lived to tell of it. The pit, I think, is shaped like a bottle; the opening before the five peaks is the neck. But how wide the bottom is I do not know—thousands of miles maybe. I had begun to catch little glints of light far down in the blue. Then I saw the tops of—trees, I suppose they are. But not our kind of trees—unpleasant, snaky kind of trees. They reared themselves on high thin trunks and their tops were nests of thick tendrils with ugly little leaves like arrow heads. The trees were red, a vivid angry red. Here and there I glimpsed spots of shining yellow. I knew these were water because I could see things breaking through their surface—or at least I could see the splash and ripple, but what it was that disturbed them I never saw.

"Straight beneath me was the—city. I looked down upon mile after mile of closely packed cylinders. They lay upon their sides in pyramids of three, of five—of dozens—piled upon each other. It is hard to make you see what that city is like—look, suppose you have water pipes of a certain length and first you lay three of them side by side and on top of them you place two and on these two one; or suppose you take five for a foundation and place on these four and then three, then two and then one. Do you see? That was the way they looked. But they were topped by towers, by minarets, by flares, by fans and twisted monstrosities. They gleamed as though coated with pale rose flame. Beside them the venomous red trees raised themselves like the heads of hydras guarding nests of gigantic, jeweled and sleeping worms!

"A few feet beneath me the stairway jutted out into a titanic arch, unearthly as the span that bridges Hell and leads to Asgard. It curved out and down straight through the top of the highest pile of carven cylinders and then it vanished through it. It was appalling—it was demonic—"

The crawling man stopped. His eyes rolled up into his head. He trembled and his arms and legs began their horrible crawling movement. From his lips came a whispering. It was an echo of the high murmuring we had heard the night he came to us. I put my hands over his eyes. He quieted.

"The Things Accursed!" he said. "The People of the Pit! Did I whisper? Yes—but they can't get me now—they can't!"

After a time he began as quietly as before.

"I crossed the span. I went down through the top of that—building. Blue darkness shrouded me for a moment and I felt the steps twist into a spiral. I wound down and then—I was standing high up in—I can't tell you in what, I'll have to call it a room. We have no images for what is in the pit. A hundred feet below me was the floor. The walls sloped down and out from where I stood in a series of widening crescents. The place was colossal—and it was filled with a curious mottled red light. It was like the light inside a green and gold flecked fire opal. I went down to the last step. Far in front of me rose a high, columned altar. Its pillars were carved in monstrous scrolls—like mad octopuses with a thousand drunken tentacles; they rested on the backs of shapeless monstrosities carved in crimson stone. The altar front was a gigantic slab of purple covered with carvings.

"I can't describe these carvings! No human being could—the human eye cannot grasp them any more than it can grasp the shapes that haunt the fourth dimension. Only a subtle sense in the back of the brain sensed them vaguely. They were formless things that gave no conscious image, yet pressed into the mind like small hot seals— ideas of hate—of combats between unthinkable monstrous things— victories in a nebulous hell of steaming, obscene jungles—aspirations and ideals immeasurably loathsome—

"And as I stood I grew aware of something that lay behind the lip of the altar fifty feet above me. I knew it was there—I felt it with every hair and every tiny bit of my skin. Something infinitely malignant, infinitely horrible, infinitely ancient. It lurked, it brooded, it threatened and it—was invisible!

"Behind me was a circle of blue light. I ran for it. Something urged me to turn back, to climb the stairs and make away. It was impossible. Repulsion for that unseen Thing raced me onward as though a current had my feet. I passed through the circle. I was out on a street that stretched on into dim distance between rows of the carven cylinders.

"Here and there the red trees arose. Between them rolled the stone burrows. And now I could take in the amazing ornamentation that clothed them. They were like the trunks of smooth-skinned trees that had fallen and had been clothed with high-reaching noxious orchids. Yes—those cylinders were like that—and more. They should have gone out with the dinosaurs. They were—monstrous. They struck the eyes like a blow and they passed across the nerves like a rasp. And nowhere was there sight or sound of living thing.

"There were circular openings in the cylinders like the circle in the Temple of the Stairway. I passed through one of them. I was in a long, bare vaulted room whose curving sides half closed twenty feet over my head, leaving a wide slit that opened into another vaulted chamber above. There was absolutely nothing in the room save the same mottled reddish light that I had seen in the Temple. I stumbled. I still could see nothing, but there was something on the floor over which I had tripped. I reached down—and my hand touched a thing cold and smooth—that moved under it. I turned and ran out of that place—I was filled with a loathing that had in it something of madness—I ran on and on blindly—wringing my hands—weeping with horror—

"When I came to myself I was still among the stone cylinders and red trees. I tried to retrace my steps; to find the Temple. I was more than afraid. I was like a new-loosed soul panic-stricken with the first terrors of Hell. I could not find the Temple! Then the haze began to thicken and glow; the cylinders to shine more brightly. I knew that it was dusk in the world above and I felt that with dusk my time of peril had come; that the thickening of the haze was the signal for the awakening of whatever things lived in this pit.

"I scrambled up the sides of one of the burrows. I hid behind a twisted nightmare of stone. Perhaps, I thought, there was a chance of remaining hidden until the blue lightened, and the peril passed. There began to grow around me a murmur. It was everywhere— and it grew and grew into a great whispering. I peeped from the side of the stone down into the street. I saw lights passing and repassing. More and more lights—they swam out of the circular doorways and they thronged the street. The highest were eight feet above the pave; the lowest perhaps two. They hurried, they sauntered, they bowed, they stopped and whispered—and there was nothing under them!"

"Nothing under them!" breathed Anderson.

"No," he went on, "that was the terrible part of it—there was nothing under them. Yet certainly the lights were living things. They had consciousness, volition, thought—what else I did not know. They were nearly two feet across—the largest. Their center was a bright nucleus—red, blue, green. This nucleus faded off, gradually, into a misty glow that did not end abruptly. It, too, seemed to fade off into nothingness—but a nothingness that had under it a—some-thingness. I strained my eyes trying to grasp this body into which the lights merged and which one could only feel was there, but could not see.

"And all at once I grew rigid. Something cold, and thin like a whip, had touched my face. I turned my head. Close behind were three of the lights. They were a pale blue. They looked at me—if you can imagine lights that are eyes. Another whiplash gripped my shoulder. Under the closest light came a shrill whispering. I shrieked. Abruptly the murmuring in the street ceased. I dragged my eyes from the pale blue globe that held them and looked out— the lights in the streets were rising by myriads to the level of where I stood! There they stopped and peered at me. They crowded and jostled as though they were a crowd of curious people—on Broadway. I felt a score of the lashes touch me—

"When I came to myself I was again in the great Place of the Stairway, lying at the foot of the altar. All was silent. There were no lights—only the mottled red glow. I jumped to my feet and ran toward the steps. Something jerked me back to my knees. And then I saw that around my waist had been fastened a yellow ring of metal. From it hung a chain and this chain passed up over the lip of the high ledge. I was chained to the altar!

"I reached into my pockets for my knife to cut through the ring. It was not there! I had been stripped of everything except one of the canteens that I had hung around my neck and which I suppose They had thought was—part of me. I tried to break the ring. It seemed alive. It writhed in my hands and it drew itself closer around me! I pulled at the chain. It was immovable. There came to me the consciousness of the unseen Thing above the altar. I groveled at the foot of the slab and wept. Think—alone in that place of strange light with the brooding ancient Horror above me—a monstrous Thing, a Thing unthinkable—an unseen Thing that poured forth horror—

"After a while I gripped myself. Then I saw beside one of the pillars a yellow bowl filled with a thick white liquid. I drank it. If it killed I did not care. But its taste was pleasant and as I drank, strength came back to me with a rush. Clearly I was not to be starved. The lights, whatever they were, had a conception of human needs.

"And now the reddish mottled gleam began to deepen. Outside arose the humming and through the circle that was the entrance came streaming the globes. They ranged themselves in ranks until they filled the Temple. Their whispering grew into a chant, a cadenced whispering chant that rose and fell, rose and fell, while to its rhythm the globes lifted and sank, lifted and sank.

"All that night the lights came and went—and all that night the chant sounded as they rose and fell. At the last I felt myself only an atom of consciousness in a sea of cadenced whispering; an atom that rose and fell with the bowing globes. I tell you that even my heart pulsed in unison with them! The red glow faded, the lights streamed out; the whispering died. I was again alone and I knew that once again day had broken in my own world.

"I slept. When I awoke I found beside the pillar more of the white liquid. I scrutinized the chain that held me to the altar. I began to rub two of the links together. I did this for hours. When the red began to thicken there was a ridge worn in the links. Hope rushed up within me. There was, then, a chance to escape.

"With the thickening the lights came again. All through that night the whispering chant sounded, and the globes rose and fell. The chant seized me. It pulsed through me until every nerve and muscle quivered to it. My lips began to quiver. They strove like a man trying to cry out in a nightmare. And at last they, too, were whispering the chant of the people of the pit. My body bowed in unison with the lights—I was, in movement and sound, one with the nameless things while my soul sank back sick with horror and powerless. While I whispered I—saw them!"

"Saw the lights?" I asked stupidly.

"Saw the Things under the lights," he answered. "Great transparent snail-like bodies—dozens of waving tentacles stretching from them—round gaping mouths under the luminous seeing globes. They were like the ghosts of inconceivably monstrous slugs! I could see through them. And as I stared, still bowing and whispering, the dawn came and they streamed to and through the entrance. They did not crawl or walk—they floated! They floated and were—gone!

"I did not sleep. I worked all that day at my chain. By the thickening of the red I had worn it a sixth through. And all that night I whispered and bowed with the pit people, joining in their chant to the Thing that brooded above me!

"Twice again the red thickened and the chant held me—then on the morning of the fifth day I broke through the worn links of the chain. I was free! I drank from the bowl of white liquid and poured what was left in my flask. I ran to the Stairway. I rushed up and past that unseen Horror behind the altar ledge and was out upon the Bridge. I raced across the span and up the Stairway.

"Can you think what it is to climb straight up the verge of a cleft-world—with hell behind you? Hell was behind me and terror rode me. The city had long been lost in the blue haze before I knew that I could climb no more. My heart beat upon my ears like a sledge. I fell before one of the little caves feeling that here at last was sanctuary. I crept far back within it and waited for the haze to thicken. Almost at once it did so. From far below me came a vast and angry murmur. At the mouth of the rift I saw a light pulse up through the blue; die down, and as it dimmed I saw myriads of the globes that are the eyes of the pit people swing downward into the abyss. Again and again the light pulsed and the globes fell. They were hunting me. The whispering grew louder, more insistent.

"There grew in me the dreadful desire to join in the whispering as I had done in the Temple. I bit my lips through and through to still them. All that night the beam shot up through the abyss, the globes swung and the whispering sounded—and now I knew the purpose of the caves and of the sculptured figures that still had power to guard them. But what were the people who had carved them? Why had they built their city around the verge and why had they set that Stairway in the pit? What had they been to those Things that dwelt at the bottom and what use had the Things been to them that they should live beside their dwelling place? That there had been some purpose was certain. No work so prodigious as the Stairway would have been undertaken otherwise. But what was the purpose? And why was it that those who had dwelt about the abyss had passed away ages gone, and the dwellers in the abyss still lived? I could find no answer—nor can I find any now. I have not the shred of a theory.

"Dawn came as I wondered and with it silence. I drank what was left of the liquid in my canteen, crept from the cave and began to climb again. That afternoon my legs gave out. I tore off my shirt, made from it pads for my knees and coverings for my hands. I crawled upward. I crawled up and up. And again I crept into one of the caves and waited until again the blue thickened, the shaft of light shot through it and the whispering came.

"But now there was a new note in the whispering. It was no longer threatening. It called and coaxed. It drew. A new terror gripped me. There had come upon me a mighty desire to leave the cave and go out where the lights swung; to let them do with me as they pleased, carry me where they wished. The desire grew. It gained fresh impulse with every rise of the beam until at last I vibrated with the desire as I had vibrated to the chant in the Temple. My body was a pendulum. Up would go the beam and I would swing toward it! Only my soul kept steady. It held me fast to the floor of the cave. And all that night it fought with my body against the spell of the pit people.

"Dawn came. Again I crept from the cave and faced the Stairway. I could not rise. My hands were torn and bleeding; my knees an agony. I forced myself upward step by step. After a while my hands became numb, the pain left my knees. They deadened. Step by step my will drove my body upward upon them.

"And then—a nightmare of crawling up infinite stretches of steps —memories of dull horror while hidden within caves with the lights pulsing without and whisperings that called and called me—memory of a time when I awoke to find that my body was obeying the call and had carried me halfway out between the guardians of the portals while thousands of gleaming globes rested in the blue haze and watched me. Glimpses of bitter fights against sleep and always, always—a climb up and up along infinite distances of steps that led from Abaddon to a Paradise of blue sky and open world!

"At last a consciousness of the clear sky close above me, the lip of the pit before me—memory of passing between the great portals of the pit and of steady withdrawal from it—dreams of giant men with strange peaked crowns and veiled faces who pushed me onward and onward and held back Roman-candle globules of light that sought to draw me back to a gulf wherein planets swam between the branches of red trees that had snakes for crowns.

"And then a long, long sleep—how long God alone knows—in a cleft of rocks; an awakening to see far in the north the beam still rising and falling, the lights still hunting, the whispering high above me calling.

"Again crawling on dead arms and legs that moved—that moved —like the Ancient Mariner's ship—without volition of mine, but that carried me from a haunted place. And then—your fire—and this— safety!"

The crawling man smiled at us for a moment. Then swiftly life faded from his face. He slept.

That afternoon we struck camp and carrying the crawling man started back south. For three days we carried him and still he slept. And on the third day, still sleeping, he died. We built a great pile of wood and we burned his body as he had asked. We scattered his ashes about the forest with the ashes of the trees that had consumed him. It must be a great magic indeed that could disentangle those ashes and draw him back in a rushing cloud to the pit he called Accursed. I do not think that even the People of the Pit have such a spell. No.

But we did not return to the five peaks to see.

H. G. WELLS

In the Avu Observatory

Unlike A. Merritt, author of the preceding tale, the British H. G. WELLS (1866–1946) was both prolific and a stylistically superior writer. Among his many novels and short stories are some of the most important tales of fantasy and science fiction written during the last century, including "The Man Who Could Work Miracles," "The Magic Shop," "Pollock and the Porroh Man," "The Red Room," "The Sea Raiders," The Invisible Man, The Island of Doctor Moreau, The Time Machine *and* The War of the Worlds.

The observatory at Avu, in Borneo, stands on the spur of the mountain. To the north rises the old crater, black at night against the unfathomable blue of the sky. From the little circular building, with its mushroom dome, the slopes plunge steeply downward into the black mysteries of the tropical forest beneath. The little house in which the observer and his assistant live is about fifty yards from the observatory, and beyond this are the huts of their native attendants.

Thaddy, the chief observer, was down with a slight fever. His assistant, Woodhouse, paused for a moment in silent contemplation of the tropical night before commencing his solitary vigil. The night was very still. Now and then voices and laughter came from the native huts, or the cry of some strange animal was heard from the midst of the mystery of the forest. Nocturnal insects appeared in ghostly fashion out of the darkness, and fluttered round his light. He thought, perhaps, of all the possibilities of discovery that still lay in the black tangle beneath him; for to the naturalist the virgin forests of Borneo are still a wonderland full of strange questions and half-suspected discoveries. Woodhouse carried a small lantern in his hand, and its yellow glow contrasted vividly with the infinite series of tints between lavender-blue and black in which the landscape was painted. His hands and face were smeared with ointment against the attacks of the mosquitoes.

Even in these days of celestial photography, work done in a purely temporary erection, and with only the most primitive appliances in addition to the telescope, still involves a very large amount of cramped and motionless watching. He sighed as he thought of the physical fatigues before him, stretched himself, and entered the observatory.

The reader is probably familiar with the structure of an ordinary astronomical observatory. The building is usually cylindrical in shape, with a very light hemispherical roof capable of being turned round from the interior. The telescope is supported upon a stone pillar in the centre, and a clockwork arrangement compensates for the earth's rotation, and allows a star once found to be continuously observed. Besides this, there is a compact tracery of wheels and screws about its point of support, by which the astronomer adjusts it. There is, of course, a slit in the movable roof which follows the eye of the telescope in its survey of the heavens. The observer sits or lies on a sloping wooden arrangement, which he can wheel to any part of the observatory as the position of the telescope may require. Within it is advisable to have things as dark as possible, in order to enhance the brilliance of the stars observed.

The lantern flared as Woodhouse entered his circular den, and the general darkness fled into black shadows behind the big machine, from which it presently seemed to creep back over the whole place again as the light waned. The slit was a profound transparent blue, in which six stars shone with tropical brilliance, and their light lay, a pallid gleam, along the black tube of the instrument. Woodhouse shifted the roof, and then proceeding to the telescope, turned first one wheel and then another, the great cylinder slowly swinging into a new position. Then he glanced through the finder, the little companion telescope, moved the roof a little more, made some further adjustments, and set the clockwork in motion. He took off his jacket, for the night was very hot, and pushed into position the uncomfortable seat to which he was condemned for the next four hours. Then with a sigh he resigned himself to his watch upon the mysteries of space.

There was no sound now in the observatory, and the lantern

waned steadily. Outside there was the occasional cry of some animal in alarm or pain, or calling to its mate, and the intermittent sounds of the Malay and Dyak servants. Presently one of the men began a queer chanting song, in which the others joined at intervals. After this it would seem that they turned in for the night, for no further sound came from their direction, and the whispering stillness became more and more profound.

The clockwork ticked steadily. The shrill hum of a mosquito explored the place and grew shriller in indignation at Woodhouse's ointment. Then the lantern went out and all the observatory was black.

Woodhouse shifted his position presently, when the slow movement of the telescope had carried it beyond the limits of his comfort.

He was watching a little group of stars in the Milky Way, in one of which his chief had seen or fancied a remarkable colour variability. It was not a part of the regular work for which the establishment existed, and for that reason perhaps Woodhouse was deeply interested. He must have forgotten things terrestrial. All his attention was concentrated upon the great blue circle of the telescope field—a circle powdered, so it seemed, with an innumerable multitude of stars, and all luminous against the blackness of its setting. As he watched he seemed to himself to become incorporeal, as if he too were floating in the ether of space. Infinitely remote was the faint red spot he was observing.

Suddenly the stars were blotted out. A flash of blackness passed, and they were visible again.

"Queer," said Woodhouse. "Must have been a bird."

The thing happened again, and immediately after the great tube shivered as though it had been struck. Then the dome of the observatory resounded with a series of thundering blows. The stars seemed to sweep aside as the telescope—which had been unclamped —swung round and away from the slit in the roof.

"Great Scott!" cried Woodhouse. "What's this?"

Some huge vague black shape, with a flapping something like a wing, seemed to be struggling in the aperture of the roof. In another moment the slit was clear again, and the luminous haze of the Milky Way shone warm and bright.

The interior of the roof was perfectly black, and only a scraping sound marked the whereabouts of the unknown creature.

Woodhouse had scrambled from the seat to his feet. He was trembling violently and in a perspiration with the suddenness of the occurrence. Was the thing, whatever it was, inside or out? It was big, whatever else it might be. Something shot across the skylight, and the telescope swayed. He started violently and put his arm up. It was in the observatory, then, with him. It was clinging to the roof, apparently. What the devil was it? Could it see him?

He stood for perhaps a minute in a state of stupefaction. The beast, whatever it was, clawed at the interior of the dome, and then something flapped almost into his face, and he saw the momentary gleam of starlight on a skin like oiled leather. His water-bottle was knocked off his little table with a smash.

The sense of some strange bird-creature hovering a few yards from his face in the darkness was indescribably unpleasant to Woodhouse. As his thought returned he concluded that it must be some night-bird or large bat. At any risk he would see what it was, and pulling a match from his pocket, he tried to strike it on the telescope seat. There was a smoking streak of phosphorescent light, the match flared for a moment, and he saw a vast wing sweeping towards him, a gleam of grey-brown fur, and then he was struck in the face and the match knocked out of his hand. The blow was aimed at his temple, and a claw tore sideways down to his cheek. He reeled and fell, and he heard the extinguished lantern smash. Another blow followed as he fell. He was partly stunned, he felt his own warm blood stream out upon his face. Instinctively he felt his eyes had been struck at, and, turning over on his face to protect them, tried to crawl under the protection of the telescope.

He was struck again upon the back, and he heard his jacket rip, and then the thing hit the roof of the observatory. He edged as far as he could between the wooden seat and the eyepiece of the instrument, and turned his body round so that it was chiefly his feet that were exposed. With these he could at least kick. He was still in a mystified state. The strange beast banged about in the darkness, and presently clung to the telescope, making it sway and the gear rattle. Once it flapped near him, and he kicked out madly and felt a soft body with his feet. He was horribly scared now. It must be a big thing to swing the telescope like that. He saw for a moment the outline of a head black against the starlight, with sharply pointed upstanding ears and a crest between them. It seemed to him to be as big as a mastiff's. Then he began to bawl out as loudly as he could for help.

At that the thing came down upon him again. As it did so his hand touched something beside him on the floor. He kicked out, and the next moment his ankle was gripped and held by a row of keen teeth. He yelled again, and tried to free his leg by kicking with the other. Then he realised he had the broken water-bottle at his hand, and, snatching it, he struggled into a sitting posture, and feeling in the darkness towards his foot, gripped a velvety ear, like the ear of a big cat. He had seized the water-bottle by its neck and brought it down with a shivering crash upon the head of the strange beast. He repeated the blow, and then stabbed and jabbed with the jagged end of it, in the darkness, where he judged the face might be.

The small teeth relaxed their hold, and at once Woodhouse pulled his leg free and kicked hard. He felt the sickening feel of fur and bone giving under his boot. There was a tearing bite at his arm, and he struck over it at the face, as he judged, and hit damp fur.

There was a pause; then he heard the sound of claws and the dragging of a heavy body away from him over the observatory floor. Then there was silence, broken only by his own sobbing breathing, and a sound like licking. Everything was black except the parallelogram of the blue skylight with the luminous dust of stars, against which the end of the telescope now appeared in silhouette. He waited, as it seemed, an interminable time.

Was the thing coming on again? He felt in his trouser pocket for some matches, and found one remaining. He tried to strike this, but the floor was wet, and it spat and went out. He cursed. He could not see where the door was situated. In his struggle he had quite lost his bearings. The strange beast, disturbed by the splutter of the match, began to move again. "Time!" called Woodhouse, with a sudden gleam of mirth, but the thing was not coming at him again. He must have hurt it, he thought, with the broken bottle. He felt a dull pain in his ankle. Probably he was bleeding there. He wondered if it would support him if he tried to stand up. The night outside was very still. There was no sound of anyone moving. The sleepy fools had not heard those wings battering upon the dome, nor his shouts. It was no good wasting strength in shouting. The monster flapped its wings and startled him into a defensive attitude. He hit his elbow against the seat, and it fell over with a crash. He cursed this, and then he cursed the darkness.

Suddenly the oblong patch of starlight seemed to sway to and fro. Was he going to faint? It would never do to faint. He clenched his fists and set his teeth to hold himself together. Where had the door got to? It occurred to him he could get his bearings by the stars visible through the skylight. The patch of stars he saw was in Sagittarius and south-eastward; the door was north—or was it north by west? He tried to think. If he could get the door open he might retreat. It might be the thing was wounded. The suspense was beastly. "Look here!" he said, "if you don't come on, I shall come at you."

Then the thing began clambering up the side of the observatory, and he saw its black outline gradually blot out the skylight. Was it in retreat? He forgot about the door, and watched as the dome shifted and creaked. Somehow he did not feel very frightened or excited now. He felt a curious sinking sensation inside him. The sharply defined patch of light, with the black form moving across it, seemed to be growing smaller and smaller. That was curious. He began to feel very thirsty, and yet he did not feel inclined to get anything to drink. He seemed to be sliding down a long funnel.

He felt a burning sensation in his throat, and then he perceived it was broad daylight, and that one of the Dyak servants was looking at him with a curious expression. Then there was the top of Thaddy's face upside down. Funny fellow, Thaddy, to go about like that! Then he grasped the situation better, and perceived that his head was on Thaddy's knee, and Thaddy was giving him brandy. And then he saw the eyepiece of the telescope with a lot of red smears on it. He began to remember.

"You've made this observatory in a pretty mess," said Thaddy.

The Dyak boy was beating up an egg in brandy. Woodhouse took this and sat up. He felt a sharp twinge of pain. His ankle was tied up, so were his arm and the side of his face. The smashed glass, red-stained, lay about the floor, the telescope seat was overturned, and by the opposite wall was a dark pool. The door was open, and he saw the grey summit of the mountain against a brilliant background of blue sky.

"Pah!" said Woodhouse. "Who's been killing calves here? Take me out of it."

Then he remembered the Thing, and the fight he had had with it.

"What *was* it?" he said to Thaddy—"the Thing I fought with?"

"*You* know that best," said Thaddy. "But, anyhow, don't worry yourself now about it. Have some more to drink."

Thaddy, however, was curious enough, and it was a hard struggle between duty and inclination to keep Woodhouse quiet until he was decently put away in bed, and had slept upon the copious dose of meat-extract Thaddy considered advisable. They then talked it over together.

"It was," said Woodhouse, "more like a big bat than anything else in the world. It had sharp, short ears, and soft fur, and its wings were leathery. Its teeth were little, but devilish sharp, and its jaw could not have been very strong or else it would have bitten through my ankle."

"It has pretty nearly," said Thaddy.

"It seemed to me to hit out with its claws pretty freely. That is about as much as I know about the beast. Our conversation was intimate, so to speak, and yet not confidential."

"The Dyak chaps talk about a Big Colugo, a Klangutang—whatever that may be. It does not often attack man, but I suppose you made it nervous. They say there is a Big Colugo and a Little Colugo, and a something else that sounds like gobble. They all fly about at night. For my own part I know there are flying foxes and flying lemurs about here, but they are none of them very big beasts."

"There are more things in heaven and earth," said Woodhouse— and Thaddy groaned at the quotation—"and more particularly in the forests of Borneo, than are dreamt of in our philosophies. On the whole, if the Borneo fauna is going to disgorge any more of its novelties upon me, I should prefer that it did so when I was not occupied in the observatory at night and alone."

C. H. SHERMAN

In the Valley
of the Shades

C. H. SHERMAN, *one of my former writing students at New York University and a frequent contributor to my anthologies, lives a schizophrenic existence as a successful stage and television actor. When not occupied working in front of a camera, "C.H." sometimes finds the time to dash off alternately grim and poignant fantasies. Two earlier Sherman tales, "Doll-Baby" and "Teacher," are set in the same backwoods territory as "In the Valley of the Shades."*

Well, she was dead.

She lay there in the coffin that Thomas had built a few years ago. That awful spring she'd been so sick with the influenza she asked him to make the box from the persimmon tree that fell two weeks before during a fearsome storm. She said she didn't want him to kill a tree on her account so whyn't he take advantage of the storm's gift. He did as she asked, as he always did ever since he'd met his gruff Harley, but he warned her not to die until the coffin was finished or bad luck would surely smite the both of them. She snarled and said, "Old man, you think you can fool me into getting well while you dawdle with your tools?" Which was exactly what Thomas's thought had been. But he answered her smartness as if she had made him mad. "You do what you have to do, little one, and I'll do what I have to do. But I sure won't appreciate your racing to Heaven and leaving me to deal with misfortune alone."

He dawdled as she knew he would. And she got well as he hoped she would.

But now the coffin that was waiting for her finally held its burden.

She'd always been frail, always tiny. That's what attracted her to Thomas in the first place. Her bones were practically child-sized, even though she was in her twenties when their marriage took place. He called her Hardly to make her laugh. Not that she ever did. When they met, she didn't look like she had even smiled since the day she was born. She wasn't so much feisty as downright ornery. Still, Thomas was taken with her and, in her own way, she was taken with him.

She never put on weight. But then she never ate with much relish, always heaping Thomas's plate to make sure he was satisfied while she merely nibbled. She was a dutiful wife, if not exactly loving.

Thomas sat in his rocking chair and watched over her. Lying there in the box Harley looked even smaller than he remembered her. He felt bad about the nickels on her eyelids. He had spent one of the silver dollars of their corpse money on medicine for her, figuring that she would surely get well again and he'd be able to sell the quilt she was working on to replace it. He tried to comfort himself with the thought that she would have smirked and said the nickels were just the right size for her weaselly little eyes.

Outside, the katydids started to sing. Vaguely, Thomas glanced at the Trillington Bank and Trust calendar tacked up near the door. First frost by October fifteenth. An ordinary year. An average year. Except that he had lost both his wife and baby child within two months.

The boy wasn't but half a year old when Harley found it dead in its cradle in mid-afternoon. Thomas came running from the field when he heard his wife screaming but the baby couldn't be revived. Harley's spirits faded after that. Her frail body, not yet recovered from the birthing, fell prey to sickness and she just wasted away. Thomas grieved for the child in silence while he struggled to revive Harley's will to live.

She died in the middle of the night. Thomas tried to keep her cool with wet rags but her fever burned so high that he could almost see steam rising from the cloths. She slipped in and out of delirium, crying sometimes, moaning, talking. Thomas held her like a baby and sang to her. Right before she died she looked him square in the face and said, "I'm sorry to leave you." She was a hard woman to like and Thomas knew deep inside she was troubled. He loved her, though, and he knew that somehow they were meant to be together. Now he tolerated his sorrow alone in the stillness of the night.

A burnt-through log tumbled close to the hearth. He had built the fire more for something to do than for the warmth or light. Thomas studied the glowing wood and the white ash clumped around it like hot snow. The air in the cabin smelled bad. He had washed her gently with soap and water, had even washed her soiled sheets and nightgown, to get rid of the smell of sickness. Now the smell of the dead tinged the night.

He would bury her himself next to the baby. Thomas wasn't a religious man and Harley never liked Pastor Dailey so there wasn't any reason to get all taken up with some funeral service. They weren't allowed to be buried in the churchyard, anyway. Thomas and Harley had refused to be married by the minister when she decided to move in with him. Each of them felt no call for some preachy know-it-all to say some words and charge them money when they knew that it was the two of them who were the important parties in this get-together. They stood under the persimmon tree out back of his shack and swore to love each other till the end of time, no matter what, and that was enough for them. Harley's father was glad of one less mouth to feed but her grandmother hated her for leaving her alone to do all the cooking and cleaning, even if it was only for two people. If her Gran hadn't made such a fuss Harley would have helped out, but the squall between them got so ugly that Harley never saw her kin again. They didn't know she'd been sick, didn't even know she'd had a child at her late age. Knowing she was dying, Harley asked Thomas to say good-bye to them for her. Thomas wasn't sure they'd believe him.

He sat quietly, not rocking, just staring at the body of his wife. The coffin sat on top of the table. With the firelight almost gone, he could just barely see the outline of her forehead and nose. A squinch owl hooted from somewhere out front. The katydids buzzed so loud it sounded like they were in the rafters. Thomas sighed. A mouse skittered in the corner and he shot a look at it even though he knew it was safe in the dark. He knew he'd better light the lamps to make sure nothing disturbed Harley's body. For the first time he wished that somebody else was there to look after her so he could sleep a little.

More than anything he wanted to close his burning eyes. But he kept watch over his wife even though his eyelids started to dip. He had better light those lamps before the dark fooled his body into thinking it needed rest. And he should poke that log further back. The air hummed in his ears. Thomas closed his eyes for a second. The comfort washed over him like water from the creek. He opened his eyes quickly, annoyed that sleep was waylaying him. He had to keep an eye on Harley. She needed him to protect her. His eyelids slid down again. Sleep nestled inside him, stroking his tired mind and body. He wanted to fight it off but sleep is a wily mistress and he was no match for her caresses. He struggled to open his eyes but his heavy lids fought a finer battle. Thomas slumped in his rocking chair and slept.

The whispers were faint, almost not there at all, muffled and hushed but willful. Sound tickled his ears like gnats heckling a flame. Thomas twitched in his sleep. The whispers stopped for a little bit, then started up again. The noise floated all around him and rustled the hairs on his neck. In his dreams Thomas could feel light strokes on the back of his hand, tiny touches that tickled his rough skin. He was powerless to brush away the words that swam in the air.

His body wanted to sink softer into sleep but something in his mind tugged at him. What was the sound that was pulling him to the surface? He knew it inside and out, this word that had so much power over him. Just listen, old man, just listen with your mind. So he let the sound he knew so well seep into his pores and into his blood until it found its way to his brain. In his mind's eye he saw Harley's face and knew that it was her name he heard all around him.

Harley.

Harley.

Someone was calling her from a long way away.

Harley.

Harley.

Harley.

Thomas dragged himself up from the depths of sleep until he broke surface behind his eyelids. All around him he could hear voices whispering his dead wife's name. Was he awake or dreaming? He was afraid to open his eyes to find out. His body felt cold, like all the blood had run out of it. Maybe that meant he was awake. And if he wasn't sleeping, then . . . he wasn't alone.

Harley.

Harley.

Thomas shivered. He didn't know any of the voices. They sounded strange, sometimes far off, sometimes real close like a cat purring on his stomach. Why were they calling to Harley? Didn't they know she was dead? Thomas's breath caught in his throat. He had to make sure that Harley was all right. He eased open his eyes. Harley was there in her coffin the same as before. Thomas took a breath and swallowed hard. She was there all right, but all around her was a silvery light. It made her look like she was glowing in the dark. Slowly Thomas turned his head to see where the light was coming from. What he saw by the door made his heart thump against his ribs so hard it hurt.

A dozen shadowy figures floated in the corner. They looked like ordinary hill folk, clothed in dresses and overalls. Thomas could see the walls of the shack right through their bodies. The female spirits were in front of the male spirits and a silver light shone from a bundle that the figure in front held in its arms.

Even if he wanted to move, Thomas couldn't so much as raise an eyebrow. The shock of seeing real live ghosts left him so dazed that he just stared in amazement. Oddly enough, he wasn't afraid.

The whispering of Harley's name got louder as the female holding the bundle of light drifted closer to the coffin. Although the spirit's features weren't real clear, Thomas could see that she was very old. She was small-boned, almost like a young girl, but her hands were gnarled and strong. She cradled the bundle in her arms and began to rock it slowly, like a baby. The silver light washed back and forth over Harley's body. After a minute the old woman stopped rocking and nuzzled the bundle. Then she held it out towards the coffin.

The whispering stopped.

Thomas, still frozen in his chair, felt the silence settle on him like a blanket. He watched the old woman lay the glowing bundle carefully on the floor and back away. The silver light grew even brighter before it faded to a soft glow.

There on the floor was a scrawny little baby, wiggling and sucking its fist. Thomas felt a tug at his heart for the puny little thing. The child had probably not lasted more than a few weeks after being born. No bigger than a minute. But what was this baby spirit doing here?

To Thomas's surprise, the baby began shifting around until it finally managed to flop over onto its stomach. For a runt it was pretty strong. The baby scooted around a little and suddenly it was on its knees. Thomas realized that the baby was unaccountably bigger. Amazed, he watched the crawling baby grow in front of his eyes. It wobbled as it tried to stand on its frail legs, failed, then tried again and succeeded. The baby balanced itself and waddled a few steps. The homely little thing was a skinny girl child. Her bloated belly made her thin arms and legs look like sticks and her face was pinched and plain to the point of ugliness. But pitiful though she was, her eyes . . . her eyes were fierce even at that young age.

Thomas watched the little girl's growth from an awkward tot to a contrary child. Her body got its strength from her stormy nature. Like lightning the girl aged through the years, but the venom in her blood carved lines in her face as her troubled life unfolded. And Thomas was caught in the whirlwind because he had no choice.

He knew he was witnessing the life of the woman he loved.

Eleven-year-old Harley tending her mother during her last confinement and placing the stillborn baby in its dead mother's arms; fourteen-year-old Harley struggling with the pneumonia that would weaken her lungs forever; sixteen-year-old Harley furiously hacking the tree stump that lamed the runaway mule; twenty-one-year-old Harley staring hard at the aged recluse Thomas Southmayd at the quail shoot on the Fourth of July; and always she railed at the world.

Thomas wept at the sight of his Harley when he first came across her. He loved the tiny girl with the wild eyes who taunted him about his scraggly gray beard. He beheld their first night together when she threw away his sack of wild sang that cost a whole five dollars and he was so mad at her that he stormed out of the shack into the rain. She followed him and threw herself upon him with such ferociousness that lying there drenched and dripping in the weeds she proved more than once that he didn't need any medicinals to help him satisfy her. There was the sight of her ripping her favorite quilt that got scorched and there were the two of them trying to grab the chickens that got swept away in the flood and there was the quiet time lying on the roof looking for shooting stars when she told him she was going to have his child. The visions of their life together rushed by so quickly that they melted together like molasses and butter. He wanted to holler at her to quit growing up, quit getting older, quit rushing to die.

The revelations idled to show a screaming Harley as she finally gave birth after thirty-nine hours of labor. There she lay close to dying, bloodied and torn and gasping with fear. Thomas physically ached as he watched scenes of her struggling day after day to care for the child while she wept with exhaustion. And then came the sight of a confused and weakened Harley trying to quiet her screeching boy, trying to shush its wails as she staggered with weariness, trying to resist the fury that boiled within her, trying and failing to stop herself from covering the baby's face with its pillow so dear God she could please get some rest.

Thomas watched in horror at the sight of his wife stumbling to the cradle as she realized what she had done. Wild-eyed, she grabbed the baby and tried to shake it back to life, blowing air into its dead mouth in a hopeless attempt to make it live again. Her screams were choked with bile as she retched over the limp body of the child she had killed. And Thomas watched his crazed wife's anguish as she lied to him about finding the baby dead.

The rest of the visions of her life slid past quickly until the image of her lying in her coffin mirrored the real Harley.

Thomas sat unmoving in his chair. The glow in the room shone with a dull brightness as the shades of the past faded in front of him. He grieved for the innocent baby boy who lived only to have his life taken away by the woman who bore him. He grieved for his dear Harley whose despair had killed her. He grieved for his wretched life that left him in such misery. And he grieved for the love that had departed his life.

He sensed rather than saw the movement in the coffin. He turned and watched the spirit of his wife rise slowly from its mortal remains. The sadness in her eyes seemed to weigh down her soul.

"Old Man, I wanted you to see what I'd done. I couldn't tell you face to face."

The woeful sound of her voice broke Thomas's heart.

"I got to come back, Old Man. I got to make amends. You were the best thing in my life and I'm sorry to bring you so much pain."

Thomas looked at Harley's spirit. The pitiable ghost was a far cry from the angry Harley he had loved. She floated toward the shadows waiting for her near the door.

"Harley." His voice sounded ancient to his ears. "I'll come back for you. Next time it'll be better."

Harley's spirit lightened just a little. She even managed a wan smile. She turned back to the spirits and began to fade. At the last moment Thomas saw that she was holding the pale figure of their baby boy. He watched the child embrace its sorrowful mother and make her laugh.

E. F. BENSON

The Thing
in the Hall

E. F. BENSON *(1867–1940) was a member of a remarkably literate family. His brother A. C. also wrote copiously, as did his other sibling, Robert Hugh Benson, author of exemplary Roman Catholic fantasies. Edward Frederic Benson is highly regarded for his recently reprinted* Lucia *novels, but genre enthusiasts remember him best for his many excellent ghost stories, including "The Room in the Tower," "How Fear Departed from the Long Gallery" and the loathsome history of "The Thing in the Hall."*

The following pages are the account given me by Dr. Assheton of the Thing in the Hall. I took notes, as copious as my quickness of hand allowed me, from his dictation, and subsequently read to him this narrative in its transcribed and connected form. This was on the day before his death, which indeed probably occurred within an hour after I had left him, and, as readers of inquests and such atrocious literature may remember, I had to give evidence before the coroner's jury. Only a week before Dr. Assheton had to give similar evidence, but as a medical expert, with regard to the death of his friend, Louis Fielder, which occurred in a manner identical with his own. As a specialist, he said he believed that his friend had committed suicide while of unsound mind, and the verdict was brought in accordingly. But in the inquest held over Dr. Assheton's body, though the verdict eventually returned was the same, there was more room for doubt.

For I was bound to state that only shortly before his death, I read what follows to him; that he corrected me with extreme precision on a few points of detail, that he seemed perfectly himself, and that at the end he used these words:

"I am quite certain as a brain specialist that I am completely sane, and that these things happened not merely in my imagination, but in the external world. If I had to give evidence again about poor Louis, I should be compelled to take a different line. Please put that down at the end of your account, or at the beginning, if it arranges itself better so."

There will be a few words I must add at the end of this story, and a few words of explanation must precede it. Briefly, they are these.

Francis Assheton and Louis Fielder were up at Cambridge together, and there formed the friendship that lasted nearly till their death. In general attributes no two men could have been less alike, for while Dr. Assheton had become at the age of thirty-five the first and final authority on his subject, which was the functions and diseases of the brain, Louis Fielder at the same age was still on the threshold of achievement. Assheton, apparently without any brilliance at all, had by careful and incessant work arrived at the top of his profession, while Fielder, brilliant at school, brilliant at college and brilliant ever afterwards, had never done anything. He was too eager, so it seemed to his friends, to set about the dreary work of patient investigation and logical deductions; he was for ever guessing and prying, and striking out luminous ideas, which he left burning, so to speak, to illumine the work of others. But at bottom, the two men had this compelling interest in common, namely, an insatiable curiosity after the unknown, perhaps the most potent bond yet devised between the solitary units that make up the race of man. Both—till the end—were absolutely fearless, and Dr. Assheton would sit by the bedside of the man stricken with bubonic plague to note the gradual surge of the tide of disease to the reasoning faculty with the same absorption as Fielder would study X-rays one week, flying machines the next, and spiritualism the third. The rest of the story, I think, explains itself—or does not quite do so. This, anyhow, is what I read to Dr. Assheton, being the connected narrative of what he had himself told me. It is he, of course, who speaks.

After I returned from Paris, where I had studied under Charcot, I set up practice at home. The general doctrine of hypnotism, suggestion, and cure by such means had been accepted even in London by this time, and, owing to a few papers I had written on the subject, together with my foreign diplomas, I found that I was a busy man almost as soon as I had arrived in town. Louis Fielder had his ideas about how I should make my début (for he had ideas on every subject, and all of them original), and entreated me to come and live not in the stronghold of doctors, "Chloroform Square," as he called it, but down in Chelsea, where there was a house vacant next his own.

"Who cares where a doctor lives," he said, "so long as he cures people? Besides you don't believe in old methods; why believe in old localities? Oh, there is an atmosphere of painless death in Chloroform Square! Come and make people live instead! And on most evenings I shall have so much to tell you; I can't 'drop in' across half London."

Now if you have been abroad for five years, it is a great deal to know that you have any intimate friend at all still left in the metropolis, and, as Louis said, to have that intimate friend next door, is an excellent reason for going next door. Above all, I remembered from Cambridge days, what Louis' "dropping in" meant. Towards bedtime, when work was over, there would come a rapid step on the landing, and for an hour, or two hours, he would gush with ideas. He simply diffused life, which is ideas, wherever he went. He fed one's brain, which is the one thing which matters. Most people who are ill, are ill because their brain is starving, and the body rebels, and gets lumbago or cancer. That is the chief doctrine of my work such as it has been. All bodily disease springs from the brain. It is merely the brain that has to be fed and rested and exercised properly to make the body absolutely healthy, and immune from all disease. But when the brain is affected, it is as useful to pour medicines down the sink, as make your patient swallow them, unless—and this is a paramount limitation—unless he believes in them.

I said something of the kind to Louis one night, when, at the end of a busy day, I had dined with him. We were sitting over coffee in the hall, or so it is called, where he takes his meals. Outside, his house is just like mine, and ten thousand other small houses in London, but on entering, instead of finding a narrow passage with a door on one side, leading into the dining-room, which again communicates with a small back room called "the study," he has had the sense to eliminate all unnecessary walls, and consequently the whole ground floor of his house is one room, with stairs leading up to the first floor. Study, dining-room and passage have been knocked into one; you enter a big room from the front door. The only drawback is that the postman makes loud noises close to you, as you dine, and just as I made these commonplace observations to him about the effect of the brain on the body and the senses, there came a loud rap, somewhere close to me, that was startling.

"You ought to muffle your knocker," I said, "anyhow during the time of meals."

Louis leaned back and laughed.

"There isn't a knocker," he said. "You were startled a week ago, and said the same thing. So I took the knocker off. The letters slide in now. But you heard a knock, did you?"

"Didn't you?" said I.

"Why, certainly. But it wasn't the postman. It was the Thing. I don't know what it is. That makes it so interesting."

Now if there is one thing that the hypnotist, the believer in unexplained influences, detests and despises, it is the whole root-notion of spiritualism. Drugs are not more opposed to his belief than the exploded, discredited idea of the influence of spirits on our lives. And both are discredited for the same reason; it is easy to understand how brain can act on brain, just as it is easy to understand how body can act on body, so that there is no more difficulty in the reception of the idea that the strong mind can direct the weak one, than there is in the fact of a wrestler of greater strength overcoming one of less. But that spirits should rap at furniture and divert the course of events is as absurd as administering phosphorus to strengthen the brain. That was what I thought then.

However, I felt sure it was the postman, and instantly rose and went to the door. There were no letters in the box, and I opened the door. The postman was just ascending the steps. He gave the letters into my hand.

Louis was sipping his coffee when I came back to the table.

"Have you ever tried table-turning?" he asked. "It's rather odd."

"No, and I have not tried violet-leaves as a cure for cancer," I said.

"Oh, try everything," he said. "I know that that is your plan, just as it is mine. All these years that you have been away, you have tried all sorts of things, first with no faith, then with just a little faith, and finally with mountain-moving faith. Why, you didn't believe in hypnotism at all when you went to Paris."

He rang the bell as he spoke, and his servant came up and cleared the table. While this was being done we strolled about the room, looking at prints, with applause for a Bartolozzi that Louis had bought in the New Cut, and dead silence over a "Perdita" which he had acquired at considerable cost. Then he sat down again at the table on which we had dined. It was round, and mahogany-heavy, with a central foot divided into claws.

"Try its weight," he said; "see if you can push it about."

So I held the edge of it in my hands, and found that I could just move it. But that was all; it required the exercise of a good deal of strength to stir it.

"Now put your hands on the top of it," he said, "and see what you can do."

I could not do anything, my fingers merely slipped about on it. But I protested at the idea of spending the evening thus.

"I would much sooner play chess or noughts and crosses with you," I said, "or even talk about politics, than turn tables. You won't mean to push, nor shall I, but we shall push without meaning to."

Louis nodded.

"Just a minute," he said, "let us both put our fingers only on the top of the table and push for all we are worth, from right to left."

We pushed. At least I pushed, and I observed his fingernails. From pink they grew to white, because of the pressure he exercised. So I must assume that he pushed too. Once, as we tried this, the table creaked. But it did not move.

Then there came a quick peremptory rap, not I thought on the front door, but somewhere in the room.

"It's the Thing," said he.

Today, as I speak to you, I suppose it was. But on that evening it seemed only like a challenge. I wanted to demonstrate its absurdity.

"For five years, on and off, I've been studying rank spiritualism," he said. "I haven't told you before, because I wanted to lay before you certain phenomena, which I can't explain, but which now seem to me to be at my command. You shall see and hear, and then decide if you will help me."

"And in order to let me see better, you are proposing to put out the lights," I said.

"Yes; you will see why."

"I am here as a sceptic," said I.

"Scep away," said he.

Next moment the room was in darkness, except for a very faint glow of firelight. The window-curtains were thick, and no street-illumination penetrated them, and the familiar, cheerful sounds of pedestrians and wheeled traffic came in muffled. I was at the side of the table towards the door; Louis was opposite me, for I could see his figure dimly silhouetted against the glow from the smouldering fire.

"Put your hands on the table," he said, "quite lightly, and—how shall I say it—expect."

Still protesting in spirit, I expected. I could hear his breathing rather quickened, and it seemed to me odd that anybody could find excitement in standing in the dark over a large mahogany table, expecting. Then—through my finger-tips, laid lightly on the table, there began to come a faint vibration, like nothing so much as the vibration through the handle of a kettle when water is beginning to boil inside it. This got gradually more pronounced and violent till it was like the throbbing of a motor-car. It seemed to give off a low humming note. Then quite suddenly the table seemed to slip from under my fingers and began very slowly to revolve.

"Keep your hands on it and move with it," said Louis, and as he spoke I saw his silhouette pass away from in front of the fire, moving as the table moved.

For some moments there was silence, and we continued, rather absurdly, to circle round keeping step, so to speak, with the table. Then Louis spoke again, and his voice was trembling with excitement.

"Are you there?" he said.

There was no reply, of course, and he asked it again. This time there came a rap like that which I had thought during dinner to be the postman. But whether it was that the room was dark, or that despite myself I felt rather excited, too, it seemed to me now to be far louder than before. Also it appeared to come neither from here nor there, but to be diffused through the room.

Then the curious revolving of the table ceased, but the intense, violent throbbing continued. My eyes were fixed on it, though owing to the darkness I could see nothing, when quite suddenly a little speck of light moved across it, so that for an instant I saw my own hands. Then came another and another, like the spark of matches struck in the dark, or like fire-flies crossing the dusk in southern gardens. Then came another knock of shattering loudness, and the throbbing of the table ceased, and the lights vanished.

Such were the phenomena at the first séance at which I was present, but Fielder, it must be remembered, had been studying, "expecting", he called it, for some years. To adopt spiritualistic language (which at that time I was very far from doing), he was the medium, I merely the observer, and all the phenomena I had seen that night were habitually produced or witnessed by him. I make this limitation since he told me that certain of them now appeared to be outside his own control altogether. The knockings would come when his mind, as far as he knew, was entirely occupied in other matters, and sometimes he had even been awakened out of sleep by them. The lights were also independent of his volition.

Now my theory at the time was that all these things were purely subjective in him, and that what he expressed by saying that they were out of his control, meant that they had become fixed and rooted in the unconscious self, of which we know so little, but which, more and more, we see to play so enormous a part in the life of a man. In fact, it is not too much to say that the vast majority of our deeds spring, apparently without volition, from this unconscious self. All hearing is the unconscious exercise of the aural nerve, all seeing of the optic, all walking, all ordinary movement seem to be done without the exercise of will on our part. Nay more, should we take to some new form of progression, skating, for instance, the beginner will learn with falls and difficulty the outside edge, but within a few hours of his having learned his balance on it, he will give no more thought to what he learned so short a time ago as an acrobatic feat, than he gives to the placing of one foot before the other.

But to the brain specialist all this was intensely interesting, and to the student of hypnotism, as I was, even more so, for (such was the conclusion I came to after this first séance), the fact that I saw and heard just what Louis saw and heard was an exhibition of thought-transference which in all my experience in the Charcot-schools I had never seen surpassed, if indeed rivalled. I knew that I was myself extremely sensitive to suggestion, and my part in it this evening I believed to be purely that of the receiver of suggestions so vivid that I visualized and heard these phenomena which existed only in the brain of my friend.

We talked over what had occurred upstairs. His view was that the Thing was trying to communicate with us. According to him, it was the Thing that moved the table and tapped, and made us see streaks of light.

"Yes, but the Thing," I interrupted, "what do you mean? Is it a great-uncle—oh, I have seen so many relatives appear at séances, and heard so many of their dreadful platitudes—or what is it? A spirit? Whose spirit?"

Louis was sitting opposite to me, and on the little table before us there was an electric light. Looking at him I saw the pupil of his eye suddenly dilate. To the medical man—provided that some violent change in the light is not the cause of the dilation—that meant only one thing, terror. But it quickly resumed its normal proportion again.

Then he got up, and stood in front of the fire.

"No, I don't think it is great-uncle anybody," he said, "I don't know, as I told you, what the Thing is. But if you ask me what my conjecture is, it is that the Thing is an Elemental."

"And pray explain further. What is an Elemental?"

Once again his eye dilated.

"It will take two minutes," he said. "But, listen. There are good things in this world, are there not, and bad things? Cancer, I take it is bad, and—and fresh air is good; honesty is good, lying is bad. Impulses of some sort direct both sides, and some power suggests the impulses. Well, I went into this spiritualistic business impartially. I learned to 'expect', to throw open the door into the soul, and I said, 'Anyone may come in.' And I think Something has applied for admission, the Thing that tapped and turned the table and struck matches, as you saw, across it. Now the control of the evil principle in the world is in the hands of a power which entrusts its errands to the things which I call Elementals. Oh, they have been seen; I doubt not that they will be seen again. I did not, and do not ask good spirits to come in. I don't want 'The Church's one foundation' played on a musical box. Nor do I *want* an Elemental. I only threw open the door. I believe the Thing has come into my house, and is establishing communication with me. Oh, I want to go the whole hog. What is it? In the name of Satan, if necessary, what is it? I just want to know."

What followed I thought then might easily be an invention of the imagination, but what I believed to have happened was this. A piano with music on it was standing at the far end of the room by the door, and a sudden draught entered the room, so strong that the leaves turned. Next the draught troubled a vase of daffodils, and the yellow heads nodded. Then it reached the candles that stood close to us, and they fluttered, burning blue and low. Then it reached me, and the draught was cold, and stirred my hair. Then it eddied, so to speak, and went across to Louis, and his hair also moved, as I could see. Then it went downwards towards the fire, and flames suddenly started up in its path, blown upwards. The rug by the fireplace flapped also.

"Funny, wasn't it?" he asked.

"And has the Elemental gone up the chimney?" said I.

"Oh, no," said he, "the Thing only passed us."

Then suddenly he pointed at the wall just behind my chair, and his voice cracked as he spoke.

"Look, what's that?" he said. "There on the wall."

Considerably startled, I turned in the direction of his shaking finger. The wall was pale grey in tone, and sharp-cut against it was a shadow that, as I looked, moved. It was like the shadow of some enormous slug, legless and fat, some two feet high by about four feet long. Only at one end of it was a head shaped like the head of a seal, with open mouth and panting tongue.

Then even as I looked it faded, and from somewhere close at hand there sounded another of those shattering knocks.

For a moment after there was silence between us, and horror was thick as snow in the air. But, somehow neither Louis nor I were frightened for more than one moment. The whole thing was so absorbingly interesting.

"That's what I mean by its being outside my control," he said. "I said I was ready for any—any visitor to come in, and by God, we've got a beauty."

Now I was still, even in spite of the appearance of this shadow, quite convinced that I was only taking observations of a most curious case of disordered brain accompanied by the most vivid and remarkable thought-transference. I believed that I had not seen a slug-like shadow at all, but that Louis had visualized this dreadful creature so intensely that I saw what he saw. I found also that his spiritualistic trash books which I thought a truer nomenclature than text-books, mentioned this as a common form for Elementals to take. He on the other hand was more firmly convinced than ever that we were dealing not with a subjective but an objective phenomenon.

For the next six months or so we sat constantly, but made no further progress, nor did the Thing or its shadow appear again, and I began to feel that we were really wasting time. Then it occurred to me, to get in a so-called medium, induce hypnotic sleep, and see if we could learn anything further. This we did, sitting as before round the dining-room table. The room was not quite dark, and I could see sufficiently clearly what happened.

The medium, a young man, sat between Louis and myself, and

without the slightest difficulty I put him into a light hypnotic sleep. Instantly there came a series of the most terrific raps, and across the table there slid something more palpable than a shadow, with a faint luminance about it, as if the surface of it was smouldering. At the moment the medium's face became contorted to a mask of hellish terror; mouth and eyes were both open, and the eyes were focused on something close to him. The Thing waving its head came closer and closer to him, and reached out towards his throat. Then with a yell of panic, and warding off this horror with his hands, the medium sprang up, but It had already caught hold, and for the moment he could not get free. Then simultaneously Louis and I went to his aid, and my hands touched something cold and slimy. But pull as we could we could not get it away. There was no firm hand-hold to be taken; it was as if one tried to grasp slimy fur, and the touch of it was horrible, unclean, like a leper. Then, in a sort of despair, though I still could not believe that the horror was real, for it must be a vision of diseased imagination, I remembered that the switch of the four electric lights was close to my hand. I turned them all on. There on the floor lay the medium, Louis was kneeling by him with a face of wet paper, but there was nothing else there. Only the collar of the medium was crumpled and torn, and on his throat were two scratches that bled.

The medium was still in hypnotic sleep, and I woke him. He felt at his collar, put his hand to his throat and found it bleeding, but, as I expected, knew nothing whatever of what had passed. We told him that there had been an unusual manifestation, and he had, while in sleep, wrestled with something. We had got the result we wished for, and were much obliged to him.

I never saw him again. A week after that he died of blood-poisoning.

From that evening dates the second stage of this adventure. The Thing had materialized (I use again spiritualistic language which I still did not use at the time). The huge slug, the Elemental, manifested itself no longer by knocks and waltzing tables, nor yet by shadows. It was there in a form that could be seen and felt. But it still— this was my strong point—was only a thing of twilight; the sudden kindling of the electric light had shown us that there was nothing there. In his struggle perhaps the medium had clutched his own throat, perhaps I had grasped Louis' sleeve, he mine. But though I said these things to myself, I am not sure that I believed them in the same way that I believe the sun will rise tomorrow.

Now as a student of brain-functions and a student in hypnotic affairs, I ought perhaps to have steadily and unremittingly pursued this extraordinary series of phenomena. But I had my practice to attend to, and I found that with the best will in the world, I could think of nothing else except the occurrence in the hall next door. So I refused to take part in any further séance with Louis. I had another reason also. For the last four or five months he was becoming depraved. I have been no prude or Puritan in my own life, and I hope I have not turned a Pharisaical shoulder on sinners. But in all branches of life and morals, Louis had become infamous. He was turned out of a club for cheating at cards, and narrated the event to me with gusto. He had become cruel; he tortured his cat to death; he had become bestial. I used to shudder as I passed his house, expecting I knew not what fiendish thing to be looking at me from the window.

Then came a night only a week ago, when I was awakened by an awful cry, swelling and falling and rising again. It came from next door. I ran downstairs in my pyjamas, and out into the street. The policeman on the beat had heard it, too, and it came from the hall of Louis' house, the window of which was open. Together we burst the door in. You know what we found. The screaming had ceased but a moment before, but he was dead already. Both jugulars were severed, torn open.

It was dawn, early and dusky when I got back to my house next door. Even as I went in something seemed to push by me, something soft and slimy. It could not be Louis' imagination this time. Since then, I have seen glimpses of it every evening. I am awakened at night by tappings, and in the shadows in the corner of my room there sits something more substantial than a shadow.

Within an hour of my leaving Dr. Assheton, the quiet street was once more aroused by cries of terror and agony. He was already dead, and in no other manner than his friend, when they got into the house.

ROBERT SOUTHEY

The Inchcape Rock

"The Inchcape Rock," a perfect example of both figurative and literal poetic justice, is one of the ballads of ROBERT SOUTHEY *(1774–1843) that, according to* The Oxford Companion to English Literature, *"had an influence in loosening the constrictions of Eighteenth Century verse." A friend and occasional collaborator of Coleridge, Southey was appointed British poet laureate in 1813. Ironically, he is remembered today mostly for the diatribes leveled against him by Lord Byron in his long narrative poem,* Don Juan.

No stir in the air, no stir in the sea—
The ship was as still as she could be;
Her sails from heaven received no motion;
Her keel was steady in the ocean.

Without either sign or sound of their shock,
The waves flowed over the Inchcape rock;
So little they rose, so little they fell,
They did not move the Inchcape bell.

The holy Abbot of Aberbrothok
Had placed that bell on the Inchcape rock;
On a buoy in the storm it floated and swung,
And over the waves its warning rung.

When the rock was hid by the surges' swell,
The mariners heard the warning bell;

And then they knew the perilous rock,
And blessed the Abbot of Aberbrothok.

The sun in heaven was shining gay—
All things were joyful on that day;
The sea-birds screamed as they wheeled around,
And there was joyance in their sound.

The buoy of the Inchcape bell was seen,
A darker speck on the ocean green;
Sir Ralph, the rover, walked his deck,
And he fixed his eye on the darker speck.

He felt the cheering power of spring—
It made him whistle, it made him sing;
His heart was mirthful to excess;
But the rover's mirth was wickedness.

His eye was on the bell and float:
Quoth he, "My men, put out the boat;
And row me to the Inchcape rock,
And I'll plague the priest of Aberbrothok."

The boat is lowered, the boatmen row,
And to the Inchcape rock they go;
Sir Ralph bent over from the boat,
And cut the warning bell from the float.

Down sank the bell with a gurgling sound;
The bubbles rose, and burst around.
Quoth Sir Ralph, "The next who comes to the rock
Will not bless the Abbot of Aberbrothok."

Sir Ralph, the rover, sailed away—
He scoured the seas for many a day;
And now, grown rich with plundered store,
He steers his course to Scotland's shore.

So thick a haze o'erspreads the sky
They cannot see the sun on high;

The wind hath blown a gale all day;
At evening it hath died away.

On the deck the rover takes his stand;
So dark it is they see no land.
Quoth Sir Ralph, "It will be lighter soon,
For there is the dawn of the rising moon."

"Canst hear," said one, "the breakers roar?
For yonder, methinks, should be the shore.
Now where we are I cannot tell,
But I wish we could hear the Inchcape bell."

They hear no sound; the swell is strong;
Though the wind hath fallen, they drift along;
Till the vessel strikes with a shivering shock—
O Christ! it is the Inchcape rock!

Sir Ralph, the rover, tore his hair;
He cursed himself in his despair.
The waves rush in on every side;
The ship is sinking beneath the tide.

But ever in his dying fear
One dreadful sound he seemed to hear—
A sound as if with the Inchcape bell
The Devil below was ringing his knell.

JOANNA RUSS

Mr. Wilde's
Second Chance

The great, tormented Irish genius Oscar Wilde is remembered today quite as much for his shameful imprisonment as for writing such superb plays, poetry and prose as The Importance of Being Earnest, Lady Windermere's Fan, Salomé, *"The Ballad of Reading Gaol," "The Fisherman and His Soul," "The Canterville Ghost" and his novel-length masterpiece,* The Picture of Dorian Gray. *In the next story, which first appeared in the September 1966 issue of* The Magazine of Fantasy and Science Fiction, *feminist author* JOANNA RUSS *affords Mr. Wilde the opportunity to reshape his tragic personal destiny.*

This is a tale told to me by a friend after the Cointreau and the music, as we sat in the dusk waiting for the night to come:

When Oscar Wilde (he said) died, his soul was found too sad for heaven and too happy for hell. A tattered spirit with the look of a debased street imp led him through miles of limbo into a large, foggy room, very like (for what he could see of it) a certain club in London. His small, grimy scud of a guide went up to a stand something like that used by ladies for embroidery or old men for chess, and there it stopped, spinning like a top.

"Yours!" it squeaked.

"Mine?"

But it was gone. On the stand was a board like the kind used for children's games, and nearby a dark lady in wine-colored silk moved pieces over a board of her own. The celebrated writer bent to watch her—she chanced to look up—it was Ada R——, the victim of the most celebrated scandal of the last decade. She had died of pneumonia or a broken heart in Paris; no one knew which. She gave him, out of her black eyes, a look so tragic, so shrinking, so haunted, that the poet (the most courteous of men, even when dead) bowed and turned away. The board before him was a maze of colored squares and meandering lines, and on top was written "O. O'F. Wilde" in coronet script, for this was his life's pattern and each man or woman in the room labored over a board on which was figured the events of his life. Each was trying to rearrange his life into a beautiful and ordered picture, and when he had done that he would be free to live again. As you can imagine, it was both exciting and horribly anxious, this reliving, this being down on the board and at the same time a dead—if not damned—soul in a room the size of all Aetna, but queerly like a London club when it has just got dark and they have lit the lamps. The lady next to Wilde was pale as glass. She was almost finished. She raised one arm—her dark sleeve swept across the board—and in an instant her design was in ruins. Mr. Wilde picked up several of the pieces that had fallen and handed them to the lady.

"If you please," she said, "you are still holding my birthday and my visits to my children."

The poet returned them.

"You are generous," said she, "but then everyone here is generous. They provide everything. They provide all of one's life."

The poet bowed.

"Of course, it is not easy," said the lady. "I try very hard. But I cannot seem to finish anything. I am not sure if it is the necessary organizing ability that I lack or perhaps the aesthetic sense; something ugly always seems to intrude . . ." She raised her colored counters in both hands, with the grace that had once made her a favorite of society.

"I have tried several times before," she said.

It was at this point that the poet turned and attempted to walk away from his second chance, but wherever he went the board preceded him. It interposed itself between him and old gentlemen in velvet vests; it hovered in front of ladies; it even blossomed briefly at the elbow of a child. Then the poet seemed to regain his composure; he began to work at the game; he sorted and matched and disposed, although with what public in view it was not possible to tell. The board—which had been heavily overlaid in black and purple (like a drawing by one of Mr. Wilde's contemporaries)—began to take on the most delicate stipple of color. It breathed wind and shadow like the closes of a park in June. It spread itself like a fan.

O. O'F. Wilde, the successful man of letters, was strolling with his wife in Hyde Park in the year nineteen-twenty-five. He was sixty-nine years old. He had written twenty books where Oscar Wilde had written one, fifteen plays where the degenerate and debauchee had written five, innumerable essays, seven historical romances, three volumes of collected verse, had given many public addresses (though not in the last few years) and had received a citation (this was long in the past) from Queen Victoria herself. The tulips of Hyde Park shone upon the Wildes with a mild and equable light. O. O'F. Wilde, who had written twenty books, and—needless to say—left his two sons an unimpeachable reputation, started, clutched at his heart and died.

"That is beautiful, sir, beautiful," said a voice in the poet's ear. A gentleman—who was not *a gentleman*—stood at his elbow. "Seldom," said the voice, "have we had one of our visitors, as you might say, complete a work in such a short time, and such a beautiful work, too. And such industry, sir!" The gentleman was beside himself. "Such enthusiasm! Such agreeable docility! You know, of course, that few of our guests display such an excellent attitude. Most of our guests—"

"Do you think so?" said Mr. Wilde curiously.

"Lovely, sir! Such agreeable color. Such delicacy."

"I see," said Mr. Wilde.

"I'm so glad you do, sir. Most of our guests don't. Most of our guests, if you'll permit me the liberty of saying so, are not genteel. Not genteel at all. But you, sir—"

Oscar Wilde, poet, dead at forty-four, took his second chance from the table before him and broke the board across his knee. He was a tall, strong man for all his weight, nearly six feet tall.

"And then?" I said.

"And then," said my friend, "I do not know what happened."

"Perhaps," said I, "they gave him his second chance, after all. Perhaps they had to."

"Perhaps," said my friend, "they did nothing of the kind . . .

"I wish I knew," he added. "I only wish I knew!"

And there we left it.

H. P. LOVECRAFT

The Dreams in the Witch-House

"The Dreams in the Witch-House" is one of the longest crypto-science-fiction tales of H. P. LOVECRAFT (1890–1937), one of twentieth-century America's most influential writers of supernatural fiction. Not nearly so well known as "The Colour Out of Space," "The Dunwich Horror," "The Music of Erich Zann," "The Rats in the Walls" or "The Thing on the Doorstep," this nightmarish novella comes closer than any of those tales to explaining the arcane mysteries that lurk on the fringes of Lovecraft's cosmos.

Whether the dreams brought on the fever or the fever brought on the dreams, Walter Gilman did not know. Behind everything crouched the brooding, festering horror of the ancient town, and of the moldy, unhallowed garret gable where he wrote and studied and wrestled with figures and formulae when he was not tossing on the meager iron bed. His ears were growing sensitive to a preternatural and intolerable degree, and he had long ago stopped the cheap mantel clock whose ticking had come to seem like a thunder of artillery. At night the subtle stirring of the black city outside, the sinister scurrying of rats in the wormy partitions, and the creaking of hidden timbers in the centuried house, were enough to give him a sense of strident pandemonium. The darkness always teemed with unexplained sound—and yet he sometimes shook with fear lest the noises he heard should subside and allow him to hear certain other, fainter noises which he suspected were lurking behind them.

He was in the changeless, legend-haunted city of Arkham, with its clustering gambrel roofs that sway and sag over attics where witches hid from the King's men in the dark, olden days of the Province. Nor was any spot in that city more steeped in macabre memory than the gable room which harbored him—for it was this house and this room which had likewise harbored old Keziah Mason, whose flight from Salem Jail at the last no one was ever able to explain. That was in 1692—the jailer had gone mad and babbled of a small white-fanged furry thing which scuttled out of Keziah's cell, and not even Cotton Mather could explain the curves and angles smeared on the gray stone walls with some red, sticky fluid.

Possibly Gilman ought not to have studied so hard. Non-Euclidean calculus and quantum physics are enough to stretch any brain; and when one mixes them with folklore, and tries to trace a strange background of multi-dimensional reality behind the ghoulish hints of the Gothic tales and the wild whispers of the chimney-corner, one can hardly expect to be wholly free from mental tension. Gilman came from Haverhill, but it was only after he had entered college in Arkham that he began to connect his mathematics with the fantastic legends of elder magic. Something in the air of the hoary town worked obscurely on his imagination. The professors at Miskatonic had urged him to slacken up, and had voluntarily cut down his course at several points. Moreover, they had stopped him from consulting the dubious old books on forbidden secrets that were kept under lock and key in a vault at the university library. But all these precautions came late in the day, so that Gilman had some terrible hints from the dreaded *Necronomicon* of Abdul Alhazred, the fragmentary *Book of Eibon,* and the suppressed *Unaussprechlichen Kulten* of von Junzt to correlate with his abstract formulae on the properties of space and the linkage of dimensions known and unknown.

He knew his room was in the old Witch-House—that, indeed, was why he had taken it. There was much in the Essex County records about Keziah Mason's trial, and what she had admitted under pressure to the Court of Oyer and Terminer had fascinated Gilman beyond all reason. She had told Judge Hathorne of lines and curves that could be made to point out directions leading through the walls of space to other spaces beyond, and had implied that such lines and curves were frequently used at certain midnight meetings in the dark valley of the white stone beyond Meadow Hill and on the unpeopled island in the river. She had spoken also of the Black Man, of her oath, and of her new secret name of Nahab. Then she had drawn those devices on the walls of her cell and vanished.

Gilman believed strange things about Keziah, and had felt a queer thrill on learning that her dwelling was still standing after more than 235 years. When he heard the hushed Arkham whispers about Keziah's persistent presence in the old house and the narrow streets, about the irregular human tooth-marks left on certain sleepers in that and other houses, about the childish cries heard near May-Eve and Hallowmass, about the stench often noted in the old house's attic just after those dreaded seasons, and about the small, furry, sharp-toothed thing which haunted the moldering structure and the town and nuzzled people curiously in the black hours before dawn, he resolved to live in the place at any cost. A room was easy to secure; for the house was unpopular, hard to rent, and long given over to cheap lodgings. Gilman could not have told what he expected to find there, but he knew he wanted to be in the building where some circumstance had more or less suddenly given a mediocre old woman of the seventeenth century an insight into mathematical depths perhaps beyond the utmost modern delvings of Planck, Heisenberg, Einstein, and de Sitter.

He studied the timber and plaster walls for traces of cryptic designs at every accessible spot where the paper had peeled, and within a week managed to get the eastern attic room where Keziah was held to have practised her spells. It had been vacant from the first—for no one had ever been willing to stay there long—but the Polish landlord had grown wary about renting it. Yet nothing whatever happened to Gilman till about the time of the fever. No ghostly Keziah flitted through the somber halls and chambers, no small furry thing crept into his dismal eyrie to nuzzle him, and no record of the witch's incantations rewarded his constant search. Sometimes he would take walks through shadowy tangles of unpaved musty-smelling lanes where eldritch brown houses of unknown age leaned and tottered and leered mockingly through narrow, small-paned windows. Here he knew strange things had happened once, and there was a faint suggestion behind the surface that everything of that monstrous past might not—at least in the darkest, narrowest, and most intricately crooked alleys—have utterly perished. He also rowed out twice to the ill-regarded island in the river, and made a sketch of the singular angles described by the moss-grown rows of gray standing stones whose origin was so obscure and immemorial.

Gilman's room was of good size but queerly irregular shape; the north wall slanting perceptibly inward from the outer to the inner end, while the low ceiling slanted gently downward in the same direction. Aside from an obvious rat-hole and the signs of other stopped-up ones, there was no access—nor any appearance of a former avenue of access—to the space which must have existed between the slanting wall and the straight outer wall on the house's north side, though a view from the exterior showed where a window had been boarded up at a very remote date. The loft above the ceiling—which must have had a slanting floor—was likewise inaccessible. When Gilman climbed up a ladder to the cob-webbed level loft above the rest of the attic he found vestiges of a bygone aperture tightly and heavily covered with ancient planking and secured by the stout wooden pegs common in Colonial carpentry. No amount of persuasion, however, could induce the stolid landlord to let him investigate either of these two closed spaces.

As time wore along, his absorption in the irregular wall and ceiling of his room increased; for he began to read into the odd angles a mathematical significance which seemed to offer vague clues regarding their purpose. Old Keziah, he reflected, might have had excellent reasons for living in a room with peculiar angles; for was it not through certain angles that she claimed to have gone outside the boundaries of the world of space we know? His interest gradually veered away from the unplumbed voids beyond the slanting surfaces, since it now appeared that the purpose of those surfaces concerned the side he was already on.

The touch of brain-fever and the dreams began early in February. For some time, apparently, the curious angles of Gilman's room had been having a strange, almost hypnotic effect on him; and as the bleak winter advanced he had found himself staring more and more intently at the corner where the down-slanting ceiling met the inward-slanting wall. About this period his inability to concentrate on his formal studies worried him considerably, his apprehensions about the mid-year examinations being very acute. But the exaggerated sense of hearing was scarcely less annoying. Life had become an insistent and almost unendurable cacophony, and there was that constant, terrifying impression of *other* sounds—perhaps from regions beyond life—trembling on the very brink of audibility. So far as concrete noises went, the rats in the ancient partitions were the worst. Sometimes their scratching seemed not only furtive but deliberate. When it came from beyond the slanting north wall it was mixed with a sort of dry rattling; and when it came from the century-closed loft above the slanting ceiling Gilman always braced himself as if expecting some horror which only bided its time before descending to engulf him utterly.

The dreams were wholly beyond the pale of sanity, and Gilman felt that they must be a result, jointly, of his studies in mathematics and in folklore. He had been thinking too much about the vague regions which his formulae told him must lie beyond the three dimensions we know, and about the possibility that old Keziah Mason—guided by some influence past all conjecture—had actually found the gate to those regions. The yellowed county records containing her testimony and that of her accusers were so damnably suggestive of things beyond human experience—and the descriptions of the darting little furry object which served as her familiar were so painfully realistic despite their incredible details.

That object—no larger than a good-sized rat and quaintly called by the townspeople "Brown Jenkin"—seemed to have been the fruit of a remarkable case of sympathetic herd-delusion, for in 1692 no less than eleven persons had testified to glimpsing it. There were recent rumors, too, with a baffling and disconcerting amount of agreement. Witnesses said it had long hair and the shape of a rat, but that its sharp-toothed, bearded face was evilly human while its paws were like tiny human hands. It took messages betwixt old Keziah and the devil, and was nursed on the witch's blood, which it sucked like a vampire. Its voice was a kind of loathsome titter, and it could speak all languages. Of all the bizarre monstrosities in Gilman's dreams, nothing filled him with greater panic and nausea than this blasphemous and diminutive hybrid, whose image flitted across his vision in a form a thousandfold more hateful than anything his waking mind had deduced from the ancient records and the modern whispers.

Gilman's dreams consisted largely in plunges through limitless abysses of inexplicably colored twilight and bafflingly disordered sound; abysses whose material and gravitational properties, and whose relation to his own entity, he could not even begin to explain. He did not walk or climb, fly or swim, crawl or wriggle; yet always experienced a mode of motion partly voluntary and partly involuntary. Of his own condition he could not well judge, for sight of his arms, legs, and torso seemed always cut off by some odd disarrangement of perspective; but he felt that his physical organization and faculties were somehow marvelously transmuted and obliquely projected—though not without a certain grotesque relationship to his normal proportions and properties.

The abysses were by no means vacant, being crowded with indescribably angled masses of alien-hued substance, some of which appeared to be organic while others seemed inorganic. A few of the organic objects tended to awake vague memories in the back of his mind, though he could form no conscious idea of what they mockingly resembled or suggested. In the later dreams he began to distinguish separate categories into which the organic objects appeared to be divided, and which seemed to involve in each case a radically different species of conduct-pattern and basic motivation. Of these categories one seemed to him to include objects slightly less illogical and irrelevant in their motions than the members of the other categories.

All the objects—organic and inorganic alike—were totally beyond description or even comprehension. Gilman sometimes compared the inorganic matter to prisms, labyrinths, clusters of cubes and planes, and cyclopean buildings; and the organic things struck him variously as groups of bubbles, octopi, centipedes, living Hindu idols, and intricate arabesques roused into a kind of ophidian animation. Everything he saw was unspeakably menacing and horrible; and whenever one of the organic entities appeared by its motions to be noticing him, he felt a stark, hideous fright which generally jolted him awake. Of how the organic entities moved, he could tell no more than of how he moved himself. In time he observed a further mystery—the tendency of certain entities to appear suddenly out of empty space, or to disappear totally with equal suddenness. The shrieking, roaring confusion of sound which permeated the abysses was past all analysis as to pitch, timbre or rhythm; but seemed to be synchronous with vague visual changes in all the indefinite objects, organic and inorganic alike. Gilman had a constant sense of dread that it might rise to some unbearable degree of intensity during one or another of its obscure, relentlessly inevitable fluctuations.

But it was in these vortices of complete alienage that he saw Brown Jenkin. That shocking little horror was reserved for certain lighter, sharper dreams which assailed him just before he dropped into the fullest depths of sleep. He would be lying in the dark fighting to keep awake when a faint lambent glow would seem to shimmer around the centuried room, showing in a violet mist the convergence of angled planes which had seized his brain so insidiously. The horror would appear to pop out of the rat-hole in the corner and patter toward him over the sagging, wide-planked floor with evil expectancy in its tiny, bearded human face; but mercifully, this dream always melted away before the object got close enough to nuzzle him. It had hellishly long, sharp, canine teeth. Gilman tried to stop up the rat-hole every day, but each night the real tenants of the partitions would gnaw away the obstruction, whatever it might be. Once he had the landlord nail tin over it, but the next night the rats gnawed a fresh hole, in making which they pushed or dragged out into the room a curious little fragment of bone.

Gilman did not report his fever to the doctor, for he knew he could not pass the examinations if ordered to the college infirmary when every moment was needed for cramming. As it was, he failed in Calculus D and Advanced General Psychology, though not without hope of making up lost ground before the end of the term.

It was in March when the fresh element entered his lighter preliminary dreaming, and the nightmare shape of Brown Jenkin began to be companioned by the nebulous blur which grew more and more to resemble a bent old woman. This addition disturbed him more than he could account for, but finally he decided that it was like an ancient crone whom he had twice actually encountered in the dark tangle of lanes near the abandoned wharves. On those occasions the evil, sardonic, and seemingly unmotivated stare of the beldame had set him almost shivering—especially the first time, when an overgrown rat darting across the shadowed mouth of a neighboring alley had made him think of Brown Jenkin. Now, he reflected, those nervous fears were being mirrored in his disordered dreams.

That the influence of the old house was unwholesome he could not deny, but traces of his early morbid interest still held him there. He argued that the fever alone was responsible for his nightly fantasies, and that when the touch abated he would be free from the monstrous visions. Those visions, however, were of absorbing vividness and convincingness, and whenever he awakened he retained a vague sense of having undergone much more than he remembered. He was hideously sure that in unrecalled dreams he had talked with both Brown Jenkin and the old woman, and that they had been urging him to go somewhere with them and to meet a third being of greater potency.

Toward the end of March he began to pick up his mathematics, though other studies bothered him increasingly. He was getting an intuitive knack for solving Riemannian equations, and astonished Professor Upham by his comprehension of fourth-dimensional and other problems which had floored all the rest of the class. One afternoon there was a discussion of possible freakish curvatures in space, and of theoretical points of approach or even contact between our part of the cosmos and various other regions as distant as the farthest stars or the trans-galactic gulfs themselves—or even as fabulously remote as the tentatively conceivable cosmic units beyond the whole Einsteinian space-time continuum. Gilman's handling of this theme filled every one with admiration, even though some of his hypothetical illustrations caused an increase in the always plentiful gossip about his nervous and solitary eccentricity. What made the students shake their heads was his sober theory that a man might—given mathematical knowledge admittedly beyond all likelihood of human acquirement—step deliberately from the earth to any other celestial body which might lie at one of an infinity of specific points in the cosmic pattern.

Such a step, he said, would require only two stages; first, a passage out of the three-dimensional sphere we know, and second, a passage back to the three-dimensional sphere at another point, perhaps one of infinite remoteness. That this could be accomplished without loss of life was in many cases conceivable. Any being from any part of three-dimensional space could probably survive in the fourth dimension; and its survival of the second stage would depend upon what alien part of three-dimensional space it might select for its re-entry. Denizens of some planets might be able to live on certain others—even planets belonging to other space-time continua—though of course there must be vast numbers of mutually uninhabitable even though mathematically juxtaposed bodies or zones of space.

It was also possible that the inhabitants of a given dimensional realm could survive entry to many unknown and incomprehensible realm of additional or indefinitely multiplied dimensions—be they within or outside the given space-time continuum—and that the converse would be likewise true. This was a matter for speculation, though one could be fairly certain that the type of mutation involved in a passage from any given dimensional plane to the next higher plane would not be destructive of biological integrity as we understand it. Gilman could not be very clear about his reasons for this last assumption, but his haziness here was more than overbalanced by his clearness on other complex points. Professor Upham especially liked his demonstration of the kinship of higher mathematics to certain phases of magical lore transmitted down the ages from an ineffable antiquity—human or pre-human—whose knowledge of the cosmos and its laws was greater than ours.

Around the first of April Gilman worried considerably because his slow fever did not abate. He was also troubled by what some of his fellow-lodgers said about his sleep-walking. It seemed that he was often absent from his bed, and that the creaking of his floor at certain hours of the night was remarked by the man in the room below. This fellow also spoke of hearing the tread of shod feet in the night; but Gilman was sure he must have been mistaken in this, since shoes as well as other apparel were always precisely in place in the morning. One could develop all sorts of aural delusions in this morbid old house—for did not Gilman himself, even in daylight, now feel certain that noises other than rat-scratching came from the black voids beyond the slanting wall and above the slanting ceiling? His pathologically sensitive ears began to listen for faint footfalls in the immemorially sealed loft overhead, and sometimes the illusion of such things was agonizingly realistic.

However, he knew that he had actually become a somnambulist; for twice at night his room had been found vacant, though with all his clothing in place. Of this he had been assured by Frank Elwood, the one fellow-student whose poverty forced him to room in this squalid and unpopular house. Elwood had been studying in the small hours and had come up for help on a differential equation, only to find Gilman absent. It had been rather presumptuous of him to open the unlocked door after knocking had failed to rouse a response, but he had needed the help very badly and thought that his host would not mind a gentle prodding awake. On neither occasion, though, had Gilman been there; and when told of the matter he wondered where he could have been wandering, barefoot and with only his nightclothes on. He resolved to investigate the matter if reports of his sleep-walking continued, and thought of sprinkling flour on the floor of the corridor to see where his footsteps might lead. The door was the only conceivable egress, for there was no possible foothold outside the narrow window.

As April advanced, Gilman's fever-sharpened ears were disturbed by the whining prayers of a superstitious loom-fixer named Joe Mazurewicz, who had a room on the ground floor. Mazurewicz had told long, rambling stories about the ghost of old Keziah and the furry, sharp-fanged, nuzzling thing, and had said he was so badly haunted at times that only his silver crucifix—given him for the purpose by Father Iwanicki of St. Stanislaus' Church—could bring him relief. Now he was praying because the Witches' Sabbath was drawing near. May-Eve was Walpurgis Night, when Hell's blackest evil roamed the earth and all the slaves of Satan gathered for nameless rites and deeds. It was always a very bad time in Arkham, even though the fine folks up in Miskatonic Avenue and High and Saltonstall streets pretended to know nothing about it. There would be bad doings, and a child or two would probably be missing. Joe knew about such things, for his grandmother in the old country had heard tales from her grandmother. It was wise to pray and count one's beads at this season. For three months Keziah and Brown Jenkin had not been near Joe's room, nor near Paul Choynski's room, nor anywhere else—and it meant no good when they held off like that. They must be up to something.

Gilman dropped in at the doctor's office on the 16th of the month, and was surprised to find his temperature was not as high as he had feared. The physician questioned him sharply, and advised him to see a nerve specialist. On reflection, he was glad he had not consulted the still more inquisitive college doctor. Old Waldron, who had curtailed his activities before, would have made him take a rest —an impossible thing now that he was so close to great results in his equations. He was certainly near the boundary between the known universe and the fourth dimension, and who could say how much farther he might go?

But even as these thoughts came to him, he wondered at the source of his strange confidence. Did all of this perilous sense of imminence come from the formulae and the sheets he covered day by day? The soft, stealthy, imaginary footsteps in the sealed loft above were unnerving. And now, too, there was a growing feeling that somebody was constantly persuading him to do something terrible which he could not do. How about the somnambulism? Where did he go sometimes in the night? And what was that faint suggestion of sound which once in a while seemed to trickle through the confusion of identifiable sounds even in broad daylight and full wakefulness? Its rhythm did not correspond to anything on earth, unless perhaps to the cadence of one or two unmentionable Sabbath-chants, and sometimes he feared it corresponded to certain attributes of the vague shrieking or roaring in those wholly alien abysses of dream.

The dreams were meanwhile getting to be atrocious. In the lighter preliminary phase the evil old woman was now of fiendish distinctness, and Gilman knew she was the one who had frightened him in the slums. Her bent back, long nose, and shrivelled chin were unmistakable, and her shapeless brown garments were like those he remembered. The expression on her face was one of hideous malevolence and exultation, and when he awaked he could recall a croaking voice that persuaded and threatened. He must meet the Black Man, and go with them all to the throne of Azathoth at the center of ultimate chaos. That was what she said. He must sign the book of Azathoth in his own blood and take a new secret name now that his independent delvings had gone so far. What kept him from going with her and Brown Jenkin and the other to the throne of Chaos where the thin flutes pipe mindlessly was the fact that he had seen the name "Azathoth" in the *Necronomicon,* and knew it stood for a primal evil too horrible for description.

The old woman always appeared out of thin air near the corner where the downward slant met the inward slant. She seemed to crystallize at a point closer to the ceiling than to the floor, and every night she was a little nearer and more distinct before the dream shifted. Brown Jenkin, too, was always a little nearer at the last, and his yellowish-white fangs glistened shockingly in that unearthly violet phosphorescence. Its shrill loathsome tittering stuck more and more in Gilman's head, and he could remember in the morning how it had pronounced the words "Azathoth" and "Nyarlathotep."

In the deeper dreams everything was likewise more distinct, and Gilman felt that the twilight abysses around him were those of the fourth dimension. Those organic entities whose motions seemed least flagrantly irrelevant and unmotivated were probably projections of life-forms from our own planet, including human beings. What the others were in their own dimensional sphere or spheres he dared not try to think. Two of the less irrelevantly moving things—a rather large congeries of iridescent, prolately spheroidal bubbles and a very much smaller polyhedron of unknown colors and rapidly shifting surface angles—seemed to take notice of him and follow him about or float ahead as he changed position among the titan prisms, labyrinths, cube-and-plane clusters and quasi-buildings; and all the while the vague shrieking and roaring waxed louder and louder, as if approaching some monstrous climax of utterly unendurable intensity.

.   .   .   .   .

During the night of April 19–20th the new development occurred. Gilman was half involuntarily moving about in the twilight abysses with the bubble-mass and the small polyhedron floating ahead, when he noticed the peculiarly regular angles formed by the edges of some gigantic neighboring prism-clusters. In another second he was out of the abyss and standing tremulously on a rocky hillside bathed in intense, diffused green light. He was barefooted and in his night-clothes, and when he tried to walk discovered that he could scarcely lift his feet. A swirling vapor hid everything but the immediate slop-ing terrain from sight, and he shrank from the thought of the sounds that might surge out of that vapor.

Then he saw the two shapes laboriously crawling toward him—the old woman and the little furry thing. The crone strained up to her knees and managed to cross her arms in a singular fashion, while Brown Jenkin pointed in a certain direction with a horribly anthro-poid fore-paw which it raised with evident difficulty. Spurred by an impulse he did not originate, Gilman dragged himself forward along a course determined by the angle of the old woman's arms and the direction of the small monstrosity's paw, and before he had shuffled three steps he was back in the twilight abysses. Geometrical shapes seethed around him, and he fell dizzily and interminably. At last he woke in his bed in the crazily angled garret of the eldritch old house.

He was good for nothing that morning, and stayed away from all his classes. Some unknown attraction was pulling his eyes in a seem-ingly irrelevant direction, for he could not help staring at a certain vacant spot on the floor. As the day advanced, the focus of his unsee-ing eyes changed position, and by noon he had conquered the im-pulse to stare at vacancy. About two o'clock he went out for lunch, and as he threaded the narrow lanes of the city he found himself turning always to the southeast. Only an effort halted him at a cafete-ria in Church Street, and after the meal he felt the unknown pull still more strongly.

He would have to consult a nerve specialist after all—perhaps there was a connection with his somnambulism—but meanwhile he might at least try to break the morbid spell himself. Undoubtedly he could still manage to walk away from the pull; so with great resolu-tion he headed against it and dragged himself deliberately north along Garrison Street. By the time he had reached the bridge over the Miskatonic he was in a cold perspiration, and he clutched at the iron railing as he gazed upstream at the ill-regarded island whose regular lines of ancient standing stones brooded sullenly in the afternoon sunlight.

Then he gave a start. For there was a clearly visible living figure on that desolate island, and a second glance told him it was certainly the strange old woman whose sinister aspect had worked itself so disastrously into his dreams. The tall grass near her was moving, too, as if some other living thing were crawling close to the ground. When the old woman began to turn toward him he fled precipitately off the bridge and into the shelter of the town's labyrinthine waterfront alleys. Distant though the island was, he felt that a monstrous and invincible evil could flow from the sardonic stare of that bent, ancient figure in brown.

The southeastward pull still held, and only with tremendous resolution could Gilman drag himself into the old house and up the rickety stairs. For hours he sat silent and aimless, with his eyes shifting gradually westward. About six o'clock his sharpened ears caught the prayers of Joe Mazurewicz two floors below, and in desperation he seized his hat and walked out into the sunset-golden streets, letting the now directly southward pull carry him where it might. An hour later, darkness found him in the open fields beyond Hangman's Brook, with glimmering spring stars shining ahead. The urge to walk was gradually changing to an urge to leap mystically into space, and suddenly he realized just where the source of the pull lay.

It was in the sky. A definite point among the stars had a claim on him and was calling him. Apparently it was a point somewhere between Hydra and Argo Navis, and he knew that he had been urged toward it ever since he had awaked soon after dawn. In the morning it had been underfoot, and now it was roughly south but stealing toward the west. What was the meaning of this new thing? Was he going mad? How long would it last? Again mustering his resolution, Gilman turned and dragged himself back to the sinister old house.

Mazurewicz was waiting for him at the door, and seemed both anxious and reluctant to whisper some fresh bit of superstition. It was about the witch-light. Joe had been out celebrating the night before—it was Patriots' Day in Massachusetts—and had come home after midnight. Looking up at the house from outside, he had thought at first that Gilman's window was dark, but then he had seen the faint violet glow within. He wanted to warn the gentleman about that glow, for everybody in Arkham knew it was Keziah's witch-light which played near Brown Jenkin and the ghost of the old crone herself. He had not mentioned this before, but now he must tell about it because it meant that Keziah and her long-toothed familiar were haunting the young gentleman. Sometimes he and Paul Choynski and Landlord Dombrowski thought they saw that light seeping out of cracks in the sealed loft above the young gentleman's room, but they had all agreed not to talk about that. However, it would be better for the gentleman to take another room and get a crucifix from some good priest like Father Iwanicki.

As the man rambled on, Gilman felt a nameless panic clutch at his throat. He knew that Joe must have been half drunk when he came home the night before; yet the mention of a violet light in the garret window was of frightening import. It was a lambent glow of this sort which always played about the old woman and the small furry thing in those lighter, sharper dreams which prefaced his plunge into unknown abysses, and the thought that a wakeful second person could see the dream-luminance was utterly beyond sane harborage. Yet where had the fellow got such an odd notion? Had he himself talked as well as walked around the house in his sleep? No, Joe said, he had not—but he must check up on this. Perhaps Frank Elwood could tell him something, though he hated to ask.

Fever—wild dreams—somnambulism—illusions of sounds—a pull toward a point in the sky—and now a suspicion of sleep-talking! He must stop studying, see a nerve specialist, and take himself in hand. When he climbed to the second story, he paused at Elwood's door but saw that the other youth was out. Reluctantly, he continued up to his garret room and sat down in the dark. His gaze was still pulled to the southward, but he also found himself listening intently for some sound in the closed loft above, and half imagining that an evil violet light seeped down through an infinitesimal crack in the low, slanting ceiling.

That night as Gilman slept, the violet light broke upon him with heightened intensity, and the old witch and small furry thing, getting closer than ever before, mocked him with inhuman squeals and devilish gestures. He was glad to sink into the vaguely roaring twilight abysses, though the pursuit of that iridescent bubble-congeries and that kaleidoscopic little polyhedron was menacing and irritating. Then came the shift as vast converging planes of a slippery-looking substance loomed above and below him—a shift which ended in a flash of delirium and a blaze of unknown, alien light in which yellow, carmine, and indigo were madly and inextricably blended.

He was half lying on a high, fantastically balustraded terrace above a boundless jungle of outlandish, incredible peaks, balanced planes, domes, minarets, horizontal disks poised on pinnacles, and number-less forms of still greater wildness—some of stone and some of metal —which glittered gorgeously in the mixed, almost blistering glare from a polychromatic sky. Looking upward, he saw three stupen-dous disks of flame, each of a different hue, and at a different height above an infinitely distant curving horizon of low mountains. Behind him, tiers of higher terraces towered aloft as far as he could see. The city below stretched away to the limits of vision, and he hoped that no sound would well up from it.

The pavement from which he easily raised himself was of a veined, polished stone beyond his power to identify, and the tiles were cut in bizarre-angled shapes which struck him as less asymmetrical than based on some unearthly symmetry whose laws he could not com-prehend. The balustrade was chest-high, delicate, and fantastically wrought, while along the rail were ranged at short intervals little figures of grotesque design and exquisite workmanship. They, like the whole balustrade, seemed to be made of some sort of shining metal whose color could not be guessed in the chaos of mixed efful-gences, and their nature utterly defied conjecture. They represented some ridged barrel-shaped object with thin horizontal arms radiat-ing spoke-like from a central ring and with vertical knobs or bulbs projecting from the head and base of the barrel. Each of these knobs was the hub of a system of five long, flat, triangularly tapering arms arranged around it like the arms of a starfish—nearly horizontal, but curving slightly away from the central barrel. The base of the bottom knob was fused to the long railing with so delicate a point of contact that several figures had been broken off and were missing. The fig-ures were about four and a half inches in height, while the spiky arms gave them a maximum diameter of about two and a half inches.

When Gilman stood up, the tiles felt hot to his bare feet. He was wholly alone, and his first act was to walk to the balustrade and look dizzily down at the endless, cyclopean city almost two thousand feet below. As he listened he thought a rhythmic confusion of faint musi-cal pipings covering a wide tonal range welled up from the narrow streets beneath, and he wished he might discern the denizens of the place. The sight turned him giddy after a while, so that he would have fallen to the pavement had he not clutched instinctively at the lustrous balustrade. His right hand fell on one of the projecting figures, the touch seeming to steady him slightly. It was too much, however, for the exotic delicacy of the metal-work, and the spiky figure snapped off under his grasp. Still half dazed, he continued to clutch it as his other hand seized a vacant space on the smooth railing.

But now his over-sensitive ears caught something behind him, and he looked back across the level terrace. Approaching him softly though without apparent furtiveness were five figures, two of which were the sinister old woman and the fanged, furry little animal. The other three were what sent him unconscious; for they were living entities about eight feet high, shaped precisely like the spiky images on the balustrade, and propelling themselves by a spider-like wriggling of their lower set of starfish-arms.

Gilman awoke in his bed, drenched by a cold perspiration and with a smarting sensation in his face, hands and feet. Springing to the floor, he washed and dressed in frantic haste, as if it were necessary for him to get out of the house as quickly as possible. He did not know where he wished to go, but felt that once more he would have to sacrifice his classes. The odd pull toward that spot in the sky between Hydra and Argo had abated, but another of even greater strength had taken its place. Now he felt that he must go north—infinitely north. He dreaded to cross the bridge that gave a view of the desolate island in the Miskatonic, so went over the Peabody Avenue bridge. Very often he stumbled, for his eyes and ears were chained to an extremely lofty point in the blank blue sky.

After about an hour he got himself under better control, and saw that he was far from the city. All around him stretched the bleak emptiness of salt marshes, while the narrow road ahead led to Innsmouth—that ancient, half-deserted town which Arkham people were so curiously unwilling to visit. Though the northward pull had not diminished, he resisted it as he had resisted the other pull, and finally found that he could almost balance the one against the other. Plodding back to town and getting some coffee at a soda fountain, he dragged himself into the public library and browsed aimlessly among the lighter magazines. Once he met some friends who remarked how oddly sunburned he looked, but he did not tell them of his walk. At three o'clock he took some lunch at a restaurant, noting meanwhile that the pull had either lessened or divided itself. After that he killed the time at a cheap cinema show, seeing the inane performance over and over again without paying any attention to it.

About nine at night he drifted homeward and shuffled into the ancient house. Joe Mazurewicz was whining unintelligible prayers, and Gilman hastened up to his own garret chamber without pausing to see if Elwood was in. It was when he turned on the feeble electric light that the shock came. At once he saw there was something on the table which did not belong there, and a second look left no room for doubt. Lying on its side—for it could not stand up alone—was the exotic spiky figure which in his monstrous dream he had broken off the fantastic balustrade. No detail was missing. The ridged, barrel-shaped center, the thin radiating arms, the knobs at each end, and the flat, slightly outward-curving starfish-arms spreading from those knobs—all were there. In the electric light, the color seemed to be a kind of iridescent gray veined with green; and Gilman could see amidst his horror and bewilderment that one of the knobs ended in a jagged break, corresponding to its former point of attachment to the dream-railing.

Only his tendency toward a dazed stupor prevented him from screaming aloud. This fusion of dream and reality was too much to bear. Still dazed, he clutched at the spiky thing and staggered downstairs to Landlord Dombrowski's quarters. The prayers of the loom-fixer were still sounding through the moldy halls, but Gilman did not mind them now. The landlord was in, and greeted him pleasantly. No, he had not seen that thing before and did not know anything about it. But his wife had said she found a funny tin thing in one of the beds when she fixed the rooms at noon, and maybe that was it. Dombrowski called her, and she waddled in. Yes, that was the thing. She had found it in the young gentleman's bed—on the side next to the wall. It had looked very queer to her, but of course the young gentleman had lots of queer things in his room—books and curios and pictures and markings on paper. She certainly knew nothing about it.

So Gilman climbed upstairs again in mental turmoil, convinced that he was either still dreaming or that his somnambulism had run to incredible extremes and led him to depredations in unknown places. Where had he got this outre thing? He did not recall seeing it in any museum in Arkham. It must have been somewhere, though; and the sight of it as he snatched it in his sleep must have caused the odd dream-picture of the balustraded terrace. Next day, he would make some very guarded inquiries—and perhaps see the nerve specialist.

Meanwhile, he would try to keep track of his somnambulism. As he went upstairs across the garret hall, he sprinkled about some flour which he had borrowed—with a frank admission as to its purpose—from the landlord. He had stopped at Elwood's door on the way, but had found all dark within. Entering his room, he placed the spiky thing on the table, and lay down in complete mental and physical exhaustion without pausing to undress. From the closed loft above the slanting ceiling he thought he heard a faint scratching and padding, but he was too disorganized even to mind it. That cryptical pull from the north was getting very strong again, though it seemed now to come from a lower place in the sky.

In the dazzling violet light of dream, the old woman and the fanged, furry thing came again and with a greater distinctness than on any former occasion. This time they actually reached him, and he felt the crone's withered claws clutching at him. He was pulled out of bed and into empty space, and for a moment he heard a rhythmic roaring and saw the twilight amorphousness of the vague abysses seething around him. But that moment was very brief, for presently he was in a crude, windowless little space with rough beams and planks rising to a peak just above his head, and with a curious slanting floor underfoot. Propped level on that floor were low cases full of books of every degree of antiquity and disintegration, and in the center were a table and bench, both apparently fastened in place. Small objects of unknown shape and nature were ranged on the tops of the cases, and in the flaming violet light Gilman thought he saw a counterpart of the spiky image which had puzzled him so horribly. On the left, the floor fell abruptly away, leaving a black triangular gulf out of which, after a second's dry rattling, there presently climbed the hateful little furry thing with the yellow fangs and bearded human face.

The evilly grinning beldame still clutched him, and beyond the table stood a figure he had never seen before—a tall, lean man of dead black coloration but without the slightest sign of Negroid features; wholly devoid of either hair or beard, and wearing as his only garment a shapeless robe of some heavy black fabric. His feet were indistinguishable because of the table and bench, but he must have been shod, since there was a clicking whenever he changed position. The man did not speak, and bore no trace of expression on his small, regular features. He merely pointed to a book of prodigious size which lay open on the table, while the beldame thrust a huge gray quill into Gilman's right hand. Over everything was a pall of intensely maddening fear, and the climax was reached when the furry thing ran up the dreamer's clothing to his shoulders and then down his left arm, finally biting him sharply in the wrist just below his cuff. As the blood spurted from this wound, Gilman lapsed into a faint.

He awoke on the morning of the 22nd with a pain in his left wrist, and saw that his cuff was brown with dried blood. His recollections were very confused, but the scene with the black man in the unknown space stood out vividly. The rats must have bitten him as he slept, giving rise to the climax of that frightful dream. Opening the door, he saw that the flour on the corridor floor was undisturbed except for the huge prints of the loutish fellow who roamed at the other end of the garret. So he had not been sleep-walking this time. But something would have to be done about those rats. He would speak to the landlord about them. Again he tried to stop up the hole at the base of the slanting wall, wedging in a candlestick which seemed of about the right size. His ears were ringing horribly, as if with the residual echoes of some horrible noise heard in dreams.

As he bathed and changed clothes, he tried to recall what he had dreamed after the scene in the violet-litten space, but nothing definite would crystallize in his mind. That scene itself must have corresponded to the sealed loft overhead, which had begun to attack his imagination so violently, but later impressions were faint and hazy. There were suggestions of the vague, twilight abysses, and of still vaster, blacker abysses beyond them—abysses in which all fixed suggestions were absent. He had been taken there by the bubble-congeries and the little polyhedron which always dogged him; but they, like himself, had changed to wisps of mist in this farther void of ultimate blackness. Something else had gone on ahead—a larger wisp which now and then condensed into nameless approximations of form—and he thought that their progress had not been in a straight line, but rather along the alien curves and spirals of some ethereal vortex which obeyed laws unknown to the physics and mathematics of any conceivable cosmos. Eventually there had been a hint of vast, leaping shadows, of a monstrous, half-acoustic pulsing, and of the thin, monotonous piping of an unseen flute—but that was all. Gilman decided he had picked up that last conception from what he had read in the *Necronomicon* about the mindless entity Azathoth, which rules all time and space from a curiously environed black throne at the center of Chaos.

When the blood was washed away, the wrist wound proved very slight, and Gilman puzzled over the location of the two tiny punctures. It occurred to him that there was no blood on the bedspread where he had lain—which was very curious in view of the amount on his skin and cuff. Had he been sleep-walking within his room, and had the rat bitten him as he sat in some chair or paused in some less rational position? He looked in every corner for brownish drops or stains, but did not find any. He had better, he thought, sprinkle flour within the room as well as outside the door—though, after all, no further proof of his sleep-walking was needed. He knew he did walk—and the thing to do now was to stop it. He must ask Frank Elwood for help. This morning, the strange pulls from space seemed lessened, though they were replaced by another sensation even more inexplicable. It was a vague, insistent impulse to fly away from his present situation, but held not a hint of the specific direction in which he wished to fly. As he picked up the strange spiky image on the table, he thought the older northward pull grew a trifle stronger; but even so, it was wholly overruled by the newer and more bewildering urge.

He took the spiky image down to Elwood's room, steeling himself against the whines of the loom-fixer which welled up from the ground floor. Elwood was in, thank heaven, and appeared to be stirring about. There was time for a little conversation before leaving for breakfast and college; so Gilman hurriedly poured forth an account of his recent dreams and fears. His host was very sympathetic, and agreed that something ought to be done. He was shocked by his guest's drawn, haggard aspect, and noticed the queer, abnormal-looking sunburn which others had remarked during the past week. There was not much, though, that he could say. He had not seen Gilman on any sleep-walking expedition, and had no idea what the curious image could be. He had, though, heard the French-Canadian who lodged just under Gilman talking to Mazurewicz one evening. They were telling each other how badly they dreaded the coming of Walpurgis Night, now only a few days off; and were exchanging pitying comments about the poor, doomed young gentleman. Desrochers, the fellow under Gilman's room, had spoken of nocturnal footsteps shod and unshod, and of the violet light he saw one night when he had stolen fearfully up to peer through Gilman's keyhole. He had not dared to peer, he told Mazurewicz, after he had glimpsed that light through the cracks around the door. There had been soft talking, too—and as he began to describe it, his voice had sunk to an inaudible whisper.

Elwood could not imagine what had set these people gossiping, but supposed their imaginations had been roused by Gilman's late hours and somnolent walking and talking on the one hand, and by the nearness of traditionally-feared May-Eve on the other hand. That Gilman talked in his sleep was plain, and it was obviously from Desrocher's keyhole-listenings that the delusive notion of the violet dream-light had got abroad. These simple people were quick to imagine they had seen any odd thing they had heard about. As for a plan of action—Gilman had better move down to Elwood's room and avoid sleeping alone. Elwood would, if awake, rouse him whenever he began to talk or rise in his sleep. Very soon, too, he must see the specialist. Meanwhile, they would take the spiky image around to the various museums and to certain professors; seeking identification and stating that it had been found in a public rubbish-can. Also, Dombrowski must attend to the poisoning of those rats in the walls.

Braced up by Elwood's companionship, Gilman attended classes that day. Strange urges still tugged at him, but he could sidetrack them with considerable success. During a free period, he showed the queer image to several professors, all of whom were intensely interested, though none of them could shed any light upon its nature or origin. That night, he slept on a couch which Elwood had had the landlord bring to the second-story room, and for the first time in weeks was wholly free from disquieting dreams. But the feverishness still hung on, and the whines of the loom-fixer were an unnerving influence.

During the next few days, Gilman enjoyed an almost perfect immunity from morbid manifestations. He had, Elwood said, showed no tendency to talk or rise in his sleep; and meanwhile the landlord was putting rat-poison everywhere. The only disturbing element was the talk among the foreigners, whose imaginations had become highly excited. Mazurewicz was always trying to make him get a crucifix, and finally forced one upon him which he said had been blessed by the good Father Iwanicki. Desrochers, too, had something to say; in fact, he insisted that cautious steps had sounded in the now vacant room above him on the first and second nights of Gilman's absence from it. Paul Choynski thought he heard sounds in the halls and on the stairs at night, and claimed that his door had been softly tried, while Mrs. Dombrowski vowed she had seen Brown Jenkin for the first time since All-Hallows. But such naive reports could mean very little, and Gilman let the cheap metal crucifix hang idly from a knob on his host's dresser.

For three days, Gilman and Elwood canvassed the local museums in an effort to identify the strange spiky image, but always without success. In every quarter, however, interest was intense; for the utter alienage of the thing was a tremendous challenge to scientific curiosity. One of the small radiating arms was broken off and subjected to chemical analysis. Professor Ellery found platinum, iron and tellurium in the strange alloy; but mixed with these were at least three other apparent elements of high atomic weight which chemistry was absolutely powerless to classify. Not only did they fail to correspond with any known element, but they did not even fit the vacant places reserved for probable elements in the periodic system.

On the morning of April 27th, a fresh rat-hole appeared in the room where Gilman was a guest, but Dombrowski tinned it up during the day. The poison was not having much effect, for scratching and scurryings in the walls were virtually undiminished.

Elwood was out late that night, and Gilman waited up for him. He did not wish to go to sleep in a room alone—especially since he thought he had glimpsed in the evening twilight the repellent old woman whose image had become so horribly transferred to his dreams. He wondered who she was, and what had been near her rattling the tin cans in a rubbish-heap at the mouth of a squalid courtyard. The crone had seemed to notice him and leer evilly at him—though perhaps this was merely his imagination.

The next day, both youths felt very tired and knew they would sleep like logs when night came. In the evening, they drowsily discussed the mathematical studies which had so completely and perhaps harmfully engrossed Gilman, and speculated about the linkage with ancient magic and folklore which seemed so darkly probable. They spoke of old Keziah Mason, and Elwood agreed that Gilman had good scientific grounds for thinking she might have stumbled on strange and significant information. The hidden cults to which these witches belonged often guarded and handed down surprising secrets from elder, forgotten eons; and it was by no means impossible that Keziah had actually mastered the art of passing through dimensional gates. Tradition emphasizes the uselessness of material barriers in halting a witch's motions, and who can say what underlies the old tales of broomstick rides through the night?

Whether a modern student could ever gain similar powers from mathematical research alone, was still to be seen. Success, Gilman added, might lead to dangerous and unthinkable situations; for who could foretell the conditions pervading an adjacent but normally inaccessible dimension? On the other hand, the picturesque possibilities were enormous. Time could not exist in certain belts of space, and by entering and remaining in such a belt one might preserve one's life and age indefinitely; never suffering organic metabolism or deterioration except for slight amounts incurred during visits to one's own or similar planes. One might, for example, pass into a timeless dimension and emerge at some remote period of the earth's history as young as before.

Whether anybody had ever managed to do this, one could hardly conjecture with any degree of authority. Old legends are hazy and ambiguous, and in historic times all attempts at crossing forbidden gaps seem complicated by strange and terrible alliances with beings and messengers from outside. There was the immemorial figure of the deputy or messenger of hidden and terrible powers—the "Black Man" of the witch-cult, and the "Nyarlathotep" of the *Necronomicon*. There was, too, the baffling problem of the lesser messengers or intermediaries—the quasi-animals and queer hybrids which legend depicts as witches' familiars. As Gilman and Elwood retired, too sleepy to argue further, they heard Joe Mazurewicz reel into the house half drunk, and shuddered at the desperate wildness of his prayers.

That night, Gilman saw the violet light again. In his dream he had heard a scratching and gnawing in the partitions, and thought that someone fumbled clumsily at the latch. Then he saw the old woman and the small furry thing advancing toward him over the carpeted floor. The beldame's face was alight with inhuman exultation, and the little yellow-toothed morbidity tittered mockingly as it pointed at the hearty-sleeping form of Elwood on the other couch across the room. A paralysis of fear stifled all attempts to cry out. As once before, the hideous crone seized Gilman by the shoulders, yanking him out of bed and into empty space. Again the infinitude of the shrieking abysses flashed past him, but in another second he thought he was in a dark, muddy, unknown alley of fetid odors with the rotting walls of ancient houses towering up on every hand.

Ahead was the robed black man he had seen in the peaked space in the other dream, while from a lesser distance the old woman was beckoning and grimacing imperiously. Brown Jenkin was rubbing itself with a kind of affectionate playfulness around the ankles of the black man, which the deep mud largely concealed. There was a dark open doorway on the right, to which the black man silently pointed. Into this the grinning crone started, dragging Gilman after her by his pajama sleeves. There were evil-smelling staircases which creaked ominously, and on which the old woman seemed to radiate a faint violet light; and finally a door leading off a landing. The crone fumbled with the latch and pushed the door open, motioning to Gilman to wait, and disappearing inside the black aperture.

The youth's over-sensitive ears caught a hideous strangled cry, and presently the beldame came out of the room bearing a small, senseless form which she thrust at the dreamer as if ordering him to carry it. The sight of this form, and the expression on its face, broke the spell. Still too dazed to cry out, he plunged recklessly down the noisome staircase and into the mud outside; halting only when seized and choked by the waiting black man. As consciousness departed he heard the faint, shrill tittering of the fanged, rat-like abnormality.

On the morning of the 29th, Gilman awoke into a maelstrom of horror. The instant he opened his eyes he knew something was terribly wrong, for he was back in his old garret room with the slanting wall and ceiling, sprawled on the now unmade bed. His throat was aching inexplicably, and as he struggled to a sitting posture he saw with growing fright that his feet and pajama bottoms were brown with caked mud. For the moment, his recollections were hopelessly hazy, but he knew at least that he must have been sleep-walking. Elwood had been lost too deeply in slumber to hear and stop him. On the floor were confused muddy prints, but oddly enough they did not extend all the way to the door. The more Gilman looked at them, the more peculiar they seemed; for in addition to those he could recognize as his there were some smaller, almost round markings—such as the legs of a large chair or a table might make, except that most of them tended to be divided into halves. There were also some curious muddy rat-tracks leading out of a fresh hole and back into it again. Utter bewilderment and the fear of madness racked Gilman as he staggered to the door and saw that there were no muddy prints outside. The more he remembered of his hideous dream the more terrified he felt, and it added to his desperation to hear Joe Mazurewicz chanting mournfully two floors below.

Descending to Elwood's room, he roused his still-sleeping host and began telling of how he had found himself, but Elwood could form no idea of what might really have happened. Where Gilman could have been, how he got back to his room without making tracks in the hall, and how the muddy, furniture-like prints came to be mixed with his in the garret chamber, were wholly beyond conjecture. Then there were those dark, livid marks on his throat, as if he had tried to strangle himself. He put his hands up to them, but found that they did not even approximately fit. While they were talking, Desrochers dropped in to say that he had heard a terrific clattering overhead in the dark small hours. No, there had been no one on the stairs after midnight, though just before midnight he had heard faint footfalls in the garret, and cautiously descending steps he did not like. It was, he added, a very bad time of the year for Arkham. The younger gentleman had better be sure to wear the crucifix Joe Mazurewicz had given him. Even the daytime was not safe, for after dawn there had been strange sounds in the house—especially a thin, childish wail hastily choked off.

Gilman mechanically attended classes that morning, but was wholly unable to fix his mind on his studies. A mood of hideous apprehension and expectancy had seized him, and he seemed to be awaiting the fall of some annihilating blow. At noon he lunched at the University Spa, picking up a paper from the next seat as he waited for dessert. But he never ate that dessert; for an item on the paper's first page left him limp, wild-eyed, and able only to pay his check and stagger back to Elwood's room.

There had been a strange kidnapping the night before in Orne's Gangway, and the two-year-old child of a laundry worker named Anastasia Wolejko had completely vanished from sight. The mother, it appeared, had feared the event for some time; but the reasons she assigned for her fear were so grotesque that no one took them seriously. She had, she said, seen Brown Jenkin about the place now and then ever since early in March, and knew from its grimaces and titterings that little Ladislas must be marked for sacrifice at the awful Sabbat on Walpurgis Night. She had asked her neighbor Mary Czanek to sleep in the room and try to protect the child, but Mary had not dared. She could not tell the police, for they never believed such things. Children had been taken that way every year ever since she could remember. And her friend Pete Stowacki would not help because he wanted the child out of the way.

But what threw Gilman into a cold perspiration was the report of a pair of revellers who had been walking past the mouth of the gangway just after midnight. They admitted they had been drunk, but both vowed they had seen a crazily dressed trio furtively entering the dark passageway. There had, they said, been a huge robed Negro, a little old woman in rags, and a young white man in his nightclothes.

The old woman had been dragging the youth, while around the feet of the Negro a tame rat was rubbing and weaving in the brown mud.

Gilman sat in a daze all the afternoon, and Elwood—who had meanwhile seen the papers and formed terrible conjectures from them—found him thus when he came home. This time, neither could doubt but that something hideously serious was closing in around them. Between the fantasms of nightmare and the realities of the objective world a monstrous and unthinkable relationship was crystallizing, and only stupendous vigilance could avert still more direful developments. Gilman must see a specialist sooner or later, but not just now, when all the papers were full of this kidnapping business.

Just what had really happened was maddeningly obscure, and for a moment both Gilman and Elwood exchanged whispered theories of the wildest kind. Had Gilman unconsciously succeeded better than he knew in his studies of space and its dimensions? Had he actually slipped outside our sphere to points unguessed and unimaginable? Where—if anywhere—had he been on those nights of demoniac alienage? The roaring twilight abysses—the green hillside—the blistering terrace—the pulls from the stars—the ultimate black vortex—the black man—the muddy alley and the stairs—the old witch and the fanged furry horror—the bubble-congeries and the little polyhedron—the strange sunburn—the wrist wound—the unexplained image—the muddy feet—the throat-marks—the tales and fears of the foreigners—what did all this mean? To what extent could the laws of sanity apply to such a case?

There was no sleep for either of them that night, but next day they both cut classes and drowsed. This was April 30th, and with the dusk would come the hellish Sabbat-time which all the foreigners and the superstitious old folk feared. Mazurewicz came home at six o'clock and said people at the mill were whispering that the Walpurgis revels would be held in the dark ravine beyond Meadow Hill where the old white stone stands in a place queerly devoid of all plant life. Some of them had even told the police and advised them to look there for the missing Wolejko child, but they did not believe anything would be done. Joe insisted that the poor young gentleman wear his nickel-chained crucifix, and Gilman put it on and dropped it inside his shirt to humor the fellow.

Late at night, the two youths sat drowsing in their chairs, lulled by the praying of the loom-fixer on the floor below. Gilman listened as he nodded, his preternaturally sharpened hearing seeming to strain for some subtle, dreaded murmur beyond the noises in the ancient house. Unwholesome recollections of things in the *Necronomicon* and the *Black Book* welled up, and he found himself swaying to infamous rhythms said to pertain to the blackest ceremonies of the Sabbat and to have an origin outside the time and space we comprehend.

Presently he realized what he was listening for—the hellish chant of the celebrants in the distant dark valley. How did he know so much about what they expected? How did he know the time when Nahab and her acolyte were due to bear the brimming bowl which would follow the black cock and the black goat? He saw that Elwood had dropped asleep, and tried to call out and waken him. Something, however, closed his throat. He was not his own master. Had he signed the black man's book, after all?

Then his fevered, abnormal hearing caught the distant, windborne notes. Over miles of hill and field and alley they came, but he recognized them none the less. The fires must be lit, and the dancers must be starting in. How could he keep himself from going? What was it that had enmeshed him? Mathematics—folklore—the house—old Keziah—Brown Jenkin . . . and now he saw that there was a fresh rat-hole in the wall near his couch. Above the distant chanting and the nearer praying of Joe Mazurewicz came another sound—a stealthy, determined scratching in the partitions. He hoped the electric lights would not go out. Then he saw the fanged, bearded little face in the rat-hole—the accursed little face which he at last realized bore such a shocking, mocking resemblance to old Keziah's—and heard the faint fumbling at the door.

The screaming twilight abysses flashed before him, and he felt himself helpless in the formless grasp of the iridescent bubble-congeries. Ahead raced the small, kaleidoscopic polyhedron, and all through the churning void there was a heightening and acceleration of the vague tonal pattern which seemed to foreshadow some unutterable and unendurable climax. He seemed to know what was coming—the monstrous burst of Walpurgis-rhythm in whose cosmic timbre would be concentrated all the primal, ultimate space-time seethings which lie behind the massed spheres of matter and sometimes break forth in measured reverberations that penetrate faintly to every layer of entity and give hideous significance throughout the worlds to certain dreaded periods.

But all this vanished in a second. He was again in the cramped, violet-litten peaked space with the slanting floor, the low cases of ancient books, the bench and a table, the queer objects, and the triangular gulf at one side. On the table lay a small white figure—an infant boy, unclothed and unconscious—while on the other side stood the monstrous, leering old woman with a gleaming, grotesque-hafted knife in her right hand, and a queerly proportioned pale metal bowl covered with curiously chased designs and having delicate lateral handles in her left. She was intoning some croaking ritual in a language which Gilman could not understand, but which seemed like something guardedly quoted in the *Necronomicon*.

As the scene grew clear, he saw the ancient crone bend forward and extend the empty bowl across the table—and unable to control his own motions, he reached far forward and took it in both hands, noticing as he did so its comparative lightness. At the same moment, the disgusting form of Brown Jenkin scrambled up over the brink of the triangular black gulf on his left. The crone now motioned him to hold the bowl in a certain position while she raised the huge, grotesque knife above the small white victim as high as her right hand could reach. The fanged, furry thing began tittering a continuation of the unknown ritual, while the witch croaked loathsome responses. Gilman felt a gnawing, poignant abhorrence shoot through his mental and emotional paralysis, and the light metal bowl shook in his grasp. A second later the downward motion of the knife broke the spell completely, and he dropped the bowl with a resounding bell-like clangor while his hands darted out frantically to stop the monstrous deed.

In an instant, he had edged up the slanting floor around the end of the table and wrenched the knife from the old woman's claws; sending it clattering over the brink of the narrow triangular gulf. In another instant, however, matters were reversed; for those murderous claws had locked themselves tightly around his own throat, while the wrinkled face was twisted with insane fury. He felt the chain of the cheap crucifix grinding into his neck, and in his peril wondered how the sight of the object itself would affect the evil creature. Her strength was altogether superhuman, but as she continued her choking he reached feebly in his shirt and drew out the metal symbol, snapping the chain and pulling it free.

At sight of the device, the witch seemed struck with panic, and her grip relaxed long enough to give Gilman a chance to break it entirely. He pulled the steel-like claws from his neck, and would have dragged the beldame over the edge of the gulf had not the claws received a fresh access of strength and closed in again. This time he resolved to reply in kind, and his own hands reached out for the creature's throat. Before she saw what he was doing he had the chain of the crucifix twisted about her neck, and a moment later he had tightened it enough to cut off her breath. During her last struggle, he felt something bite at his ankle, and saw that Brown Jenkin had come to her aid. With one savage kick he sent the morbidity over the edge of the gulf and heard it whimper on some level far below.

Whether he had killed the ancient crone he did not know, but he let her rest on the floor where she had fallen. Then, as he turned away, he saw on the table a sight which nearly snapped the last thread of his reason. Brown Jenkin, tough of sinew and with four tiny hands of demoniac dexterity, had been busy while the witch was throttling him, and his efforts had been in vain. What he had prevented the knife from doing to the victim's chest, the yellow fangs of the furry blasphemy had done to a wrist—and the bowl so lately on the floor stood full beside the small lifeless body.

In his dream-delirium, Gilman heard the hellish alien-rhythmed chant of the Sabbat coming from an infinite distance, and knew the black man must be there. Confused memories mixed themselves with his mathematics, and he believed his subconscious mind held the *angles* which he needed to guide him back to the normal world alone and unaided for the first time. He felt sure he was in the immemorially sealed loft above his own room, but whether he could ever escape through the slanting floor or the long-stopped egress he doubted greatly. Besides, would not an escape from a dream-loft bring him merely into a dream-house—an abnormal projection of the actual place he sought? He was wholly bewildered as to the relation betwixt dream and reality in all his experiences.

The passage through the vague abysses would be frightful, for the Walpurgis-rhythm would be vibrating, and at last he would have to hear that hitherto-veiled cosmic pulsing which he so mortally dreaded. Even now he could detect a low, monstrous shaking whose tempo he suspected all too well. At Sabbat-time, it always mounted and reached through to the worlds to summon the initiate to nameless rites. Half the chants of the Sabbat were patterned on this faintly overheard pulsing which no earthly ear could endure in its unveiled spatial fullness. Gilman wondered, too, whether he could trust his instincts to take him back to the right part of space. How could he be sure he would not land on that green-litten hillside of a far planet, on the tessellated terrace above the city of tentacled monsters somewhere beyond the galaxy, or in the spiral black vortices of that ultimate void of Chaos where reigns the mindless demon-sultan Azathoth?

Just before he made the plunge, the violet light went out and left him in utter blackness. The witch—old Keziah—Nahab—that must have meant her death. And mixed with the distant chant of the Sabbat and the whimpers of Brown Jenkin in the gulf below he thought he heard another and wilder whine from unknown depths. Joe Mazurewicz—the prayers against the Crawling Chaos now turning to an inexplicably triumphant shriek—worlds of sardonic actuality impinging on vortices of febrile dream—Ia! Shub-Niggurath! The Goat with a Thousand Young . . .

They found Gilman on the floor of his queerly-angled old garret room long before dawn, for the terrible cry had brought Desrochers and Choynski and Dombrowski and Mazurewicz at once, and had even wakened the soundly sleeping Elwood in his chair. He was alive, and with open, staring eyes, but seemed largely unconscious. On his throat were the marks of murderous hands, and on his left ankle was a distressing rat-bite. His clothing was badly rumpled, and Joe's crucifix was missing. Elwood trembled, afraid even to speculate on what new form his friend's sleep-walking had taken. Mazurewicz seemed half dazed because of a "sign" he said he had in response to his prayers, and he crossed himself frantically when the squealing and whimpering of a rat sounded from beyond the slanting partition.

When the dreamer was settled on his couch in Elwood's room, they sent for Doctor Malkowski—a local practitioner who would repeat no tales where they might prove embarrassing—and he gave Gilman two hypodermic injections which caused him to relax in something like natural drowsiness. During the day, the patient regained consciousness at times and whispered his newest dream disjointedly to Elwood. It was a painful process, and at its very start brought out a fresh and disconcerting fact.

Gilman—whose ears had so lately possessed an abnormal sensitiveness—was now stone-deaf. Doctor Malkowski, summoned again in haste, told Elwood that both ear-drums were ruptured, as if by the impact of some stupendous sound intense beyond all human conception or endurance. How such a sound could have been heard in the last few hours without arousing all the Miskatonic Valley was more than the honest physician could say.

Elwood wrote his part of the colloquy on paper, so that a fairly easy communication was maintained. Neither knew what to make of the whole chaotic business, and decided it would be better if they thought as little as possible about it. Both, though, agreed that they must leave this ancient and accursed house as soon as it could be arranged. Evening papers spoke of a police raid on some curious revellers in a ravine beyond Meadow Hill just before dawn, and mentioned that the white stone there was an object of age-long superstitious regard. Nobody had been caught, but among the scattering fugitives had been glimpsed a huge Negro. In another column it was stated that no trace of the missing child Ladislas Wolejko had been found.

The crowning horror came that very night. Elwood will never forget it, and was forced to stay out of college the rest of the term because of the resulting nervous breakdown. He had thought he heard rats in the partitions all the evening, but paid little attention to them. Then, long after both he and Gilman had retired, the atrocious shrieking began. Elwood jumped up, turned on the lights, and rushed over to his guest's couch. The occupant was emitting sounds of veritably inhuman nature, as if racked by some torment beyond description. He was writhing under the bedclothes, and a great red stain was beginning to appear on the blankets.

Elwood scarcely dared to touch him, but gradually the screaming and writhing subsided. By this time Dombrowski, Choynski, Desrochers, Mazurewicz, and the top-floor lodger were all crowding into the doorway, and the landlord had sent his wife back to telephone for Doctor Malkowski. Everybody shrieked when a large rat-like form suddenly jumped out from beneath the ensanguined bedclothes and scuttled across the floor to a fresh, open hole close by. When the doctor arrived and began to pull down those frightful covers Walter Gilman was dead.

It would be barbarous to do more than suggest what had killed Gilman. There had been virtually a tunnel through his body—something had eaten his heart out. Dombrowski, frantic at the failure of his rat-poisoning efforts, cast aside all thought of his lease and within a week had moved with all his older lodgers to a dingy but less ancient house in Walnut Street. The worst thing for a while was keeping Joe Mazurewicz quiet; for the brooding loom-fixer would never stay sober, and was constantly whining and muttering about spectral and terrible things.

It seems that on that last hideous night, Joe had stooped to look at the crimson rat-tracks which led from Gilman's couch to the near-by hole. On the carpet they were very indistinct, but a piece of open flooring intervened between the carpet's edge and the baseboard. There Mazurewicz had found something monstrous—or thought he had, for no one else could quite agree with him despite the undeniable queerness of the prints. The tracks on the flooring were certainly vastly unlike the average prints of a rat, but even Choynski and Desrochers would not admit that they were like the prints of four tiny human hands.

The house was never rented again. As soon as Dombrowski left it, the pall of its final desolation began to descend, for people shunned it both on account of its old reputation and because of the new fetid odor. Perhaps the ex-landlord's rat-poison had worked after all, for not long after his departure the place became a neighborhood nuisance. Health officials traced the smell to the closed spaces above and beside the eastern garret room, and agreed that the number of dead rats must be enormous. They decided, however, that it was not worth their while to hew open and disinfect the long-sealed spaces; for the fetor would soon be over, and the locality was not one which encouraged fastidious standards. Indeed, there were always vague local tales of unexplained stenches upstairs in the Witch-House just after May-Eve and Hallowmass. The neighbors acquiesced in the inertia—but the fetor none the less formed an additional count against the place. Toward the last, the house was condemned as a habitation by the building inspector.

Gilman's dreams and their attendant circumstances have never been explained. Elwood, whose thoughts on the entire episode are sometimes almost maddening, came back to college the next autumn and graduated in the following June. He found the spectral gossip of the town much diminished, and it is indeed a fact that—notwithstanding certain reports of a ghostly tittering in the deserted house which lasted almost as long as that edifice itself—no fresh appearances either of Old Keziah or of Brown Jenkin have been muttered of since Gilman's death. It is rather fortunate that Elwood was not in Arkham in that later year when certain events abruptly renewed horrors. Of course, he heard about the matter afterward and suffered untold torments of black and bewildered speculation; but even that was not as bad as actual nearness and several possible sights would have been.

In March, 1931, a gale wrecked the roof and great chimney of the vacant Witch-House, so that a chaos of crumbling bricks, blackened, moss-grown shingles, and rotting planks and timbers crashed down into the loft and broke through the floor beneath. The whole attic story was choked with debris from above, but no one took the trouble to touch the mess before the inevitable razing of the decrepit structure. That ultimate step came in the following December, and it was when Gilman's old room was cleared out by reluctant, apprehensive workmen that the gossip began.

Among the rubbish which had crashed through the ancient slanting ceiling were several things which made the workmen pause and call in the police. Later, the police in turn called in the coroner and several professors from the university. There were bones—badly crushed and splintered, but clearly recognizable as human—whose manifestly modern date conflicted puzzlingly with the remote period at which their only possible lurking place, the low, slant-floored loft overhead, had supposedly been sealed from all human access. The coroner's physician decided that some belonged to a small child, while certain others—found mixed with shreds of rotten brownish cloth—belonged to a rather undersized, bent female of advanced years. Careful sifting of debris also disclosed many tiny bones of rats caught in the collapse, as well as older rat-bones gnawed by small fangs in a fashion now and then highly productive of controversy and reflection.

Other objects found included the mangled fragments of many books and papers, together with a yellowish dust left from the total disintegration of still older books and papers. All, without exception, appeared to deal with black magic in its most advanced and horrible forms; and the evidently recent date of certain items is still a mystery as unsolved as that of the modern human bones. An even greater mystery is the absolute homogeneity of the crabbed, archaic writing found on a wide range of papers whose conditions and watermarks suggest age differences of at least 150 to 200 years. To some, though, the greatest mystery of all is the variety of utterly inexplicable objects —objects whose shapes, materials, types of workmanship, and purposes baffle all conjecture—found scattered amidst the wreckage in evidently diverse states of injury. One of these things—which excited several Miskatonic professors profoundly—is a badly damaged monstrosity plainly resembling the strange image which Gilman gave to the college museum, save that it is larger, wrought of some peculiar bluish stone instead of metal, and possessed of a singularly angled pedestal with undecipherable hieroglyphics.

Archeologists and anthropologists are still trying to explain the bizarre designs chased on a crushed bowl of light metal whose inner side bore ominous brownish stains when found. Foreigners and credulous grandmothers are equally garrulous about the modern nickel crucifix with broken chain mixed in the rubbish and shiveringly identified by Joe Mazurewicz as that which he had given poor Gilman many years before. Some believe this crucifix was dragged up to the sealed loft by rats, while others think it must have been on the floor in some corner of Gilman's old room all the time. Still others, including Joe himself, have theories too wild and fantastic for sober credence.

When the slanting wall of Gilman's room was torn out, the once sealed triangular space between that partition and the house's north wall was found to contain much less structural debris, even in proportion to its size, than the room itself; though it had a ghastly layer of older materials which paralyzed the wreckers with horror. In brief, the floor was a veritable ossuary of the bones of small children —some fairly modern, but others extending back in infinite gradations to a period so remote that crumbling was almost complete. On this deep bony layer rested a knife of great size, obvious antiquity, and grotesque, ornate, and exotic design—above which the debris was piled.

In the midst of this debris, wedged between a fallen plank and a cluster of cemented bricks from the ruined chimney, was an object destined to cause more bafflement, veiled fright, and openly superstitious talk in Arkham than anything else discovered in the haunted and accursed building. This object was the partly crushed skeleton of a huge diseased rat, whose abnormalities of form are still a topic of debate and source of singular reticence among the members of Miskatonic's department of comparative anatomy. Very little concerning this skeleton has leaked out, but the workmen who found it whisper in shocked tones about the long, brownish hairs with which it was associated.

The bones of the tiny paws, it is rumored, imply prehensile characteristics more typical of a diminutive monkey than of a rat, while the small skull with its savage yellow fangs is of the utmost anomalousness, appearing from certain angles like a miniature, monstrously degraded parody of a human skull. The workmen crossed themselves in fright when they came upon this blasphemy, but later burned candles of gratitude in St. Stanislaus' Church because of the shrill, ghostly tittering they felt they would never hear again.

ISAAC ASIMOV
and FREDERIK POHL

The Little Man
on the Subway

What a delight it is to find yet another first-rate fantasy by ISAAC ASIMOV, *who was, of course, best known for such award-winning science fiction as the Foundation series, the interlinked Robot tales and novels and literally hundreds of nonfiction books that brilliantly explain science to the layman. This early Asimov short story first appeared as a collaboration with James Mac-Creigh, a pseudonym for* FREDERIK POHL, *another important science-fiction writer (and editor, agent and anthologist).*

Subway stations are places where people usually get out, so when no one left the first car at Atlantic Avenue station, Conductor Cullen of the I.R.T. began to get worried. In fact, no one had left the first car from the time the run to Flatbush had begun—though dozens were getting on all the time.

Odd! Very odd! It was the kind of proposition that made well-bred conductors remove their caps and scratch their heads. Conductor Cullen did so. It didn't help, but he repeated the process at Bergen Street, the next station, where again the first car lost not one of its population. And at Grand Army Plaza, he added to the headscratching process a few rare old Gaelic words that had passed down from father to son for hundreds of years. They ionized the surrounding atmosphere, but otherwise did not affect the situation.

At Eastern Parkway, Cullen tried an experiment. He carefully refrained from opening the first car's doors at all. He leaned forward eagerly, twisted his head and watched—and was treated to nothing short of a miracle. The New York subway rider is neither shy, meek, nor modest, and doors that do not open immediately or sooner are helped on their way by sundry kicks. But this time there was not a kick, not a shriek, not even a modified yell. Cullen's eyes popped.

He was getting angry. At Franklin Avenue, where he again contacted the Express, he flung open the doors and swore at the crowd. Every door spouted commuters of both sexes and all ages, except that terrible first car. At those doors, three men and a very young girl got on, though Cullen could plainly see the slight bulging of the walls that the already supercrowded condition of the car had caused.

For the rest of the trip to Flatbush Avenue, Cullen ignored the first car completely, concentrating on that last stop where everyone would *have* to get off. Everyone! President, Church, and Beverly Road were visited and passed, and Cullen found himself counting the stations to the Flatbush terminus.

They seemed like such a nice bunch of passengers, too. They read their newspapers, stared into the whirling blackness out the window, or at the girl's legs across the way, or at nothing at all, quite like ordinary people. Only, they didn't want to get out. They didn't even want to get into the next car, where empty seats filled the place. Imagine New Yorkers resisting the impulse to pass from one car to the other, and missing the chance to leave the doors open for the benefit of the draft.

But it was Flatbush Avenue! Cullen rubbed his hands, slammed the doors open and yelled in his best unintelligible manner, "Lasstop!" He repeated it two or three times hoarsely and several in that damned first car looked up at him. There was reproach in their eyes. Have you never heard of the Mayor's anti-noise campaign, they seemed to say.

The last other passenger had come out of the train, and the scattered new ones were coming in. There were a few curious looks at the jammed car, but not too many. The New Yorker considers everything he cannot understand a publicity stunt.

Cullen fell back on his Gaelic once more and dashed up the platform toward the motorman's booth. He needed moral assistance. The motorman should have been out of his cab, preparing for his next trip, but he wasn't. Cullen could see him through the glass of the door, leaning on the controls and staring vacantly at the bumper-stop ahead.

"Gus!" cried Cullen. "Come out! There's a hell of—"

At this point, his tongue skidded to a halt, because it wasn't Gus. It was a little old man, who smiled politely and twiddled his fingers in greeting.

Patrick Cullen's Irish soul rebelled. With a yelp, he grabbed the edge of the door and tried to shove it open. He should have known that wouldn't work. So, taking a deep breath and commending said Irish soul to God, he made for the open door and ploughed into the mass of haunted humans in that first car. Momentum carried him six feet, and then there he stuck. Behind him, those he had knocked down picked themselves up from the laps of their fellow-travelers, apologized with true New York courtesy (consisting of a growl, a grunt, and a grimace) and returned to their papers.

Then, caught helplessly, he heard the Dispatcher's bell. It was time for his own train to be on its way. Duty called! With a superhuman effort, he inched towards the door, but it closed before he could get there, and the train commenced to move.

It occurred to Cullen that he had missed a report for the first time, and he said, "Damn!" After the train had travelled some fifty feet, it came to him that they were going the wrong way, and this time he said nothing.

After all, what was there to say—even in the purest of Gaelic.

How *could* a train go the wrong way at Flatbush Ave. There were no further tracks. There was no further tunnel. There was a bumper-stop to prevent eccentric motormen from trying to bore one. It was absurd. Even the Big Deal couldn't do it.

But there they were!

There were stations in this new tunnel, too—cute little small ones just large enough for one car. But that was all right, because only one car was travelling. The rest had somehow become detached, presumably to make the routine trip to Bronx Park.

There were maybe a dozen stations on the line—with curious names. Cullen noticed only a few, because he found it difficult to keep his eyes from going out of focus. One was Archangel Boulevard; another Seraph Road; still another Cherub Plaza.

And then, the train slid into a monster station, that looked uncommonly like a cave, and stopped. It was huge, about three hundred feet deep, and almost spherical. The tracks ran to the exact center, without trusses, and the platform at its side likewise rested comfortably upon air.

The conductor was the only person left in the car, the rest having mostly gotten off at Hosannah Square. He hung limply from the porcelain hand-grip, staring fixedly at a lipstick advertisement. The door of the motorman's cabin opened and the little man came out. He glanced at Cullen, turned away, then whirled back.

"Hey," he said, "who are you?"

Cullen rotated slowly, still clutching the hand-grip. "Only the conductor. Don't mind me. I'm quitting anyway. I don't like the work."

"Oh, dear, dear, this is unexpected." The little man waggled his head and tch-tched. "I'm Mr. Crumley," he explained. "I steal things. People mostly. Sometimes subway cars—but they're such big, clumsy things, don't you think?"

"Mister," groaned Cullen. "I quit thinking two hours ago. It didn't get me anywhere. Who are you, anyway?"

"I told you—I'm Mr. Crumley. I'm practicing to be a god."

"A gob?" said Cullen. "You mean a sailor?"

"Dear, no," frowned Mr. Crumley. "I said, 'god,' as in Jehovah. Look!" He pointed out the window to the wall of the cave. Where his finger pointed, the rock billowed and rose. He moved his finger and there was a neat ridge of rock describing a reversed, lower case "h."

"That's my symbol," said Crumley modestly. "Mystic, isn't it? But that's nothing. Wait till I really get things organized. Dear, dear, will I give them miracles!"

Cullen's head swivelled between the raised-rock symbol and the simpering Mr. Crumley, until he began to get dizzy, and then he stopped.

"Listen," he demanded hoarsely. "How did you get that car out of Flatbush Avenue? Where did that tunnel come from? Are some of them foreigners—"

"Oh, my, no!" answered Mr. Crumley. "I made that myself and willed it so that no one would notice. It was quite difficult. It just wears the ectoplasm right out of me. Miracles with people mixed up in it are much harder than the other kind, because you have to fight their wills. Unless you have lots of Believers, you can't do it. Now that I've got over a hundred thousand, I can do it, but there was a time," he shook his head reminiscently, "when I couldn't even have levitated a baby—or healed a leper. Oh, well, we're wasting time. We ought to be at the nearest factory."

Cullen brightened. Factory was more prosaic. "I once had a brother," he said, "who worked in a sweater factory, but—"

"Oh, goodness, Mr. Cullen. I'm referring to my Believers' Factories. I have to educate people to believe in me, don't I, and preaching is such slow work. I believe in mass production. Some day I intend to be called the Henry Ford of Utopia. Why, I've got twelve

Factories in Brooklyn alone and when I manufacture enough Believers, I'll just cover the world with them."

He sighed, "Gracious me, if I only had enough Believers. I've got to have a million before I can let things progress by themselves and until then I have to attend to every little detail myself. It is so boring! I even have to keep reminding my Believers who I am—even the Disciples. Incidentally, Cullen—I read your mind, by the way, so that's how I know your name—you want to be a Believer, of course."

"Well, now," said Cullen nervously.

"Oh, come now. *Some* gods would have been angry at your intrusion and done away with you," he snapped his fingers, "like that. Not I, though, because I think killing people is messy and inconsiderate. Just the same, you'll have to be a Believer."

Now Patrick Cullen was an intelligent Irishman. That is to say, he admitted the existence of banshees, leprechauns, and the Little Folk, and kept an open mind on poltergeists, werewolves, vampires and such-like foreign trash. At mere supernaturalities, he was too well-educated to sneer. Still, Cullen did not intend to compromise his religion. His theology was weak, but for a mortal to claim godship smacked of heresy, not to say sacrilege and blasphemy, even to him.

"You're a faker," he cried boldly, "and you're headed straight for Hell the way you're going."

Mr. Crumley clicked his tongue, "What terrible language you use. And so unnecessary! Of course you Believe in me."

"Oh, yeah?"

"Well, then, if you are stubborn, I'll pass a minor miracle. It's inconvenient, but now," he made vague motions with his left hand, "you Believe in me."

"Certainly," said Cullen, hurt. "I always did. How do I go about worshipping you? I want to do this properly."

"Just Believe in me, and that's enough. Now you must go to the factories and then we'll send you back home—they'll never know you were gone—and you can live your life like a Believer."

The conductor smiled ecstatically, "Oh, happy life! I *want* to go to the factories."

"Of course you would," replied Mr. Crumley. "You'd be a fine Crumleyite otherwise, wouldn't you? Come!" He pointed at the door of the car, and the door slid open. They walked out and Crumley kept on pointing. Rock faded away in front, and bit down again behind. Through the wall Cullen walked, following that little figure who was his god.

That *was* a god, thought Cullen. Any god that could do that was one hell of a damn good god to believe in.

And then he was at the factory—in another cave, only smaller. Mr. Crumley seemed to like caves.

Cullen didn't pay much attention to his surroundings. He couldn't see much anyway on account of the faint violet mist that blurred his vision. He got the impression of a slowly moving conveyor belt, with men stationed at intervals along it. Disciples, he thought. And the parts being machined on that belt were probably non-Believers, or such low trash.

There was a man watching him, smiling. A Disciple, Cullen thought, and quite naturally made the sign to him. He had never made it before, but it was easy. The Disciple replied in kind.

"He told me you were coming," said the Disciple. "He made a special miracle for you, he said. That's quite a distinction. Do you want me to show you around the belt?"

"You bet."

"Well, this is Factory One. It's the nerve center of all the factories of the country. The others give preliminary treatment only; and make only Believers. *We* make Disciples."

Oh, boy, Disciples! "Am I going to be a Disciple?" asked Cullen eagerly.

"After being miraculated by *him*, of course! You're a *somebody*, you know. There are only five other people he ever took personal charge of."

This was a glorious way to do things. Everything Mr. Crumley did was glorious. What a god! What a god!

"You started that way, too."

"Certainly," said the Disciple, placidly, "I'm an important fellow, too. Only I wish I were more important, even."

"What for?" said Cullen, in a shocked tone of voice. "Are you murmuring against the dictates of Mr. Crumley? (may he prosper). This is sacrilege."

The Disciple shifted uncomfortably, "Well, I've got ideas, and I'd like to try them out."

"You've got ideas, huh?" muttered Cullen balefully. "Does Mr. Crumley (may he live forever) know?"

"Well—frankly, no! But just the same," the Disciple looked over each shoulder carefully and drew closer, "I'm not the only one. There are lots of us that think Mr. Crumley (on whom be blessings) is just a trifle old-fashioned. For instance, take the lights in this place."

Cullen stared upwards. The lights were the same type as those in the terminal-cave. They might have been stolen from any line of the IRT subway. Perfect copies of the stop-and-go signals and the exit markers.

"What's wrong?" he asked.

The Disciple sneered, "They lack originality. You'd think a grade A god would do something new. When he takes people, he does it through the subway, and he obeys subway rules. He waits for the Dispatcher to tell him to go; he stops at every station; he uses crude electricity and so on. What we need," the Disciple was waving his hands wildly and shouting, "is more enterprise, more git-and-go. We've got to speed up things and run them with efficiency and vim."

Cullen stared hotly, "You are a heretic," he accused. "You are doomed to damnation." He looked angrily about for a bell, whistle, gong, or drum wherewith to summon the great Crumley, but found nothing.

The other blinked in quick thought. "Say," he said, bluffly, "look at what time it is. I'm behind schedule. You better get on the belt for your first treatment."

Cullen was hot about the slovenly assistance Mr. Crumley was getting from this inferior Disciple, but a treatment is a treatment, so making the sign devoutly, he got on. He found it fairly comfortable despite its jerky motion. The Disciple motioned to Cullen's first preceptor—another Disciple—standing beside a sort of blackboard. Cullen had watched others while discussing Crumley and he had noticed the question and answer procedure that had taken place. He had noticed it particularly.

Consequently, he was surprised, when the second Disciple, instead of using his heavy pointer to indicate a question on the board, reversed it and brought it down upon his head.

The lights went out!

When he came to, he was under the belt, at the very bottom of the cave. He was tied up, and the Rebellious Disciple and three others were talking about him.

"He couldn't be persuaded," the Disciple was saying. "Crumley must have given him a double treatment or something."

"It's the last double treatment Crumley'll ever give," said the fat little man.

"Let's hope so. How's it coming?"

"Very well. Very well, indeed. We teleported ourselves to Section Four about two hours ago. It was a perfect miracle."

The Disciple was pleased. "Fine! How're they doing at Four?"

The fat little man clucked his lips. "Well, now, not so hot. For some reason, they're getting odd effects over there. Miracles are just happening. Even ordinary Crumleyites can pass them, and sometimes they—just happen. It's extremely annoying."

"Hmm, that's bad. If there are too many hitches, Crumley'll get suspicious. If he investigates there first, he can reconvert all of them in a jiffy, before he comes here and then without their support we might not be strong enough to stand up against him."

"Say, now," said the fat man apprehensively, "we're not strong enough *now*, you know. None of this going off half-cocked."

"We're strong enough," pointed out the Disciple stiffly, "to weaken him long enough to get us a new god started, and after that—"

"A new god, eh?" said another. He nodded wisely.

"Sure," said the Disciple. "A new god, created by us, can be destroyed by us. He'd be completely under our thumb and then instead of this one-man tyranny, we can have a sort of—er—council."

There were general grins and everyone looked pleased.

"But we'll discuss that further some other time," continued the Disciple briskly. "Let's Believe just a bit. Crumley isn't stupid, you know, and we don't want him to observe any slackening. Come on, now. All together."

They closed their eyes, concentrated a bit, and then opened them with a sigh.

"Well," said the little fat man, *"that's* over. I'd better be getting back now."

From under the belt, Cullen watched him. He looked singularly like a chicken about to take off for a tree as he flexed his knees and stared upwards. Then he added to the resemblance not a little when he spread his arms, gave a little hop and fluttered away.

Cullen could follow his flight only by watching the eyes of the three remaining. Those eyes turned up and up, following the fat man to the very top of the cave, it seemed. There was an air of self-satisfaction about those eyes. They were very happy over their miracles.

Then they all went away and left Cullen to his holy indignation. He was shocked to the very core of his being at this sinful rebellion, this apostasy—this—this— There weren't any words for it, even when he tried Gaelic.

Imagine trying to create a god that would be under the thumbs of the creators. It was anthropomorphic heresy (where had he heard that word, now?) and struck at the roots of all religion. Was he going to lie there and watch anything strike at the roots of all religion? Was he going to submit to having Mr. Crumley (may he swim through seas of ecstasy) deposed?

Never!

But the ropes thought otherwise, so there he stayed.

And then there was an interruption in his thoughts. There came a low, booming sound—a sound which would have been a voice if it had not been pitched so incredibly low. There was a menace to it that got immediate attention. It got attention from Cullen, who quivered in his bonds; from the others in the cave, who quivered even harder, not being restrained by ropes; from the belt itself, which stopped dead with a jerk, and quivered mightily.

The Rebellious Disciple dropped to his knees and quivered more than any of them.

The voice came again, this time in a recognizable language, "WHERE IS THAT BUM, CRUMLEY?" it roared.

There was no wait for an answer. A cloud of shadow gathered in the center of the hall and spat a black bolt at the belt. A spot of fire leaped out from where the bolt had touched and spread slowly outward. Where it passed, the belt ceased to exist. It was far from Cullen, but there were humans nearer, and among those scurrying pandemonium existed.

Cullen wanted very much to join the flight, but unfortunately the Disciple who had trussed him up had evidently been a Boy Scout. Jerking, twisting, and writhing had no effect upon the stubborn ropes, so he fell back upon Gaelic and wishing. He wished he were free. He wished he weren't tied. He wished he were far away from that devouring flame. He wished lots of things, some unprintable, but mainly those.

And with that he felt a gentle slipping pressure and down at his feet was an untidy pile of hempen fibre. Evidently the forces liberated by the rebellion were getting out of control here as well as in Section Four. What had the little fat man said? "Miracles are just happening. Even ordinary Crumleyites can pass them, and sometimes they—just happen."

But why waste time? He ran to the rock wall and howled a wish at it to dissolve into nothing. He howled several times, with Gaelic modifications, but the wall didn't even slightly soften. He stared wildly and then saw the hole. It was on the side of the cave, diametrically across from Cullen's position at the bottom of the hall, and about three loops of the belt up. The upward spiral passed just below it.

Somehow he made the leap that grabbed the lower lip of the spiral, wriggled his way onto it and jumped into a run. The fire of disintegration was behind him and plenty far away, but it was making time. Up the belt to the third loop he ran, not taking time to be dizzy from the circular trip. But when he got there, the hole, large, black and inviting, was just the tiniest bit higher than he could jump.

He leaned against the wall panting. The spot of fire was now two spots, crawling both ways from a twenty foot break in the belt. Everyone in the cavern, some two hundred people, was in motion, and everyone made some sort of noise.

Somehow, the sight stimulated him. It nerved him to further efforts to get into the hole. Wildly, he tried walking up the sheer wall, but this didn't work.

And then Mr. Crumley stuck his head out of the hole and said, "Oh, mercy me, what a perfectly terrible mess. Dear, dear! Come up here, Cullen! Why do you stay down there!"

A great peace descended upon Cullen. "Hail, Mr. Crumley," he cried. "May you sniff the essence of roses forever."

Mr. Crumley looked pleased, "Thank you, Cullen." He waved his hand, and the conductor was beside him—a simple matter of levitation. Once again, Cullen decided in his inmost soul that here was a *god*.

"And now," said Mr. Crumley, "we must hurry, hurry, hurry. I've lost most of my power when the Disciples rebelled, and my subway car is stuck half-way. I'll need your help. Hurry!"

Cullen had no time to admire the tiny subway at the end of the tunnel. He jumped off the platform on Crumley's heels and dashed about a hundred feet down the tube to where the car was standing idle. He wafted into the open front door with the grace of a chorusboy. Mr. Crumley took care of that.

"Cullen," said Mr. Crumley, "start this thing and take it back to the regular line. And be careful; *he* is waiting for me."

"Who?"

"He, the new god. Imagine those fools—no, idiots—thinking they could create a controllable god, when the very essence of godship is uncontrollability. Of course, when they made a god to destroy me, they made a Destroyer, and he'll just destroy everything in sight that I created, including my Disciples."

Cullen worked quickly. He knew how to start car 30990; any conductor would. He raced to the other end of the car for the control lever, snatched it off, and returned at top speed. That was all he needed. There was power in the rail; the lights were on; and there were no stop signals between him and God's Country.

Mr. Crumley lay himself down on a seat, "Be very quiet. *He* may let you get past him. I'm going to blank myself out, and maybe he won't notice me. At any rate, he won't harm you—I *hope*. Dear, dear, since this all started in section four, things are *such* a mess."

Eight stations passed before anything happened and then came Utopia Circle station and—well, nothing really *happened*. It was just an impression—an impression of people all around him for a few seconds watching him closely with a virulent hostility. It wasn't exactly people, but a person. It wasn't exactly a person either, but just a huge eye, watching—watching—watching.

But it passed, and almost immediately Cullen saw a black and white "Flatbush Avenue" sign at the side of the tunnel. He jammed on his brakes in a hurry, for there was a train waiting there. But the controls didn't work the way they should have, and the car edged up until it was in contact with the cars before. With a soft click, it coupled and 30990 was just the last car of the train.

It was Mr. Crumley's work, of course. Mr. Crumley stood behind him, watching. "He didn't get you, did he? No—I see he didn't."

"Is there any more danger?" asked Cullen, anxiously.

"I don't think so," responded Mr. Crumley sadly. "After he has destroyed all my creation, there will be nothing left for him to destroy, and, deprived of a function, he will simply cease to exist. That's the result of this nasty, slipshod work. I'm disgusted with human beings."

"Don't say that," said Cullen.

"I will," reported Mr. Crumley savagely, "Human beings aren't fit to be god of. They're too much trouble and worry. It would give any self-respecting god grey hairs and I suppose you think a god looks very dignified all grey. Darn all humans! They can get along without me. From now on, I'm going to go to Africa and try the chimpanzees. I'll bet they make *much* better material."

"But wait," wailed Cullen. "What about me? I *believe* in you."

"Oh, dear, that would never do. Here! Return to normal."

Mr. Crumley's hand caressed the air, and Cullen, once more a God-fearing Irishman, let loose a roar in the purest Gaelic and made for him.

"Why, you blaspheming spalpeen—"

But there was no Mr. Crumley. There was only the Dispatcher, asking very impolitely—in English—what the blankety-blank hell was the matter with him.

RAY BRADBURY

The Poems

In 1958, while visiting relatives in California, my mother sought out my favorite writer, RAY BRADBURY, and had him autograph my treasured copy of his out-of-print short story collection, Dark Carnival. *After asking a few questions about me, Ray told my mother that someday I would be a writer, which seemed an astonishing prediction since at that time I had no such ambition. Now that I'm older and have taught many fledgling writers, I think I understand why he thought so. Thanks, Ray . . . though we "wear our rue with a difference." The following story was first published in the January 1945 issue of* Weird Tales, *but for some reason, Ray did not include it in* Dark Carnival *nor any of his subsequent collections. I am honoured, therefore, to offer this remarkable Bradbury fantasy for the first time in nearly fifty years!*

It started out to be just another poem. And then David began sweating over it, stalking the rooms, talking to himself more than ever before in the long, poorly-paid years. So intent was he upon the poem's facets that Lisa felt forgotten, left out, put away until such time as he finished writing and could notice her again.

Then, finally—the poem was completed.

With the ink still wet upon an old envelope's back, he gave it to her with trembling fingers, his eyes red-rimmed and shining with a hot, inspired light. And she read it.

"David—" she murmured. Her hand began to shake in sympathy with his.

"It's *good*, isn't it?" he cried. "Damn good!"

The cottage whirled around Lisa in a wooden torrent. Gazing at the paper she experienced sensations as if words were melting, flowing into animate things. The paper was a square, brilliantly sunlit casement through which one might lean into another and brighter amber land! Her mind swung pendulum-wise. She had to clutch, crying out fearfully, at the ledges of this incredible window to support herself from being flung headlong into three-dimensional impossibility!

"David, how strange and wonderful and—*frightening.*"

It was as if she held a tube of light cupped in her hands, through which she could race into a vast space of singing and color and new sensation. Somehow, David had caught up, netted, skeined, imbedded reality, substance, atoms—mounting them upon paper with a simple imprisonment of ink!

He described the green, moist verdure of the dell, the eucalyptus trees and the birds flowing through their high, swaying branches. And the flowers cupping the propelled humming of bees.

"It *is* good, David. The very finest poem you've ever written!" She felt her heart beat swiftly with the idea and urge that came to her in the next moment. She felt that she must see the dell, to compare its quiet contents with those of this poem. She took David's arm. "Darling, let's walk down the road—now."

In high spirits, David agreed, and they set out together, from their lonely little house in the hills. Half down the road she changed her mind and wanted to retreat, but she brushed the thought aside with a move of her fine, thinly sculptured face. It seemed ominously dark for this time of day, down there toward the end of the path. She talked lightly to shield her apprehension:

"You've worked so hard, so long, to write the perfect poem. I knew you'd succeed some day. I guess this is it."

"Thanks to a patient wife," he said.

They rounded a bend of gigantic rock and twilight came as swiftly as a purple veil drawn down.

"David!"

In the unexpected dimness she clutched and found his arm and held to him. "What's happened? Is this the dell?"

"Yes, of course it is."

"But, it's so dark!"

"Well—yes—it is—" He sounded at a loss.

"The flowers are gone!"

"I saw them early this morning; they can't be gone!"

"You wrote about them in the poem. And where are the grape vines?"

"They *must* be here. It's only been an hour or more. It's too dark. Let's go back." He sounded afraid himself, peering into the uneven light.

"I can't find anything, David. The grass is gone, and the trees and bushes and vines, all gone!"

She cried it out, then stopped, and it fell upon them, the unnatural blank spaced silence, a vague timelessness, windlessness, a vacuumed sucked out feeling that oppressed and panicked them.

He swore softly and there was no echo. "It's too dark to tell now. It'll all be here tomorrow."

"But what if it *never* comes back?" She began to shiver.

"What are you raving about?"

She held the poem out. It glowed quietly with a steady pure yellow shining, like a small niche in which a candle steadily lived.

"You've written the perfect poem. Too perfect. That's what you've done." She heard herself talking, tonelessly, far away.

She read the poem again. And a coldness moved through her.

"The dell is here. Reading this is like opening a gate upon a path and walking knee-high in grass, smelling blue grapes, hearing bees in yellow transits on the air, and the wind carrying birds upon it. The paper dissolves into things, sun, water, colors and life. It's not symbols or reading any more, it's LIVING!"

"No," he said. "You're wrong. It's crazy."

They ran up the path together. A wind came to meet them after they were free of the lightless vacuum behind them.

In their small, meagerly furnished cottage they sat at the window, staring down at the dell. All around was the unchanged light of mid-afternoon. Not dimmed or diffused or silent as down in the cup of rocks.

"It's not true. Poems don't work that way," he said.

"Words are symbols. They conjure up images in the mind."

"Have I done more than that?" he demanded. "And how did I do it, I ask you?" He rattled the paper, scowling intently at each line. "Have I made more than symbols with a form of matter and energy? Have I compressed, concentrated, dehydrated life? Does matter pass into and through my mind, like light through a magnifying glass to be focused into one narrow, magnificent blazing apex of fire? Can I etch life, burn it onto paper, with that flame? Gods in heaven, I'm going mad with thought!"

A wind circled the house.

"If we are not crazy, the two of us," said Lisa, stiffening at the sound of the wind, "there is one way to prove our suspicions."

"How?"

"Cage the wind."

"Cage it? Bar it up? Build a mortar of ink around it?"

She nodded.

"No, I won't fool myself." He jerked his head. Wetting his lips, he sat for a long while. Then, cursing at his own curiosity, he walked to the table and fumbled self-consciously with pen and ink. He looked at her, then at the windy light outside. Dipping his pen, he flowed it out onto paper in regular dark miracles.

Instantly, the wind vanished.

"The wind," he said. "It's caged. The ink is dry."

Over his shoulder she read it, became immersed in its cool heady current, smelling far oceans tainted on it, odors of distant wheat acres and green corn and the sharp brick and cement smell of cities far away.

David stood up so quickly the chair fell back like an old thin woman. Like a blind man he walked down the hill toward the dell, not turning, even when Lisa called after him, frantically.

When he returned he was by turns hysterical and immensely calm. He collapsed in a chair. By night, he was smoking his pipe, eyes closed, talking on and on, as calmly as possible.

"I've got power now no man ever had. I don't know its extensions, its boundaries or its governing limits. Somewhere, the enchantment ends. Oh, my god, Lisa, you should see what I've done to that dell. It's gone, all gone, stripped to the very raw primordial bones of its former self. And the beauty is here!" He opened his eyes and stared at the poem, as at the Holy Grail. "Captured forever, a few bars of midnight ink on paper! I'll be the greatest poet in history! I've always dreamed of that."

"I'm afraid, David. Let's tear up the poems and get away from here!"

"Move away? Now?"

"It's dangerous. What if your power extends beyond the valley?"

His eyes shone fiercely. "Then I can destroy the universe and immortalize it at one and the same instant. It's in the power of a sonnet, if I choose to write it."

"But you *won't* write it, promise me, David?"

He seemed not to hear her. He seemed to be listening to a cosmic music, a movement of bird wings very high and clear. He seemed to be wondering how long this land had waited here, for centuries perhaps, waiting for a poet to come and drink of its power. This valley seemed like the center of the universe, now.

"It would be a magnificent poem," he said, thoughtfully. "The most magnificent poem ever written, shamming Keats and Shelley and Browning and all the rest. A poem about the universe. But no." He shook his head sadly. "I guess I won't ever write that poem."

Breathless, Lisa waited in the long silence.

Another wind came from across the world to replace the one newly imprisoned. She let out her breath, at ease.

"For a moment I was afraid you'd overstepped the boundary and taken in all the winds of the earth. It's all right now."

"All right, hell," he cried, happily. "It's marvelous!"

And he caught hold of her, and kissed her again and again.

Fifty poems were written in fifty days. Poems about a rock, a stem, a blossom, a pebble, an ant, a dropped feather, a raindrop, an avalanche, a dried skull, a dropped key, a fingernail, a shattered light bulb.

Recognition came upon him like a rain shower. The poems were bought and read across the world. Critics referred to the masterpieces as "—chunks of amber in which are caught whole portions of life and living—" "—each poem a window looking out upon the world—"

He was suddenly a very famous man. It took him many days to believe it. When he saw his name on the printed books he didn't believe it, and said so. And when he read the critics columns he didn't believe them either.

Then it began to make a flame inside him, growing up, climbing and consuming his body and legs and arms and face.

Amidst the sound and glory, she pressed her cheek to his and whispered:

"This is your perfect hour. When will there ever be a more perfect time than this? Never again."

He showed her the letters as they arrived.

"See? This letter. From New York." He blinked rapidly and couldn't sit still. "They want me to write more poems. Thousands more. Look at this letter. Here." He gave it to her. "That editor says that if I can write so fine and great about a pebble or a drop of water, think what I can do when I—well experiment with real life. Real life. Nothing big. An amoeba perhaps. Or, well, just this morning, I saw a bird—"

"A bird?" She stiffened and waited for him to answer.

"Yes, a hummingbird—hovering, settling, rising—"

"You didn't . . . ?"

"Why NOT? Only a bird. One bird out of a billion," he said self-consciously. "One little bird, one little poem. You can't deny me that."

"One amoeba," she repeated, tonelessly. "And then next it will be one dog, one man, one city, one continent, one universe!"

"Nonsense." His cheek twitched. He paced the room, fingering back his dark hair. "You dramatize things. Well, after all, what's one dog, even, or to go one step further, one man?"

She sighed. "It's the very thing you talked of with fear, the danger we spoke of that first time we knew your power. Remember, David, it's not really yours, it was only an accident our coming here to the valley house—"

He swore softly. "Who cares whether it was accident or Fate? The thing that counts is that I'm here, now, and they're—they're—" He paused, flushing.

"They're what?" she prompted.

"They're calling me the greatest poet who ever lived!"

"It'll ruin you."

"Let it ruin me, then! Let's have silence, now."

He stalked into his den and sat restlessly studying the dirt road. While in this mood, he saw a small brown dog come patting along the road, raising little dust-tufts behind.

"And a damn good poet I am," he whispered angrily, taking out pen and paper. He scratched out four lines swiftly.

The dog's barking came in even shrill intervals upon the air as it circled a tree and bounded a green bush. Quite unexpectedly, half over one leap across a vine, the barking ceased, and the dog fell apart in the air, inch by inch, and vanished.

Locked in his den, he composed at a furious pace, counting pebbles in the garden and changing them to stars simply by giving them mention, immortalizing clouds, hornets, bees, lightning and thunder with a few pen flourishes.

It was inevitable that some of his more secret poems should be stumbled upon and read by his wife.

Coming home from a long afternoon walk he found her with the poems lying all unfolded upon her lap.

"David," she demanded. "What does this mean?" She was very cold and shaken by it. "This poem. First a dog. Then a cat, some sheep and—finally—a man!"

He seized the papers from her. "So what!" Sliding them in a drawer, he slammed it, violently. "He was just an old man, they were old sheep, and it was a microbe-infested terrier! The world breathes better without them!"

"But here, THIS poem, too." She held it straight out before her, eyes widened. "A woman. Three children from Charlottesville!"

"All right, so you don't like it!" he said, furiously. "An artist has to experiment. With everything! I can't just stand still and do the same thing over and over. I've got greater plans than you think. Yes, really good, fine plans. I've decided to write about everything. I'll dissect the heavens if I wish, rip down the worlds, toy with suns if I damn please!"

"David," she said, shocked.

"Well, I will! I will!"

"You're such a child, David. I should have known. If this goes on, I can't stay here with you."

"You'll have to stay," he said.

"What do you mean?"

He didn't know what he meant himself. He looked around, helplessly and then declared, "I mean. I mean—if you try to go all I have to do is sit at my desk and describe you in ink . . ."

"You . . ." she said, dazedly.

She began to cry. Very silently, with no noise, her shoulders moved, as she sank down on a chair.

"I'm sorry," he said, lamely, hating the scene. "I didn't mean to say that, Lisa. Forgive me." He came and laid a hand upon her quivering body.

"I won't leave you," she said, finally.

And closing her eyes, she began to think.

It was much later in the day when she returned from a shopping trip to town with bulging grocery sacks and a large gleaming bottle of champagne.

David looked at it and laughed aloud. "Celebrating, are we?"

"Yes," she said, giving him the bottle and an opener. "Celebrating you as the world's greatest poet!"

"I detect sarcasm, Lisa," he said, pouring drinks. "Here's a toast to the—the universe." He drank. "Good stuff." He pointed at hers. "Drink up. What's wrong?" Her eyes looked wet and sad about something.

She refilled his glass and lifted her own. "May we always be together. Always."

The room tilted. "It's hitting me," he observed very seriously, sitting down so as not to fall. "On an empty stomach I drank. Oh, Lord!"

He sat for ten minutes while she refilled his glass. She seemed very happy suddenly, for no reason. He sat scowling, thinking, looking at his pen and ink and paper, trying to make a decision. "Lisa?"

"Yes?" She was now preparing supper, singing.

"I feel in a mood. I have been considering all afternoon and—"

"And what, darling?"

"I am going to write the greatest poem in history—NOW!"

She felt her heart flutter.

"Will your poem be about the valley?"

He smirked. "No. No! Bigger than that. Much bigger!"

"I'm afraid I'm not much good at guessing," she confessed.

"Simple," he said, gulping another drink of champagne. Nice of her to think of buying it, it stimulated his thoughts. He held up his pen and dipped it in ink. "I shall write my poem about the universe! Let me see now . . ."

"David!"

He winced. "What?"

"Oh, nothing. Just, have some more champagne, darling."

"Eh?" He blinked fuzzily. "Don't mind if I do. Pour."

She sat beside him, trying to be casual.

"Tell me again. What is it you'll write?"

"About the universe, the stars, the epileptic shamblings of comets, the blind black seekings of meteors, the heated embraces and spawnings of giant suns, the cold, graceful excursions of polar planets, asteroids plummeting like paramecium under a gigantic microscope, all and everything and anything my mind lays claim to! Earth, sun, stars!" he exclaimed.

"No!" she said, but caught herself. "I mean, darling, don't do it all at once. One thing at a time—"

"One at a time." He made a face. "That's the way I've been doing things and I'm tied to dandelions and daisies."

He wrote upon the paper with the pen.

"What're you doing?" she demanded, catching his elbow.

"Let me alone!" He shook her off.

She saw the black words form:

"Illimitable universe, with stars and planets and suns—"

She must have screamed.

"No, David, cross it out, before it's too late. Stop it!"

He gazed at her as through a long dark tube, and her far away at the other end, echoing. "Cross it out?" he said. "Why, it's GOOD poetry! Not a line will I cross out. I want to be a GOOD poet!"

She fell across him, groping, finding the pen. With one instantaneous slash, she wiped out the words.

"Before the ink dries, before it dries!"

"Fool!" he shouted. "Let me alone!"

She ran to the window. The first evening stars were still there, and the crescent moon. She sobbed with relief. She swung about to face him and walked toward him. "I want to help you write your poem—"

"Don't need your help!"

"Are you blind? Do you realize the power of your pen!"

To distract him, she poured more champagne, which he welcomed and drank. "Ah," he sighed, dizzily. "My head spins."

But it didn't stop him from writing, and write he did, starting again on a new sheet of paper:

"UNIVERSE—VAST UNIVERSE—BILLION STARRED AND WIDE—"

She snatched frantically at shreds of things to say, things to stave off his writing.

"That's poor poetry," she said.

"What do you mean 'poor'?" he wanted to know, writing.

"You've got to start at the beginning and build up," she explained logically. "Like a watch spring being wound or the universe starting with a molecule building on up through stars into a stellar cartwheel—"

He slowed his writing and scowled with thought.

She hurried on, seeing this. "You see, darling, you've let emotion run off with you. You can't start with the big things. Put them at the end of your poem. Build to a climax!"

The ink was drying. She stared at it as it dried. In another sixty seconds—

He stopped writing. "Maybe you're right. Just maybe you are." He put aside the pen a moment.

"I know I'm right," she said, lightly, laughing. "Here. I'll just take the pen and—there—"

She had expected him to stop her, but he was holding his pale brow and looking pained with the ache in his eyes from the drink.

She drew a bold line through his poem. Her heart slowed.

"Now," she said, solicitously, "you take the pen, and I'll help you. Start out with small things and build, like an artist."

His eyes were gray-filmed. "Maybe you're right, maybe, maybe."

The wind howled outside.

"Catch the wind!" she cried, to give him a minor triumph to satisfy his ego. "Catch the wind!"

He stroked the pen. "Caught it!" he bellowed, drunkenly, weaving. "Caught the wind! Made a cage of ink!"

"Catch the flowers!" she commanded, excitedly. "Every one in the valley! And the grass!"

"There! Caught the flowers!"

"The hill next!" she said.

"The hill!"

"The valley!"

"The valley!"

"The sunlight, the odors, the trees, the shadows, the house and the garden, and the things inside the house!"

"Yes, yes, yes," he cried, going on and on and on.

And while he wrote quickly she said, "David, I love you. Forgive me for what I do next, darling—"

"What?" he asked, not having heard her.

"Nothing at all. Except that we are never satisfied and want to go on beyond proper limits. You tried to do that, David, and it was wrong."

He nodded over his work. She kissed him on the cheek. He reached up and patted her chin. "Know what, lady?"

"What?"

"I think I like you, yes, sir, I think I like you."

She shook him. "Don't go to sleep, David, don't."

"Want to sleep. Want to sleep."

"Later, darling. When you've finished your poem, your last great poem, the very finest one, David. Listen to me—"

He fumbled with the pen. "What'll I say?"

She smoothed his hair, touched his cheek with her fingers and kissed him, tremblingly. Then, closing her eyes, she began to dictate:

"There lived a fine man named David and his wife's name was Lisa and—"

The pen moved slowly, achingly, tiredly forming words.

"Yes?" he prompted.

"—and they lived in a house in the garden of Eden—"

He wrote again, tediously. She watched.

He raised his eyes. "Well? What's next?"

She looked at the house, and the night outside, and the wind returned to sing in her ears and she held his hands and kissed his sleepy lips.

"That's all," she said, "the ink is drying."

The publishers from New York visited the valley months later and went back to New York with only three pieces of paper they had found blowing in the wind around and about the raw, scarred, empty valley.

The publishers stared at one another, blankly:

"Why, why, there was nothing left at all," they said. "Just bare rock, not a sign of vegetation or humanity. The home he lived in— gone! The road, everything! *He* was gone! His wife, *she* was gone, too! Not a word out of them. It was like a river flood had washed through, scraping away the whole countryside! Gone! Washed out! And only three last poems to show for the whole thing!"

No further word was ever received from the poet or his wife. The Agricultural College experts traveled hundreds of miles to study the starkly denuded valley, and went away shaking their heads and looking pale.

But it is all simply found again.

You turn the pages of his last small thin book and read the three poems.

She is there, pale and beautiful and immortal; you smell the sweet warm flash of her, young forever, hair blowing golden upon the wind.

And next to her, upon the opposite page, he stands gaunt, smiling, firm, hair like raven's hair, hands on hips, face raised to look about him.

And on all sides of them, green with an immortal green, under a sapphire sky, with the odor of fat wine-grapes, with the grass knee-high and bending to touch of exploring feet, with the trails waiting for any reader who takes them, one finds the valley, and the house, and the deep rich peace of sunlight and of moonlight and many stars, and the two of them, he and she, walking through it all, laughing together, forever and forever.

PATRICK LoBRUTTO

Vision Quest

PATRICK LoBRUTTO *was recently named Best Editor in the coveted World Fantasy Awards, and about time, too! One of my closest friends, Pat, who cofounded the Foundation science-fiction imprint, was for many years the head of Doubleday's trade science-fiction department (as well as their Western line). He edited* The Masters of Solitude *and* Wintermind, *"cult classics" I wrote in collaboration with Parke Godwin, as well as the novelized editions of my "Incredible Umbrella" stories. Now a publications editor with the American Association of Advertising Agencies, Pat, like me and Parke, is both an iconoclast and a Laurel and Hardy enthusiast. Believe it or not, these tendencies surface in the next wacky adventure, which its author claims is partly based on fact. Honest!*

Solomon Gunya was from one of those wild warrior tribes out there in the Southwest. Great sky-scrapper, sky-walkers, and horseplayers they were and baptized to the magic with the Drink, too.

Mom, Dad, teachers, and friends in San Kelton, Texas, thought of him as just good ole Solly the Boy. He was a hot outfielder with a rocket arm just like Joltinjoe, and he had a great social life. He lived with his folks and grandfolks in one of those finer double-wide mobile condos within easy commuting distance of everything. He did real fine in school, and one day, everyone knew, he would have Stuff. He wasn't too different from you, or me, even. He did have dreams, though, BIG dreams. Solly wanted more Stuff than his parents had, he wanted people to know he had more Stuff than his parents had; Solly wanted to stop being the Boy; Solly needed to be a Real Man, a Bimac.

GrandMother and GrandFather came home from the University of SoSoCal just itching to use everything they learned about their Native American Heritage. They were ready to build—and live in—a wickiup right in Mother Nature's face. They were going to forecast troubled times and the hogs' futures. They were going back to Nature and Nature would never be the same.

Minute they got back from graduation they were waving their sheeps' skins in Solly's cute little face. They talked about the Land and the Spirits every chance they got, blue bouffants shaking in excitement. "Please pass the milk" could segue into how to dress a buffalo, or how to influence the weather. Solly was damned impressed. Solly never had a chance.

It was only a matter of time before he asked them what he'd been asking everyone since he learned to speak: "Who am I?"

"Since he's Lucky Seven, he's been asking that," said Mom. "What the hell does he mean?"

GrandMa and GrandPa ignored Mom and stared deep into each other's eyes. They looked at Sol and they knew they had them a volunteer.

"He's ready," said the old man.

"Ready for what?" Sol wanted to know.

"Vision Quest."

"That's right," said GrandMa. "You'll have to leave this world to learn how to live in it, dear heart. You can be the one to lead us back to the good old days, Solomon. Power and Wisdom can be yours. Now. Say your mantra, dear."

They quick filled him up with tales of derring done once upon a time, and especially the derring he could do right now.

Solomon the Boy was hooked, line and sincronzada.

Mom and Dad were too wrapped up in the here and now and cash flow to notice anything until it was too late.

Mom chewed on a cheroot and said, "This is all our fault, Ward. We never taught the Boy an alternative system of beliefs, and the time we spent on him wasn't of the right quality."

"Bullshitbullshitbullshit," he replied. "No one cares about that crap anymore. Our oldtimers have filled that boy with voodoo doodoo. *We've* given him every advantage." He scooped up the brunch dishes and tossed them into the sink, viciously stuffing them into the disposal piece by piece. "He's spoiled for sure by now."

Mom rolled the little cigar to the other side of her mouth, stood up, put a leg on the chair, smoothed her stocking, changed legs, did the same. She always did that when there was a problem; she said it helped her to think. She looked at her husband and said, "I'm going to talk to that boy, right away. This can't go on."

"I'll feed the Venus Flytrap while you do that, then meet you in ten minutes at the Exchange. Market in Djakarta should be open about now."

Well, they did great in the market that day. And Mom gave Sol whatfer—and GrandMa and GrandPa, too. She gave it to them a couple of few times, at that. Solly smiled and the two old ones nodded during each lecture. "Oh yeah! We'll be good. Oh yeah! We hear ya, Mom." Sol's parents were satisfied, they felt they nipped Lou n' Bud damnstraight. Unfortunately the market in fish went belly up soon after; Mom and Dad just didn't have the time to follow through. The Venus Flytrap died; Solly went back to the research with his two mentors. They hit the library and checked out a wad of tapes, books, and vids. They held meetings. They shook feathers in dusty corners. They did lunch.

Solly listened to GrandMa and GrandPa like it was Godspell. Before he knew it, he was about to put Childhood aside and go out and grab the Big Banana. And then, there he was at the final briefing—threeD blackboard and nice crisp khakis and whatall.

Now, all of us know that once upon a time there were some fairly strict rules about Vision Quests and such. Lots of folks followed those rules for quite a long while, too.

Things change.

Over a lot of time, rules have a way of getting confused. Somebody shoulda been watching that. Nobody was. Solomon's oldtimers shoulda been more thorough. They weren't. Sol shoulda stripped nekkid and gone weaponless into that good wilderness until Big Time Magic found him. . . . He went with shades, beanshorts, and hiking boots, a loaded Magnum, a condom, money, dried health food, a canteen full of fancy frogwater, a flashlight, and, what must have been the last straw for the Ancestors, a cap with the smiley face of Crazy Eddie, the Cleveland Indian, on the front for luck.

The Ancestors, let's be honest, were really pissed. "Gramma an Grampa fullashit," they said. "Solly the pivot man for this whole deal. How come we spend so much time makin' sure People's all in right place and we got fullashit Trojans teachin' pivot man bogus stuff? Whose job was this, anyway?" Everything blamed everybody else . . . and another long argument began on Olympus, and while that rages on—another story, altogether, from this one—the setup tried to work itself out. And Solly didn't even know he was the pivot person.

They drove out to the middle of the desert and let Sol out. "We'll do Vegas for a while and wait for you. After a week, we'll figure you're probably not coming back. But we'll wait around another week just to be sure." GrandPa wouldn't look him in the eye.

Sol looked out into the shimmering wasteland all around him.

GrandMa said, "Don't worry, dear, we'll come back here every day to look for you. We have every confidence that you can do it."

Gulp.

They all thought about Death for a while. Sol suddenly realized that it was miles to anything.

Pretty soon, his grandparents were wondering what was at the Feelies in the hotel. And they were gone.

Solomon couldn't stop thinking about the Grim Ripper. He watched their dust a long, long time.

Picture this: a shimmering wasteland with little food and less water glued to the anvil of the sun. Picture this: Solly using up his dried food and his water much faster than he thought possible. Picture this: the Boy stumbling around wildly. Picture this: Solly's head in a very weird place.

Even though he was out of food and water, Sol never let go of the sack. After all, it had his Stuff. He dragged it around behind him in the dirt and sand his feet plodding forward always forward and then he was pulling himself up up up. He stopped when he could go no higher.

By the time he got to the mountaintop, our Boy didn't know where the hell he was. He was dizzy and gasping and just hanging on . . . and wishing he'd never got involved in this foolishness in the first place.

"Who the hell is *he?*" asked the Raven.

"Fuck if I know," said the Snake.

"What did he say?" Solly asked.

"She said, who the fuck are you?" replied the Snake.

"Fuck if I know," Sol said giddily. "And I don't know where I am, either, or who you guys are."

"Well, what *do* you know, Boy?" Raven demanded.

"I'm on a quest!" shouted Sol. "I'm on a quest for knowledge and power, for strength and old injun wisdom. I'm gonna learn who I am, and then I'm gonna go back and ride right over anything gets in my way. I'm gonna get plenty of Stuff."

Snake and Raven looked at each other for a long moment. Then Snake whispered, "Topeka! I think he's the one." Raven rolled her eyes: "You always say that. Look at him, he can't be the one. *Look* at him!"

Snake looked the Boy up and down. "Yeah, but," he said. "This *is* the Mountain at the center of the world. This *is* just the right time. He's certainly an empty enough vessel. And he *is* decked out for a vision quest . . . sort of." Raven just stared at our hero.

"Besides," Snake continued, "there ain't been anyone around here on a vision quest in ever so long. He's gotta be the one I tell ya!"

No one noticed the speck of dust rolling down the mountain at their feet.

No one noticed what looked like a speck of dust rolling down the mountain miles away across the valley floor.

Solomon had listened, swaying and blinking with his mouth open. He decided abruptly to gain control of the situation. He collapsed onto his backside, pulling his knapsack around. After rummaging for a minute, he pulled out the Magnum, thumbed the safety and waved at the two animals.

He stood and demanded, "I want some answers and I want 'em now. Are you two my Spirit Guides?" Silence. "Look, you gonna tell me what I need to know, or do I have to get tough?"

Raven sniffed contemptuously and turned her back, head shaking from side to side. Mr. Snake screamed theatrically, "Look out! He's got a gun!" Shaking his head, he said, "What a rube."

Sol dropped the gun and started in whining. He jumped and stomped around, kicking stones. He realized that both his compan-

ions were intently watching something, and it wasn't him. He followed their eyes across the valley floor to the foot of the mountain
and saw the truck for the first time.

Raven turned to Snake. "You were right, I guess." And then to
Solly, "Something's coming. We don't know what to expect either,
boy. We're just along for your ride."

The sun was heavy on the seated boy. The Raven stood. The Snake
lay, belly in the dust. They could see the pickup truck from a great
distance in the dry air. Since nobody knew what to think, there was
nothing to do but wait. Solomon dreamed of counting beaucoup on
the world when he returned a Man. Snake and Raven knew it was
possible that one of those rare changes was about to be made in the
Dreams. Only humans could do that. And not very often, either.
They knew, also, that it was possible for the change to fizzle or become perverted. That had happened many times in the great past. It
meant that the schedule would be screwed up, and that meant trouble for the Ancestors and bad karma for everybody.

Everything, now, depended on Sol. The rules, which both Raven
and Snake knew very well—and had agreed to abide by quite some
time ago—only allowed the two a minimal influence on the Boy.
Only the least little encouragement, or the most cryptic advice. Their
own performance would be judged, and they knew that if they
wanted to look good, they should be conservative and laconic—
which, after all, is the way we're used to seeing most animals. On the
other hand, if they were too close-mouthed, then Solly would be too
confused and blow the whole deal. And then it was bad karma for
everybody. Stress. Stress. Stress.

Even so, Raven and Snake felt growing excitement as they
watched the pickup coming across the desert straight as an arrow.
Change and survive; change and survive, they thought. What a plan.

They stayed a long time watching the truck. They could see it
flying over boulders, smashing back into the ground, careening on
two wheels, shooting toward them across the valley floor at an amazing speed. Sol just sat swaying, shokl'n in the still air. Unable to
concentrate on anything, his mind wandered back and forth between conscious and unconscious . . . Snake and Raven murmured
gently to him the while, ". . . Change and Survive . . ."

Solomon allowed later that he must have fallen asleep for a little
while there on the mountain. He wasn't sure, for no boy knows when

he falls asleep. All he knew was that, at one point, all, or much, was about to be revealed to him; then he was in the lotus position just like one of the Wise Wogs, but lying on his side. With the world horizontal, he watched the pickup—which bore the name BILLY SUE in a ridiculously fancy script on a piece of plastic over the radiator, and decals of the Bleeding Liberal Heart on each headlight—lurch up the dusty rhodes.

The Snake and Raven watched the truck headed straight for them and jumped over to the Boy. Frantically checking the oncoming BILLY SUE, they pulled, nudged, and pecked at Solomon again and again. When it was clear Sol wasn't going to move anytime soon, and when BILLY SUE was as close as your chicken, the Raven and the Snake jumped clear.

Solly didn't have his shit together at all. This explains why he didn't twitch a muscle as BILLY SUE rushed closer and closer. Great Allah! It was a juggernaut, and Solly was a goner sure.

Not to worry. The indistinct form behind the dusty windows was one hell of a drivin' man. The pickup veered at the last moment. The brakes jammed on, and in a hail of gravel BILLY SUE was lost for a few minutes. The truck slid past Sol turning one complete spin, ending just about twenty feet from the Boy and the Animals. Just a hair from the peak's edge. Nothing moved anywhere. The only sound was the gentle *pik pink* of falling dirt and rock. Even after the final pieces of earth fell BILLY SUE sat motionless for a few minutes.

Suddenly the door slammed open banged closed and opened again. Softly, then, what could only have been Billy Sue leapt out onto little cat feet. Long, low muscles rippled along a lithe body over six and a half feet tall. A short curly beard formed a tight cover over the lower half of his face. A mass of elaborately teased blond hair . . . cascaded . . . over her head and around graceful, perfectly formed classic features.

"My Aunt Lenore, that's one fine lookin' cuss," said Sol from the heart and from the ground.

"Best you ever seen," said Billy Sue in a high tenor.

Solomon just lay there, staring.

Quoth the raven, "Showtime."

"Up, Solly! Up! It's time. He's here." Snake took a look at Billy Sue. "C'mon, talk to her."

Billy Sue looked at Sol with genuine concern. "Aww, honey, why you look so discombobulated?" He paused, then frowned and said, "But don't try anything funny, Jim, or I'll rip your lungs out." She bent and patted the long dagger sheathed on the side of her high, fringed boots.

Billy Sue walked over, and Solly began to come out of his coma watching her move. "Look," she said. "Can I help? You look like you're about to come all dislaminated."

Solomon just stared.

Billy Sue leaned over and a good deal of bosom bulged over his low-cut leopardskin dress. A blue and red rose tattoo, thorns dripping, separated the two firm globes. Hard nipples were clearly imprinted on the thin covering fabric. Muscles moved up and down her arms and legs with the slightest movement; long, slow waves flowing under deeply tanned skin. Sol began to get pretty scared; this was weirder than he'd imagined it could ever get.

Billy Sue stood and walked back to the pickup, then returned. Yep, watching her walk was doing something to Sol . . . in addition to scaring the shit out of him. Billy Sue bent again, cradled Solly's head, and gave him water from a canteen and a cracker. Sol felt a bit of strength returning as he chewed. His eyes moved down slowly. Above the boots, Billy Sue's legs were covered by black mesh stockings. Sol's eyes moved up. Billy Sue's legs closed abruptly. "Everything you ever wanted is up there, pal. But no peeking," he said.

Gentle hands lifted Sol off the ground, easily. He stared at Billy Sue for a moment and then seemed to come to his senses. The instant he was set down, Solly jumped for his knapsack, pulled his roscoe out, rolled, stood up, and held the weapon out in front of his body with both hands. Just like in the Feelies. Considering everything he'd been through, Sol was as smooth as milk; not a wasted movement and quick as a flash.

But a split second after Sol had jumped, Billy Sue moved. He twisted and spun in an amazing series of graceful arcs. Both figures intersected perfectly—ending with Billy Sue kicking the gun out of Sol's hand just as it was held out in front of his body.

Solomon stood, still in position, and watched his gun sail away. Billy Sue, eyes closed, stood just in front of him, in the Horse Stance. Sol threw a quick punch with his right and then his left. Both were hard efficient blows. Billy Sue deflected each without opening her eyes. His eyes stayed closed when Sol charged her a moment later. She spun like a toreador just out of Sol's way, gently pushing his back. Solly stumbled, turned, and charged again, hoping to tackle her and bring him to earth. Our hero never laid a hand on her. Ten minutes later, completely frustrated, almost too tired to sprawl, the boy once again gaped at Billy Sue from the ground.

Billy Sue hadn't drawn a deep breath, broken a sweat, or opened an eye through the whole thing. He just turned his back and walked away, hips swinging. Oops, there was that walk again. About ten feet from poor Sol, Billy Sue stopped and began smoothing her skirt, running his hands down along his body starting at a point just below the chest. Sol sat watching as the slender, large hands cupped a breast and ran along a flat stomach and over rounded hips. Sol couldn't stop watching those hands, that firm body . . . those breasts, those nipples, thighs. . . . Something real strange was happening to Solomon the Boy.

The Raven whistled in appreciation. "Hubba, Hruba Ralston," she said.

Maybe it was the lack of food and water. It could have been no sleep for days. It could be the heat. Like a dreamwalker, he stood shakily and began to walk towards Billy Sue. "Something very weird is moving in me," he said.

Billy Sue and the Boy looked deep into each other's eyes. Solomon *knew* what she wanted; he walked right up to her and slowly reached out his right hand toward her apple breast. Billy Sue slapped his hand away. "And no touching, either."

The world began to spin ever so gently faster . . . just enough to be felt. Sol opened his mouth to ask—

And Billy Sue cut him off, "I ask the questions. And I get three just like Sabu in the fairytales."

In GrandMother's voice, Snake said, "Myths are dreams, dear."

"That's right," said Raven in GrandFather's voice. "The dreams of the People."

Suddenly it was night. The Full Moon, moving slowly across the sky, swept silvery light over everything. Vincent's stars wheeled against blue velvet. Sol opened his mouth again.

And Billy Sue cut him off again. "Who are you? That's Love. What do you want to do? That's Life. How much is it worth to you? That's Death." Billy Sue turned and walked to the pickup. Dawn was a thin light on the horizon.

"I get it now," said Snake.

"This could be good for us," said the Raven, laying a wing alongside her beak knowingly.

Solomon watched. He only understood when Billy Sue opened the door of the truck.

"Wait a goddamn minute!" he shouted. "That's it? I came all the way out here for *you* to ask *me* questions? I could've stayed home and watched videos!" Sol looked over to his animal friends and said, pleadingly, "I wanted strength, I wanted to be shown the way, I wanted answers, goddamn it!"

"Let's chance it," said Snake to Raven.

His feathered friend agreed, "It could be worth it."

Billy Sue watched.

"Yin," said Snake.

"Yang," said Raven.

"Shazam!" said Raven and Snake together.

The spinning world slowed to normal speed.

Billy Sue hopped into the driver's seat. With the door open, he folded his hands in her lap and looked down demurely. Then, with her head just turned towards Solomon, Billy Sue smiled the barest of smiles and looked up into Sol's eyes.

A moment later, he slammed the door, then slammed the truck into gear. With a mighty roar and a hearty, "Heidy Heidy Heidy Ho!" BILLY SUE leapt off. Three times the truck roared around Raven, Sol, and Snake, then blew off into a cloud of dust and the rising sun and the shimmering desert air.

Sol still had his mouth open. He stumbled a few steps after the pickup and fell into unconsciousness. Snake and Raven turned around in time to see a little fat man in a red suit with white fur trim. The jolly fellow was smoking sharp, pungent tobacco in a feathered tomahawk pipe. "Call for Snake and Raven! Telegram from the Ancestors!" he boomed. "Ho, Ho, Ho. Telegram!" Walking up to the pair, he presented them with a small golden plate which he held between the thumb and forefinger of each hand. A Western Onion Telegram was opened on the paten.

Snake and Raven read aloud, *"You're covered*STOP*We're all covered-*STOP*Chiao Bella*STOP ANCESTORS."

The man tipped his little cap with the tinkling bell, then turned and waddled off. Snake and Raven gave each other an emphatic nod. Snake slithered into a hole in the ground, and Raven, she flew into the Sun. The Ancestors sighed and smiled big grins.

Solly awoke tired and hungry and thirsty. Alone except for a blinding migraine, he sat in the sand under the sun and thought about what happened and what was told him. He sat a long time.

When he was sure he didn't understand, he got up and went from the mountain a changed man. He thought about his vision quest every day for the rest of his life. He told everyone who would listen about Snake and Raven and Billy Sue. No one understood. He told his children and grandchildren and his great-grandchildren. Generations after he died, many people knew the story of Solomon the Mensch and His Vision Quest, and they understood.

Contes Cruelles

I have never been a fan of American or Gallic *cinéma noir*, which puzzles me since I have a special fondness for those hard-edged works of fiction that the French, with their genius for classifying the unclassifiable, collectively describe as *contes cruelles:* cruel stories.

Most of the twelve selections that comprise the next subsection of this book are unremittingly nasty, and even the few pieces that contain traces of humor are still edged in mortuary black.

GUSTAV MEYRINK

The Man
in the Bottle

Though generally regarded as one of Germany's most important fantasy-horror writers, GUSTAV MEYRINK is little known in America, perhaps because, according to Jessica Amanda Salmonson, he is difficult to translate. Meyrink, who was a friend of Franz Kafka, is best remembered for his 1915 novel, The Golem. *The gruesome tale of "The Man in the Bottle" first appeared in English in 1912 in an edition edited by Julian Hawthorne, son of Nathaniel Hawthorne.*

Melanchthon was dancing with the Bat, whose costume represented her in an inverted position. The wings were folded close to the body, and in the claws she held a large gold hoop upright, which gave the impression that she was hanging, suspended from some imaginary point. The effect was grotesque, and it amused Melanchthon very much, for he had to peep through this gold hoop, which was exactly on a level with his face, while dancing with the Bat.

She was one of the most original masks—and at the same time one of the most repelling ones—at the fête of the Persian prince. She had even impressed his highness, Mohammed Darasche-Koh, the host.

"I know you, pretty one," he had nodded to her, much to the amusement of the bystanders.

"It is certainly the little marquise, the intimate friend of the princess," declared a Dutch councilor in a Rembrandt costume.

He surmised this because she knew every turn and corner of the palace, to judge by her conversation. And but a few moments ago, when some cavalier had ordered felt boots and torches so that they might go down into the courtyard and indulge in snowballing, the

Bat joined them and participated wildly in the game. It was then—
and the Dutchman was quite ready to back it with a wager—that he
had seen a well-known bracelet on her wrist.

"Oh, how interesting," exclaimed a Blue Butterfly. "Couldn't Melanchthon discover whether or not Count Faast is a slave of the princess?"

"Don't speak so loud," interrupted the Dutch councilor. "It is a
mighty good thing that the orchestra played the close of that waltz
fortissimo, for the prince was standing here only a moment since."

"Better not speak of such things," whispered an Egyptian, "for the
jealousy of this Asiatic prince knows no bounds, and there are probably more explosives in the palace than we dream. Count de Faast has
been playing with fire too long, and if Darasche-Koh suspects—"

A rough figure representing a huge knot dashed by them in wild
flight to escape a Hellenic warrior in shimmering armor.

"If you were the Gordian knot, Mynherr, and were pursued by
Alexander the Great, wouldn't you be frightened?" teased the inverted Bat, tapping the Dutchman coquettishly on the end of the
nose with her fan.

"The sharp wit of the pretty Marquise Bat betrays her," smiled a
lanky Satan with tail and cloven foot. "What a pity that only as a Bat
are you to be seen with your feet in the air."

The dull sound of a gong filled the room as an executioner appeared, draped in a crimson robe. He tapped a bronze gong, and
then, resting his weight on his glittering cudgel, posed himself in the
center of the big hall.

Out of every niche and lobby the maskers streamed toward him—
harlequins, cannibals, an ibis, and some Chinese, Don Quixotes, Col-
umbines, bayaderes and dominoes of all colors.

The crimson executioner distributed tablets of ivory inscribed with
gold letters.

"Oh, programmes for the entertainment!" chorused the crowd.

THE MAN IN THE BOTTLE

Marionette Comedy in the Spirit of Aubrey Beardsley
By Prince Mohammed Darasche-Koh

Characters:

The Man in the Bottle . . . . Miguel, Count de Faast
The Man on the Bottle . . . . . Prince Mohammed Darasche-Koh
The Lady in the Sedan Chair
Vampires, Marionettes, Hunchbacks, Apes, Musicians
Scene of Action: A Tiger's Maw

"What! The prince is the author of this marionette play?"

"Probably a scene out of the 'Thousand and One Nights.' "

"But who will play the part of the Lady in the Sedan Chair?"

"Oh, there is a great surprise in store for us," twittered a seductive Incroyable, leaning on the arm of an Abbé. "Do you know, the Pierrot with whom I danced the tarantelle was the Count de Faast, who is going to play The Man in the Bottle; and he confided a lot of things to me: the marionettes will be very gruesome—that is, for those who appreciate the spirit of the thing—and the prince had an elephant sent down from Hamburg—but you are not listening to me at all!" And the little one dropped the arm of her escort and bolted into the swirling crowd.

New groups of masks constantly poured out of the adjoining rooms through the wide doorways into the big hall, making a kaleidoscopic play of colors, while files of costumed guests stood admiring the wonderful mural frescoes that rose to the blue, star-dotted ceiling. Attendants served refreshments, sorbets and wines in the window niches.

With a rolling sound the walls of the narrow end of the hall separated and a stage was pushed slowly into view. Its setting, in red brown and a flaming yellow proscenium, was a yawning tiger's maw, the white teeth glittering above and below.

In the middle of the scene stood a huge glass bottle in the form of a globe, with walls at least a foot thick. It was about twice the height of an average man and very roomy. The back of the scene was draped with pink silk hangings.

Then the colossal ebony doors of the hall opened and admitted a richly caparisoned elephant, which advanced with majestic tread. On its head sat the crimson executioner guiding the beast with the butt of his cudgel. Chains of amethysts dangled from the elephant's tusks, and plumes of peacock feathers nodded from its head. Heavily embroidered gold cloths streamed down from the back of the beast, skirting the floor; across its enormous forehead there was a network of sparkling jewels.

The maskers flocked around the advancing beast, shouting greetings to the gay group of actors seated in the palanquin; Prince Darasche-Koh with turban and aigrette, Count de Faast as Pierrot, marionettes and musicians, stiff as wooden puppets. The elephant reached the stage, and with its trunk lifted one man after another from its back. There was much applause and a yell of delight as the beast seized the Pierrot and sliding him into the neck of the bottle, closed the metal top. Then the Persian prince was placed on top of the bottle.

The musicians seated themselves in a semicircle, drawing forth strange, slender instruments. The elephant gazed at them a moment, then turned about and strode toward the door. Like a lot of happy children the maskers clung to its trunk, ears, and tusks and tried to hold it back; but the animal seemed not to feel their weight at all.

The performance began, and somewhere, as if out of the ground, there arose weird music. The puppet orchestra of marionettes remained lifeless and waxen; the flute player stared with glassy, idiotic eyes at the ceiling; the features of the rococo conductor in peruke and plumed hat, holding the baton aloft and pressing a pointed finger mysteriously to his lips, were distorted by a shrewd, uncanny smile.

In the foreground posed the marionettes. Here were grouped a humpbacked dwarf with chalky face, a gray, grinning devil, and a sallow, rouged actress with carmine lips. The three seemed possessed of some satanic secret that had paralyzed their movements. The semblance of death brooded over the entire motionless group.

The Pierrot in the bottle now began to move restlessly. He doffed his white felt hat, bowed and occasionally greeted the Persian prince, who with crossed legs sat on the cap of the bottle. His antics amused the audience. The thick walls of glass distorted his appearance curiously; sometimes his eyes seemed to pop out of his head; then again they disappeared, and one saw only forehead and chin; sometimes he was fat and bloated, then again slender, with long legs like a spider's.

In the midst of a motionless pause the red silk hangings of the background parted, and a closed sedan chair was carried on by two Moors, who placed it near the bottle. A ray of pale light from above now illuminated the scene. The spectators had formed themselves into two camps. The one was speechless under the spell of this vampiric, enigmatic marionette play that seemed to exhale an atmosphere of poisoned merriment; the other group, not sensitive enough to appreciate such a scene, laughed immoderately at the comical capering of the man in the bottle.

He had given up his merry dancing and was trying by every possible means to impart some information or other to the prince sitting on the cap. He pounded the walls of the bottle as though he would smash them; and to all appearances he was screaming at the top of his voice, although not the slightest sound penetrated the thick glass.

The Persian prince acknowledged the movements of the Pierrot with a smile, pointing with his finger at the sedan chair.

The curiosity of the audience reached its climax when it saw that the Pierrot had pressed his face against the glass and was staring at something in the window of the sedan chair. Then suddenly, like one gone mad, he beat his face with his hands, sank on his knees and tore his hair. Then he sprang furiously up and raced around the bottle at such speed that the audience saw only a fluttering cloth in his wake.

The secret of the Lady in the Sedan Chair puzzled the audience considerably—they could only see that a white face was pressed against the window of the chair and was staring over at the bottle. Shadows cut off all further view.

Laughter and applause rose to a tumult. Pierrot had crouched on the bottom of the bottle, his fingers clutching his throat. Then he opened his mouth wide and pointed in wild frenzy to his chest and then to the one sitting above. He folded his hands in supplication, as though he were begging something from the audience.

"He wants something to drink! Such a large bottle and no wine in it? I say, you marionettes, give him a drink," cried one of the maskers.

Everybody laughed and applauded.

Then the Pierrot jumped up once more, tore his garments from his chest and staggered about until he measured his length on the bottom of the bottle.

"Bravo, bravo, Pierrot! Wonderfully acted! *Da capo, da capo!*" yelled the maskers.

When the man in the bottle did not stir again and made no effort to repeat his scene, the applause gradually subsided and the attention of the spectators was drawn to the marionettes. They still remained motionless in the poses they had assumed, but in their miens there was now a sense of expectancy that had not been there before. It seemed as if they were waiting for a cue.

The humpbacked dwarf, with the chalked face, turned his eyes carefully and gazed at the Prince Darasche-Koh. The Persian did not stir.

Finally two figures advanced from the background, and one of the Moors haltingly approached the sedan chair and opened the door.

And then something very remarkable occurred—the body of a

woman fell stiffly out on the stage. There was a moment of deathly silence and then a thousand voices arose: "What has happened?"

Marionettes, apes, musicians—all leaped forward; maskers climbed up on the stage.

The princess, wife of Darasche-Koh, lay there strapped to a steel frame. Where the ropes had cut into her flesh were blue bruises, and in her mouth there was a silk gag.

A nameless horror took possession of the audience.

"Pierrot!" a voice suddenly shrilled. "Pierrot!" Like a dagger, indescribable fear penetrated every heart.

"Where is the prince?"

During the tumult the Persian had disappeared.

Melanchthon stood on the shoulders of Mephisto, but he could not lift the cap of the bottle, and the air valve was screwed tightly shut.

"Break the walls of the bottle! Quick!"

The Dutch councilor tore the cudgel from the hand of the crimson executioner and with a leap landed on the stage.

A gruesome sound arose, like the tolling of a cracked bell. Like streaks of white lightning the cracks leaped across the surface of the glass. Finally the bottle was splintered into bits. And within lay, suffocated, the corpse of the Count de Faast, his fingers clawing his breast.

The bright hall seemed to darken.

Silently and with invisible pinions the gigantic ebon birds of terror streaked through the hall of the fête.

AMBROSE BIERCE

A Diagnosis of Death

Medical horror is the subject of "A Diagnosis of Death" by AMBROSE BIERCE
(1842–?), the cynical American journalist and author of such savagely horri-
ble short stories as "The Damned Thing," "Oil of Dog," "One Summer
Night," "My Favorite Murder" and the often-copied "An Occurrence at Owl
Creek Bridge." Bierce went to Mexico at the height of its civil war and was
never heard of again.

"I am not so superstitious as some of your physicians—men of science, as you are pleased to be called," said Hawver, replying to an
accusation that had not been made. "Some of you—only a few, I
confess—believe in the immortality of the soul, and in apparitions
which you have not the honesty to call ghosts. I go no further than a
conviction that the living are sometimes seen where they are not, but
have been—where they have lived so long, perhaps so intensely, as
to have left their impress on everything about them. I know, indeed,
that one's environment may be so affected by one's personality as to
yield, long afterward, an image of one's self to the eyes of another.
Doubtless the impressing personality has to be the right kind of personality as the perceiving eyes have to be the right kind of eyes—
mine, for example."

"Yes, the right kind of eyes, conveying sensations to the wrong
kind of brain," said Dr. Frayley, smiling.

"Thank you; one likes to have an expectation gratified; that is
about the reply that I supposed you would have the civility to make."

"Pardon me. But you say that you know. That is a good deal to say, don't you think? Perhaps you will not mind the trouble of saying how you learned."

"You will call it an hallucination," Hawver said, "but that does not matter." And he told the story.

"Last summer I went, as you know, to pass the hot weather term in the town of Meridian. The relative at whose house I had intended to stay was ill, so I sought other quarters. After some difficulty I succeeded in renting a vacant dwelling that had been occupied by an eccentric doctor of the name of Mannering, who had gone away years before, no one knew where, not even his agent. He had built the house himself and had lived in it with an old servant for about ten years. His practice, never very extensive, had after a few years been given up entirely. Not only so, but he had withdrawn himself almost altogether from social life and become a recluse. I was told by the village doctor, about the only person with whom he held any relations, that during his retirement he had devoted himself to a single line of study, the result of which he had expounded in a book that did not commend itself to the approval of his professional brethren, who, indeed, considered him not entirely sane. I have not seen the book and cannot now recall the title of it, but I am told that it expounded a rather startling theory. He held that it was possible in the case of many a person in good health to forecast his death with precision, several months in advance of the event. The limit, I think, was eighteen months. There were local tales of his having exerted his powers of prognosis, or perhaps you would say diagnosis; and it was said that in every instance the person whose friends he had warned had died suddenly at the appointed time, and from no assignable cause. All this, however, has nothing to do with what I have to tell; I thought it might amuse a physician.

"The house was furnished, just as he had lived in it. It was a rather gloomy dwelling for one who was neither a recluse nor a student, and I think it gave something of its character to me—perhaps some of its former occupant's character; for always I felt in it a certain melancholy that was not in my natural disposition, nor, I think, due to loneliness. I had no servants that slept in the house, but I have always been, as you know, rather fond of my own society, being much addicted to reading, though little to study. Whatever was the cause, the effect was dejection and a sense of impending evil; this was especially so in Dr. Mannering's study, although that room was the lightest and most airy in the house. The doctor's life-size portrait in oil hung in that room, and seemed completely to dominate it. There was nothing unusual in the picture; the man was evidently rather good looking, about fifty years old, with iron-gray hair, a smooth-shaven face and dark, serious eyes. Something in the picture always drew and held my attention. The man's appearance became familiar to me, and rather 'haunted' me.

"One evening I was passing through this room to my bedroom, with a lamp—there is no gas in Meridian. I stopped as usual before the portrait, which seemed in the lamplight to have a new expression, not easily named, but distinctly uncanny. It interested but did not disturb me. I moved the lamp from one side to the other and observed the effects of the altered light. While so engaged I felt an impulse to turn round. As I did so I saw a man moving across the room directly toward me! As soon as he came near enough for the lamplight to illuminate the face I saw that it was Dr. Mannering himself; it was as if the portrait were walking!

" 'I beg your pardon,' I said, somewhat coldly, 'but if you knocked I did not hear.'

"He passed me, within an arm's length, lifted his right forefinger, as in warning, and without a word went on out of the room, though I observed his exit no more than I had observed his entrance.

"Of course, I need not tell you that this was what you will call an hallucination and I call an apparition. That room had only two doors, of which one was locked; the other led into a bedroom, from which there was no exit. My feeling on realizing this is not an important part of the incident.

"Doubtless this seems to you a very commonplace 'ghost story'—one constructed on the regular lines laid down by the old masters of the art. If that were so I should not have related it, even if it were true. The man was not dead; I met him today in Union street. He passed me in a crowd."

Hawver had finished his story and both men were silent. Dr. Frayley absently drummed on the table with his fingers.

"Did he say anything today?" he asked—"anything from which you inferred that he was not dead?"

Hawver stared and did not reply.

"Perhaps," continued Frayley, "he made a sign, a gesture—lifted a finger, as in warning. It's a trick he had—a habit when saying something serious—announcing the result of a diagnosis, for example."

"Yes, he did—just as his apparition had done. But, good God! did you ever know him?"

Hawver was apparently growing nervous.

"I knew him. I have read his book, as will every physician some day. It is one of the most striking and important of the century's contributions to medical science. Yes, I knew him; I attended him in an illness three years ago. He died."

Hawver sprang from his chair, manifestly disturbed. He strode forward and back across the room; then approached his friend, and in a voice not altogether steady, said: "Doctor, have you anything to say to me—as a physician?"

"No, Hawver; you are the healthiest man I ever knew. As a friend I advise you to go to your room. You play the violin like an angel. Play it; play something light and lively. Get this cursed bad business off your mind."

The next day Hawver was found dead in his room, the violin at his neck, the bow upon the strings, his music open before him at Chopin's funeral march.

JOAN VANDER PUTTEN

Remember Me

My friend JOAN VANDER PUTTEN *is a promising fantasy writer whose work has appeared in numerous periodicals and anthologies, including Kathryn Ptacek's* Women of Darkness *and my own* Devils & Demons *and* Lovers and Other Monsters. *"Remember Me" is one of her latest and most remarkable stories, a compassionate yet ultimately horrifying modern tale that takes place in the Tower of London.*

The restaurant Nick sat at in London's Heathrow Airport wasn't that busy; there was no reason the waitress should be taking so long to bring his food. The meal on the flight from Chicago had been godawful, and he was starving. He drummed his fingers on the Formica table, waiting for her to reemerge from the kitchen.

"Miss?" he called, raising his hand tentatively when she appeared. The tray she balanced did *not* hold his hamburger.

Smiling vaguely and holding up her index finger, she placed the food on the table of a couple who'd come in well after Nick had.

"Yes, sir," she said when she finally came over. "What would you like to order?"

Nick contained his rage. He should be used to this by now, but he still felt his anger surge every time it happened. "I *did* order, and I'm waiting for my hamburger," he said, controlling his voice.

"Sorry, sir," the waitress apologized. "I must have forgotten all about you!"

She scurried off, and Nick shook his head in disgust. Everybody *always* forgot all about him. He had one of those nondescript, forgettable faces, he knew, and had tried his whole life to fight living in the anonymous zone. But, as of his twentieth year, he still hadn't succeeded.

An attractive girl, near his own age, entered and sat at a table facing him. He thought about smiling, dreamed of a witty conversation that would end in something like *"My place or yours?"* before he looked down and adjusted his silverware.

From past experience, he knew she'd look right through him if he smiled at her. Hadn't Karen done so at school last semester, when he'd met her at the student rally for Pro-Choice? Oh, he'd finally managed to get her to speak to him—and at length, too—but when he'd worked up the nerve to call her for a date . . .

Who? I don't remember meeting a Nick Hammond that day.

I was the guy who was carrying the banner. . . . I really believe women have a right to do what they want with their own bodies. . . . Remember our discussion?

No.

And so he'd hung up, unable to take the pain of further embarrassment. Nick often thought being the middle child of eleven had contributed greatly to his becoming a clone of *The Invisible Man.*

The waitress carelessly plopped the plate with his food on it in front of him. Looking at the gray, nondescript circle of meat, he suddenly lost his appetite.

He had to transfer and double back on the bus: the driver forgot he'd asked to be told when his stop came. He alighted at Tower Bridge, dragging his suitcase after him.

When his Uncle Charlie suggested to Nick that he come for an extended visit to England, to stay with him and his wife, Julie, Nick halfheartedly agreed to go. Whether he stayed on Long Island or went to London made no difference. Who would care? He could use a break from school—had decided on taking a semester or two off, anyway, before Uncle Charlie had even called—so he'd made his arrangements and left.

Strolling over Tower Bridge, he gazed at the anachronism before him. The Tower of London hunkered down on the bank of the Thames river like an ancient, sleeping beast amidst a modern civilization that hedged its sides boldly, unafraid, knowing the beast would never again awaken.

From the bridge he had a splendid view of its eighteen acres, which were enclosed by stone walls and punctuated with towers both round and square. Nick stopped for a moment, opened his guide-book, and read that the White Tower in the center, built in 1066 by William the Conqueror, dominated the compound. Surrounding it was the square Inner Ward, with buildings that once housed either guests or prisoners of rank, depending on their fate. And protecting both of these was the final, Outer Ward, from whose towers and battlements archers once hurled their arrows at attacking enemies.

Names he remembered from history books leapt off the pages at him, coming alive. He envied anyone who had caused enough of a stir in life to become immortalized in the annals of history, regardless of the reasons.

Continuing on, he followed the stone wall along its course until he reached the Tower's main gate. There he mingled with the tourists crowding around a Beefeater, who was collecting tickets.

"I have a pass," he said, brandishing the scrap of white, "to visit my aunt and uncle." The gray-bearded figure exuding authority looked at the pass, then back at Nick. "Ah yes," he said, voice thick as bread pudding. "Your uncle said you'd be coming in today. Welcome." He smiled briefly and hitched thumb over broad shoulder. "Go directly through."

Nick doubted the man would remember his face next time he tried to get in, so he stuffed the pass back in his pocket for future use, nodded his thanks, and blended into the crowd.

From another pocket he pulled a crumpled map of the Tower's buildings, sent to him by his uncle. Uncle Charlie had penciled in a line from the main gate in Middle Tower to the casemate where his flat was, and Nick stopped after he'd passed through the portcullis of Byward Tower to get his bearings. Easy enough—straight ahead to Salt Tower, then left, second door on the right before Broad Arrow Tower.

Once inside the confines of the Tower, an unexpected excitement filled Nick. He dared to hope that perhaps here he could make a new beginning, meet people who were more . . . *aware* of him than the ones he knew back home. He certainly had time . . . the invitation from his uncle was open-ended, and Nick sensed that the childless couple would enjoy having him around, should he decide to move to London permanently.

Yet as he scanned the ancient stone curtain hedging him on all sides, he sensed that in here time stood still. He shivered. The centuries of tortures and murders committed within these walls seemed to have left their mark in the very air trapped between them.

A muffled scream, a harsh laugh reached his ears. The tourists? He wasn't sure. . . .

Nick suddenly felt an inexplicable uneasiness steal over him, as if the Tower's ghosts found in him a likely victim to haunt.

"Idiot," he muttered.

He switched his suitcase to his other hand, ran his fingers through the lock of blond hair that always fell into his eyes, and headed down Water Lane.

The early December sun was thin, sickly, the pale stripes it cast on the stone walls reminding him of prison bars. Apt, he thought, given the Tower's history.

At the corner of Salt Tower, another Beefeater stood watch. As Nick approached, the man said, "Sorry, sir. This area's private. You'll have to—"

"—My uncle is one of you Yeoman Warders of the Tower," he said, using the Beefeaters' proper title to show respect. He smiled and extended his hand. "I'm Nick Hammond, Charlie Hammond's nephew."

The red-and-black-garbed man smiled warmly, took Nick's hand and shook it heartily. "Right-o. Nice to meet you." He pointed down a narrow walkway. "Your uncle's flat is in the casemate on the right, two doors before—"

"Broad Arrow Tower," Nick finished, saving him the trouble. "Thanks." Leaving the Beefeater to ward off tourists who had followed him like mindless sheep, he walked to his uncle's door and knocked.

His Aunt Julie opened it, her smile as broad as the Thames. "Welcome to England, Nick!" He bent to hug the diminutive aunt he hadn't seen in nine years. Her hair had grayed, but her complexion was as rosy as ever. "Thanks, Aunt Julie. It's good to be here."

She had to reach up to pat him on the back. "Come in, come in. You're just in time for tea."

He entered, stooping so as not to hit his head on the lintel. These doors—this whole place, he realized—had been built for people who lived in centuries past, and were obviously much shorter. He felt like an awkward giant.

His suitcase dropped with a soft thud on the highly polished wooden floor and he sniffed the air. "Umm, something smells great."

"Thought I'd bake some fresh scones today in honor of your arrival," Julie said. She spoke rapidly, voice high, words tumbling over themselves, just as he'd remembered her always doing. "Give me your coat, Nick, and go into the kitchen. Take the clotted cream from the fridge for me, would you? There's a dear. The jam's next to it. How was your trip? Did you get lost in the compound? I thought your uncle's directions were clear, you shouldn't have had any trouble."

"I didn't," he answered, then took for himself the breath he thought she needed. He moved to the refrigerator while she hung up his coat. She joined him, brought the scones from the oven, and sat opposite him. The hot biscuits filled the air with fragrant warmth. He rubbed his hands together and took a scone, then smeared it with cream and bit in.

"Is Uncle Charlie working?" he asked, after he'd swallowed. "Yes," she answered, patting his free hand. "He's pulled duty guarding the royal jewels today—boring work, he says. All he does is tell the gawking tourists, 'Move along, please, move along.'" She laughed and Nick joined her, realizing it was the first time he'd laughed in a long while.

"He'll be in for dinner, though," Julie continued. "P'raps you'd enjoy a stroll around the grounds after you get settled into your room. Or would you rather rest from your trip?"

The word *rest* affected Nick the way a bell did Pavlov's dogs. He yawned reflexively.

Julie laughed again. "There's my answer. A nap it is for you, lad, as soon as you're done."

He gave her all the news of his family at home. It took a while, with ten brothers and sisters to account for. When he finally finished and drained the fragile china cup of its last drop, he yawned again.

Julie stood and crooked her finger. "Follow me. You'll feel better for a long nap."

Nick took his suitcase and followed his aunt up a narrow staircase. The room she led him to was surprisingly modern in decor, with a cheerful, flower print on comforter and draperies.

"The loo is down the hall," she said. "Is there anything else you'd like?"

Nick shook his head and smiled. "Thanks, no. Just make sure I'm up in time for dinner."

"No fear of sleeping through," she said, then chuckled. "Your uncle makes enough noise to rouse the Tower's ghosts when he comes home. I'm sure you'll hear him."

"Ghosts?" Nick said. "Is your flat haunted like the rest of this place?"

Julie shook her head. "Oh, no. The casements are too boring for our specters. They prefer the more historical places," she said as she pulled down the shades at the small, leaden window. Turning, she clasped her hands in front of her. "We're proud of our ghosts, we are. None more famous in the world. P'raps you'll get to meet some of them before you leave!" Wishing him a good rest, she left.

He threw himself across the bed and soon slept dreamlessly, only awakening when he heard the heavy front door slam loudly shut hours later. Uncle Charlie was home.

Nick grinned at the thought of finally seeing his favorite relative again. It had been too many years between visits. Feeling refreshed, he hurried down to greet his uncle.

The large frame of Charlie Hammond blocked the dining room doorway. "Nick!" the older man thundered when he saw him. Too British to hug his nephew in a greeting, Charlie grasped both of Nick's hands in his own and shook them until Nick's arms ached.

Nick thought his uncle had aged quite a bit since they'd last met. He was almost bald, and deep grooves skittered down his cheeks, veering off in all directions before hiding under the neatly trimmed white beard. "Good to see you, Uncle Charlie. What's new?"

His question set Charlie off on a monologue until dinner. When it was ready Charlie led him to the table, where Julie and her delicious pasties waited. "I remember how you loved them last time you were here," she said as his eyes lit up at the sight of them.

Nick dug in, savoring the tender lamb and gravy in the pasties. After they'd finished eating, and while he was helping his aunt clear the table, a trumpet sounded somewhere nearby. He looked his question at her.

"The Ceremony of the Keys," she answered. "It means the tourists are gone and the gates are locked for the night." While they worked, she told him how the residents of the Tower could get in and out after the main gates had been locked, and gave him his own key for the small side door they used in the north wall.

When Uncle Charlie was snoring in front of the television, Nick turned to his aunt. The nap he'd taken had left him feeling wide awake and restless. Stretching, he said, "Think I'll take a look around the grounds. I only remember this place from the one time we came here on vacation."

His aunt smiled wistfully at the memory as she added another cross stitch to a growing line of them on her needlepoint. "You were twelve, and so taken with the ravens."

Nick suddenly remembered the huge black birds. "Are they still here?"

Julie smiled. "Of course! They're as much a part of the Tower as the stones and the ghosts. Legend says that if the ravens ever leave the Tower it will fall, and the kingdom with it. But they're locked up at night."

"Well then, I think I'll take my trusty guidebook and familiarize myself with the buildings. I suppose they're all locked up, too?"

"Yes, dear, but at least you can learn your way around. It should only take a few days."

Taking his coat from the closet, he stepped out into the dark London night.

The late-evening fog wound around his ankles like twin ropes, pulled him into the obscurity of its soupy whiteness. Jack the Ripper hid his evil deeds on nights like this, Nick thought with a small shiver as he let the historic atmosphere of the country enfold him. *Even murderers get to be remembered,* he thought, and the names of some American murderers came instantly to mind. Although the reasons for their infamy were not to be envied, Nick found himself doing so anyway. He was beginning to think that being remembered for *anything* was better than being one of the nameless mass lumped under the term humanity.

He studied the map of the Tower's layout and headed for White Tower; originally the home of monarchs, it now housed the armories.

The mist surrounded him, allowing him only occasional glimpses of a seemingly alien world through its shroud. Nick followed the map to the steps of the armories and halted. The fog suddenly parted long enough for him to notice someone, dressed in white, slip inside the armory door. How could that be? They were locked. It must have been a tail of mist, not a person at all . . . and yet, he heard the quiet *click* of a door closing. Perhaps it was one of the Tower guards making rounds. . . .

Curious, he tiptoed up the steps and tried the handle. Open. Why not take a private tour, and see who the late-night visitor was? He stepped inside. The door snickered shut quietly behind him. The full moon flooded through the large windows, illuminating the room and casting an eerie, silver glow on the polished suits of armor whose metal had transcended their original wearers in longevity and memory.

Clink.

Metal hitting metal.

Clink clank.

Sounding like hollow armor, rusty from centuries of disuse, squeaking to renewed life.

Sweat beaded on Nick's brow.

He swallowed, balled his fists.

Whoever had come in made no noise now, and he sensed an unidentifiable threat reach for him from somewhere in the room.

Then, from the semi-darkness at the end of the room, he saw a white form. It flitted from behind a particularly large suit of armor and raced through a doorway. He waited a moment until his eyes adjusted to the dimness, then followed. No one was going to terrorize him, intentionally or *not*.

Just before he reached the doorway through which the form had disappeared, he stopped. Perhaps he should call out, alert the guard or whoever it was to his presence. He almost *halloed* then, but something . . . some nebulous feeling, which he denied was fear, choked off his voice. He inched his way closer to the darkness beyond the opening . . . and summoned courage to peek around the doorframe.

A white form stepped into a beam of moonlight in the next room, and Nick felt a shout building in his throat.

"Hello," a friendly voice said. "I am Jane Trickett, the reincarnation of Lady Jane Grey. In this life I am daughter to the Tower's Ravenmaster, Jack Trickett. Who art thou, pray tell?"

Nick studied the girl before him. She was no more than fifteen, he guessed, and wore a white dress as wispy as thin fog. Her face was almost as white, or perhaps it only looked that way because of the silver light, or the way it contrasted with her long, unencumbered, black hair. She was young, but so very beautiful . . . and nutty as a fruitcake, he judged from her introduction.

He stepped closer. "I'm Nick Hammond, Charlie Hammond's nephew." When he saw no sign of recognition in her pale face, he explained further. "He's a Yeoman Warder, like your father."

She smiled. "Like my father in *this* life, you mean. How do you do, Nick Hammond?" Her small chin lifted and she extended her hand in a regal manner, as if for a kiss.

He decided to play along and took the slender fingers in his, placing his lips to them. Although she was barely out of childhood in Nick's estimation, there was an indefinable quality about this girl that made her appear much older, he thought.

"You may call me *Lady* Jane, instead of Your Royal Highness." She smiled her pleasure at him, and Nick couldn't help but smile back.

"What are you doing in here?" he asked.

"I might inquire the same of you." Her voice was playful, her head cocked to the side as she spoke. "If thou must know, Nick Hammond, I am looking for the ghosts of my former guards, those loyal and protective souls who mourned their powerlessness to prevent my fate."

Oh boy. *Nuttier* than a fruitcake. Asylum material, beyond a doubt . . . but damn friendly. He needed a friend. "Have you found them?" he asked, instantly thinking of the metallic sounds of a few minutes ago. Impossible. It must have been Jane, knocking against the armor with one of her long, slender arms in her flight. Her beauty mesmerized him more by the second.

She sighed. "Alas, none walk in here tonight, I fear. Other ghosts might be found about the grounds, though. The Tower has spawned many, all given equal importance due to their death within these walls, and all walk . . . occasionally."

"I see." Nick's hands clasped and unclasped of their own will, wanting to do nothing more than stroke the white softness of her long neck. What an odd effect she was having on him!

She startled him by a quick jump in the air. Her hands clapped and then grabbed his, swinging him around in a circle. "I have a splendid idea. Wouldst thou like to accompany me on my search, this eve?"

Although he found her lapses into medieval English unsettling, the feel of her small hands curled inside of his was anything but. It felt damn good. "Sure, let's go scare up some ghosts," he said, allowing her to pull him down the corridor and out the door, which she locked behind them.

"You have a key?" he asked. No one in their right mind would have given this delightful candidate for the booby-hatch a key.

"I . . . borrow it, sometimes," she answered before flitting down the stairs.

Steal it, more than likely, he thought, and smiled to himself. He hurried after her, almost losing sight of her in the fog. But it was thinning, and he saw her slight form ahead of him, flying across the stones. The chill air made him shiver in his coat, but the girl wore none and seemed not to notice the temperature. He raced, caught up to her, and grasped her hand. "Slow down, Jane." She shot him a quick look of displeasure. *"Lady* Jane," he corrected. "The ghosts will wait for us."

She stopped and turned to him, her white face a mask of deadly earnest. "Ghosts cater to no man's whims. They walk when they must, *do* what they must, for eternity. Humans can only observe their rituals, if they be in luck." She smiled, then, a smile that chilled him more than the cool night. "I know, you see," she added. "For I have been a ghost."

She really believed what she said. He should leave now, continue his explorations alone, forget about this beautiful, strange girl and her insane delusions. But as he saw the quick rise and fall of her small breasts, felt her hand curled trustingly in his, he knew he couldn't leave her. Not now, not yet.

Maybe not ever.

That last thought made him realize how quickly he'd fallen under the spell of this fairylike child-woman. What was happening to him? Could he be falling in love this quickly?

The thought was too delicious to dwell on now. It could be savored when he was alone, in his room. For the moment, he would just enjoy her company. He steered the conversation back to reality and away from Jane's talk of having been a ghost. "You said you're the Ravenmaster's daughter."

"In this incarnation, yes."

He ignored that. "When I was a kid, I came here once. Nothing interested me as much as the ravens. Could we go see them now?"

"They are caged for the night."

"But I'm sure you have the key—or can get it."

Her face clouded with uncertainty. "Will you search for the ghosts with me after you've seen them?"

"Sure," he promised. He hoped he could convince her, before the night was out, that reality was a better place to live than the world which she inhabited. Maybe even get her to agree to a date. Would her parents let her go out with someone as old as he?

She seemed satisfied by his answer and led him across the stone courtyard in the direction of Wakefield Tower. Her hands skillfully undid the lock on one cage and disappeared within. When they emerged, a raven perched on her arm. "Nick Hammond, meet Lenore. In *her* former life she was my personal maid."

The large black bird was calm and silent, obviously used to Jane.

Its head cocked to one side and the beady black gaze riveted on Nick. Jane nuzzled the bird with her head. He couldn't tell where her black hair ended and the raven's ebony feathers began. He didn't know what he found so compelling about these birds when he was young, but whatever it was, their attraction for him still held. He stretched out his hand to pet Lenore.

"Don't!" Jane whispered, to avoid startling the raven. "She'll give you a nasty bite. They're vicious birds by nature." Then she gave a small laugh. "I always tease Lenore that she's nasty now to pay for how grumpy she sometimes was in our former life together. But I tease her in love's name, because we were so much alike—both in our nastiness and our pleasantness—that I believe we are two halves of the same soul, with the same longings and desires."

Nick withdrew his hand and watched the bird stretch its wings—or what there was of them. "I remember hearing that they clip the ravens' wings so they don't fly away—is that right?"

Jane was silent for so long that Nick thought she hadn't heard his question. He was about to repeat it when he was amazed to see tears cascade down her cheeks in moonlit streams. "What's wrong, Lady Jane?" Slowly, so as not to frighten the bird, he stroked Jane's free arm. It was warm, despite the fact that she wore no coat. The bird eyed Nick's motions, but thankfully didn't attack.

"I cry because I am sad," Jane said. "Sad for the ravens, who were born to fly, and can only mate in the air. Because their wings are clipped they cannot breed . . . and poor Lenore always wanted children, as did I. In that we were alike as well, and together would often bemoan our childlessness before my death. Although innocent of wrongdoing, my young husband and I—I, who was only fifteen— were beheaded before we could conceive a child." She sighed deeply. "That is how it was in those days. Look at someone crooked and some monarch or other would shout 'Off with her head!' "

Nick almost burst out laughing as Jane's brow furrowed and her hand sliced across her throat, but he managed not to. He decided that besides English history she'd read *Alice in Wonderland* as well. He found her entrancing.

"Lenore was hanged soon after, for her loyalty to me. And in none of our following incarnations have we borne children. Perhaps this incarnation will be different—for me, at least." She stroked the raven's clipped wing. "But not, I fear, for my loyal Lenore, who is denied the joy of mating, due to her mutilation."

Grateful for the semi-darkness, Nick smiled benignly. Batty, batty,

batty. But so beautiful, and sensitive. "I'd like to have kids someday, too," he said. They sort of . . . help you live on, after you die."

She turned her face to his and he saw her expression—not exactly a smile, but something close, before she returned the bird to its cage and relocked it. "Now I will introduce you to some ghosts, Nick Hammond, if any walk this night."

She took his hand and they were off, running over stones that made their footsteps echo hollowly in the silence of the night, across grass that gleamed wet and whispered promises as they trod it. Jane stopped suddenly. "This is the Bloody Tower," she said, pointing to a square building in the Inner Ward. "It is so named because it was here that twelve-year-old King Edward V and his younger brother Richard were imprisoned and later murdered by their uncle Richard, Duke of Gloucester, who then ascended the throne."

"That their uncle actually killed them was never proven, was it?" Nick asked, remembering a bit of history himself.

"Not in this world, no. But when the boys and I were spirits together in the other world, they told me so. And their uncle admitted it."

"Oh really?" he asked, playing her game again. "So the spirits talk to each other over there, do they?"

"Of course." As if his question was a stupid one not worth further discussion, she settled down on the grass. "Let us sit quietly and see if the boys are about this evening."

Nick humored her and sat down, then summoned up all his courage to snake his arm around her waist. She did not move, or protest. A beginning, at least, and he felt happier than he'd ever felt before.

Suddenly Jane gripped his hand with hers, her nails biting into his wrist like a claw. "Look," she whispered, excitement edging her voice. "There are the boys!"

Nick looked to where she pointed only to please her. December nights were not the time to go ghost hunting, he decided as he shivered. Any sensible ghost would wait until it was warmer out to do his haunting. Jane still didn't seem to feel the cold. He decided ghosts and crazy people both lived in the same world. He squinted into the gloom at the base of the tower. "I don't see anything," he said.

"Over there," she whispered, pointing a bit to the right of where he'd been looking.

Two small tornadoes of fog whirled in a dark corner, then were pushed closer to Nick and Jane by the night's strong breath.

When the two separate clots of fog were within a few feet of them, Nick swore he could make out the faces of two young boys. Before he had time to be frightened, he heard Jane's voice: calm, friendly. "Hello, Edward. Hello, Richard. How art thou both this eve?"

"You spoke to them," Nick whispered, when the now faceless, opaque mists eventually passed them by.

Jane's laugh was as silvery as the moonlight, as melodious as a bird's song. "Yes, I did. But they didn't reply—they never do. They are too intent on re-creating some scene from their lives, or their deaths. The ghosts are the haunted ones, not us. Their passions—good or evil—live on forever, and they are cursed to continue trying to fulfill them for all eternity . . . as am I." She stood with a light spring and pulled him to his feet. Facing her, he could see something in her eyes, a sanity he hadn't noticed before, and he suddenly wondered if all this Lady Jane stuff was an act put on for his benefit. Her voice carried a kernel of knowledge beyond her years and experience when next she spoke. "Ghosts are not to be feared. It is the living we must fear."

Before he could respond she flew away into the mist, crossing the courtyard as soundlessly as the recent apparitions. "Jane! Wait!" But she was gone, and her absence left a strange, empty place inside of him.

Unnatural.

And considering their age difference, unhealthy. She was jail bait, and he wasn't about to get himself in trouble with the law.

The night felt colder than ever, suddenly, and Nick shivered again. Like water shaken from a dog's coat, so did the shiver seem to release Nick from Jane's spell. He went home feeling foolish, determined to avoid Jane if he saw her again.

When he reached his uncle's flat, the lights were out. Noiselessly he climbed to his room and slipped into bed, hoping for a restful sleep. But black wings fluttered over his head in his dreams, black wings that became soft, black hair caressing his face, and in the morning he woke exhausted.

After breakfast Nick went in search of his uncle, who had gone out, Julie said, on his "morning constitutional." He found Charlie in conversation with another warder, and his uncle waved him over.

"Jack, this is my nephew Nick," he said. "Nick, Jack Trickett, the Ravenmaster."

Nick's pulse quickened and he extended his hand. "Nice to meet you, sir. I met your daughter last night."

His father and the Ravenmaster exchanged quick glances, then the Ravenmaster's gaze sought the ground. "Yes, well, *harumph*, nice to meet you, Nick." The man whirled suddenly and strode off.

Puzzled, Nick turned to his uncle. "What did I say?"

Charlie's face took on a decidedly uncomfortable look. "The Tricketts had to send Jane away to a hospital this morning."

Nick pointed to his temple. "I noticed she was a bit strange. . . ."

"Fey, your aunt calls it. And sometimes a bit dangerous. Jack and his wife are upset, but the doctors say Jane might be well enough to come home in a month or two." He clapped Nick on the back. "How about a tour? I've today off, and would like nothing better than to show off the Tower."

"Great," Nick said, but his mind was on Jane as he followed his uncle. So she really *had* been crazy. A sadness welled up in him, a disappointment at the thought of not seeing her again that was disproportionate for such a brief encounter as they'd had.

As the days slid into weeks and the weeks clumped into a month—then two—Nick found himself unsuccessful in putting Jane out of his mind. And when he wasn't thinking of her, he was thinking of his future. What could he do with his life that would make him be *remembered*, make him more than just another person who lived and eventually died, make him special in this world full of the ordinary and mundane? One profession after another got considered and discarded; till, at the end, Nick was no closer to an answer than he had been at the beginning of his search.

He toured the city during the cold winter days, finding himself strangely drawn to the grislier parts of its history, and almost obsessed by Jack the Ripper. Who had the man been? Why had he killed . . . and why had he stopped? The Tower's Dungeon fascinated him as well, and he never grew tired of visiting it. After a while, he even began believing it might be possible to see some of the Tower's ghosts, as Jane believed she had; as he had convinced himself, that night, that he *hadn't*. Lately, he wasn't so sure. His solitary lifestyle was affecting him, he decided.

One February night after dinner, while Nick and his uncle were playing a game of chess and his aunt worked at her needlepoint, she said conversationally, "Today is the anniversary of the beheading of Lady Jane Grey. February 12th, 1554. Poor child was beheaded on Tower Green just because she was unlucky enough to be born a rival to the throne in the eyes of her cousin, Mary the First."

Nick suddenly saw Jane's face before him, with her haunting eyes and dark hair, and felt an inexplicable aching start deep in his heart. If Jane Trickett were home tonight, he'd bet a ten-spot she'd be at the patch of grass called Tower Green, trying to speak to the ghost of Lady Jane Grey.

Suddenly restless, he decided to go for a walk. The night was bitter and dead grass blanketed in hoarfrost snapped beneath his feet. The air was clear, his breath the only mist as he wandered across courtyards and between ancient buildings. No one was about, and Nick almost felt as if he had somehow stepped back in time. Was this how Jane often felt as she'd prowled the grounds, looking for her ghosts? Tonight, as he walked on the ground once trod by kings and beggars alike, he believed in Jane's ghosts.

Realizing he was near Tower Green, he glanced in the direction of the innocent-looking patch of grass that lent its name to where the famous—or infamous—chopping block had once stood, the place where so many had lost their heads to the executioner's ax—including Lady Jane Grey. The block was gone now, replaced by a small marker that seemed to huddle in shame at what it commemorated.

Because of the almost shattering clarity of the air, Nick knew it couldn't be fog when he saw a white form sitting on the marker, a form he was sure he recognized. Jane was home for a visit!

Blood throbbed in his chest, pounded in his ears. Urged him onward. When he reached the place where she sat, he stopped. "Hello, Lady Jane," he said, praying that she would remember him, unlike all the other girls he'd ever met.

"Why hello, Nick Hammond. Why art thou here, the eve of my first earthly demise, on such a cold night?"

He smiled in joy. *She hadn't forgotten him!* Even though they'd met only once, he was obviously more than just another face to her. The need to become someone—to pull himself out of the crowd and be remembered in some way—grew stronger in him at her greeting.

For a second, he thought he saw a gaping wound across her neck . . . and then the illusion was gone.

He decided to fit his mood to hers, win her back to reality gently. He even decided to try the medieval accent, hoping that might help. "I couldst not stay away. I have loved thee since first we met, my lady, and I sensed thou wouldst be here this eve, in mourning. I have come to be with thee."

Jane's eyes burned fiercely, seemed to look through him, or beyond him. He turned to see if there was anyone else present. They were alone . . . except for the invisible ghosts in her mind.

Her voice was a jubilant sigh of rapture. "Husband! You have come at last! All these centuries I have awaited our union, for the fruit of your loins to make me swell with child. Come to me!"

Before Nick knew what was happening Jane was in his arms and he closed his eyes, felt the warmth of her body against his. He reveled at how she moved under his hands as he sought to touch every part of her at once. Let her think him to be anyone she wanted; nothing mattered now but that she was his, and he vowed to cherish and protect her for eternity.

"Lenore and I desire children, husband," she whispered.

Nick felt one quick twinge of guilt—he saw himself as taking advantage of her—but it disappeared the moment she kissed him, and he lost himself in their lovemaking.

Afterward, when their breathing had slowed and they lay wrapped in one another's arms, Nick pulled her gently to him. His tongue parted her soft lips, met hers in a lovers' embrace. He opened his eyes, wanting to see the love he expected to be in hers.

But instead of her luminous eyes he saw beads of black, a sharp beak where her lips had been, and her tongue was no longer gently twined around his but pulling, as if to yank it from his mouth, and the pain, oh *God*, he couldn't stand the sweet, horrible pain . . .

His hands were too small a cup for the river of blood that burbled between his lips when she released him.

The black hair that brushed his cheek a moment ago was still soft, but hair no longer. Feathers, black as the starless sky, flew from clipped wings that beat at his face.

Her mouth—

that silver beak, so like a knife—

stung his eyes with sharp kisses, then started on the skin over his heart.

Through a red haze of agony, he heard her whisper.

"I told you, Nick Hammond, that it's not the ghosts one must fear but the living . . ."

Tonight, he knew, London Tower would have one more harmless ghost . . . but then, a sudden thought made him smile, regardless of his pain.

A harmless ghost, yes.

But, because he had died in the Tower, he would be at last—and forever—remembered.

EMILIA PARDO-BAZAN

The Pardon

How many American book collectors recall Big Little Books, those small, fragile paperbound novels, short story and nonfiction collections once sold through the mails by the Johnson Smith Company? Last summer, while browsing through a used-book store in upstate New York, I uncovered a cache of them. One which I bought contained "The Pardon", a tragic tale by the Spanish novelist Emilia Pardo Bazan *(1852–1921), who lived and wrote in Madrid.*

Of all the women busily engaged in lathering soiled linen in the public laundry of Marineda, their arms stiff with the biting cold of a March morning, Antonia the charwoman was the most bowed down, the most disheartened, the one who wrung the clothes with the least energy, and rinsed them with the greatest lassitude. From time to time she would interrupt her work in order to pass the back of her hand across her reddened eyelids; and the drops of water and soapy bubbles glistened like so many tears upon her withered cheeks.

Antonia's companions at the tubs eyed her compassionately, and every now and again, in the midst of the confusion of gossip and of quarrels, a brief dialogue would ensue in lowered tones, interrupted by exclamations of astonishment, indignation, and pity. The entire laundry knew, down to the smallest details, the poor washerwoman's misfortunes, which furnished occasion for unending comment. No one was unaware that, after her marriage a few years ago with a young butcher, she had kept house together with her mother and husband in one of the suburbs outside the town wall, and that the family lived in comfortable circumstances, thanks to Antonia's steady industry, and to the frugal savings of the older woman in her former capacity of huckster, second-hand dealer, and money-lender.

Still less had anyone forgotten the tragic evening when the old woman was found assassinated, with nothing but splinters left of the lid of the chest in which she kept her money and a few earrings and trinkets of gold; still less, the horror that spread through the neighborhood at the news that the thief and assassin was none other than Antonia's husband, as she herself declared, adding that for some time past the guilty man had been tormented with a desire for his mother-in-law's money, with which he wished to set up a butcher's shop of his own. The accused, to be sure, attempted to establish an alibi, relying on the testimony of two or three boon companions, and so far confused the facts, that, instead of going to the gallows, he got off with twenty years in prison.

Public opinion was less indulgent than the law; in addition to the wife's testimony, there was one overwhelming piece of evidence, namely, the wound itself which had caused the old woman's death, an accurate, clean-cut wound, delivered from above downward, like the stroke used in slaughtering hogs, evidently with a broad, keen blade, like that of a meat knife. Among the people, there was no question but that the culprit should have paid for his deed upon the scaffold. And Antonia's destiny began to evoke a holy horror when the rumor was circulated that her husband had *sworn to get even with her*, on the day of his release, for having testified against him. The poor woman was expecting soon to have a child; yet none the less, he left her with the assurance that, as soon as he should come back, she might count herself among the dead.

When Antonia's son was born, she was unable to nurse him, because of her enfeebled and wasted condition, and the frequent attacks of prostration from which she had suffered since the commission of the crime. And since the state of her purse did not permit her to pay for a nurse, the women of the neighborhood who had nursing children took turns in caring for the poor little thing, which grew up sickly, suffering the consequences of all its mother's anguish. Before she had fully got back her strength, Antonia was hard at work again, and although her cheeks continually showed that bluish pallor which is characteristic of a weak heart, she recovered her silent activity and her placid manner.

Twenty years of prison! In twenty years, she told herself, either he might die, or she might die, and from now until then was, in any case, a long time. The idea of a natural death did not disturb her; but the mere thought of her husband's return filled her with horror. In vain her sympathetic neighbors tried to console her, suggesting the possibility that the guilty wretch might repent and mend his ways, or, as they expressed themselves, "think better of it"; but Antonia would only shake her hand, murmuring gloomily:

"What, he? Think better of it? Not unless God Himself came down from Heaven to tear his dog's heart out of him and give him another!"

And at the mere mention of the criminal, a shudder would run throughout Antonia's body.

After all, twenty years contain a good many days, and time alleviates even the cruelest pain. Sometimes it seemed to Antonia as though all that had happened was a dream, or that the wide gates of the prison, having once closed upon the condemned man, would never again reopen; and that the law, which in the end had inflicted punishment for the first crime, would have the power to prevent a second. The law! that moral entity, of which Antonia formed a mysterious and confused conception, was beyond doubt a terrible force, yet one that offered protection; a hand of iron that would sustain her upon the brink of an abyss. Accordingly she added to her illimitable fears a sort of indefinable confidence, founded chiefly upon the time that had already elapsed and that which remained before the expiration of the sentence.

Strange, indeed, is the conception of human events! Certainly it would never have occurred to the king, when, clad in the uniform of general-in-chief and with his breast covered over with decorations, he gave his hand to a princess before the altar, that this solemn act would cost pangs beyond number to a poor washerwoman in the capital of a distant province. When Antonia learned that her husband had been one of the convicts singled out for royal clemency, she spoke not a word; and the neighbors found her seated on the sill of her doorway, with her fingers interlocked and her head drooping forward on her breast; while the boy, raising his sad face, with its stamp of chronic invalidism, kept moaning:

"Mother, mother, warm me some soup, for God's sake, for I am starving!"

The kind-hearted and chattering chorus of neighbors swooped down upon Antonia; some busied themselves in preparing the child's dinner; others tried as best they could to instil courage into the mother. She was very foolish to distress herself like this! Holy

Virgin! It wasn't as though the brute had nothing to do but just walk in and kill her! There was a government, God be thanked, and the law courts, and the police; she could appeal to the authorities, to the mayor—

"The mayor's no good!" she answered, with a gloomy look, in a hopeless tone.

"Or to the governor, or the regent, or the chief of the city council; you ought to go to a lawyer and find out what the law says."

One kind-hearted girl, married to a policeman, offered to send for her husband, "to give the scoundrel a good scare"; another, a swarthy, dauntless sort of woman, insisted on coming every night to sleep at the charwoman's house; in short, so many and so varied were the signs of interest shown by her neighbors that Antonia made up her mind to take a bold step, and without waiting for her counselors to adjourn, decided to consult a lawyer and find out what he advised.

When Antonia returned from the consultation, paler even than usual, from every basement and ground floor disheveled women emerged to hear the news, and exclamations of horror arose. Instead of protecting her, the law required the daughter of the murdered woman to live under the same roof with the assassin, as his wife!

"What laws, divine Lord of Heaven! That's how the brigands who make them carry them out!" clamored the indignant chorus. "And is there no help for it, my dear, no help at all?"

"He says that I could leave him after I got what they call a divorce."

"And what is a divorce, my dear?"

"It's a lawsuit that takes a long time."

All the women let their arms fall hopelessly. Lawsuits never came to an end, or if they did it was all the worse, because they were always decided against the innocent and the poor.

"And to get it," continued the charwoman, "I should have to prove that my husband had ill-treated me."

Lord of mercy! Hadn't the beast killed her own mother? And if that wasn't ill treatment, then what was? And didn't the very cats in the street know that he had threatened to kill her, too?

"But since no one heard him— The lawyer says the proof has to be very clear."

Something akin to a riot ensued. Some of the women insisted that they would certainly send a petition to the king himself, asking to have the pardon revoked; and they took turns at spending the night at the charwoman's house, so that the poor thing could get a chance to sleep. Fortunately, it was only three days later that the news arrived that the pardon was only a partial remission of the sentence, and that the assassin still had some years to drag his chains behind prison bars. The night after Antonia had learned this was the first that she did not suddenly start up in bed, with her eyes immeasurably wide open, and scream for help.

After this first alarm, more than a year passed, and the charwoman recovered her tranquillity and was able to devote herself to her humble labors. One day the butler in one of the houses where she worked thought that he was doing a kindness to the poor, white-faced thing who had a husband in prison, by telling her that there was soon to be an heir to the throne, and that this would undoubtedly mean some more pardons.

The charwoman was in the midst of scrubbing the floor, but on hearing this announcement she dropped her scrubbing-brush and, shaking down her skirt, which had been gathered up around her waist, she left the house, moving like an automaton, as cold and silent as a statue. To all inquiries from her various employers, she replied that she was ill; although, in reality, she was merely suffering from a sort of general prostration, an inability to raise her arms to any work whatever. On the day of the royal birth, she counted the number of salutes, whose reverberations seemed to jar through to the center of her brain; and when someone told her that the royal child was a girl, she began to take heart at the thought that a male child would have been the occasion of a larger number of pardons.

Besides, why should one of the pardons be for her husband? They had already remitted part of his sentence once, and his crime had been a shocking one. To kill a defenseless old woman, just for the sake of a few wretched pieces of gold! The terrible scene once more unrolled itself before her eyes. How did they dare to pardon the beast who had inflicted that fearful knife-thrust? Antonia remembered that the lips of the wound were livid, and it seemed as though she could still see the coagulated blood at the foot of the narrow bed.

She locked herself into her house, and passed the hours seated in a low chair before the hearth. Bah! If they were bound to kill her, they might as well come and do it!

Nothing but the plaintive voice of the little boy aroused her from her self-absorption.

"Mother, I am hungry! Mother, who is at the door? Who is coming?"

But at last, on a beautiful, sunny morning, she roused herself and, taking a bundle of soiled clothing, made her way towards the public washing place. To the many affectionate inquiries she answered only in slow monosyllables, and her eyes rested in unseeing absorption on the soapy water that now and again splashed in her face.

Who was it that brought to the laundry the unlooked-for news? It happened just as Antonia was gathering up her washing and preparing to start for home. Did someone invent the story, meaning to be kind, or was it one of those mysterious rumors, of unknown origin, which on the eve of momentous happenings, whether personal or public, palpitate and whisper through the air? The actual facts are that poor Antonia, upon hearing it, raised her hand instinctively to her heart and fell backward upon the wet flooring of the laundry.

"But is he really dead?" demanded the early comers of the more recent arrivals.

"Indeed he is!"

"I heard it in the market-place."

"I heard it in the shop."

"Well, and who told you?"

"Me? Oh, I heard it from my husband."

"And who told your husband?"

"The captain's mate."

"Who told the mate?"

"His foster-father."

At this point the matter seemed to be sufficiently authenticated, and no one sought to verify it further, but assumed that the news was valid and beyond question. The culprit dead, on the eve of pardon, and before completing the term of his sentence! Antonia, the charwoman, raised her head, and for the first time her cheeks tooks on the color of health, and the fountain of her tears was opened. She wept to her heart's content, and of all who saw her, there was not one that blamed her. It was she who had received her release, and her gladness was justified. The tears chased each other from the corners of her eyes, and as they flowed her heart expanded; because, from the day of the murder she had been under a weight too heavy for relief in tears. Now once more she could breathe freely, released from her nightmare fear. The hand of Providence had so plainly intervened that it never even occurred to the poor charwoman that the news might be false.

That evening, Antonia returned home later than usual, because she stopped at the primary school for her boy, and bought him some spice cakes and other dainties that he had long been wanting; and the two wandered from street to street, lingering before the shop windows. She forgot the dinner hour, and thought of nothing but of drinking in the air, and feeling herself alive, and little by little taking possession of herself.

So great was Antonia's self-absorption that she did not notice that her outer door was unlatched. Still holding the child by the hand, she entered the narrow quarters that served as parlor, kitchen and dining-room all in one, then recoiled in amazement at seeing that the candle was lighted. A huge, dark bulk raised itself from the table, and the scream which rose to the charwoman's lips was strangled in her throat.

It was he. Antonia, motionless, riveted to the ground, stared unseeingly at him, although the sinister image was mirrored in her dilated pupils. Her rigid body was for the moment paralyzed; her icy hands relaxed their hold upon the boy, who clung in terror to her skirts. The husband spoke:

"You were not counting on me today!" he murmured in a hoarse but tranquil tone; and at the sound of that voice, in which Antonia fancied that she could hear the echo of maledictions and threats of death, the poor woman, waking from her daze, came to life, emitted one shrill wail, and snatching her boy up in her arms, started to run to the door. The man intercepted her.

"Come, come! Where are you off to, my lady?" he asked her, with harsh irony. "Rousing the neighborhood at this time of night? Stay home and stop your noise!"

The last words were spoken without any accompanying gesture of intimidation, but in a tone that froze Antonia's blood. Her first stupefaction had by this time given place to fever, the lucid fever of the instinct of self-preservation. A sudden thought flashed through her mind: she would appeal to him through the child. The father had never seen him, but after all he was his father. Catching the boy up, she carried him over to the light.

"Is that the kid?" murmured the convict, and taking up the candle he held it close to the boy's face. The latter, dazzled, blinked his eyes and covered his face with his hands, as if trying to hide from this unknown father whose name he had never heard pronounced excepting with universal fear and condemnation. He shrank back against his mother, and she at the same time nervously held him close, while her face grew whiter than wax.

"What an ugly kid!" muttered the father, setting the candle down again. "He looks as if the witches had sucked him dry."

Antonia, still holding the boy, leaned against the wall, half fainting. The room seemed to be circling around her, and the air was full of tiny flecks of blue light.

"Look here, isn't there anything to eat in the house?" demanded her husband. Antonia set the boy on the floor in a corner, where he sat, crying from fear and stifling his sobs, while she proceeded to hurry about the room, setting the table with trembling hands; she brought out some bread and a bottle of wine, and removed the pot of codfish from the fire, making herself a willing slave in the hope of placating the enemy. The convict took his seat and proceeded to eat voraciously, helping himself to repeated draughts of wine. She remained standing, staring in fascination at the hard, parchment-like face, with close-clipped hair, and the unmistakable prison pallor. He filled his glass again and reached it towards her.

"No, I don't want it," stammered Antonia, for the wine, where the candlelight fell upon it, seemed to her imagination like a pool of blood.

He drank it himself, with a shrug of his shoulders, and replenished his plate with the codfish, which he consumed, greedily, feeding himself with his fingers and devouring huge slices of bread. His wife watched him as he ate, and a faint hope began to dawn in her heart. As soon as he had finished his meal, he might go out without killing her; in that case, she would lock and bar the door, and if he tried to come back to kill her, it would rouse the neighbors and they would hear her screams. Only it was quite likely that she would find it impossible to scream! She hawked repeatedly in order to clear her voice. Her husband, having eaten his fill, drew a cigar from his pocket, pinched off the tip with his finger nail, and tranquilly lighted it with the candle.

"Here, where are you going?" he called, seeing that his wife made a furtive movement towards the door. "Let's enjoy ourselves in peace."

"I must put the boy to bed," she answered, scarcely knowing what she said, and she took refuge in the adjoining room, carrying the child in her arms. She felt sure that the murderer would not dare to enter there. How could he have the dreadful courage to do so? It was the room where the crime was committed, her mother's room;

the room that she had shared before her marriage. The poverty that followed the old woman's death had forced Antonia to sell her own bed and use that of the deceased. Believing herself in security, she proceeded to undress the child, who now ventured to sob aloud, and with his face buried on her breast. All at once the door opened and the ex-convict came in.

Antonia saw him cast a side glance around the room; then he proceeded tranquilly to remove his shoes, to undress, and finally stretch himself in the murdered woman's bed. The charwoman felt that she must be dreaming; if her husband had drawn a knife, he would have frightened her less than by this horrible show of tranquillity. He meanwhile stretched and turned between the sheets, sighing with the contentment of a weary man who has obtained the luxury of a soft, clean bed.

"And you?" he exclaimed, turning towards Antonia, "what are you sitting there for, as dumb as a post? Aren't you coming to bed?"

"No, I—I am not sleepy," she temporized, with her teeth chattering.

"What if you aren't sleepy? Are you going to sit up all night?"

"No—no—there isn't room. You go to sleep. I'll get on here, some way or other."

He uttered two or three coarse words.

"Are you afraid of me, do you hate me, or what on earth is the trouble? We'll see whether you aren't coming to bed! If you don't—"

He sat up, reached out his hands, and prepared to spring from the bed to the floor. But Antonia, with the fatalistic docility of a slave, had already begun to undress. Her hurrying fingers broke the strings, violently tore off the hooks and eyes, ripped her skirts and petticoats. In one corner of the room could still be heard the smothered sobbing of the boy.

It was the boy who summoned the neighbors the following morning by his desperate cries. They found Antonia still in bed, stretched out as if dead. A doctor, summoned in haste, declared that she was still alive, and bled her, but he could not draw from her one drop of blood. She passed away at noon, by a natural death, for there was no mark of violence upon her. The boy insisted that the man who had passed the night there had called her several times to get up, and seeing that she didn't answer, had gone away, running like a madman.

JACK LONDON

The One Thousand Dozen

JACK LONDON *(1876–1916) was born in San Francisco, the son of a spiritualist and a traveling astrologer. Author of such popular tales and novels of high adventure as* "To Build a Fire," The Call of the Wild *and* The Sea Wolf, *London had many careers, some respectable, some less so, before he took his own life. His castle, Wolf House, in Sonoma Valley, California, was destroyed by fire, but its ruins are allegedly haunted.*

David Rasmunsen was a hustler, and like many a greater man, a man of the one idea. Wherefore, when the clarion call of the North rang on his ear, he conceived an adventure in eggs and bent all his energy to its achievement. He figured briefly and to the point, and the adventure became iridescent-hued, splendid. That eggs would sell at Dawson for five dollars a dozen was a safe working premise. Whence it was incontrovertible that one thousand dozen would bring, in the Golden Metropolis, five thousand dollars.

On the other hand, expense was to be considered, and he considered it well, for he was a careful man, keenly practical, with a hard head and a heart that imagination never warmed. At fifteen cents a dozen, the initial cost of his thousand dozen would be one hundred and fifty dollars, a mere bagatelle in face of the enormous profit. And suppose, just suppose, to be wildly extravagant for once, that transportation for himself and eggs should run up eight hundred and fifty more; he would still have four thousand clear cash and clean when the last egg was disposed of and the last dust had rippled into his sack.

"You see, Alma"—he figured it over with his wife, the cozy dining room submerged in a sea of maps, government surveys, guidebooks, and Alaskan itineraries—"you see, expenses don't really begin till you make Dyea; fifty dollars'll cover it with a first-class passage thrown in. Now, from Dyea to Lake Linderman, Indian packers take your goods over for twelve cents a pound, twelve dollars a hundred, or one hundred and twenty dollars a thousand. Say I have fifteen hundred pounds, it'll cost one hundred and eighty dollars—call it two hundred and be safe. I am creditably informed by a Klondiker just come out that I can buy a boat for three hundred. But the same man says I'm sure to get a couple of passengers for one hundred and fifty each, which will give me the boat for nothing, and further, they can help me manage it. And—that's all; I put my eggs ashore from the boat at Dawson. Now let me see, how much is that?"

"Fifty dollars from San Francisco to Dyea, two hundred from Dyea to Linderman, passengers pay for the boat—two hundred and fifty all told," she summed up swiftly.

"And a hundred for my clothes and personal outfit," he went on happily; "that leaves a margin of five hundred for emergencies. And what possible emergencies can arise?"

Alma shrugged her shoulders and elevated her brows. If that vast Northland was capable of swallowing up a man and a thousand dozen eggs, surely there was room and to spare for whatever else he might happen to possess. So she thought, but she said nothing. She knew David Rasmunsen too well to say anything.

"Doubling the time because of chance delays, I should make the trip in two months. Think of it, Alma! Four thousand in two months! Beats the paltry hundred a month I'm getting now. Why, we'll build further out, where we'll have more space, gas in every room, and a view, and the rent of the cottage'll pay taxes, insurance, and water and leave something over. And then there's always the chance of my striking it and coming out a millionaire. Now tell me, Alma, don't you think I'm very moderate?"

And Alma could hardly think otherwise. Besides, had not her own cousin—though a remote and distant one to be sure, the black sheep, the harum-scarum, the ne'er-do-well—had not he come down out of that weird North country with a hundred thousand in yellow dust, to say nothing of a half ownership in the hole from which it came?

David Rasmunsen's grocer was surprised when he found him weighing eggs in the scales at the end of the counter, and Rasmunsen himself was more surprised when he found that a dozen eggs weighed a pound and a half—fifteen hundred pounds for his thousand dozen! There would be no weight left for his clothes, blankets, and cooking utensils, to say nothing of the grub he must necessarily consume by the way. His calculations were all thrown out, and he was just proceeding to recast them when he hit upon the idea of weighing small eggs. "For whether they be large or small, a dozen eggs is a dozen eggs," he observed sagely to himself; and a dozen small ones he found to weigh but a pound and a quarter. Thereat the city of San Francisco was overrun by anxious-eyed emissaries, and commission houses and dairy associations were startled by a sudden demand for eggs running not more than twenty ounces to the dozen.

Rasmunsen mortgaged the little cottage for a thousand dollars, arranged for his wife to make a prolonged stay among her own people, threw up his job, and started North. To keep within his schedule he compromised on a second-class passage, which because of the rush was worse than steerage; and in the late summer, a pale and wobbly man, he disembarked with his eggs on the Dyea beach. But it did not take him long to recover his land legs and appetite. His first interview with the Chilkoot packers straightened him up and stiffened his backbone. Forty cents a pound they demanded for the twenty-eight-mile portage, and while he caught his breath and swallowed, the price went up to forty-three. Fifteen husky Indians put the straps on his packs at forty-five, but took them off at an offer of forty-seven from a Skaguay Croesus in dirty shirt and ragged overalls who had lost his horses on the White Pass Trail and was now making a last desperate drive at the country by way of Chilkoot.

But Rasmunsen was clean grit, and at fifty cents found takers who two days later set his eggs down intact at Linderman. But fifty cents a pound is a thousand dollars a ton, and his fifteen hundred pounds had exhausted his emergency fund and left him stranded at the Tantalus point, where each day he saw the fresh-whipsawed boats departing for Dawson. Further, a great anxiety brooded over the camp where the boats were built. Men worked frantically, early and late, at the height of their endurance, caulking, nailing, and pitching in a frenzy of haste for which adequate explanation was not far to seek. Each day the snow line crept farther down the bleak, rock-shouldered peaks, and gale followed gale, with sleet and slush and snow, and in the eddies and quiet places young ice formed and thickened through the fleeting hours. And each morn, toil-stiffened men turned wan faces across the lake to see if the freeze-up had come. For the freeze-up heralded the death of their hope—the hope that they would be floating down the swift river ere navigation closed on the chain of lakes.

To harrow Rasmunsen's soul further, he discovered three competitors in the egg business. It was true that one, a little German, had gone broke and was himself forlornly back-tripping the last pack of the portage; but the other two had boats nearly completed and were daily supplicating the god of merchants and traders to stay the iron hand of winter for just another day. But the iron hand closed down over the land. Men were being frozen in the blizzard, which swept Chilkoot, and Rasmunsen frosted his toes ere he was aware. He found a chance to go passenger with his freight in a boat just shoving off through the rubble, but two hundred, hard cash, was required, and he had no money.

"Ay tank you yust wait one leedle w'ile," said the Swedish boatbuilder, who had struck his Klondike right there and was wise enough to know it. "One leedle w'ile und I make you a tam fine skiff boat, sure Pete."

With this unpledged word to go on, Rasmunsen hit the back trail to Crater Lake, where he fell in with two press correspondents whose tangled baggage was strewn from Stone House, over across the Pass, and as far as Happy Camp.

"Yes," he said with consequence. "I've a thousand dozen eggs at Linderman, and my boat's just about got the last seam caulked. Consider myself in luck to get it. Boats are at a premium, you know, and none to be had."

Whereupon and almost with bodily violence the correspondents clamored to go with him, fluttered greenbacks before his eyes, and spilled yellow twenties from hand to hand. He could not hear of it, but they overpersuaded him, and he reluctantly consented to take them at three hundred apiece. Also they pressed upon him the passage money in advance. And while they wrote to their respective journals concerning the good samaritan with the thousand dozen eggs, the good samaritan was hurrying back to the Swede at Linderman.

"Here, you! Gimme that boat!" was his salutation, his hand jingling the correspondents' gold pieces and his eyes hungrily bent upon the finished craft.

The Swede regarded him stolidly and shook his head.

"How much is the other fellow paying? Three hundred? Well, here's four. Take it."

He tried to press it upon him, but the man backed away.

"Ay tank not. Ay say him get der skiff boat. You yust wait—"

"Here's six hundred. Last call. Take it or leave it. Tell'm it's a mistake."

The Swede wavered. "Ay tank yes," he finally said, and the last Rasmunsen saw of him his vocabulary was going to wreck in a vain effort to explain the mistake to the other fellows.

The German slipped and broke his ankle on the steep hogback above Deep Lake, sold out his stock for a dollar a dozen, and with the proceeds hired Indian packers to carry him back to Dyea. But on the morning Rasmunsen shoved off with his correspondents, his two rivals followed suit.

"How many you got?" one of them, a lean little New Englander, called out.

"One thousand dozen," Rasmunsen answered proudly.

"Huh! I'll go you even stakes I beat you in with my eight hundred."

The correspondents offered to lend him the money, but Rasmunsen declined, and the Yankee closed with the remaining rival, a brawny son of the sea and sailor of ships and things, who promised to show them all a wrinkle or two when it came to cracking on. And crack on he did, with a large tarpaulin squaresail which pressed the bow half under at every jump. He was the first to run out of Linderman, but disdaining the portage, piled his loaded boat on the rocks in the boiling rapids. Rasmunsen and the Yankee, who likewise had two passengers, portaged across on their backs and then lined their empty boats down through the bad water to Bennett.

Bennett was a twenty-five-mile lake, narrow and deep, a funnel between the mountains through which storms ever romped. Rasmunsen camped on the sandpit at its head, where were many men and boats bound north in the teeth of the Arctic winter. He awoke in the morning to find a piping gale from the south, which caught the chill from the whited peaks and glacial valleys and blew as cold as north wind ever blew. But it was fair, and he also found the Yankee staggering past the first bold headland with all sail set. Boat after boat was getting under way, and the correspondents fell to with enthusiasm.

"We'll catch him before Cariboo Crossing," they assured Rasmunsen as they ran up the sail and the *Alma* took the first icy spray over her bow.

Now, Rasmunsen all his life had been prone to cowardice on water, but he clung to the kicking steering oar with set face and determined jaw. His thousand dozen were there in the boat before his eyes, safely secured beneath the correspondents' baggage, and somehow before his eyes were the little cottage and the mortgage for a thousand dollars.

It was bitter cold. Now and again he hauled in the steering sweep and put out a fresh one while his passengers chopped the ice from the blade. Wherever the spray struck, it turned instantly to frost, and the dipping boom of the spritsail was quickly fringed with icicles. The *Alma* strained and hammered through the big seas till the seams and butts began to spread, but in lieu of bailing the correspondents chopped ice and flung it overboard. There was no letup. The mad race with winter was on, and the boats tore along in a desperate string.

"W-w-we can't stop to save our souls!" one of the correspondents chattered, from cold, not fright.

"That's right! Keep her down the middle, old man!" the other encouraged.

Rasmunsen replied with an idiotic grin. The iron-bound shores were in a lather of foam, and even down the middle the only hope was to keep running away from the big seas. To lower sail was to be overtaken and swamped. Time and again they passed boats pounding among the rocks, and once they saw one on the edge of the breakers about to strike. A little craft behind them, with two men, jibed over and turned bottom up.

"W-w-watch out, old man!" cried he of the chattering teeth.

Rasmunsen grinned and tightened his aching grip on the sweep. Scores of times had the send of the sea caught the big square stern of the *Alma* and thrown her off from dead before it till the after-leach of the spritsail fluttered hollowly, and each time, and only with all his strength, had he forced her back. His grin by then had become fixed, and it disturbed the correspondents to look at him.

They roared down past an isolated rock a hundred yards from shore. From its wave-drenched top a man shrieked wildly, for the instant cutting the storm with his voice. But the next instant the *Alma* was by, and the rock growing a black speck in the troubled froth.

"That settles the Yankee! Where's the sailor?" shouted one of his passengers.

Rasmunsen shot a glance over his shoulder at a black squaresail. He had seen it leap up out of the gray to windward and for an hour, off and on, had been watching it grow. The sailor had evidently repaired damages and was making up for lost time.

"Look at him come!"

Both passengers stopped chopping ice to watch. Twenty miles of Bennett were behind them—room and to spare for the sea to toss up its mountains toward the sky. Sinking and soaring like a storm god, the sailor drove by them. The huge sail seemed to grip the boat from the crests of the waves, to tear it bodily out of the water and fling it crashing and smothering down into the yawning troughs.

"The sea'll never catch him!"

"But he'll r-r-run her nose under!"

Even as they spoke the black tarpaulin swooped from sight behind a big comber. The next wave rolled over the spot, and the next, but the boat did not reappear. The *Alma* rushed by the place. A little riffraff of oars and boxes was seen. An arm thrust up and a shaggy head broke surface a score of yards away.

For a time there was silence. As the end of the lake came in sight, the waves began to leap aboard with such steady recurrence that the correspondents no longer chopped ice but flung the water out with buckets. Even this would not do, and after a shouted conference with Rasmunsen, they attacked the baggage. Flour, bacon, beans, blankets, cooking stove, ropes, odds and ends, everything they could get hands on, flew overboard. The boat acknowledged it at once, taking less water and rising more buoyantly.

"That'll do!" Rasmunsen called sternly, as they applied themselves to the top layer of eggs.

"The h-hell it will!" answered the shivering one savagely. With the exception of their notes, films, and cameras, they had sacrificed their outfit. He bent over, laid hold of an egg box, and began to worry it out from under the lashing.

"Drop it! Drop it, I say!"

Rasmunsen had managed to draw his revolver, and with the crook of his arm over the sweep head, was taking aim. The correspondent stood up on the thwart, balancing back and forth, his face twisted with menace and speechless anger.

"My God!"

So cried his brother correspondent, hurling himself face downward into the bottom of the boat. The *Alma*, under the divided attention of Rasmunsen, had been caught by a great mass of water and whirled around. The after-leach hollowed, the sail emptied and jibed, and the boom, sweeping with terrific force across the boat, carried the angry correspondent overboard with a broken back. Mast and sail had gone over the side as well. A drenching sea followed, as the boat lost headway, and Rasmunsen sprang to the bailing bucket.

Several boats hurtled past them in the next half hour—small boats, boats of their own size, boats afraid, unable to do aught but run madly on. Then a ten-ton barge, at imminent risk of destruction, lowered sail to windward and lumbered down upon them.

"Keep off! Keep off!" Rasmunsen screamed.

But his low gunwale ground against the heavy craft, and the remaining correspondent clambered aboard. Rasmunsen was over the eggs like a cat and in the bow of the *Alma*, striving with numb fingers to bend the hauling lines together.

"Come on!" a red-whiskered man yelled at him.

"I've a thousand dozen eggs here," he shouted back. "Gimme a tow! I'll pay you!"

"Come on!" they howled in chorus.

A big whitecap broke just beyond, washing over the barge and leaving the *Alma* half swamped. The men cast off, cursing him as they ran up their sail. Rasmunsen cursed back and fell to bailing. The mast and sail, like a sea anchor, still fast by the halyards, held the boat head on to wind and sea and gave him a chance to fight the water out.

Three hours later, numbed, exhausted, blathering like a lunatic, but still bailing, he went ashore on an ice-strewn beach near Cariboo Crossing. Two men, a government courier and a half-breed voyageur, dragged him out of the surf, saved his cargo, and beached the *Alma*. They were paddling out of the country in a Peterborough and gave him shelter for the night in their stormbound camp. Next morning they departed, but he elected to stay by his eggs. And thereafter the name and fame of the man with the thousand dozen eggs began to spread through the land. Gold seekers who made in before the freeze-up carried the news of his coming. Grizzled old-timers of Forty Mile and Circle City, sourdoughs with leathern jaws and bean-calloused stomachs, called up dream memories of chickens and green things at mention of his name. Dyea and Skaguay took an interest in his being and questioned his progress from every man who came over the passes, while Dawson—golden, omeletless Dawson—fretted and worried and waylaid every chance arrival for word of him.

But of this, Rasmunsen knew nothing. The day after the wreck he patched up the *Alma* and pulled out. A cruel east wind blew in his teeth from Tagish, but he got the oars over the side and bucked manfully into it, though half the time he was drifting backward and chopping ice from the blades. According to the custom of the country, he was driven ashore at Windy Arm; three times on Tagish saw him swamped and beached; and Lake Marsh held him at the freeze-up. The *Alma* was crushed in the jamming of the floes, but the eggs were intact. These he back-tripped two miles across the ice to the shore, where he built a cache, which stood for years after and was pointed out by men who knew.

Half a thousand frozen miles stretched between him and Dawson, and the waterway was closed. But Rasmunsen, with a peculiar tense look in his face, struck back up the lakes on foot. What he suffered on that lone trip, with naught but a single blanket, an ax, and a handful of beans, is not given to ordinary mortals to know. Only the Arctic adventurer may understand. Suffice that he was caught in a blizzard on Chilkoot and left two of his toes with the surgeon at Sheep Camp. Yet he stood on his feet and washed dishes in the scullery of the *Pawona* to the Puget Sound, and from there passed coal on a P. S. boat to San Francisco.

It was a haggard, unkempt man who limped across the shining office floor to raise a second mortgage from the bank people. His hollow cheeks betrayed themselves through the scraggly beard, and his eyes seemed to have retired into deep caverns, where they burned with cold fires. His hands were grained from exposure and hard work, and the nails were rimmed with tight-packed dirt and coal dust. He spoke vaguely of eggs and ice packs, winds and tides; but when they declined to let him have more than a second thousand, his talk became incoherent, concerning itself chiefly with the price of dogs and dog food, and such things as snowshoes and moccasins and winter trails. They let him have fifteen hundred, which was more than the cottage warranted, and breathed easier when he scrawled his signature and passed out the door.

Two weeks later he went over Chilkoot with three dog sleds of five dogs each. One team he drove, the two Indians with him driving the others. At Lake Marsh they broke out the cache and loaded up. But there was no trail. He was the first in over the ice, and to him fell the task of packing the snow and hammering away through the rough river jams. Behind him he often observed a campfire smoke trickling thinly up through the quiet air, and he wondered why the people did not overtake him. For he was a stranger to the land and did not understand. Nor could he understand his Indians when they tried to explain. This they conceived to be a hardship, but when they balked and refused to break camp of mornings, he drove them to their work at pistol point.

When he slipped through an ice bridge near the White Horse and froze his foot, tender yet and oversensitive from the previous freezing, the Indians looked for him to lie up. But he sacrificed a blanket, and with his foot encased in an enormous moccasin big as a water bucket, continued to take his regular turn with the front sled. Here was the cruelest work, and they respected him, though on the side they rapped their foreheads with their knuckles and significantly shook their heads. One night they tried to run away, but the zip-zip of his bullets in the snow brought them back, snarling but convinced. Whereupon, being only savage Chilkat men, they put their heads together to kill him; but he slept like a cat, and waking or sleeping, the chance never came. Often they tried to tell him the import of the smoke wreath in the rear, but he could not comprehend and grew suspicious of them. And when they sulked or shirked, he was quick to let drive at them between the eyes, and quick to cool their heated souls with sight of his ready revolver.

And so it went—with mutinous men, wild dogs, and a trail that broke the heart. He fought the men to stay with him, fought the dogs to keep them away from the eggs, fought the ice, the cold, and the pain of his foot, which would not heal. As fast as the young tissue renewed, it was bitten and seared by the frost, so that a running sore developed, into which he could almost shove his fist. In the mornings, when he first put his weight upon it, his head went dizzy, and he was near to fainting from the pain; but later on in the day it usually grew numb, to recommence when he crawled into his blankets and tried to sleep. Yet he, who had been a clerk and sat at a desk all his days, toiled till the Indians were exhausted and even outworked the dogs. How hard he worked, how much he suffered, he did not know. Being a man of the one idea, now that the idea had come, it mastered him. In the foreground of his consciousness was Dawson, in the background his thousand dozen eggs, and midway between the two his ego fluttered, striving always to draw them together to a glittering golden point. This golden point was the five thousand dollars, the consummation of the idea and the point of departure for whatever new idea might present itself. For the rest, he was a mere automaton. He was unaware of other things, seeing them as through a glass darkly and giving them no thought. The work of his hands he did with machinelike wisdom; likewise the work of his head. So the look on his face grew very tense, till even the Indians were afraid of it and marveled at the strange white man who had made them slaves and forced them to toil with such foolishness.

Then came a snap on Lake Le Barge, when the cold of outer space smote the tip of the planet, and the frost ranged sixty and odd degrees below zero. Here, laboring with open mouth that he might breathe more freely, he chilled his lungs, and for the rest of the trip he was troubled with a dry, hacking cough, especially irritable in smoke of camp or under stress of undue exertion. On the Thirty Mile River he found much open water, spanned by precarious ice bridges and fringed with narrow rim ice, tricky and uncertain. The rim ice was impossible to reckon on, and he dared it without reckoning, falling back on his revolver when his drivers demurred. But on the ice bridges, covered with snow though they were, precautions could be taken. These they crossed on their snowshoes, with long poles held crosswise in their hands, to which to cling in case of accident. Once over, the dogs were called to follow. And on such a bridge, where the absence of the center ice was masked by the snow, one of the Indians met his end. He went through as quickly and neatly as a knife through thin cream, and the current swept him from view down under the stream ice.

That night his mate fled away through the pale moonlight, Rasmunsen futilely puncturing the silence with his revolver—a thing that he handled with more celerity than cleverness. Thirty-six hours later the Indian made a police camp on the Big Salmon.

"Um—um—um funny mans—what you call?—top um head all loose," the interpreter explained to the puzzled captain. "Eh? Yep, clazy, much clazy mans. Eggs, eggs, all a time eggs—savvy? Come bime-by."

It was several days before Rasmunsen arrived, the three sleds lashed together and all the dogs in a single team. It was awkward, and where the going was bad he was compelled to back-trip it sled by sled, though he managed most of the time through herculean efforts to bring all along on the one haul. He did not seem moved when the captain of police told him his man was hitting the high places for Dawson and was by that time probably, halfway between Selkirk and Stewart. Nor did he appear interested when informed that the police had broken the trail as far as Pelly, for he had attained to a fatalistic acceptance of all natural dispensations, good or ill. But when they told him that Dawson was in the bitter clutch of famine, he smiled, threw the harness on his dogs, and pulled out.

But it was at his next halt that the mystery of the smoke was explained. With the word at Big Salmon that the trail was broken to Pelly, there was no longer any need for the smoke wreath to linger in his wake; and Rasmunsen, crouching over his lonely fire, saw a motley string of sleds go by. First came the courier and the half-breed who had hauled him out from Bennett; then mail carriers for Circle City, two sleds of them, and a mixed following of ingoing Klondikers. Dogs and men were fresh and fat, while Rasmunsen and his brutes were jaded and worn down to the skin and bone. They of the smoke wreath had traveled one day in three, resting and reserving their strength for the dash to come when broken trail was met with, while each day he had plunged and floundered forward, breaking the spirit of his dogs and robbing them of their mettle.

As for himself, he was unbreakable. They thanked him kindly for his efforts in their behalf, those fat, fresh men—thanked him kindly, with broad grins and ribald laughter; and now, when he understood, he made no answer. Nor did he cherish silent bitterness. It was immaterial. The idea—the fact behind the idea—was not changed. Here he was and his thousand dozen; there was Dawson; the problem was unaltered.

At the Little Salmon, being short of dog food, the dogs got into his grub, and from there to Selkirk he lived on beans—coarse, brown beans, big beans, grossly nutritive, which griped his stomach and doubled him up at two-hour intervals. But the factor at Selkirk had a notice on the door of the post to the effect that no steamer had been up the Yukon for two years, and in consequence grub was beyond price. He offered to swap flour, however, at the rate of a cupful for each egg, but Rasmunsen shook his head and hit the trail. Below the post he managed to buy frozen horse hide for the dogs, the horses having been slain by the Chilkat cattlemen, and the scraps and offal preserved by the Indians. He tackled the hide himself, but the hair worked into the bean sores of his mouth and was beyond endurance.

Here at Selkirk he met the forerunners of the hungry exodus of Dawson, and from there on they crept over the trail, a dismal throng. "No grub!" was the song they sang. "No grub, and had to go." "Everybody holding candles for a rise in the spring." "Flour dollar'n a half a pound, and no sellers."

"Eggs?" one of them answered. "Dollar apiece, but they ain't none."

Rasmunsen made a rapid calculation. "Twelve thousand dollars," he said aloud.

"Hey?" the man asked.

"Nothing," he answered, and "mushed" the dogs along.

When he arrived at Stewart River, seventy miles from Dawson, five of his dogs were gone, and the remainder were falling in the traces. He also was in the traces, hauling with what little strength was left in him. Even then he was barely crawling along ten miles a day. His cheekbones and nose, frostbitten again and again, were turned bloody black and hideous. The thumb, which was separated from the fingers by the gee pole, had likewise been nipped and gave him great pain. The monstrous moccasin still encased his foot, and strange pains were beginning to rack the leg. At Sixty Mile, the last beans, which he had been rationing for some time, were finished; yet he steadfastly refused to touch the eggs. He could not reconcile his mind to the legitimacy of it and staggered and fell along the way to Indian River. Here a fresh-killed moose and an openhanded old-timer gave him and his dogs new strength, and at Ainslie's he felt repaid for it all when a stampede, ripe from Dawson in five hours, was sure he could get a dollar and a quarter for every egg he possessed.

He came up the steep bank by the Dawson barracks with fluttering heart and shaking knees. The dogs were so weak that he was forced to rest them, and waiting, he leaned limply against the gee pole. A man, an eminently decorous-looking man, came sauntering by in a great bearskin coat. He glanced at Rasmunsen curiously, then stopped and ran a speculative eye over the dogs and the three lashed sleds.

"What you got?" he asked.

"Eggs," Rasmunsen answered huskily, hardly able to pitch his voice above a whisper.

"Eggs! Whoopee! Whoopee!" He sprang up into the air, gyrated madly, and finished with half a dozen war steps. "You don't say—all of 'em?"

"All of 'em?"

"Say, you must be the Egg Man." He walked around and viewed Rasmunsen from the other side. "Come, now, ain't you the Egg Man?"

Rasmunsen didn't know, but supposed he was, and the man sobered down a bit.

"What d'ye expect to get for 'em?" he asked cautiously.

Rasmunsen became audacious. "Dollar'n a half," he said.

"Done!" the man came back promptly. "Gimme a dozen."

"I-I mean a dollar'n a half apiece," Rasmunsen hesitatingly explained.

"Sure. I heard you. Make it two dozen. Here's the dust."

The man pulled out a healthy gold sack the size of a small sausage and knocked it negligently against the gee pole. Rasmunsen felt a strange trembling in the pit of his stomach, a tickling of the nostrils, and an almost overwhelming desire to sit down and cry. But a curious, wide-eyed crowd was beginning to collect, and man after man was calling out for eggs. He was without scales, but the man with the bearskin coat fetched a pair and obligingly weighed in the dust while Rasmunsen passed out the goods. Soon there was a pushing and shoving and shouldering, and a great clamor. Everybody wanted to buy and to be served first. And as the excitement grew, Rasmunsen cooled down. This would never do. There must be something behind the fact of their buying so eagerly. It would be wiser if he rested first and sized up the market. Perhaps eggs were worth two dollars apiece. Anyway, whenever he wished to sell, he was sure of a dollar and a half. "Stop!" he cried when a couple of hundred had been sold. "No more now. I'm played out. I've got to get a cabin, and then you can come and see me."

A groan went up at this, but the man with the bearskin coat approved. Twenty-four of the frozen eggs went rattling in his capacious pockets and he didn't care whether the rest of the town ate or not. Besides, he could see Rasmunsen was on his last legs.

"There's a cabin right around the second corner from the Monte Carlo," he told him, "the one with the sody-bottle window. It ain't mine, but I've got charge of it. Rents for ten a day and cheap for the money. You move right in, and I'll see you later. Don't forget the sody-bottle window.

"Tra-la-loo!" he called back a moment later. "I'm goin' up the hill to eat eggs and dream of home."

On his way to the cabin, Rasmunsen recollected he was hungry and bought a small supply of provisions at the N.A.T.&T. store, also a beefsteak at the butcher shop and dried salmon for the dogs. He found the cabin without difficulty and left the dogs in the harness while he started the fire and got the coffee under way.

"A dollar'n a half apiece—one thousand dozen—eighteen thousand dollars!" He kept muttering it to himself over and over as he went about his work.

As he flopped the steak into the frying pan the door opened. He turned. It was the man with the bearskin coat. He seemed to come in with determination, as though bound on some explicit errand, but as he looked at Rasmunsen an expression of perplexity came into his face.

"I say—now I say—" he began, then halted.

Rasmunsen wondered if he wanted the rent.

"I say, damn it, you know, them eggs is bad."

Rasmunsen staggered. He felt as though someone had struck him an astounding blow between the eyes. The walls of the cabin reeled and tilted up. He put out his hand to steady himself and rested it on the stove. The sharp pain and the smell of the burning flesh brought him back to himself.

"I see," he said slowly, fumbling in his pocket for the sack. "You want your money back."

"It ain't the money," the man said, "but hain't you got any eggs—good?"

Rasmunsen shook his head. "You'd better take the money."

But the man refused and backed away. "I'll come back," he said, "when you've taken stock, and get what's comin'."

Rasmunsen rolled the chopping block into the cabin and carried in the eggs. He went about it quite calmly. He took up the hand ax and, one by one, chopped the eggs in half. These halves he examined carefully and let fall to the floor. At first he sampled from the different cases, then deliberately emptied one case at a time. The heap on the floor grew larger. The coffee boiled over and the smoke of the burning beefsteak filled the cabin. He chopped steadfastly and monotonously till the last case was finished.

Somebody knocked at the door, knocked again, and let himself in.

"What a mess!" he remarked as he paused and surveyed the scene.

The severed eggs were beginning to thaw in the heat of the stove, and a miserable odor was growing stronger.

"Must a-happened on the steamer," he suggested.

Rasmunsen looked at him long and blankly.

"I'm Murray, Big Jim Murray, everybody knows me," the man volunteered. "I'm just hearin' your eggs is rotten, and I'm offerin' you two hundred for the batch. They ain't good as salmon, but still they're fair scoffin's for dogs."

Rasmunsen seemed turned to stone. He did not move. "You go to hell," he said passionlessly.

"Now just consider. I pride myself it's a decent price for a mess like that, and it's better'n nothin'. Two hundred. What you say?"

"You go to hell," Rasmunsen repeated softly, "and get out of here."

Murray gaped with a great awe, then went out carefully, backward, with his eyes fixed on the other's face.

Rasmunsen followed him out and turned the dogs loose. He threw them all the salmon he had bought and coiled a sled lashing up in his hand. Then he reentered the cabin and drew the latch in after him. The smoke from the cindered steak made his eyes smart. He stood on the bunk, passed the lashing over the ridgepole, and measured the swing-off with his eye. It did not seem to satisfy, for he put the stool on the bunk and climbed upon the stool. He drove a noose in the end of the lashing and slipped his head through. The other end he made fast. Then he kicked the stool out from under.

JESSICA AMANDA SALMONSON

Carmanda

JESSICA AMANDA SALMONSON, *scholar, bookseller and publisher of* Fantasy Macabre *magazine, is the author of such sophisticated fantasies as the* Tomoe Gozen Saga, *"The Trilling Princess" (in my anthology* Devils & Demons*), and the short story collections* A Silver Thread of Madness *and* John Collier and Fredric Brown Went Quarreling Through My Head, *from which comes the following haunting variation on Keats's "La Belle Dame sans Merci."*

for Theodore Sturgeon

She was slender, too slender, almost skeletal, yet somehow properly and sensuously proportioned: tall, lithe, sleek, graceful as a frond of gently swaying sea-grass. McCord passed this strange woman on the street and he turned, almost against his will, to watch her walking away as might a specter into the night.

Like a moth to a flame, he had been attracted and, unable to resist, he followed her along the concrete walk, keeping a safe distance behind. Her passing had been swift and he had not clearly pictured her face, so he tried to sort out the features of her profile in the imperfect reflections in the plate glass windows she passed. The reflections were distorted, and he could not properly interpret her appearance. All the same, his heart beat rapidly with unnatural desire. He increased his pace. Still, she remained ever the same distance ahead of him.

For a second he stopped, turned to flee, but came face to face with a reflection that was his own. Looking back at him from the darkness of a department store window was a man young and reasonably handsome, with a well trimmed, light brown beard and longish styled hair. He was fashionably dressed. He glared at himself as though he'd never seen that fellow before, as though it were new revelations and not a reflection staring him in the face.

Why, he wondered, couldn't he run away? He looked back down the street. The tall, thin, so thin woman was out of view. Near to panic, he cursed himself for his cowardice and hesitation and began running down the street, almost colliding with pedestrians who eyed him cautiously. Had she gone into one of the buildings? If so, which one? Had she only turned the corner? Which way, then?

It was a short sprint to the corner, but he stopped all out of breath, scanning the whole intersection until he saw, unmistakably, her long night-blue dress nearly dragging the sidewalk, the backs of her heels peeking out from under the hem with each step, her hair so long and grey as stone—grey not with age but with a naturally unnatural color promising softness and pleasant scents of mysterious places.

There were park benches ahead. The woman turned from the concrete path, crossed an expanse of green lawn, turned with underwater slowness and seated herself not on the bench but on the grass beside one, apparently not caring if her beautiful gown were stained or moistened. Passers seemed not to notice her sitting there. Perhaps her long dress, her hueless crown of hair, her sleek slenderness, were not so unusual here in the city's laughable semblance of nature: a block-wide park where long-haired young men and individualistically clad young women met and collected with regularity; where old widows fed pigeons and the men of another age walked slow, ailing dogs. All the same, even with the human variety in a jaded, populated city, Ken McCord found it strange that people did not stop to gaze upon her, worshiping her unique loveliness even as Kenneth found himself doing.

From a mailbox at the edge of the street, he stood studying her cold, discompassionate face. Hers was a dreadful beauty—could a skull truly be beautiful? Her face was so thin, sallow, her lids naturally blue and half closed over eyes as shimmering green and enigmatic as unknown seas, not so much sultry in their lethargy as seeming far away on some opium journey.

If Death were a woman, She would look like this: unforgettably beautiful, yet inimically frightening.

Her emerald eyes slowly opened and met those of the man at the park's boundary. Buses and cars and people moved along paths of concrete and asphalt like discordant notes across bars of sheet music. Ken was frozen in her glance.

It seemed to him she smiled, but it was impossible to know what that face-without-emotion intended to express. She raised a pale hand, as colorless as her face and slim neck but for the long blood-red nails. She beckoned him with a slow motion of the wrist.

Apprehensive but without hesitation he crossed the lawn, as in a dream—her dream, not his—and sat beside her. For a while they did not speak. He wondered if perhaps he were mad and that he had become infatuated with a marble-white piece of statuary, living only in his demented mind. Then he said, "Tell me your name is Lilith."

She did smile then and it was like silent, mocking laughter. Her teeth were perfect within thin, wide lips and Ken was somehow disappointed not to see the canines pronounced.

"Would you settle for Carmanda?" she asked, her voice deep and resonant and almost, but not quite, masculine, exciting McCord's flesh by its quality.

"Why did I follow you?" he asked, whispering.

"Should I know that?" her deeply sombre voice parried.

"My name is Ken," he said, and held out his hand in greeting. She stared a moment at his outheld hand as if not understanding the gesture. Then she took it, pulled it down into her lap. Her touch was cool, but gentle and nice. McCord looked at their joined hands, her red and perfect nails tipping long fingers, almost like talons. Hers were spidery hands, yet once again exciting in their uncommon beauty.

"I'm mad," he whispered with conviction, more to himself than to her; for he knew only madmen followed women in the streets.

"And I," she said aloud, as though it were the simplest of small facts.

His fear was intense, though he told himself he was thinking irrationally. For a moment, he shivered all over with a feeling of impending danger. But a soft squeeze of his hand calmed him enough to ask her, "What do you want from me?"

"A cure for loneliness."

"Can a beautiful woman be lonely?"

"Am I beautiful?"

"Did you not know you were?"

"I know. But not all men can see beauty in what they fear."

"How do you know I fear you?"

"All men fear women. Could you find bravery enough to run to the ends of the universe to find another such as I?"

"I could walk."

"I could wait."

Silence fell about them. The sounds of the city, the passing of people, barking dogs, all seemed distant as Ken tried to make sense of the dizzying words that had passed between her and himself. Was there subtle warning in her tone? Profound meaning in her words? Or were the things she said not really obscure, meaning nothing more than their face value? She didn't move as he thought these matters out; she was waiting.

"If I made love to you," he asked at last, "would I die?"

"You would slowly waste away," she said calmly, unemotionally. Then she smiled the first smile which did not seem sinister, and he realized that she was teasing him. "Am I that strange to you, Kenneth?"

"I'm strange to myself," he replied, shaking his head, lost in confusion. "I've never been drawn to a perfect stranger so strongly, so utterly. It doesn't seem natural. I don't feel sane. What have I been asking you? Mad questions! Have I fallen in love with you, Carmanda? Is that impossible? Can you love, Carmanda?"

"I can love," she said simply, nearly committally.

"Can you deny," he begged to know, "that you are evil?"

"It is evil to kill a tree that a mandolin might be fashioned from its wood, or to flay some beast that the mandolin might have strings. But would it be less evil to go without song?"

"Is that a riddle?"

"It is."

"I can't answer it."

"Carmanda is the answer."

"I knew that."

In his head a hammer pounded and an aura limited his vision so that he could see nothing but the alluring creature sitting before him. He sat in limbo, somehow knowing he had only to let go of her hand to be free and go his way. She would not stop him. But would he ever be truly free if left with the wonder of what might have been tugging eternally at his mind? If he fled now, would he not spend his life wandering the city streets, himself a daylight spectre, searching for one such as he now beheld?

This time, Carmanda broke the silence. "I could gladly take one as you to where I live; but it might disappoint you to find it no dark cavern or sinister castle. Dear Kenneth, yes I am strange, but born of man and woman like you. No demon I; no spell is upon you, or none of my doing. I knew when you began to follow, but I did not willfully make myself irresistible. Believing this, will you still fear to come with me?"

"Yes," he confessed, "but I would not try to stop myself. I'm not certain it was all in jest you named yourself a succubus; but it is a thing I must risk for what love we might share."

"Then help me up," she bid, tugging on the hand still in her lap. Ken stood, pulling her up after, and when he did, the city street was vanished and the park stretched wild forever. Beyond, a black cottage with thorn fencing and lightless windows sat like a grim sentinel toad in the shadows of high trees by an unreflective pond.

As they neared the black cottage hand in hand, Ken asked his last mad question:

"Will I ever return?"

All she answered was, "Not to me if you leave." And he knew he would never leave.

SARALEE TERRY

The Spirit
of Hospitality

"The Spirit of Hospitality," written and set to music by the pseudonymous poet
SARALEE TERRY, *was featured in* The Lighter Side of Darkness, *a show*
produced in 1991 by The Open Book, New York's first professional readers'
theatre ensemble.

A stormy night, a lonely house. She whispered: "Sir, come in.
I'll lead ye to a cozy bed, and there ye'll meet m' kin—
I mean the spooks that walk these halls and visit folk within."

"I'll gladly rest on warm, dry sheets, but I do sore bethink
That ghosties are the kind of host that drives a man to drink,
And if they flit within these walls, I shall not sleep a wink."

She led me up a dusty stair. "Ah, lad, don't gawp so queer!
Our ghostly clan, nor dam or man, are aught that you maun fear,
For once ye get to know them, ye'll find them rather dear.

Our spectres ain't some raffish crew who utter dire wails;
They play at draughts and vingt-et-un, and tell each other tales.
Ye'll never meet a merrier bunch, though they be dead as nails!"

She led me to my bed. I said, "O lass, you're very brave,
But if tonight I'm visited by something from the grave,
I cannot positively pledge that I won't foam and rave."

"O, in that case, I fear they'd find your company a bore,
And thus I guarantee ye, lad, your chamber they'll ignore."
With that she turned and vanishèd, passing through the floor.

I clutched my chest, I gasped for breath, I shook my fevered
head.
My brain did whirl and churn and twirl. I fell across the bed,
And when I woke the morrow morn, I found that I was dead.

A stormy night, a lonely house. He whispered: "Lass, come in.
I'll lead you to a cozy bed, and there you'll meet my kin—
I mean the spooks who walk these halls and visit folk within . . ."

MAURICE LEVEL

The Cripple

MAURICE LEVEL *(1875–1926), according to the Library of Congress catalog card, was the pseudonym for Jeanne Mareteux-Level. "He" wrote numerous horrific* contes cruelles, *three of which were printed in* Weird Tales *magazine. The first, "Night and Silence," appeared in my anthology* Masterpieces of Terror and the Supernatural, *and the third, "The Look," is in* Weird Tales: The Magazine that Never Dies. *Here is the middle member of that horrific trio.*

Because he knew good manners, and although there was no one present but Farmer Galot, Trache said on entering:

"Good day, gentlemen!"

"You again!" growled Galot, without turning round.

"To be sure," replied Trache.

He raised his two maimed hands, as if explaining, by their very appearance, his instructions.

Two years ago, in harvest-time, a threshing-machine had caught him up and, by a miracle, dashed him to the ground again instead of crushing him to death. They had borne him off, covered with blood, shrieking, with arms mangled, a rib smashed in, and spitting out his teeth. There remained from the accident a certain dullness of intellect, short breath, a whistling sound which seemed to grope for words at the bottom of his chest, scrape them out of his throat and jumble them up as they passed his bare gums, and a pair of crooked hands which he held out before him in an awkward and apprehensive manner.

"Well, what is it you want?" snapped Galot.

"My compensation money," answered Trache with a weak smile.

"Compensation money! I haven't owed you anything for a long time. There's nothing the matter with you now but laziness and a bad disposition. To begin with, you were drunk when the thing happened. I needn't have given you anything."

"I was *not* drunk," said Trache quietly.

The farmer lost all patience.

"At this moment you can use your hands as well as anybody. You keep up the sham before people, but when you are alone you do what you like with them."

"I don't move them then; I can't," mumbled Trache.

"I tell you, you are an impostor, a trickster, a rascal; I say that you are fleecing me because I have not been firmer with you, that you are making a little fortune out of my money, but that you shall not have another cent. There, that's final. Do you understand?"

"Yes, from your point of view," assented Trache without moving.

Galot flung his cap on the table and began to pace the room with long strides.

Trache shook his head and hunched up his shoulders. At last Galot squared up before him.

"How much do you want to settle for good and all? Suppose we say five hundred francs and make an end of it?"

"I want what is due to me according to the judgment of the court."

Galot became transported with rage:

"Ne'er-do-well, lazy-bones, good-for-nothing; I know what you told the court through the mouth of your doctor, and why you would not let mine examine you."

"It was upon the sworn evidence of the doctors that the case was decided," observed the cripple.

"Ah, it isn't they who have to pay!" sneered Galot. "Let me see your hands. . . . Let me look, I say: I know something about injuries."

Trache stretched out his arms and presented the wrists. Galot took them between his heavy hands, turned them over, turned them back, feeling the bones and the fleshy parts, as he would have done with cattle at a fair. Now and then Trache made a wry face and drew back his shoulder. At last Galot pushed him away with brutal force.

"You are artful, cunning. But look out for yourself: I am keeping my eye on you, and when I have found you out, look out for yourself! You will end by laughing on the other side of your face, and to get your living you will have to work—you hear what I say?—to work."

"I should like nothing better," sighed the cripple.

Pale with wrath, Galot emptied a purse of silver money on the table, counted it and pushed it toward him.

"There's your money; now be off."

"If you would be so good as to put it in my blouse," suggested Trache, "seeing that I can't do it myself. . . ."

Then he said, as on entering: "Good day, gentlemen," and with stuffed pocket, shaking head and unsteady step, he took his departure.

To return to his lodging he had to pass along the riverside. In the fields the patient oxen trudged on their way. Laborers were binding the sheaves amid the shocks of corn; and across the flickering haze of the sultry air the barking of dogs came with softened intonation.

Near a bend of the river, where it deepened into a little pool, a woman was washing linen. The water ran at her feet, flecked with foam and in places clouded with a pearly tint.

"Well, are things going as you wish, Françoise?" asked Trache.

"Oh, well enough," said she. "And you?"

"The same as usual . . . with my miserable hands."

He sighed, and the coins jingled under his blouse. Françoise winked at him.

"All the same it isn't so bad—what the threshing-machine has done for you, eh? . . . And then, to be sure, it's only right; Galot can well afford to pay."

"If I wasn't crippled for life, I wouldn't ask for anything."

Thereupon she began to laugh, with shoulders raised and mallet held aloft. She was a handsome girl, and even a good girl, and more than once he had talked to her in the meadow, but now he reddened with anger.

"What is the matter with you all—dropping hints and poking your fun at me?"

She shrugged her shoulders.

"If I gossip it's only for the fun of gossiping."

He sat down near her, mollified, and listened as she beat her linen. Then, wanting to smoke, and unable to use his helpless hands, he asked her:

"Would you mind getting my pouch out of my pocket and filling my pipe for me?"

She wiped her hands on her apron, searched in his blouse, filled his pipe, struck a match and, shielding it with her hand, said jokingly:

"You're lucky in meeting me."

He bent forward to light his pipe. At the same moment she slipped on the bank, lost a sabot, threw up her arms and fell backward into the water.

Seeing her fall, Trache sprang up. She had sunk immediately, dragging her wash-tub after her, in a place where the water was deep and encumbered with weeds. Then her head reappeared, stretched out into the air, and she cried, already half choking:

"Your hand! Your hand!"

Trache stopped short, his pipe shaking in the corner of his mouth. Shriller, more despairingly came the cry:

"Your hand; I'm drowning. . . . Help! . . ."

Some men in a neighboring field were running. But they were at a great distance, and could only be seen as shadows moving over the corn.

Françoise sank again, rose, sank, rose once more. No sound came from her lips now: her face was terrible in its agony of supplication. Then she sank finally; the weeds, scattered in all directions, closed up again; their tangled network lay placid as before under the current. And that was all.

It was only after an hour's search that the body was found, enmeshed in the river growth, the clothes floating over the head. Trache stamped on the ground.

"I, a man, and powerless to do anything! . . . Curses, curses on my miserable hands!"

They tried to calm him as they condoled with him on his wretched lot, accompanying him to his cottage in their desire to soothe. Seeing him approach in this way, his wife uttered a piercing cry. What new disaster had befallen her husband? . . . They told her of the catastrophe, and of his anguish at not being able to save Françoise, whereupon she joined her lamentations to his.

But when they were alone behind closed doors, taking off his hat with a brisk movement, Trache rubbed his benumbed hands, stretched out his fingers, worked his joints, drew forth his pouch full of coins, flung it on the table and said:

"No, damn it. A fine business if I had given her my hand and she had gone and chattered to Galot! . . . No! damn it . . ."

BRAM STOKER

The Squaw

Anthropomorphizing cat owners will have scant affection for the following grisly narrative by BRAM STOKER *(1847–1912), the Irish-born author of* Dracula, The Lair of the White Worm *and other horror tales and novels.* "The Squaw" *was first published in* Holly Leaves, *the 1893 Christmas issue of the British* Illustrated Sporting and Dramatic News, *and was later collected in the posthumous volume* Dracula's Guest and Other Weird Stories.

Nürnberg at the time was not so much exploited as it has been since then. Irving had not been playing *Faust*, and the very name of the old town was hardly known to the great bulk of the travelling public. My wife and I, being in the second week of our honeymoon, naturally wanted someone else to join our party, so that when the cheery stranger, Elias P. Hutcheson, hailing from Isthmian City, Bleeding Gulch, Maple Tree County, Neb., turned up at the station at Frankfort, and casually remarked that he was going on to see the most all-fired old Methusaleh of a town in Yurrup, and that he guessed that so much travelling alone was enough to send an intelligent, active citizen into the melancholy ward of a daft house, we took the pretty broad hint and suggested that we should join forces. We found, on comparing notes afterwards, that we had each intended to speak with some diffidence or hesitation so as not to appear too eager, such not being a good compliment to the success of our married life; but the effect was entirely marred by our both beginning to speak at the same instant—stopping simultaneously and then going on together again. Anyhow, no matter how, it was done; and Elias P. Hutcheson became one of our party. Straightway Amelia and I found the pleasant benefit; instead of quarrelling, as we had been doing, we found that the restraining influence of a third party was such that we now took every opportunity of spooning in odd corners. Amelia declares that ever since she has, as the result of that experience, advised all her friends to take a friend on the honeymoon. Well, we "did" Nürnberg together, and much enjoyed the racy remarks of our transatlantic friend, who, from his quaint speech and his wonderful stock of adventures, might have stepped out of a novel. We kept for the last object of interest in the city to be visited the Burg, and on the day appointed for the visit strolled round the outer wall of the city by the eastern side.

The Burg is seated on a rock dominating the town, and an immensely deep fosse guards it on the northern side. Nürnberg has been happy in that it was never sacked; had it been it would certainly not be so spick and span perfect as it is at present. The ditch has not been used for centuries, and now its base is spread with tea-gardens and orchards, of which some of the trees are of quite respectable growth. As we wandered round the wall, dawdling in the hot July sunshine, we often paused to admire the views spread before us, and in especial the great plain covered with towns and villages and bounded with a blue line of hills, like a landscape of Claude Lorraine. From this we always turned with new delight to the city itself, with its myriad of quaint old gables and acre-wide red roofs dotted with dormer windows, tier upon tier. A little to our right rose the towers of the Burg, and nearer still, standing grim, the Torture Tower, which was, and is, perhaps, the most interesting place in the city. For centuries the tradition of the Iron Virgin of Nürnberg has been handed down as an instance of the horrors of cruelty of which man is capable; we had long looked forward to seeing it; and here at last was its home.

In one of our pauses we leaned over the wall of the moat and looked down. The garden seemed quite fifty or sixty feet below us, and the sun pouring into it with an intense, moveless heat like that of an oven. Beyond rose the grey, grim wall seemingly of endless height, and losing itself right and left in the angles of bastion and counterscarp. Trees and bushes crowned the wall, and above again towered the lofty houses on whose massive beauty Time has only set the hand of approval. The sun was hot and we were lazy; time was our own, and we lingered, leaning on the wall. Just below us was a pretty sight—a great black cat lying stretched in the sun, whilst round her gambolled prettily a tiny black kitten. The mother would wave her tail for the kitten to play with, or would raise her feet and push away the little one as an encouragement to further play. They were just at the foot of the wall, and Elias P. Hutcheson, in order to help the play, stooped and took from the walk a moderate sized pebble.

"See!" he said. "I will drop it near the kitten, and they will both wonder where it came from."

"Oh, be careful," said my wife; "you might hit the dear little thing!"

"Not me, ma'am," said Elias P. "Why, I'm as tender as a Maine cherry-tree. Lor bless ye, I wouldn't hurt the poor pooty little critter more'n I'd scalp a baby. An' you may bet your variegated socks on that! See, I'll drop it fur away on the outside so's not to go near her!" Thus saying, he leaned over and held his arm out at full length and dropped the stone. It may be that there is some attractive force which draws lesser matters to greater; or more probably that the wall was not plumb but sloped to its base—we not noticing the inclination from above; but the stone fell with a sickening thud that came up to us through the hot air, right on the kitten's head, and shattered out its little brains then and there. The black cat cast a swift upward glance, and we saw her eyes like green fire fixed an instant on Elias P. Hutcheson; and then her attention was given to the kitten, which lay still with just a quiver of her tiny limbs, whilst a thin red stream trickled from a gaping wound. With a muffled cry, such as a human being might give, she bent over the kitten, licking its wound and moaning. Suddenly she seemed to realise that it was dead, and again threw her eyes up at us. I shall never forget the sight, for she looked the perfect incarnation of hate. Her green eyes blazed with lurid fire, and the white, sharp teeth seemed to almost shine through the blood which dabbled her mouth and whiskers. She gnashed her teeth, and her claws stood out stark and at full length on every paw. Then she made a wild rush up the wall as if to reach us, but when the momentum ended fell back, and further added to her horrible appearance for she fell on the kitten, and rose with her black fur smeared with its brains and blood. Amelia turned quite faint, and I had to lift her back from the wall. There was a seat close by in shade of a spreading plane-tree, and here I placed her whilst she composed herself. Then I went back to Hutcheson, who stood without moving, looking down on the angry cat below.

As I joined him, he said:

"Wall, I guess that air the savagest beast I ever see—'cept once when an Apache squaw had an edge on a half-breed what they nick-named 'Splinters' 'cos of the way he fixed up her papoose which he stole on a raid just to show that he appreciated the way they had given his mother the fire torture. She got that kinder look so set on her face that it jest seemed to grow there. She followed Splinters more'n three year till at last the braves got him and handed him over to her. They did say that no man, white or Injun, had ever been so long a-dying under the tortures of the Apaches. The only time I ever see her smile was when I wiped her out. I kem on the camp just in time to see Splinters pass in his checks, and he wasn't sorry to go either. He was a hard citizen, and though I never could shake with him after that papoose business—for it was bitter bad, and he should have been a white man, for he looked like one—I see he had got paid out in full. Durn me, but I took a piece of his hide from one of his skinnin' posts an' had it made into a pocket-book. It's here now!" and he slapped the breast pocket of his coat.

Whilst he was speaking the cat was continuing her frantic efforts to get up the wall. She would take a run back and then charge up, sometimes reaching an incredible height. She did not seem to mind the heavy fall which she got each time but started with renewed vigour; and at every tumble her appearance became more horrible. Hutcheson was a kind-hearted man—my wife and I had both no-ticed little acts of kindness to animals as well as to persons—and he seemed concerned at the state of fury to which the cat had wrought herself.

"Wall, now!" he said, "I du declare that that poor critter seems quite desperate. There! there! poor thing, it was all an accident—though that won't bring back your little one to you. Say! I wouldn't have had such a thing happen for a thousand! Just shows what a clumsy fool of a man can do when he tries to play! Seems I'm too darned slipperhanded to even play with a cat. Say, Colonel!" it was a pleasant way he had to bestow titles freely—"I hope your wife don't hold no grudge against me on account of this unpleasantness? Why, I wouldn't have had it occur on no account."

He came over to Amelia and apologised profusely, and she with her usual kindness of heart hastened to assure him that she quite understood that it was an accident. Then we all went again to the wall and looked over.

The cat missing Hutcheson's face had drawn back across the moat, and was sitting on her haunches as though ready to spring. Indeed, the very instant she saw him she did spring, and with a blind unreasoning fury, which would have been grotesque, only that it was so frightfully real. She did not try to run up the wall, but simply launched herself at him as though hate and fury could lend her wings to pass straight through the great distance between them. Amelia, womanlike, got quite concerned, and said to Elias P. in a warning voice:

"Oh! you must be very careful. That animal would try to kill you if she were here; her eyes look like positive murder."

He laughed out jovially. "Excuse me, ma'am," he said, "but I can't help laughin'. Fancy a man that has fought grizzlies an' Injuns bein' careful of bein' murdered by a cat!"

When the cat heard him laugh, her whole demeanour seemed to change. She no longer tried to jump or run up the wall, but went quietly over, and sitting again beside the dead kitten began to lick and fondle it as though it were alive.

"See!" said I, "the effect of a really strong man. Even that animal in the midst of her fury recognises the voice of a master, and bows to him!"

"Like a squaw!" was the only comment of Elias P. Hutcheson, as we moved on our way round the city fosse. Every now and then we looked over the wall and each time saw the cat following us. At first she had kept going back to the dead kitten, and then as the distance grew greater took it in her mouth and so followed. After a while, however, she abandoned this, for we saw her following all alone; she had evidently hidden the body somewhere. Amelia's alarm grew at the cat's persistence, and more than once she repeated her warning; but the American always laughed with amusement, till finally, seeing that she was beginning to be worried, he said:

"I say, ma'am, you needn't be skeered over that cat. I go heeled, I du!" Here he slapped his pistol pocket at the back of his lumbar region. "Why sooner'n have you worried, I'll shoot the critter, right here, an' risk the police interferin' with a citizen of the United States for carryin' arms contrary to reg'lations!" As he spoke he looked over the wall, but the cat, on seeing him, retreated, with a growl, into a bed of tall flowers, and was hidden. He went on: "Blest if that ar critter ain't got more sense of what's good for her than most Christians. I guess we've seen the last of her! You bet, she'll go back now to that busted kitten and have a private funeral of it, all to herself!"

Amelia did not like to say more, lest he might, in mistaken kindness to her, fulfil his threat of shooting the cat: and so we went on and crossed the little wooden bridge leading to the gateway whence ran the steep paved roadway between the Burg and the pentagonal Torture Tower. As we crossed the bridge we saw the cat again down below us. When she saw us her fury seemed to return, and she made frantic efforts to get up the steep wall. Hutcheson laughed as he looked down at her, and said:

"Good-bye, old girl. Sorry I in-jured your feelin's, but you'll get over it in time! So long!" And then we passed through the long, dim archway and came to the gate of the Burg.

When we came out again after our survey of this most beautiful old place which not even the well-intentioned efforts of the Gothic restorers of forty years ago have been able to spoil—though their restoration was then glaring white—we seemed to have quite forgotten the unpleasant episode of the morning. The old lime tree with its great trunk gnarled with the passing of nearly nine centuries, the deep well cut through the heart of the rock by those captives of old, and the lovely view from the city wall whence we heard, spread over almost a full quarter of an hour, the multitudinous chimes of the city, had all helped to wipe out from our minds the incident of the slain kitten.

We were the only visitors who had entered the Torture Tower that morning—so at least said the old custodian—and as we had the place all to ourselves were able to make a minute and more satisfactory survey than would have otherwise been possible. The custodian, looking to us as the sole source of his gains for the day, was willing to meet our wishes in any way. The Torture Tower is truly a grim place, even now when many thousands of visitors have sent a stream of life, and the joy that follows life, into the place; but at the time I mention it wore its grimmest and most gruesome aspect. The dust of ages seemed to have settled on it, and the darkness and the horror of its memories seem to have become sentient in a way that would have satisfied the Pantheistic souls of Philo or Spinoza. The lower chamber where we entered was seemingly, in its normal state, filled with incarnate darkness; even the hot sunlight streaming in through the door seemed to be lost in the vast thickness of the walls, and only showed the masonry rough as when the builder's scaffolding had come down, but coated with dust and marked here and there with patches of dark stain which, if walls could speak, could have given their own dread memories of fear and pain. We were glad to pass up the dusty wooden staircase, the custodian leaving the outer door open to light us somewhat on our way; for to our eyes the one long-wick'd, evil-smelling candle stuck in a sconce on the wall gave an inadequate light. When we came up through the open trap in the corner of the chamber overhead, Amelia held on to me so tightly that I could actually feel her heart beat. I must say for my own part that I was not surprised at her fear, for this room was even more gruesome than that below. Here there was certainly more light, but only just sufficient to realise the horrible surroundings of the place. The builders of the tower had evidently intended that only they who should gain the top should have any of the joys of light and prospect. There, as we had noticed from below, were ranges of windows, albeit of medieval smallness, but elsewhere in the tower were only a very few narrow slits such as were habitual in places of medieval defence. A few of these only lit the chamber, and these so high up in the wall that from no part could the sky be seen through the thickness of the walls. In racks, and leaning in disorder against the walls, were a number of headsmen's swords, great double-handed weapons with broad blade and keen edge. Hard by were several blocks whereon the necks of the victims had lain, with here and there deep notches where the steel had bitten through the guard of flesh and shored into the wood. Round the chamber, placed in all sorts of irregular ways, were many implements of torture which made one's heart ache to see—chairs full of spikes which gave instant and excruciating pain; chairs and couches with dull knobs whose torture was seemingly less, but which, though slower, were equally efficacious; racks, belts, boots, gloves, collars, all made for compressing at will; steel baskets in which the head could be slowly crushed into a pulp if necessary; watchmen's hooks with long handle and knife that cut at resistance—this a specialty of the old Nürnberg police system; and many, many other devices for man's injury to man. Amelia grew quite pale with the horror of the things, but fortunately did not faint, for being a little overcome she sat down on a torture chair, but jumped up again with a shriek, all tendency to faint gone. We both pretended that it was the injury done to her dress by the dust of the chair, and the rusty spikes which had upset her, and Mr. Hutcheson acquiesced in accepting the explanation with a kind-hearted laugh.

But the central object in the whole of this chamber of horrors was the engine known as the Iron Virgin, which stood near the centre of the room. It was a rudely-shaped figure of a woman, something of the bell order, or, to make a closer comparison, of the figure of Mrs. Noah in the children's Ark, but without that slimness of waist and perfect *rondeur* of hip which marks the aesthetic type of the Noah family. One would hardly have recognised it as intended for a human figure at all had not the founder shaped on the forehead a rude semblance of a woman's face. This machine was coated with rust without, and covered with dust; a rope was fastened to a ring in the front of the figure, about where the waist should have been, and was drawn through a pulley, fastened on the wooden pillar which sustained the flooring above. The custodian pulling this rope showed that a section of the front was hinged like a door at one side; we then saw that the engine was of considerable thickness, leaving just room enough inside for a man to be placed. The door was of equal thickness and of great weight, for it took the custodian all his strength, aided though he was by the contrivance of the pulley, to open it. This weight was partly due to the fact that the door was of manifest purpose hung so as to throw its weight downwards, so that it might shut of its own accord when the strain was released. The inside was honeycombed with rust—nay more, the rust alone that comes through time would hardly have eaten so deep into the iron walls; the rust of the cruel stains was deep indeed! It was only, however, when we came to look at the inside of the door that the diabolical intention was manifest to the full. Here were several long spikes, square and massive, broad at the base and sharp at the points, placed in such a position that when the door should close the upper ones would pierce the eyes of the victim, and the lower ones his heart and vitals. The sight was too much for poor Amelia, and this time she fainted dead off, and I had to carry her down the stairs, and place her on a bench outside till she recovered. That she felt it to the quick was afterwards shown by the fact that my eldest son bears to this day a rude birthmark on his breast, which has, by family consent, been accepted as representing the Nürnberg Virgin.

When we got back to the chamber we found Hutcheson still opposite the Iron Virgin; he had been evidently philosophising, and now gave us the benefit of his thought in the shape of a sort of exordium.

"Wall, I guess I've been learnin' somethin' here while madam has been gettin' over her faint. 'Pears to me that we're a long way behind the times on our side of the big drink. We uster think out on the plains that the Injun could give us points in tryin' to make a man oncomfortable; but I guess your old medieval law-and-order party could raise him every time. Splinters was pretty good in his bluff on the squaw, but this here young miss held a straight flush all high on him. The points of them spikes air sharp enough still, though even the edges air eaten out by what uster be on them. It'd be a good thing for our Indian section to get some specimens of this here play-toy to send round to the reservations jest to knock the stuffin' out of the bucks, and the squaws too, by showing them as how old civilisation lays over them at their best. Guess but I'll get in that box a minute jest to see how it feels!"

"Oh no! no!" said Amelia. "It is too terrible!"

"Guess, ma'am, nothin's too terrible to the explorin' mind. I've been in some queer places in my time. Spent a night inside a dead horse while a prairie fire swept over me in Montana Territory—an' another time slept inside a dead buffler when the Comanches was on the war path an' I didn't keer to leave my kyard on them. I've been two days in a caved-in tunnel in the Billy Broncho gold mine in New Mexico, an' was one of the four shut up for three parts of a day in the caisson what slid over on her side when we was settin' the foundations of the Buffalo Bridge. I've not funked an odd experience yet, an' I don't propose to begin now!"

We saw that he was set on the experiment, so I said: "Well, hurry up, old man, and get through it quick."

"All right, General," said he, "but I calculate we ain't quite ready yet. The gentlemen, my predecessors, what stood in that thar canister, didn't volunteer for the office—not much! And I guess there was some ornamental tyin' up before the big stroke was made. I want to go into this thing fair and square, so I must get fixed up proper first. I dare say this old galoot can rise some string and tie me up accordin' to sample?"

This was said interrogatively to the old custodian, but the latter, who understood the drift of his speech, though perhaps not appreciating to the full the niceties of dialect and imagery, shook his head. His protest was, however, only formal and made to be overcome. The American thrust a gold piece into his hand, saying, "Take it, pard! it's your pot; and don't be skeer'd. This ain't no necktie party that you're asked to assist in!" He produced some thin frayed rope and proceeded to bind our companion with sufficient strictness for the purpose. When the upper part of his body was bound, Hutcheson said:

"Hold on a moment, Judge. Guess I'm too heavy for you to tote into the canister. You jest let me walk in, and then you can wash up regardin' my legs!"

Whilst speaking he had backed himself into the opening which was just enough to hold him. It was a close fit and no mistake. Amelia looked on with fear in her eyes, but she evidently did not like to say anything. Then the custodian completed his task by tying the American's feet together so that he was now absolutely helpless and fixed in his voluntary prison. He seemed to really enjoy it, and the incipient smile which was habitual to his face blossomed into actuality as he said:

"Guess this here Eve was made out of the rib of a dwarf! There ain't much room for a full-grown citizen of the United States to hustle. We uster make our coffins more roomier in Idaho territory. Now, Judge, you jest begin to let this door down, slow, on to me. I want to feel the same pleasure as the other jays had when those spikes began to move toward their eyes!"

"Oh no! no! no!" broke in Amelia hysterically. "It is too terrible! I can't bear to see it!—I can't! I can't!"

But the American was obdurate. "Say, Colonel," said he, "Why not take Madame for a little promenade? I wouldn't hurt her feelin's for the world; but now that I am here, havin' kem eight thousand miles, wouldn't it be too hard to give up the very experience I've been pinin' an' pantin' fur? A man can't get to feel like canned goods every time! Me and the Judge here'll fix up this thing in no time, an' then you'll come back, an' we'll all laugh together!"

Once more the resolution that is born of curiosity triumphed, and Amelia stayed holding tight to my arm and shivering whilst the custodian began to slacken slowly inch by inch the rope that held back the iron door. Hutcheson's face was positively radiant as his eyes followed the first movement of the spikes.

"Wall!" he said, "I guess I've not had enjoyment like this since I left Noo York. Bar a scrap with a French sailor at Wapping—an' that warn't much of a picnic neither—I've not had a show fur real pleasure in this dod-rotted Continent, where there ain't no b'ars nor no Injuns, an' wheer nary man goes heeled. Slow there, Judge! Don't you rush this business! I want a show for my money this game—I du!"

The custodian must have had in him some of the blood of his predecessors in that ghastly tower, for he worked the engine with a deliberate and excruciating slowness which after five minutes, in which the outer edge of the door had not moved half as many inches, began to overcome Amelia. I saw her lips whiten, and felt her hold upon my arm relax. I looked around an instant for a place whereon to lay her, and when I looked at her again found that her eye had become fixed on the side of the Virgin. Following its direction I saw the black cat crouching out of sight. Her green eyes shone like danger lamps in the gloom of the place, and their colour was heightened by the blood which still smeared her coat and reddened her mouth. I cried out:

"The cat! look out for the cat!" for even then she sprang out before the engine. At this moment she looked like a triumphant demon. Her eyes blazed with ferocity, her hair bristled out till she seemed twice her normal size, and her tail lashed about as does a tiger's when the quarry is before it. Elias P. Hutcheson when he saw her was amused, and his eyes positively sparkled with fun as he said:

"Darned if the squaw hain't got on all her war paint! Jest give her a shove off if she comes any of her tricks on me, for I'm so fixed everlastingly by the boss, that durn my skin if I can keep my eyes from her if she wants them! Easy there, Judge! don't you slack that ar rope or I'm euchered!"

At this moment Amelia completed her faint, and I had to clutch hold of her round the waist or she would have fallen to the floor. Whilst attending to her I saw the black cat crouching for a spring, and jumped up to turn the creature out.

But at that instant, with a sort of hellish scream, she hurled herself, not as we expected at Hutcheson, but straight at the face of the custodian. Her claws seemed to be tearing wildly as one sees in the Chinese drawings of the dragon rampant, and as I looked I saw one of them light on the poor man's eye, and actually tear through it and down his cheek, leaving a wide band of red where the blood seemed to spurt from every vein.

With a yell of sheer terror which came quicker than even his sense of pain, the man leaped back, dropping as he did so the rope which held back the iron door. I jumped for it, but was too late, for the cord ran like lightning through the pulley-block, and the heavy mass fell forward from its own weight.

As the door closed I caught a glimpse of our poor companion's face. He seemed frozen with terror. His eyes stared with a horrible anguish as if dazed, and no sound came from his lips.

And then the spikes did their work. Happily the end was quick, for when I wrenched open the door they had pierced so deep that they had locked in the bones of the skull through which they had crushed, and actually tore him—it—out of his iron prison till, bound as he was, he fell at full length with a sickly thud upon the floor, the face turning upward as he fell.

I rushed to my wife, lifted her up and carried her out, for I feared

for her very reason if she should wake from her faint to such a scene.
I laid her on the bench outside and ran back. Leaning against the
wooden column was the custodian moaning in pain whilst he held
his reddening handkerchief to his eyes. And sitting on the head of
the poor American was the cat, purring loudly as she licked the
blood which trickled through the gashed socket of his eyes.

I think no one will call me cruel because I seized one of the old
executioner's swords and shore her in two as she sat.

IRVING WERNER

Pictures

IRVING WERNER, *formerly the comptroller of New York City's famous Plaza Hotel, is the author of many exquisitely crafted and gently understated tales of contemporary urban and suburban angst.*

Arthur sprawled in an orange plastic chair in the Jacksonville airport, eyes closed, wondering what the hell he was doing there. It drove him crazy that the bureaucrats thought it perfectly reasonable to drag in five guys from all over the country, who had to spend long hours traveling and being away from home, for a really dumb one-hour conference that could have been handled better by phone.

His right lid began fluttering. He tried to decide whether it was just weariness or nerves again, then opened his eyes to rid himself of the disconcerting sensation.

On a Wednesday afternoon the terminal was less than crowded, with sizable gaps between such groupings of families, lovers, and uniformed airline employees as could be found in every airport. Arthur wondered if airports retained interior decorators with a sharp eye for the usual to blend the groups and position them according to a standard layout approved by the Federal Aviation Administration.

He let his eyes roam in lazy arcs over the banal vista. It was not until they had followed her for some seconds that the image registered in his mind and hoisted him by the collar.

At the far end, she strode back and forth across the entire width of the lounge, toting two pieces of luggage. Each time she reached the doorway at either side she disappeared, as if exiting a stage, and each time reappeared after a short interval, as if for an encore in response to Arthur's applauding gaze.

A man's gray felt hat failed to contain all of the golden hair spilling onto her shoulders. Arthur thought the hat, whether idiosyncrasy or fad, strikingly at odds with the rest of her. Her dress, an unadorned gray, high-necked and nominally demure, was cunningly sculpted to reveal a supporting structure that might easily have provoked another war among the ancient Greeks.

He shut his eyes again, chasing her persistent image with lines that had served him well over the years, "If she be not fair for me, What care I how fair she be?"

He was in the midst of erecting a structure of calm around himself, with his mantra as the bricks and slow deep breaths as the mortar, when the crash brought his walls tumbling down.

His eyes sprang open. Pointing to the luggage dumped onto the chair next to his, she commanded, "Could you keep an eye on this for me?" and without waiting for a response marched away, bottom twitching, high heels clicking, hem twirling.

He was still mulling over equations to account for the long and elliptical trajectory bringing her to a halt in front of his chair, out of all those in the huge room, when she startled him with, "Okay, I'm back. Thanks."

Assuming the transaction completed, he nodded acknowledgment but said nothing. She asked impatiently, "Okay if I sit here?"

"Please." Arthur leaped up to help her transfer her luggage one seat further on.

"So," she said with a little sigh as they sat down. "Where are you headed?"

He was surprised to find her not quite so young as he had at first thought. "New York," he answered. There was a fine webbing at the corners of her eyes, adding interest to skin that was otherwise smooth and unblemished, or at least successfully made up.

"Oh yes. Spent a couple of weeks there once," she said. "The Big Apple. God, what a time! Of course," she added, reaching back to touch the overflow of hair, "that was quite a while ago. When I was still young and attractive."

Arthur gave her his best shy smile. "How could you have possibly been any more attractive than you are right now?"

He liked the way she laughed at that clumsy transparency, unstinted, full-throated. With the laugh still hanging around her eyes and mouth, she said, "The minute I spotted you across the room I knew you for a liar."

They grinned at each other, accomplices in the small verbal misdemeanor. But then the subject seemed exhausted. When the silence began to swell, he punctured it with, "I don't really live in New York, by the way. That's just where the plane lands. Then I still have to go on up to Connecticut."

"Say no more," she said. "The picture is becoming quite clear. A four-bedroom colonial. White with green shutters. Flower garden in front. Am I right? A wife, three kids, and a dog?"

"Not exactly. To begin with," Arthur corrected her, "just two kids."

"Boy and girl?"

"Alicia, ten and Jeremy, twelve." He changed his opinion of the man's hat. He now found it saucily attractive, underscoring the femininity rather than detracting from it. Perhaps, he thought, because of all that golden hair flooding out of it.

"I'm from Atlanta, myself," she explained. "Came out here to look at some real estate. What I do is, I buy old houses, fix them up, and then resell them." In the unhurried voice with the round soft accent it sounded like a cultural activity for gentil ladies.

Actually, her hair was darker than gold. Maybe copper shot through with gold. He liked the way it peeped out of the hat in front, delicately crosshatching part of the forehead.

"What time does your plane take off?" she asked.

"Four-thirty." He glanced at his watch. "Three quarters of an hour to go."

"Why I ask is, I still have a couple of hours to hang around this godforsaken place."

Their eyes met again, but this time bounced off. Each searched the large room, as if hunting for something remarkable. Something worth talking about.

Then she asked, "Got any pictures? Of the kids, I mean."

Arthur looked down at his hands. "I haven't had a chance to take any recently." He glanced up at her. "What about you? Got any of yours?"

"Nope. No kids. No kids, no husband, no pictures." She wilted momentarily, then pulled her shoulders back. "So tell me: Are you down here on business?"

"A totally unnecessary meeting is what I'm down here for."

"My plane doesn't take off for two hours and . . . ," she peered down at her wristwatch, ". . . and ten minutes."

The loudspeaker announced the boarding of an unintelligibly numbered Eastern Airlines flight to an unintelligible city. They watched an airliner taxi in slowly over the tarmac right up to the glass wall.

She crossed her legs. A finely honed ankle swung close to his. "Actually," she said, "the reason I asked when your plane leaves is I wanted to find out if we have enough time to be friends."

Arthur, brow rising, weighed, measured, evaluated, then shrugged. "Sure," he said tentatively, "we can be friends."

"Oh no," she said. "Not if you answer like that. Trying to decide if you're humoring a crazy lady or accepting an invitation for a roll in the hay."

"That's not at all what I was thinking."

"Yes? So then why are we blushing?"

Arthur, feeling the blood in his face, smiled a sheepish admission.

"What I mean is," she said, "everyone has something they need to get off their chest. But maybe there's no one to listen, or else it's too embarrassing. Right now, we have the chance to open up about the most personal things, or to say the craziest things, or anything at all. Like real good friends. And no worry, no embarrassment. Because probably, we'll never meet again."

Arthur hesitated, then permitted a grin to show. "Well, why not? But only if you go first."

"Oh, don't you worry about me. Once I get started, my mouth will go on flapping for three days without any encouragement whatever, and no stopping to even draw breath. Hon, if I were you I'd grab this opportunity while it lasts."

"No, the idea was yours, so the honor should be yours." He had a momentary vision of his head in her lap, with her coppery hair hanging down over him, tickling his face.

With a rueful smile she shook her head, slowly back and forth, pityingly. "That's right, keep it buttoned down and bottled up." She reached out, then, and lightly touched the sleeve above his wrist. "Friend," she said softly, "are you aware how much pain shows? Even when you're smiling?"

Arthur, looking at her carefully, felt himself inching closer. But her calm brown-flecked irises only reflected his own image. He said, "Sorry, I don't know what you mean."

"The hurt is flooding right out through your eyes. It's there for anyone to see who wants to. But you're married, poor fellow, so you probably don't have anyone to talk to about it."

"Wait." He raised an open hand part way in a stop signal. "I don't remember saying I'm married."

"Aren't you?"

"Used to be."

"Is that why you don't carry a picture of the kids?"

"They change too fast at that age."

She reached out and took Arthur's hand in hers. She held it in the palm of the hand resting on her thigh.

"She tells them lies," he said, not knowing he would say it, "and then they don't want to be with me."

She pressed his hand and he averted his face, shaking his head as if impatient with himself. After an interval he turned back to her, smiling thinly. "How about yourself?"

She placed her free hand over his already held in her lap, making a sandwich of it. "I'll talk your ears off, if you'll let me. But perhaps we could do it somewhere else? Over a drink or a quick bite?"

He stifled a vision of the two of them entwined, weaving the tapestry of an illicit afternoon. "They'll be calling my plane in a few minutes."

She said, "Don't you agree we're getting along pretty well?"

"Oh yes." He nodded vigorously. "Very well."

"What would happen if you missed your flight? If you took a later one? Would anyone be harmed?"

Arthur's gaze dropped to his hands. He studied the fantastically complex system of tendons and delicate bones making precise movement possible. He clenched and unclenched his fists; turned his hands palm up and then palm down; bent his fingers to bring the nails into closer view. He could feel the shape of his mouth change, the corners melt upward.

He lifted his head. "No," he said, as if pleased at having solved a knotty problem, "there'd be no harm." He stood up. "Let me help you with that luggage."

She smiled up at him hopefully. "You're with me?"

"Yes," he said, "I'm with you."

She sprang up. He tucked her overnight bag under the arm that held his own case. She picked up her attaché case, then offered her free hand. He grasped it tightly in his.

They started down the corridor. Arthur tried to imagine what they would do when they got outside, but couldn't, and quickly gave it up as irrelevant. He was game for anything at all; this was the beginning of a new chapter. No, he corrected himself, not a new chapter, a whole new book.

Hand in hand, they walked briskly across the lounge. The clack of her heels on the polished floor seemed to Arthur a drum roll, a flourish accompanying a brave explorer's departure for unknown worlds. He intercepted the glances of male passersby, lasers flashing desire at her and envy at him. And then he gave himself up to her fragrance, to the feel of her smooth cool fingers. To the idea of her.

They were through the lounge. Then they were past the ticketing area. Through the plate-glass outer wall they could see the taxis lined up just beyond, waiting.

It was then that the clatter of her heels slowed. He heard them falter.

"Is anything wrong?" he asked.

They stopped. Puzzlement on her face, she asked, "Didn't you realize you were holding me back? Pulling on my hand?"

"No," he said, defending himself. Even more adamantly, "No." Then, conceding somewhat, he asked, more gently, "Did I really?" And at the same moment he posed the question the answer became clear to him. His shoulders sagged and he bent to set his briefcase on the floor. Still looking down, he shook his head mournfully. "I really wanted to. But I guess I just can't do it."

"Can't do what?" she asked coolly. "Skip the plane? Have a drink with me? Talk?"

He peered up at her. "Go with you."

She reached for her case. Straightening up quickly, he lifted it and held it away from her. "Please don't," he said, touching her arm. "Sit down with me. Please."

Grudgingly, she allowed him to steer her to an empty seat. Almost immediately she jumped up again. "No. I'm going to leave you alone to enjoy your pain."

"Don't go," he pleaded. "I want to explain. Something I'm not sure I understand myself."

With a quick little shrug of exasperation she dropped back into her seat. She lifted off the hat and let it fall onto her lap. Her hair, cascading, was a living thing. He seated himself facing her. He took a deep breath, and she turned her ear toward him as if to better concentrate on the disembodied voice.

He said, "There's no picture in my wallet, but there is one I carry in my mind. Alicia and Jeremy sitting at the kitchen table, doing their homework. The dog's poking her head into Jeremy's lap and he's petting her with one hand and writing with the other. Supper's cooking, and the heat from the oven fogs the windows. Alicia asks me to help her multiply fractions."

They stared at each other through a departure announcement. Arthur marveled at how quickly her features and facial expressions were becoming familiar to him: the faint quarter-inch tomboy scar on her temple, the way she had of worrying her lower lip when thinking.

He said, as if mulling over the inexplicable, "Whenever something good comes along, I get scared. That it'll remove me from that picture."

She nodded slowly, comprehending. "Oh, my dear," she smiled ruefully, telling a joke on herself, "I was wanting to help mend your wings and you're still imagining you can fly."

He couldn't tell if she intended contempt or pity or regret, but he heard only caring when she softly added, "We have met too soon."

He pushed himself to his feet. "I think they've already called my flight."

"Yes," she said. "Good luck. Don't forget your briefcase."

"Good luck," he said, gazing down at her shining copper hair. Its naked center part, not quite straight, seemed touchingly vulnerable. When she glanced up at him he hesitated, then said shyly, "Goodbye, friend."

He took a dozen steps before he heard her call after him, "What's your name?"

He turned, backpedaling, still moving away from her. "Arthur," he yelled.

She stood up, as if to make herself better heard. She shouted back at him, presumably her name, but already he was too far away to hear it distinctly. Then a group of travelers came between, and he lost sight of her.

GUY DE MAUPASSANT

The Necklace

"The Necklace," one of the most famous tales-with-a-twist ever written, is by the great French novelist and short story writer GUY DE MAUPASSANT *(1850–1893). Normally, I would consider this too familiar a composition to include in one of my anthologies, but it is a necessary prelude to the selection which follows immediately afterward.*

She was one of those pretty, charming young women, born, as if through an error of destiny, into a family of clerks. She had no dowry, no hopes, no means of becoming known, appreciated, loved and married by a man either rich or distinguished; so she allowed herself to marry a petty clerk in the office of the Board of Education.

She was simple, not being able to adorn herself; and she was unhappy, as one out of her class; for women belong to no caste, no race —their grace, their beauty and their charm serving them in the place of birth and family. Their inborn finesse, their instinctive elegance, their suppleness of wit are their only aristocracy, making some daughters of the people the equals of great ladies.

She suffered incessantly, feeling herself born for all delicacies and luxuries. She suffered from the poverty of her apartment, the shabby walls, the worn chairs, and the faded fabrics. All these things, which another woman in her position would not have noticed, tortured and angered her.

The sight of the little maid, who kept their humble home, awoke in her sad regrets and desperate dreams. She thought of quiet antechambers, with their Oriental hangings, lighted by high, bronze torches, and of the two great footmen in fine livery who slept in the large armchairs, made drowsy by the heavy air from the heating apparatus.

She thought of large drawing rooms, hung in old silks, of graceful pieces of furniture carrying bric-à-brac of inestimable value, and of the little perfumed coquettish apartments, made for five o'clock chats with one's most intimate friends, men known and sought after, whose attention all women envied and desired.

When she seated herself for dinner, before the round table where the tablecloth had been used three days, her husband would uncover the tureen with a delighted air, saying, "Oh! the good potpie! I know nothing better than that—"

Then she would think of elegant dinner parties, of the shining silver, of the tapestries peopling the walls with ancient personages and rare birds in the midst of fairy forests; she thought of the exquisite food served on marvelous dishes, of the whispered gallantries, listened to with the smile of the sphinx, while eating the rose-colored flesh of trout or a chicken's wing.

She had neither frocks nor jewels, nothing. And she loved only those things. She felt that she was made for them. She had such a desire to please, to be sought after, to be clever, and courted.

She had a rich friend, a schoolmate at the convent, whom she did not like to visit; she suffered so much when she returned home again. And she wept for whole days from chagrin, from regret, from despair, and disappointment.

One evening her husband returned elated, bearing in his hand a large envelope.

"Here," said he, "here is something for you."

She quickly tore it open and drew out a printed card on which were inscribed these words:

The Minister of Public Instruction and Madame George Ramponneau ask the honor of Mr. and Mrs. Loisel's company Monday evening, January 18, at the Minister's residence.

Instead of being delighted, as her husband had hoped, she threw the invitation spitefully upon the table murmuring, "What do you suppose I want with that?"

"But, my dear, I thought it would make you happy. You never go out, and this is an occasion, and a fine one! I had a great deal of trouble to get it. Everybody wants one, and it is very select; not many are given to employees. You will see the whole official world there."

She looked at him with an irritated eye and declared impatiently, "What do you suppose I have to wear to such a thing as that?"

He had not thought of that; he stammered, "Why, the dress you wear when we go to the theater. It seems very pretty to me—"

He was silent, stupefied, in dismay, at the sight of his wife weeping. Two great tears fell slowly from the corners of her eyes toward the corners of her mouth.

"What is the matter? What is the matter?" he implored her.

By a violent effort, she controlled her vexation and responded in a calm voice, wiping her moist cheeks, "Nothing. Only I have no dress and consequently I cannot go to this affair. Give your card to some colleague whose wife is better fitted out than I."

He was grieved, but answered, "Let us see, Mathilde. How much would a suitable costume cost, something that would serve for other occasions, something reasonable?"

She reflected for some seconds, making estimates and thinking of a sum that she could ask for without bringing with it an immediate refusal and a frightened exclamation from the economical clerk.

Finally she said, in a hesitating voice, "I cannot tell exactly, but it seems to me that four hundred francs ought to cover it."

He turned a little pale, for he had saved just this sum to buy a gun that he might be able to join some hunting parties the next summer with some friends who went to shoot larks on the plains on Sunday.

Nevertheless, he answered, "Very well. I will give you four hundred francs. But try to have a pretty dress."

The day of the ball approached and Madame Loisel seemed sad, disturbed, anxious. Nevertheless, her dress was nearly ready.

Her husband said to her one evening, "What is the matter with you? You have acted strangely for two or three days."

And she responded, "I am miserable not to have a jewel, not one stone, nothing to adorn myself with. I shall have such a poverty-laden look. I would prefer not to go to this party."

He replied, "You can wear some natural flowers. At this season they look very chic. For ten francs you can have two or three magnificent roses."

She was not convinced. "No," she replied, "there is nothing more humiliating than to have a shabby air in the midst of rich women."

Then her husband cried out, "How stupid we are! Go and find

your friend Madame Forestier and ask her to lend you her jewels. You are well enough acquainted with her to do this."

She uttered a cry of joy. "It is true!" she said, "I had not thought of that."

The next day she went to her friend's house and related her story of distress. Madame Forestier went to her cabinet with the glass doors, took out a large jewel case, brought it, opened it, and said, "Choose, my dear."

She saw at first some bracelets, then a collar of pearls, then a Venetian cross of gold and jewels and of admirable workmanship. She tried the jewels before the glass, hesitated, but could neither decide to take them nor leave them.

Then she asked, "Have you nothing more?"

"Why, yes. Look for yourself. I do not know what will please you."

Suddenly she discovered, in a black satin box, a superb necklace of diamonds, and her heart beat fast with an immoderate desire. Her hands trembled as she picked them up. She placed them around her throat against her dress, and remained in ecstasy before them.

Then she asked, in a hesitating voice, full of anxiety, "Could you lend me this? Only this?"

"Why, yes, certainly."

She fell on her friend's neck, embraced her with passion, then went away with her treasure.

The day of the ball arrived. Madame Loisel was a great success. She was the prettiest of all, elegant, gracious, smiling, and full of joy. All the men noticed her, asked her name, and wanted to be presented. All the members of the cabinet wished to waltz with her. The Minister of Education paid her some attention.

She danced with enthusiasm, with passion, intoxicated with pleasure, thinking of nothing, in the triumph of her beauty, in the glory of her success, in a kind of cloud of happiness that came of all this homage, and all this admiration, of all these awakened desires, and this victory so complete and sweet to the heart of a woman.

She went home toward four o'clock in the morning. Her husband had been half asleep in one of the little salons since midnight, with three other gentlemen whose wives were enjoying themselves very much.

He threw the wrap they had carried for the return home around her shoulders—a modest garment for everyday wear, whose poverty clashed with the elegance of the ball costume. She felt this and wished to hurry away in order not to be noticed by the other women who were wrapping themselves in rich furs.

Loisel detained her. "Wait," he said. "You will catch cold out there. I am going to call a cab."

But she would not listen and descended the steps rapidly. When they were in the street, they began to seek a cab, hailing the coachmen whom they saw at a distance, but they could not find an empty one.

They walked along toward the Seine, hopeless and shivering. Finally they found on the quai one of those old, nocturnal *coupés* that one sees in Paris after nightfall, as if they were ashamed of their misery by day.

It took them to their door in Martyr Street, and they went wearily up to their apartment. It was all over for her. And on his part, he remembered that he would have to be at the office by ten o'clock.

She removed the wrap from her shoulders before the mirror, for a final view of herself in her glory. Suddenly she uttered a cry. Her necklace was not around her neck!

Her husband, already half undressed, asked, "What is the matter?"

She turned toward him excitedly, "I have—I have—I no longer have Madame Forestier's necklace."

He cried in dismay, "What! How is that? It is not possible."

And they looked in the folds of her dress, in the folds of the wrap, in the pockets, everywhere. They could not find it.

He asked, "You are sure you still had it when we left the ball?"

"Yes, I felt it in the vestibule as we came out."

"But if you had lost it in the street, we should have heard it fall. It must be in the cab."

"Yes. It is probable. Did you take the number?"

"No. And you, did you notice what it was?"

"No."

They looked at each other utterly downcast. Finally, Loisel dressed himself again.

"I am going," he said, "over the route where we went on foot, to see if I can find it."

And he went. She remained in her evening gown, not having the strength to go to bed, stretched on a chaise lounge, without ambition or thoughts.

Toward seven o'clock that morning her husband returned. He had found nothing.

He went to the police and to the cab offices, and put an advertisement in the newspapers, offering a reward; he did everything that afforded them a suspicion of hope.

She waited all day in a state of bewilderment before this frightful disaster. Loisel returned at evening with his face harrowed and pale; he had discovered nothing.

"It will be necessary," said he, "to write to your friend that you have broken the clasp of the necklace and that you will have it repaired. That will give us time to turn around."

She wrote as he dictated.

At the end of a week, they had lost all hope. And Loisel, older by five years, declared, "We must take steps to replace this necklace."

The next day they took the box which had enclosed it, to the jeweler whose name was on the inside. He consulted his books.

"It is not I, madame," he said, "who sold this necklace; I only furnished the box."

Then they went from jeweler to jeweler seeking a necklace like the other one, consulting their memories, both of them ill with chagrin and anxiety.

In a shop on the Palais-Royal, they found a chaplet of diamonds which seemed to them exactly like the one they had lost. It was valued at forty thousand francs. They could get it for thirty-six thousand.

They begged the jeweler not to sell it for three days and made an arrangement by which they could return it for thirty-four thousand francs if they found the other one before the end of February.

Loisel possessed eighteen thousand francs which his father had left him. He borrowed the rest.

He borrowed it, asking for a thousand francs of one, five hundred of another, five louis of this one, and three louis of that one. He gave notes, made ruinous promises, and borrowed money from usurers. He compromised his whole existence; in fact, risked his signature, without even knowing whether he could make it good or not. Harassed by anxiety for the future, by the black misery which surrounded him, and by the prospect of all physical privations and moral torture, he went to get the new necklace, depositing on the merchant's counter thirty-six thousand francs.

When Madame Loisel took back the jewels to Madame Forestier, the latter said to her in a frigid tone, "You should have returned them to me sooner, for I might have needed them."

She did not open the jewel box as her friend feared she would. But if she should notice the substitution, what would she think? What should she say? Would she take her for a robber?

Madame Loisel now knew the horrible life of necessity. However, she did her part completely, heroically. It was necessary to pay this frightful debt. She would pay it. They dismissed the maid; they changed their lodgings; they rented some rooms under a mansard roof.

She learned the heavy cares of a household, the tedious work of a kitchen. She washed the dishes, using her rosy nails upon the greasy pots and the bottoms of the stewpans. She washed the soiled linen, the chemises, and dishcloths, which she hung on the line to dry; she took the refuse down to the street each morning and brought up the water, stopping at each landing for breath. And, frugally clothed, she went to the grocer's, the butcher's, and the fruiterer's, with her basket on her arm, shopping, haggling, defending to the last sou her miserable money.

Every month it was necessary to renew some notes, thus obtaining time, and to pay others.

The husband worked in the evenings, auditing the books of some merchants, and at night he often did copying at five sous a page.

And this life lasted for ten years.

At the end of ten years, they had restored all, all, with the usurer's interest, and accumulated interest besides.

Madame Loisel seemed old now. She had become a strong, hard woman, the crude woman of the poor household. Her hair badly dressed, her skirts awry, her hands red, she spoke in a loud tone, and scrubbed the floors. But sometimes, when her husband was at the office, she would seat herself before the window and think of that evening party of former times, of that ball where she was so beautiful and so flattered.

How would it have been if she had not lost that necklace? Who knows? How singular is life, and how full of changes! How small a thing can ruin or save one!

One Sunday, as she was taking a walk in the Champs-Élysées to rid herself of the cares of the week, she suddenly noticed a woman walking with a child. It was Madame Forestier, still young, still pretty, still attractive. Madame Loisel was disturbed. Should she speak to her? Yes, certainly. And now that she had paid, she would tell her all. Why not?

She approached her. "Good morning, Jeanne."

Her friend did not recognize her and was astonished to be so familiarly addressed by this common personage.

She stammered, "But, madame—I do not know—You must be mistaken—"

"No, I am Mathilde Loisel."

Her friend uttered a cry of astonishment: "Oh! My poor Mathilde! How you have changed—"

"Yes, I have had some hard days since I saw you, and some miserable ones—and all because of you—"

"Because of me? How is that?"

"You remember the diamond necklace that you lent me to wear to the Commissioner's ball?"

"Yes, indeed."

"Well, I lost it."

"How is that possible, since you returned it to me?"

"I returned another to you exactly like it. And it has taken us ten years to pay for it. You can understand that it was not easy for us who have nothing. But it is over and I am satisfied."

Madame Forestier stopped short. She said, "You say that you bought a diamond necklace to replace mine?"

"Yes. You did not notice it then? They were exactly alike." And she smiled with a proud and simple joy.

Madam Forestier was touched and took both Mathilde's hands as she replied, "Oh! my poor Mathilde! Mine was false. It was not worth over five hundred francs!"

JACK MOFFITT

The Necklace
(A Sequel to DE Maupassant's "The Necklace")

JACK MOFFITT *was a Hollywood screenwriter who, during the 1940s, astonished the editors of* Ellery Queen's Mystery Magazine *(EQMM) by writing the perfect sequel to Frank R. Stockton's riddle tale "The Lady or the
Tiger," an enigma long deemed unsolvable. (Moffitt's brilliant solution appears in my 1992 Doubleday Book and Music Club anthology,* Lovers &
Other Monsters.*) Moffitt told the editors at EQMM that he intended to
solve such other literary mysteries as Cleveland Moffett's "The Mysterious
Card," but there is no record that he ever did. However, Moffitt did write a
sequel to Guy de Maupassant's preceding "The Necklace," and here it is.*

Women live in a secret world. They will share their beds much more
readily than their thoughts. A husband may know every contour of
his wife's body and still be ignorant of what goes on in her mind.
Sometimes a great emotional climax breaks down this barricade and
a man who has lived with the most commonplace of females finds
himself shocked as he looks across the spiritual wreckage at things
that are both terrifying and inspired.

I am thinking of the case of Mathilde Loisel. Her story has waited
a century to be told. De Maupassant told half of it in his little masterpiece called "The Necklace." But there was a second half that
stemmed from the first.

It is this that I propose to tell you. I found the story among the
memoirs of a long dead priest. He had been Madame Loisel's confessor—and it is certain that he enjoyed the confidence of the Paris

police officers who were assigned to the Loisel case. By means of a curious collaboration, in which they considered both criminal and spiritual clues, they seem to have arrived at a solution which had its overtones of disconcerting human truth.

As you undoubtedly remember, de Maupassant tells of a pretty and vain young woman, Madame Loisel, who borrowed a diamond necklace to wear to a ball. On the way home, she lost it. The author goes on to explain how she returned a duplicate of the lost piece of jewelry and to describe the miserable ten years of poverty and drudgery by which she and her husband, a small-salaried clerk, managed to pay for it. Then, after the struggle was over, Madame Loisel saw the woman from whom she had borrowed the necklace walking in the Champs-Élysées on a Sunday afternoon. Her name was Madame Jeanne Forestier and, except for the child by her side, the years had brought few changes to this prosperous matron. The unfortunate Madame Loisel went up to her.

De Maupassant brings his narrative to its dénouement as his heroine says:

"Good morning, Jeanne."

Her friend did not recognize her and was astonished to be so familiarly addressed by this common personage.

She stammered, "But, madame—I do not know—You must be mistaken—"

"No, I am Mathilde Loisel."

Her friend uttered a cry of astonishment: "Oh! My poor Mathilde! How you have changed—"

"Yes, I have had some hard days since I saw you, and some miserable ones—and all because of you—"

"Because of me? How is that?"

"You remember the diamond necklace that you lent me to wear to the Commissioner's ball?"

"Yes, indeed."

"Well, I lost it."

"How is that possible, since you returned it to me?"

"I returned another to you exactly like it. And it has taken us ten years to pay for it. You can understand that it was not easy for us who have nothing. But it is over and I am satisfied."

Madame Forestier stopped short. She said, "You say that you bought a diamond necklace to replace mine?"

"Yes. You did not notice it then? They were exactly alike." And she smiled with a proud and simple joy.

Madam Forestier was touched and took both Mathilde's hands as she replied, "Oh! my poor Mathilde! Mine was false. It was not worth over five hundred francs!"

That is where de Maupassant ends his narrative. But life cannot conclude with a paragraph. Ten minutes after the tragic revelation, Madame Forestier had called her carriage and the horses were drawing them smartly through the shaded elegance of the Champs-Élysées. Jeanne was crying. She kept exclaiming piteously over the tragedy of Mathilde's wasted ten years.

Mathilde said nothing. She sat with her big hands limp in her lap and her eyes expressionless.

What could this flighty woman with her ostrich feathers and her smell of mignonette know of toil and poverty? Her words lacked meaning.

Jeanne's child sat silently in a corner of the carriage. Her little feet did not touch the floor. Her soft eyes regarded Mathilde with uncomprehending awe; as though she were rendering homage to the heroine of some grownup play—a play she found impressive but whose plot she did not understand.

Without realizing it, Mathilde responded to the look of the child. It gave her a certain pleasure. She had not been the center of admiring attention for such a long time. Not since the night of the ministerial ball—when her husband had dozed, with other unimportant guests, in an anteroom while she danced until four in the morning with fashionable young men!

When they reached the home of the Forestiers, this sense of pleasure increased. Madame Forestier was so full of what had happened that she started blurting out the story to the old man-servant who opened the door. She told more of it to the maid as she took their wraps. Both servants followed them up the stairs.

Jeanne's husband was dozing in a worn silk chair, as they entered the boudoir sitting room. He removed a silk handkerchief from his face and arose to blink at his wife as she crossed to the wardrobe with a rustle of flounces and opened the mirrored door. He yawned as though expecting neither his wife's chatter nor her guest to be very interesting. Mathilde felt herself a nobody in his presence. A high bald brow and a magnificent yellow beard gave him a Jovian appearance. The newspapers sometimes mentioned him as one of the court physicians.

He listened owlishly as Madame Forestier brought out her jewel box and unlocked it. Mathilde did not see the pearls which she had been tempted to borrow on that momentous visit ten years before. But some new trinkets had been added and the Venetian cross of intricate workmanship still was there. It now occurred to Mathilde to wonder if these treasures were artificial, too.

But such doubts were forgotten when Madame Forestier reached into the bottom of her coffer and brought out the black satin necklace case. It was worn. Its stitches were broken and, from beneath the ruined fabric, a soiled white showed through—like sickly flesh within a ruined stocking. It was a miserable container for a fortune. Mathilde found herself choking with disappointment.

But her breath came quicker and her heart pounded noisily when Madame Forestier snapped the catch and the frayed lid sprang back, revealing the glittering necklace.

How bright they were! How dazzling! Thirty-six thousand francs' worth of brilliant luxury. How could the Forestiers ever have mistaken them for imitations? How pure and stainless they were! Unsmirched by the ten years of filth and poverty that had paid for them.

Mathilde held her breath like a stalking animal. She scarcely dared look at her host and hostess. She must not communicate her anxiety. This was the critical moment.

Would the necklace be returned to her? If the Forestiers refused to surrender it, how could she prove it was hers? Ten years of haggling economy had left her suspicious of everyone. These people were supposed to be rich, but the threadbare upholstery of their fashionable furniture was in a suspicious contrast to their carriage and their clothing. They might be keeping up appearances. Anyway, no one was ever too rich to stop loving money. In her ten years of poverty, Mathilde had yet to meet a generous landlord or an open-handed shopkeeper. No one gave anything away.

Of course Mathilde now had witnesses. When Jeanne had chattered, like a fool, in front of the servants, it had seemed to be too good to be true. Yet servants are at the mercy of their masters. They can be bribed or intimidated. And, if their masters are politically prominent, the police are willing to dismiss their testimony as malicious tale-bearing. Most of Dr. Forestier's patients had positions in the government.

Mathilde glanced at him from the corners of wary eyes. He was eyeing the necklace as though he never had seen it before. One large pink hand clutched his yellow beard—paralyzed in the midst of a stately gesture. He seemed both thinking and listening, making a befuddled effort to force the sleep from his eyes. He wheezed. His whole being appeared to be struggling with some idea too startling to be readily absorbed.

Then his wife laughed and placed the jewel case in Mathilde's hands.

"This now belongs to you, my dear."

Mathilde couldn't smile. She wasn't sure yet. It had been too easy. She turned her full shrewd look on the woman's husband.

He failed to meet her eyes. His gaze was fixed enigmatically on the servants who loitered breathlessly by the door. For this domestic drama, they were an avid audience.

Benevolent wrinkles appeared at the corners of Dr. Forestier's eyes. A smile bloomed in the depths of the yellow beard.

"Of course the necklace belongs to you, Madame Loisel," he said. "There can be no question about it."

Ten years before, when her imagination glamorized such gentle folk, she would have taken his graciousness for granted. But now she found it unnatural. She heard herself sobbing most unpleasantly and she wished that she could stop. She wanted to take this treasure of hers and run out of the house.

It was hers. She wanted to be alone with it!

But she was afraid.

After ten years, Mathilde's husband still was an unimportant little clerk. He had achieved three promotions during the interval of struggle, each with its infinitesimal salary increase. His insignificance was, perhaps, fortunate. Had he been more important, he never would have survived the shifting tides of politics at the Ministry of Public Instruction where he was employed.

As it was, he had become a respected fixture in that gray world of copyists wherein distinction is won by the mastery of petty routine and where valor consists of a patient and uncomplaining ability to hang on.

And he was not unhappy. On the contrary, he felt a tremendous sense of accomplishment over having, several months before, repaid the last loan necessitated by the necklace catastrophe—down to the final fraction of compound interest. He regarded himself as a man of amply proven honor. And he looked back on the enormity of his debt with the same pride which misers reserve for their savings.

At first this triumph was accompanied by a sort of purposeless bewilderment. During the years of unremitting industry, he had lost all ability to enjoy leisure. Indeed, his bleak surroundings made work a blessing which permitted squalor to be ignored.

So Monsieur Loisel set for himself a new ambition. If he and his good wife continued to work and economize they might, within the not too distant future, return to such an attractive apartment as they, during their early wedded years, had occupied in the Rue des Martyrs. Everything, or nearly everything, might be as it once was.

And so, on that fateful Sunday afternoon, he was alone in his garret, bent over the rickety table, still intent on making extra money by copying manuscripts for five sous a page—and smiling at his work.

He was aroused from his happy musings by the soup kettle. After simmering all afternoon, it had suddenly come to a boil. Sniffing the appetizing smell of meat and vegetables, Monsieur Loisel put down his pen and shuffled to the stove. It was wonderful to have meat twice a week now. Without waiting for his wife to come home, Monsieur Loisel popped a tiny bit of beef into his mouth and felt a delightful guilt. He smacked his lips. When Mathilde had something to work with, she was an excellent cook.

But the soup needed a little more salt. Or perhaps it didn't. He wouldn't want to ruin it. Mathilde should be home now to decide such questions. An annoyed uneasiness took possession of him as he looked out the window, and realized that it was late. It was well past the dinner hour. Half the chimneys had stopped smoking as householders let their kitchen fires go out. Monsieur Loisel had been uncomplaining over a ten-year interruption of his life. But he wanted his dinner on time.

He polished his spectacles and peered down at the figures on the pavement. As they moved in and out through the patches of street light they looked like grotesque foreshortened toys. He could distinguish no one from this height. Hurrying to the alcove, he kicked off his carpet slippers and fumbled for his gaiters. He must go out and look for her. Mathilde was long overdue.

He was beginning to worry now. He remembered newspaper stories of robbers and footpads; ruffians who leapt from alleyways and stole women's rings by slashing off their fingers. Monsieur Loisel shuddered. Mathilde had devoured such stories. The women, she maintained, were more to blame than the criminals. Was not their vanity a constant temptation to violence as they walked abroad displaying their useless jewels?

Monsieur Loisel fumbled for the buttons of his waistcoat. He knew his fears were foolish. The newspapers made one's imagination too vivid. What was there about his wife clumping homeward on ungainly shoes to arouse the cupidity of a footpad?

Then why did he keep seeing the leaping figure, the menacing hands, and hearing the running footsteps?

And why, upon the moist and dimly shining cobblestones, did he keep seeing Mathilde sprawled like a broken jumping jack with her limbs at crazy angles? Could this be the end of the bride who had come to him so lovely? He remembered her cool slenderness when he first knew her. Her romantic imaginings, and her dainty embarrassments when, as bride and groom, they first had shared their awkward passion. What if she had been vain and frivolous? Life had been hard to her. She was a creature too beautiful to have been born into a world of clerks.

Filled with an unreasoning sadness, he blew out the candle and went through the door toward the stairs. Keeping close to the rickety banister, he felt his way down to the fourth floor landing. The stairs were cluttered with refuse. Since a month ago when he made Mathilde give up her job as janitress, the place had been a disgrace.

Tonight one of the tenants had taken the trouble to light the lamp on the fourth floor. By its faint flicker, he suddenly saw the angular figure of Madame Loisel plodding toward him up the stairs.

"Mathilde!"

She looked up at him and seemed surprised. Both surprised and resentful. She glared at him as she clutched her old cracked patent leather pocketbook to her bosom with both hands. Two small parcels were tucked beneath her elbows.

"Where have you been?" Anxiety made his voice irritable.

She stared at him as though trying to think of an answer.

He took a step toward her and asked, "Is anything wrong?"

"No—no—can't a woman rest in the park without being cross-examined? Is it a sin to enjoy the sunshine? You'd try the patience of a saint!"

"I was worried." He tried to kiss her but she pushed past him.

"No, no! Not here on the public stairway! Stop acting the fool!"

"Can I help you?" He reached for the parcels. "What did you buy?"

"Nothing that concerns you—can't a woman have any privacy . . . ? Let them alone."

But he persisted and, as she jerked away from him, one of the parcels crashed from her arms.

"Now see what you've done!"

Like an angry spirit, she vanished into the gloom of the upper stairs.

Hoping to soothe her, he stooped to retrieve the parcel. It was wrapped in colored paper and tied with fancy two-colored string such as was used by the fashionable chemists and hairdressers. He could see that it had contained a bottle of expensive cold cream. The paper wrappings were cut by the broken glass and a film of fragrant grease was oozing over the stairs.

Monsieur Loisel straightened up. The parcel was ruined beyond salvage. He trudged thoughtfully up the stairs.

What was happening to Mathilde? That jar of ointment must have cost all of her week's shopping money. It was her first extravagance since the night she lost the necklace. The night on which she had disdained the public omnibus and had insisted upon going to the ball in a cab.

When he re-entered the garret, he saw her other parcel on the table, but she had retired behind the alcove curtains. And he knew better than to follow her.

He crossed the room and lifted the lid on the soup kettle. He sniffed and reached for the wooden spoon.

"Don't be too long," he said, "the good soup is getting cold."

"The good soup!" Behind the flimsy curtains, Mathilde remembered ironically how that phrase of his had plagued her. Even when they were first married. It was so ambitionless. It still irritated her. He accepted the commonplace. He had no knack for elegance. He was a man for whom wealth could do no good.

Mathilde took off her cape and bonnet. She fumbled clumsily with the knots, trying to untie them with one hand. With the other she clutched the pocketbook.

Not once, since the Forestiers handed her the necklace, had she permitted it to leave her hands. She had clutched it during Jeanne's sentimental babble and the undisciplined congratulations of the servants. Dr. Forestier had offered to see her home in his carriage, but she had refused. She had scarcely been able to restrain her impatience when he had insisted upon presenting her with a bottle of vintage wine from the Forestiers' own table—or to wait while he had rushed off to see that it was properly wrapped.

"Take this," he said, "and promise us that you will drink it with your husband tonight. Soon Jeanne and I will visit you to help celebrate your happiness. But tonight should be for you two alone. Have you given Jeanne your address?"

Mathilde made a hasty promise and muttered her humble address. Then, as they smiled at her and patted her arms affectionately, she finally succeeded in getting down the stairs and out the door.

She wanted to be alone with her treasure. Without thinking of where she was going, moving like a somnambulist through the occasional cross-currents of traffic, she walked heedlessly up one street and down the other, rejoicing in the knowledge that she was wealthy —and that wealth can make one free.

It was some time before she realized that she had retraced her steps to the Champs-Élysées—to a spot near where she had met Jeanne.

She sat down on a bench. Then moved to another—nearer to a gendarme and placed closer to a lamppost, for daylight was beginning to fade. A few hours ago she had entered the park a drudge, almost a pauper. Now she was a rich woman. It was time to take inventory.

She and her husband paid thirty-six thousand francs for the necklace ten years ago. It should be worth more now. All Paris knew the current government was shaky. For some weeks the editorial writers had been denouncing the increasing tendency of the rich to convert their wealth into movable assets. Those close to the court of Louis Philippe were getting ready to run. And they were reluctant to leave empty-handed. The gazettes said jewelers were doing a rushing business. Today the necklace might bring fifty or sixty thousand francs.

All her life Mathilde had wanted to be rich. She had been born poor and beautiful, a maddening combination. She might have made a wonderful match had her father been able to provide her with a dowry. What a dowry sixty thousand francs would have been!

Mathilde sat under the street light, holding the pocketbook that contained the necklace, and permitted herself to daydream.

She was rich now. The future swung dazzlingly before her, like the bright pendant that hung from the necklace, outshining the stones that supported it. She was only thirty-two years old. The life before her would be so brilliant that it would totally eclipse the feeble sparkle of all previous hopes and years.

A laugh cut in on her reverie and in its harshness it seemed to be the mockery of her own conscience. She had no reason to feel triumphant over a dowry. She was irrevocably married to a little clerk. A pettyfogging nonentity. And her beauty was gone.

Mathilde was self-centered enough to be a realist. She knew her skin had coarsened and her voice had become strident. She had neither looks nor charm. It was too late now.

The laugh was repeated and she turned to see where it came from. A horse-faced woman was making her way from one of the sidewalk restaurants followed by a swarm of stylish young men. She had prominent discolored teeth and her hair was inaccurately dyed beneath a bonnet of expensive and garish plumes. Her hands were large and her eyes were bold and her skin had become more roughened on the hunting field than Mathilde's had become among her clotheslines.

But the tight-waisted young man in the cocoa-colored coat was calling her "Duchess," and an officer of the Garde Royale was jostling to kiss her hand as they helped her into her cabriolet, laughing and simpering at everything she said.

To Mathilde, the woman's ugliness was a benediction. As she rose from the bench, she shook out her old skirts as though they were made of taffeta. She found a chemist's shop that was open even on Sunday to cater to court belles. To the clerk, who mistook her for somebody's servant, she gave most of her week's shopping money for a jar of cold cream. And as she boarded the crowded omnibus, it was as though invisible fops were kissing her hands.

As Mathilde came out of the alcove she saw that Monsieur Loisel had laid the table. He looked up from filling the new soup tureen.

"How nice you look!" he exclaimed.

"It is nothing," she replied shortly. "Must you make a scene over it when I wash my face and straighten my hair?"

"But the collar and cuffs."

"They are old relics, I found them in the bottom of a drawer." She looked at the table and spoke accusingly, "You unwrapped my parcel, the wine."

"Yes, I hoped it was wine. It made me thirsty to hear the gurgling."

"It was supposed to be a surprise."

"The whole evening is a surprise," he drew back her chair. "I will attend to the stove. You might soil your cuffs."

He handed her one of his large clean handkerchiefs. It was a long time since they had used napkins.

"What foolery are you up to?" she demanded.

"Not foolery—elegance." He sat opposite her. "When my wife brings home a jar of cold cream and a bottle of wine, I know where her thoughts are heading, and I hasten to conform." He reached for her glass and polished it with the handkerchief. "And may I tell you, my dear, that you have made me very glad?"

"Glad?" She looked at him curiously. "What have you to be glad about?"

He put down the glass and regarded her with quizzical amusement.

"Because these things have given me the answer to a question— the question of your character."

As she returned his look, her voice was guarded. "You have had eleven years of me. You should know me pretty thoroughly by now."

"One cannot always be sure. Your sudden interest in cosmetics gave me quite a start just now." He removed the cover from the tureen and started to fill the soup bowls. "I have been asking myself, ever since we paid the last usurer, how much these last ten years had changed you. I see now that they have changed you very little."

"And you are glad?" she asked incredulously.

"Decidedly. I have thought over this matter of the cold cream and I have decided that I am exhilarated. During all these hard years, do you know what kept me going?"

"Necessity, I suppose."

"No. I could have run away. After all, you were the one who borrowed the necklace. And the one who lost it. All our neighbors knew that I did not have to be involved." He put down his spoon and assumed a tone of bantering reproach. "My dear, I hope you do not mistake me for a saint. Or for one of those dull fellows of completely thoughtless nobility. I could be a rogue if I chose."

"You are talking like a book," she said. "You have been copying too many manuscripts. But why didn't you run off if you felt that way?"

He leaned toward her. "Because I knew I could never find anything I wanted as much as you. You were my only chance to be more than God made me. I never felt proud in my life until I had a woman who was too fine to be the wife of a clerk."

She looked down at her soup plate and saw that he had given her the largest piece of meat.

"Drink your wine," she said, "and let me have some."

He reached the bottle toward her glass.

"Did you notice that this bottle had been uncorked?" he asked.

"Of course it has! Do you think I could bring home a luxury if it were not cheap!" She was lying frantically and finding the task difficult. "I was passing a sidewalk restaurant in the Champs-Élysées. A diner was leaving the table with his wine scarcely touched. I made a bargain with the waiter who was cleaning up."

"And a fine bargain," he said, sipping his glass. "If we are to return to the Rue des Martyrs, we must reacclimatize ourselves to little comforts. I am sorry about the cold cream. I tried to save some of it, but it was full of broken glass."

She pushed back her chair. "I had better go clean it up."

"Stop, Madame!" he cried with humorous emphasis. "On the day our last debt was paid, you were through being a janitress. I gave our landlord a piece of my mind, I can tell you! All those years you slaved for him—for a few sous deducted from our rent. If you touch those stairs now he may think I am weakening. I absolutely forbid it."

She made an ironic gesture with her lips and started to get up.

"Please!" he said. "I have begun to feel like a husband again. Do not deny me my self-respect."

She shrugged and sipped her wine.

"If we hurry, we can go to vespers," she said.

"Not tonight." He drank deeply. "Tonight let us sit and talk. Next month we shall be back in our old parish. We will ask for a pew in the middle aisle, and you will have a new bonnet and a new dress."

She made her voice scornful. "Even if our savings would pay for it, the parish would laugh at me. And it would have a right to—a janitress got up in clothes like that."

"Nonsense! How will they know you were a janitress? One appears in a new neighborhood. One makes no reference to a former life. If you look prosperous, you are taken at face value! No questions asked."

She looked at him sharply. Was he reading her thoughts? She had been thinking about this all the way home in the omnibus. There were other cities beside Paris—Lyons or Bordeaux. They would accept her as a rich widow if she appeared there with the money from the necklace. No questions would be asked. After he went to work tomorrow, she would sell the necklace and never come back.

She looked at him again and saw him wool-gathering. No chance of his reading anyone's thoughts! The whole thing would be easy. She became angered at his guilelessness.

"I know why you go to vespers no more," she sneered. "And why you sneak in at the back of the church for mass. It is because you feel guilty."

"Guilty?" His look was troubled. "Why should I feel guilty?"

"Because we have no children. We've been too poor to risk it! You think that's a sin—you know you do and you hate me for it."

"No—I don't think it's a sin."

"I wake up at night," she continued cruelly, "to see you telling your beads—you're begging God to forgive you, aren't you?"

He shoved back his chair with a loud clatter. He came toward her around the table. And he strove to control his voice.

"I ask God to understand," he said gently, "and I think He does. I wish that you could."

"You want me to have a child—" Her voice was edged with fear, "now that the debt is paid. Is that it?"

"No. It would be too dangerous. You are past thirty and that is much too late in life for the first child. So I have made myself forget it."

She wanted to strike him. He was too good. Too sanctimonious.

Some uncontrollable impulse made her want to goad him, to break his smugness; so that, when the blow fell, he would know all that he was missing.

"Oh, no, I'm not! Not if we had money enough! Childbearing is no problem at the new English hospital in the Rue de Villiers! They have made it perfectly safe! Not one death from child-bed fever! But they won't let you in the door for less than four thousand francs!"

"Mathilde! Be quiet! I know you are as disappointed as I am, but don't excite yourself."

"I am not excited! You are! I can see it in your face. Shall we go to the loan sharks? We have slaved for my vanity, now we can slave for yours. For four thousand francs you can have your precious son—"

He struck her a hard stinging blow, right across the mouth. She looked up at him in amazement.

"I had not thought of a son," he said, "but once I hoped for a daughter."

The hysteria had gone out of her. But she still contradicted him.

"I cannot understand you. All men want sons."

It was the first sarcastic smile she ever had seen on his face.

"Perhaps I have been deficient in vanity," he said, "but I found little about myself to perpetuate. The world is never short of clerks. But you always seemed different to me. Even when I tried to look at you realistically, when I admitted that the years have brought changes and that your petulance had soured into surliness, I was still proud of your narrow waist and straight back. Every man needs some vanity. I told myself I would be happy when we returned to the Rue de Martyrs and I could compare my hostess with the wives of the other clerks. Now, I am not so sure. The faces of those other women are flabby and stupid—but, for the most part, they are kind.

"For a long time," he said, "I told myself I had wronged you. You seemed too good to be the wife of a clerk. I hoped some day I could see your youth and prettiness repeated in a daughter. I felt that if I could work for her, and provide her with a dowry, something like the amount we saved for the necklace, I would somehow be making things right, and paying for a blessing I had not deserved."

There was a long silence in the room before he turned to her and added, without bitterness, "You see, in spite of the fact that you read the novels, while I only copied them, I am the one who has been the sentimentalist and the fool. I tried to give you something you had no use for—something you didn't want—the knowledge that there was one person out of all humanity who cared whether you lived or died. The feeling that there was one person in this world who would always remember your beauty and want to see it preserved. . . . Instead of helping you pay for the necklace, I should have given you what money I had ten years ago, and told you to go away."

She got up and spoke in a flat voice.

"I am tired," she said, "I am going to bed. It has been an exhausting day."

For a long time he sat looking at the stars, waiting until he was sure she would be asleep. Then he undressed silently and turned out the lamp.

He moved softly into the curtained alcove and reached for his worn rosary.

But as he touched it, his hand drew back and he gasped a choked exclamation of surprise.

There on the bedpost, intertwined with the smoothly-worn prayer beads, he saw the diamond necklace shining softly like the tears of a Magdalene.

Mathilde lay beside her sleeping husband and her face was misty with tears. She had forced herself to one great moment of unselfishness and she asked God, desperately, to somehow make it last. She prayed with anxiety and humility. For she finally knew herself.

· · · ·

When their neighbors found them on Monday morning, there was a look of tranquillity upon the faces of Monsieur Loisel and his bride. After much discussion, the priest of their parish finally decided that they should be buried in consecrated soil, side by side. Despite the fact the police found poison in their wine bottle, the priest was not quite willing to call it suicide. He felt that their deaths might be somehow linked with the mystery of the big blond man who was found that same morning at the foot of the tenement stairs. Apparently there had been an accident. Investigation revealed a smear of cold cream on his right boot—and in his pocket, a necklace valued at sixty thousand francs.

He was a very fashionable physician, but he couldn't cure his own broken neck.

Fiends and Creatures

In the final group of eleven stories and one poem, the minions of Hell rub knobby shoulders with various nightmarish critters, none of whom is particularly schooled in the social graces.

As I mentioned at the beginning of *Masterpieces of Terror and the Supernatural,* Friedrich Nietzsche once stated that the will to power leads the ethically superior being to perform acts of great benevolence, but the ogres, monsters, vampires and beasties you are about to meet obviously do not possess a philosophical bent.

JACK SNOW

Midnight

I am not one of those editors who automatically scorn deal-with-the-Devil stories, so long as the author has a new twist up his sleeve, as does JACK SNOW *(1907–1956), a National Broadcasting Company executive who wrote a number of excellent weird fantasy tales, as well as two of the best post–L. Frank Baum* Oz *books,* The Magical Mimics of Oz *and* The Shaggy Man of Oz.

Between the hour of eleven and midnight John Ware made ready to perform the ceremony that would climax the years of homage he had paid to the dark powers of evil. Tonight he would become a part of that essence of dread that roams the night hours. At the last stroke of midnight his consciousness would leave his body and unite with that which shuns the light and is all depravity and evil. Then he would roam the world with this midnight elemental and for one hour savor all the evil that this alien being is capable of inspiring in human souls.

John Ware had lived so long among the shadows of evil that his mind had become tainted, and through the channel of his thoughts his soul had been corrupted by the poison of the dark powers with which he consorted.

There was scarcely a forbidden book of shocking ceremonies and nameless teachings that Ware had not consulted and pored over in the long hours of the night. When certain guarded books he desired were unobtainable, he had shown no hesitation in stealing them. Nor had Ware stopped with mere reading and studying these books.

He had descended to the ultimate depths and put into practice the ceremonies, rites and black sorceries that stained the pages of the volumes. Often these practices had required human blood and human lives, and here again Ware had not hesitated. He had long ago lost count of the number of innocent persons who had mysteriously vanished from the face of the earth—victims of his insatiable craving for knowledge of the evil that dwells in the dark, furtively, when the powers of light are at their nadir.

John Ware had traveled to all the strange and little-known parts of the earth. He had tricked and wormed secrets out of priests and dignitaries of ancient cults and religions of whose existence the world of clean daylight has no inkling. Africa, the West Indies, Tibet, China—Ware knew them all and they held no secret whose knowledge he had not violated.

By devious means Ware had secured admission to certain private institutions and homes behind whose facades were confined individuals who were not mad in the outright sense of the everyday definition of the word, but who, given their freedom, would loose nightmare horror on the world. Some of these prisoners were so curiously shaped and formed that they had been hidden away since childhood. In a number of instances their vocal organs were so alien that the sounds they uttered could not be considered human. Nevertheless, John Ware had been heard to converse with them.

In John Ware's chamber stood an ancient clock, tall as a human being, and abhorently fashioned from age-yellowed ivory. Its head was that of a woman in an advanced state of dissolution. Around the skull, from which shreds of ivory flesh hung, were Roman numerals, marked by two death's-head beetles, which, engineered by intricate machinery in the clock, crawled slowly around the perimeter of the skull to mark the hours. Nor did this clock tick as does an ordinary clock. Deep within its woman's bosom sounded a dull, regular thud, disturbingly similar to the beating of a human heart.

The malevolent creation of an unknown sorcerer of the dim past, this eerie clock had been the property of a succession of warlocks, alchemists, wizards, Satanists and like devotees of forbidden arts, each of whom had invested the clock with something of his own evil existence, so that a dark and revolting nimbus hung about it and it seemed to exude a loathsome animus from its repellently human form.

It was to this clock that John Ware addressed himself at the first stroke of midnight. The clock did not announce the hour in the fashion of other clocks. During the hour its ticking sounded faint and dull, scarcely distinguishable above ordinary sounds. But at each hour the ticking rose to a muffled thud, sounding like a human heartbeat heard through a stethoscope. With these ominous thuds it marked the hours, seeming to intimate that each beat of the human heart narrows that much more the span of mortal life.

Now the clock sounded the midnight hour. "Thud, thud, thud—" Before it stood John Ware, his body traced with cabalistic markings in a black pigment which he had prepared according to an ancient and noxious formula.

As the clock thudded out the midnight hour, John Ware repeated an incantation, which, had it not been for his devouring passion for evil, would have caused even him to shudder at the mere sounds of the contorted vowels. To his mouthing of the unhuman phrases, he performed a pattern of motions with his body and limbs which was an unearthly grotesquerie of a dance.

"Thud, thud, thud—" The beat sounded for the twelfth time and then subsided to a dull, muffled murmur which was barely audible in the silence of the chamber. The body of John Ware sank to the thick rug and lay motionless. The spirit was gone from it. At the last stroke of the hour of midnight it had fled.

With a great thrill of exultation, John Ware found himself outside in the night. He had succeeded! That which he had summoned had accepted him! Now for the next hour he would feast to his fill on unholy evil. Ware was conscious that he was not alone as he moved effortlessly through the night air. He was accompanied by a being which he perceived only as an amorphous darkness, a darkness that was deeper and more absolute than the inky night, a darkness that was a vacuum or blank in the color spectrum.

Ware found himself plunging suddenly earthward. The walls of a building flashed past him and an instant later he was in a sumptuously furnished living room, where stood a man and a woman. Ware felt a strong bond between himself and the woman. Her thoughts were his, he felt as she did. A wave of terror was enveloping him, flowing to him from the woman, for the man standing before her held a revolver in his hand. He was about to pull the trigger. John Ware lived through an agony of fear in those few moments that the helpless woman cringed before the man. Then a shapeless darkness settled over the man. His eyes glazed dully. Like an automaton he pressed the trigger and the bullet crashed into the woman's heart. John Ware died as she died.

Once again Ware was soaring through the night, the black being close at his side. He was shaken by the experience. What could it mean? How had he come to be identified so closely with the tortured consciousness of the murdered woman?

Again Ware felt himself plummeting earthward. This time he was in a musty cellar in the depths of a vast city's tenement section. A man lay chained to a crude wooden table. Over him stood two creatures of loathsome and sadistic countenance. Then John Ware *was* the man on the table. He knew, he thought, he felt everything that the captive felt. He saw a black shadow settle over the two evil-looking men. Their eyes glazed, their lips parted slightly as saliva drooled from them. The men made use of an assortment of crude instruments, knives, scalpels, pincers and barbed hooks, in a manner which in ten short minutes reduced the helpless body before them from a screaming human being to a whimpering, senseless thing covered with wounds and rivulets of blood. John Ware suffered as the victim suffered. At last the tortured one slipped into unconsciousness. An instant later John Ware was moving swiftly through the night sky. At his side was the black being.

It had been terrible. Ware had endured agony that he had not believed the human body was capable of suffering. Why? Why had he been chained to the consciousness of the man on the torture table? Swiftly Ware and his companion soared through the night moving ever westward.

John Ware felt himself descending again. He caught a fleeting glimpse of a lonely farmhouse, with a single lamp glowing in one window. Then he was in an old-fashioned country living room. In a wheelchair an aged man sat dozing. At his side, near the window, stood a table on which burned an oil lamp. A dark shape hovered over the sleeping man. Shuddering in his slumber, the man flung out one arm, restlessly. It struck the oil lamp, sending it crashing to the floor, where it shattered and a pool of flame sprang up instantly. The aged cripple awoke with a cry, and made an effort to wheel his chair from the flames. But it was too late. Already the carpet and floor were burning and now the man's clothing and the robe that covered his legs were afire. Instinctively the victim threw up his arms to shield his face. Then he screamed piercingly, again and again. John Ware felt everything that the old man felt. He suffered the inexpressible agony of being consumed alive by flames. Then he was outside in the night. Far below and behind him the house burned like a torch in the distance. Ware glanced fearfully at the shadow that accompanied him as they sped on at tremendous speed, ever westward.

Once again Ware felt himself hurtling down through the night. Where to this time? What unspeakable torment was he to endure now? All was dark about him. He glimpsed no city or abode as he flashed to earth. About him was only silence and darkness. Then, like a wave engulfing his spirit, came a torrent of fear and dread. He was striving to push something upward. Panic thoughts consumed him. He would not die—he wanted to live—he would escape! He writhed and twisted in his narrow confines, his fists beating on the surface above him. It did not yield. John Ware knew that he was linked with the consciousness of a man who had been prematurely buried. Soon the victim's fists were dripping with blood as he ineffectually clawed and pounded at the lid of the coffin. As time is measured it didn't last long. The exertions of the doomed man caused him quickly to exhaust the small amount of air in the coffin and he soon smothered to death. John Ware experienced that, too. But the final obliteration and crushing of the hope that burned in the man's bosom probably was the worst of all.

Ware was again soaring through the night. His soul shuddered as he grasped the final, unmistakable significance of the night's experiences. *He, he* was to be the victim, the sufferer, throughout this long hour of midnight.

He had thought that by accompanying the dark being around the earth, he would share in the savoring of all the evils that flourish in the midnight hour. He *was* participating—but not as he had expected. Instead, *he* was the victim, the cringing, tormented one. Perhaps this dark being he had summoned was jealous of its pleasures, or perhaps it derived an additional intensity of satisfaction by adding John Ware's consciousness to those of its victims.

Ware was descending again. There was no resisting the force that flung him earthward.

He was completely helpless before the power he had summoned. What now? What new terror would he experience?

On and on, ever westward through the night, John Ware endured horror after horror. He died again and again, each time in a more fearsome manner. He was subjected to revolting tortures and torments as he was linked with victim after victim. He knew the frightening nightmare of human minds tottering on the abyss of madness. All that is black and unholy and is visited upon mankind he experienced as he roamed the earth with the midnight being.

Would it never end? Only the thought that these sixty minutes must pass sustained him. But it did not end. It seemed an eternity had gone by. Such suffering could not be crowded into a single hour. It must be days since he had left his body.

Days, nights, sixty minutes, one hour? John Ware was struck with a realization of terrific impact. It seemed to be communicated to him from the dark being at his side. Horribly clear did that being make the simple truth. John Ware was lost. Weeks, even months, might have passed since he had left his body. Time, for him, had stopped still.

John Ware was eternally chained to the amorphous black shape, and was doomed to exist thus horribly forever, suffering endless and revolting madness, torture and death through eternity. He had stepped into that band of time known as midnight, and was caught, trapped hoplessly—doomed to move with the grain of time endlessly around the earth.

For as long as the earth spins beneath the sun, one side of it is always dark and in the darkness midnight dwells forever.

MARVIN KAYE

Ms. Lipshutz
and the Goblin

The chutzpah-laden rationale by which I include one of my own stories in a book with the word "Masterpieces" in the title is that "Ms. Lipshutz and the Goblin" found its way into the fifth DAW Books Year's Best Fantasy Stories. *(Nevertheless, I've still got one hell of a nerve!)*

Lipshutz, Daphne A., Ms. (age: 28; height: 5'2"; weight: 160 lbs.; must wear corrective lenses), had frizzy brown hair, buck teeth, and an almost terminal case of acne. Though her mother frequently reassured her she had a Very Nice Personality, that commodity seemed of little value in Daphne's Quest for The Perfect Mate.

According to Daphne A. (for Arabella) Lipshutz, The Perfect Mate must be 30, about 5'9" in height, weigh approximately 130 pounds, have wavy blond hair (1st preference), white teeth, a gentle smile and peaches-and-cream complexion. He must like children and occasional sex, or if necessary, the other way around.

Daphne's Quest for The Perfect Mate was hampered by her job as an interviewer (2nd grade) for the State of New York, Manhattan division of the Labor Department's Upper West Side office of the Bureau of Unemployment. The only men she met there were sour-stomached married colleagues, or the people she processed for unemployment checks, "and them," her mother cautioned, "you can do without. Who'd buy the tickets, tip the cabbie, shmeer the head-waiter, pick up the check?"

Ms. Lipshutz worked in a dingy green office around the corner from a supermarket. To get there, she had to take a southbound bus from The Bronx, get off at 90th and Broadway and walk west past a narrow, dark alley. Next to it was a brick building with a doorway providing access to steep wooden stairs that mounted to her office. The stairs were worn smooth and low in the middle of each step by innumerable shuffling feet. Daphne noticed that unemployed feet frequently shuffle.

Late one October afternoon, just before Hallowe'en, Ms. Lipshutz was about to take her final coffee-break of the day when an unusual personage entered the unemployment bureau and approached her window. He was six feet eight inches tall and thin as a breadstick. There were warts all over his body, and the color of his skin was bright green.

Ms. Lipshutz thought he looked like the Jolly Green Pickle or an elongated cousin of Peter Pain. He was certainly the ugliest thing she'd ever set her soulful brown eyes on.

Leaning his pointy elbows on her window-shelf, the newcomer glanced admiringly at her acne-dimpled face and asked whether he was in the correct line. He addressed her as Miss.

Bridling, Daphne told him to address her as *Ms.* The tall green creature's eyebrows rose.

"Miz?" he echoed, mystified. "What dat?"

"I am a liberated woman," she said in the clockwork rhythm of a civil servant or a missioned spirit. Her vocal timbre was flat and nasal, pure Grand Concourse. "I do not like to be called Miss. If I were married—" (here she betrayed her cause with a profound sigh) "—I would not call myself Mrs. So please call me Ms."

The green one nodded. "Me once had girlfriend named Miz. Shlubya Miz. She great big troll. You troll?"

"This," said Ms. Lipshutz, "is an immaterial conversation. Please state your name and business."

"Name: Klotsch."

"Would you repeat that?" she asked, fishing out an application form and poising a pencil.

"Klotsch."

"First or last?"

"Always!"

Unusual names were common at the unemployment office, and so was unusual stupidity. Ms. Lipshutz patiently explained she wanted to know whether Klotsch was a first or last name.

"Only name. Just Klotsch."

"How do you spell it? Is that C as in Couch?"

"K as in Kill!" Klotsch shouted. "Kill-LOTSCH!"

"Kindly lower your voice," she said mechanically. "I presume you wish to apply for unemployment checks?"

Spreading his warty hands, the big green thing grinned. "Klotsch not come to count your pimples, Miz."

Not realizing the remark was meant flirtatiously, Daphne, who was extremely sensitive about her acne, took offense. "That was a cru-el thing to say!"

"How come?" Klotsch was puzzled. "Me no understand. Klotsch like pimples. You lots cuter than Shlubya the troll!"

Daphne, not very reassured, found it wise to retreat into the prescribed formulae of the State of New York for dealing with an unemployment insurance applicant.

"Now," she began. "Mister Klotsch—"

He waved a deprecatory claw. "No Mister."

"I beg your pardon?"

"You liberated, so okay, Klotsch liberated, too. If you Miz, me *Murr*."

"I see," she said primly, unable to determine whether she was being made fun of. Inscribing Klotsch's name on Form NYS204-A, Ms. Lipshutz requested his address.

"No got."

"You are a transient?"

He shook his shaggy head. "Me are a goblin."

"No, no, Murr Klotsch, we are not up to Employment History yet. Simply state your address."

"Me don't got. Landlady kick me out of cave."

"Oh, dear. Couldn't you pay your rent?"

"Ate landlord," Klotsch glumly confessed.

Daphne suddenly noticed that Klotsch had two lower incisors which protruded three inches north of his upper lip. Civic conscience aroused, she told him eating the landlord was a terrible thing to do.

"Telling me! Klotsch sick three days."

"Do you go round eating people all the time?"

The goblin drew himself erect, his pride hurt. "Klotsch no eat people! Only landlords!"

Ms. Lipshutz conceded the distinction. Returning to the form, she asked Klotsch for his last date of employment.

He sighed gloomily. "October 31, 1877."

Time to be firm: "The unemployment relief act, Murr Klotsch, does *not* cover cases prior to 1932."

"So put down 1932," he suggested. In an uncharacteristic spirit of compromise, Daphne promptly complied. (It was eight minutes before five o'clock.)

"Place of previous employment?"

"Black Forest."

"Is that in New York State?"

"Is Germany."

"You may not be aware that the State of New York does not share reciprocity with overseas powers."

Klotsch thought about it briefly, then raised a crooked talon in recollection. "Once did one-night gig in Poughkeepsie."

"Check." She wrote it down. "Previous employer's name?"

"Beelzebub."

Ms. Lipshutz stuck pencil and application in Klotsch's paws. "Here —*you* tackle that one!" While he wrote, she studied him, deciding that, after all, Klotsch wasn't *so* bad looking. He had a kind of sexy expression in his big purple eye.

"And where does this Mist—uh, Murr Beelzebub conduct his business?"

The goblin shrugged. "Usually hangs around Times Square."

"Then he does not maintain a permanent place of business?"

"Oh, yeah: further south." Klotsch shook his large head, scowling. "He no good boss, got all goblins unionized. Me no like. Klotsch work for self."

Ms. Lipshutz muttered something about scabs. Klotsch, misunderstanding, beamed toothily. "Klotsch got plenty scabs. You like?"

Eye on the clock (four of five), Ms. Lipshutz proceeded with her routine. "Have you received any recent employment offers?"

"Just Beelzebub."

"Do you mean," she inquired with the frosty, lofty disapproval of an accredited representative of the State of New York, "that you have refused a job offer?"

"Me no going to shovel coal!" Klotsch howled, eyes glowing like the embers he disdained.

Ms. Lipshutz understood. "So long as the position was not in your chosen professional line." She ticked off another question on the form. "That brings us, Murr Klotsch, to the kind of work you are seeking. What precisely do you do?"

He replied in a solemn guttural tone. "Me goblin."

"What does that entail?"

By way of demonstration, Klotsch uttered a fearful yell, gnashed his teeth and dashed up and down the walls. He panted, snorted, whistled, screamed, swung from the light fixtures and dripped green on various desks. Ms. Lipshutz's colleagues paid no attention. Worse things happen in Manhattan.

Gibbering his last gibber, Klotsch returned to Ms. Lipshutz's window. "That my Class A material. You like?"

"Interesting," she conceded. "Do you get much call for that sort of thing?"

"Plenty work once! Double-time during day! Klotsch used to frighten farmers, shepherds, even once in a while, genuine hero." He sighed, shrugging eloquently. "But then scare biz go down toilet. They bust me down to kids, then not even them. Too many other scary things nowadays, goblins outclassed."

She nodded, not without hasty sympathy (two of five). "And have you ever considered changing your profession?"

"Got plenty monsters already in TV, movies, comics."

"What about the armed services?"

Klotsch shook his big green head. "All the best jobs already got by trolls."

Ms. Lipshutz sighed. She would have liked to assist Klotsch, but it was 4:59 and she did not want to miss the 5:03 bus. Setting his form aside for processing the following day, she asked him to return in one week.

The hapless goblin shambled out without another word.

Ms. Lipshutz hurried on her coat and hat, locked up her desk, pattered swiftly down the old stairs to catch the 5:03.

Turning east, she heel-clicked toward Broadway. There was a dark alleyway separating the corner supermarket from the building that housed the unemployment bureau. As she passed it, a great green goblin leaped out at her, whoofling, snorting and howling in outrageous menace.

Daphne nearly collapsed with laughter. She snickered, tittered, chortled and giggled for nearly a minute before gaining sufficient self-control to speak. "Murr Klotsch . . . it's you!"

His face was sad and long. "Miz no scared, she laugh."

"Oh . . . oh, *no!*" Daphne consolingly reached out her hand and touched him. "Murr Klotsch . . . I was so, *so* frightened!"

"Then why you laugh?"

"I was positively . . . uh . . . hysterical with fear!"

The goblin grinned shyly, hopefully. "No kidding?"

"Truly," she declared firmly, coyly adding, "I don't believe my heart will stop pounding until I've had a drink."

So she missed the 5:03 and Klotsch took her to a nearby Chinese restaurant where the bartender mixed excellent zombies. Just as her mother always warned, Daphne was stuck paying the bar bill. But somehow, she didn't mind.

Ms. Daphne Arabella Lipshutz (age: 28½; weight: 110 lbs., wears contact lenses) wedded Klotsch the following spring despite her mother's protests that she surely could have found a nice Jewish goblin somewhere.

"And what about the children?" she shrilled. "Suppose they resemble their father?"

Daphne shrugged. "He's not bad once you get used to him."

With the combined aid of his wife and the New York State Department of Labor, Klotsch found work in an amusement park fun house, where he made such a hit that a talent scout caught his act and signed him up. Since then, the goblin has made several horror films, appears on TV talk shows (as guest host on one of them), endorses a brand of green toothpaste and is part owner of a line of Hallowe'en masks. The couple moved to the suburbs, where Mrs. Lipshutz often visits her illustrious son-in-law.

The only unfortunate result of their marriage is that it has worked wonders with Daphne's complexion. But Klotsch is too considerate to mention his disappointment.

EDWARD LUCAS WHITE

Amina

Once a popular historical novelist (for such works as El Supremo, The Unwilling Vestal *and* Andivius Hedulio*),* EDWARD LUCAS WHITE *is best remembered today for* Lukundoo, *a collection of weird fantasies mostly based on the author's own nightmares. "Amina" is such a story.*

Waldo, brought face to face with the actuality of the unbelievable—as he himself would have worded it—was completely dazed. In silence he suffered the consul to lead him from the tepid gloom of the interior, through the ruinous doorway, out into the hot, stunning brilliance of the desert landscape. Hassan followed, with never a look behind him. Without any word he had taken Waldo's gun from his nerveless hand and carried it, with his own and the consul's.

The consul strode across the gravelly sand, some fifty paces from the southwest corner of the tomb, to a bit of not wholly ruined wall from which there was a clear view of the doorway side of the tomb and of the side with the larger crevice.

"Hassan," he commanded, "watch here."

Hassan said something in Persian.

"How many cubs were there?" the consul asked Waldo.

Waldo stared mute.

"How many young ones did you see?" the consul asked again.

"Twenty or more," Waldo made answer.

"That's impossible," snapped the consul.

"There seemed to be sixteen or eighteen," Waldo asserted. Hassan smiled and grunted. The consul took from him two guns, handed

Waldo his, and they walked around the tomb to a point about equally distant from the opposite corner. There was another bit of ruin, and in front of it, on the side toward the tomb, was a block of stone mostly in the shadow of the wall.

"Convenient," said the consul. "Sit on that stone and lean against the wall, make yourself comfortable. You are a bit shaken, but you will be all right in a moment. You should have something to eat, but we have nothing. Anyhow, take a good swallow of this."

He stood by him as Waldo gasped over the raw brandy.

"Hassan will bring you his water-bottle before he goes," the consul went on; "drink plenty, for you must stay here for some time. And now, pay attention to me. We must extirpate these vermin. The male, I judge, is absent. If he had been anywhere about, you would not now be alive. The young cannot be as many as you say, but, I take it, we have to deal with ten, a full litter. We must smoke them out. Hassan will go back to camp after fuel and the guard. Meanwhile, you and I must see that none escape."

He took Waldo's gun, opened the breech, shut it, examined the magazine and handed it back to him.

"Now watch me closely," he said. He paced off, looking to his left past the tomb. Presently he stopped and gathered several stones together.

"You see these?" he called.

Waldo shouted an affirmation.

The consul came back, passed on in the same line, looking to his right past the tomb, and presently, at a similar distance, put up another tiny cairn, shouted again and was again answered. Again he returned.

"Now you are sure you cannot mistake those two marks I have made?"

"Very sure indeed," said Waldo.

"It is important," warned the consul. "I am going back to where I left Hassan, to watch there while he is gone. You will watch here. You may pace as often as you like to either of those stone heaps. From either you can see me on my beat. Do not diverge from the line from one to the other. For as soon as Hassan is out of sight I shall shoot any moving thing I see nearer. Sit here till you see me set up similar limits for my sentry-go on the farther side, then shoot any moving thing not on my line of patrol. Keep a lookout all around you. There is one chance in a million that the male might return in daylight—

mostly they are nocturnal, but this lair is evidently exceptional. Keep a bright lookout.

"And now listen to me. You must not feel any foolish sentimentalism about any fancied resemblance of these vermin to human beings. Shoot, and shoot to kill. Not only is it our duty, in general, to abolish them, but it will be very dangerous for us if we do not. There is little or no solidarity in Mohammedan communities, but on the comparatively few points upon which public opinion exists it acts with amazing promptitude and vigor. One matter as to which there is no disagreement is that it is incumbent upon every man to assist in eradicating these creatures. The good old Biblical custom of stoning to death is the mode of lynching indigenous hereabouts. These modern Asiatics are quite capable of applying it to anyone believed derelict against any of these inimical monsters. If we let one escape and the rumor of it gets about, we may precipitate an outburst of racial prejudice difficult to cope with. Shoot, I say, without hesitation or mercy."

"I understand," said Waldo.

"I don't care whether you understand or not," said the consul, "I want you to act. Shoot if needful, and shoot straight." And he tramped off.

Hassan presently appeared, and Waldo drank from his water-bottle as nearly all of its contents as Hassan would permit. After his departure Waldo's first alertness soon gave place to mere endurance of the monotony of watching and the intensity of the heat. His discomfort became suffering, and what with the fury of the dry glare, the pangs of thirst and his bewilderment of mind, Waldo was moving in a waking dream by the time Hassan returned with two donkeys and a mule laden with brushwood. Behind the beasts straggled the guard.

Waldo's trance became a nightmare when the smoke took effect and the battle began. He was, however, not only not required to join in the killing, but was enjoined to keep back. He did keep very much in the background, seeing only so much of the slaughter as his curiosity would not let him refrain from viewing. Yet he felt all a murderer as he gazed at the ten small carcasses laid out a row, and the memory of his vigil and its end, indeed of the whole day, though it was the day of his most marvelous adventure, remains to him as the broken recollections of a phantasmagoria.

On the morning of his memorable peril Waldo had waked early. The experiences of his sea-voyage, the sights at Gibraltar, at Port

Said, in the canal, at Suez, at Aden, at Muscat, and at Basrah had formed an altogether inadequate transition from the decorous regularity of house and school life in New England to the breathless wonder of the desert immensities.

Everything seemed unreal, and yet the reality of its strangeness so besieged him that he could not feel at home in it, he could not sleep heavily in a tent. After composing himself to sleep, he lay long conscious and awakened early, as on this morning, just at the beginning of the false-dawn.

The consul was fast asleep, snoring loudly. Waldo dressed quietly and went out; mechanically, without any purpose or forethought, taking his gun. Outside he found Hassan, seated, his gun across his knees, his head sunk forward, as fast asleep as the consul. Ali and Ibrahim had left the camp the day before for supplies. Waldo was the only waking creature about; for the guards, camped some little distance off, were but logs about the ashes of their fire. Meaning merely to enjoy, under the white glow of the false-dawn, the magical reappearance of the constellations and the short last glory of the star-laden firmament, that brief coolness which compensated a trifle for the hot morning, the fiery day and the warmish night, he seated himself on a rock, some paces from the tent and twice as far from the guards. Turning his gun in his hands he felt an irresistible temptation to wander off by himself, to stroll alone through the fascinating emptiness of the arid landscape.

When he had begun camp life he had expected to find the consul, that combination of sportsman, explorer and archaeologist, a particularly easy-going guardian. He had looked forward to absolutely untramelled liberty in the spacious expanse of the limitless wastes. The reality he had found exactly the reverse of his preconceptions. The consul's first injunction was:

"Never let yourself get out of sight of me or of Hassan unless he or I send you off with Ali or Ibrahim. Let nothing tempt you to roam about alone. Even a ramble is dangerous. You might lose sight of the camp before you knew it."

At first Waldo acquiesced, later he protested. "I have a good pocket-compass. I know how to use it. I never lost my way in the Maine woods."

"No Kourds in the Maine woods," said the consul.

Yet before long Waldo noticed that the few Kourds they encountered seemed simple-hearted, peaceful folk. No semblance of danger or even of adventure had appeared. Their armed guard of a dozen greasy tatterdemalions had passed their time in uneasy loafing.

Likewise Waldo noticed that the consul seemed indifferent to the ruins they passed by or encamped among, that his feeling for sites and topography was cooler than lukewarm, that he showed no ardor in the pursuit of the scanty and uninteresting game. He had picked up enough of several dialects to hear repeated conversations about "them." "Have you heard of any about here?" "Has one been killed?" "Any traces of them in this district?" And such queries he could make out in the various talks with the natives they met; as to what "they" were he received no enlightenment.

Then he had questioned Hassan as to why he was so restricted in his movements. Hassan spoke some English and regaled him with tales of Afrits, ghouls, specters and other uncanny legendary presences; of the jinn of the waste, appearing in human shape, talking all languages, ever on the alert to ensnare infidels; of the woman whose feet turned the wrong way at the ankles, luring the unwary to a pool and there drowning her victims; of the malignant ghosts of dead brigands, more terrible than their living fellows; of the spirit in the shape of a wild-ass, or of a gazelle, enticing its pursuers to the brink of a precipice and itself seeming to run ahead upon an expanse of sand, a mere mirage, dissolving as the victim passed the brink and fell to death; of the sprite in the semblance of a hare feigning a limp, or of a ground-bird feigning a broken wing, drawing its pursuer after it till he met death in an unseen pit or well-shaft.

Ali and Ibrahim spoke no English. As far as Waldo could understand their long harangues, they told similar stories or hinted at dangers equally vague and imaginary. These childish bogy-tales merely whetted Waldo's craving for independence.

Now, as he sat on a rock, longing to enjoy the perfect sky, the clear, early air, the wide, lonely landscape, along with the sense of having it to himself, it seemed to him that the consul was merely innately cautious, over-cautious. There was no danger. He would have a fine leisurely stroll, kill something perhaps and certainly be back in camp before the sun grew hot. He stood up.

Some hours later he was seated on a fallen coping-stone in the shadow of a ruined tomb. All the country they had been traversing is full of tombs and remains of tombs, prehistoric, Bactrian, old Persian, Parthian, Sassanian, or Mohammedan, scattered everywhere in groups or solitary. Vanished utterly are the faintest traces of the cities, towns, and villages, ephemeral houses or temporary huts, in which had lived the countless generations of mourners who had reared these tombs.

The tombs, built more durably than mere dwellings of the living, remained. Complete or ruinous, or reduced to mere fragments, they were everywhere. In that district they were all of one type. Each was domed and below was square, its one door facing eastward and opening into a large empty room, behind which were the mortuary chambers.

In the shadow of such a tomb Waldo sat. He had shot nothing, had lost his way, had no idea of the direction of the camp, was tired, warm and thirsty. He had forgotten his water-bottle.

He swept his gaze over the vast, desolate prospect, the unvaried turquoise of the sky arched above the rolling desert. Far reddish hills along the skyline hooped in the less distant brown hillocks which, without diversifying it, hummocked the yellow landscape. Sand and rocks with a lean, starved bush or two made up the nearer view, broken here and there by dazzling white or streaked, grayish, crumbling ruins. The sun had not been long above the horizon, yet the whole surface of the desert was quivering with heat.

As Waldo sat viewing the outlook a woman came round the corner of the tomb. All the village women Waldo had seen had worn yashmaks or some other form of face-covering or veil. This woman was bareheaded and unveiled. She wore some sort of yellowish-brown garment which enveloped her from neck to ankles, showing no waist line. Her feet, in defiance of the blistering sands, were bare.

At sight of Waldo she stopped and stared at him as he at her. He remarked the un-European posture of her feet, not at all turned out, but with the inner lines parallel. She wore no anklets, he observed, no bracelets, no necklace or earrings. Her bare arms he thought the most muscular he had ever seen on a human being. Her nails were pointed and long, both on her hands and feet. Her hair was black, short and tousled, yet she did not look wild or uncomely. Her eyes smiled and her lips had the effect of smiling, though they did not part ever so little, not showing at all the teeth behind them.

"What a pity," said Waldo aloud, "that she does not speak English."

"I do speak English," said the woman, and Waldo noticed that as she spoke, her lips did not perceptibly open. "What does the gentleman want?"

"You speak English!" Waldo exclaimed, jumping to his feet. "What luck! Where did you learn it?"

"At the mission school," she replied, an amused smile playing about the corners of her rather wide, unopening mouth. "What can be done for you?" She spoke with scarcely any foreign accent, but very slowly and with a sort of growl running along from syllable to syllable.

"I am thirsty," said Waldo, "and I have lost my way."

"Is the gentleman living in a brown tent, shaped like half a melon?" she inquired, the queer, rumbling note drawling from one word to the next, her lips barely separated.

"Yes, that is our camp," said Waldo.

"I could guide the gentleman that way," she droned; "but it is far, and there is no water on that side."

"I want water first," said Waldo, "or milk."

"If you mean cow's milk, we have none. But we have goat's milk. There is to drink where I dwell," she said, sing-songing the words. "It is not far. It is the other way."

"Show me," said he.

She began to walk, Waldo, his gun under his arm, beside her. She trod noiselessly and fast. Waldo could scarcely keep up with her. As they walked he often fell behind and noted how her swathing garments clung to a lithe, shapely back, neat waist and firm hips. Each time he hurried and caught up with her, he scanned her with intermittent glances, puzzled that her waist, so well-marked at the spine, showed no particular definition in front; that the outline of her from neck to knees, perfectly shapeless under her wrappings, was without any waistline or suggestion of firmness or undulation. Likewise he remarked the amused flicker in her eyes and the compressed line of her red, her too red lips.

"How long were you in the mission school?" he inquired.

"Four years," she replied.

"Are you a Christian?" he asked.

"The Free-folk do not submit to baptism," she stated simply, but with rather more of the droning growl between her words.

He felt a queer shiver as he watched the scarcely moved lips through which the syllables edged their way.

"But you are not veiled," he could not resist saying.

"The Free-folk," she rejoined, "are never veiled."

"Then you are not a Mohammedan?" he ventured.

"The Free-folk are not Moslems."

"Who are the Free-folk?" he blurted out incautiously.

She shot one baleful glance at him. Waldo remembered that he had to do with an Asiatic. He recalled the three permitted questions.

"What is your name?" he inquired.

"Amina," she told him.

"That is a name from the 'Arabian Nights,' " he hazarded.

"From the foolish tales of the believers," she sneered. "The Free-folk know nothing of such follies." The unvarying shutness of her speaking lips, the drawly burr between the syllables, struck him all the more as her lips curled but did not open.

"You utter your words in a strange way," he said.

"Your language is not mine," she replied.

"How is it that you learned my language at the mission school and are not a Christian?"

"They teach all at the mission school," she said, "and the maidens of the Free-folk are like the other maidens they teach, though the Free-folk when grown are not as town-dwellers are. Therefore they taught me as any townbred girl, not knowing me for what I am."

"They taught you well," he commented.

"I have the gift of tongues," she uttered enigmatically, with an odd note of triumph burring the words through her unmoving lips.

Waldo felt a horrid shudder all over him, not only at her uncanny words, but also from mere faintness.

"Is it far to your home?" he breathed.

"It is there," she said, pointing to the doorway of a large tomb just before them.

The wholly open arch admitted them into a fairly spacious interior, cool with the abiding temperature of thick masonry. There was no rubbish on the floor. Waldo, relieved to escape the blistering glare outside, seated himself on a block of stone midway between the door and the inner partition-wall, resting his gun-butt on the floor. For the moment he was blinded by the change from the insistent brilliance of the desert morning to the blurred gray light of the interior.

When his sight cleared he looked about and remarked, opposite the door, the ragged hole which laid open the desecrated mausoleum. As his eyes grew accustomed to the dimness he was so startled that he stood up. It seemed to him that from its four corners the room swarmed with naked children. To his inexperienced conjecture they seemed about two years old, but they moved with the assurance of boys of eight or ten.

"Whose are these children?" he exclaimed.

"Mine," she said.

"All yours?" he protested.

"All mine," she replied, a curious suppressed boisterousness in her demeanor.

"But there are twenty of them," he cried.

"You count badly in the dark," she told him. "There are fewer."

"There certainly are a dozen," he maintained, spinning round as they danced and scampered about.

"The Free-people have large families," she said.

"But they are all of one age," Waldo exclaimed, his tongue dry against the roof of his mouth.

She laughed, an unpleasant, mocking laugh, clapping her hands. She was between him and the doorway, and as most of the light came from it he could not see her lips.

"Is not that like a man! No woman would have made that mistake."

Waldo was confused and sat down again. The children circulated around him, chattering, laughing, giggling, snickering, making noises indicative of glee.

"Please get me something cool to drink," said Waldo, and his tongue was not only dry but big in his mouth.

"We shall have to drink shortly," she said, "but it will be warm."

Waldo began to feel uneasy. The children pranced around him, jabbering strange, guttural noises, licking their lips, pointing at him, their eyes fixed on him, with now and then a glance at their mother.

"Where is the water?"

The woman stood silent, her arms hanging at her sides, and it seemed to Waldo she was shorter than she had been.

"Where is the water?" he repeated.

"Patience, patience," she growled, and came a step near to him.

The sunlight struck upon her back and made a sort of halo about her hips. She seemed still shorter than before. There was a something furtive in her bearing, and the little ones sniggered evilly.

At that instant two rifle shots rang out almost as one. The woman fell face downward on the floor. The babies shrieked in a shrill chorus. Then she leapt up from all fours with an explosive suddenness, staggered in a hurled, lurching rush toward the hole in the wall, and, with a frightful yell, threw up her arms and whirled backward to the ground, doubled and contorted like a dying fish, stiffened, shuddered and was still. Waldo, his horrified eyes fixed on her face, even in his amazement noted that her lips did not open.

The children, squealing faint cries of dismay, scrambled through the hole in the inner wall, vanishing into the inky void beyond. The last had hardly gone when the consul appeared in the doorway, his smoking gun in his hand.

"Not a second too soon, my boy," he ejaculated. "She was just going to spring."

He cocked his gun and prodded the body with the muzzle.

"Good and dead," he commented. "What luck! Generally it takes three or four bullets to finish one. I've known one with two bullets through her lungs to kill a man."

"Did you murder this woman?" Waldo demanded fiercely.

"Murder?" the consul snorted. "Murder! Look at that."

He knelt down and pulled open the full, close lips, disclosing not human teeth, but small incisors, cusped grinders, wide-spaced; and long, keen, overlapping canines, like those of a greyhound: a fierce, deadly, carnivorous dentition, menacing and combative.

Waldo felt a qualm, yet the face and form still swayed his horrified sympathy for their humanness.

"Do you shoot women because they have long teeth?" Waldo insisted, revolted at the horrid death he had watched.

"You are hard to convince," said the consul sternly. "Do you call that a woman?"

He stripped the clothing from the carcass.

Waldo sickened all over. What he saw was not the front of a woman, but more like the underside of an old fox-terrier with puppies, or of a white sow, with her second litter; from collar-bone to groin ten lolloping udders, two rows, mauled, stringy and flaccid.

"What kind of a creature is it?" he asked faintly.

"A Ghoul, my boy," the consul answered solemnly, almost in a whisper.

"I thought they did not exist," Waldo babbled. "I thought they were mythical; I thought there were none."

"I can very well believe that there are none in Rhode Island," the consul said gravely. "This is in Persia, and Persia is in Asia."

ESTHER M. FRIESNER

Simpson's Lesser Sphynx

Earlier in this volume, Ray Russell contributed an excellent pastiche of that literary subgenre known as "the club story," popular examples of which have been written by such disparate male writers as Arthur C. Clarke, L. Sprague DeCamp & Fletcher Pratt and Lord Dunsany. "Simpson's Lesser Sphynx" is a delightful send-up of the tradition by the witty and prolific fantasy novelist ESTHER M. FRIESNER, *who lives with her husband and children in Madison, Connecticut.*

Later we all agreed to share the blame. We should have known Simpson was just not our kind. On the basis of blood alone we admitted him to the Club. His father was good stock: Boston, Choate, and Yale; his mother similarly Philadelphia, Miss Devon's, and Skidmore. But nature delights in sports. Who can depend on biology? We are still writing notes to next of kin, and the Club Secretary claims he will resign if those *Enquirer* reporters don't cease hanging around the Pro Shop, putting him off his game.

It was August and we were bored. The market had been sluggish, and so were we. Sterling went so far as to suggest a trip to the local massage parlor to take our minds off our portfolios before he was hissed down and sent to the bar for another round of G&Ts. As he shuffled from the room, he bumped into Simpson.

That is, he afterwards learned it was Simpson he'd encountered. The man's face was hidden behind the bulky wooden crate he bore before him. He heaved it onto the sideboard, scraping the mahogany ruinously, and blew like a draft horse.

"There!" He wiped his brow. "That's done."

We stared at the crate. It was riddled with air holes, and through these a pungent, unpleasant reek began to fill the room. Something inside hissed.

"Simpson," said Dixwell severely, "no pets."

Simpson's eyes crinkled. "Pets?" he echoed, laughing. The thing in the crate hissed again, and we heard a scrabbling sound. The smell was stronger, overwhelming the room's comfortable aura of oiled leather and good burley.

"Here I am, back from Greece with something a sight more interesting to show than slides, and what happens?" Simpson went on. "Dixie quotes Club scripture at me. Well, it's *not* a pet I've got in here. It's a present; a present to the dear old Club. Now, I'll need a hammer."

Wilkes was at his elbow on the moment, hammer graciously proffered. Wilkes is—or was—such an integral part of the Club that old members have long forgotten whether he was hired as butler, waiter, confessor, or handyman. New members were wisely too overawed to ask.

Simpson pried the lid off the crate. Hard pine splinters flew everywhere, and the feral stench intensified. When the lid lay grinding sawdust into the Aubusson, Simpson stood back, made a dramatic flourish, and was actually heard to remark, "Ta-*daah!*"

She did not respond to vulgar fanfare. Simpson had to rap sharply on the side of the crate before the tiny, exquisitely modelled head peeped over the wooden rim. It was no bigger than a man's hand, a head with the face of a Tanagra figurine framed by clusters of dark curls such as old Cretan priestesses wore. She opened her delicate lips and a third, more tentative hiss escaped.

"Come on, Bessie," cried Simpson, seizing the crate and dropping it to the floor with a jarring thud. "Don't make me look bad. Come out and show yourself." He tipped it over and the sphynx spilled out in a tumble of feline body, bare breasts, and goshawk's wings.

"Isn't she a beauty?" Simpson demanded. The sphynx looked at each of us in turn as he spoke, her bosom heaving and her eyes wild. You could trace the ripples of fear on her tawny flanks. Her eyes were blue. "Don't ask me how I got her through customs. Trade secret. The things I do for the Club! Wilkes, bring me a Scotch. I want to toast our new mascot."

"Simpson, you're mad," objected Haskins. "This . . . this creature is a miracle! A myth come to life! It can't—it *shouldn't* exist, and yet . . ." He stretched out a hesitant hand. The sphynx sniffed it warily, cat-fashion, then allowed him to stroke her fur. Slowly an enchanting smile spread across her face; she closed her eyes and thrummed.

"Where did you find it? How? . . ." demanded Dixwell.

Simpson shrugged. "That's a story I'm saving to dine out on."

It was Chapin, as usual, who cast a sopping-wet blanket over the whole affair. "We cannot keep it . . . her . . . here," he decreed from the height of three hundred years of Puritan ancestry. "Quite aside from an obvious violation of U.S. Customs law, we cannot. This is a dangerous animal, Simpson. A monster!"

"Don't you know what sphynxes eat?" put in Hobbs.

Well, of course we'd all suffered through the Oedipus tale in the original Greek at prep school. However, none of us really liked Chapin, and it was hard to ignore how prettily the little sphynx purred and snuggled when Haskins scratched between her wings.

"Oh, for God's sake!" Simpson spat in exasperation. "She's never taken a bite out of me, if that's what you mean. Besides, this one's purebred; can't eat manflesh unless it's gotten according to the code. I watched them for at least a week before I nabbed Bessie, and the only time I saw one of them chow down on a local boy was when he got stupid and arrogant enough to try his hand at the Riddle." You could tell Simpson meant the Riddle to be capitalized by the way he said it.

"What riddle?" Chapin asked in minuscule. We had long suspected his education lacking. Who has not heard of the immortal riddle the sphynx propounds? What is it that goes on four legs at morning, two at noon, three at night? We also had to supply Chapin with the answer: man.

"So you see," Simpson went on, "she's harmless. A, she can only ask the Riddle in Greek—doesn't speak a word of English, besides making cat sounds. B, she can't hurt a fly with it since every school-child knows the answer to that old chestnut. And C, unless the victim's willing to be questioned, she can't touch him. *Now* have we got a mascot?"

We did. We all grew rather fond of Oenone, as she was renamed. Only Simpson would call a sphynx "Bessie." She lived in a kennel in the woodsy clump off the eleventh tee and never needed leashing. It was great fun to do a round of golf and stop by to visit our unique Club pet. She bounded from the kennel or the woods when called and perched on a large boulder, like her famous man-eating ancestress. There she would jabber at us in flawless Greek, cocking her head expectantly, her rose-petal tongue darting out to lick needle-sharp fangs.

"Sorry, Oenone"—we all chuckled—"no riddles today; and the answer is man." This sent her slinking back to the kennel where Wilkes fed her 9-Lives mackerel and changed the newspapers lining the floor.

When winter came, it was Wilkes who offered to take Oenone to live with him in the groundsman's cottage. We saw little of her until spring, although I once surprised the two of them in the Club library. Wilkes was reading, and Oenone, perched on the wing chair's back, almost appeared to be following the text. When he turned a page too quickly, she hissed. He became aware of me and hastily stood up.

"Just relaxing a bit. I do enjoy a good book," he said. I glanced at the book, a paperback mystery. Despite his polished facade, Wilkes was hopelessly addicted to tales of ruthless women, spies, and black-mailers.

Oenone leaped from the chairback and rubbed against his legs. "She looks well. You're taking good care of her, Wilkes," I remarked.

"Oh, she's no trouble. Very affectionate, she is. And smart? Per-sonally"—he lowered his voice—"I've never cared much for cats. But she's different."

I looked at Oenone's human face and pert breasts. Wilkes was innocent to the obvious. So were we all.

That spring the disappearances began.

The first to go were Reynolds and Kramer, a pair of busboys, to be followed in rapid succession by Thomson, Jones, and Green, cad-dies. At first no one missed them; a certain turnover in personnel is expected at any club.

Then it was Wilkes.

The police were little help. Theories flew, but the Club remained beyond implication. Or so it did until the bright May morning when Dixwell announced he was going out to cure his slice and did not return.

"This is atrocious," fumed Chapin, consulting his watch every five minutes as we sat in the bar. "Dixie swore he'd give me advice on my IBM holdings; said he had private news. Must be keeping it to him-self, make a killing and leave his friends out in the cold."

Wearily I stepped down from the stool. "If it's so important to you, we can seek him out on the greens."

Chapin took a cart; I opted to walk. It was better for my health, especially in view of Chapin's driving. So it was natural that he got to the eleventh tee ahead of me by nearly ten minutes. When I came trudging over the bank shielding the sand trap I heard the whine of Chapin's voice from the woods and assumed he'd found Dixwell. Only when I came nearer did I realize that the second voice was female.

"I'll tell you honestly, Chapin," she said, "I don't like you; never have. Don't think I don't know who proposed feeding me generic tuna at the last Club board meeting. Why should I tell you if Dixie's come this way?"

"You're doing just fine on 9-Lives, from the look of you." Chapin's voice was harsh. "Mackerel's brain food; how long have you known English?"

Oenone's reply—who else could it be but Oenone?—came calm and measured. "I don't owe you answers. You have it all wrong. It's you who must play with me; by the old rules."

Chapin's barking laugh was so loud I thought I'd come upon them soon, but I only found the golf cart. They were deeper in the woods, and as I pressed on I heard him say, "And if I don't, you won't help me find Dixie before the market closes, is that it? Dying to ask that stupid riddle after all these years, aren't you?"

"Call it an ethnic whim."

"I call it blackmail; but okay." I could imagine Chapin's fatuous grin. "Ask. What have I got to lose? But the answer is man."

"Is it?" Oenone purred. The rumbling shook the blackberry bushes. I was at the edge of her kennel-clearing, about to announce myself, when I tripped over something and sprawled out of sight just as the sphynx propounded her riddle. "Who was that lady I saw you with last night?"

"Man!" snapped Chapin automatically, then goggled. "*What* did you say?"

I raised myself on my elbows and saw her. She had grown, our sweet Oenone. She was as big as a Siberian tiger, and her steel grey wings fanned out suddenly with a clap of thunder. There were blots of dried blood on her breasts.

"I said," she replied sweetly, "you lose." She pounced before he could utter another word.

I lunged away, sickened by the scream that ended in gurgles and then silence. Something snagged my feet a second time, and I went down in a deafening dry clatter, falling among Oenone's well-gnawed leftovers. I spied Dixwell's nine iron among them. Gorging, she ignored me as I tottered off.

We mounted an armed hunt, but in vain. Sphinxes are smart, as witness Oenone's quiet scholarship, learning English and—no doubt —a more suitable set of riddles. She knew she'd never make her full growth on 9-Lives mackerel. She was gone; literally flown the coop. Where she went is anyone's guess. America is larger than Greece, and there is wilderness still.

Perhaps there will come reports of backpackers unaccounted for, campers gone too long in the high country, mysterious vanishments of hunters and fishermen. Will they chuckle, as we did, and dare her to ask her silly riddle? Arrogance is never the answer to the sphinx's question. Oedipus himself was never educated at Yale.

Of course, look where it got him.

Simpson has been blackballed from the Club. Under the circumstances it was the least we could do.

RICHARD MATHESON

Dress of White Silk

In my opinion, Californian RICHARD MATHESON *is the uncrowned King of American Horror Writers. He is the author of such novels as* I Am Legend, The Incredible Shrinking Man, A Stir of Echoes, Bid Time Return *and the most nerve-wracking ghost story I've ever read,* Hell House. *Some of Matheson's many superb horror stories include "Blood Son," "Born of Man and Woman," "Graveyard Shift," "Nightmare at 20,000 Feet," "Slaughter House" and the following deceptively poignant* guignol.

Quiet is here and all in me.

Granma locked me in my room and wont let me out. Because its happened she says. I guess I was bad. Only it was the dress. Mommas dress I mean. She is gone away forever. Granma says your momma is in heaven. I dont know how. Can she go in heaven if shes dead?

Now I hear granma. She is in mommas room. She is putting mommas dress down the box. Why does she always? And locks it too. I wish she didnt. Its a pretty dress and smells sweet so. And warm. I love to touch it against my cheek. But I cant never again. I guess that is why granma is mad at me.

But I amnt sure. All day it was only like everyday. Mary Jane came over to my house. She lives across the street. Everyday she comes to my house and play. Today she was.

I have seven dolls and a fire truck. Today granma said play with your dolls and it. Dont you go inside your mommas room now she said. She always says it. She just means not mess up I think. Because she says it all the time. Dont go in your mommas room. Like that.

But its nice in mommas room. When it rains I go there. Or when granma is doing her nap I do. I dont make noise. I just sit on the bed and touch the white cover. Like when I was only small. The room smells like sweet.

I make believe momma is dressing and I am allowed in. I smell her white silk dress. Her going out for night dress. She called it that I dont remember when.

I hear it moving if I listen hard. I make believe to see her sitting at the dressing table. Like touching on perfume or something I mean. And see her dark eyes. I can remember.

Its so nice if it rains and I see eyes on the window. The rain sounds like a big giant outside. He says shushshush so every one will be quiet. I like to make believe that in mommas room.

What I like almost best is sit at mommas dressing table. It is like pink and big and smells sweet too. The seat in front has a pillow sewed in it. There are bottles and bottles with bumps and have colored perfume in them. And you can see almost your whole self in the mirror.

When I sit there I make believe to be momma. I say be quiet mother I am going out and you can not stop me. It is something I say I dont know why like hear it in me. And oh stop your sobbing mother they will not catch me I have my magic dress.

When I pretend I brush my hair long. But I only use my own brush from my room. I didnt never use mommas brush. I dont think granma is mad at me for that because I never use mommas brush. I wouldnt never.

Sometimes I did open the box up. Because I know where granma puts the key. I saw her once when she wouldnt know I saw her. She puts the key on the hook in mommas closet. Behind the door I mean.

I could open the box lots of times. Thats because I like to look at mommas dress. I like best to look at it. It is so pretty and feels soft and like silky. I could touch it for a million years.

I kneel on the rug with roses on it. I hold the dress in my arms and like breathe from it. I touch it against my cheek. I wish I could take it to sleep with me and hold it. I like to. Now I cant. Because granma says. And she says I should burn it up but I loved her so. And she cries about the dress.

I wasnt never bad with it. I put it back neat like it was never touched. Granma never knew. I laughed that she never knew before. But she knows now I did it I guess. And shell punish me. What did it hurt her? Wasnt it my mommas dress?

What I like the real best in mommas room is look at the picture of momma. It has a gold thing around it. Frame is what granma says. It is on the wall on top the bureau.

Momma is pretty. Your momma was pretty granma says. Why does she? I see momma there smiling on me and she *is* pretty. For always.

Her hair is black. Like mine. Her eyes are even pretty like black. Her mouth is red so red. I like the dress and its the white one. It is all down on her shoulders. Her skin is white almost white like the dress. And so too are her hands. She is so pretty. I love her even if she is gone away forever I love her so much.

I guess I think thats what made me bad. I mean to Mary Jane.

Mary Jane came from lunch like she does. Granma went to do her nap. She said dont forget now no going in your mommas room. I told her no granma. And I was saying the truth but then Mary Jane and I was playing fire truck. Mary Jane said I bet you havent no mother I bet you made up it all she said.

I got mad at her. I have a momma I know. She made me mad at her to say I made up it all. She said Im a liar. I mean about the bed and the dressing table and the picture and the dress even and every thing.

I said well Ill show you smarty.

I looked into granmas room. She was doing her nap still. I went down and said Mary Jane to come on because granma wont know.

She wasnt so smart after then. She giggled like she does. Even she made a scaredy noise when she hit into the table in the hall upstairs. I said youre a scaredy cat to her. She said back well *my* house isnt so dark like this. Like that was so much.

We went in mommas room. It was more dark than you could see. So I took back the curtains. Just a little so Mary Jane could see. I said this is my mommas room I suppose I made up it all.

She was by the door and she wasnt smart then either. She didnt say any word. She looked around the room. She jumped when I got her arm. Well come on I said.

I sat on the bed and said this is my mommas bed see how soft it is. She didnt say nothing. Scaredy cat I said. Am not she said like she does.

I said to sit down how can you tell if its soft if you dont sit down.

She sat down by me. I said feel how soft it is. Smell how like sweet it is.

I closed my eyes but funny it wasnt like always. Because Mary Jane was there. I told her to stop feeling the cover. You said to she said. Well stop it I said.

See I said and I pulled her up. Thats the dressing table. I took her and brought her there. She said let go. It was so quiet and like always. I started to feel bad. Because Mary Jane was there. Because it was in my mommas room and momma wouldnt like Mary Jane there.

But I had to show her the things because. I showed her the mirror. We looked at each other in it. She looked white. Mary Jane is a scaredy cat I said. Am not am not she said anyway nobodys house is so quiet and dark inside. Anyway she said it smells.

I got mad at her. No it doesnt smell I said. Does so she said you said it did. I got madder too. It smells like sugar she said. It smells like sick people in your mommas room.

Dont say my mommas room is like sick people I said to her.

Well you didnt show me no dress and youre lying she said there isnt no dress. I felt all warm inside so I pulled her hair. Ill show you I said and dont never say Im a liar again.

She said Im going home and tell my mother on you. You are not I said youre going to see my mommas dress and youll better not call me a liar.

I made her stand still and I got the key off the hook. I kneeled down. I opened the box with the key.

Mary Jane said pew that smells like garbage.

I put my nails in her and she pulled away and got mad. Dont you pinch me she said and she was all red. Im telling my mother on you she said. And anyway its not a white dress its dirty and ugly she said.

Its not dirty I said. I said it so loud I wonder why granma didnt hear. I pulled out the dress from the box. I held it up to show her how its white. It fell open like the rain whispering and the bottom touched on the rug.

It is too white I said all white and clean and silky.

No she said she was so mad and red it has a hole in it. I got more madder. If my momma was here shed show you I said. You got no momma she said all ugly. I hate her.

I have. I said it way loud. I pointed my finger to mommas picture. Well who can see in this stupid dark room she said. I pushed her hard and she hit against the bureau. See then I said mean look at the picture. Thats my momma and shes the most beautiful lady in the whole world.

Shes ugly she has funny hands Mary Jane said. She hasnt I said shes the most beautiful lady in the world!

Not not she said *she has buck teeth.*

I dont remember then. I think like the dress moved in my arms. Mary Jane screamed. I dont remember what. It got dark and the curtains were closed I think. I couldnt see anyway. I couldnt hear nothing except buck teeth funny hands buck teeth funny hands even when no one was saying it.

There was something else because I think I heard some one call *dont let her say that!* I couldnt hold to the dress. And I had it on me I cant remember. Because I was like grown up strong. But I was a little girl still I think. I mean outside.

I think I was terrible bad then.

Granma took me away from there I guess. I dont know. She was screaming god help us its happened its happened. Over and over. I dont know why. She pulled me all the way here to my room and locked me in. She wont let me out. Well Im not so scared. Who cares if she locks me in a million billion years? She doesnt have to even give me supper. Im not hungry anyway.

Im full.

TOBY SANDERS

The Palace of the Mountain Ogre
A Chinese Hansel and Gretel

Author of the definitive study of the clowning art, How to Be a Compleat Clown *(Stein & Day, 1978),* TOBY SANDERS *is a native Pennsylvanian now employed as a New York City schoolteacher. A fluent scholar of Chinese culture, language and literature, Mr. Sanders is currently engaged in rendering into English a series of Asian fantasy stories analogous to Western fairy tales. One of his first efforts is "The Palace of the Mountain Ogre," which corresponds to "Hansel and Gretel."*

Once there was a poor, hard-working farmer and his wife who lived in the shadow of a large mountain. Though their lives were not easy, they lived comfortably with their two children, a boy named Xiao Di Di and a girl, Da Jie.

One day, the children's mother became seriously ill. Her husband did not know what to do. He carried the burden of the farm and raising the children, at the same time caring for his wife. But at last, the woman knew she was going to die, so she called her family to her bedside.

"My babies," she said, "soon I will have to leave you. I no longer will be able to take care of you morning and night. You must rely on your father for that. Remember to stay together always, because there is nothing sadder in this world than the lot of a motherless child." With her last ounce of strength, she raised her hand and pointed to her son, her daughter and then her husband. "The days ahead of you will be hard and full of grief." With a sigh, her hand fell as she quietly passed away.

The family buried her in a clearing behind the house and the farmer taught his children how to take care of the grave. He instructed them in the proper rituals for honoring their mother and told them when during the year they must perform them. He showed them which foods and objects made the best offerings to her memory.

As time passed, the children faithfully honored the memory of their mother. Their father did so, too, for a while, but he longed for a companion and someone to help him with the duties of the farm and household, so he finally decided to take another wife.

The woman he chose was beautiful and practical, but she was also mean-spirited and devious. From the moment she set foot in the house, the children knew she hated them. She was always quick to scold and criticize the work they did, and she constantly thought up chores for them. She would send them to fetch firewood and as soon as they were finished, she would send them to carry water. When they were done with the water, she sent them to thresh the grain. Their work was never done. She denied them warm clothes during the winter and refused to let them have new shoes. When they walked through the snow, they were virtually barefoot. The meaning of their dead mother's last words became all too clear to them: there *was* nothing sadder in this world than the lot of a motherless child.

The farmer was unaware of his children's hardships. He was very busy tending the farm and since his new wife was pleasant to him, it never occurred to him that she might be treating his offspring cruelly. The children were more afraid of their stepmother than they were of snakes, slugs or other slimy things, but though their father noticed that they were unhappy, he thought this was because they missed their real mother.

Before long, the stepmother began worrying that when she had a family of her own, there would not be enough to go around. Furthermore, she wanted to be sure that if the farmer died, she and her children would inherit the farm and house. She kept these thoughts to herself while she laid her plans.

One morning, instead of getting out of bed, she moaned, groaned, shook and cried out. The farmer ran to her in alarm.

"What is the matter?" he asked. "Are you sick?"

"I *am* sick, my husband," said the stepmother, overacting so badly that it is a wonder he believed her. "I do not think anything will make me feel well again. There is only one hope . . ."

"Tell me! I will do anything to help you get better."

"Then you must seek guidance at the Temple Where the Enlightened Mother Dwells. Go quickly, for I am almost beyond hope!"

The farmer ran from the house, jumped on a horse and galloped down the road.

As soon as he was gone, the stepmother hurried outside and got on another horse, but did not follow the main road her husband took. She threaded her way along a mountain path and through the old forest. She arrived at the temple long before the farmer. The women there were her friends. Together they helped disguise her as the Mother Superior.*

When the farmer reached the shrine, he devoutly prepared himself, solemnly lighting the revival lamp, reverently laying out offerings of silk and food, humbly praying for assistance. Before he finished his prostrations, the false Mother Superior spoke to him with solemn severity.

"Your wife's illness cannot be cured by ordinary means. She will certainly die unless you eliminate the offspring of your previous marriage. Doing so will prove your love for your wife, and she may begin to heal. You may keep her or your children, but not both. Choose quickly, for it soon will be too late to save your wife."

The farmer was struck dumb. Sadly, he rose and began the journey home. How could he choose between his new wife and his children? As he pondered his choice, he began to cry.

His trip home was much slower than the one he had made to the temple. This gave the stepmother plenty of time to change out of her disguise and hurry back to the farmhouse.

When the farmer arrived home, he heard her in bed crying out even louder than before. This decided him on what he must do. Still, he loved his children too much to destroy them himself, so, first preparing two bags by undoing their bottom stitching, he called his daughter and his son to him.

"We are going to collect herbs to help your new mother get well," he told them, "but we must hurry."

The three set off through the mountains, turning and twisting, going up hills and down valleys. After walking winding paths for half

* The words "Mother Superior" generally reflect the function of this notary. There is really no accurate English translation.—TS

a day, the farmer was sure the boy and girl could not possibly find their way home.

He handed them the bags he had prepared and said, "My children, you are my own flesh and blood." He wanted to tell them good-bye, but the sadness welling up within his heart forced him to stop. Instead, he instructed them, "I want you to go into the woods and pick as many herbs as you can. Put them all in the bags I have given you. Don't come back until the bags are full. I will stay here and prepare supper. When your bags are stuffed, you can find your way back by walking towards the smoke of the fire I'll make to cook our food."

The innocent children hung on every word their father said. The farmer watched them turn with their bags and enter the woods. When they were out of sight, he sat upon a log and wept bitterly. He was sure he would never see them again. At length, he changed his mind and called for them to come back, but by that time they were too far away to hear his cries.

The children kept on walking through the forest picking herbs and putting them into their bags. The little girl thought about their stepmother's illness. She was sure that helping collect the herbs to cure her would help change the way the woman treated her and her brother. So when the boy said, "Da Jie, I'm hungry," his sister replied that he must work faster so they could return to their father. A little later, her brother complained that he was tired. She scolded him, saying, "Xiao Di Di, you shouldn't think about yourself all the time. Think about our poor sick stepmother. She needs our help." Thus they continued picking herbs all day long.

When the sun began to dip below the horizon, the children examined their bags and discovered that they were empty. They also saw that they were in a strange part of the forest. The little boy began to cry, "How will we find our way back to Daddy?"

His sister tried to comfort him. "Don't cry, Xiao Di Di. Our father would never leave us alone in the woods. He'd wait for us all night and keep his fire burning." She started collecting leaves and branches to make a bed for them beneath a large tree. "Let's sleep here tonight. In the morning, we'll follow the herbs that fell out of our bags till they lead us to our father."

Quieting her brother in this fashion, she settled down with him for the night. But the deep woods in the mountains were full of strange sounds and soon they were shivering with fright. Finally, they moved to one of the branches in a large tree for safety.

As soon as the sun rose, they climbed down and followed the trail of herbs, every now and then stopping to see if they could spot their father's campfire. After walking for several hours, the boy shouted, "Da Jie, I can see the fire! Daddy didn't leave us!" The little boy began to run through the woods toward a pillar of smoke rising above the treetops.

His sister noticed that the smoke came from a direction that led them away from the path of herbs. But remembering her mother's stern warning that they must "stay together always," Da Jie knew she could not allow her brother to wander away without her, so she followed after him.

Before long, the children entered a clearing at the foot of a large mountain. In front of them towered an immense palace, its walls carved from the mountainside. Its doors and balconies glittered gold and silver in the sunlight. Never in their lives had they seen a building so great and magnificent. They walked hesitantly toward it. Suddenly, the front door of the palace swung open. Standing on the threshold was a woman about the same age as their own mother. For a few moments, she watched them greedily, and then she smiled at them.

The strange woman frightened the children. Dropping their bags, they turned to run away, but she called, "Don't flee, my little treasures. You look tired and hungry. Inside, I've got a big fireplace and many good things to eat. Come in and rest a while." As they hesitated, she stepped forward and gently urged them into the palace.

They exchanged worried glances. On the one hand, they felt afraid, but on the other, since their real mother died, no other person had ever treated them so kindly. The children decided to follow her.

Inside the palace, she sat them before a huge fireplace in an immense room and fed them reviving cups of tea, delicious vegetables and savory meats. The blaze warmed them. As they ate, they glanced all about at their surroundings. At the other end of the hall, three staircases ascended to other rooms in the palace. One was made of pure gold, a second was formed from silver, while the third stairs were built of rather plain-looking wood.

Once the children had eaten, the woman asked, "My little treasures, do you like it here in my palace?"

Da Jie, who was still afraid of the woman, did not like the palace, but politely replied, "Auntie, I admire the golden stairs."

"I like the silver staircase," said her brother.

The woman cackled loudly. "My little treasures," she said, "since you fancy my palace so much, from this day forth, it shall be your home! Here there is plenty for you to eat and lots of room to play."

The woman began to clear the table. "Soon, my children, I will go away for a little while. I want to fetch my sons to meet you. Until I get back, you must not move from this room. Stay by the fireplace and make sure the fire does not go out." She pointed to a large covered pot by the fireplace. "Above all, if you wish to remain safe, you must not disturb that pot or lift its lid."

She went outside and saddled a horse, but just before she left, she produced a large key and locked the palace door securely. Cackling three times at the door, she mounted her steed and raced off through the woods.

Da Jie, by now very frightened, asked her brother, "Xiao Di Di, tell me truly, do you think this lady who has treated us so well is a good woman?"

"No," he answered, "I think she is very bad. I'm afraid of her. I want to go home!"

Without another word, Da Jie took her brother's hand. Disobeying the woman's instructions, she led him through the palace, hoping to find a way out. They crossed the main hall and tiptoed upstairs.

The first room they came to was horrifying. From its lofty rafters hung the bodies of their hostess's victims. Shocked and frightened, Da Jie, pulling her brother by the hand, forced her legs to carry her away from the terrible chamber. Now she knew the kind of place they'd stumbled into—they were in the lair of a mountain ogre!

The little girl led her brother to the roof where the ogre's clothes were drying. Its edge dropped off suddenly like a steep cliff. Da Jie pulled her brother with her as she ran from one end of the roof to the other, but there was no way down. Xiao Di Di was still too young to understand completely what was happening, but tears began to flow down his cheeks, so his sister gave up and led him back downstairs to the fireplace.

Da Jie settled herself next to the fire-blackened, greasy kettle that the ogre warned her not to touch. As she lowered herself onto the hearth, her hand accidentally bumped against the pot's lid. An icy chill shot up her arm, but at first she paid no attention. She was too worried about what would happen when the ogre returned with her family. Probably the only reason she and her brother were still alive was because they'd come to the palace in the morning. The ogre must have dined already and was saving them for supper.

As Da Jie pondered their predicament, she leaned closer to the pot and again felt a chill. Cautiously, she lifted its lid. Inside she saw nothing but seven gigantic black beetles with huge pincers crawling about.

The girl was surprised. Why wouldn't the ogre want her to know about the beetles? Of what importance could they possibly be? Da Jie thought hard about the insects in the pot and what they meant. She remembered something that her mother once told her about ogres.

Ogres are evil, magical creatures, the little girl recalled. *Mother said the reason they are so hard to destroy is because they never keep their power in their own bodies. Perhaps these beetles are where this mountain ogre stores her power.*

As soon as Da Jie came to this conclusion, she began stoking the fire until it was a roaring blaze. Then, seizing a pair of large tongs near the hearth, the child carefully picked up the squirming beetles, one at a time, and began to throw them into the flames.

Suddenly, the children heard roars of pain coming from the forest outside the palace. Every time Da Jie threw another beetle into the fire, the howling grew louder. When there was only one beetle left, the little girl ran to the window to see what was making such a racket. Outside, she saw six young ogres, the sons of the older woman, turning into charcoal and crumbling to ash.

Out of the woods burst the mother of the six ogres. Her face was no longer kindly. It was terrifying. She ran shrieking toward her palace with the key to the front door held out before her.

Da Jie knew that she and her brother would perish horribly if the ogre got her hands on them, so, hurrying back to the fireplace, she fought her own fear and grabbed the last beetle. Great coldness shot up her arms, she could hardly move them. She heard the click of the key in the lock. Crying out in terror, the child thrust her hands toward the fireplace. As the door shook in its frame and swung open violently, the last beetle tumbled end over end, dropped into the blaze and burst into flames. Behind her, Da Jie heard the ogre utter one last hideous howl and then there was silence.

The girl waited, trembling, not sure if her plan had worked. Beside her, Xiao Di Di sobbed softly. Utter silence. No ogre's hand clamped over her shoulder. At last, she turned to look at the door. It hung open, a large key firmly fixed in the lock. On the doorstep outside was a dwindling pile of ash being blown away by the wind. The ogres and her sons were no more.

After calming herself, Da Jie comforted her brother. Evening was approaching and she did not want to leave the palace, for she knew that though the forest was quiet, other monsters besides ogres roamed the sides of mountains and lurked in the woods. The girl took the key and locked the door.

Next morning when they went outside, the children were surprised to see that the palace was really made up of two sections, one with a wooden door, the other golden. Conquering their fear, they decided to explore some more. They opened the golden door and found a pantry full of fruits and vegetables and other good things to eat. Inside, they also discovered two more staircases. A golden one led to rooms full of gold objects, while a pair of silver stairs brought them to silver-laden chambers.

"Daddy has had such a hard life," Xiao Di Di said. "If we could find him and bring him here, we could all be happy together again."

His sister instantly made a decision. "We will stay here together while we hunt for father. When we find him, we'll bring him here to live with us."

They did so. Every day, Da Jie went with her brother to find their father, walking through the woods and searching the mountains for the smoke from his fire. They hunted goats so they would have milk and meat to go with the fruits and vegetables in the palace, and they also took time out to play together. Their life was much better than when they lived with their stepmother.

Meanwhile, their father, unable to forgive himself for tricking his youngsters, often returned to the place where he'd left them. He would build a fire, hoping they would see the smoke and come back to him. As he sat by the burning logs, his tears sputtered into the fire and made it smoke all the more. After months of waiting, he despaired that he would ever see them again.

But his children never gave up. They remembered their father had told them, "I will be on this mountainside by the fire waiting for you." One day, Da Jie at last noticed a column of smoke rising above the trees.

She called to her brother, "Xiao Di Di, come and look! Father must still be waiting for us. I think I see his fire!"

They ran through the woods toward the smoke. There was no path in that direction, so they made their own, trampling through bushes, wading brooks, clambering over huge logs. At last, they reached the clearing where their father stood feeding the flames.

The farmer did not see his children at the edge of the clearing. He had a sad expression on his face. They heard him say, "Spirits of the forests, please watch after my daughter and my baby son. Don't let them be eaten by the monsters that prowl these mountains." He sank down slowly, sobbing bitterly.

The children stared at him. During the months since they'd gone away, his hair had turned completely white. "Da Jie," the boy asked, "is this really our father?"

"Yes," she nodded, "but he has grown much older."

The two called out to him, but he was crying so loudly he did not hear, so they ran to his side to comfort him. When the farmer saw that his children were alive and safe, his tears of sadness turned to tears of happiness. Springing to his feet, he hugged them. They all wept for joy.

The children excitedly told their father about their adventure and, describing the magnificent place where they now lived, led him through the forest to the palace of the mountain ogre. It sparkled gold and silver in the sunlight.

Da Jie led the farmer to the palace's doors and asked, "Father, would you like to go in by the golden door or the wooden door?"

The farmer hesitated. He seemed reluctant to enter. He shook his head and said with embarrassment, "I have let both of you down. How may I use the golden stairs?" He approached the wooden steps, but when he set his foot on them, they changed to gold.

Inside, the children showed their father all the treasures in all the rooms. They begged him to stay there with them. He happily agreed. But after many days passed, he began to worry that nobody was tending to the duties of his farm. It was time to plant the crops, and the animals needed someone to care for them. Finally, he told his children he must go back home for a while, but he promised to return.

When the time came for him to leave, his daughter gave him a walking stick to help him on the road and a bag of multicolored stones from the palace's main hall.

The farmer walked for one whole day, but could not reach his farm before the sky turned dark, so he found a cave to sleep in. When he woke the following morning, his walking stick was gone and in its place was a spirited horse. As he leaped upon the horse with the bag his daughter had given him, he noticed that the bag felt heavier. He looked inside and found that the colored stones had turned into silver. He put the bag of silver on the horse and rode proudly and happily home.

His wife, amazed by her husband's good fortune, immediately

started nagging him until he told her all about the palace that his children found. She was angry that they should have such luck, and she was greedy to get a share of the treasure for herself, so before long she forced her mate to stop working on the farm long enough to lead her into the mountains.

Taking her to the place where he'd found his children, he built a fire and then went back to his farm. The boy and girl saw the smoke rising above the trees from the roof of the palace. They ran through the woods to meet their father, but when they reached the clearing, the only person they saw was their stepmother.

The boy said, "Da Jie, let's go. We don't have to be nice to her."

"Yes, we do," his sister replied. "She is still our father's wife."

Unhappily, the children led their stepmother down the mountain and through the woods. On the way, she asked many questions about all the treasures of their new home. When they arrived at the clearing, the stepmother's eyes grew wide when she saw the sparkling palace.

Da Jie pointed to the building's two entrances. "Stepmother, would you like to go through the gold door or the wooden one?"

The woman, drooling in anticipation, said, "Even though I haven't treated you very well, I am still your mother. I will go through the golden door." But as soon as she touched it, the door turned to wood. This angered the stepmother, but she did not show it, for she was hoping for greater riches than a golden door.

Inside, the girl pointed to the two staircases and asked her stepmother which one she wished to ascend. Again the woman chose the gold one, but the touch of her feet changed the stairs to wood.

The children took their stepmother to the fireplace and offered her many good things to eat. But no matter what food she raised to her lips, it immediately rotted.

The woman was very upset. She wanted the same kinds of treasures her husband received, but nothing she touched remained unspoiled. After a single night in the mountain ogre's palace, she was so unhappy that she told the children she wanted to go back to the farm. To send her on her way, they gave her a walking stick and a bag of many-colored pebbles just like the ones they'd given their father.

The stepmother walked a whole day without reaching the farm. When the sky grew dark, she found a cave to sleep in. Next morning, her walking stick was gone. In its place was a huge poisonous snake. She grabbed her bag and tried to get away from the serpent's fangs, but when she leaped up, the colored stones spilled out of the bag and as soon as they hit the earth, they changed into great spotted leopards. The leopards and snake circled the stepmother, then tore her apart.

Days later, the farmer returned to the palace. When he asked about his wife, his children told him all they knew, but none of them ever saw her again. This was just as well, for without her, they all lived most fortunate lives in the palace of the mountain ogre.

ADÈLE SLAUGHTER

Snow White Waking

Speaking of fairy tales, here is a strikingly offbeat footnote to the Snow White legend. ADÈLE SLAUGHTER *is a professional poet from Long Island, New York, where she is consultant and coordinator of a series of poetry readings at the Heckscher Museum in Huntington. Her poetry has appeared in numerous periodicals, including the "Long Island Quarterly," "Earthwise" and the "Princeton Spectrum," and she has also edited twelve anthologies of adolescent writings.*

Slam your fist through the glass coffin.
I have been lying here for so long,
my body dark, my mind blank.
I have forgotten touch.
Does red lick milk from a bowl,
does black caw or is that the night?
What's that buzz in my ears—
ice thawing or a fly?

I am so relieved you are here
but cannot speak or move.
You reach between the sheets.
My hands clutch an apple to my breast.
That witch meant it to be forever,
but you are here now and it is not forever.
Come hold me. My arms are stiff,

Has frost bit my fingers?
A weak pulse throbs through my body.

Black is the hair on my head and curls
between my legs. Hair, black like
night next to the day of my white skin.
come hold both the day and the night.
The flies, dogs, cats and parakeets
are buzzing back to life and yes
the ice is melting. I can almost feel you.
Come closer, breathe your milk-breath on my face.
Red is a color, red is blood and rushes to my lips
and flows from my legs. Come kiss me.

MILDRED CLINGERMAN

The Little Witch of Elm Street

MILDRED CLINGERMAN, *a resident of Tucson, Arizona, is the author of many charming fantasy stories published in* "F&SF" . . . The Magazine of Fantasy and Science Fiction. *"The Little Witch of Elm Street," one of her most delightful tales, first appeared in the April, 1957 edition of* F&SF.

Nina hit our neighborhood hard. Of course we'd been warned, but for the first day or two we found it impossible to believe that such a beautiful child could be seven kinds of unmitigated hell. My first introduction to Nina came one day late in the spring. I was visiting Mrs. Pritchett, who lives next door. I'd made the mistake of telling Mrs. Pritchett that I never seemed to get caught up on my housework. She insisted that I come right over to see just how she organized her day. I never could resist expert demonstrations. Every year at the county fair I buy little kitchen thingumbobs that look perfectly easy to operate. Under my hand, though, they turn into Awful Mysteries.

For two hours I'd been watching Mrs. Pritchett squaring corners and quieting ruffled surfaces and in every room obliterating evidence that Mr. Pritchett or any living thing had ever passed that way. Poor Mr. Pritchett, I thought. On Elm Street Mrs. Pritchett's living room was referred to as "the living reproach"—to the rest of us. Neither Mr. Pritchett nor the Pritchett infant was allowed to impede the smooth progress of her day. All of Mrs. Pritchett's days clicked and purred, turning out nice square little compartments labeled "cleaning," "baking," "baby," "marketing." In the nursery I watched her bend over the baby's pram and tuck in another half inch of blanket on the right hand side. This exactly centered the knot of blue-ribbon trimming under Master Pritchett's chins.

Master Pritchett himself remained inert, except for the slow blinking of his eyelids. After seven and one half months of perfect, ordered existence the Pritchett infant had taken on the exact look and deportment of a justice of a superior court. Mrs. Pritchett wheeled him out to the sunny porch and left him to his judicial contemplation of a world that might, or might not, show cause.

I recalled how my own children at that age had screamed for attention. Just the same, I thought, they didn't in the least resemble stuffed sausages. Back in the living room Mrs. Pritchett was lifting the taut sofa cushions and narrowly inspecting the crevices along the sofa arms. Once, two years ago, she told me, she'd found an orange seed buried there—damning proof, I gathered, that in her brief absences Mr. Pritchett's besetting sin still twitched in him. I was glad to hear it. He would eat oranges in the living room, she said, though he no longer piled the ashtrays high with orange peels. He couldn't. Mrs. Pritchett had made him stop smoking and removed the ashtrays. Poor Mr. Pritchett.

Even expert demonstrations pall, especially when accompanied by little lectures in miniature, calculated to imbue me with the Pritchett Housekeeping Doctrine, which I knew very well was as alien to me as Druidic rites, and about as likely to be put into practice. I was ready to go when the doorbell rang.

Two figures confronted us. One was a thin, spectacled girl of about twelve, whose hair straggled out of careless braids to hang curtain-like over her high forehead. She maintained a firm hold on a leather leash which was attached to a four-year-old beauty, a dimpled dumpling in a blue pinafore. The dumpling's smile was enchanting. Here, I thought, is perfection. One simply overlooked the fact that the tiny girl's elbows were bandaged (so were both knees) and that a yellow-and-green bruise lay like a slap along one round cheek.

The older girl blew at a bothersome strand of hair and wrapped another loop of the leash around her arm.

"This," she said, pointing to the Vision, "is Nina. We've just moved into that new house in the next block and I'm calling on all the neighbors to warn them—it's only fair. Especially those with children."

She peered curiously past the astonished Mrs. Pritchett into the Pritchett living room.

"Mind if I come in? It's quite safe, really. It's a new leash, you see, and in any case Nina has a thing about me. She always has had. Isn't it lucky? But of course," she said, "I can't be with her constantly. There's school and all. . . . That's what I'd like to explain to you if I may? Thank you, we'd love to come in."

Mrs. Pritchett and I fell back before this determined advance. I sat down again. The morning began to look like fun.

"What a neat room!" the child said. "Is the whole house like this? You must have a compulsion or something. I know all about the beastly subconscious, you see. My brother, *her* father," she jerked the leash indicating Nina, "is a professor at the University. By the way, my name is Garnet Bayard." She stuck out a rather dirty little hand first to Mrs. Pritchett, then to me. The handshake was quick and down, as the French do it. She seated herself composedly in the best chair, with the radiant Nina leaning against her bony knees.

"It's this way," she said, bending confidentially toward us. "Nina expresses her aggressions very readily without any regard for painful consequences. For herself, I mean. Hence the bandages. Naturally she doesn't care how painful the consequences are for her victim. They—that is, her parents and the psychiatrist—believe that this is simply a phase and that it is up to them to try to provide her with 'inanimate objects' to vent her aggressions on. Personally, I've grown a little bored with this phase. I've been with my brother and his wife since Nina's birth and, frankly, she was ever thus. I loathe sounding reactionary but until psychiatry becomes more of a science"—Garnet lifted her eyebrows and shrugged her shoulders—"one may as well resort to witchcraft. As a matter of fact, I find the study of witchcraft a fascinating one. My brother has a very nice collection of old books on the subject—"

But Mrs. Pritchett, whose mouth had been opening and closing without any sounds emerging, finally found her voice.

"I don't understand. What was it you came to . . . *warn* us of?"

Garnet looked at her in surprise. "Why, I came to warn you about Nina. She bites. She kicks. She pinches babies. She aims her tricycle at the behinds of nice old ladies and never misses the target. She's hell on wheels." Garnet turned to smile at me. "I am addicted to plays on words. I think even bad puns are delightful, don't you?"

Mrs. Pritchett was sputtering. "You . . . you mean she attacks people without any provocation? What are her parents thinking of? Have they no control over her at all?"

"They've got me," Garnet said, "and the leash. As to what they're thinking, does one ever know? About anybody, I mean. Pamela—Nina's mother—is lying down at this moment reading Proust. One would suppose reading Proust would set her to dithering around in half-forgotten, somewhat mucky old impressions. What it actually does to Pamela is put her to sleep. She's rather tired with the moving, and the sight of all those un-unpacked boxes and barrels simply drove her to Proust. It's that kind of day."

Mrs. Pritchett, I saw, had reached the hand-wringing stage. "But what do you expect us—the neighbors—to do about it?"

Garnet studied her for a moment and then spoke soothingly.

"About Nina? Nothing, except for keeping your gate closed and latched. And when you're out walking look behind you frequently. She's amazingly quiet when approaching her prey."

It was almost lunchtime. I had to run along, much as I hated to, but I went away cherishing the picture of Mrs. Pritchett's face as she listened to Garnet in horrified fascination. Mrs. Pritchett's eyes, I thought, looked as if she were suddenly confronted by far, disorderly vistas. I decided this was an even nicer spring than usual. Of course, our neighborhood wasn't exactly dull before Nina's and Garnet's arrival, but there wasn't much scope for righteous indignation. True, we women always reacted when the Pritchetts were mentioned. Some of us clucked our tongues and some of us grinned, but we all joined in the chorus to murmur, "Poor Mr. Pritchett . . ." Living next door to them, I saw a good deal more than most. Like Mrs. Pritchett sweeping the front walk right behind Mr. Pritchett every morning as he left the house, as if she were determined to erase his irresolute footsteps. I could hear her delivering firm lectures—not miniature ones, either—yet I had never once heard Mr. Pritchett answer back.

At parties I'd heard ribald speculations as to just how Master Pritchett happened. They had been childless for the six or seven years of their marriage, and when Mrs. P. began to appear in neat, dark maternity dresses some of the gayer couples insisted she was about to deliver herself of New Man—a robot-like creature somewhat resembling an efficiency expert, but minus vocal cords.

I'm afraid we were all disappointed that the baby hadn't upset the rigid routine of that household. Some of the women had begun to say, "Yes, but wait till he starts walking or trying to feed himself!" As for me, I had no such hopes. I was certain Mrs. Pritchett was more than a match for her son. I had watched the slow metamorphosis in Mr. Pritchett. He hadn't always been an object of half-scornful pity to his neighbors. Years ago he had exchanged books with me and sometimes a few words at twilight, standing on his neat patch of lawn, gazing wistfully at our toy-littered yard, tumbling children, cats and dogs. We talked then of beer and pigeons and amateur painting in oils. He was fond of all three but Mrs. Pritchett banned them as "messy." He said lovely, unexpected things sometimes, like the evening I told him about my struggles to measure our windows correctly for new curtains. I had tried it four times, I told him, and the inches came out exasperatingly different each time.

"Yes," he smiled at me warmly, "there's something queer about measuring tapes. I believe they hate us, and sometimes they can't resist making fools of us—for being so silly as to imagine we can tame even a small chunk of space or fence it in."

I went inside my house and looked at my measuring tape with new eyes. Mr. Pritchett's words only served to deepen my own conviction that the world was a fearful and wonderful place, and that in it anything could happen and the very best thing for me to do was to stay limber enough to enjoy it.

I harbored the uncharitable wish that Nina's first attack would be on Mrs. P. but the initial assault, unhappily, was directed toward my own two children. While I bandaged and soothed, the story emerged between sobs. Nina had ridden them down on her "trike" while they were kneeling unaware, playing marbles. The severest injury, I saw, was to their pride. It was unthinkable that a four-year-old girl should dare assail boys of eight and ten. And, by George, she wouldn't catch them that way again. The sobbing stopped while they showed each other just how they'd show her. Here I stepped in to separate them before they forgot that this was a mere demonstration and to point out how extreme my scorn would be if they ever stooped to fighting a four-year-old girl.

"But what'll we do?" they wailed. "You want us just to lie down and let her ride that old trike all over us? Be smashed to smithereens?"

I remembered Garnet's words. "Keep looking behind you. If you see her coming, get out of the way. Run!"

I got nothing but rebellious looks for this advice but in two weeks it was standard operating procedure for every child in the neighborhood and for most of the adults. The adults who didn't use evasive tactics soon learned to. She bit the postman on the thumb, hanging on like a terrier. She butted fat Mr. Simpson in the belly. Twice. She broke up every knot of children she found by pedaling furiously into their midst. I became accustomed to the sound of terrified shrieks and pounding feet. I knew Nina had appeared on the block. And throughout all the commotion and blood, Nina kept smiling her entrancing smile. We mothers began to long for summer when school would be dismissed and Garnet could take full charge.

We all agreed that Nina suffered as many injuries as anybody. More, really. I rarely saw her when she wasn't swathed in bandages. She didn't talk much, even in Garnet's care, and of course nobody paused to converse with her otherwise. We hesitated to call on her parents, since some of the first callers had been a little put off by the Bayards' reception of them. Nina's mother, I heard, was a languid woman who lived in a welter of books and dust and who, at the mention of Nina's crimes, either bristled or laughed heartily. Professor Bayard's laughter at his daughter was rather hollow and it was remarked that he had several bruises on his shins. That was one of the things that made the callers uncomfortable: the professor at home wore nothing but a pair of shorts and one or two of the older ladies disliked the sight of his peaked, naked little chest. And the talk, they said, was like nothing they'd ever heard before. Very erudite, but also full of very strong Anglo-Saxon words. I thought the Bayards sounded like fun, but I was too busy just then to seek them out.

And anyway Garnet sought me out often enough to keep me informed about the Bayards, though mostly, to my delight, her talk ranged farther afield. Nina was never a menace when Garnet brought her. She sat playing with the boys' outgrown toys and picture books, the perfect picture, herself. I was charmed. Garnet, however, pointed out that even bulldozers occasionally run out of gas.

Garnet's talk had much the same effect on me that Mr. Pritchett's once had. I recognized the fact that she was some kind of genius and might one day startle the world with her originality and fire. But at twelve she was content to startle me—her quick mind grasping, sorting, and discarding, her tongue curling around new words she'd just learned, framing her newest thoughts in mint condition. I liked her because she was interested in almost everything: people, cats, pies, stars, or the way to scrub a floor. I just this minute realized that Garnet, all along, was meant to be a poet. There was a time, though, when I saw her as retributive justice or just plain witch.

It began—this period—the day Garnet came rushing in to tell me that she had finally, in her study of witchcraft, discovered a possible cure for Nina.

"I am convinced," she said, "that she is, in old-fashioned terminology, harboring a devil. Why not? Isn't that what the psychiatrist is trying to lure out of her with his little dolls and toy furniture? He gives them to her so she'll build a world in miniature and then react to it, while he watches. She reacts, all right. Smash. Crash. But why? He could have come over here and watched her in this one for all he's learned. Do you know what our bill for bandages alone amounts to? She'll kill herself if we don't do something quick." Garnet pushed excitedly at her hair. "Why, any day now she may begin attacking people in automobiles.

"I have to get back. I left Pamela at her eternal bandaging. No, Nina hasn't attacked anybody today. Not yet. Pam and I decided last week that Nina adores being bandaged. . . . She'd just intercepted a man on a bicycle and afterwards she apparently felt she rated an extra big bandage, though all she needed was a small piece of tape. *How* she howled! So we're experimenting—wrapping her like a mummy several times a day. I haven't much faith in it, and Nina keeps protesting there isn't any 'red.' Have you got a bottle of ketchup? We don't keep it on hand. Pamela thinks people who eat ketchup ought to be cast into outer darkness, but I like it. . . ."

I found a bottle of ketchup and humbly passed it on to Garnet.

"I hope you're on the track of her trouble," I said. "This bandage idea sounds good to me. Maybe she hurts herself so her mother will fuss over her."

Garnet shook her head impatiently. "That's too simple," she said. "Besides it's too utterly dull. By the way, I need a few . . . uh . . . herbs. For the spell, you know—the exorcism. I've been collecting stuff for two days now, and what a pile of junk. Have you got any rosemary? Good. I'll take some of those poppy seeds, too. I haven't told Pam about this witchcraft thing. My brother wouldn't care, I know. He'd laugh. But Pam can be very primitive-mother about Nina at times. You'd be surprised. They're going to a faculty party tonight, so just as soon as I wave them on their way, I'm going to set the scene and do the deed."

I was alarmed. "Garnet! You're sure you won't hurt her? You aren't going to feed Nina any queer messes or potions?"

"Of course not. I'm simply going to seat her in the middle of a chalked pentacle and then work my abracadabra. Actually, I'm combining three different spells—just the best features of each." She turned to go, then hesitated. "The thing is, you aren't likely to be in the vicinity of our house this evening, are you? It has occurred to me that Nina's devil might hunt for another host. The book doesn't say anything about that. Just to be on the safe side, why don't you keep your family in the house between seven and seven thirty P.M.?"

I promised and Garnet left.

As the witching half-hour approached that evening I felt a little nervous. I believe I half-expected the sound of a great explosion, followed by a mushroom-shaped cloud.

It wasn't till a little after eight o'clock that I received the first hint that Nina's devil had perhaps found a new host, though neither Garnet nor I can ever be certain.

Garnet phoned me immediately after her "ceremony."

"Of course it worked. Nina was sitting there calmly trying to mash her fingers with her rubber hammer, smiling like an angel. I was dashing around rather madly, you know, lighting incense, waving my hands and chanting, flinging little bags of herbs hither and yon, when suddenly the blinds on the big picture window fell with a dreadful clatter. Nina began to scream like crazy. I felt a little shaky, myself, but all the lights were on and I still had a few details to attend to. Nina kept screaming her piercing screams and drumming her heels on the floor—a perfect devil's tattoo. Just as I finished the spell, somebody rang the doorbell. When I answered it Mr. Pritchett dashed over and picked up Nina before I could explain anything. He was passing by, you see, and heard her screaming and was afraid she'd hurt herself again.

"He couldn't help seeing me through the window and I guess he thought I'd panicked or something. But, listen . . . the thing is, Nina stopped crying *immediately*, and she hugged him instead of kicking him . . . and, well, Mr. Pritchett was breathing hard and looking rather pale, so I offered him a drink of Pam's gin and he took it! Not only that, when he left just now he was murmuring something about beer and pigeons and every man's right to express himself! Now, really, what do you think?"

When I hung up, I thought, Poor Mr. Pritchett—one drink of gin bringing out all those stifled little loves. I felt so sad I left the warm peacefulness of our lived-in living room and went out back to look at the stars. After a while I was sure I heard Mr. Pritchett singing a rollicking drinking song and was astonished to see him standing in his kitchen doorway, pitching empty beer cans out into the darkness.

Behind him I could see Mrs. Pritchett clutching her chest, her mouth open, her voice silent.

Of course, Elm Street these days isn't exactly dull. But there's no longer much scope for righteous indignation. Some of us cluck our tongues over that mischievous Pritchett boy and some of us grin. And there are people, I hear, who object to Mr. Pritchett's pigeons as a messy nuisance, but I like to see them wheeling against the sky.

Yesterday when I ran over to see poor Mrs. Pritchett for a moment, I found the living room ashtrays (as usual) full of orange peels. There was an empty beer can on the floor, too, half hidden by the ruffle on the easy chair. But there was also a new look in Mrs. Pritchett's eyes, as if she was contemplating some long, exciting vista and finding she rather liked it.

"Mr. Pritchett," she told me proudly, "has just received an important promotion. I'm not a bit surprised—he's such a forceful man!"

The Bayards, I'm sorry to say, have moved away. The bandage idea must have worked its magic on Nina, or perhaps it was the psychiatrist. The people around here still miss her. There isn't, after all, so much beauty in the world that one grows resigned to parting with it, particularly when it's accompanied, as it was these last few years, by Nina's kind of sweetness.

But it's Garnet I miss most. So stout of heart, so original and altogether delightful. Though there was a time when I looked on her with a feeling akin to fear. For who wants retributive justice loose in his neighborhood, or even a witch?

W. W. JACOBS

The Brown Man's Servant

W. W. JACOBS (1863–1943), a native of Wapping, England, was a civil service clerk who began contributing stories to the Strand Magazine and other periodicals in the 1890s. Much of his fiction is concerned with nautical themes, but Jacobs also penned some remarkable chillers, such as "The Interruption," "The Well" and what may well be the most anthologized fantasy story in English, "The Monkey's Paw." For many years, I've owned a copy of his humorous novel The Skipper's Wooing, but only recently noticed that there is a second story at the back of the volume, a forgotten tale I've never seen anthologized anywhere else. "The Brown Man's Servant," vaguely reminiscent of Lord Dunsany's "A Night at an Inn," contains a mild degree of racial stereotyping, but the reader able to tolerate this flaw will be rewarded by a virtually unknown and truly nasty little horror story.

The shop of Solomon Hyams stood in a small thoroughfare branching off the Commercial Road. In its windows unredeemed pledges of all kinds, from old-time watches to seamen's boots, appealed to all tastes and requirements. Bundles of cigars, candidly described as "wonderful," were marked at absurdly low figures, while silver watches endeavored to excuse the clumsiness of their make by describing themselves as "strong workmen's." The side entrance, up a narrow alley, was surmounted by the usual three brass balls, and here Mr. Hyams' clients were wont to call. They entered as optimists, smiled confidently upon Mr. Hyams, argued, protested shrilly, and left the establishment pessimists of a most pronounced and virulent type.

None of these things, however, disturbed the pawnbroker. The drunken client who endeavored to bail out his Sunday clothes with a tram ticket was accommodated with a chair, while the assistant went to hunt up his friends and contract for a speedy removal; the old woman who, with a view of obtaining a higher advance than usual, poured a tale of grievous woe into the hardened ears of Mr. Hyams found herself left to the same invaluable assistant, and, realizing her failure, would at once become cheerful and take what was offered. Mr. Hyams' methods of business were quiet and unostentatious, and rumor had it that he might retire at any time and live in luxury.

It was a cold, cheerless afternoon in November as Mr. Hyams, who had occasional hazy ideas of hygiene, stood at his door taking the air. It was an atmosphere laden with soot and redolent of many blended odors, but after the fusty smell of the shop it was almost health-giving. In the large public-house opposite, with its dirty windows and faded signboards, the gas was already being lit, which should change it from its daylight dreariness to a resort of light and life.

Mr. Hyams, who was never in a hurry to light up his own premises, many of his clients preferring the romantic light which comes between day and night for their visits, was about to leave the chilly air for the warmth inside, when his attention was attracted by a seaman of sturdy aspect stopping and looking in at his window. Mr. Hyams rubbed his hands softly. There was an air of comfort and prosperity about this seaman, and the pawnbroker had many small articles in his window, utterly useless to the man, which he would have liked to have sold him.

The man came from the window, made as though to pass, and then paused irresolute before the pawnbroker.

"You want a watch?" said the latter genially. "Come inside."

Mr. Hyams went behind his counter and waited.

"I don't want to buy nothing, and I don't want to pawn nothing," said the sailor. "What do you think o' that?"

Mr. Hyams, who objected to riddles, especially those which seemed to be against business, eyed him unfavorably from beneath his shaggy eyebrows.

"We might have a little quiet talk together," said the seaman, "you an' me; we might do a little bit o' business together, you an' me. In the parler, shall we say, over a glass o' something hot?"

Mr. Hyams hesitated. He was not averse to a little business of an illicit nature, but there rose up vividly before him the picture of another sailor who had made much the same sort of proposal, and, after four glasses of rum, had merely suggested to him that he should lend him twenty pounds on the security of an I.O.U. It was long since, but the memory of it still rankled.

"What sort of business is it?" he inquired.

"Business that's too big for you, p'raps," said the sailor with a lordly air. "I'll try a bigger place. What's that lantern-faced swab shoving his ugly mug into the daylight for?"

"Get off," said the pawnbroker to the assistant, who was quietly and unobtrusively making a third. "Mind the shop. This gentleman and I have business in the parlor. Come this way, sir."

He raised the flap of the counter, and led the way to a small, untidy room at the back of the shop. A copper kettle was boiling on the fire, and the table was already laid for tea. The pawnbroker, motioning his visitor to a dingy leather armchair, went to a cupboard and produced a bottle of rum, three parts full, and a couple of glasses.

"Tea for me," said the seaman, eyeing the bottle wistfully.

The pawnbroker pricked up his ears. "Nonsense," he said, with an attempt at heartiness, "a jolly fellow like you don't want tea. Have some o' this."

"Tea, confound yer!" said the other. "When I say tea, I mean tea."

The pawnbroker, repressing his choler, replaced the bottle, and, seating himself at the table, reached over for the kettle, and made the tea. It was really a pleasing picture of domestic life, and would have looked well in a lantern slide at a temperance lecture, the long, gaunt Jew and the burly seaman hobnobbing over the blameless teapot. But Mr. Hyams grew restless. He was intent upon business; but the other, so far as his inroads on the teapot and the eatables gave any indication, seemed to be bent only upon pleasure. Once again the picture of the former sailor rose before Mr. Hyams' eyes, and he scowled fiercely as the seaman pushed his cup up for the fourth time.

"And now for a smoke," said his visitor, as he settled back in his chair. "A good 'un, mind. Lord, this is comfort! It's the first bit o' comfort I've 'ad since I come ashore five days ago."

The pawnbroker grunted, and producing a couple of black, greasy-looking cigars, gave one to his guest. They both fell to smoking, the former ill at ease, the latter with his feet spread out on the small fender, making the very utmost of his bit of comfort.

"Are you a man as is fond of asking questions?" he said at length.

"No," said the pawnbroker, shutting his lips illustratively.

"Suppose," said the sailor, leaning forward intently—"suppose a man came to you an' ses— There's that confounded assistant of yours peeping through the door."

The pawnbroker got up almost as exasperated as the seaman, and, after rating his assistant through the half-open door, closed it with a bang, and pulled down a small blind over the glass.

"Suppose a man came to you," resumed the sailor, after the pawnbroker had seated himself again, "and asked you for five hundred pounds for something. Have you got it?"

"Not here," said the pawnbroker suspiciously. "I don't keep any money on the premises."

"You could get it, though?" suggested the other.

"We'll see," said the pawnbroker; "five hundred pounds is a fortune—five hundred pounds, why it takes years of work—five hundred pounds—"

"I don't want no blessed psalms," said the seaman abruptly; "but, look here, suppose I wanted five hundred pounds for something, and you wouldn't give it. How am I to know you wouldn't give information to the police if I didn't take what you offered me for it?"

The pawnbroker threw up his huge palms in virtuous horror.

"I'd mark you for it if you did," said the seaman menacingly, through his teeth. "It 'ud be the worst day's work you ever did. Will you take it or leave it at my price, an' if you won't give it, leave me to go as I came?"

"I will," said the pawnbroker solemnly.

The seaman laid his cigar in the tray, where it expired in a little puddle of tea, and, undoing his coat, cautiously took from his waist a canvas belt. In a hesitating fashion he dangled the belt in his hands, looking from the Jew to the door, and from the door back to the Jew again. Then from a pocket in the belt he took something wrapped in a small piece of dirty flannel, and, unrolling it, deposited on the table a huge diamond, whose smouldering fires flashed back in many colors the light from the gas.

The Jew, with an exclamation, reached forward to handle it, but the sailor thrust him back.

"Hands off," he said grimly. "None of your ringing the changes on me."

He tipped it over with his finger-nail on the table from side to side, the other, with his head bent down, closely inspecting it. Then, as a great indulgence, he laid it on the Jew's open palm for a few seconds.

"Five hundred pounds," he said, taking it in his own hands again.

The pawnbroker laughed. It was a laugh which he kept for business purposes, and would have formed a valuable addition to the goodwill of the shop.

"I'll give you fifty," he said, after he had regained his composure.

The seaman replaced the gem in its wrapper again.

"Well, I'll give you seventy, and risk whether I lose over it," continued the pawnbroker.

"Five hundred's my price," said the seaman calmly, as he placed the belt about his waist and began to buckle it up.

"Seventy-five," said the pawnbroker persuasively.

"Look here," said the seaman, regarding him sternly, "you drop it. I'm not going to haggle with you. I'm not going to haggle with any man. I ain't no judge o' diamonds, but I've 'ad cause to know as this is something special. See here."

He rolled back the coat sleeve from his brawny arm, and revealed a long, newly healed scar.

"I risked my life for that stone," he said slowly. "I value my life at five hundred pounds. It's likely worth more than as many thousands, and you know it. However, good-night to you, mate. How much for the tea?"

He put his hand contemptuously in his trouser pocket, and pulled out some small change.

"There's the risk of getting rid of the stone," said the pawnbroker, pushing aside the proffered coin. "Where did it come from? Has it got a history?"

"Not in Europe it ain't," said the seaman. "So far as I know, you an' me an' one other are the only white men as know of it. That's all I'm going to tell you."

"Do you mind waiting while I go and fetch a friend of mine to see it?" inquired the pawnbroker. "You needn't be afraid," he added hastily. "He's a respectable man and as close as the grave."

"I'm not afraid," said the seaman quietly. "But no larks, mind. I'm not a nice man to play them on. I'm pretty strong, an' I've got something else besides."

He settled himself in the armchair again, and accepting another cigar, watched his host as he took his hat from the sideboard.

"I'll be back as soon as I can," said the latter somewhat anxiously. "You won't go before I come?"

"Not me," said the seaman bluntly. "When I say a thing I stick to it. I don't haggle, and haggle, and—" he paused a moment for a word—"and haggle," he concluded.

Left to himself, he smoked on contentedly, blandly undisturbed by the fact that the assistant looked in at the door occasionally, to see that things were all right. It was quite a new departure for Mr. Hyams to leave his parlor to a stranger, and the assistant felt a sense of responsibility so great that it was a positive relief to him when his master returned, accompanied by another man.

"This is my friend," said Mr. Hyams, as they entered the parlor and closed the door. "You might let him see the stone."

The seaman took off his belt again, and placing the diamond in his hand held it before the stranger who, making no attempt to take it, turned it over with his finger and examined it critically.

"Are you going to sea again just yet?" he inquired softly.

"Thursday night," said the seaman, "Five hundred is my price; p'raps he told you. I'm not going to haggle."

"Just so, just so," said the other quietly. "It's worth five hundred."

"Spoke like a man," said the seaman warmly.

"I like to deal with a man who knows his own mind," said the stranger, "it saves trouble. But if we buy it for that amount you must do one thing for us. Keep quiet and don't touch a drop of liquor until you sail, and not a word to anybody."

"You needn't be afraid o' the licker," said the sailor grimly. "I shan't touch that for my own sake."

"He's a teetotaler," explained the pawnbroker.

"He's not," said the seaman indignantly.

"Why won't you drink, then?" asked the other man.

"Fancy," said the seaman dryly, and closed his mouth.

Without another word the stranger turned to the pawnbroker, who, taking a pocket-book from his coat, counted out the amount in notes. These, after the sailor had examined them in every possible manner, he rolled up and put in his pocket, then without a word he took out the diamond again and laid it silently on the table. Mr. Hyams, his fingers trembling with eagerness, took it up and examined it delightedly.

"You've got it a bargain," said the seaman. "Goodnight, gentlemen. I hope, for your sakes, nobody'll know I've parted with it. Keep your eyes open, and trust nobody. When you see black, smell mischief. I'm glad to get rid of it."

He threw his head back, and, expanding his chest as though he already breathed more freely, nodded to both men, and, walking through the shop, passed out into the street and disappeared.

Long after he had gone, the pawnbroker and his friend, Levi, sat with the door locked and the diamond before them, eagerly inspecting it.

"It's a great risk," said the pawnbroker. "A stone like that generally makes some noise."

"Anything good is risky," said the other somewhat contemptuously. "You don't expect to get a windfall like that without any drawback, do you?"

He took the stone in his hand again, and eyed it lovingly. "It's from the East somewhere," he said quietly. "It's badly cut, but it's a diamond of diamonds, a king of gems."

"I don't want any trouble with the police," said the pawnbroker, as he took it from him.

"You are talking now as though you have just made a small advance on a stolen overcoat," said his friend impatiently. "A risk like that—and you have done it before now—is a foolish one to run; the game is not worth the candle. But this—why it warms one's blood to look at it."

"Well, I'll leave it with you," said the pawnbroker. "If you do well with it I ought not to want to work any more."

The other placed it in an inside pocket, while the owner watched him anxiously.

"Don't let any accident happen to you to-night, Levi," he said nervously.

"Thanks for your concern," said Levi, grimacing. "I shall probably be careful for my own sake."

He buttoned up his coat, and, drinking a glass of hot whisky, went out whistling. He had just reached the door when the pawnbroker called him back.

"If you like to take a cab, Levi," he said, in a low voice so that the assistant should not hear, "I'll pay for it."

"I'll take an omnibus," said Levi, smiling quietly. "You're getting extravagant, Hyams. Besides, fancy the humor of sitting next to a pickpocket with this on me."

He waved a cheery farewell, and the pawnbroker, watching him from the door, scowled angrily as he saw his light-hearted friend hail an omnibus at the corner and board it. Then he went back to the shop, and his everyday business of making advances on flat-irons and other realizable assets of the neighborhood.

At ten o'clock he closed for the night, the assistant hurriedly pulling down the shutters that his time for recreation might not be unduly curtailed. He slept off the premises, and the pawnbroker, after his departure, made a slight supper, and sat revolving the affairs of the day over another of his black cigars until nearly midnight. Then, well contented with himself, he went up the bare, dirty stairs to his room and went to bed, and, despite the excitement of the evening, was soon in a loud slumber, from which he was aroused by a distant and sustained knocking.

II

At first the noise mingled with his dreams, and helped to form them. He was down a mine, and grimy workers with strong picks were knocking diamonds from the walls, diamonds so large that he became despondent at the comparative smallness of his own. Then he awoke suddenly and sat up with a start, rubbing his eyes. The din was infernal to a man who liked to do a quiet business in an unobtrusive way. It was a knocking which he usually associated with the police, and it came from his side door. With a sense of evil strong upon him, the Jew sprang from his bed, and, slipping the catch, noiselessly opened the window and thrust his head out. In the light of a lamp which projected from the brick wall at the other end of the alley he saw a figure below.

"Hulloa!" said the Jew harshly.

His voice was drowned in the noise.

"What do you want?" he yelled. "Hulloa, there! What do you want, I say?"

The knocking ceased, and the figure, stepping back a little, looked up at the window.

"Come down and open the door," said a voice which the pawnbroker recognized as the sailor's.

"Go away," he said, in a low, stern voice. "Do you want to rouse the neighborhood?"

"Come down and let me in," said the other. "It's for your own good. You're a dead man if you don't."

Impressed by his manner the Jew, after bidding him shortly not to make any more noise, lit his candle, and, dressing hurriedly, took the light in his hand and went grumbling downstairs into the shop.

"Now, what do you want?" he said through the door.

"Let me in and I'll tell you," said the other, "or I'll bawl it through the keyhole, if you like."

The Jew, placing the candle on the counter, drew back the heavy bolts and cautiously opened the door. The seaman stepped in, and, as the other closed the door, vaulted on to the counter and sat there with his legs dangling.

"That's right," he said, nodding approvingly in the direction of the Jew's right hand. "I hope you know how to use it."

"What do you want?" demanded the other irritably, putting his hand behind him. "What time o' night do you call this for turning respectable men out of their beds?"

"I didn't come for the pleasure o' seeing your pretty face again, you can bet," said the seaman carelessly. "It's good nature what's brought me here. What have you done with that diamond?"

"That's my business," said the other. "What do you want?"

"I told you I sailed in five days," said the seaman. "Well, I got another ship this evening instead, and I sail at 6 A.M. Things are getting just a bit too thick for me, an' I thought out o' pure good nature I'd step round and put you on your guard."

"Why didn't you do so at first?" said the Jew, eyeing him suspiciously.

"Well, I didn't want to spoil a bargain," said the seaman carelessly. "Maybe you wouldn't have bought the stone if I had told you. Mind that thing don't go off; I don't want to rob you. Point it the other way."

"There was four of us in that deal," he continued, after the other had complied with his request. "Me an' Jack Ball and Nosey Wheeler and a Burmese chap; the last I see o' Jack Ball he was quiet and peaceful, with a knife sticking in his chest. If I hadn't been a very careful man I'd have had one sticking in mine. If you ain't a very careful man, and do what I tell you, you'll have one sticking in yours."

"Speak a little more plainly," said the Jew. "Come into the parlor, I don't want the police to see a light in the shop."

"We stole it," said the seaman, as he followed the other into the little back parlor, "the four of us, from—"

"I don't want to know anything about that," interrupted the other hastily.

The sailor grinned approvingly, and continued: "Then me an' Jack being stronger than them, we took it from them two, but they got level with poor Jack. I shipped before the mast on a barque, and they came over by steamer an' waited for me."

"Well, you're not afraid of them?" said the Jew interrogatively. "Besides, a word to the police—"

"Telling 'em all about the diamond," said the seaman. "Oh, yes. Well, you can do that now if you feel so inclined. They know all about *that*, bless you, and, if they were had, they'd blab about the diamond."

"Have they been dogging you?" inquired the pawnbroker.

"Dogging me!" said the seaman. "Dogging's no word for it. Wherever I've been they've been my shadders. They want to hurt me, but they're careful about being hurt themselves. That's where I have the pull of them. They want the stone back first, and revenge afterwards, so I thought I'd put you on your guard, for they pretty well guess who's got the thing now. You'll know Wheeler by his nose, which is broken."

"I'm not afraid of them," said the Jew, "but thank you for telling me. Did they follow you here?"

"They're outside, I've no doubt," said the other; "but they come along like human cats—leastways, the Burma chap does. You want eyes in the back of your head for them almost. The Burmese is an old man and soft as velvet, and Jack Ball just afore he died was going to tell me something about him. I don't know what it was; but, pore Jack, he was a superstitious sort o' chap, and I know it was something horrible. He was as brave as a lion, was Jack, but he was afraid o' that little shrivelled-up Burmese. They'll follow me to the ship tonight. If they'll only come close enough, and there's nobody nigh, I'll do Jack a good turn."

"Stay here till the morning," said the Jew.

The seaman shook his head. "I don't want to miss my ship," said he; "but remember what I've told you, and mind, they're villains, both of them, and if you are not very careful, they'll have you, sooner or later. Good-night!"

He buttoned up his coat, and leading the way to the door, followed by the Jew with the candle, opened it noiselessly, and peered carefully out right and left. The alley was empty.

"Take this," said the Jew, proffering his pistol.

"I've got one," said the seaman. "Goodnight!"

He strode boldly up the alley, his footsteps sounding loudly in the silence of the night. The Jew watched him to the corner, and then, closing the door, secured it with extra care, and went back to his bedroom, where he lay meditating upon the warning which had just been given to him until he fell asleep.

Before going downstairs next morning he placed the revolver in his pocket, not necessarily for use, but as a demonstration of the lengths to which he was prepared to go. His manner with two or three inoffensive gentlemen of color was also somewhat strained. Especially was this the case with a worthy Lascar, who, knowing no English, gesticulated cheerfully in front of him with a long dagger which he wanted to pawn.

The morning passed without anything happening, and it was nearly dinner-time before anything occurred to justify the sailor's warning. Then, happening to glance at the window, he saw between the articles which were hanging there a villainous face, the principal feature of which being strangely bent at once recalled the warning of the sailor. As he looked the face disappeared, and a moment later its owner, after furtively looking in at the side door, entered quietly.

"Morning, boss," said he.

The pawnbroker nodded and waited.

"I want to have a little talk with you, boss," said the man, after waiting for him to speak.

"All right, go on," said the other.

"What about 'im?" said the man, indicating the assistant with a nod.

"Well, what about him?" inquired the Jew.

"What I've got to say is private," said the man.

The Jew raised his eyebrows.

"You can go in and get your dinner, Bob," he said. "Now, what do you want?" he continued. "Hurry up, because I'm busy."

"I come from a pal o' mine," said the man, speaking in a low voice, "him what was 'ere last night. He couldn't come himself, so he sent me. He wants it back."

"Wants what back?" asked the Jew.

"The diamond," said the other.

"Diamond? What on earth are you talking about?" demanded the pawnbroker.

"You needn't try to come it on me," said the other fiercely. "We want that diamond back, and, mind you, we'll have it."

"You clear out," said the Jew. "I don't allow people to come threatening me. Out you go."

"We'll do more than threaten you," said the man, the veins in his forehead swelling with rage. "You've got that diamond. You got it for five 'undred pound. We'll give you that back for it, and you may think yourself lucky to get it."

"You've been drinking," said the Jew, "or somebody's been fooling you."

"Look here," said the man with a snarl, "drop it. I'm dealing fair an' square by you. I don't want to hurt a hair of your head. I'm a peaceable man, but I want my own, and, what's more, I can get it. I got the shell, and I can get the kernel. Do you know what I mean by that?"

"I don't know, and I don't care," said the Jew. He moved off a little way, and, taking some tarnished spoons from a box, began to rub them with a piece of leather.

"I daresay you can take a hint as well as anybody else," said the other. "Have you seen that before?"

He threw something on the counter, and the Jew started, despite himself, as he glanced up. *It was the sailor's belt.*

"That's a hint," said the man with a leer, "and a very fair one."

The Jew looked at him steadily, and saw that he was white and nervous; his whole aspect that of a man who was running a great risk for a great stake.

"I suppose," he said at length, speaking very slowly, "that you want me to understand that you have murdered the owner of this."

"Understand what you like," said the other with sullen ferocity. "Will you let us have that back again?"

"No," said the Jew explosively. "I have no fear of a dog like you; if it was worth the trouble I'd send for the police and hand you over to them."

"Call them," said the other; "do; I'll wait. But mark my words, if you don't give us the stone back you're a dead man. I've got a pal what half that diamond belongs to. He's from the East, and a bad man to cross. He has only got to wish it, and you're a dead man without his raising a finger at you. I've come here to do you a good turn; if he comes here it's all up with you."

"Well, you go back to him," jeered the Jew; "a clever man like that can get the diamond without going near it seemingly. You're wasting your time here, and it's a pity; you must have got a lot of friends."

"Well, I've warned you," said the other, "you'll have one more warning. If you won't be wise you must keep the diamond, but it won't be much good to you. It's a good stone, but, speaking for myself I'd sooner be alive without it than dead with it."

He gave the Jew a menacing glance and departed, and the assistant having by this time finished his dinner, the pawnbroker went to his own with an appetite by no means improved by his late interview.

III

The cat, with its fore-paws tucked beneath it, was dozing on the counter. Business had been slack that morning, and it had only been pushed off three times. It had staked out a claim on that counter some five years before, and if anything was required to convince it of the value of the possession it was the fact that it was being constantly pushed off. To a firm-minded cat this alone gave the counter a value difficult to overestimate, and sometimes an obsequious customer fell into raptures over its beauty. This was soothing, and the animal allowed customers of this type to scratch it gently behind the ear.

The cat was for the time the only occupant of the shop. The assistant was out, and the pawnbroker sat in the small room beyond, with the door half open, reading a newspaper. He had read the financial columns, glanced at the foreign intelligence, and was just about to turn to the leader when his eye was caught by the headline, "Murder in Whitechapel."

He folded the paper back, and, with a chilly feeling creeping over him, perused the account. In the usual thrilling style it recorded the finding of the body of a man, evidently a sailor, behind a hoarding placed in front of some shops in course of erection. There was no clue to the victim, who had evidently been stabbed from behind in the street, and then dragged or carried to the place in which the body had been discovered.

The pockets had been emptied, and the police who regarded the crime as an ordinary one of murder and robbery, entertained the usual hopes of shortly arresting the assassins.

The pawnbroker put the paper down, and drummed on the table with his fingers. The description of the body left no room for doubt that the victim of the tragedy and the man who had sold him the diamond were identical. He began to realize the responsibilities of the bargain, and the daring of his visitor of the day before, in venturing before him almost red-handed, gave him an unpleasant idea of the lengths to which he was prepared to go. In a pleasanter direction it gave him another idea; it was strong confirmation of Levi's valuation of the stone.

"I shall see my friend again," said the Jew to himself, as he looked up from the paper. "Let him make an attempt on me and we'll see."

He threw the paper down, and, settling back in his chair, fell into a pleasing reverie. He saw his release from sordid toil close at hand. He would travel and enjoy his life. Pity the diamond hadn't come twenty years before. As for the sailor, well, poor fellow, why didn't he stay when he was asked?

The cat, still dozing, became aware of a strong, strange odor. In a lazy fashion it opened one eye, and discovered that an old, shrivelled-up little man, with a brown face, was standing by the counter. It watched him lazily, but warily, out of a half-closed eye, and then, finding that he appeared to be quite harmless, closed it again.

The intruder was not an impatient type of customer. He stood for some time gazing round him; then a thought struck him, and he approached the cat and stroked it with a masterly hand. Never, in the course of its life, had the animal met such a born stroker. Every touch was a caress, and a gentle thrum, thrum rose from its interior in response.

Something went wrong with the stroker. He hurt. The cat started up suddenly and jumped behind the counter. The dark gentleman smiled an evil smile, and, after waiting a little longer, tapped on the counter.

The pawnbroker came from the little room beyond, with the newspaper in his hand, and his brow darkened as he saw the customer. He was of a harsh and dominant nature, and he foresaw more distasteful threats.

"Well, what do you want?" he demanded abruptly.

"Morning, sir," said the brown man in perfect English; "fine day."

"The day's well enough," said the Jew.

"I want a little talk with you," said the other suavely, "a little, quiet, reasonable talk."

"You'd better make it short," said the Jew. "My time is valuable."

The brown man smiled, and raised his hand with a deprecatory gesture. "Many things are valuable," said he, "but time is the most valuable of all. And time to us means life."

The Jew saw the covert threat, and grew more irritable still.

"Get to your business," he said sharply.

The brown man leant on the counter, and regarded him with a pair of fierce brown eyes, which age had not dimmed.

"You are a reasonable man," he said slowly, "a good merchant. I can see it. But sometimes a good merchant makes a bad bargain. In that case what does the good merchant do?"

"Get out of here," said the Jew angrily.

"He makes the best of it," continued the other calmly, "and he is a lucky man if he is not too late to repair the mischief. *You are not too late.*"

The Jew laughed boisterously.

"There was a sailor once made a bad bargain," said the brown man, still in the same even tones, "and he died—of grief."

He grinned at this pleasantry until his face looked like a cracked mask.

"I read in this paper of a sailor being killed," said the Jew, holding it up. "Have you ever heard of the police, of prison, and of the hangman?"

"All of them," said the other softly.

"I might be able to put the hangman on the track of the sailor's murderer," continued the Jew grimly.

The brown man smiled and shook his head. "You are too good a merchant," he said; "besides, it would be very difficult."

"It would be a pleasure to me," said the Jew.

"Let us talk business like men, not nonsense like children," said the brown man suddenly. "You talk of hangmen. I talk of death. Well, listen. Two nights ago you bought a diamond from a sailor for five hundred pounds. Unless you give me that diamond back for the same money I will kill you."

"What?" snarled the Jew, drawing his gaunt figure to its full height. "You, you miserable mummy!"

"I will kill you," repeated the brown man calmly. "I will send death to you—death in a horrible shape. I will send a devil, a little artful, teasing devil, to worry you and kill you. In the darkness he will come and spring out on you. You had better give back the diamond, and live. If you give it back I promise you your life."

He paused, and the Jew noticed that his face had changed, and the sardonic good-humor which had before possessed it was now distorted by a devilish malice. His eyes gleamed coldly, and he snapped them quickly as he spoke.

"Well, what do you say?" he demanded.

"This," said the Jew.

He leant over the counter, and, taking the brown man's skinny throat in his great hand, flung him reeling back to the partition, which shook with his weight. Then he burst into a laugh as the being who had just been threatening him with a terrible and mysterious death changed into a little weak old man, coughing and spitting as he clutched at his throat and fought for breath.

"What about your servant, the devil?" asked the Jew maliciously.

"He serves when I am absent," said the brown man faintly. "Even now I give you one more chance. I will let you see the young fellow in your shop die first. But no, he has not offended. I will kill—"

He paused, and his eye fell on the cat, which at that moment sprang up and took its old place on the counter. "I will kill your cat," said the brown man. "I will send the devil to worry it. Watch the cat, and as its death is so shall yours be—unless—"

"Unless?" said the Jew, regarding him mockingly.

"Unless tonight before ten o'clock you mark on your door-post two crosses in chalk," said the other. "Do that and live. Watch your cat."

He pointed his lean, brown finger at the animal, and, still feeling at his throat, stepped softly to the door and passed out.

With the entrance of other customers, the pawnbroker forgot the annoyance to which he had been subjected, and attended to their wants in a spirit made liberal by the near prospect of fortune. It was certain that the stone must be of great value. With that and the money he had made by his business, he would give up work and settle down to a life of pleasant ease. So liberal was he that an elderly Irishwoman forgot their slight differences in creeds and blessed him fervently with all the saints in the calendar.

His assistant being back in his place in the shop, the pawnbroker returned to the little sitting-room, and once more carefully looked through the account of the sailor's murder. Then he sat still trying to work out a problem; to hand the murderers over to the police without his connection with the stolen diamond being made public, and after considerable deliberation, convinced himself that the feat was impossible. He was interrupted by a slight scuffling noise in the shop, and the cat came bolting into the room, and, after running round the table, went out at the door and fled upstairs. The assistant came into the room.

"What are you worrying the thing for?" demanded his master.

"I'm not worrying it," said the assistant in an aggrieved voice. "It's been moving about up and down the shop, and then it suddenly started like that. It's got a fit, I suppose."

He went back to the shop, and the Jew sat in his chair half ashamed of his nervous credulity, listening to the animal, which was rushing about in the rooms upstairs.

"Go and see what's the matter with the thing, Bob," he cried.

The assistant obeyed, returning hastily in a minute or two, and closing the door behind him.

"Well, what's the matter?" demanded his master.

"The brute's gone mad," said the assistant, whose face was white. "It's flying about upstairs like a wild thing. Mind it don't get in, it's as bad as a mad dog."

"Oh, rubbish," said the Jew. "Cats are often like that."

"Well, I've never seen one like it before," said the other, "and, what's more, I'm not going to see that again."

The animal came downstairs, scuffling along the passage, hit the door with its head, and then dashed upstairs again.

"It must have been poisoned, or else it's mad," said the assistant. "What's it been eating, I wonder?"

The pawnbroker made no reply. The suggestion of poisoning was a welcome one. It was preferable to the sinister hintings of the brown man. But even if it had been poisoned it was a very singular coincidence, unless indeed the Burmese had himself poisoned it. He tried to think whether it could have been possible for his visitor to have administered poison undetected.

"It's quiet now," said the assistant, and he opened the door a little way.

"It's all right," said the pawnbroker, half ashamed of his fears, "get back to the shop."

The assistant complied, and the Jew, after sitting down a little while to persuade himself that he really had no particular interest in the matter, rose and went slowly upstairs. The staircase was badly lighted, and half way up he stumbled on something soft.

He gave a hasty exclamation and, stooping down, saw that he had trodden on the dead cat.

IV

At ten o'clock that night the pawnbroker sat with his friend Levi discussing a bottle of champagne, which the open-eyed assistant had procured from the public-house opposite.

"You're a lucky man, Hyams," said his friend, as he raised his glass to his lips. "Thirty thousand pounds! It's a fortune, a small fortune," he added correctively.

"I shall give this place up," said the pawnbroker, "and go away for a time. I'm not safe here."

"Safe?" queried Levi, raising his eyebrows.

The pawnbroker related his adventures with his visitors.

"I can't understand that cat business," said Levi when he had finished. "It's quite farcical; he must have poisoned it."

"He wasn't near it," said the pawnbroker, "it was at the other end of the counter."

"Oh, hang it," said Levi, the more irritably because he could not think of any solution to the mystery. "You don't believe in occult powers and all that sort of thing. This is the neighborhood of the Commercial Road; time, nineteenth century. The thing's got on your nerves. Keep your eyes open, and stay indoors; they can't hurt you here. Why not tell the police?"

"I don't want any questions," said the pawnbroker.

"I mean, just tell them that one or two suspicious characters have been hanging round lately," said the other. "If this precious couple see that they are watched they'll probably bolt. There's nothing like a uniform to scare that sort."

"I won't have anything to do with the police," said the pawnbroker firmly.

"Well, let Bob sleep on the premises," suggested his friend.

"I think I will tomorrow," said the other. "I'll have a bed fixed up for him."

"Why not tonight?" asked Levi.

"He's gone," said the pawnbroker briefly. "Didn't you hear him shut up?"

"He was in the shop five minutes ago," said Levi.

"He left at ten," said the pawnbroker.

"I'll swear I heard somebody only a minute or two back," said Levi, staring.

"Nerves, as you remarked a little while ago," said his friend, with a grin.

"Well, I thought I heard him," said Levi. "You might just secure the door, anyway."

The pawnbroker went to the door and made it fast, giving a careless glance round the dimly-lighted shop as he did so.

"Perhaps you could stay tonight yourself," he said, as he returned to the sitting-room.

"I can't possibly, tonight," said the other. "By the way, you might lend me a pistol of some kind. With all these cut-throats hanging round, visiting you is a somewhat perilous pleasure. They might take it into their heads to kill me to see whether I have got the stone."

"Take your pick," said the pawnbroker, going to the shop and

returning with two or three secondhand revolvers and some car-
tridges.

"I never fired one in my life," said Levi dubiously, "but I believe
the chief thing is to make a bang. Which'll make the loudest?"

On his friend's recommendation he selected a revolver of the service pattern, and, after one or two suggestions from the pawnbroker,
expressed himself as qualified to shoot anything between a chimney-
pot and a paving-stone.

"Make your room-door fast tonight, and tomorrow let Bob have a
bed there," he said earnestly, as he rose to go. "By the way, why not
make those chalk marks on the door just for the night? You can
laugh at them tomorrow. Sort of suggestion of the Passover about it,
isn't there?"

"I'm not going to mark my door for all the assassins that ever
breathed," said the Jew fiercely, as he rose to see the other out.

"Well, I think you're safe enough in the house," said Levi.
"Beastly dreary the shop looks. To a man of imagination like myself
it's quite easy to fancy that there is one of your brown friend's pet
devils crouching under the counter ready to spring."

The pawnbroker grunted and opened the door.

"Poof, fog," said Levi, as a cloud streamed in. "Bad night for pistol
practice. I shan't be able to hit anything."

The two men stood in the doorway for a minute, trying to peer
through the fog. A heavy, measured tread sounded in the alley; a
huge figure loomed up, and, to the relief of Levi, a constable halted
before them.

"Thick night, sir," said he to the pawnbroker.

"Very," was the reply. "Just keep your eye on my place tonight,
constable. There have been one or two suspicious-looking characters
hanging about here lately."

"I will, sir," said the constable, and moved off in company with
Levi.

The pawnbroker closed the door hastily behind them and bolted it
securely. His friend's jest about the devil under the counter occurred
to him as he eyed it, and for the first time in his life, the lonely
silence of the shop became oppressive. He half thought of opening
the door again and calling them back, but by this time they were out
of earshot, and he had a very strong idea that there might be somebody lurking in the fog outside.

"Bah!" said he aloud, "thirty thousand pounds."

He turned the gas-jet on full—a man that had just made that sum could afford to burn a little gas—and, first satisfying himself by look-ing under the counter and round the shop, reentered the sitting-room.

Despite his efforts, he could not get rid of the sense of loneliness and danger which possessed him. The clock had stopped, and the only sound audible was the snapping of the extinguished coals in the grate. He crossed over to the mantelpiece, and, taking out his watch, wound the clock up. Then he heard something else.

With great care he laid the key softly on the mantelpiece and listened intently. The clock was now aggressively audible, so that he opened the case again, and putting his finger against the pendulum, stopped it. Then he drew his revolver and cocked it, and, with his set face turned towards the door, and his lips parted, waited.

At first—nothing. Then all the noises which a lonely man hears in a house at night. The stairs creaked, something moved in the walls. He crossed noiselessly to the door and opened it. At the head of the staircase he fancied the darkness moved.

"Who's there?" he cried in a strong voice.

Then he stepped back into the room and lit his lamp. "I'll get to bed," he said grimly; "I've got the horrors."

He left the gas burning, and with the lamp in his left hand and the pistol in his right slowly ascended the stairs. The first landing was clear. He opened the doors of each room, and, holding the lamp aloft, peered in. Then he mounted higher, and looked in the rooms, crammed from floor to ceiling with pledges, ticketed and placed on shelves. In one room he thought he saw something crouching in a corner. He entered boldly, and as he passed along one side of a row of shelves could have sworn that he heard a stealthy footfall on the other. He rushed back to the door, and hung listening over the shaky balusters. Nothing stirred, and, satisfied that he must have been mistaken, he gave up the search and went to his bedroom. He set the lamp down on the drawers, and turned to close the door, when he distinctly heard a noise in the shop below. He snatched up the lamp again and ran hastily downstairs, pausing halfway on the lowest flight as he saw a dark figure spreadeagled against the side door, standing on tiptoe to draw back the bolt.

At the noise of his approach, it turned its head hastily, and re-vealed the face of the brown man; the bolt shot back, and at the same moment the Jew raised his pistol and fired twice.

From beneath the little cloud of smoke, as it rose, he saw that the door stood open and that the figure had vanished. He ran hastily down to the door, and, with the pistol raised, stood listening, trying to peer through the fog.

An unearthly stillness followed the deafening noise of the shots. The fog poured in at the doorway as he stood there hoping that the noise had reached the ears of some chance passer-by. He stood so for a few minutes, and then, closing the door again, resolutely turned back and went upstairs.

His first proceeding upon entering his room was to carefully look beneath and behind the heavy, dusty pieces of furniture, and, satisfied that no foe lurked there, he closed the door and locked it. Then he opened the window gently, and listened. The court below was perfectly still. He closed the window, and, taking off his coat, barricaded the door with all the heaviest furniture in the room. With a feeling of perfect security, he complacently regarded his handiwork, and then, sitting on the edge of the bed, began to undress. He turned the lamp down a little, and reloading the empty chambers of his revolver, placed it by the side of the lamp on the drawers. Then, as he turned back the clothes, he fancied that something moved beneath them. As he paused, it dropped lightly from the other side of the bed to the floor.

At first he sat, with knitted brows, trying to see what it was. He had only had a glimpse of it, but he certainly had an idea that it was alive. A rat, perhaps. He got off the bed again with an oath, and, taking the lamp in his hand, peered cautiously about the floor. Twice he walked round the room in this fashion. Then he stooped down, and, raising the dirty bed hangings, peered beneath.

He almost touched the wicked little head of the brown man's devil, and with a stifled cry, sprang hastily backward. The lamp shattered against the corner of the drawers, and, falling in a shower of broken glass and oil about his stockinged feet, left him in darkness. He threw the fragment of glass stand which remained in his hand from him, and, quick as thought, gained the bed again, and crouched there, breathing heavily.

He tried to think where he had put the matches, and remembered there were some on the window-sill. The room was so dark that he could not see the foot of the bed, and in his fatuity he had barricaded himself in the room with the loathsome reptile which was to work the brown man's vengeance.

For some time he lay listening intently. Once or twice he fancied that he heard the rustle of the snake over the dingy carpet, and he wondered whether it would attempt to climb on to the bed. He stood up, and tried to get his revolver from the drawers. It was out of reach, and as the bed creaked beneath his weight, a faint hiss sounded from the floor, and he sat still again, hardly daring to breathe.

The cold rawness of the room chilled him. He cautiously drew the bedclothes towards him, and rolled himself up in them, leaving only his head and arms exposed. In this position he began to feel more secure, until the thought struck him that the snake might be inside them. He fought against this idea, and tried to force his nerves into steadiness. Then his fears suggested that two might have been placed in the bed. At this his fears got the upper hand, and it seemed to him that something stirred in the clothes. He drew his body from them slowly and stealthily, and taking them in his arms, flung them violently to the other end of the room. On his hands and knees he now travelled over the bare bed, feeling. There was nothing there.

In this state of suspense and dread, time seemed to stop. Several times he thought that the thing had got on the bed, and to stay there in suspense in the darkness was impossible. He felt it over again and again. At last, unable to endure it any longer, he resolved to obtain the matches, and stepped cautiously off the bed; but no sooner had his feet touched the floor than his courage forsook him, and he sprang hurriedly back to his refuge again.

After that, in a spirit of dogged fatalism, he sat still and waited. To his disordered mind it seemed that footsteps were moving about the house, but they had no terrors for him. To grapple with a man for life and death would be play; to kill him, joy unspeakable. He sat still, listening. He heard rats in the walls and a babel of jeering voices on the staircase. The whole blackness of the room with the devilish, writhing thing on the floor became invested with supernatural significance. Then, dimly at first, and hardly comprehending the joy of it, he saw the window. A little later he saw the outlines of the things in the room. The night had passed and he was alive!

He raised his half-frozen body to its full height, and, expanding his chest, planted his feet firmly on the bed, stretching his long body to the utmost. He clenched his fist, and felt strong. The bed was unoccupied except by himself. He bent down and scrutinized the floor for his enemy, and set his teeth as he thought how he would tear it and mangle it. It was light enough, but first he would put on his boots. He leant over cautiously, and lifting one on to the bed, put it on. Then he bent down and took up the other, and, swift as lightning, something issued from it, and, coiling round his wrist, ran up the sleeve of his shirt.

With starting eyeballs the Jew held his breath, and, stiffened into stone, waited helplessly. The tightness round his arm relaxed as the snake drew the whole of its body under the sleeve and wound round his arm. He felt its head moving. It came wriggling across his chest, and with a mad cry, the wretched man clutched at the front of his shirt with both hands and strove to tear it off. He felt the snake in his hands, and for a moment hoped. Then the creature got its head free, and struck him smartly in the throat.

The Jew's hold relaxed, and the snake fell at his feet. He bent down and seized it, careless now that it bit his hand, and, with blood-shot eyes, dashed it repeatedly on the rail of the bed. Then he flung it to the floor, and, raising his heel, smashed its head to pulp.

His fury passed, he strove to think, but his brain was in a whirl. He had heard of sucking the wound, but one puncture was in his throat, and he laughed discordantly. He had heard that death had been prevented by drinking heavily of spirits. He would do that first, and then obtain medical assistance.

He ran to the door, and began to drag the furniture away. In his haste the revolver fell from the drawers to the floor. He looked at it steadily for a moment, and then, taking it up, handled it wistfully. He began to think more clearly, although a numbing sensation was already stealing over him.

"Thirty thousands pounds!" he said slowly, and tapped his cheek lightly with the cold barrel.

Then he slipped it in his mouth, and, pulling the trigger, crashed heavily to the floor.

ALVIN VOGEL

Poppa Bear

ALVIN VOGEL, *a resident of Great Neck, New York, is a consultant for the North American Company for Life and Health. "Poppa Bear," which was first published in the April 1989 issue of* Beyond Science Fiction and Fantasy, *is the second adventure of a private EYE whose cases are both supernatural and slapstick. The first Nick Merlin story, "The Party Animal," appeared in my GuildAmerica Books anthology* Witches & Warlocks.

It's been what, six years now, since the Bendith Y Mamau kidnapped a child? Yep, six years, and now the pale and visibly shaken couple is telling me that their little boy was kidnapped two days ago. Even though the Bendith have been inactive for so long, if the little fella *were* kidnapped, you can bet your bottom dollar that they did it.

I can imagine a plane where there are Others beside the Bendith who kidnap human children. If I really stretch my imagination I can conceive of a plane where a Human could commit such an act. But I can tell you, from my long experience as a P.I., that in *this* plane, if there's a kidnapping, it's the Bendith.

I said to the couple, "Have you contacted the P.D.?"

The young woman stopped trying to tear her handkerchief in two and said, "No, Intervenor, we were afraid to."

"Call me Nick, Mrs. Brodie."

She started to weep quietly. Her husband said, "Our friends all warned us that the Public Defenders are very gung-ho with Others. We're afraid for Paulie. We read about how you deplaned the Belarivo thing—you and the Eskimo Shaman. We thought it'd be safer for Paulie if we hired a Private Intervenor."

Mrs. Brodie broke off her weeping with a sob. She said, very earnestly, "We can pay you. We can afford it. Will you take the case? Will you get our Paulie back?" Her husband sat there tensely, holding his breath.

It didn't take me long. I'm a sucker for kids. "Yeah, I'll take it on, so you try not to worry, okay?"

"You'll get our little boy back?"

"If it can be done, I'll do it. Now I'll need all the information you can give me."

Mr. Brodie said, "There's not much to tell. We moved out of the city after Paulie was born. We thought it would be better to live in the country, closer to nature, you know?"

Mrs. Brodie interrupted, "We never should have moved. If I'd only known!"

"Please, dear, let me tell the Intervenor," Brodie said to his wife. She went back to destroying her handkerchief. "Yesterday we left Paulie in his playpen on the back porch. It was such a beautiful day. When we went to see if he needed changing he was gone." Mrs. Brodie sobbed pitifully.

I waited. They sat silently. "That's it?"

"That's all we know."

"Was anything left?" I asked.

"What do you mean?"

"If it was the Bendith Y Mamau, they'd leave behind an offspring of their own—a defective one." I added, understating the situation as best I could.

"No. We didn't see anything."

Good, I thought. You guys were traumatized enough. "I'll be up to your place in the morning and take a look around. I'd like you to stay at a hotel in the city tonight."

Mrs. Brodie said, "Oh, no. I couldn't do that. I must be home in case—"

I interrupted her. "There is no 'in case.' I hate to be so brutally frank, but if I don't find their lair and come up with the right spell, you'll never see the child again."

She broke down completely. Her husband gently pulled her to her feet and guided her toward the door. "We'll stay," he said. "You know how to get to our place?" I nodded.

Brodie said, "Our caretaker, Harry, will show you around." They nodded to me and left quietly.

I rang for my secretary. "Yes, Boss?"

"Get me Ms. Coulis. If she's not home, try her coven." I sat back and pinched the bridge of my nose. I was tired. I hated this case. I'm beginning to hate all my cases lately, I thought. Maybe it's time to pack it in and go live on the beach somewhere. It was a pleasant thought, but since we adepts were given human status by the Magica Carta we've been committed to serve and protect all Humans.

The intercom buzz cut off my reverie. "I have Ms. Coulis on line three."

"Cass? It's Nick. How're you doing?"

"You have some nerve calling me."

Oh, oh—I thought. What did I do to deserve that response?

She said, "Do you know what today's date is?" Without giving me a chance to show her how aware I was, she said, "It's May second." Then she said, "Two days ago you were supposed to escort me to the Walpurgisnacht Ball. My coven was honoring me for my work with handicapped children. I sat on the dais alone, while Nicodemus Merlin, the great Intervenor, was out getting drunk with that smelly Eskimo Shaman. It was humiliating!"

Yep, I blew it. "Now Cassie, honey—"

"Don't 'Cassie honey' me, Nick. We're finished. That's the last time you stand me up."

"Cassie, I'm really sorry. Please listen. I need you. I just took on a new case, a kidnapping. A little baby—a darling little baby boy . . ."

"Oh, Nick. How terrible! The Bendith?"

"I can't imagine who else."

Her personal pique forgotten, Cassie asked about the details. I told her what little I knew and asked her if she'd come upstate with me to the Brodie house. She agreed, as I knew she would. Cassie adored children, but like so many adepts, she was sterile and could have none of her own. Her coven, Delta Theta Pi, was known for its pediatric witchcraft.

Cassie said she'd meet me at my office in the morning. I asked her, "Are you coming by broom?"

"Of course! You want me to use a dog sled like Angakuk?" She hung up. I glanced at my window. If my office were in a modern building, the windows wouldn't open manually and my visitors would have to use the lobby like the other tenants' visitors. Oh, well, she *was* coming with me. I really didn't want to look for what I knew the Bendith must have left. Not alone, anyway.

I unlocked my cabinet and took out my thirty-eight. I normally carry a twenty-two, but I felt I might need more stopping power. I checked it out. I was very short on mandrake root powder. I had absolutely no whitethorn, having given it all to the Loa, Amelia Ougun, in exchange for information on the Belarivo case. The other thirty-six potions were in good order. I wished for the old days when a silver bullet and a wooden stake were all I needed.

The next morning I was having coffee at my desk when a shadow slid across my wall. I looked over my shoulder at the window. It was Cassie on her broom, legs crossed, showing a lot of inner thigh. She was busily smoothing microscopic flaws on her exquisite nails with an emery board. Her cat, Wendigo, sat on the brush end—very nonchalant. But the way his claws were dug in belied his image. I opened the window and they floated in. Cassie folded her broom and stowed it in her fitted Vuitton carrying case. I noticed her jar of flying ointment was low and resolved to whip up a batch for her when I had some time to spare. Wendigo stalked around the room, tail in the air, sniffing disdainfully.

2

We took the Thruway to the Northway and arrived at the Brodie place. It was once a farm, about fourteen acres and a few more acres of apple orchard. The main house was nicely restored, but everything else had been allowed to revert to nature. Almost obscured by a grove of willows were a barn and a few utility sheds.

"Where should I set up?" Cassie asked.

"How about the front porch?" I suggested. "There's a table you can use for your VIEWING, and chairs. While you get set I'll look around a bit." Cassie got busy and I went through the house looking for Harry. I couldn't find him so I looked around by myself but found nothing out of the ordinary. I went back to the front porch.

Cassie was sitting in front of her crystal ball. Wendigo was perched on her shoulder looking interested. His sleek black fur contrasted beautifully with Cassie's red mane. "You ready?" she asked.

I peeled the square of plastiflesh from my forehead and opened my EYE slowly. First the reds, then the spectrum, then the ultraviolets. I achieved stasis and the busy intersecting lines of the planes became clearly visible. Cassie had removed her MacMahon head-band and was focusing her EYE on her crystal. Her EYE functioned differently from mine. She couldn't SEE the myriad planes, nor did she have the power to move objects from our plane to a confluent one. Hers enhanced her intuition and empathetic sense and enabled her to communicate with her familiar, Wendigo.

We tuned frequencies. She said, "Your best estimate is that the baby was stolen about sixty hours ago?"

"Yes, about that."

She muttered some numbers to herself, calculating the speed of light during that period. "Around thirty-three and a half billion miles should do it." She thought nothing of rushing through black space to VIEW a past event, but VIEWING plane lines with me made her ill.

It took a bit of jockeying around, but she got a fix. She locked on and we LOOKED at the scene of the kidnapping and rode with it as the creature took the baby from the playpen and disappeared into the tangle of the apple orchard. It was a Bendith, all right. But this one was a real monster. Excuse the profanity. The Bendith Y Mamau are a very unpleasant clan of Welsh Other. They are genetic sports—results of interbreeding between true fairie and goblin. Brothers customarily rape their sisters, or fathers their daughters, when the girls come of age. The incestuous inbreeding produces many monst— defective offspring. These crimbils are left in place of a kidnapped Human child. At times these crimbils have been known to cause great harm to their unwilling adoptive parents before being killed or deplaned. The thing that really worried me was that the Bendith in Cassie's crystal had a rudimentary EYE! An adept Bendith was nothing I wanted to even *think* about. I hated this case.

Cassie closed her EYE and the crystal went dark. She rested for a moment, then raised her lid and LOOKED at Wendigo. They talked for a while and then Cassie turned to me, paler than she should have been from her VIEWING, and said tonelessly, "The barn."

I drew my thirty-eight and selected my fountainpent. I moved Cassie's crystal aside and sketched a quick pentagram on the table top, inscribing a stasis spell. I held it carefully in my eidetic image center and started toward the barn. I hoped my reflexes were still sharp. If I spotted the crimbil, I'd have to recall the sign and LOOK at the creature to cast a spell that would hold it in stasis till I figured out what the next step was to be.

Wendigo led the way, fur bristling and tail weaving. At the barn door he sat down and yeowed a few times. I looked at Cassie. She said, "He says, 'If you want to be an idiot and go in there, you can—but without him.'" Wendigo grinned at me and began to wash his face with his paw.

I opened the wide door and stepped just inside. The interior was dim, but as soon as my eyes adjusted to the light I could see well enough. The smells of an old barn trickled by my senses. And something else. Something overripe and something I've smelled too often in my career—the salty, coppery tang of spilled blood. A crumpled form lay in the shadows to the right of the door. I approached it gingerly, my eyes scanning the barn for any movement or sign of the crimbil. I didn't need to be a P.I. to figure out I had found Harry. His clothes had been shredded down the front, from collar to inseam. His genitals were gone and his intestines, what was left of them, shimmered out in silvery slime from the crater chewed from his belly. The wood planking of the floor around him was stained with congealed blood. His eyes stared sightlessly upward.

There was a sudden leathery rustling, and scuttling clicks rushed toward me. I whirled around. My EYE had no time to target the crimbil. It was the size of a Doberman and moved with the speed of a tarantula. It leaped at my throat and I reflexively wrapped my arms around it, pinning it to my chest. The convulsive energy of the thing as it struggled upward in my arms was like living electricity. With a cry of mingled fear and disgust, I flung the crimbil away from me and managed a LOOK. It froze in place, red eyed, rodent toothed. Even in stasis it vibrated with contained nervous movement. Something brushed my leg. I let out a startled yelp and jumped a mile. Wendigo walked a slow circle around the crimbil and sat down facing it. I had a barely suppressed desire to free the crimbil from its spell. See how far *you'd* jump, you rotten cat!

Cassie poked her head into the door and, seeing everything under control, walked in and stood by my side. The crimbil crouched in front of us glaring balefully—a pulsing, vibrating, evil statue. I tuned into the planes and judged that one was heading into confluence. At the moment of confluence, I LOOKED and sent the crimbil on its way. A neat, quick deplaning, Nick, I congratulated myself. I turned to Cassie and said, "No rest for the weary. We've got to track Poppa Bear to his lair and find Paulie. You game?"

"I'll go, of course. But I'm not walking on these heels," she said. "I'm going back to the house for my broom. I'll meet you at the orchard where we SAW the Bendith go."

"You don't have much flying ointment left, you know," I told her.

"At an average altitude of three feet, I've got enough."

I paced the edge of the line of trees looking fruitlessly for some sign of our quarry. Cassie floated up, gracefully balanced sidesaddle. Wendigo sat easily on the brush end. He wasn't worried about the altitude this time. "Any luck, Nick?"

"'Fraid not, honey. I'm too much the city slicker to track spoor in the woods, I guess."

She spoke to Wendigo for a while, but he remained aloof and motionless. Cassie turned to me and asked, "Did you threaten to turn the crimbil loose on Wendigo?"

"Me? Absolutely not! Well . . . I *thought* about it. But just for a minute."

"He wants you to apologize before he'll help."

"What? Apologize? Me? To him?"

"Do it, Nick, or we'll never find Paulie."

"Okay. I'm sorry I thought about scaring you with the crimbil. I'm very sorry. Okay?"

"He also wants you to apologize for calling him a rotten cat."

"Oh, Jeez! I'm very sorry about that too, Wendigo. Now will you please help us?" Wendigo landed lightly and began to look around, sniffing here and there, batting away some forest debris, purring songs to himself. He stopped suddenly, looked straight ahead and began to trot purposefully in the direction of his gaze.

"He's on it!" Cassie said excitedly and floated after him. I followed, stumbling awkwardly on the uneven ground. The orchard merged into forest and the terrain became rocky and rose into the first foothills of the Catskills—an appropriate place for Wendigo, I thought. The cat stopped in his tracks and jumped back on the broom. Cassie said, "Up there. A cave. Wendy says the whole clan is there." She took a scrap of Paulie's blanket from her bag, rubbed it between her palms and LOOKED. "Paulie is there, too."

"All right! You guys have been great. Wait here for me. I'm going in."

Cass shook her head. "I don't think you should. Witches have always been the traditional go-between with the Bendith. They'll have something that will need the right spells to fix. They usually deal. Let me try."

"Ordinarily I would, sweetheart, but Poppa Bear is a monst— an unusual Other. He has an EYE."

"A rudimentary one."

"Rudimentary or not, he's got one, and he's almost five feet tall."
"Nick, please! Don't be such a chauvinist. I can handle myself."
I saw the signs. Her green eyes were flashing dangerously. Her
familiar's back was arched, his hairs standing out like a porcupine's
quills. "All right. But if you're not back in half an hour, I'm coming
after you." It was all I could do. I watched her float up the hill to the
place indicated by Wendigo and disappear behind a pile of brush. I
assumed that it was camouflage for the cave entrance.

3

I sat there compulsively checking my thirty-eight, as if there were
something in it I could use against an entire clan of Bendith Y
Mamau. I rechecked, bit my nails and walked in circles for almost an
hour before I came to believe what I didn't want to believe. They
wouldn't deal. Cassie was in trouble!

As I walked up the hill toward their lair, I had a vision of myself as
Randolph Scott, marshal of Tombstone, marching into a saloon
crowded with rowdy criminals and announcing, "You're all under
arrest!" Cowered by my steely stare, they march meekly to the
hoosegow. Sure. Just like that. I pushed aside the shrubbery curtain.
The mouth of the cave was framed in bones. All kinds, from all parts
of the anatomy, stuck together in a macabre cornice. The keystone
was a large, grinning human skull. I shouted into the dark interior,
"Hey! You in there! I am the Intervenor, Nicodemus Merlin. I seek
entry to speak with the adept."

A rasping voice from within said, "Cover your EYE, Intervenor,
then enter." I slapped a square of plastiflesh on and entered the
cave. It was more than a cave. It was a huge limestone cavern carved
out by an ancient river, long since diverted by a receding glacier.
There were several hundred Bendith sitting on the floor and lining
the ledges to the thirty-foot vaulted ceiling. Sitting on a throne of
skulls was Poppa Bear himself. Cassie lay sprawled at his feet, bound
and BLINDfolded with filthy rags. The throne occupied a pentagram with a shielding spell inscribed upon it. I immediately noticed
the gap he left at the third point. You've got to complete the pentagram in one continuous movement. It's very difficult to do with
brush and paint. Maybe I could trade my fountainpent. Never mind
that now, just so long as I know I can get to him.

Poppa Bear said, "My name is Manawydan, first of the Bendith

Kings. This is the fortress of Annoeth, named for my mother. Why are you here?"

"I've come to bargain for the Human child and to find my woman, Cassandra Coulis, Witch of the Coven Delta Theta Pi." *And to put you all under arrest,* I said to myself.

"You are in no position to bargain for the child nor to retrieve your woman." I didn't like the direction this was going. I pulled off the plastiflesh and opened my EYE. Manawydan cackled his laughter. "You cannot magic me, Intervenor. It would be a capital offense. I am as human as you."

"Wrong. You are Bendith Y Mamau. The Magica Carta of 1215 classified you as Other."

"Adepts were classified as Human. *I* am an adept. You have no doubt noticed my magnificent EYE." I noticed it all right—more of a magnificent wart, but I said nothing. "I was born of a Human girl my father exchanged for his crimbil. It is because of her that I rule." I was scanning the planes while he spoke, but luck was not with me. I didn't see anything nearing confluence. I thought I'd better keep him talking.

"You do seem unlike ordinary Bendith. Your mother, Annoeth, was Welsh?"

"Yes, of the original folk, but brought to this foul land by her ancestors. Some of my brethren came with them, hidden with the rats in the dark places of the ship. My father stole Annoeth as a baby and when she was twelve and came into blood, he impregnated her. She was afraid I would be a crimbil, but when she saw my EYE she told me I would be a king. Her prophesy came true, and now I have the means to carry forward my dynasty." He patted Cassie's head. "She will bear my child and like Annoeth, when her milk runs dry, she will give her blood until the end, and then her flesh. The one contained in the other shall pass immortal to the next generation as Annoeth has within me."

A wave of murmuring and rustling swept the cavern as the Bendith exulted. I LOOKED at Manawydan and stepped through the gap in the third point. Manawydan made a gesture and a Bendith above me dropped a hundred-ton boulder on my head and the lights went out.

I awoke hanging by my heels, like a side of beef. The cave was dim, lit only by the smoky fires at the cave mouth. The Bendith were sleeping. I looked up and saw I was suspended alongside the cave wall from a rope attached to a spiny rock protuberance above me.

Cassie was sitting with her back against the wall, knees drawn up and still trussed up with twisted lengths of rags. We had never been face to face in this position. She was beautiful, even upside down. I tried to open my EYE to do a spell or two, but couldn't. Cassie must have seen the wrinkling forehead and said, "Forget it."

"My EYE! I can't open my EYE," I cried in panic. "What did they do?"

"They put a pat of mud over your EYElid, and then Poppa Bear, who may be an adept after all, cast a neat little spell."

"What spell? What? For God's sake!"

"He changed the mud."

"Changed? How changed?"

"Ethyl alpha cyanoacrylate."

"Ethyl alpha cyanoacrylate?"

"Krazy Glue."

"Oh, shit!"

Cassie giggled. "You look so funny!"

Surely, this girl had gone mad. I couldn't blame her. The new Queen of the Bendith. Ugh! "Cassie," I said sharply, "cut that out. We've got to get out of here." Hysteria tinged my voice.

"I'm working on it," she said.

"You are? What's the plan?" Relief flooded my mind.

"I sent Wendigo to get my nail polish remover from my carrying case."

The relief ebbed as fast as it had come. She clearly had lost her mind. A shadow, blacker than black, more silent than silence, brushed past me. Wendigo. He reached up and clawed the BLIND-fold down from Cassie's forehead. She opened her EYE and they talked for a while. Cassie said, "Nick, Wendy will give you the bottle. You'll have to open it for him."

"Why the hell do I want to open your nail polish remover? Your nails look good enough for the Queen of Monsters."

"Nick! You know I hate it when you use such vulgar language. Just do as I say!"

My loosely bound hands dangled a few inches off the floor. They felt the touch of an object. I grasped it. It was a flask-type plastic bottle. I held it firmly and managed to twist off the top. "It's open."

"Fine. Now put it down."

I did and wondered what this was all about. I soon understood. Wendigo dipped his tail in the nail polish remover and swabbed at the infuriating patch over my EYE. Nail polish remover—the sharp smell of acetone! That should do for the glue, I rhymed in my head. Wendigo flicked me across the nose, twice. I sneezed explosively. That rot— nice kitty. I could feel the wad softening. Wendigo slathered it again. It began to ooze, stickily. My EYElid snapped open and I immediately levitated upright. The blood rushing from my head put me in syncope for a minute. When it passed I undid the rope and released my spell. I untied Cassie and asked her if she knew where Paulie was.

She nodded and pointed to a wide ledge on the opposite wall. "In back of that ledge there's an entrance to another, smaller cave. Manawydan is holding some sort of ceremony preparing Paulie's initiation to the Bendith clan. I'm next."

"Okay. Let's get over there. I'll have to wait for the right time to go in and deplane that mon—Bendith. He won't know what hit him. I just hope I'm right and that he's not human. I'd be committing a capital offense otherwise."

"Don't worry, darling. To quote Wendigo, 'If Poppa Bear was Human, he was Clark Kent.'"

That cat is such a smartass. We silently threaded our way across the cave floor, undetected by dozing Bendith. My null spell covered Cassie as well as myself. Wendigo didn't need it. He flowed from shadow to shadow. He was kin to them.

On the ledge with our backs to the wall we peeked around the entrance into the chapel-like cave. A Human baby lay on a crude stone altar, arms and legs making vague swimming motions. Acolytes in crude robes crouched in a semicircle around the altar watching Manawydan paint an elaborate pentagram around the baby.

I couldn't make out the details of the design but I didn't like the looks of what was going on. I had a feeling that if Manawydan completed his spell, getting Paulie back to his parents might not be in their best interests. I LOOKED at the plane lines, hoping for a confluent situation. The planes were difficult tonight, like a million electrocardiogram readouts, all busily rushing toward and receding from each other in a maelstrom of kinetic energy. I concentrated and spotted a possibility. I narrowed my focus and began following a promising vector. Yep, I might luck out. I didn't have a reinforcing sign in my eidetic imagery to back my play this time. It was going to be *mano a mano* with Manawydan. The planes rushed into confluence and I sprang into the room and shouted, "Manawydan!" He looked up, startled. I LOOKED and snarled, "You're outta here." His EYE opened and for a moment we were in rapport. I knew instantly I had made the right choice. He wasn't Human. Not even close. I fought down my disgust and my fear. His EYE was weak and untutored. I could blow him away. The planes intersected and I felt myself fading. He had deflected my LOOK and was deplaning me! The adrenaline electrified me and I achieved stability with a burst of concentration. He started to move toward me followed by his acolytes. In desperation, I invoked the stasis design I used on the crimbil. Manawydan froze in his tracks.

Cassie sent her broom spinning like a helicopter rotor and bowled over the acolytes. I grabbed Paulie and ran toward the cave mouth. I didn't have time for a null spell so I removed the oxygen around the fires and the cave went dark. "Wendigo," I yelled. "Lead us out of here." No Wendigo. "Cassie, where's that lous— nice cat of yours?"

"He's right here."

"Well, get him on the ball. We've got to *move*."

"He says the reason that there are no Seeing Eye Cats is that it's dog work. He further says you called him a smartass, so find your own way out."

"Oh, Jeez! Look Wendigo, I'm really sorry. We'd all be in deep trouble if it weren't for you. I'm really sorry, I guess I'm just jealous about how familiar—I'm sorry, how close you are with Cassie. But please, if not for me, then for Paulie, get us out of here." I was already being pulled along by Cassie. I had Paulie tucked under my arm and I went through the cave like a running back, brushing off grasping leathery arms. It was much lighter outside the cave. I handed off Paulie to Cassie and drew my fountainpent. I inscribed a no-pass spell at the cave entrance. A molecule couldn't get through that sign. "That should hold them till the P.D. gets here," I said.

"What will be done with them?" Cassie asked.

"They'll deplane Poppa Bear for sure and probably deport the clan to Wales. There's a Bendith reservation outside Merthyr Tydfil where there's still plenty of room. The Bendith have a little trouble with reproduction, you know."

Cassie looked at me. I could see her face, pale in the moonlight. She had tears in her eyes. "Do tell," she said softly, hugging Paulie to her bosom.

GASTON LEROUX

In Letters of Fire

A dreadful night in the forest, a mysterious castle, a doomed nobleman with a Hellish secret . . . these are the Gothic trappings of "In Letters of Fire," one of six stories featured in Weird Tales *magazine that were written by* GASTON LEROUX *(1868–1927), the prolific French novelist best known today for* Murder in the Yellow Room *and* The Phantom of the Opera. *Another of this Leroux sextet, "The Woman in the Velvet Collar," is included in my collection* Weird Tales: The Magazine that Never Dies.

We had been out hunting wild boar all day when we were overtaken by a violent storm, which compelled us to seek refuge in a deep cavern. It was Makoko, our guide, who took upon himself to give utterance to the thought which haunted the minds of the four of us who had sought safety from the fury of the tempest—Mathis, Allan, Makoko, and myself.

"If the gentleman who lives in yonder house, which is said to be haunted by the devil, does not grant us the shelter of his roof to-night, we shall be compelled to sleep here."

Hardly had he uttered the words when a strange figure appeared at the entrance of the cavern.

"It is *he!*" exclaimed Makoko, grasping my arm.

I stared at the stranger.

He was tall, lanky, of bony frame, and melancholy aspect. Unconscious of our presence, he stood leaning on his fowling-piece at the entrance of the cavern, showing a strong aquiline nose, a thin mustache, a stern mouth, and lackluster eyes. He was bareheaded; his hair was thin, while a few gray locks fell behind his ears. His age might have been anywhere between forty and sixty. He must have been strikingly handsome in the days when the light shone in those time-dimmed eyes and those bitter lips could still break into a smile —but handsome in a haughty and forbidding style. A kind of terrible energy still lurked beneath his features, spectral as those of an apparition.

By his side stood a hairless dog, low on its legs, which was evidently barking at us. Yet we could hear nothing! The dog, it was plain, was dumb, and *barked at us in silence!*

Suddenly the man turned toward us.

"Gentlemen," he said in a voice of the most exquisite politeness, "it is out of the question for you to return to La Chaux-de-Fonds tonight. Permit me to offer you my hospitality."

Then, bending over his dog, he said: "Stop barking, Mystère."

The dog closed his jaws at once.

Makoko emitted a grunt. During the five hours that we had been enjoying the hunt, Mathis and Makoko had told Allan and me, who were strangers to the district, some strange and startling stories about our host, whom they represented as having had, like Faust, dealings with the Evil Spirit.

It was not without some trepidation, therefore, that we all moved out of the cavern.

"Gentlemen," said the stranger, with a melancholy smile, "it is many a long year since my door was thrown open to visitors. I am not fond of society, but I must tell you that one night, six months ago, a youth who had lost his way came and knocked at that door and begged for shelter till the morning. I refused him his request. Next day a body was found at the bottom of the big marl-pit—a body partly devoured by wolves."

"Why, that must have been Petit-Ledue!" cried Makoko. "So you were heartless enough to turn the poor boy away, at night and in the midst of winter! You are his murderer!"

"Truly spoken," replied the man, simply. "It was I who killed him. And now you see, gentlemen, that the incident has rendered me hospitable."

"Would you tell us why you drove him from your door?" growled Makoko.

"Because," he replied, quietly, "my house brings misfortune."

"I would rather risk meeting the powers of darkness than catching a cold," I retorted, laughing, and without further parley we set off, and in a short while had reached the door of the ancient mansion, which stood among the most desolate surroundings, on a shelf of barren rock swept by all the winds of heaven.

The huge door, antique, iron-barred, and studded with enormous nails, revolved slowly on its hinges, and opened noiselessly. A shrunken little old woman was there to welcome us.

From the threshold we could see a large, high room, somewhat similar to the room formerly styled the retainers' hall. It certainly constituted a part of what remained of the castle, on the ruins of which the mansion had been erected some centuries before. It was fully lighted by the fire on the enormous hearth, where a huge log was burning, and by two petrol lamps hanging by chains from the stone roof. There was no furniture except a heavy table of white wood, a large armchair upholstered in leather, a few stools, and a rude sideboard.

We walked the length of the room. The old woman opened a door. We found ourselves at the foot of a worm-eaten staircase with sunken steps. This staircase, a spiral one, led to the second story of the building, where the old woman showed us to our rooms.

To this day I can recall our host—were I to live a hundred years I could not forget that figure such as it appeared to me, as if framed by the fireplace—when I went into the hall where Mother Appenzel had spread our supper.

He was standing in front of my friends, on the stone hearth of the enormous fireplace. He was in evening dress—but such evening dress! It was in the pink of fashion, but a fashion long since vanished. The high collar of the coat, the broad lapels, the velvet waistcoat, the silken knee-breeches and stockings, the cravat, all seemed to possess the elegance of days gone by.

By his side lay his dog Mystère, his massive jaws parted in a yawn —yawning, just as he had barked, *in silence.*

"Has your dog been dumb for long?" I ventured to ask. "What strange accident has happened to him?"

"He has been dumb from his birth," replied my host, after a slight pause, as if this topic of conversation did not please him.

Still, I persisted in my questions.

"Was his father dumb?—or perhaps his mother?"

"His mother, and his mother's mother," he replied still coldly, "and *her* mother also."

"So you were the master of Mystère's great-grandmother?"

"I was, sir. She was indeed a faithful creature, and one who loved me well. A marvelous watch-dog," added my host, displaying sudden signs of emotion which surprised me.

"And she also was dumb from her birth?"

"No, sir. No, she was not born dumb—*but she became so one night when she had barked too much!*"

There was a world of meaning in the tone with which he spoke these words that at the moment I did not understand.

Supper was served. During the meal the conversation did not languish. Our host inquired whether we liked our rooms.

"I have a favor to beg of you," I ventured to say. "I should like to sleep in the haunted room!"

No sooner had I uttered the sentence than our host's pale face became still paler.

"Who has told you that there was a haunted room in this house?" he asked, striving with difficulty to restrain an evident irritation.

Mother Appenzel, who had just entered, trembled violently.

"It was you, Mother Appenzel?"

"Pray do not scold the good woman," I said; "my indiscreet behavior alone must bear the blame. I was attempting to enter a room the door of which was closed, when your servant forbade me to do so. 'Do not go into the haunted chamber,' she said."

"And you naturally did not do so?"

"Well, yes; I did go in."

"Heaven protect us!" wailed Mother Appenzel, letting fall a tumbler, which broke into pieces.

"Begone!" cried her master. Then, turning to us, he added, "You are indeed full of curiosity, gentlemen!"

"Please pardon us if we are so," I said. "Moreover, permit me to remind you that it was you yourself who alluded to the rumors current on the mountainside. Well, it would afford me much pleasure if your generous hospitality should be the occasion of dispersing them. When I have slept in the room which enjoys so evil a reputation, and have rested there peacefully, it will no longer be said that, to use your own expression, 'your house brings misfortune'."

Our host interrupted me: "You shall not sleep in that room; it is no longer used as a bedroom. No one has slept there for fifty years past."

"Who, then, was the last one to sleep in it?"

"I myself—and I should not advise anyone to sleep in it after me!"

"Fifty years ago, you say! You could only be a child at the time, at an age when one is still afraid at nights—"

"Fifty years ago I was twenty-eight!"

"Am I committing an indiscretion when asking you what happened to you in that room? I have just come from visiting it, and nothing whatever happened to me. The room seems to me the most natural of rooms. I even attempted to prop up a wardrobe which seemed as if it were about to fall."

"You laid hands on the wardrobe!" cried the man, throwing down his table-napkin and coming toward me with the gleam of madness in his eyes. "You actually laid hands on the wardrobe?"

"Yes," was my quiet answer; "as I say, it seemed about to fall."

"But it cannot fall! It will never fall! Never again will it stand upright! It is its nature to be in that position for all time to come, trembling with fear for all eternity!"

We had all risen. The man's voice was harsh as he spoke these most mysterious words. Heavy drops of perspiration trickled down his face. Those eyes of his, which we had thought dimmed forever, flashed with fury. He was indeed awful to look at. He grasped my wrist and wrung it with a strength of which I would have deemed him incapable.

"You did not open it?"

"No."

"Then you do not know what is in it? No? Well, all the better! By heaven, I tell you, sir, it is all the better for *you!*"

Turning toward his dog, he shouted: "To your kennel! When will you find your voice again, Mystère? Or are you going to die like the others—*in silence?*"

He had opened the door leading to a tower, and went out, driving the dog before him.

We were deeply moved at this unexpected scene. The man had disappeared in the darkness of the tower, still pursuing his dog.

"What did I tell you?" remarked Makoko, in a scarcely audible tone. "You may all please yourselves, but, as for me, I do not intend to sleep here tonight. I shall sit up here in this hall until daybreak."

"And so shall I," added Mathis.

Makoko, bending over us, his eyes staring out of their sockets, continued: "Don't you see that he is crazy?"

"You two fellows with your death-mask faces," exclaimed Allan, "are not going to prevent us from enjoying ourselves. Supposing we start a game of écarté. We will ask our host to take a hand; it will divert his thoughts."

An extraordinary fellow was Allan. His fondness for card-playing amounted to a mania. He pulled out a pack of cards, and had hardly done so when our host reentered the hall. He was now comparatively calm, but no sooner had he perceived the pack of cards on the table than his features became transformed and assumed such an expression of fear and fury that I myself was terrified.

"Cards!" he cried. "You have cards!"

Allan rose and said, pleasantly, "We have decided not to retire for the night. We are about to have a friendly little game of écarté. Do you know the game?"

Allan stopped. He also had been struck with the fearful expression on our host's face. His eyes were bloodshot, the sparse hairs of his mustache stood out bristling, his teeth gleamed, while his lips hissed out the words: "Cards! Cards!"

The words escaped with difficulty from his throat, as if some invisible hand were clutching it.

"Who sent you here with cards? What do you want with me? The cards must be burnt—they must be burnt!"

Of a sudden he grasped the pack and was about to cast it into the flames, but he stopped just on the point of doing so, his trembling fingers let drop the cards, and he sank into the armchair, exclaiming hoarsely: "I am suffocating; I am suffocating!"

We rushed to his help, but with a single effort of his bony fingers he had already torn off his collar and his tie; and now, motionless, holding his head erect, and settling down in the huge armchair, he burst into tears.

"You are good fellows," he said at last, in milder tones. "You shall know everything. You shall not leave this house in ignorance, taking me for a madman—for a poor, miserable, melancholy madman.

"Yes, indeed," he continued; "yes, you shall know everything. It may be of use to you."

He rose, paced up and down, then halted in front of us, staring at us with the dimmed look that had given way to the momentary flash.

"Sixty years ago I was entering upon my eighteenth year. With all the overweening presumption of youth, I was skeptical of everything. Nature had fashioned me strong and handsome. Fate had endowed me with enormous wealth. I became the most fashionable youth of my day. Paris, gentlemen, with all its pleasures, was for ten years at my feet. When I had reached the age of twenty-eight I was on the brink of ruin. There remained to me between two and three hundred thousand francs and this manor, with the land surrounding it.

"Just at that time, gentlemen, I fell madly in love with an angelic creature. I could never have dreamt of the existence of such beauty and purity. The girl whom I adored was ignorant of the passionate love which was consuming me, and she remained so. Her family was one of the wealthiest in all Europe. For nothing in this world would I have had her suspect that I aspired to the honor of her hand in order to replenish my empty coffers. So I went the way of the gambling dens, in the vain hope of recovering my vanished millions. I lost all, and one fine evening I left Paris to come and bury myself in this old mansion, my sole refuge.

"I found here an old man, Father Appenzel; his granddaughter, of whom later on I made a servant; and his grandson, a child of tender years, who grew up to manhood on the estate, and who is now my steward. I fell a prey, on the very evening of my arrival, to despair and ennui. The astounding events that followed took place that very evening.

"When I went up to my room—the room which one of you has asked to be allowed to occupy tonight—I had made up my mind to take my own life. A brace of pistols lay on the chest of drawers. Suddenly, as I was putting my hand on one of the pistols, my dog began to howl in the courtyard—to howl as I have never heard the wind howl, unless it be tonight.

" 'So,' thought I, 'here is Mystère raising a death-howl. She must know that I am going to kill myself tonight.'

"I toyed with the pistol, recalling of a sudden what my past life had been, and wondering for the first time what my death would be like. Suddenly my eye lighted on the titles of a few old books which stood on a shelf hanging above the chest of drawers. I was surprised to see that all of them dealt with sorcerers and matters appertaining to the powers of evil. I took up a book, *The Sorcerers of the Jura*, and, with the skeptical smile of the man who has defied fate, I opened it. The first two lines, printed in red, at once caught my eye:

" '*He who seriously wishes to see the devil has but to summon him with his whole heart, and he will come.*'

"Then followed the story of an individual who, like myself, a lover in despair—like myself, a ruined man—had in all sincerity summoned to his help the Prince of Darkness, and who had been assisted by him; for, a few months later, he had once more become incredibly rich and had married his beloved. I read the story to the end.

" 'Well, here was a lucky fellow!' I exclaimed, tossing the book on to the chest of drawers. Mystère was still howling in the grounds. I parted the window-curtains, and could not help shuddering when I saw the dog's shadow dancing in the moonlight. It really seemed as if the slut was possessed of some evil spirit, for her movements were inexplicably eccentric. She seemed to be snapping at some invisible form!

"I tried to laugh over the matter, but the state of my mind, the story I had just read, the howling of the dog, her strange leaps, the sinister locality, the old room, the pistols which I myself had loaded, all had contributed to take a greater hold of my imagination than I dared confess.

"Leaving the window I strolled about the room for awhile. Of a sudden I saw myself in the mirror of the wardrobe. My pallor was such that I thought that I was dead. Alas, no! The man standing before the wardrobe was not dead. It was, on the contrary, a living man who, with all his heart, was summoning the King of Lost Souls.

"Yes, then, in the mirror, side by side with my form, something superhuman—a pale object—a mist, a terrible little cloud which was soon transformed into eyes—eyes of fearful loveliness. Another form was standing resplendent beside my haggard face; a mouth—a mouth which said to me, 'Open!' At this I recoiled. But the mouth was still saying to me, 'Open, open, if you dare!'

"Then something knocked three times upon the door inside the wardrobe—and the door flew open of its own accord!"

Just at that instant the old man's narrative was interrupted by three knocks on the door, which suddenly opened, and a man entered.

"Was it you who knocked like that, Guillaume?" asked our host, striving in vain to regain his composure.

"Yes, master."

"I had given you up for tonight. You saw the notary?"

"Yes; and I did not care to keep so great a sum of money about my person."

We gathered that Guillaume was the gentleman's steward. He came to the table, took a little bag from the folds of his cloak, extracted some documents from it, and laid them on the table. Then he drew an envelope from his bag, emptied its contents on the table, and counted out twelve one-thousand-franc notes.

"There's the purchase-money for Misery Wood."

"Good, Guillaume," said our host, picking up the bank-notes and replacing them in the envelope. "You must be hungry. Are you going to sleep here tonight?"

"No; it is impossible. I have to call on the farmer. We have some business to transact together early in the morning. However, I do not mind having a bit of supper."

"Go to Mother Appenzel, my good fellow; she will take good care of you," adding, as the steward strode toward the kitchen, "Take away all those rubbishy papers."

The man picked up the documents, while the gentleman, taking a pocketbook out of his pocket, placed in it the envelope containing the twelve notes and returned the book to his pocket. Then, resuming his narrative in reply to a request from Makoko, he continued:

"You wish to know what the wardrobe contained? Well, I am going to tell you. There was something which I saw—something which scorched my eyes. There shone within the recess of the wardrobe, written in letters of fire, three words:

" *'Thou Shalt Win!'*

"Yes," he continued, in a gloomy tone, "the devil had, in three words, expressed in characters of fire, in the depths of the wardrobe, the fate that awaited me. He had left behind him his sign-manual, the irrefutable proof of the hideous pact into which I had entered with him on that tragic night. 'Thou shalt win!' In three short words he granted me the world's wealth. 'Thou shalt win!'

"Next morning old Appenzel found me lying unconscious at the foot of the wardrobe. Alas! when I had recovered my senses I had forgotten nothing. I was fated never to forget what I had seen. Wherever I go, wherever I wend my steps, be it night, be it day, I read the fiery phrase, 'Thou shalt win!'—on the walls of darkness, on the resplendent orb of the sun, on the earth and in the skies; within myself when I close my eyes, on your faces when I look at you!"

The old man, exhausted, ceased speaking, and fell back, moaning, into the armchair.

"I must tell you," he resumed, after a few moments, "that my experience had had so terrifying an effect on me that I had been compelled to keep my bed, where Father Appenzel brought me a soothing potion of 11 herbs. Addressing me, he said: 'Something incredible has happened, sir. Your dog has become dumb. *She barks in silence!'*

" 'Oh, I know, I understand!' I exclaimed. 'She will not recover her voice until *he* shall have returned!'

Father Appenzel looked at me in amazement and fright, for my hair was standing on end. In spite of myself, my gaze was straying toward the wardrobe. Father Appenzel, as alarmed and agitated as myself, went on to say:

" 'When I found you, sir, on the floor this morning the wardrobe was inclined as it is now, while its door was open. I closed it, but I was unable to get it to stand upright. It seems always on the point of falling forward.'

"I begged old Appenzel to leave me to myself. I got out of bed, went to the wardrobe, and opened its door. Conceive, I pray you, my feelings when I had done so. The sentence, that sentence written in characters of fire, was still there! It was graven in the boards at the back; it had burnt the boards with its imprint; and by day I read what I had ready by night—the words: 'Thou shalt win.'

"I flew out of the room. I called for help. Father Appenzel returned. I said to him: 'Look into the depths of that wardrobe, and tell me what you see there!'

"My servant did as I bade him, and said to me: 'Thou shalt win!'

"I dressed myself. I fled like a madman from the accursed house, and wandered in the mountains. The mountain air did me good. When I came home in the evening I was perfectly calm; I had thought matters over; my dog might have become dumb through some perfectly natural physiological phenomenon. With regard to the sentence in the wardrobe, it had not come there of itself, and, as I had not had any previous acquaintance with that piece of furniture, it was probable that the three fatal words had been there for countless years, inscribed by someone addicted to the black art, following upon some gambling affair which was no concern of mine.

"I ate my supper, and went to bed in the same room. The night passed without incident.

"Next day I went to La Chaux-de-Fonds, to call on a notary. All that this adventure with the wardrobe had succeeded in doing was to imbue me with the idea of tempting fate, in the shape of cards, one last time, ere putting into execution my idea about suicide. I borrowed a few thousand francs on the security of the estate, and went to Paris. As I ascended the staircase of the club I recalled my nightmare, and remarked to myself ironically, for I placed no faith in the success of this supreme attempt: 'We shall now see whether, if the devil helps me—' I did not finish the sentence.

"The bank was being put up to auction when I entered the salon. I secured it for two thousand francs. I had not reached the middle of my deal when I had already won two hundred and fifty thousand francs! But no longer would any of the players stake against me. *I was winning every game!*

"I was jubilant; I had never dreamt that such luck would be mine. I threw up the bank; that is, what remained of it for me to hold. I next amused myself at throwing away chances, just to see what would happen. In spite of this I continued winning. Exclamations were heard on all sides. The players swore I had the devil's own luck. I collected my winnings and left.

"No sooner had I reached the street than I began to think and to become alarmed. The coincidence between the scene of the wardrobe and of my extraordinary success as a banker troubled me. Of a sudden, and to my surprise, I found myself wending my way back to the club. I was determined to probe the matter to the bottom. My short-lived joy was disturbed by the fact that I had not lost once. So it was that I was anxious to lose just once.

"When I left the club for the second time, at six o'clock in the morning, I had won, in money and on parole, no less than a couple of millions. But I had not once lost—not a single, solitary time! I felt myself becoming a raving madman. When I say that I had not lost once, I speak with regard to money, for when I had played for nothing, without stakes, to see, just for the fun of the matter, I lost inexorably. But no sooner had a punter staked even as low as half a franc against me, I won his money. It mattered little, a cent or a million francs. I could no longer lose. 'Thou shalt win!' Oh, that terrible curse! that curse! For a whole week did I try. I went into the worst gambling-halls. I sat down to card-tables presided over by card-sharpers; I won even from them; I won from one and all against whom I played. I did nothing but win!

"So, you no longer laugh, gentlemen! You scoff no more! You see now, good sirs, that one should never be in a hurry to laugh! I told you I had seen the devil! Do you believe me now? I possessed then the certainty, the palpable proof, visible to one and all, the natural and terrestrial proof of my revolting compact with the devil. The law of probabilities no longer existed as far as I was concerned. There remained only the supernatural certainty of winning eternally—until the day of death. Death! I could no longer dream of it as a desire. For the first time in my life I dreaded it. The terrors of death haunted me, because of what awaited me at the end!

"My uppermost thought was to redeem my soul—my wretched, my lost soul. I frequented the churches. I saw priests. I prostrated myself at the foot of church steps. I beat my delirious head on the sacred flagstones! I prayed to God that I might lose, just as I had prayed to the devil that I might win. On leaving the holy place I was wont to hurry to some low gambling-den and stake a few louis on a card. But I continued winning for ever and ever! 'Thou shalt win!'

"Not for a single second did I entertain the idea of owing my happiness to those accursed millions. I offered up my heart to God as a burnt-offering, I distributed the millions I had won to the poor, and I came here, gentlemen, to await the death which spurns me— the death I dread!"

"You have never played since those days?" I asked.

"I have never played from that time until now."

Allan had read my thoughts. He too was dreaming that it might be possible to rescue from his monomania the man whom we both persisted in considering insane.

"I feel sure," he said, "that so great a sacrifice has won you pardon. Your despair has been undoubtedly sincere, and your punishment a terrible one. What more could heaven require of you? In your place, *I should try*—"

"You would try—what?" exclaimed the man, springing from his seat.

"I should try whether I were still doomed to win!"

The man struck the table a violent blow with his clenched fist.

"And so this is all the remedy you can suggest! So this is all that the narrative of a curse transcending all things earthly has inspired you with? You seek to induce an old lunatic to play, with the object of demonstrating to him that he is not insane! For I read full well in your eyes what you think of me: 'He is mad, mad, mad!' You do not believe a single word of all I have told you. You think I am insane, young man! And you, too," he added, addressing Allan, "you think I am insane—mad, mad, mad! I tell you that I have seen the devil! Yes, your old madman has seen the devil! And he is going to prove it to you. The cards! Where are the cards?"

Espying them on the edge of the table, he sprang on them.

"It is you who have so willed it. I had harbored a supreme hope that I should die without having again made the infernal attempt, so that when my hour had come I might imagine that heaven had forgiven me. They are yours. Shuffle them—deal me which you please—stack them as you will. I tell you that I shall win. Do you believe me now?"

Allan had quietly picked up the cards.

The man, placing his hand on his shoulder, asked, "You do not believe me?"

"We shall see," replied Allan.

"What shall the stakes be?" I inquired.

"I do not know, gentlemen, whether you are well off or not, but I feel bound to inform you—you who have come to destroy my last hope—that you are ruined men."

Thereupon he took out his pocket-book and laid it on the table, saying: "I will play you five straight points at écarté for the contents of this pocket-book. This just by way of a beginning. After that, I am willing to play you as many games as you see fit, until I cast you out of doors picked clean, your friends and yourself, ruined for the rest of your lives—yes, picked bare."

"Picked bare?" repeated Allan, who was far less moved than myself. "Do you want even our shirts?"

"Even your souls," cried the man, "which I intend to present to the devil in exchange for my own."

Allan winked at me, and asked: "Shall we say 'Done,' and go halves in this?"

I agreed, shuffled the pack, and handed it to my opponent.

He cut. I dealt. I turned up the knave of hearts. Our host looked at his hand and led. Clearly he ought not to have played the hand he held—three small clubs, the queen of diamonds, and the seven of spades. He took a trick with his queen, I took the four others, and, as he had led, I marked two points. I entertained not the slightest doubt that he was doing his utmost to lose.

It was his turn to deal. He turned up the king of spades. He could not restrain a shudder when he beheld that black-faced card, which, in spite of himself, gave him a trick.

He scanned his hand anxiously. It was my turn to call for cards. He refused them, evidently believing that he held a very poor hand; but my own was as bad as his, and he had a ten of hearts, which took my nine—I held the nine, eight, and seven of hearts.

He then played diamonds, to which I could not respond, and two clubs higher than mine. Neither of us held a single trump. He scored a point, which, with the one secured to him by his king, gave him two. We were "evens," either of us being in a position to end matters at once if we made three points.

The deal was mine. I turned up the eight of diamonds. This time both of us called for cards. He asked for one, and showed me the one he had discarded—the seven of diamonds. He was anxious not to hold any trumps. His wish was gratified, and he succeeded in making me score another two points, which gave me four.

In spite of ourselves, Allan and I glanced toward the pocket-book. Our thoughts ran: "There lies a small fortune which is shortly to be ours, one which, in all conscience, we shall not have had much trouble in winning."

Our host dealt in his turn, and when I saw the cards he had given me I considered the matter as good as settled. This time he had not turned up a king, but the seven of clubs. I held two hearts and three trumps—the ace and king of hearts, the ace, ten, and nine of clubs. I led the king, my opponent followed with the queen; I flung the ace on the table, my opponent being compelled to take it with the knave of hearts, and he then played a diamond, which I trumped. I played the ace of trumps; he took it with the queen, but I was ready for him with my last card, the ten of clubs. He had the knave of trumps! As I had led he scored two, making "four all." Our host smothered a curse which was hovering on his lips.

"No need for you to worry," I remarked; "no one has won yet."

"We are about to prove to you," said Allan, in the midst of a deathly silence, "that you can lose just like any ordinary mortal."

Our host groaned, "I cannot lose."

The interest in the game was now at its height. A point on either side, and either of us would be the winner. If I turned up the king the game was ended, and I won twelve thousand francs from a man who claimed that he could not lose. I had dealt. I turned up the king —the king of hearts. I had won!

My opponent uttered a cry of joy. He bent over the card, picked it up, considered it attentively, fingered it, raised it to his eyes, and we thought he was about to press it to his lips. He murmured:

"Great heavens, can it be? Then—then I have lost!"

"So it would seem," I remarked.

Allan added, "You now see full well that one should not place any faith in what the devil says."

The gentleman took his pocket-book and opened it.

"Gentlemen," he sighed, "bless you for having won all that is in this book. Would that it contained a million! I should gladly have handed it over to you."

With trembling hands he searched the pocket-book, emptying it of all its contents, with a look of surprise at not finding at once the twelve thousand francs he had deposited in its folds. They were not there!

The pocket-book, searched with feverish hands, lay empty on the table. *There was nothing in the pocket-book! Nothing!*

We sat dumfounded at this inexplicable phenomenon—the empty pocket-book! We picked it up and fingered it. We searched it carefully, only to find it empty. Our host, livid and as one possessed, was searching himself, and begging us to search him. We searched him—we searched him, because it was beyond our power to resist his delirious will; but we found nothing—nothing!

"Hark!" exclaimed our host. "Hark, hark! Does it not seem to you tonight that the wind sounds like the voice of a dog?"

We listened, and Makoko answered, "It is true! The wind really seems to be barking—there, behind the door!"

The door was shaking strangely, and we heard a voice calling, "Open!"

I drew the bolts and opened the door. A human form rushed into the room.

"It is the steward," I said.

"Sir, sir!" he began.

"What is it?" we all exclaimed, breathlessly, and wondering what was about to follow.

"Sir, I thought I had handed you your twelve thousand francs. Indeed, I am positive I did so. Those gentlemen doubtless saw me."

"Yes, indeed," from all of us.

"Well, I have just discovered them in my bag. I can not understand how it has happened. I have returned to bring them back to you—*once more*. Here they are."

The steward again pulled out the identical envelope, and a second time counted the twelve one-thousand-franc notes, adding:

"I know not what ails the mountainside tonight, but it terrifies me. I shall sleep here."

The twelve thousand francs were now lying on the table. Our host cried:

"This time we see them there, there before us! Where are the cards? Deal them. The twelve thousand in five straight points, to see, to know for certain. I tell you that I wish to know—*to know*."

I dealt. My opponent called for cards; I refused them. He had five trumps. He scored two points. He dealt the cards. He turned up the king. I led. He again had five trumps. Three and two are five! He had won!

Then he howled; yes, howled like the wind which had the voice of a dog. He snatched the cards from the table and cast them into the flames. "Into the fire with the cards! Let the fire consume them!" he shrieked.

Suddenly he strode toward the door. Outside a dog barked—a dog raising a death-howl.

The man reached the door, and speaking through it asked:

"Is that you, Mystère?"

To what phenomenon was it due that both wind and dog were silent simultaneously?

The man softly drew the bolts and half opened the door. No sooner was the door ajar than the infernal yelping broke out so prolonged and so lugubrious that it made us shiver to our very marrow. Our host had now flung himself upon the door with such force that we could almost think he had smashed it. Not content with having pushed back the bolts, he pressed with his knees and arms against the door, without uttering a sound. All we heard was his panting respiration.

Then, when the death-like yelping had ceased, and silence reigned both within and without, turning toward us and tottering forward he said:

"He has returned! Beware!"

Midnight. We have gone our respective ways. Makoko and Mathis have remained below beside the dying embers. Allan has sought his bedroom, while, driven by some unknown inner force controlling me absolutely, I find myself in the haunted room. I am repeating the doings of the man whose story we had heard that night; I select the same book, open it at the same page; I go to the same window; I pull the curtain aside; I gaze upon the same moonlit landscape, for the wind has long since driven off the tempest-clouds and the fog. I only see bare rocks, shining like steel under the rays of the bright moon, and on the desolate plateau a weirdly dancing shadow—the shadow of Mystère, with her formidable jaws wide apart—jaws that I can see barking. Do I hear the barking? Yes, it seems to me that I hear it. I let the curtain drop. I take my candlestick from the chest of drawers. I step toward the wardrobe. I look at myself in its mirrored panel. I dream of *him* who wrote the words which lie concealed within. Whose face is it that I see in the mirror? It is my own! But is it possible that the face of our host on the fatal night could have been more pallid than mine is now? In all truth, my face is that of a dead man. On one side—there—there—that little cloud—that misty cloudlet in the mirror—cheek by jowl with my face—those fearful eyes—those lips! Oh, if I could but scream! I can not. I am powerless to cry out, *when suddenly I hear three knocks.* And—and my hand strays of its own accord toward the door of the wardrobe—my inquisitive hand—my accursed hand.

Of a sudden my hand is gripped in the vise I know so well. I look round. I am face to face with our host, who says to me in a voice which seems to come from another world:

"Do not open it!"

Next morning we did not ask our host to give us the opportunity of winning back our money. We fled from his roof without even taking leave of him. Twelve thousand francs were sent that evening to our strange host through Makoko's father, to whom we had told our adventure. He returned them to us, with the following note:

"We are quits. When we played, both the first game, which you won, and the second one, which you lost, we *believed,* you and I, that we were staking twelve thousand francs. That must be sufficient for us. The devil has my soul, but he shall not possess my honor."

We were not at all anxious to keep the twelve thousand francs, so we presented them to a hospital in La Chaux-de-Fonds which was in sore need of money. Following upon urgent repairs, to which our donation was applied, the hospital, one winter's night, was so thoroughly burned to the ground that at noon the following day nothing but ashes remained of it.

JACK VANCE

Green Magic

I always reserve the final spot in my anthologies for the selection that I consider to be the most remarkable, and this time it is undoubtedly "Green Magic," a nonpareil by JACK VANCE, *a San Francisco science-fantasy and mystery writer whose stylish prose and genius for inventive settings and alien cultures have garnered him both the Hugo and Nebula awards, as well as the Mystery Writers of America's "Edgar." Author of* The Dragon Masters, The Dying Earth, Galactic Effectuator, The Languages of Pao, The Man in the Cage, To Live Forever *and many other superb novels and stories, Mr. Vance was guest of honor at "Magicon," the 1992 World Science Fiction Convention in Orlando, Florida.*

Howard Fair, looking over the relics of his great uncle Gerald McIntyre, found a large ledger entitled:

WORKBOOK & JOURNAL
Open at Peril!

Fair read the journal with interest, although his own work went far beyond ideas treated only gingerly by Gerald McIntyre.

"The existence of disciplines concentric to the elementary magics must now be admitted without further controversy," wrote McIntyre. "Guided by a set of analogies from the white and black magics (to be detailed in due course), I have delineated the basic extension of purple magic, as well as its corollary, Dynamic Nomism."

Fair read on, remarking the careful charts, the projections and expansions, the transpolations and transformations by which Gerald

McIntyre had conceived his systemology. So swiftly had the technical arts advanced that McIntyre's expositions, highly controversial sixty years before, now seemed pedantic and overly rigorous.

"Whereas benign creatures: angels, white sprites, merrihews, sandestins—are typical of the white cycle; whereas demons, magners, trolls and warlocks are evinced by black magic; so do the purple and green cycles sponsor their own particulars, but these are neither good nor evil, bearing, rather, the same relation to the black and white provinces that these latter do to our own basic realm."

Fair re-read the passage. The "green cycle?" Had Gerald McIntyre wandered into regions overlooked by modern workers?

He reviewed the journal in the light of this suspicion, and discovered additional hints and references. Especially provocative was a bit of scribbled marginalia: "More concerning my latest researches I may not state, having been promised an infinite reward for this forbearance."

The passage was dated a day before Gerald McIntyre's death, which had occurred on March 21, 1898, the first day of spring. McIntyre had enjoyed very little of his "infinite reward," whatever had been its nature . . . Fair returned to a consideration of the journal, which, in a sentence or two, had opened a chink on an entire new panorama. McIntyre provided no further illumination, and Fair set out to make a fuller investigation.

His first steps were routine. He performed two divinations, searched the standard indexes, concordances, handbooks and formularies, evoked a demon whom he had previously found knowledgeable: all without success. He found no direct reference to cycles beyond the purple; the demon refused even to speculate.

Fair was by no means discouraged; if anything, the intensity of his interest increased. He re-read the journal, with particular care to the justification for purple magic, reasoning that McIntyre, groping for a lore beyond the purple, might well have used the methods which had yielded results before. Applying stains and ultraviolet light to the pages, Fair made legible a number of notes McIntyre had jotted down, then erased.

Fair was immensely stimulated. The notes assured him that he was on the right track, and further indicated a number of blind alleys which Fair profited by avoiding. He applied himself so successfully that before the week was out he had evoked a sprite of the green cycle.

It appeared in the semblance of a man with green glass eyes and a thatch of young eucalyptus leaves in the place of hair. It greeted Fair with cool courtesy, would not seat itself, and ignored Fair's proffer of coffee.

After wandering around the apartment inspecting Fair's books and curios with an air of negligent amusement, it agreed to respond to Fair's questions.

Fair asked permission to use his tape-recorder, which the sprite allowed, and Fair set the apparatus in motion. (When subsequently he replayed the interview, no sound could be heard.)

"What realms of magic lie beyond the green?" asked Fair.

"I can't give you an exact answer," replied the sprite, "because I don't know. There are at least two more, corresponding to the colors we call rawn and pallow, and very likely others."

Fair arranged the microphone where it would more directly intercept the voice of the sprite.

"What," he asked, "is the green cycle like? What is its physical semblance?"

The sprite paused to consider. Glistening mother-of-pearl films wandered across its face, reflecting the tinge of its thoughts. "I'm rather severely restricted by your use of the word 'physical.' And 'semblance' involves a subjective interpretation, which changes with the rise and fall of the seconds."

"By all means," Fair said hastily, "describe it in your own words."

"Well—we have four different regions, two of which floresce from the basic skeleton of the universe, and so subsede the others. The first of these is compressed and isthiated, but is notable for its wide pools of mottle which we use sometimes for deranging stations. We've transplanted club-mosses from Earth's Devonian and a few ice-fires from Perdition. They climb among the rods which we call devil-hair—" He went on for several minutes but the meaning almost entirely escaped Fair. And it seemed as if the question by which he had hoped to break the ice might run away with the entire interview. He introduced another idea.

" 'Can we freely manipulate the physical extensions of Earth?' " The sprite seemed amused. "You refer, so I assume, to the various aspects of space, time, mass, energy, life, thought and recollection."

"Exactly."

The sprite raised its green corn-silk eyebrows. "I might as sensibly ask can you break an egg by striking it with a club? The response is on a similar level of seriousness."

Fair had expected a certain amount of condescension and impatience, and was not abashed. "How may I learn these techniques?"

"In the usual manner: through diligent study."

"Ah, indeed—but where could I study? Who would teach me?"

The sprite made an easy gesture, and whorls of green smoke trailed from his fingers to spin through the air. "I could arrange the matter, but since I bear you no particular animosity, I'll do nothing of the sort. And now, I must be gone."

"Where do you go?" Fair asked in wonder and longing. "May I go with you?"

The sprite, swirling a drape of bright green dust over its shoulders, shook his head. "You would be less than comfortable."

"Other men have explored the worlds of magic!"

"True: your uncle Gerald McIntyre, for instance."

"My uncle Gerald learned green magic?"

"To the limit of his capabilities. He found no pleasure in his learning. You would do well to profit by his experience and modify your ambitions." The sprite turned and walked away.

Fair watched it depart. The sprite receded in space and dimension, but never reached the wall of Fair's room. At a distance which might have been fifty yards, the sprite glanced back, as if to make sure that Fair was not following, then stepped off at another angle and disappeared.

Fair's first impulse was to take heed and limit his explorations. He was an adept in white magic, and had mastered the black art—occasionally he evoked a demon to liven a social gathering which otherwise threatened to become dull—but he had by no means illuminated every mystery of purple magic, which is the realm of Incarnate Symbols.

Howard Fair might have turned away from the green cycle except for three factors.

First was his physical appearance. He stood rather under medium height, with a swarthy face, sparse black hair, a gnarled nose, a small heavy mouth. He felt no great sensitivity about his appearance, but realized that it might be improved. In his mind's eye he pictured the personified ideal of himself: he was taller by six inches, his nose thin and keen, his skin cleared of its muddy undertone. A striking figure, but still recognizable as Howard Fair. He wanted the love of women, but he wanted it without the interposition of his craft. Many times he had brought beautiful girls to his bed, lips wet and eyes shining; but purple magic had seduced them rather than Howard Fair, and he took limited satisfaction in such conquests.

Here was the first factor which drew Howard Fair back to the green lore; the second was his yearning for extended, perhaps eternal, life; the third was simple thirst for knowledge.

The fact of Gerald McIntyre's death, or dissolution, or disappearance—whatever had happened to him—was naturally a matter of concern. If he had won to a goal so precious, why had he died so quickly? Was the "infinite reward" so miraculous, so exquisite, that the mind failed under its possession? (If such were the case, the reward was hardly a reward.)

Fair could not restrain himself, and by degrees returned to a study of green magic. Rather than again invoke the sprite whose air of indulgent contempt he had found exasperating, he decided to seek knowledge by an indirect method, employing the most advanced concepts of technical and cabalistic science.

He obtained a portable television transmitter which he loaded into his panel truck along with a receiver. On a Monday night in early May, he drove to an abandoned graveyard far out in the wooded hills, and there, by the light of a waning moon, he buried the television camera in graveyard clay until only the lense protruded from the soil.

With a sharp alder twig he scratched on the ground a monstrous outline. The television lens served for one eye, a beer bottle pushed neck-first into the soil the other.

During the middle hours, while the moon died behind wisps of pale cloud, he carved a word on the dark forehead; then recited the activating incantation.

The ground rumbled and moaned, the golem heaved up to blot out the stars.

The glass eyes stared down at Fair, secure in his pentagon.

"Speak!" called out Fair. *"Enteresthes, Akmai Adonai Bidemgir! Elohim, pa rahulli! Enteresthes, HVOI! Speak!"*

"Return me to earth, return my clay to the quiet clay from whence you roused me."

"First you must serve."

The golem stumbled forward to crush Fair, but was halted by the pang of protective magic.

"Serve you I will, if serve you I must."

Fair stepped boldly forth from the pentagon, strung forty yards of green ribbon down the road in the shape of a narrow V. "Go forth into the realm of green magic," he told the monster. "The ribbons reach forty miles, walk to the end, turn about, return, and then fall back, return to the earth from which you rose."

The golem turned, shuffled into the V of green ribbon, shaking off clods of mold, jarring the ground with its ponderous tread.

Fair watched the squat shape dwindle, recede, yet never reach the angle of the magic V. He returned to his panel truck, tuned the television receiver to the golem's eye, and surveyed the fantastic vistas of the green realm.

Two elementals of the green realm met on a spun-silver landscape. They were Jaadian and Misthemar, and they fell to discussing the earthen monster which had stalked forty miles through the region known as Cil; which then, turning in its tracks, had retraced its steps, gradually increasing its pace until at the end it moved in a shambling rush, leaving a trail of clods on the fragile moth-wing mosaics.

"Events, events, events," Misthemar fretted, "they crowd the chute of time till the bounds bulge. Or then again, the course is as lean and spare as a stretched tendon . . . But in regard to this incursion . . ." He paused for a period of reflection, and silver clouds moved over his head and under his feet.

Jaadian remarked, "You are aware that I conversed with Howard Fair; he is so obsessed to escape the squalor of his world that he acts with recklessness."

"The man Gerald McIntyre was his uncle," mused Misthemar. "McIntyre besought, we yielded; as perhaps now we must yield to Howard Fair."

Jaadian uneasily opened his hand, shook off a spray of emerald fire. "Events press, both in and out. I find myself unable to act in this regard."

"I likewise do not care to be the agent of tragedy."

A Meaning came fluttering up from below: "A disturbance among the spiral towers! A caterpillar of glass and metal has come clanking; it has thrust electric eyes into the Portinone and broke open the Egg of Innocence. Howard Fair is the fault."

Jaadian and Misthemar consulted each other with wry disinclination. "Very well, both of us will go; such a duty needs two souls in support."

They impinged upon Earth and found Howard Fair in a wall booth at a cocktail bar. He looked up at the two strangers and one of them asked, "May we join you?"

Fair examined the two men. Both wore conservative suits and carried cashmere topcoats over their arms. Fair noticed that the left thumb-nail of each man glistened green.

Fair rose politely to his feet. "Will you sit down?"

The green sprites hung up their overcoats and slid into the booth. Fair looked from one to the other. He addressed Jaadian. "Aren't you he whom I interviewed several weeks ago?"

Jaadian assented. "You have not accepted my advice."

Fair shrugged. "You asked me to remain ignorant, to accept my stupidity and ineptitude."

"And why should you not?" asked Jaadian gently. "You are a primitive in a primitive realm; nevertheless not one man in a thousand can match your achievements."

Fair agreed, smiling faintly. "But knowledge creates a craving for further knowledge. Where is the harm in knowledge?"

Misthemar, the more mercurial of the sprites, spoke angrily. "Where is the harm? Consider your earthen monster! It befouled forty miles of delicacy, the record of ten million years. Consider your caterpillar! It trampled our pillars of carved milk, our dreaming towers, damaged the nerve-skeins which extrude and waft us our Meanings."

"I'm dreadfully sorry," said Fair. "I meant no destruction."

The sprites nodded. "But your apology conveys no guarantee of restraint."

Fair toyed with his glass. A waiter approached the table, addressed the two sprites. "Something for you two gentlemen?"

Jaadian ordered a glass of charged water, as did Misthemar. Fair called for another highball.

"What do you hope to gain from this activity?" inquired Misthemar. "Destructive forays teach you nothing!"

Fair agreed. "I have learned little. But I have seen miraculous sights. I am more than ever anxious to learn."

The green sprites glumly watched the bubbles rising in their glasses. Jaadian at last drew a deep sigh. "Perhaps we can obviate toil on your part and disturbance on ours. Explicitly, what gains or advantages do you hope to derive from green magic?"

Fair, smiling, leaned back into the red imitation-leather cushions. "I want many things. Extended life—mobility in time—comprehensive memory—augmented perception, with vision across the whole spectrum. I want physical charm and magnetism, the semblance of youth, muscular endurance . . . Then there are qualities more or less speculative, such as—"

Jaadian interrupted. "These qualities and characteristics we will confer upon you. In return you will undertake never again to disturb the green realm. You will evade centuries of toil; we will be spared the nuisance of your presence, and the inevitable tragedy."

"Tragedy?" inquired Fair in wonder. "Why tragedy?"

Jaadian spoke in a deep reverberating voice. "You are a man of Earth. Your goals are not our goals. Green magic makes you aware of our goals."

Fair thoughtfully sipped his highball. "I can't see that this is a disadvantage. I am willing to submit to the discipline of instruction. Surely a knowledge of green magic will not change me into a different entity?"

"No. And this is the basic tragedy!"

Misthemar spoke in exasperation. "We are forbidden to harm lesser creatures, and so you are fortunate; for to dissolve you into air would end all the annoyance."

Fair laughed. "I apologize again for making such a nuisance of myself. But surely you understand how important this is to me?"

Jaadian asked hopefully, "Then you agree to our offer?"

Fair shook his head. "How could I live, forever young, capable of extended learning, but limited to knowledge which I already see bounds to? I would be bored, restless, miserable."

"That well may be," said Jaadian. "But not so bored, restless and miserable as if you were learned in green magic."

Fair drew himself erect. "I must learn green magic. It is an opportunity which only a person both torpid and stupid could refuse."

Jaadian sighed. "In your place I would make the same response." The sprites rose to their feet. "Come then, we will teach you."

"Don't say we didn't warn you," said Misthemar.

Time passed. Sunset waned and twilight darkened. A man walked up the stairs, entered Howard Fair's apartment. He was tall, unobtrusively muscular. His face was sensitive, keen, humorous; his left thumb-nail glistened green.

Time is a function of vital processes. The people of Earth had perceived the motion of their clocks. On this understanding, two hours had elapsed since Howard Fair had followed the green sprites from the bar.

Howard Fair had perceived other criteria. For him the interval had been seven hundred years, during which he had lived in the green realm, learning to the utmost capacity of his brain.

He had occupied two years training his senses to the new conditions. Gradually he learned to walk in the six basic three-dimensional directions, and accustomed himself to the fourth-dimensional short-cuts. By easy stages the blinds over his eyes were removed, so that the dazzling over-human intricacy of the landscape never completely confounded him.

Another year was spent training him to the use of a code-language —an intermediate step between the vocalizations of Earth and the meaning-patterns of the green realm, where a hundred symbol-flakes (each a flitting spot of delicate iridescence) might be displayed in a single swirl of import. During this time Howard Fair's eyes and brain were altered, to allow him the use of the many new colors, without which the meaning-flakes could not be recognized.

These were preliminary steps. For forty years he studied the flakes, of which there were almost a million. Another forty years was given to elementary permutations and shifts, and another forty to parallels, attenuation, diminishments and extensions; and during this time he was introduced to flake patterns, and certain of the more obvious displays.

Now he was able to study without recourse to the code-language, and his progress became more marked. Another twenty years found him able to recognize more complicated Meanings, and he was introduced to a more varied program. He floated over the field of moth-wing mosaics, which still showed the footprints of the golem. He sweated in embarrassment, the extent of his wicked willfulness now clear to him.

So passed the years. Howard Fair learned as much green magic as his brain could encompass.

He explored much of the green realm, finding so much beauty that he feared his brain might burst. He tasted, he heard, he felt, he sensed, and each one of his senses was a hundred times more discriminating than before. Nourishment came in a thousand different forms: from pink eggs which burst into a hot sweet gas, suffusing his entire body; from passing through a rain of stinging metal crystals; from simple contemplation of the proper symbol.

Homesickness for Earth waxed and waned. Sometimes it was insupportable and he was ready to forsake all he had learned and abandon his hopes for the future. At other times the magnificence of the green realm permeated him, and the thought of departure seemed like the threat of death itself.

By stages so gradual he never realized them he learned green magic.

But the new faculty gave him no pride: between his crude ineptitudes and the poetic elegance of the sprites remained a tremendous gap—and he felt his innate inferiority much more keenly than he ever had in his old state. Worse, his most earnest efforts failed to improve his technique, and sometimes, observing the singing joy of an improvised manifestation by one of the sprites, and contrasting it to his own labored constructions, he felt futility and shame.

The longer he remained in the green realm, the stronger grew the sense of his own maladroitness, and he began to long for the easy environment of Earth, where each of his acts would not shout aloud of vulgarity and crassness. At times he would watch the sprites (in the gossamer forms natural to them) at play among the pearl-petals, or twining like quick flashes of music through the forest of pink spirals. The contrast between their verve and his brutish fumbling could not be borne and he would turn away. His self-respect dwindled with each passing hour, and instead of pride in his learning, he felt a sullen ache for what he was not and could never become. The first few hundred years he worked with the enthusiasm of ignorance, for the next few he was buoyed by hope. During the last part of his time, only dogged obstinacy kept him plodding through what now he knew for infantile exercises.

In one terrible bitter-sweet spasm, he gave up. He found Jaadian weaving tinkling fragments of various magics into a warp of shining long splines. With grave courtesy, Jaadian gave Fair his attention, and Fair laboriously set forth his meaning.

Jaadian returned a message. "I recognize your discomfort, and extend my sympathy. It is best that you now return to your native home."

He put aside his weaving and conveyed Fair down through the requisite vortices. Along the way they passed Misthemar. No flicker of meaning was expressed or exchanged, but Howard Fair thought to feel a tinge of faintly malicious amusement.

Howard Fair sat in his apartment. His perceptions, augmented and sharpened by his sojourn in the green realm, took note of the surroundings. Only two hours before, by the clocks of Earth, he had found them both restful and stimulating; now they were neither. His

books: superstition, spuriousness, earnest nonsense. His private
journals and workbooks: a pathetic scrawl of infantilisms. Gravity
tugged at his feet, held him rigid. The shoddy construction of the
house, which heretofore he never had noticed, oppressed him. Everywhere he looked he saw slipshod disorder, primitive filth. The
thought of the food he must now eat revolted him.

He went out on his little balcony which overlooked the street. The
air was impregnated with organic smells. Across the street he could
look into windows where his fellow humans lived in stupid squalor.

Fair smiled sadly. He had tried to prepare himself for these reac-
tions, but now was surprised by their intensity. He returned into his
apartment. He must accustom himself to the old environment. And
after all there were compensations. The most desirable commodities
of the world were now his to enjoy.

Howard Fair plunged into the enjoyment of these pleasures. He
forced himself to drink quantities of expensive wines, brandies, li-
queurs, even though they offended his palate. Hunger overcame his
nausea, he forced himself to the consumption of what he thought of
as fried animal tissue, the hypertrophied sexual organs of plants. He
experimented with erotic sensations, but found that beautiful
women no longer seemed different from the plain ones, and that he
could barely steel himself to the untidy contacts. He bought libraries
of erudite books, glanced through them with contempt. He tried to
amuse himself with his old magics; they seemed ridiculous.

He forced himself to enjoy these pleasures for a month; then he
fled the city and established a crystal bubble on a crag in the Andes.
To nourish himself, he contrived a thick liquid, which, while by no
means as exhilarating as the substances of the green realm, was innocent of organic contamination.

After a certain degree of improvisation and make-shift, he arranged his life to its minimum discomfort. The view was one of aus-
tere grandeur; not even the condors came to disturb him. He sat
back to ponder the chain of events which had started with his discovery of Gerald McIntyre's workbook. He frowned. Gerald McIntyre?
He jumped to his feet, looked far off over the crags.

He found Gerald McIntyre at a wayside service station in the heart
of the South Dakota prairie. McIntyre was sitting in an old wooden
chair, tilted back against the peeling yellow paint of the service station, a straw hat shading his eyes from the sun.

He was a magnetically handsome man, blond of hair, brown of

skin, with blue eyes whose gaze stung like the touch of icicle. His left thumb-nail glistened green.

Fair greeted him casually; the two men surveyed each other with wry curiosity.

"I see you have adapted yourself," said Howard Fair.

McIntyre shrugged. "As well as possible. I try to maintain a balance between solitude and the pressure of humanity." He looked into the bright blue sky where crows flapped and called. "For many years I lived in isolation. I began to detest the sound of my own breathing."

Along the highway came a glittering automobile, rococo as a hybrid goldfish. With the perceptions now available to them, Fair and McIntyre could see the driver to be red-faced and truculent, his companion a peevish woman in expensive clothes.

"There are other advantages to residence here," said McIntyre. "For instance, I am able to enrich the lives of passers-by with trifles of novel adventure." He made a small gesture; two dozen crows swooped down and flew beside the automobile. They settled on the fenders, strutted back and forth along the hood, fouled the windshield.

The automobile squealed to a halt, the driver jumped out, put the birds to flight. He threw an ineffectual rock, waved his arms in outrage, returned to his car, proceeded.

"A paltry affair," said McIntyre with a sigh. "The truth of the matter is that I am bored." He pursed his mouth and blew forth three bright puffs of smoke: first red, then yellow, then blazing blue. "I have arrived at the estate of foolishness, as you can see."

Fair surveyed his great-uncle with a trace of uneasiness. McIntyre laughed. "No more pranks. I predict, however, that you will presently share my malaise."

"I share it already," said Fair. "Sometimes I wish I could abandon all my magic and return to my former innocence."

"I have toyed with the idea," McIntyre replied thoughtfully. "In fact I have made all the necessary arrangements. It is really a simple matter." He led Fair to a small room behind the station. Although the door was open, the interior showed a thick darkness.

McIntyre, standing well back, surveyed the darkness with a quizzical curl to his lip. "You need only enter. All your magic, all your recollections of the green realm will depart. You will be no wiser than the next man you meet. And with your knowledge will go your boredom, your melancholy, your dissatisfaction."

Fair contemplated the dark doorway. A single step would resolve his discomfort.

He glanced at McIntyre; the two surveyed each other with sardonic amusement. They returned to the front of the building.

"Sometimes I stand by the door and look into the darkness," said McIntyre. "Then I am reminded how dearly I cherish my boredom, and what a precious commodity is so much misery."

Fair made himself ready for departure. "I thank you for this new wisdom, which a hundred more years in the green realm would not have taught me. And now—for a time, at least—I go back to my crag in the Andes."

McIntyre tilted his chair against the wall of the service station. "And I—for a time, at least—will wait for the next passerby."

"Goodby then, Uncle Gerald."

"Goodby, Howard."

Acknowledgments